# Celestial Harmonies

# Celestial Harmonies

A NOVEL

# PÉTER ESTERHÁZY

*Translated by Judith Sollosy*

ecco
An Imprint of HarperCollinsPublishers

FIRST EDITION

*Designed by Cassandra J. Pappas*

Printed on acid-free paper

Library of Congress Cataloging-in-Publication Data

Esterházy, Péter, 1950–
[Harmonia cælestis. English]
Celestial harmonies : a novel / Péter Esterházy ; translated by Judith Sollosy.—1st ed.
p. cm.
ISBN 0-06-050104-9 (alk. paper)
I. Sollosy, Judith. II. Title.
PH3241.E85H3713 2004
894'.511334—dc21
2003053139

04  05  06  07  08   FFG   10  9  8  7  6  5  4  3  2  1

# Contents

*A Brief Introduction*
{ *vii* }


BOOK ONE

Numbered Sentences from the Lives of the
Esterházy Family
{ I }


BOOK TWO

Confessions of an Esterházy Family
{ 393 }


*Comments*
{ 843 }

# A Brief Introduction

As a rule, the writer chooses his subject. But as Péter Esterházy said in a recent interview, he knew that sooner or later, his subject would choose him. The result is *Celestial Harmonies,* first published in Hungary in 2001.

Princes, counts, military commanders, diplomats, bishops and patrons of the arts, the Esterházy family were among the greatest aristocrats in Hungarian history, and certainly the best loved, revered, and respected. *Celestial Harmonies* stands as a tribute to them—but above all, to Mátyás Esterházy, the author's father, who was born into great wealth and privilege in 1919, worked as a field hand and parquet floor layer under the hard-line Communists, then later on, as a translator making a meager living. But regardless of what the vagaries of fortune held in store, he never relinquished the humanist values that were his birthright, nor his defiance of any regime or ideology, whether sacred or secular, that tried to temper with the dignity and love of life that—as we learn from the book—were typical Esterházy traits. It is, perhaps, this thought that has helped give this work its intriguing structure.

*Celestial Harmonies* is composed of two parts, which the author likes to characterize as the "hard core" and the "soft core" versions of the story he has to tell. Of the two, Book One is the philosophical, reflexive take on the author's subject; Book Two is the straight narrative—provided we do not insist on the even, one-directional flow of time. The former, which rests on a complex philosophical system, works with indirection and has no narrative action, no one main character; the latter, which approximates a biography of sorts, tells the story of the author's immediate family, first and foremost, his father.

Both histories are as complex as the history of Hungary itself, from which the story of the Esterházys cannot be severed. There's a joke about an old man—let's call him Uncle Kovács—who was born in the Austro-Hungarian Empire, spent his childhood in Hungary, studied in Czechoslovakia, was married in Hungary, worked in the USSR, and retired in the Ukraine, all without having left the town of Ungvár.

The thousand-year history of Hungary is anything if not lively, buzzing with stir and movement. In the more distant past it is especially linked to the 150 years of Turkish occupation, followed by the subjugation of the Austrian Empire which, as a result of the freedom fights of 1848–49, in 1867 became the Austro-Hungarian Empire. The rest, as we say, is history (a short spell of independence, a short spell of the Soviet Commune followed by White Terror, the Horthy regime, and Soviet-type Communism, in that order, followed by a republic). And since turbulence came so hard upon turbulence, a man—provided he was blessed with a long life—could have his share of both elation and woe. It is this circumstance that has allowed the author to make free and easy with his characters, especially his father, who is seen galloping off into "the discriminating seventeenth-century landscape" at one moment, and suggesting to Haydn that he compose a string-triplet in the next. Family is family; father or great-great-great-grandfather, it is all the same. At one point in the book, the father is seen fighting the Turks and writing psalms; at another he is described as herding geese and feathering his already well-feathered nest. In the nineteenth century he is caught cavorting with his mistress while looking after matters of state, in the 1940s and 1950s he is seen helping to organize a number of conspiracies, then reporting it to the secret police. Conversely, he is also seen apprehended and tortured by them. On the first page of the novel, the father is seen as a baroque *grand seigneur;* on the last, he is seated by his typewriter, bereft of everything except for the one word, "homeland." Any resemblance to James Joyce's *Finnegans Wake* may not be purely coincidental.

Indeed, *Celestial Harmonies* is monumental in scope. The author pays tribute to his father not by reductionism ("this is what my father was like") but by expansion ("my father was all fathers and all men whose lives collided with Hungarian history"). He is a monster, and he is an angel, but above all, he is man wrestling with the meaning of God. At least, this is one of the recurrent themes of Book One, which the father leaves ambling along, bent, like a straightened-out saxophone, his head lowered to prevent him from banging it into the heavenly spheres.

Often, the stories of the father—and the mother, too—appear as parable, which is one of the main tools of indirection used by the author—to great effect, one might add. He is a master of telling one story while shedding light on another. The more "naïve" a story, the more certain it is to be "about" something else—the nature of man, God, Communism, love, hate. The list is endless. There is always something more behind the raised curtain; there is always yet another surprise, another revelation. To fully understand *Celestial Harmonies* is the work of a lifetime.

The image of a revolving lighthouse comes to mind, a strong, clear beam of crystal light illuminating everything in its path. Often couched within a story—and hardly ever directly, which is part of the fun—the author launches into elaborate discourses and snappy critiques of everything that crosses his path from identity, time, old age, integrity, forgetting and remembering, faith, atheism, being and non-being. We are even offered a hilarious take on the second law of thermodynamics, cloning, quantum mechanics, the particle theory, and Schrödinger's cats. The text is interspersed with off-the-cuff comments about kings and lowly servants, Party members and class aliens, culinary know-how, and what it is like to be a prince in the morning and the scum of the earth at night. It makes one's head reel.

The author also critiques art (with special attention to the baroque), music, words, style, the predicament of the contemporary writer caught in the trap of his own self-awareness, and modern crowd-control. *Celestial Harmonies,* whose author holds that literature is a dialogue between good books, abounds in references to world literature and great thinkers—and even, playfully, to his own previous works. There are overt and covert references, even snippets, from the works of Friedrich Nietzsche, Immanuel Kant, Ludwig Wittgenstein, Martin Heidegger, Walter Benjamin, E. M. Cioran, Danilo Kis, Witold Gombrowicz, Leszek Kolakowski, Homer (one word), Goethe (several), Natalia Ginzburg, Joseph Roth, Vladimir Nabokov, Albert Camus, Samuel Beckett, Mary Daly, James Joyce, Saul Bellow, John Updike, Donald Barthelme, Frank McCourt—and oh, yes, the Bible. If asked what happens if one glides over these things, the author grins and says, nothing. The *text* knows it is there, and that is enough.

Indeed, *Celestial Harmonies* is so replete with reflections of all kinds and a sleight-of-hand juggling with language and literary form, and the various elements are so expertly fused, that it is perhaps best read as if it were a musical score. Every word, every comma, every gesture serves a complex philosophical system. Nothing is done in a random way. Nothing.

Still, though the orchestration of the whole is admirable, we mustn't expect to hear the whole symphony in one bar. A word or phrase crops up unexpectedly, is gradually elaborated, until we recognize it as a theme. Form and content are one, and beyond their separation, we can sit back and enjoy ourselves, allowing the work to unfold at its own pace, giving ourselves over to the roller-coaster ride of the flow of ideas and emotions. The manner in which the author pulls at our heartstrings, the quick, unexpected *frissons* and smiles, the tears and laughter, makes you want to cry out, Péter, you devil, it's not fair!

*Celestial Harmonies* is exuberantly playful. It is the work of a great philosopher-clown, a rarity in European literature. The author gives free rein to his imagination (he can't help himself); the spirit of unencumbered fun and *joie de vivre* informs every part of the book. We read a story, and suddenly, interrupting the flow of the narrative, the authorial voice cries out in joy, anger, or despair. Or the literary narration is curtailed, if for an instant, by the surfacing of everyday speech. The written word is sequential, the spoken quick and implicit. As we speak, we even react to our own act of speaking. The content of speech is always an actual process of thought. In *Harmonia Caelestis,* speech is used as an effective element of spontaneity. Esterházy is in full control, and he won't let us forget it. Each of his pieces, which he calls "sentences" (the subtitle of Book One is Numbered Sentences from the Lives of the Esterházy Family), builds up to a clincher.

This authorial presence goes hand in hand with the dizzying kaleidoscope of words and styles, from narrative to authorial interjection, from the most florid of baroques to the lowest proletarian jargon. At times, a sudden switch in style will tell the reader not to take what is being said at face value; at other times the introduction of another style acts as a commentary on the text by another consciousness (sometimes the author's, sometimes one or another of his character's). Certain words act as leitmotifs pointing to some profound subterranean spring of meanings. Of these, "bright," "brightness," "baroque," "everything," and "nothing" come most readily to mind. The unexpected appearance of such words and expressions brings another time plane or consciousness onto the scene.

At times, one feels that a story is told for the sake of a pun on which it relies for its meaning, or that a word is used only because the writer can't let it go to waste, or because, as he'd put it, "the word wanted in." Still, it all hangs together. The structure of the book is orchestrated with the expertise of a mathematician. (Péter Esterházy was, in fact, trained as a mathematician.) From the first page to the last, it oscillates between the comic and the tragic. (It is in this sense, too, that the Esterházy family is all families, and that the main character, referred to as "my father," is all fathers.) The text is replete with paradox. The message: if we are willing to look paradox in the eye, it will restore our sense of balance.

No question could be more embarrassing than this: "What is *Celestial Harmonies* about?" Or, as the author asks at one point in the book, "What gives?" The question has no easy answer. With its multiplicity of dovetailing concerns and radical departure from traditional narrative structure, ultimately, it is what it is—a book that has brought European literature of age, bridging the embarrassing gap that has prevailed between literature and modern art for nearly a century now. Having dropped the illusion of the objective, invisible author in favor of the controlling authorial presence and, along with it, the illusion of a piece of literature as a closed entity, finished before it is read, Esterházy's *Celestial Harmonies* is "cool" in the best McLuhanese sense of the term. It is literature as a twenty-first-century happening.

I can't help thinking that when the Good Lord created the world in six days and took off for the Bahamas on the seventh, He made a bad mistake. And He knows it. And once in a while, in His infinite boredom, He looks down on us, feels sorry for our plight, and He sends us a Shakespeare, or a Mozart—or a book like *Celestial Harmonies*.

*Judith Sollosy*
*April 2003*

BOOK ONE

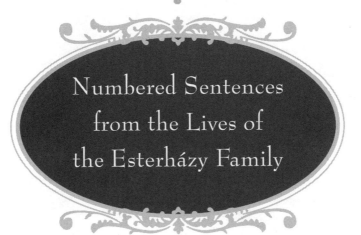

Numbered Sentences
from the Lives of
the Esterházy Family

*"Few of us can deal with the recent past. Either our present lives have too strong a hold on us, or else we are plunged into the troubled waters of the past, trying our utmost to bring back and retrieve something vanished beyond recall. Even in large and wealthy families who owe much to their ancestors, it is the custom to remember the grandfathers rather than the fathers."*

1.  It is deucedly difficult to tell a lie when you don't know the truth.

2.  To kick off a text with a ferocious-looking baroque *grand seigneur* is gratifying; a thrilling, tingling sensation thrills our bosom, our computers greet us in passing, and our cook, because why shouldn't we have a cook (*who* we?) serves us—a surprise!—breaded lamb's tail, which is like calf's foot except it's more savory because it's more fragile and tender; my father, this ferocious-looking baroque *grand seigneur* who was in a position, nay under obligation, to raise his eyes to Emperor Leopold, raised his eyes to Emperor Leopold, on his countenance an expression of solemnity, though his eyes, twinkling and mischievous, belied him as always, and he said, It is deucedly difficult, Sire, to tell a lie when you don't know the truth. Having said that, he leaped upon his chestnut steed, Challenger, and galloped off into the discriminating seventeenth-century landscape (or description thereof).

3.  My father, it was presumably my father who, with his painter's palette under his coat, sneaked back into the museum, stole back in, to retouch the paintings he'd hung on the wall or, at the very least, to effectuate certain emendations thereof.

· · ·

4. It seems to me, my father said wracking his brain long and in vain, that nothing is as sacred as that which we do not remember.

5. My father was one of the most generously endowed figures of seventeenth-century Hungarian culture and history. At the peak of his political career, he bore the title of Palatine and Prince of the Empire. He turned the palace of Kismarton into a magnificent residence, building several churches and keeping sculptors and painters in his employ at Court. Several members of the family learned to play musical instruments. My father "clapped out" his favorite pieces on the virginal, Prince Pál Antal had mastered several instruments (some say the violin, flute and lute, others the violin and the cello), while it is commonly accepted that Haydn composed his pieces expressly for Prince Miklós the Magnificent, who loved the baryton and magnificence in equal measure. My father wrote several volumes of poetry, most of which testify to the influence of the great baroque poet and military commander, Miklós Zrínyi. He also published works on religion, as well as prayer books. His collection of religious psalms, *Celestial Harmonies,* was published in Vienna in 1711. Furthermore, until recently, Hungarian musicologists have considered him a composer of some note. Latest findings, however, suggest that his contributions are somewhat limited, not only because a number of the melodies in the book can be shown not to have originated with him (most contemporary composers worked with borrowed melodies), but because, it seems, he did not compose the pieces, or adapt existing melodies, himself. His scores are not only rudimentary and tentative on the surface, they are incorrect, too. Judging by the extant documents, the schism between my father's mental faculties and his erudition and *Celestial Harmonies* is so wide, especially its more intricate layers, that it would take a great leap of the imagination to span. (To mention only the most important types of suspension bridges pertaining hereof, there's the

6

plain, the specially anchored, the self-anchored, and also the cable bridge, the slant-cable harp-bridge, the slanted star-cable bridge, the slanted fan-shaped, and the single-pylon slanted harp-cable varieties. My father played on the harp as well as the star.)

6.  For the second movement of a symphony, said the youthful Haydn for the benefit of my no longer youthful, but once again impatient (overeager) father, you must be of a certain age.

7.  The—*here my father's name follows*—stands for a dream. It stands for a Hungarian dream about a prodigally rich man, a lord palming inside his purse with both hands, sifting through his bank notes like chaff. It stands for a landowner, whose figure could have been taken from a folktale, weighing his silver and gold by the bushel. It stands for the wealthy Hungarian. In the popular imagination, my father's name conjured up all the things that can make life a heaven here on earth. It stood for a petty monarchy, not like the kind you'll find in folklore that stops at the village outskirts, but a demesne that is just a jot smaller than the old king's very own. It stood for fields so vast, the wild geese could not traverse them in one night's flight, let alone a man of dreams and fantasies reduced to hearing only the ephemeral screech of these nocturnal creatures. It stood for palaces with swirling towers and flapping banners gazing at their reflections in the mirror of the lake out of boredom, because their master had no time to spare for them. Palaces by the street full, uninhabited except by a gate-keeper, sitting and growing his beard, while in the locked rooms, the portraits of those who had once loved each other or had turned their backs on each other in enmity now live their private lives. The unoccupied servants are into their cups at the Ivkoff Inn on József Street, a favorite haunt of those serving the idle rich. The—*here my father's name follows*—name is legendary. At the close of the nineteenth century, when the great Hungarian manor

houses began their decline in earnest, only two names could still be heard in the hours when, dreamy-eyed, Hungarians gazed through the smoke rings of their pipes. One was my father's, the other Rothschild's. There were other names every Hungarian schoolboy knew, one was Francis Joseph, another old man Tisza. Those of the weaker sex would sigh when the name of Jókai's godson, the long-mustachioed sailor Mihály Tímár, passed their lips, even if in their dreams. But when engaging in its own reveries, the judicious, sober-minded populace of the nation insisted on just two names, my father's and that certain Rothschild's. Under the shade of ancient, all-knowing willows, how often would itinerant youths recall how one of my forebears had covered the highway with a pristine blanket of white salt as far as the eye could see so that in midsummer Empress Maria Theresa could be conveyed from Vienna to Kismarton on a Russian sleigh drawn by reindeer! And how often would travelers to Transdanubia, whom the landscape had accustomed to reveries to begin with, turn their heads for a last lingering look when the coachman flicked his whip toward fairy-tale palaces, huge, sprawling parks slumbering peacefully under the gentle sun's rays, or the silvery lakes and ponds rippling languidly as far as the horizon, their surface pierced now and then by a goldfish's head, and deer parks, too, from whose depths gentle fawns poked out their timid heads as in some children's book. And the driver would mumble under his reddish mustache, this too belongs to—*here my father's name followed.* And the smithy where we'll have the horses shoed, that too belongs to, *and here too my father's name followed.* By way of summation, who could tally the many sweet associations that a Hungarian of old entertained when my father's name passed his lips by way of summation?

8. My father refused to succumb without a struggle, for he did not trust his son, who kept striking him.

. . .

9. Our family received its name from the Evening Star. The Morning Star. The star of Even-Morn. At first, we didn't have a name. During the first centuries of the second millennium, the petty officials whose names appear in the documents and their attendant clauses are mentioned only by their first names or, occasionally, by the names of their clans. If there's no name, there's no family. (A family is a group of individuals related by a common ancestry, a commonality of blood, and a shared history. Respect and reverence for one's ancestors form the basis of family love, and also of patriotism. Accordingly, the family that disregards its past and does not honor the memory of its ancestors prunes off a root of the tree of life of the nation, et cetera.) For what makes a family a family? ("I will decide who is a cousin and who is not.") What makes a family a family is that they can and dare say: we. Also, they want to. It comes trippingly on the tongue. In which case, they will also need a name. Without a name, they'll just gape like a fish. We . . . gape. Go on, son, gape, oxygen is essential to life . . . A name is of the essence. We, the Baradlays. In the countryside, amid the mud holes of Csallóköz, which was our Donaueschling, they (we) were called the princes Bluebeard. *Blaubart.* It's not such a good name, because others had blue beards, too, while certain bluebeard princes didn't have one, either because it wouldn't grow, or else, it wasn't blue. In short, they were neither princes, nor bluebeards—which is no way to land yourself an illustrious family. The very idea of bluebearding, too, proved far too concrete, nebulously unequivocal, as if in fact the entire *mishpocheh* were out for pussy, whereas obviously this happened on a one-on-one basis, *if* at all, though for lack of pertinent documents, we must consider this, too, an unsolved mystery. The name had been moseying up to us for some time. It issued from the sky, it issued from the earth, it issued from ourselves, from our beards. What star could have been the star of the bluebeards if not

9

Venus, the fifth planet, the star of love, the mistress of earthly delights, of song and the violin, of trumpet and flute melodies, of fabulous fancies, expensive jewels, and other refinements? The color green is hers, too, and so is the smell of sage. She wanders closest to the Sun, one year proceeding before it, and then she is called Lucifer, or Morning Star, and the next year following in its wake, when she is called Hesperus, or the Evening Star. The star of Even-Morn. Anyone who falls ill in the hour of this star is clearly the victim of a woman. Any boy or girl born in her hour will never have children of their own, and it is to be feared lest they turn out to be lascivious into the bargain. A person of the Evening (Morning) Star is exceedingly gentle, in matters of consequence a prey to doubt, doubting where he should not, and cutting the tree from under himself. Cutting and planting, cutting and planting, that's him. My father: Any man who stands in the house of the Evening (Morning) Star is surely vertiginous and terrified, for he stands in the midst of emptiness—neither here nor there. For him, it is neither day nor night, and the sky is empty. Only one star is visible, and there is nothing but this tremulous glimmer, this vibrant void that suddenly becomes richer, dense yet light, like salmon soufflé, luminous and severe, in motion, yet constant. The hour of melancholy. He who stands under the Evening (Morning) Star may rejoice and celebrate, for he stands in the present, in the eternal—oh, that Faustian moment, be it ever so banal!—he is not dragged under by the slimy dangle-weed of the past, and he is not oppressed by the irresponsible future. There is no where and no where to, only the present, the golden moment, the silvery now, iron existence, and there is nothing left to him but this iron, the rust, the beauty of the rust, the roughness, this real, solid *crumbling away,* this substantiality within the insubstantial: my father.

10. The huge tome, *Trophaeum Nobilissimae ac Antiquissimae Domus Estorasianae,* published in 1700, this "unsavory fabrication," this

"offense against common sense," contains my father's genealogy along with 171 full-figure etchings of his real and imagined ancestors. Some of the illustrations are the handiwork of a certain Petrus, a court painter to the Prince. My father's cult of Mary and the family spring from one root, beautifully symbolized by the etching on the title page, an allegory showing Courage (Fortitude) in the shape of Hercules and the Aristocracy (Generosity) in the shape of Mars guarding the hall where an Angel offers Honor a crown perched atop a pillow—*this is where my father's name follows*—on which Honor appears almost certainly in the shape of the Virgin Mary with the crown of Hungary on her head. According to the testimony of the *Trophaeum*, my father's origin goes back not only to Adam, Noah, et cetera, but more recently Attila the Hun, and even more recently, to Csaba, Prince Csaba, ancestor of the kings of the House of Árpád, or so the manuscript says. Further, the origin goes back to Chieftain Eurs who, according to this fabrication, settled in the Carpathians and was rumored to have lived longer than any other Magyar chieftain. An independent monarch in his time, he was also a cousin of the sainted kings of the Magyars. Our ancestor Estoras, whose mother, *noch dazu,* was Decebal's granddaughter, the Dacian princess Ida, is also descended from him. And as we know, the reannexation of Transylvania was among my father's cherished but unrealized dreams. Estoras would settle for nothing less than St. Stephen (István), and so he also had himself baptized by St. Adalbert, who bestowed upon him, what else?, the name of Paul (Pál). And so the ancestors march on in long, packed lines all the way up to the real-live Benedek, who lived in the fifteenth century. The portfolio devotes a separate chapter to the royal charters, fictitious from *a to z,* that allegedly came down from St. Ladislas, Andrew of Jerusalem. Louis the Great, King Sigismund, King Mátyás, et cetera, and that bestowed various privileges on our illustrious but phantom ancestors. According to one of the fictitious deeds, St.

11

Ladislas expresses great satisfaction that his beloved relative is descended from a family that had already made a name for itself in the time of Jesus Christ. My father, I might add, had taken pains to point out the fictitious nature of such "proof," in Persian, but still . . . He also provided a new etymology for our name. It appears, for instance, that the Hungarian *sárkány,* or dragon, comes from the Persian *Ezder.* The family is really Sárkányházi, and this *sárkány,* or dragon, is the same as the griffin on our coat of arms shown protecting the homeland with its drawn sword. And that's not all, because having said this, my father launches into a lengthy disquisition, to wit, that not all families have such ancient, document-authenticated roots. Some families run helter-skelter around the country and, or so my father (!) says, they go back a mere two or three thousand years since thanks to the many strokes of misfortune the country has suffered, the archives have been reduced to ashes. But no matter—only nobility allied with virtue is worth anything, ha-ha, and not one's origin, which in itself is very like a whitewashed coffin, hollow, and full of loathsomeness within.

•  •  •  •  •

11. Once I had a distant, fascinating and intriguing father—let's call my father by this name—around whose crib there danced the last moon rays of the old century and the first shimmering light of a new dawn—the Evening Star, the Morning Star, the Star of Even-Morn. That's where our name comes from.

12. My father rode a magic steed, a *táltos*. Táltos, that was the name of his horse. It was coal black with a white mark on its left hind leg. It lived on sugar and wheat, and nothing else. It truly was a real magic steed, for it understood my father's words. It even gave him advice. Once it suggested that my father should have it shoed backward, because that way the enemy would take up the chase in the opposite direction and not find them. (Later, when all the horses had their shoes put on backward, my father surprised the enemy and effectuated his escape by having the horseshoes point in the traditional direction.) When it sensed danger, Táltos whinnied and scraped, and when my father mounted it, it galloped so swiftly, its legs did not touch the ground. It'd even fly up into the clouds with my father on its back. When the enemy approached, it pounded with its foot to indicate how many regiments of soldiers to expect. Once my father lost the battle and the enemy went in pursuit. The magic steed took him to a hiding place,

while it lay down among the dead horses and hid its head under the neck of the horse lying next to it. The enemy passed them by. This happened twice, once in August 1652, and once in the spring of 1969.

13. If someone is careless with the goods or moneys confined to his care or does damage to someone else's fortune, people say. "What do you think that is? Csáky's straw?" What is the origin of this saying, you ask? By nature, the Csákys were kindhearted, generous, happy-go-lucky farmers. The poor people were quick to discover this chink in the feudal pyramid, and concocted the following mischief: they had the horses tread the wheat out only partially, leaving some of the grain in the ear, meaning that some of the grain did and some did not, but some did remain all the same, and since his lordship let them have the straw, they could take home the above-mentioned grains of wheat as well. At home, they thrashed the straw again with a hand thresher. You lose some, you gain some; this sort of husbandry went on without a hitch, and both his lordship and the peasants were satisfied with what they'd threshed. My father's family inherited the Csáky estate, and they had severe stewards, either because they were severe to begin with, and were expected to be severe, or else, they became severe in the employ of the estate. They refused to turn a blind eye to the partially threshed wheat and said: What do you think that is? Csáky's straw? This straw here happens to belong to, *and here my father's name followed.* Well, now, this is how the saying, which also preserves the memory of the former manner of husbandry, was born.

14. My father spared the people of the land and he even prohibited his men from plundering them. (He punished us, his children, personally.) But when we ran out of food, there was nothing to do but to take the poor people's cattle. The poor people howled—a

fate that befell my father's old wet nurse, too, when my father's men took her only cow. Poor old woman, she started off on foot, and came to Kismarton. At the palace gate, the turnkey asked, What do you want, old woman? I want to speak to the Count. Impossible. Come back tomorrow. And she did for several days, just like in the Kafka story. At last, the poor woman gave him her last penny, and so he let her in. Before you could say Jack Robbins, there she was, standing before my father. Though she stood there humbly, an officer shouted at her, Kneel in front of his lordship! You mean me?, the old woman asked much surprised, you want me to kneel to my little Micu, me, who nursed him and gave him of my milk?! Having heard these loud words, my father called the old woman over to him. The old woman took out a parcel. She opened it, and wouldn't you know, it was a tiny little dolman. Do you recognize it, Micu dear?, she asked, sinking to her knees and kissing my father's fox-trimmed cloak. My father had never seen the dolman, he helped the wet nurse to her feet, planted a kiss on her forehead, God bless you, he said, and sent her on her way.

15.   For fifty fillérs my father would eat a fly, for one forint you could take a picture of the cadaver on his tongue, for five forints and an apple (Starking), he'd bite a mouse in two. He never worked with outsourced mice, he liked to catch his own.

16.   My father respected Haydn, personally as well as artistically. He had him (Haydn) sit at his (my father's) table a number of times for the midday meal. But when he (my father) was entertaining guests, he (Haydn) was served in an adjoining room, just like us children. One day two illustrious English gentlemen came to visit, the delicate, exotic perfumes heralding their arrival from a distance. They were making arrangements for Admiral Nelson's visit, and as soon as they took their places at the table, they

inquired after Haydn's whereabouts. Haydn is dining in his quarters today, my father lied without batting an eye. But the English enthusiasts were so up and up about sitting at the same table with Haydn, my father had no choice. Gritting his teeth, he dragged Joseph from the side room, and flashing one of his most endearing smiles, he had him (Haydn) sit at his (my father's) table. The foolish English were in seventh heaven, while for him (Haydn), well, he couldn't have cared less. On a sudden whim (out of revenge), my father ordered that the mustard kidneys reserved for the evening meal should be served up, which for someone with gout, like him (Haydn), is veritably fatal, figuratively speaking. Thus, everyone was satisfied with the midday meal. (According to the saying, servants have rheumatism, while their masters have gout. Which just goes to show you how well we did by him (Haydn).)

17. If there were something, if there could be something about which he, my father, could know everything, my father pleaded (Plead *giaour dog!*, came the frightening advice whistling past my father's ear from the direction of the riverbank), everything down to the last detail about catastrophe genesis, sheep breeding, or Haydn—no, Bartók, if only he knew everything about Bartók, his life would change in many ways. What's more, the change would be sudden. Right after the stuffed fillet of sole or in the middle of the second inning, just prior to planting a kiss on a lady's hand, and instead of the second Jewish law. Something like that. And he'd have to say, oh, no, it is out of the question, it couldn't have been in '25 because (he'd sigh), by then Kodály had stopped chain-smoking, even though he wouldn't know *everything* about Kodály, just a great deal. But with these flimsy but factual sentences he'd win the acknowledgment and admiration of his friends, colleagues and (in a certain sense) his family, and attaining to a certain financial equilibrium, if not security, he could hold a so-called popular lecture series (unselfishly, even in the outlying

towns and villages). The title would be "Addenda to a Bartók Harmony." Furthermore, his life would change not only in this way but, as he would soon realize, fundamentally. He'd have new emotions and new sentiments, new yearnings and new fears, and new passions, too. First he'd feel an irresistible urge to try Bartók's favorites, *puliszka* and Wiener schnitzel. Bored and indifferent, he'd push the fillet of sole away. What's more, his indifference would continue to gain ground. He'd mean less and less to himself, his gestures, his face, his face in the mirror, his smell, his name. All this would appear more and more incidental, inconsequential and petty compared to Bartók, to his, Bartók's, intake of breath. The truth is he'd like to turn into Bartók. Béla Bartók, this is what he'd like to be body and soul, if only he could have his wish. Of course, this plan of his is not easy to comprehend. You have to be a child, or a romantic. There's nothing that he, my father, knows everything about, everything down to the last detail. There is nothing about which his knowledge is exhaustive. His knowledge isn't even sufficient. In short, everything in existence is characterized by the fact that he doesn't know enough about it, as if this were the precondition for its existence, its *sine qua non*. You'd think that this was the fabric of the world, binding things together and putting things in order, this insufficient knowledge of his. And this thought, or line of reasoning, made the reeds rustle all the more threateningly from the direction of the river, and my father continued to pray. He felt that this was the logical thing to do. He felt that this logic, this quiescent horror or buoyant sense of freedom, once this, then that, was forcing him . . . forcing him to blur the distinction between these two things, the everything about Bartók and the nothing about everything, not seeing them as different, but as two sides of the same coin. But if it's two sides of the same coin, this and that side of the coin, it'd still make no sense to draw a distinction between them because, having taken sides, we'd be back where we started from, i.e., on the *other* side of the coin, in a state of exaggeration. And since it's Bartók's person that brings these things together, it follows that he, Bartók, is everything, in this sense, at least. He divides and he binds. In short, my father prayed, continuing his prayer, he'd have to turn into Bartók in either case, whether it's everything or it's nothing. And he's not saying this because it would be *comme il faut* or convenient, but because there is no other eventuality. This is where he ended up, at this point, with this *being Bartók*. And since he did not rely on anything personal in his line of reasoning, everyone else too would end up drawing the same conclusion, surely. Everyone would have to become someone. Bartók, Haydn, sheep breeding, catastrophe genesis. Which would mean, furthermore, that everything would have to be given a new name, or else the old name once again, which would call for a new Babylon. He, my father, would be Béla Bartók. Whatsoever man called every living creature, that was the name thereof. Except he, my father, is not Béla Bartók. In which case, what does all this mean? For all he knows, if he hadn't started praying, perhaps he wouldn't have gotten himself into this muddle. Or could it be that the world is the way it is because of how we see it? Bartók. Blame it on Bartók. Or the bossanova.

18. So what's it like in heaven, Béla?, my father asked abruptly. He was trying to put a good face on things.

19. Béla Bartók made my father king of Hungary. Micu, my angel, your puny little country needs you. I will make you king. May your reign be peaceful and wise. I can't promise much, you gonna get a piano, chorus girls and a lancer division. The lancer division will put your family's mind at rest. It always has, hasn't it? And the king will put the country's mind at rest. It always has. And so it came to pass. Organically speaking, my father made especially good use of the piano and the chorus girls. ("Spread your black

wings!" or: "Thrill to the savage strokes of my little hammer!" or: "Piano! piano!, fortissimo! fortissimo!") The lancer division, on the other hand, proved to be a nuisance. First he put them to work around the house (dirty dishes, shopping, gardening, and especially weeding, because nobody wanted to do the weeding). Later, he assigned them to Haydn to copy scores. Later still, having gotten the better of the anti-Habsburg Kuruc versus pro-Habsburg Labanc dichotomy, they attacked Austria, because it seemed the logical thing to do. Romania was spared, thanks to Béla's love of folk music. Even though he was very busy, plus he had to go to the office every day, my father stood at the head of his troop, his proud chestnut steed prancing squeamishly. My father was not a good rider, but he cut a dashing figure atop his horse between two falls, his head always bent slightly to the side, as if attending to something.

20.  The people of Kanizsa suffered something awful under the Turkish yoke. They yearned for freedom with all their hearts, but for some unfathomable reason, they would have liked the Turks to leave the country without the Germans marching in (while no one imagined, not even in their wildest dreams, that the Germans would be followed by the Russians, or that after the Russians, no one would march in, and yet it'd be almost as if they had). They wanted to be masters of their own town. At last, my father and General Zichy called upon the Turkish infidels to relinquish the castle. The Turks refused to negotiate, and countered by launching an assault on the Christian camp just outside of Kanizsa, my father and his men being Christians, more specifically, Catholics. They were hoping to lay their hands on the cannons. My father and his men countered in no uncertain terms and sent the Turk back to his lair with bleeding heads, i.e., the ones they sent back and did not slay on the spot, because they'd slain five hundred of them. When my father and his men saw that the Turk was not

19

about to yield the town with anything like good grace, they laid such a tight siege to them that not so much as a bird could fly through, not even a common fillet of sole or *puliszka* or a slice of Wiener schnitzel. There was one hell of a famine, as you can imagine, and the hunger was such that the Turks reeled. In the end they were so hungry that having grown tipsy from all the reeling, they surrendered the castle. Their troops marched off with four hundred carts, but at least, off they marched! However, a new peril followed in their stead when in their eagerness, my father and Zichy galloped up to the fort in such haste that they nearly trampled to death the aged and ailing agha of the janissaries, who'd come forward to greet them. Greetings, gentlemen. How are you? Wouldn't you like to alight from your horses? asked the janissary, who was old and honorable, whereupon my father made the following response, We're fine, but we're not alighting from no horse, 'cause the prestige and majesty of our all-powerful king wouldn't stand for it. From which Turk and Magyar alike understood that the gentlemen had liberated Kanizsa for themselves. History is an alternating series of frying pans and fires, my father announced, that's the nature of history. He did not mean to dismiss the theoretical possibility of freedom offhand, especially because he refused to comment on who or what the frying pan and the fire might be, and who or what was about to fall from one into the other. Raising his pewter cup, he smiled cunningly and slapped his old pal Zichy on the back. The point is, he said with a drunken nod, that you shouldn't count your chickens before they hatch. Spent with fatigue, the people of Kanizsa slept on.

21. Maria Theresa asked my father if he would stand in for her as Prince-Elector of Bohemia at the coronation of her son Joseph in Frankfurt. (Was she otherwise engaged? Or was she trying to please my father?) My father did not like Joseph, and vice versa. He's not an emperor, he's not a king, he's just a clever clerk, my

father said of him condescendingly. Later, when Joseph became king of Hungary, their relationship went from bad to worse. How *unheimlich* that the King is not an aristocrat, grumbled my father, whom not even his most virulent distractors could accuse of being liberal or enlightened. On the other hand, he had a sense of style. On that particular evening in April, the city of Frankfurt was awash in light. The quarters of the delegates who'd gathered for the coronation were sumptuously illuminated (the delegate's from Pfalz even more so than the others), casting them in a glow bright as day. The delegates vied to outdo one another. But my father outdid them all. In honor of the occasion, he abandoned his ill-situated lodgings and its neighborhood and instead chose to decorate the beautiful linden alley of the Rossmarkt. The portal up front was awash in sublime color and the background was even more exquisite yet. Situated among the trees, pyramids and globes of light were perched atop translucent pedestals, rows of luminous garlands were strung up between the boughs with hanging chandeliers. My father also handed out bread and sausage to the people, and the wine never ran short. All at once, he spotted a youth with a face bright as a button who, with his maiden friend, was admiring my father's handiwork. The youth was showing the girl around with expansive gestures when my father thought he heard his name, which surprised him. He called them over. Well, well, he reflected, here is a scene that can be pinpointed in time with relative certainty, I wonder if I can come up with a quick description of the young man . . . He shrugged. He was a great lord; he could do anything he liked. He decided what that anything was, and he decided so that he could do anything he liked. What was that you said, son? The youth flushed, then awkward but proud, proclaimed that the idea of a, *and here my father's name followed*, type of fantasyland has now become reality. Not bad, my father nodded, and told someone to make a note of it, though he then also said to the youth in his most friendly manner, this here is merely *dichtung und wahrheit,* poetry and reality, and nobody knows the difference between *dichtung* and *wahrheit* better than he. This time, it was the youth who made a note of it. What is your name? my father asked absentmindedly. The youth told him. Fine. I shall remember it, he said as he turned away, and promptly forgot.

22. My father met a troop of anti-Habsburg Kuruc soldiers on the road. The soldiers asked him, What might you be? Kuruc, or Labanc? My meek father didn't know whom he was up against and said, Labanc. At which the anti-Habsburg Kuruc gave him a thorough thrashing. My father continued his journey and came upon a group of pro-Habsburg Labanc soldiers. They, too, asked, What might you be? Kuruc, or Labanc? My father still did not know whom he was up against, nor did he know who were up against those whom he was now up against. But he remembered the previous troop of solders and said, Kuruc. At which the pro-Habsburg Labanc also gave him a thorough thrashing. Then they let him go on his way. As he continued his journey, he met another troop of anti-Habsburg Kuruc soldiers. But this time, before they could say anything, my father said, Don't ask, just strike. And so it went. My father, the "handsome count," continues his solitary gallop atop his horse Challenger over the volatile seventeenth century, et cetera.

23. General Heister knew full well that my father was a trusted subject of Prince Rákóczi, so he was the first to be sent to the scaffold. My father didn't bat an eye when he was told that he must die. He'd locked eyes with death many times before on the battlefield, they were familiars, so he wouldn't be frightened now. When he was led up to the scaffold, he pulled a fine kerchief from the pocket of his dolman, *a snow white Turkish hand-kerchief edged in gold,* unfolded it and extracted ten gold coins. The soldiers mar-

veled at it, and the headsman was also inordinately surprised, but my father ignored their surprise and, taking the ten gold coins, presented them to the headsman. The headsman broke into disconsolate sobs. Pull yourself together, son, my father said softly, then stepped up to the block, silently pushed aside the executioner's assistant, who wanted to blindfold him, and looked death intrepidly in the eye. The executioner took my father's advice, one of the last he ever gave, and pulled himself together. My father was forty-nine when he died, which is as much as he could do for us (i.e., the nation).

24. When, at dawn of the day set by imperial decree for his execution, the guards entered his cell, they found my father kneeling on the floor, his hands tightly clasped in prayer. His head was bent low and his light hair fell to either side, revealing a long, thin neck and jagged backbone that disappeared under a collarless linen shirt, as if offering themselves, naked, to the eye. The guards paused, considering a count's conversation with God sufficient reason to disregard, for a moment, the strict rules of Spanish etiquette. The priest also shrank back, mutely clenching the hands he had brought together in prayer. His palms were sweaty and had left a telltale stain on the ivory covers of his breviary; his rosary, its beads the size of olives, clicked softly together. The only other sound came from an enormous ring of keys, which was held by one of the guards and clanked two or three times, unrhythmically. Amen, my father whispered, coming to the end of his morning prayer. Then he added, for all to hear, Forgive me, Father! At that moment, as if by command, the drums began to beat, ominous, and monotonous like pounding rain. A ruddy-faced, bushy-mustachioed Hussar officer framed by the long rifles of two Croatian uhlans, one on each side, started reading out the sentence. He had a hoarse voice that echoed through the cell with a hollow ring. The sentence was harsh and implacable: death by hanging.

My father, weapon in hand, had taken part in one of the mass up-risings—sudden and unforeseen, bloody, brutal, and hopeless—that shook the Empire from time to time only to be just as suddenly, brutally, and hopelessly crushed. His origins and the eminence of his line had been treated by the court as aggravating circumstances, as a betrayal not only of the monarch but also of his own estate. The punishment was meant to set an example. My father could make out scarcely a word among the string of monotonous syllables throbbing in his ears like so many drumbeats. Time had stopped. Past, present, and future had merged, the drums beat on, and his temples, like a frantic pulse, pounded with the far-off sounds of victorious assaults and battles, triumphal processions, and with the beating of other drums, drums draped in black, no longer announcing *his* death but the death of another, a stranger. His youth notwithstanding (he looked more like a boy too tall for his age than like a mature young man), he had seen blood flow and come face-to-face with death, though never yet at such close range. And the very proximity of death, the sensation of it breathing on his bare neck, distorted the view of reality reaching his consciousness, just as for an astigmatic the proximity of an object serves only to make it appear more misshapen. All that mattered to him—because what his world valued most beside an honorable life was an honorable death—was to preserve the dignity required of a, *and here my father's name followed,* at such a moment. He had spent the night awake, but with his eyes shut and without so much as a sigh, so that the guard, whose eye was glued to the peephole, might testify that the condemned man had slept soundly, as if he were going to the altar rather than to his death. And, in a strange inversion of time, he could *already* hear the guard telling the others in the officers' club, Gentlemen, the young, *and here my father's name followed,* slept quite soundly that night, without so much as a sigh, as if going to his wedding rather than to his hanging. I give you my word as an officer! Gentlemen, let us render him his due! After which was heard—he heard—the crystal ping of glasses. Prosit! Prosit! This vision of his death, this struggle ending in victory, bolstered my father's courage the entire morning. He maintained his composure through prayer, he steeled his manhood by recourse to family legend. Thus it was that when, in accordance with compassionate protocol, he was vouchsafed a last request, he did not ask for a glass of water, though his insides were on fire; he asked for a cigarette, like an ancestor who had once, long before, requested a pinch of tobacco, which he had then chewed and spit in the face of his executioner. The officer clicked his heels and offered him his silver cigarette case. (Gentlemen, I give you my word as an officer. His hand did not tremble any more than mine trembles now as I hold this glass. Prosit! Prosit!) In the rays of the early-morning sun, which cut diagonally across the cell as across the cells of saints in old paintings, the cigarette smoke rose purple like the dawn. My father sensed that the smoke, a resplendent illusion, had momentarily sapped his strength, broken him, as if he had heard the sound of a flageolet pouring out over the Great Plains, and he quickly tossed the cigarette to the floor and crushed it with a spurless Hussar boot. Gentlemen, I am ready. Chosen for its military starkness, as brief as a command, as bare as an unsheathed saber, and as cold, the phrase was meant to be pronounced like a password, without emotion, as one says, Good night, gentlemen! at the end of a drinking bout. But now he felt it did not sound at all worthy of history. His voice was pure and sonorous, the syllables distinct, the sentence straightforward but a bit flaccid and cracked somehow. Since the day his mother visited him he had realized that despite a wild hope, wild and secret, his life was henceforth no more than a tragic farce written by people nearly as powerful as gods. She had stood before him, stolid, strong, with a veil over her face, filling the cell with her being, her person, her character, her large plumed hat, and her skirts, which swished though she made not

the slightest movement. She refused the simple prison stool pro-
ferred by the uhlans, who thereby accorded her an honor they
had surely never accorded anyone else there; she pretended not to
notice them placing the simple wooded seat, appallingly simple
beside her silk flounces, next to her. She thus remained standing
throughout her visit. She spoke French with Father, so as to rattle
the Hussar officer stationed off to one side at an appropriate distance, his unsheathed sword by his side, in what was more an
honor guard's salute to the aristocrat (whose nobility was as ancient as that of the Emperor himself) than a precaution or threat to
the proud visitor to the imperial catacombs. I shall throw myself at
his feet, my grandmother whispered. I am ready to die, Mother,
my father said. Grandmother cut him off with a stern, perhaps too
stern, *Mon fils, reprenez courage!* Then for the first time she turned
her head slightly in the direction of the guard. Her voice, still no
more than a whisper, fused with the whisper of her flounces. I
shall be standing on the balcony, she said, all but inaudibly. If I am
in white, it means that I have succeeded in . . . No, Mother, you
will be in black, I fear . . . The drums began to roll again, and this
startled my father from his reveries, nearer now, it seemed, and he
realized, from the sudden animation of a scene which had
theretofore stood immobile before him in a kind of mute permanence, that the reading of the sentence was over: the officer rolled
up the scroll; the priest leaned over him and blessed him with the
sign of the cross; the guards took hold of his arms. He did not allow the two uhlans to lift him, but rose lightly to his feet, barely
supported by them. Then, even before he had crossed the threshold of the cell, he experienced a sudden feeling of certainty—appearing first in his breast, then suffusing his entire body—that it
would all end as the logic of life demanded. Because everything
was now arrayed against death, everything in the nightmare stood
on the side of life: his youth, his origins, his family's eminence, his
mother's love, the Emperor's mercy, and the very sun streaming

down on him as he stepped into the carriage, his arms bound behind his back as if he were a common thief. But that lasted only for a moment, only until the carriage reached the boulevard, where a boisterous mob, gathered from all over the Empire, stood waiting for him. Through the intermittent drumrolls he heard the buzz of the crowd, its threatening murmur; he saw fists raised in hate. The crowd was cheering imperial justice, because the mob always cheers the victor. That realization crushed my father's spirit. His head sank a bit on his chest, his shoulders drew slightly together as if warding off blows (a stone or two was hurled at him), his back bent a little more. But the difference was enough for the rabble to sense that his courage had left him and his pride was shattered; it elicited cheers of something akin to jubilation. (Because the mob loves to see the proud and the brave brought low.) When he came to the head of the boulevard, where the residences of the nobility began and the crowd thinned out a bit, he raised his eyes. In the light of the morning sun he glimpsed a blinding white spot on the balcony. Leaning over the railing, all in white, stood Grandmother, and behind her—as if to enhance the lily-white brilliance of her dress—the enormous dark green leaves of a philodendron. (My father knew that dress well: it was an heirloom; one of his ancestors had worn it to an imperial wedding.) Immediately, almost insolently, my father straightened up, wishing to make clear to the threatening mob that a *(here my father's name followed)* could not die like that, he can't be hanged like a common thief. And thus he stood beneath the gallows. Even as the hangman removed the stool from under his feet, he awaited the miracle. Then his body twisted at the end of the rope and his eyes bulged out of their sockets, as if he had just seen something awful and terrifying. I stood only a few paces away from him, gentlemen, the Hussar with the bushy mustache told his fellow officers in the officers' dining hall. When the rope went down over his neck, he watched the hangman's hands as calmly as if they were

27

tying a brocade scarf for him . . . I give you my word as an officer, gentlemen! Two assumptions present themselves. Either my father died a brave and noble death, fully conscious of the certainty thereof, his head held high, or the whole thing was merely a cleverly planned puppet show whose strings ran together in the hands of a proud mother. The first, heroic, version was upheld and promulgated—orally, and then in writing, in their chronicles—by the *sans-culottes* and Jacobins; the second, according to which my father hoped to the very end for some magical sleight of hand, was recorded by the official historians of the powerful Habsburg dynasty to prevent the birth of a legend. History belongs to the victors, legends to the people, fantasy to literature. Only death is certain.

25. During the fights against the Habsburgs, Ferenc Rákóczi went to get help. While he was away, he entrusted my father, whom he considered a faithful follower and a steadfast friend, with the command of the troops. (Later in his disappointment, Rákóczi wrote: My soul weeps, my heart is heavy with pain and sorrow . . . that he whose honor and reputation we ourselves spread abroad, whose sins we kept hidden, and whose credit with the people we encouraged, he whom we took into our utmost confidence, opening our heart and soul to him . . . should now endanger our true and legitimate cause.) For his part, my father came to an understanding with János Pálffy, the emissary of the Viennese Court. He agreed to the imperial peace conditions, and made arrangements for the anti-Habsburg Kuruc army under his command to lay down its arms. He gathered the Kuruc cavalry, over ten thousand men, and had them line up in a long row just outside of Majtény. When General Pálffy arrived, he surveyed the infantry brigade. When he gave the signal, the 149 standard-bearers formed a circle, and my father and his officers swore allegiance to the Emperor in the middle of the circle. My father swore the fol-

lowing: I, *here my father's name followed,* swear by Almighty God, Creator of heaven and the earth, since our merciful lord His Majesty, Emperor and crowned King did fully pardon us and left us all our chattels, that I shall from here on henceforth be His Majesty's most loyal subject to my dying breath. The other officers also took the oath, and when they finished, my father delivered a fine speech, thanking the King His Majesty for the amnesty and the pardon, and General János Pálffy for his mediation. János Pálffy also delivered a speech, and with that, the work of treachery was complete. People say that my father betrayed Rákóczi because he wanted to get his hands on Rákóczi's fortune. Balderdash. (Later he did get his hands on it, but that's not why.) He was inspired by revenge because Rákóczi had assaulted his vanity. Once they were in company somewhere, Indian cooking school, and the conversation turned to what it means to be brave. My father said a brave man is one who does not think about the outcome of the battle but charges at the enemy and fights to the death. A brave man does not abscond but lays down his life on the field of battle. The gentlemen in attendance cheered and the accolade was much to my father's liking. But then the prince spoke up. The bravest is he who thinks before the battle. (He who thinks is the bravest.) He thinks about the orphans, the widows' tears, the ransacked villages. He learns his enemy's weaknesses and considers them and goes into the fray only afterward, and wins with as few casualties as possible. There was nothing to be said to this, and not only because these words were spoken by Prince Rákóczi, but because they were true. We do not value other people's truth when it stands in opposition to our falsehood. My father never forgave Rákóczi for teaching him a lesson in this way in front of illustrious gentlemen in illustrious company, and so he took revenge.

26. After Rákóczi had gone into hiding and Károlyi had laid down his arms, my father and his men refused to believe that freedom

was dead. They'd gotten used to it, or whatnot. A mistake. They waited and waited for Rákóczi and Bercsényi to liberate them. But neither came. Instead, General Pálffy (who'd seen to the work of betrayal with Károlyi) came, and immediately began negotiations with my father and his men. They had no choice. They agreed to join the imperial army and wear the Hussar uniforms with the yellow frogging, and place the tall, wide shako hats on their heads. My father had a change of uniforms, but not of heart, which that traitor Pálffy was soon to learn firsthand. This happened when he presented the new cavalrymen to the Chief of Staff. A whole slew of German soldiers were keeping watch over my father and his men when the Chief of Staff, accompanied by Pálffy, rode past them to review the troops. But the Chief of Staff was so used to the clean-shaven German faces that he couldn't abide the large-mustachioed Kuruc men. He halted in front of them and began upbraiding them. He reviled and abused them for a long time, while they (my father and his men) listened. You deserve to have your heads chopped off!, he screamed, at which my father twirled his long drooping mustache, unable to keep his peace. Tell us, he said, if you were ta chop off our heads, where would ya put 'em crazy Labanc shakos, foolish German that you are! These words made Count Pálffy smile, because he still had something of the Hungarian in him, too, and acting as an unsolicited interpreter, he spoke thus: This brave warrior says that they're real sorry for having turned against the Emperor. At which what was the Chief of Staff to do? He nodded in agreement.

27. My father refused to have himself cloned. He simply would not hear of it. He hollered at the clone master, too, and did his best to pillory the whole idea at Court. He threw the full weight of his authority and influence, which was considerable, into the fray. But then, things turned out differently all the same.

•   •   •

30

28. The God of the Magyars smiled down on them. Prince Rákóczi graciously offered the Emperor a peace deal, and entrusted the delicate negotiations to my father, saying that he had a way with words. What can one say? Our Lady of Hungary, help us, even if they're not my own. He was brought up multilingual, German mam'selle, French mam'selle, English mam'selle, (Hungarian mam'selle, ha-ha!), while Italian is something you know as a matter of course, which makes learning Spanish a cinch, and Portuguese practically inevitable. He did not think that being Hungarian posed a particular challenge to learning foreign languages, or that an Indo-European does not gouge out the eyes of another Indo-European. On the other hand, he'd always say that he never learned them. (Meaning that he did not have to learn them, as he knew them.) For instance, he didn't know the difference between weak and strong conjugation, he couldn't have explained it or defined it, he could only conjugate. He never even took a state exam. (What for? During the 1950s, half of the nobility included in the *Gotha Almanac* worked for the State Translation and Authentication Office under pseudonyms and thus, by definition, a language certificate would have been of precious little use to them. Knowing a language sufficed.) He had an unpleasant way of correcting people. He corrected Hungarians, too. Squeamishly, it was said. Also patronizingly, as if from the peak of knowledge to the desolate valley of ignorance. Also, he made faces. Which is not true. Just the opposite. He trembled with fear. The thought that so-called bad sentences might be left lying around uncorrected horrified him, and he swooped down on the offender. My mother would often jump up weeping, seeking and finding shelter in the nearby furze thicket, because even in company, my father kept correcting her French, not *la, le, le* saucisson, *die* Wurst, surely, that's what confused you, dear. (At the time, half the country was hiding in the furze thickets, while the other half was in hot pursuit, and the third half—this is how the mathematics worked

out—was living in harsh captivity.) No doubt, my mother said retching, making for the thicket. Mortifying, she sobbed. My father blinked as innocent as a newborn, looking about him as if for help: at the Spanish ambassador, at the Prussian ambassador, at the Vatican's ambassador. (Rumor had it that his name had come up for the Vatican post, but was dropped, regretfully, due to a "in all probability presumable concubinic attachment," which constituted a formal and thus a very real stumbling block.) Also, she never knows when she should be using the subjunctive, my father explained to the ambassadors, never, whimpering, his glance full of disappointment, as if it were they and not my mother who'd spoiled his little game. *The false friends,* he shouted in English, the false friends! In Dutch, *bellen* does not mean to bellow but to ring the bell, still, who could suppress a smile upon seeing the sign at the veterinarian in Amsterdam, 3 × *bellen,* and he let out a long, plaintive, acrimonious—and need we add—grade A bellow. My father negotiated through mediators, and the English and Dutch ambassadors had taken the task upon themselves. The Dutch ambassador felt that under the circumstances, the anti-Habsburg Kuruc rebels were making far too many demands. He started bargaining with my father. Except, my father was a vehement and straightforward diplomat—for fifty fillérs he'd eat a fly, for one forint you could take a picture of the cadaver on his tongue. For five forints and an apple (Starking), he'd bite a mouse in two. He never worked with outsourced mice, he liked to catch his own—and when he saw what the Dutchman was up to (bargaining), he said disdainfully, We will not haggle any further, sir, it's freedom not cheese we want, whereupon the Dutch ambassador, who was not ashamed of their trade in cheese, which brought wealth to his nation, answered my belligerent father thus: If it's freedom you want, you shouldn't give your soldiers worthless copper coins, but cut all those gold and silver buttons off your *mente* jackets, forge them into currency, and pay the soldiers with that, so they'll fight with more vigor and courage! ("To go Dutch." This means that each man pays his own way.) My father, on the other hand, dressed with an opulence that put crowned heads of state to shame. He was famous for this throughout the continent. *Sehr nobel und ein Grandseigneur,* Count Starhemberg wrote in his diary, though he described his features as lacking in expression, his intellect as average, if well founded, a man who is educated and speaks languages, yet is sparing with his words. Nothing came of the lead buttons. Facing history's tribunal, my father said that he understands the problem. It is indeed a sin, he said, to do less than one can or to jeopardize the common weal. Still, he can't be the only one wearing lead buttons, it'd make no sense, because lead buttons are symbolic, unlike diamond buttons, which he can wear as an *individual,* because a diamond is concrete. The idea that one single solitary plebeian is not a definable category, while a wily, good-for-nothing solitary aristocrat is won't hold water, my father is dead wrong if he thinks that poverty is symbolic, while wealth is concrete. My father blinked as innocent as a newborn and looked around, as if for help. I'm so subtle, he chuckled. Not always, history's tribunal replied. No, not always so subtle.

29. On Good Friday, on the road to Szombat, he (my father) is admiring the tread of angels.

30. On the road to Szombat, on Saturday, my father was accosted by a young thing who said she'd like to give him a blow job. My father was forty-something, closer to fifty; back then, he was considered an old man. He'd never really mastered Hungarian. He knew it, but his knowledge was like a blind man's who finds his way around in the world he knows nothing about; an all-knowing not-knowing. My father threw the young thing a bemused look who, after she's said this sentence, stood in front of him silent and pugnacious. You know, I never really mastered Hungarian, he

said to the girl kindly, I know it well, but I'm like a blind man who finds his way around in a world he knows nothing about. An all-knowing not-knowing, he laughed. To give someone a blow job, that's oral gratification, is it not? The girl waited without batting an eye. Come, my father said graciously, let's go, I'm busy. (He was always busy.) Maybe our ways coincide. For a while they walked in silence, the girl swinging her school bag by her side. Did she accost him on a bet, my father asked. Or for lack of money? Or the novena? Or is she sad? Or on the contrary, happy? Because she's happy? I wanted to hear your opinion, the girl said unexpectedly. Is that so? my father said disappointed, and all the time, here I was thinking you wanted to give me a blow job. ( . . . ) You talk too much. Now I don't know *what* I want. I see, my father said with a nod, in that case, thank you for the pleasant chat. And this is how my father met my mother and my mother my father.

31. My father was a great warrior, an eminent commander, who had no peer in a duel or warfare. (No peer in warfare, et cetera, I know! My mother.) Prince Rákóczi had a great affection for him, as once he had slaughtered forty-two of the enemy in front of his very eyes. When the Prince was told that my father was planning to betray him, he refused to believe it. But he had to, because it was my mother who had denounced him, after he'd told her about his plan. My father ended up in front of a military tribunal, and the tribunal sentenced him to death for high treason. My mother didn't shed a tear. Unlike the Prince, she'd stopped loving my father, practically instantaneously. In retrospect, she couldn't understand how she could have had anything to do with him. It was something she didn't even like to think about. (Everything she had once loved about my father she now saw in a new light. My father became an embarrassment. His hips were too wide, and he swayed them like a hussy. His lips too thick, and his thinking

obtuse. His backside flat, his breath sour. The quick thinking just clever. The astute assessment of a situation selfish jockeying for position. The many-sidedness capriciousness. The tartness of the rare and expensive perfumes a cesspool. His love of joking around buffoonery. His refined sense of humor cheap joking. His kindness fawning. His severity rude, his high spirits childish and inane, his low spirits surly, his lively glance vulgar, and so on and so forth, anything, everything. For instance, from time to time, my father spoke as if he were not of this world, a bit blunt, a bit lacking in humor, a bit passé—admirably, my mother had said with admiration. Beautifully. Like the angels. Now these same virtues sounded sanctimonious to her ears. As my mother tells it, when they ran into each other at the Nagyszombat fair, my father crept about among the tents and wagons for some time, deliberately not noticing her. Then he leapt out at her, pulling a book from his knapsack, but the corners of his lips drooped from hatred all the while, so that my mother, according to my mother, refused to listen. Before the betrayal, the selfsame lips seemed to her rosy and highly kissable.) But what she found really unpleasant, even irksome, was not this, but his sentences. My father had said so many beautiful things to my mother, and now my mother was bereft of these, in retrospect one might say, along with her own timorous responses. There came to be holes in my life, my mother said. What I'm saying is that I loved your father in earnest, and now I do not love him in earnest. The condemned cell was at Sárospatak, that's where they took my father before his execution. They asked him what his last wish might be. He asked for a mirror. His former friends asked, What do you need a mirror for? (A quicksilver scheme.) I want to see if I'm still as brave as when I was brave. Then he asked the officers to listen to his farewell poem, then they left him alone. Then Someone wrestled with him until the break of dawn. But he saw that he could not prevail against Him, and he touched the hollow of his thigh, and the

35

hollow of his thigh was out of joint as he wrestled with Him. The poem went as follows: *I must go, I must die, / My life is at an end. / I am guilty, death draws near, / No more mercy for me / I fear.* Indeed, there was none. The next day the executioner finished with him, i.e., he blinded him so that he should never be able to look in the mirror again and see that brave man. The executioner didn't reckon that from then on, my father would also have had to see a coward. May eternal darkness be your guiding light, said the executioner in accordance with the regulations. His voice was respectful. My father soon learned to get his bearings in the eternal darkness. His honor was gone, even the thieves spit on him. He had nothing left, neither a home, nor a country (homeland), neither a family, no *Sohn*, no *Vaterland*. Suddenly he had nothing, not even someone to remind him of everything. This too was so baroque in him, this oscillation between nothing and everything, earth and sky (the earth being everything, the sky nothing). The baroque as the absolute void: my father. Why is it that he is so difficult to get close to, more than classical art, and is at a much greater remove than the Middle Ages, which is far more removed in time, or even contemporary art, abstract as it may be? Why is this? Could it be because the ideological content of the baroque is no longer valid? Or because during the fashion for the neo-baroque they imitated the original model with so much fervor that we are wont to reject it? The feudal way of life came back to haunt them; they would have liked to live in palaces, to live with great refinement and ease, beautifully, comfortably, like the nobility of the French Court at one time, and reflect upon the lost estates of their ancestors and their undying virtues, if indeed they had any. But affectation and dreams have no place within the framework of reality. Throughout the world, the liveried servant and the palace were replaced by homes with utilities, the mechanized home, and the reality of the unions. Where is—and where was—Maria Theresa's visit to Kismarton by then? From pardonable vanity, my father wished to greet his Empress with full royal pomp. The palace was enlarged with a huge hall (everything), but even before she arrived, the entire wing burned to the ground (nothing). At this, my father quickly ordered a small palace to be erected for Her Majesty in the park—the garden parties were held in this gorgeous little palace. Maria Theresa asked how much it cost. Eighty thousand forints. *O, das ist für einen Fürsten, and here my father's name followed, eine Bagatelle!* (Oh, for a, *here my father's name followed,* prince it is bagatelle!), the Empress smiled. And in no time at all, there it stood, in gleaming gold letters, on the gate of the palace, *Bagatelle,* and from then on this is how the magnificent residence was called. Like a stray dog my father wandered around his estates, i.e., himself, going from castle to castle, from palace to palace, Frakno, Kismarton, Lánzsér, Lakompak, Léka, Keresztúr, Szarvkő, Feketevár, Csobánc and Hegyesd, Köpecsény, Simontornya, Kapos, Ozora, Tamási, Koppány, Alsólendva, Nempti, Léva, Szádvár, Végles, Tata, Árva, Létava, Kabolt, Kapuvár, whose estimated value came to 2,780,000 gold forints. For a hundred forints you could buy a decent house in town. My father had the church of Nagyszombat built for the Jesus Society for thirty thousand forints, while the yearly taxes of the burghers of Nagyszombat came to eleven hundred forints. In short, my father tumbled from the earth to the sky, and as he went from everything to nothing, he asked if he could jump on a wagon that was just heading for Kismarton. At this, a gray-haired wise man asked to be heard, and he voiced the opinion that the unfortunate man my father should sit down, because even though the distance is short, anything might happen. The people nodded in agreement. My father's face was partly covered by a mask, because the two wounds where his eyes had been were hideous to behold. It was my mother who told him before she left him. Hideous, believe me, just this once, at least, believe something I say, simply hideous, she said, and left. The people on the wagon reflected

upon the vicissitudes of life, the hopelessness of existence, the vagaries of fortune. Since they had compared the infinite to the
eleven hundred, they suddenly had an oppressive, nightmarish
feeling, but naturally, they couldn't have possibly imagined the
blind man's former life. No wonder. The difference is infinite. At
this juncture, my father fixed the mask on his face and said, Why?
What can happen? Only the rattling of the wagon could be heard.
The snow will melt, and spring will come. This was on February
13, after noon, at three-sixteen p.m., that's when my father said
that it will melt, and it will come.

*     *     *     *     *

32. The inventory of my father's belongings, written in Hungarian on five folios sewn together with red silk cord and the ends of said cords sealed with black ring seals. Cista prima ex Hebano: Pendant set with 114 bulky and minikin diamonds and an Anchora with a crucifix with two wings and two hands. Another pendant set with 25 rubies, 9 diamonds and 3 pearls, with Justice in the middle. Item: a Cupid pendant set with 4 bulky and 22 minikin rubies and 14 minikin diamonds therein, one emerald and 17 seed pearls. Item: a small bird pendant, chipped, with 4 × 4 minikin rubies set therein, a colorless chipped sapphire in its heart and a small emerald in its tail. Item: a large anthropomorphic pendant with the likeness of Adam and Eve with three rubies set therein, one brilliant-diamond and sapphire and one pearl being therein. Item: an agraffe, half of which be in the shape of a feather, the bottom be in that of a rose, set with 47 bulky and minikin diamonds and 3 pearls pendant from it. Item: an old and cracked coronet set with 9 rosets [sic!], seven set with two minikin rubies and three pearls each therein, but the upper part of two being chipped, one pearl and one ruby there be missing therein and also of the 7 rosettes also one be missing a minikin ruby on top. Spanish bodice ornament of gold and emeralds (flat-cut, 13 in all) and diamonds, enamelled flowers and stylized insects set on springs.

Amatory locket of enamelled gold, glass, mother-of-pearl and seed pearls depicting a pair of doves drinking at a fountain, inscribed "L'Amour et l'Amitié." Another amatory locket of enamelled gold, glass, mother-of-pearl and seed pearls set with a miniature of a woman with a dove and a crane, converted from a bracelet clasp. Item: an old figural crucifix from large, common stones, also seven pearls, set in gold. Item: a stomacher brooch of brilliant-cut diamonds and pearls set in silver-gilt, in two parts. Item: a hair-pin of gold, on it a pendant with a bulky Hungarian diamond and a pendant on it also with a minikin diamond of high quality. Another hair-pin, cangaroo [?] shaped, with a large uncut sapphire pendant from it and a minikin cabochon ruby and on it two tiny uncut rubies. Item: a third small hair-pin with a brilliant-cut diamond at the end; next to said pin, on a narrow flesh-colored ribband, 5 small pendants with 5 large table-cut diamonds and a large pearl bead also on it. One pair of bangles for the arm with 88 pearls and 6 beagle [bugle?] -shaped rosettes worked therein, each with 3 rubies at either end being set therein, also two rosettes each adorned with five rubies and at the other two ends clasps. One pair of ear-ornaments with heart-shaped pendants with twenty-two minikin diamonds in each and in the middle also there be a pearl in each. Item: an ear-ornament set with 8 minikin brilliant-cut diamonds therein and a pearl pendant from it. Item: a cross-shaped agraffe of gold set with a green stone in the middle therein and also a set pearl pendant from it. Item: wreath tiara with hinged sections of enamelled gold set with a paste cameo, 22 diamonds, also pearls and emeralds. Item: chatelaine of pinchbeck with scissors case flanked by a needle case, an étui and two thimble cases therein. Item: necklace of 8 colorful pietra dura panels connected by delicate golden chains. Item: yet another necklace with 41 gold rosettes enamelled in black with 2 × 2 small-size brilliant-cut diamonds each in 6 and in the twenty-first 2 × 2 pearls, but of the diamonds two be missing therein. In a small frayed black velvet box 13 rings for the fingers, of which 4 are seal-rings, the fifth set with a heart-shaped rough-cut ruby therein, the sixth and seventh with a small brilliant-cut diamond set therein, the eighth be set with a small lattice-shaped enamelled and a small purple-blue stone, the ninth be adorned with a moose [elk] claw. The tenth finger-ring is enamelled in white and green with a monogram, sans stones. The twelfth finger-ring has a white enamelled crucifix therein. The thirteenth is a silver finger ring set with an unlevelled rough stone therein. Item: in another small marcescent black box of velvet 11 finger-rings, five Giardinetti rings of gold set with small brilliant-cut diamonds, rubies, emeralds, amethysts and pastes in silver collets, the sixth in the shape of a serpent with a minikin diamond set therein; two are set with turquoise all around, again another has a minikin diamond therein, another a minikin ruby; the last is adorned with brass and glass therein. Item: in a third black velvet box there be 23 finger-rings of gold, one in the shape of a rose inlaid with a large square table-cut diamond, and a pyramid encircled by ten minikin table-cut diamonds. Another finger-ring is in the shape of a star with 7 large brilliant-cut diamonds and 19 table-cut diamonds. The third is set with a handsome uncut ruby. The fourth is set with a faceted ruby. The fifth is in the shape of a rose with 7 minikin turquoise stones therein. The sixth is enamelled in white and black and set with a diamond of little luster. The seventh is in the shape of a rose set with 5 small-faceted rubies and 4 small rubies. The eighth is enamelled in black set with a handsome flat-cut diamond. The ninth is enamelled in black with a faceted sapphire. The tenth is an enamelled finger-ring in the shape of a heart with a large heart-shaped diamond set in the middle and 14 small rubies. The eleventh is a finger-ring in the shape of a cross set with seven large diamonds. The twelfth is an old Spanish finger-ring wrought in the shape of a cross set with seven large diamonds. The thirteenth is an old Spanish finger-ring wrought in the shape of an ostrich feather set with 19 table-cut emeralds therein. The sixteenth[1] is set with a large cabochon emerald. The seventeenth is an old Spanish-type finger-ring with 13 faceted rubies therein.[2] The nineteenth has 19 diamonds encircling it. The twentieth is an old Spanish finger-ring set with 9 turquoise stones therein. The twenty-first is set with a large square diamond in the middle and 8 diamonds of lesser size below. The twenty-second is a carved memento mori ring of gold. The twenty-third is a finger-ring of gold, no stones, enamelled in green. There is also in the same box an old ring of silver, gilt with gold, Turkish, set with a large red stone. Item, ibidem: a hair-pin wrought in the shape of a serpent with 3 minikin diamonds. Pyrite, ungarite, rose quartz, lapis lazuli, achate!, jade! Item: an old parure of rosettes and stones with 19 rosettes therein, the middle being adorned with a diamond, and four set with a ruby each, another four with an emerald each, and a large pearl adorning each of the remaining ten. Item: another old parure of rosettes with 8 rosettes, four with a diamond set therein, the other four with a ruby set therein, with four seed pearls also in each rosette, and also 9 large, round pearls. Item: a third old parure with gold rosettes with 7 large rosettes set with a ruby and two pearls each. Item: a fourth parure with 14 small rosettes with rubies and again 13 small pearl rosettes and around it 270 manoken [sic!] pearls. Remarkably, they actually took the trouble to count them! In the fifth head-dress there be 14 large gold rosettes set with a small ruby each therein and also 36 pearls interspersed therein. The sixth head-dress has 22 thin gold rosettes, low and worn with a small ruby each with 36 pearls interspersed therein, but four rubies be missing therein; item: among them 46 pearls, minikin. On the seventh green and white silken ribbon head-dress there be 12 golden rosettes, the middle

[1] The description of the fourteenth and fifteenth is missing.
[2] The eighteenth is not mentioned.

one being enamelled in white, wrought in the shape of a heart; each with 9 rubies; interspersed among them, 26 small pearls. The eighth is a much-worn ribband head-dress, on it 14 rosettes with enamel and gold, no stones, interspersed with 36 pearls therein. The ninth is a much-worn head-dress, red and flesh-colored, with 7 gold rosettes of various shapes, the ribband adorned with pearls, two with Bohemian diamonds. The tenth is a Spartan diadem of diamonds, the top band containing 2 × 16 pear-shaped diamonds, the lower 2 × 18 multi-faceted briolettes with a central pink diamond. Item: a small necklace of pearls in which there be 652 medium-size Oriental pearls and in between 500 seed pearls. Item: a hair-ribbon on a green ribband of tiny corals with stones and pearls. Item: a necklace with eye-shaped corals for the neck with a black pearl. Item: a coral necklace with 234 eyes therein. In a black velvet box a handsome necklace with a large pendant adorned with two large diamonds, 18 minikin diamonds, 7 large table-cut rubies, and also 8 minikin rubies. In this necklace also there be 18 big gold rosettes in the lap of which there be one large and four small diamonds each; item: four minikin rubies each; also 4 rosettes with rubies, in the middle of each one ruby encircled by 4 smaller rubies; item: four small diamonds each; 9 more rosettes with five big pearls and four minikin rubies in each, though one pearl bead be missing thereof. Item: a large gold chain, heavy. Item: 3 beaded materials, 14 skeins in toto. Item: 4 skeins and one half-skein thin cloth. Item: two pcs. old fur with beads shaped like lace, appr. one skein. Item: 20 battered gold rosettes on cardboard, each set in the middle with a ruby and also adorned with two pearls therein. Item: various gold fragments in a small box carved of ivory. *Monthly tram ticket with a photograph in an aluminum frame.* Item: in another small white and motley-black box, a pair of sapphire ear-rings. Item: a pair of ear-ornaments, pearl set in gold, 4 sapphires, 3 minikin diamonds and a small table-cut ruby. Item: bodice ornament in the cosse-de-pois style, of enamelled gold and diamonds, fragile, in a small ivory box. Item: 12 gold buttons, enamelled, one missing an emerald from the middle. Item: 12 smaller gold buttons, enamelled, black, set with a small ruby each. Item: another 23 buttons, shaped in the round and set with blue jasper-ware plaques, except for two. Item: a thin necklace, on it 42 rosettes sewn onto a blue ribbon band. In a black case a jasper goblet encased in gold. Item: in two elephant boxes, two small gilt locks and and old seal-ring. Item: in a round silver box a French reliquary pendant portraying St. Catherine of Alexandria, of silver-gilt and basse-taille enamel. Item: in another small silver box, a French reliquary pendant made from an Islamic rock crystal flask shaped like a fish, with silver-gilt mounts. Item: in a small silver case in the shape of a book an arm band made of deer claws. Item: a small long-shaped box, empty of its contents. Item: a gilt box empty of its contents. Item: a gold cup with enamelled decoration. Item: a silver basket with various silver fragments and some stones, for the neck of a child. Item: a gilt box, blue, empty of its contents. One and a half fauz-claws [sic!], a dragon's tongue, a piece from the heart of a moose, an eagle stone and nearly an entire big, Persian Bezoar stone. Item: in a small ivory box some gold and silver commemorative coins gifted at a coronation. Cista secunda nigra, a writing desk, vulgo Schreib-Tisch, on it a winter hat made in Copenhagen. Cista seu Schreib-Tisch tertia: in which there be especially silk threads of various colors for embroidery, some small silks for buttons, a handsome rosary with one large coral, also sundry other rosaries and two large Spanish crosses. In the same box, a rich-spun cloth wrought with silver and gold for a velum. Item: *a checked flannel shirt,* a colorful Turkish silk cloth for the table, stuff for the middle of five cotton coverlets and various pieces of lace. Cista quarta: a small black box cum instrumentis scriptorijs, in concreto, *a fountain pen wrapped round with Scotch tape.* But this be found in the tenth walnut box. Cista quinta: a small apothecary's box cum instrumentis suis, *a pair of eyeglasses, broken.* Cista sexta: an old credentialis box, red leather on the outside, gilt, inside lined in red velvet in which there be the following dishes, i.e., silver centerpiece dishes 30, plates 58, cups for fruit 28, six-sided bottles 4, two large, gold inside and zielgolt (Ziergold) on the outside. A blister-jug gilt inside and out. Item: *a Hermes Baby portable typewriter.* Item: a blister-bucket, gilt, with gold inside and out. 5 3 ½ dl. tumblers, inside washed with gold. A large blister-cup for drinking, gilt inside and out. 6 Ziergold candle sticks. 12 knives, 10 forks with silver handles washed in gold, also 12 silver spoons washed in gold. Three knives and two forks for Fürschneider. Two ash receptacles and accompanying silver candle stick. A bed warmer, a drier. A pan washed inside with gold. A cane-sugar shaker, 6 small Ziergold bowls for vinegar. A credentia cup. A dish for salt-boiled meat and two old plates in the lower case. Cista septima, continens res argenteas: Antal Losonczi's toilet set with bowl (Inv. No. 35), György Báthori's silver toilet set with bowl (Inv. No. 13), a rounded, oblong-shaped toilet set with bowl, pounded, richly gilt (Inv. No. 7/2), item: another similar wash-set with bowl (Inv. No. 63), a third similar set with bowl (Inv. No. 5/b), a smallish wash set with bowl, gilt, with 13 silver plates, silver with gilt edge and the Báthori coat-of-arms (Inv. No. 162). 14 tankards in pounded silver, richly gilt (Inv. No. 25), item: a richly gilt wash set with bowl of medium quality, in a black case, a square-shaped gilt clock for the table, Krasnaya Zhvezda. 9 blistered and round, richly gilt tankards, one unlided, richly gilt tankard, two richly gilt cups (Inv. No. 281), one silver ink well. One bottle. Two wolves; one horse; one gondola. Two cans, one frying pan (Inv. No.. 21/c). A round, old, blistered, large pitcher-shaped bottle with silver, gilt stand (Inv. No. 15). Item: a small white wash bowl with pitcher. Besides of which 3 ostrick [sic!] eggs; 3 nutmeg cups, one gállya [?], one bucket, two unworked crystals in cup casings. In the old box a cut-crystal pitcher, encased in gold. A cut-crystal cup, encased in gold. A conch with mother-of-pearl, one cup wrought in the shape of an ostrich. A silver pitcher wrought in the shape of a bottle for rose water. A silver teacup for under glass. A silver bed-warmer, white. A silver case for drinking. A small white ink well which was in the big ink well of poor Milord. 3 pendulum clocks for the table with cases. Item: 9 much-used and chipped center-piece serving plates. Item: an old serving plate. Two mechanical gilt watches for round the neck. Cista octava, 6 rich silvered hinplö [sic!], washed in gold. A sword with turquoise. A sword with a richly gilt sheath. *A tchaika with bullet hole.* Item: Hussar helmet of the kettle hat type with breastplate, Hussar cuirass, crawfish. Item: lobster-tailed helmet, cuirass, protection for the bridle arm and buff coat. Item: a hanchar broad sword with gold, uncut rubies and turquoise. Item: two more Turkish hanchar with silver sheaths and white bone handles. Item: a hunting case with one big wide, 3 medium and 3 small knives with silver sheaths; the sheath is also set with silver. Two flag harnesses, one of which was won from the Bosnian pasha Ibrahim Sokolovich. One silver bridle washed in gold, attached to a red silken belt. A curb, silver, washed with gold and ornamented with turquoise on a belt woven of gold silk thread, beautifully ornate, with breast-strap. One pair of handguns with black handles, with spun-gold and silver case. One aigrette. A tassel for horse-gear sewn with pure spun-gold. Another tassel for horse-gear worked with spun-gold, gold and silver. A third tassel for horse-gear wrought with red satin, spun-gold and silk, also 3 flowers. A crimson bit encased in silver and a number of turnquois [sic!] stones. A crimson bit superimposed in silver and a number of turquoise stones. The common sword of Milord, my poor Father, encased in a black velvet sheath, silver with gold wash. Item: a shark skin sheathed, silver-gilt sharp poignard worn round the neck, with black taffeta.[3] Item: besides the boxes there

---

[3] On the margin to this item, in the hand of the chief signee of authentication of the inventory stands: "Milord László doth gift it to Milord Palatine Pál Pálffy."

be in this repository a black silvery Hebanum altar with the birth of Christ in the middle, also ducats in their cases.[4] In the inner repository, cista nona, there be: a table cloth, for one table, 19. Item: Jewish table cloth, 4. Item: sets of three cloths for the table, 4. Item: long kerchief for under a table cloth, 10. Simple *kucsma* cap, brown (fur). Serviettes for the table, six and a half ducet. Two white, embroidered hand-kerchiefs. Three reticulated hand-kerchiefs. 4 fancy embroidered hand-kerchiefs. 3 lace and one peasant hand-kerchiefs. 3 pairs lace and knitted sheets. One pair white embroidered sheets. One pair fancy-bordered sheets. One Italian-embroidered sheet. One pair of sheets wrought in gold, with Polish embroidery. One long pillowcase with Polish embroidery. A third, long pillow case embroidered after folk motifs. One Turkish pillow case with black print. 20 aprons for cooks. Two under-table-cloths with yellow fringe for a long table. 3 pieces fringed superlat. Two Turkish hand-kerchiefs, fine white linen, with gold fringe. 8 skeins fine white Turkish linen cloth. A stitched pattern for a sheet, half with gold thread. 6 patterned face-cloths and two serviettes. A superlat wreath lined with green taffeta, wrought with gold Turkish embroidery. One white embroidery for a sheet. One red linen cloth pinned with pearls and lined with green velvet Stuczen. A skirt with a long train, richly shot in gold, royal blue, white silver flowered, with fur and pearls of medium size, 4 rows up front and two rows in the back. Another long-trained skirt shot with silver and adorned with gold flowers, on it 33 large rosettes, a diamond and two pearls being set in each. A small *suba* coat of black velvet whose collar is bedecked of pearls, with one set of pearl adornments on the front and 3 sets and 3 fingers' wide on the bottom. A high fur cap, Polish, adorned with large pearls and 5 rosettes with a ruby in three of the five, it having fallen out of the other two; two vertigals, old, torn.

---

[4] Or: *deux chats*, illegible.

One white, heavily stitched, flesh-colored feather cover lined with double taffeta which had belonged to King István Báthory. Another feather coverlet, Turkish, with golden flowers, red linen, lined with green taffeta. Cista decima, there be within table covers with fur and blue silk. Item: *a packet of unopened Munkás cigarettes.* Leg warmer for a coach, black damask with flowers and gold fringe, of 12 pieces. A set of pillows for a coach made of black velvet, of 8 pieces, gold-fringed. A small apothecary's case, of walnut, lined in red velvet, with tools of silver, some partially gilt. A feather cover of linen, light gray with golden flowers. 5 Schreib-Tisch. One Turkish chest. One iron-girded chest. One small case, with silver mounting at the four corners, and a small ink well. A mirror adorned with silver and gold flowers. Item: 4 small black cases, empty of content. Item: one Italian umbrella, small. Cista undecima. A walnut storage chest with therein ex lapide serpentino 10 cups, 9 plates, 10 serving plates, *paper clip.* Cista duodecima. In a simple pine chest, painted, 13 chalices, three of which be wrought of pure gold inside and out, cum patellis; seven are gold inside, outside gold only in spots, cum patellis, three of which patellae are only white silver and two of the chalices also only white silver and one of copper shot with gold inside and out, with silver-gilt patella; and one is without patella. Item: wafer-holder, silver, three guilt, inside and out, with case; the fourth is gilt inside only, outside it is white, with case. The fifth is beaten, gilt inside and also the circumference. Item: three pieces for the altar ornamented with pearls, two Agnus DEI, the third differently shaped, with pearls, in a box; garnets on two. Item: a gold pendant weighing half a shekel, two arm bands weighing 10 gold shekels (Moses). Item: an old head-dress mixtim shot with gold on threadbare black velvet; the bottom is black broad-cloth. Item: a mottled black-yellow mottled [sic!] lined in white. Item: a reticulated antipendium for the altar, its inside areas red taffeta. Item: a chasuble of red linen with stole. Item: 15 kerchiefs for the altar, ten of which are of silk and some have ornate gold-embroidered flowers, gold reticulation, the rest with peasant reticulation. Item: two cherry-colored aprons of taffeta, one entirely of gold lace, the other linen. Item: 3 damask table cloths and one long kerchief. Item: table cloth for the altar sewn in silk, with gold, reticulated lace. Item: one long table cloth of cambric, combined with knit. Cista decima tertia. Leather chest for the back of a coach. Within it: one infantry banner, red and yellow. Item: one cavalry banner, red and yellow, with black streamer. Item: red taffeta shirts spotted with gold, from fine taffeta, 62, and of common taffeta, 62. Item: bagazia shirt, red, 14. A worn corneta, black, worn by Milord (my Father). Item: breast-plates 3, one of which is of silver, the other of copper, the third of iron, shot with gold. One red damask, the gilt banner of the nation. Another red damask, the gilt banner of the nation. A third of blue taffeta, the gilt banner of the nation. A fourth red damask, the banner of Milord István when he was a captain at Pápa. The fifth is a green damask small banner. The sixth is a flesh-colored taffeta, battered, gilt banner.[5] Worn leather upholstery, shot with gold, for a palace, of 12 pieces. Leather upholstery, royal blue, for the home, of 12 pieces. A third leather upholstery, blue, shot with gold, for the home, of 16 pieces. A fourth upholstery for the home, green with gold, of 6 pieces. A fifth upholstery for the home, red and yellow with large flowers, of damask, of 7 pieces. A sixth upholstery for the home, red and blue in color, with old-style flowers from Brudagelj, in 7 pieces, and two other red and yellow upholstery materials from Brudagelj. A seventh, red and yellow Steiczel cloth for upholstery, partly of silk, 14 pieces, timeworn, for the home. In the inner repository Milord's colorful cornette, with gilt shield, for the Court. Also yet another gold cornette, with redding, gilt iron shield. Item, two arms-belts with helmet, gilt. In the new compartment by the big

---

[5] Handwritten note to item: "It be outside of the crates, on the table."

window on the long desk there be: a new Flanders rug in 8 pieces, new, shiny, with sulk [silk?], with the story of Actaeon and Diana. *One pair of old dungarees.* Another Flanders rug, in 6 pcs. A third Flanders rug, old, for the home, in 7 pcs., with the story of Noah. A fourth Flanders rug, for the home, in 8 pieces, worn, with the story of Abraham on it. 3 long white divan rugs, timeworn. 6 other old timeworn divan rugs. *On the other table, a worn briefcase, glistening with grease, bulging like an expectant bitch.* Five old Persian rugs, silken. 9 Persian rugs for a table, silken. One worn rug of rounded shape and one white scarlet rug. In this storehouse there be also an old cup of terra sigilla, encased in silver, with a gilt hinge-lid, that Milord (my Father) hath commissioned for a Bilicum chalice for the town. Item, in the same storehouse, 4 tiger skins and 4 leopard skins. Item, 10 pcs. stitched fur rugs, embroidered in colors. In the house above the new warehouse-receptacle blue, colorful half-silk damask upholstery cloths, 7 pcs. Silver receptacles that be on the person of the cup-bearer and plate-bearer. The cup-bearer hath: a silver gilt goblet, with lid 3, shot with gold, unlided, set of 2, silver white, cups 5, small white cups 3, a handbowl with jug 1, small silver bowls 12, alpaca egg holders 6, silver plates 6, silver spoons 18, silver forks 8, knives with silver handles 8, gilt salt cellars 2, gold-plated cups 2, for cane-sugar 1, silver candlesticks 5. The food-bearer hath 24 silver trays. My poor Father, my poor, poor Father. . . .

•   •   •   •   •

33. When the Anthem was playing, when God blessed the Magyars with plenty and good cheer, we all had to stand. For instance, during the broadcast of select-team games, my father stood up, solemn and ceremonious, while his sons resisted as best they could, each and every time. They certainly waited until my father, wavering between severity and simple annoyance, would turn his head slightly, before hauling themselves to their feet. *Their fe-ro-cious fo-o-o-es,* around them. Also, they made faces, hoping my father wouldn't catch them at it. At such times, if the phone rang or the teakettle whistled, my father's sons took it as incontrovertible proof that they were right. The National Anthem lifts us out of our everyday lives, raises us into the timelessness of eternity, while television takes us nowhere. This is the contradiction the two generations embodied. My father's touching insistence sheds light on the resentment and indignation with which my father reacted to my father's eldest son's relativism. Let's not beat about the bush, he reacted hysterically. For instance, when my father's eldest son happened to mention how happy he was that theirs was such a big family, we've got one-humped and two-humped, hero and traitor and so on, indignant, my father immediately protested, What traitor?! Who exactly?! How dare you?! You could tell that he considered the existence of a person *like that* theoretically

51

impossible. My father's son shrugged. He couldn't understand my father. What's the big deal if there's a traitor in the family or not? In the past. The past belongs to us not because it is glorious, but because it is ours. We are rich, and this sort of wealth is an aid to freedom. All the same, my father is the perfect example of a so-called traitorous father. Being a hairsbreadth more of a pro-Habsburg Labanc than was prescribed by etiquette (no wonder: the younger Csesznek branch was the most Labanc offshoot to begin with), many people looked down their noses on him. As the colonel in command of the Styrum, the Forgách, and then of the Ebergényi Labanc regiments, my father had no scruples about attacking his own relatives (Antal, Dániel, et cetera), for which they looked down on him, especially those on the anti-Habsburg Kuruc side. What's more, even the members of the family who espoused neutrality were known to have made faces behind his back. My father was an obese, brown-skinned man, his cheeks lively and flushed. You felt like stroking them. All the time. He was appointed lieutenant colonel to serve under Pálffy at the age of thirty-five, but he was not motivated by the need to make a career; he was simply short on patience. He grew tired of perpetually having to consider things that one couldn't avoid (couldn't get by without, even at the end of the seventeenth century). He had to consider the Habsburgs and consider the Turks, he had to consider Transylvania and the kingship, the good of the nation, the good of the family, and he had to consider his own good. He got fed up. He threw himself into soldiering, receiving orders which he then carried out to the best of his ability. He did not hate the anti-Habsburg Kuruc, he merely considered their aims short-sighted. Rákóczi is no doubt a great man. But it would be terrible if he were to win. A Turkish pact, renewed coquetries with the French. And what then? The Kuruc is the glorious moment, what came before him and after, the cat's meow. My father is one of the most hateful members of the family. His portrait has survived at

Frakno. To this day, his sons stand up when a soccer game is telecast. There's a spring inside them that makes them jump to their feet. My father's sons' sons slowly heave themselves up to their feet after them.

34. My father could not abide Kossuth. He considered Kossuth vain, superficial, capricious. In every conflict, he took Széchenyi's side. A cheering crowd on Broadway?, ridiculous. Burying him again? Yes, he's eminently suited for that. As a rule, he didn't like the Protestants. They were too uncompromising for his taste, too much of this world. For whom, he said, God is just a phrase, though an important phrase. They're trying to spy out their fate through it. But even as they do so, they're offended, as always. That grave, manly gloom, the way it hovers overhead! He (my father) had no liking for this plebeian arrogance, as if suffering were Luther's prerogative and the exclusive privilege of his followers. As a rule, my father didn't like the Kuruc. Too many bonfires, flashes in the pan and songs, and not nearly enough reflection and labor. Kitsch! Kitsch and sentimentality and self-pity. He didn't like Kossuth—but I've already said that—and yet, they still hanged him as a traitor to the Habsburg cause on that tragic day in October. Grandmother sent men to Arad to bring back the body from under the gallows. She said that my father was easily recognizable by his long beard. But Lahner and Damjanics also had long beards, so they were brought back, too, and now all three are there, in the castle garden at Mácsa, Arad County, sleeping the sleep of the just.

35. Great lords. My father was a great lord. He was chief inspector at the State Waterworks Bureau. He and five others. But let that be our little secret. ◆ My father was a great lord. Truly great. Even greater than that. What I mean is, not greater than that, but great just the same, immensely great. Because if, for the moment, we

confine ourselves to the Earth, what is considered great in a village, for example, a peasant who has so much power that he can manage everything, for instance, and there is nothing greater than everything, and he decides the life of the village, for instance, and so on, and I do mean and so on, just imagine what it means if this power and influence is multiplied by a hundred. Or a thousand. In which case, of course, it comes to mean nothing. ♦ The common folk are so prejudiced in favor of great lords, in favor of my father, in favor of his facial expression, tone of voice and conduct in general, that indeed it would amount to idolatry if only once, just once, it ever entered my father's head to be a good man. ♦ My father has a tremendous advantage over other people: fine foods, rich furnishings, hunting dogs, horses, monkeys, dwarfs, fools, courtiers. Let him have them. ("It won't cost me.") But nothing is more enviable than having people in his service (at his service, his beck and call) who in heart and intellect are on par with him, and at times even surpass him. ♦ My father is proud when he has an alley cut through the ancient pine woods, when he ensures territories with tall, long protective walls, when he has a ceiling covered in gold, when he has some water gadget contraption put up or a spacious winter garden built. But to make a devoted heart happy, to bring happiness, to lend a helping hand in times of famine, to head off trouble, these are not among his favorite pastimes. ♦ To make promises, to pay with beautiful words, costs my father—a great lord—nothing. His high office releases him so completely from the obligation of keeping his word, that it is considered outright humble if he promises only as much as he promises, and no more. ♦ Old as the hills and worn to a frazzle, my powerful father said of Uncle Feri Dienst, *nomen est omen,* old man Service. He worked his hands to the bone in my employ, what the dickens am I supposed to do with him now? The other, who will rob the old man of his last hope, is younger. Which is why he's getting the job. Though let's be frank, Uncle Feri Dienst, old man

Service, did a great job himself. ♦ It is often wiser to walk out on my father than to complain about him. ♦ My father looks down on the man of intellect because he's got nothing but intellect. The man of intellect looks down on my father because he's got nothing but illustrious rank. The honest man looks down on all those houses where intellect or rank dwell without virtue. ♦ The scorn my father feels for the people renders my father indifferent to the praise and flattery showered upon him by the people. It also holds my father's arrogance in check. If the king or God did not scorn my old man, he, the king or God, would also be more arrogant than they are. ♦ If my father ever wished to come to know himself and his subjects, perhaps he would be ashamed to play the lord. ♦ It's no good when a person has (can have) the same name as the common folk. The name of the people (and the apostles): Peter, John, Luke. My father's, on the other hand, is Hannibal, Caesar, Pompeius, Lucrecia, and who is to prevent him (my father) from being called Jupiter, Mercury, Venus, or Adonis? ♦ The pleasures of life, plenty, leisure, indulgence, unbounded joy—all this makes my father so gay, he'll laugh at a dwarf, a monkey, a half-wit or a practical joke at the drop of a hat. Those who are less gay laugh only where appropriate, where it is called for. ♦ My father likes champagne and scorns cheap, doctored wine, which is as much as to say that he intoxicates himself with better nectar than the simple folk—the only difference revelry allows between a nobleman and a stable boy. ♦ To discover someone's merit, to ferret it out and give it its due—taking these two big steps, which must be taken in quick succession—is something my father is rarely capable of. It's his feet, poor man . . . ♦ You're great and you're mighty, my father said, but that won't suffice. Act so that I will respect you, so that it should pain me, unravel me, if I should fall out of your good graces. ♦ All my father's fortune is not enough to repay the smallest service if we take what said service had cost the person he (my father) wishes to reward as the standard of measurement. My father's might, too, is just barely enough to punish an offense against him if we take the measure of the offense as the standard of measurement. ◆ For my father not to jump at the high office that is his due, and which the world, too, considers his due, would be pure hypocrisy. It costs him nothing to be humble and mix with the crowd, which draws back immediately, or to be last, because even when he's last, he's soon first. For a mere mortal, self-effacement is a bitter indulgence. If he mixes with the crowd, he is immediately crushed, and if he sits at the end of the table, he is ignored. ◆ My father didn't like the times after the Garden of Eden, the days of yore. However reluctantly, he couldn't help but admit that we're all brothers, younger sister, older sister, younger brother, older brother. We're all one big family. The more or less depends only on one's family tree. ◆ My father must not be spoken of. To speak well of him almost always amounts to flattery. To speak ill of him is fraught with danger if he is alive, while is an act of cowardice if he is dead.

36. You can be sure—cocksure—that my father and his family spent more money on food than the Habsburgs. A family with digestive problems, what the Habsburgs lost to the Spanish they tried to make up for in the kitchen. They never had a decent cook, or if they did, they never knew it, as the head quota was so strictly set. Still, one must eat. (One must do what one must do.) They were saying around the King's table that in the vicinity of Teplice, the practitioners of the oldest profession had grown so profuse, they were veritably treading on one another's heels. Hearing this, my father leaned over the Queen's hand and allowed himself the luxury of a light joke, Sweetheart, the competition, or something to that effect. Flippant, endearing, just a whisper, yet every word could be distinctly heard at the farthest end of the room. Sweetheart, competition, et cetera. The Princess of Nassau sprang to her feet, and screaming, ran from the room. And my father right

after her! Count, the King whispered as if to himself, but so that every word could be distinctly heard at the farthest corner of the room, Count. My father stopped in his tracks, like a wax doll. He'd have liked to undo what he'd done, but it was too late, and he was overwhelmed by the cowardly fear of solitude. Thinking of the centuries, the nineteenth, the sixteenth, the eighteenth, he turned up, from the last, a saying that he liked: Grief, Sir, is a species of idleness. In that infinite moment of misery, all eyes were upon him. Her Majesty's sobs filtered in from outside. The King too was looking at him. His fear passed and the tingling sensation of warmth flooded his heart. What is beautiful is also ethical, he shouted merrily, and would have liked to take off after the beautiful. But he did not move. He, my father, stood rooted to the spot.

37. My father was born blind. He is just standing there.

38. Corruption: My father was born blind, in place of his eyes, two horrible holes. He is standing there. (He is standing on the corner, playing his violin, atrocious, obstinate, defiant. It's the Internationale, soft, sweet, lingering, as if it were a waltz.)

39. One morning, after he'd seduced my mother away from her husband and the two of them perfidiously killed that great, meek man, my father looked around, Well I'll be!, and noted, with surprise, disbelief and jubilation, that everything but everything was now his. Who would have thought that the dead man's rich estate would so suddenly fall into his lap? Oh, happy fortune, how blessed thou art, that on this day you did bestow on my father such pleasure and joy, for he doth possess all of Transdanubia in consort with his wife, rich lords, great princes, mighty kings dancing attendance upon him. My father luxuriates in fortified castles and wealthy cities; or, to put it another way, everything the body could want. A cornucopia of pleasures. He abounds in fabu-

lous hunting grounds, and he is laden with treasure that he sought neither with an excess of arms, nor of blood, nor of sweat, nor great trials and tribulations. It came to him with ease, and he is dipping into it with ease. *Carpe diem,* this was our motto, and my father declared he'd have a new court, and he'd have it proclaimed far and wide. His first care would be to have countless lute players and pipe players and drum players and trumpet players on hand, so that everyone should be merry, the young full of joy, and the beautiful should dance for the pleasure of my father's eyes. He'd have everything renovated and refurbished, thereby illustrating his privileges. He'd shower great lords with gifts. He'd fling out whatever was old and put in nothing but new things. He'd cover his palaces with gold and expensive tapestries, and also velvets shot with gold. My father wants everyone to fear and respect him as if he were a king. If that other man didn't know how to turn his wealth to his advantage, he would!

40. One morning, when my father staggered out of the kitchen because he nearly passed out at the sight of the horrendous, inert mass of unwashed dishes, especially a silver (alpaca) tray with the yellowed leftover of an egg plastered to it, he stepped into the bathroom and couldn't find his toothbrush, cup, razor and the toilet bowl. He couldn't even find his face in the mirror, and reeling, he went to the bedroom and saw his bed in disarray. In it was a bleached blonde curled up like a cat. He went to his writing desk, partly leaning, partly supporting himself on it, and he looked his son fixedly in the eye (on the picture, the boy's glance was severe, his lips pursed), and he said, Get off your high horse, son!

41. You are cheerful and understanding and loving and forgiving, a brilliant conversationalist, a fascinating person who looks for karma in everything, who does not wish to change the world, but accepts it, accepts everything that *is,* and it never occurs to you

that the world could be otherwise. What I mean is, this is what does not occur to you. You are satisfied with the cornucopia life has to offer, this is what you accept, this cornucopia of richness, where the bad and the ugly do not destroy what is good and beautiful. It does not neutralize it but enhances it. What I mean is, not it, but each other, they do not neutralize each other, and this is the way it is because you never had to stand before a firing squad before, said the commander of the firing squad to my father, during working hours.

42. My father had been palatine for some time, golden fleece and privy, when he admitted that he could never rid himself of the suspicion that the aim of Creation is not ethical in nature. It can't be. He could never rid himself of this thought for good; in short, he did not conduct himself like the Lord in the case of the first pair of humans, though to tell the truth, they did not approach their affairs from identical platforms.

43. One must paint from the heart, the painter said, pointing to his heart. Later on in the argument, which gradually seemed to turn in his favor, playing out his last trump card, as it were, aiming a boomerang, as it were, aiming it at the painter's heart, as it were, my father repeated the sentence. One must paint from the heart, and pointed to his heart. A silence ensued. Then with an inimitable, tender and sagacious gesture, the painter took hold of my father's wrist, gingerly, with two fingers, soft and sad, like some old family jewel, a lavalière, the cavalier!, and with a mocking, primitive smile, moved my father's hand to the left side of his chest. My father, the eternal loser, blushed.

44. My father was playing a short ditty by Purcell. He was elated when he'd finished, A cathedral! A cathedral! And now I will show you the stones, because every cathedral is made of stones!

Stones and God, my mother said, we know. Technically speaking, my father did not play especially well, but he was playing the music, from the music, and according to the music. When my father played it, the music stood to gain. He was humming like Gould, a lament. This here is utterly naïve, is it not, question, response, question, response, hoop-la, look at this, the same question, but an entirely different response! Is that a nice thing to do? and then, hoop-la, he takes a leap, and what a leap!, this here is a triple sharp, is it not?, and this a B, and he leaps over it, and he does so in 1691, don't forget! And with what ease. With ease, with ease, with ease! And here, here's an overstrain, practically atonal, what an accord!, Bach would have never dared attempt it, ever. But then, Purcell is English, don't forget. And here, at the end, he adds a note that hasn't been used before, he'd been preparing for this one note all along, this is what he'd been nursing all along, saving it, this small piece of Purcell tells us what composition is all about, don't you think? My mother's interjection that there is a difference between 1691 and the present clearly went over his head. Her next objection, that God has become a private matter, he clearly didn't even understand; my mother's allowance that he, my father, is in no position to declare that God either is or is not, but in either case, He is dead, and besides, whatever he says, it's about him, my father, and no one else, and certainly not about his neighbor—this, too, left him cold. He wept as he played, *o Wort, du Wort, das mir fehlt*—oh, if only I could find the words! He wept and played as my mother talked, and he nodded with satisfaction. My mother was annoyed, but tried not to show it. A capital performance, my dear Joseph!

45. My father went bananas. He actually suggested to Haydn, string triplet. But Haydn demurred. One of God's little mysteries why he did so, but he held his ground.

• • •

46. The eighteenth century: My father is herding geese by the roadside (my father never herded geese by the roadside). He is picking grass in the moat (he never picked grass in the moat). He is hanging a jug on the fence (a jug, no), he is drawing water from the well (no; yes, eventually, he did everything (nothing)). He is drawing water from the well, he is sharpening a hoe in the shed (he is sharpening a hoe). He is feeding the pig in the pigpen, he is helping a cow calve in the barn, he is burning coal in the kiln, he is sweeping the stone floor in the church, he is leveling a grave in the graveyard, he is heating up a piece of iron in the smithy. He is covering a mare with a stud, he is throwing a carcass into the stream. He is ordering a moccasin at the shoemaker. He is guzzling brandy at the Jew's. He is buying salt from an itinerant merchant. He is looking for justice at the judge's. He is beating his wife in the house. He is stashing away tobacco leaves in his bed. He is chasing a dog in the yard. He is threshing rye in the barn. He is rolling a girl in the haystack. He is carting the tithe to the landlord. He is eating beans in the shade. He is letting out gas in his pants. And all the while, during the busiest time of day, history, like a half-wit, is wandering round and round the village streets.

47. Let's see now. Some people have accused my father of feathering his nest steadily and appreciably after the debacle of the Wesselényi anti-Habsburg conspiracy. How true. With the death of Miklós Zrínyi, the situation got so garbled up, even my old man couldn't ungarble it. Sense and sensibility had a parting of the ways (back then, in the second half of the seventeenth century). The homeland had lost its great son, its only hope of deliverance from under the Turkish and Habsburg yoke. Bereft of hope, Wesselényi felt so helpless, he turned to a remedy more dangerous even than the disease, an alliance with the Turks, in the hopes that they would stop distressing the nation, stop picking away at its castles and villages and oppressing the subjugated people. Zrínyi's

younger brother Péter was a man of limited intellect, and being aware of his own shortcoming, he gladly took other people's advice, and was willing to be guided by them. Accordingly, though Leopold I had appointed him viceroy of Croatia (January 24), when it came to fulfilling the nation's hopes, he was no match for his dead brother. Thus, the brief period of hope resounding with the proud, encouraging words "Hands off the Magyar!" was followed by dark years of domestic strife, horrible years when one would have thought that there were no Magyars left, just anti-Habsburg Kuruc and pro-Habsburg Labanc. (He who sees past the picket fence and attempts to grasp the affairs of the nation with the mind, and not in isolation, he who considers *usus* and not scheming of greater benefit to politics, is an empty-hearted traitor to his country. He who would love his country with a natural passion is an antiquated leftover from the days of yore. This sort of approach is infantile, and a country like this is infantile, and so it has remained, because it is incapable of reconciling its dreams with its waking hours, its past with its present; it has failed to find a path from defeat to victory, from victory to defeat. Also, its feelings are hurt, and it sulks, like a child. Later, as palatine, my father would have liked to do away with this duality. He'd have liked to forge a bridge, except there was no riverbank. Neither his Hungarians nor his king believed in him. The slander and favors showered upon him in equal measure diminished confidence in his person. It is little wonder that the unthinkable came to pass, and not he, the palatine in office, but Pálffy was put in charge of the peace negotiations with Rákóczi. But never mind. My father was not offended, he just got the blues, plus the gout. Family matters came to occupy the foreground of his activities, i.e., personal well-being and prosperity, which further diminished confidence in his person. But let's not jump that far ahead.) This horrible crisis found my father in military service, supervising the fortresses on this side of the Danube. After the Wesselényi conspiracy, as captain general of Hegyalja, he was ordered to confiscate the goods of the so-called "discontents," which he carried out, however reluctantly. He was made a gift of a portion of the estates of his brother-in-law Ferenc Nádasdy, who'd been beheaded, namely, Szarvkő, contingent upon the payment of twenty thousand forints security which, being paid back to him later, he again put the estate in pledge for two hundred thousand forints, until on August 13 (one day before the death of my mother) he was granted it contingent upon a payment of sixty-five thousand forints; also Kapuvár, for which he had to pay fifty thousand forints, which he owed from before, and also the Pottendorf estate; for which acquisitions he brought great ire upon his head. But he couldn't get his hands on the Homonnay estate. My father's most cherished dream, to marry off one of his sons to the daughter of his older sister Mária, a descendant of the Homonnay clan that died out through the male branch, ran afoul due to the stubborn resistance of his staunch enemy, Bishop Kollonics. (Kollonics's militant, nation-disrupting tone became the norm at Court, making my father's role as "mediator" ineffective all around; this preposterous "trend" played national reaction into the hands of Rákóczi, whom Kollonics had personally educated in his youth, though this was of precious little comfort to my father.) There were other acquisitions and other jaundiced eyes, too. But it behooves us to remember that during this particular epoch, men of eminence who could hardly be said to have sympathized with my father were first and foremost looking to satisfy their aspirations, too—this despite all the praise and the hiding behind national aspirations. Seeing the resistance, my father advocated the principle of the "invisible hand" (committing both a logical and sentimental *faux pas* thereby, insofar as he was attempting to resolve a sentimental quandary by resorting to logic). According to this principle, every individual—while looking to satisfy only and exclusively his own gain—is guided by a benevolent, invisible hand, as it were, toward the best possible service to the common good. It is in this light that it is true to say that he did all this "not from irresponsibility or for his own pomp and circumstance, but for his country." My father was no penny-pincher; on the contrary, he relied rather heavily on credit, easily obtained on the strength of his luxurious home life. But he also enriched his ancient family estates with acquisitions so impressive that with his death he left not just one or two domains to his progeny, but a veritable principality fit for a king. Still, his enemies would not let him rest in peace even then, and spread the rumor that he was supposed to have died when his hunting dogs tore him limb from limb. (I might add that something of the kind was spread abroad about my grandmother as well. Namely, that she was supposed to have lain unconscious for days on the cold kitchen floor, and her cats, because she had many cats, would pitch into her when they were hungry.)

.  .  .  .  .

48. The Turks had long departed Kismarton and had marched through Hungary, when two richly garbed gentlemen appeared in the village. They knocked on the first house they came to. God be with you! And you too! What brings you here?, the master of the house, who was no other than my father, asked. At which one of the Turkish gentlemen said, It's a long, sad story. Isn't there talk in the village about a woman the Turks dragged off, but she got away? People say all sorts of things around here, my father answered, giving them the once-over with his eye. Well, it so happened that the Turks hoisted the woman's two children up in their cart, but tied her to the back. Unnoticed, the woman severed the rope, slid into a ditch, and made off. How did she have the heart to leave her two little babies behind? Maybe because she left two even smaller babies back in the village, and was sneaking back to them. Haven't you heard of her? We'll pay handsomely for information about her. Even though they persisted, nobody in the village could tell them anything about the woman. *Was verborgen ist, interessiert uns nicht,* they said, having had equally good command of German and Hungarian. (There were also Jews and Croats living there.) What's hidden should stay hidden. She must have died. Nobody knows anything about her or her family. At this the two Turkish gentlemen's hearts grew very heavy. One of

them said, We came all this way from distant Constantinople just to find out what happened to her. But why did you make the journey, if you don't mind me asking? the master of the house in Kismarton, my father, inquired, giving them another probing look. Because, sir, that woman was our mother. Ever since we heard this story, we've searched all over, but now we know that we shall never find her. Hold your horses, my father said, not so fast, and offered the two ponytailed men a seat, then sent for my mother. Maria Josepha Hermengilde, Prinzessin von und zu Lichtenstein, was a stolid, strong woman with a veil over her face who filled up the room with her being, her person, her character, her large plumed hat, and her skirts, which swished though she made not the slightest movement. The Turks jumped to their feet and kissed her hand, probably never having shown so much respect to any living soul in all their lives. Never mind that, my father barked irritably, is she your mother or is she not? Then he spun my mother around, so they should see her from the front, from the back, and also from the side. No, the Turks said shaking their heads, that's not Mommy. Deeply saddened, they took their leave and headed back to Constantinople. My father bid his time until his guests, uninvited, I hasten to add, left the house, then brutally and unexpectedly gave my mother, a stolid, strong woman with a veil over her face who filled up the room with her being, her person, her character, her large plumed hat, and her shirts, which swished though she made not the slightest movement, a backhanded slap she would not soon forget. The corner of her lip split open and the blood trickled to the floor. The sight of blood maddened my father (he took it as a personal offense, as if my mother were doing it just to annoy him), and he struck her again. My mother slipped to the floor, skidding on the blood. In short, she was no longer motionless. She cringed with fear. She was afraid of the beating, she was afraid of the pain (when he drank, my father respected neither God nor man), but above all, she was afraid that in the wake of losing her two beloved children she would also lose my father. That would have been too much to bear. My father kicked my mother, who was lying on the floor, then ran out to the yard. He was panting. The day was drawing to a close. Gradually, he (my father) regained his composure, but he was not in a good mood. The door of the house was swaying to and fro in the late-night breeze.

49. My father had come back once again. His face was black with stubble, his eyes were held in place by fine blood vessels. One of his teeth seemed to be missing, and he was stinking from drink. He looked around him. He was in a jolly good mood. The Viennese Court, the Hungarian lords, the office of the Prime Minister, the domestic staff, half of Transdanubia and my mother looked on with apprehension. The servants were carrying fourteen traveling cases behind him, fourteen English valises made of pigskin, of various shapes and functions, but all parts of one set, Richardson & Dumble, London. What's all that, asked the Viennese Court, the Hungarian lords, the office of the Prime Minister, the domestic staff, half of Transdanubia and my mother, raising their eyebrows. I got a lot of stuff to lug around with me, he said, and bowed his head. (I'm schlepping things around, he said.)

50. My father couldn't get enough of the sunset at Braunschweig. He got hooked on his way home from the ill-fated siege of Brandenburg, and after that, if he saw a Braunschweig sunset anywhere, in the morning, at noon, at night, at any time, he would immediately whoop, Lookie there, ain't that a sight?! He could not avert his gaze and tried relentlessly to make others feel the same exaltation. What's so special about it, my mother asked, indifferent, nonchalant. The incredible dance of purple, yellow, red, et cetera, its drama and cosmic farewell, et cetera. A Braunschweig sunset reminds you of the savanna, and since primeval

man was at home on the savanna, anthropologically speaking, we feel that affinity at the core of our being, and that's why we find it beautiful. Mother pouted, I'd never been near a savanna. My father liked to see the world according to his school curriculum. It's a shame he'd forgotten so much since his graduation. For instance, he could not understand how an airplane could fly when it's so heavy. Here's this knife, for instance, he demonstrated for our benefit many times during meals, imitating the sound of the engine, *brrrr*, then he let go of the knife, *bang, voilà*, or the other way around, *voilà, bang*. It plunges, doesn't it? Well, doesn't it?! he shouted with satisfaction, yet desperate for confirmation. If he read in the papers that an ocean liner sank, the *Estonia*, for instance, with friends aboard, an attractive young blonde among them, he would still rejoice, because the horrible event proved his point. Didn't I tell you, he said. It's too heavy. He pouted as if he'd bitten into birthwort. Every body, quoth he, immersed in water loses as much in weight as the weight of the water it displaces, sweetheart. Silence. My father nods. Not enough replaced, that was the problem, this not enough. I said so. Helen. The face that launched a thousand ships (tenth-grade school text, John M. Prausnitz). Let's make the degree of the beauty of the woman for whom they'd launch one ship 1 millihelen. A vector by nature. In which case a negative millihelen means that one ship's got to be sunk, she's so beautiful. Did I not say so? ("My wife is dead. Now I know what it is like. I am grateful that I will never have to know the like of it again, and I am much relieved. It is also comforting to know that I can count on your sympathy as on the sympathy of our other friends in Braunschweig." End of story.)

51. After thorough and tactful preparations, my father got up early so that prior to cutting a slice of bread, prior to burning down the bridge at Eszék and initiating criminal proceedings against the management of the Agrobank, he could go to Bratislava, the

scene of the National Assembly, the smelting works of the new, emerging Hungary, and visit his paramour. In the bathroom, however, by accident as it were, he ran into my mother, who was taking a leak, and who, half asleep, kneeled atop the toilet seat and pleasured my father. My father shrugged. Maybe it's for the best. He didn't like getting up early anyway, and he wasn't too crazy about the road to Bratislava either, where he'd have to endure numerous potholes and the sweat of horses. Besides, his appearance in town would give cause for speculation. Never mind, he said, climbing back between the covers, and he dispatched a messenger to Bratislava with elaborate excuses. Grinning from ear to ear, my mother brought him breakfast in bed. She was suffused *to the quick* with joy. So was my father. In that case, what's the problem, my mother asked. Or my father. It's boring, the other replied.

52. My father kept thinking of my mother. For instance, he'd cut a slice of bread, and then. He'd burn down the bridge at Eszék, and then. He'd start criminal proceedings against the management of the Agrobank, and then. On Thursday, in front of his house, he was attacked by strangers with baseball bats, and then. They've spent untold millions in this country on consolidation, but they never consolidated the people, and until they do, we might as well forget about social consensus, and then. In the years just prior to the French Revolution, he turned, once and for all, toward classicism, and then. His style lost some of its previous ease (abridged), and then. Where are the Hungarian ships headed, and then. Tomorrow's weather, and then. My father had a huge flat-top superstructureless late-baroque desk popular in the eighteenth century. It was there that he took care of the affairs of state, and then, too, he thought about my mother. He imagined what it would be like if she were to crawl under the table and, quietly, without so much as a how-de-do, so to speak, playful as a puppy, were to part my father's knees and thighs with her puppy head—while the affairs

of the empire would be shifted back and forth atop the table, fates shoved about, plus sentences and the daily mail!—et cetera, et cetera, and no hands, just the teeth or the nose or the chin and, to make a long story short, she (my mother) would go to the outer limits of the imaginable, but would not titillate to the outer limits but keep him (my father) in a state, reminding him of existence the whole cockamamie day. (Apropos a certain state: when my father accused the management of the young theatrical troupe (Kecskemét) partly of breeding geese and partly of holding their provincial audiences in disdain, many of the illustrious representatives of the profession took their side. Also, being a miser with his time, he ate his meals at his desk, amusing himself by passing a bite under the table now and then. Talking and touching, though, were out.) My dear, you are perverse, my mother concluded, resigned and saddened as she listened to the schedule for the day. But my father would not relent. He kept at it until, wonder of wonders, miracle of miracles, he expanded my mother's sensual horizons so dramatically that she became practically ungovernable. At this point, my father reminded her in a joking manner that she's a mother of four, after all, and Catholic into the bargain. Yes, dear, my mother nodded, but would not be curbed. It was too late. The genie had been let out of the bottle.

53. My father is a komondor. The dog that barks doesn't bite. My father barks and also bites. Another way of saying the same thing is that he feels closer to Stalin and Genghis Khan than to the romantic Grillparzer. He feels the new challenge of the times in his guts. The caravan must roll on! He'd like to turn this feeling into a method, to dislodge it from the realm of the heart. Meanwhile, my mother is translating from six languages and feeding the livestock, Polish, et cetera, Bessie the cow, et cetera. My father insists that we are living in the age of communication which, both in essence and quality, differs in every respect from anything we've

seen before. Also, its development is exponential, not like the development of agrarian and industrial societies. The change comes by leaps and bounds. A kangaroo! The situation is brand new. Perfect simultaneity. If time has ceased to be, man has also ceased to be, my mother interjects simultaneously with emptying a sack of oats. Are you saying that thanks to CNN, man has taken a giant step toward heaven? Are you suggesting that I have become an angel? He, my father, sees this as a process, the thing itself as this process. Just think of the esthetic, moral and religious implications of perfect simultaneity! What are you talking about, my mother asks softly. She was forty when she had her fourth child. What counts is not the discourse itself, but the *method* by which we approach the other person's thinking, as a result of which the simultaneity forced on us by technology is replaced by quality. What we are talking about would require a different conceptual field, of course . . . but we gotta make do with what we gotta make do with. Again and again, we are compelled to talk, or good manners compel us to talk, about things we cannot talk about. Silence is not golden. Are you saying that the thing is identical with the discourse on the thing? We're living in an age of transition, sweetheart, my father says with a nod. What about discourse on discourse, and the discourse about that? Man! Man is repeatedly forced to pull himself up by the roots of his own hair. If he does not succeed, then that's the miracle, and if he does, then that's the miracle. I'm also considering taking up letter writing. My father has a pimple stick, he carries it around with him, and if a pimple-like red anything appears, or bursts out, et cetera on him in some visible, socially determinable spot, he makes it disappear. He filched it from my mother. Of course she knows, and it drives her round the bend. Okay, but apart from the pimple stick, don't you think that Braque is great because he captures the *Ding an sich* of every object, because he turns every object back into its essence? Could be, my father admits reluctantly. On the other hand, in

71

every line by Goethe you feel the heartbeat of the entire universe, the fate of every human being. Ah, so that's it, my mother says, slapping her forehead, so that's what you're getting at. Mysticism! Unabashed mysticism! My father slams the door and scurries out to the garden, while my mother apologizes to him inside, I keep forgetting he's nuts. He's got an intimation of the madness of the times and has decided to offer his help to humanity. He knows that we're not living in the world we think we see. He knows that seeing the light of a star that had died thousands of years ago is true for other things besides stars. This is why he keeps saying to me, you are the sunshine of my life. I know that this is why he says it. Still, it makes me blush, and at my age!

54. What is the difference between my father and God? The difference is there for all to see: God is everywhere, while my father too is everywhere, except here.

55. Generally, until he was beaten to a pulp, my father conducted himself like a real man, consistent with a model he imagined for himself. But when the beating passed certain limits, the ripping out of the nails, for instance, he got scared shitless, and like a pitiful coward, started begging for his life. Fortunately, he didn't know anything about anything, which he kept repeating until the break of day. We're a big country. One way or another, we all end up as heroes.

56. My father caught himself a troublesome Turk, a Turkish girl, her name is Leila; her black hair is as robust as horsehair, as shiny as ebony, and it chimes when she tosses it; it reaches down to her bottom; her skin is elegantly pale, and she taints her lips with black mulberries, just like some punk. My father is head over heels. He has her sit in his lap and just looks and looks. Leila lowers her head. My father gently raises her chin, they quickly glance at each

other, then the girl lowers her eyes again. They are solemn, they do not speak. It's been like this for about a year now. But today the girl spoke up. She said something in Turkish. My father said something in Hungarian. They are talking now, and another year will pass, this time, like this. Before he died, my father, who'd been living alone for a long time, sour and shuddering—my mother, Thököly's younger sister, moved to Mariazell, and the Court had a field day—wondered: What could she have said?

57. My father had all sorts of principles. He had as many principles as he had cats. Most were ethical in nature, but there were also quite a number based on esthetic, practical everyday and hygienic considerations. Also gastronomic (garlic powder, for one). And pecuniary. And what's the secret of everlasting love? Is it marriage? Is it love? Or a third? He even had principles for managing low-grade soccer clubs. For driving fast but safe. Eight criteria for knowledgeable lovemaking. Geraniums and plant lice. He could pull a principle out of anywhere at all, from the pocket of his jacket, from the pocket of his pants, from under his shirt, from beside the salt shaker at lunch, from the opera glasses at the opera, the bag of pumpkin seeds at soccer games, his glass of spritzer at the inn, the library, the church, the barracks, school rooms, the Houses of Parliament, anywhere and everywhere, at the drop of a hat. A man of principles who is honorable besides is always right. The contrary cannot be posited. He is right because he cannot *not* be right. Either you agree with him, or you don't understand him. Which made life with my father a pain. He'd accept only what he could accept. He was considered successful in his profession. Consequently, when suddenly he was nowhere, neither in his pants, nor at the dinner table, nor the opera, nor the intermission at the opera, nor at the soccer games, inns, libraries, churches or barracks or the Houses of Parliament, nor in any other part of space filled with people, in an office of sorts or a

glass cubicle, and he had neither a coat nor a shirt nor a jacket on him, and could not pull out a principle either from behind his ear or his hair or from between his ribs or any other secret recess of the body, meaning he was naked and he was nowhere, i.e., when there was some hope at last for a proper exchange of views, he wasn't himself anymore. He wasn't my father, and in that case, what was the use, because, even if it were possible, what could we have talked about, and who would have been doing the talking?

58. My father's mother taught him nothing but fine notions. She taught him that in the final analysis people are good and our Heavenly Father is watching over us. We must trust the world, and if someone throws a stone at us, we should repay him with bread. What follows from all this? The fact—and this lay at the heart of my grandmother's teaching—that bad words make no sense. They're empty. The bad that they posit does not exist. When my father learned "bad" words from his village playmates, Grandmother dragged him into the bathroom and, with some sadness and anger, would wash his mouth out with soap. My father couldn't eat for days, and if he did, it came right back up. Then, when my father wasn't even five yet, Grandmother passed away amid terrible suffering, her intestines got all tangled up and began to putrefy as if a horribly stinking animal were living inside her, like in a horror movie, and she became more and more one with this animal. They even had to move out of the house because of the smell. My grandfather was ashamed of Grandmother dying, so they moved to another country, and my father was left high and dry with his torso of a vocabulary. He was incapable of saying anything bad about anyone because he lacked the words, and because he lacked them, he couldn't think anything bad about them either. As a result, he was helpless. Others played tricks on him and laughed behind his back. When he said, for instance—

this happened on March 13, by the way, when after two radiantly beautiful, sunny days the rain came down in a nasty, pinprick manner as if it were fall or Argentina—that spring had taken flight (something my father had intended as an objective statement of fact, saying what he meant which, of course, was not quite in keeping with custom), the others slapped him on the back, laughing, that's right, old boy!, it sure has, it's taken flight, you betcha!, and now we're stuck with you instead! My father looked at them with his foolish, pleased-as-punch smile, as if he'd heard his mother speaking to him—who, for her part, had taken flight by then, presumably like spring. That's right, old boy!, it's taken flight all right, and now we're stuck with you instead! And suddenly, my father was at a loss. Who is this "you" they are talking about? He looked into their belly laughs, but couldn't find the answer there either.

59. My father fucking refused to pay the fucking alimony. He sent word to my mother, fuck you, you filthy bitch. How about your sons, don't you care about your sons?! my mother screeched. They should fuckin' go fuck themselves, my father hollered, something my mother construed as a ray of hope. An encouraging sign because to go fuck yourself is not half as bad as, let's say, go drop dead. True enough. Still, my father refused to pay. My mother got fed up and hired two professionals to scare that scumbag, my father. My mother was selling neckties next to the tobacconist, gorgeous silks and whatnot, one piece costing nearly as much as the monthly wages of a construction worker on the new metroline. All sorts of people came to buy from her, a guy called Zoli, and also the Farkasevics brothers. Zoli had one of those shoulders, as distinctive as a separate organ, a limb, a separate entity. Just looking at it took my mother's breath away. It's not muscle, children, but a wonder of wonders, it's not bone or flesh, but a miracle of miracles. Where my shoulder ends is where his

75

begins. What's eating you, sweetheart, this Zoli asked. Though my mother tried to put a good face on things, this what's eating you was written all over her. And then the younger Farkasevics mentioned the prospect of him and his brother paying their respects to my father, who shat in his pants. They didn't lay a hand on him; they just let on that they think it's him they're looking for, that's what they think. Something's telling them. Why is my father such a shit ass he's not paying? It's a matter of daily bread for the children, is it not? Bread, family, responsibility. What the fuck business is it of theirs, he asked, because he wasn't scared shitless yet. We're talkin' real nice to you, you little prick, so try ta tune into da problem, right? You go fuckin' fuck up your life and we all has to get up at dawn to come all da way out here to Kispest. And that ain't right. But I'm gonna help you, you little prick, and say it like it is. It ain't right. Go give the little woman a ring-a-ding on da phone, little prick, and get this thing solved, 'cause it's their daily bread, family, responsibility, remember? It's your own little problem, if you get my drift, but we got up early. Not enough sleep. Then he walked up to my father and planted a kiss on his cheek, right and left. Which did it. Now, scared shitless, he hired two hefties of his own for five whopping thou a day. Both sides took their men to the meeting with them at the Flórián Square shopping center. Since the men, two on each side, knew each other, they held a short consultation, and my father's men called up their boss from the post office at the Flórián, but the younger Farkasevics took the receiver and talked to their boss the way their boss had talked with them. They all knew where they stood. My father's meatheads retreated to the food department for a short tête-à-tête with my father, who cried in his rage but paid through the nose, even if only two hundred instead of the three hundred thousand he was supposed to. Of this, my mother gave her boys one hundred. My mother was exceptionally pleased. If you ever forget to pay again, I'm sending my little angels after you, she communicated to my father. Drop dead, you fuckin' bitch, came my father's response. Which is how my father and my mother met.

60. The police headquarters of Győr-Moson-Sopron County arrested my fifty-two-year-old father on suspicion of manslaughter. Being under the influence, my father had gotten embroiled in an argument with his twenty-eight-year-old son. My father pressed his point not through discourse, but through rage, with a lard knife with a ten-centimeter blade. His son, who received three stab wounds, was rushed to the hospital in critical condition, where he underwent immediate surgery.

61. From the moral standpoint, my father is surely the original and ultimate temptation. There is within him what we call "necessity," the necessity that exists beyond the realm of ideas. This makes my father the means of expression, realization, communication. The difference between what "is" and what "must be" comes to fruition within him. Where my father is absent, this "must" is absent. This "must" (but first my father) is what needs to be defined.

62. Like most Turks, my father also had two wives, an obese winter wife, and a lean summer wife. He was working at the time in his capacity as a structural engineer for the Austrians, who were identical with the Habsburgs, but different countries number their sovereigns differently, Rudolph, for instance, which was initially problematic for him, and led to a number of misunderstandings; accordingly, he first had to renumber the emperors, *beziehungsweise* the kings, for instance, Rudolph. But regardless of his calculations, he'd neglected the affairs of his countries and immersed himself in the study of astronomy and alchemy instead in the castle of Hradčany until his madness got the better of him.

•  ▪  •

63. My father teaches history. During spring break he tells fortunes from cards, during winter break he sleeps, during summer break he draws conclusions from events that never happened. "I am Endre Lovag, 170 cm. in summer, 169 in winter. I will be twenty-nine years old this fall." His favorite food: alphabet soup. *(Sacré vieux.)*

64. Besides diddling, which my father considered an important aspect of hygiene and would engage in at every opportunity (What did he engage in?!—It!)—after lunch he would have his *leibdiener* go to the kitchen to tell one or another crisp young kitchen maid, *"Mari, waschn's ihnen, Seine Durchlaucht möchte unmittelbar nach dem Essen a'Hupferl machen!,"* in short, that she should go wash because directly after the meal His Excellency would like, how should we put it, a roll in the hay, to feather her back, to cohort with her. He held that keeping concubines was a good thing because all the hysteria, misunderstandings, emotional outbursts and jealousies, the natural and unavoidable concomitants of the situation, kept him (my father) alert, as it were. But being alert meant that he himself would end up taking offense! His own hysterics, misunderstandings, emotional outbursts and jealousies would unfold. The result: two equals stood face-to-face. A mirror of cosmic proportions for his egoism had risen in front of him. He looked at his lover—his paramour—and saw himself. Which is why he loved her and the others that followed. My father's lovers brought news of my virtual father, and my mother of my real father. My father's uniqueness lay in his inability to distinguish between virtual and real. Accordingly, he treated his lovers as he treated his wife, and he treated his wife, my mother, as if she were a strumpet with fire in her eyes. My father entertained equally poetic notions about himself as well.

65. During recess at the National Assembly in Bratislava, my father sent for his Parisian lady friend, Madame Shell. Organizing the

trip proved more difficult and costly than the couple had expected, not that money was an object with my father. On the other hand, his political status and the assertive presence of his permanent Viennese mistress, Gräfin Sau, in Bratislava demanded the utmost circumspection, while the lack of hotel availability thanks to the National Assembly called for not a little ingenuity. My father, however, would stop at nothing. He loved this lover of his, he loved her in every which way. He'd even talk to her. She felt the same way about my father. She was willing to talk to him, too. After everything was finally arranged—tickets for a Haydn concert in Vienna for Gräfin Sau and the Batthyány hunting lodge ready to receive them—it struck my father like a bolt from the blue, what if it's that time of the month for the mademoiselle? What if it's that time of the month just *then*? Because, granted the every which way, which goes without saying, and granted the talking, but still. He dispatched a swift-footed messenger to Paris to find out the facts bearing upon the case. The messenger, one of my father's young, ambitious men, was there and back in no time. The demoiselle began by offering me a slap right here, Your Excellency—and he pointed, and wouldn't you know, the spot was still red. Then she said she hopes her count doesn't think that she'd take a stagecoach for nothing, considering the expense, because the travel expenses were not provided by my father. I'd be hard put to say why. Possibly because money was no object to him. Anyway, he purred like a cat when he heard the news. Oh, I almost forgot: he also slapped the young man behind the ear, lest he conclude that he, my father, didn't love the woman as much as she loved him.

66. The Prince (or count or city council president) sent my father to his mistress (his, not my father's), to find out what's what. The Prince and his mistress used a secret language, and in this language the Prince wanted to know if it was spring. The Prince was a

cautious fellow. He wanted to invite the mademoiselle for the weekend, but if, as they say, she happened to have company, then, or so the Prince calculated, he'd rather spend the weekend *en famille*. God, country, family (weekend). The lady first gave my father a gay-hearted slap. I hope your muddle-headed master doesn't think I'd take my nookie all the way there for nothing, considering the expense. My father turned back, hurrying with the good news to His Excellency, who slapped him behind the ear, also lightheartedly. Everyone was satisfied, even my father, even though he had to spend the entire Sunday afternoon playing he who laughs last with the Prince's numerous offspring.

67. My father's wife, who was his for better or for worse, in sickness and in health, till death do them part—in short, my mother—was distinguished from my father's lovers by the fact that though my father was not constantly with her, and though he didn't think about this constantly often, when it came to my mother, he did not consider the idea of constantly absurd. On the other hand, even in the early, passionate stages of an affair, the very idea that he might be together with his lover constantly, before, after, and instead of, made my father scream with laughter.

68. My father was just the opposite. No, that won't suffice like this. He stood on a different footing, or, better yet, the other way around with my mother and his, my father's, lovers, than you would expect. He was surly with his lovers. He kept glancing at his wristwatch, a present from his father-in-law, and when they were sitting outside on the narrow balcony behind which the purple horizon was spreading over them, he wore a long face. He was bored. When his lovers rested their naked feet on my father's oaken thighs under the small rickety wrought-iron table (they put their feet in a variety of places, in fact), he didn't even notice, or else, with an involuntary gesture of tedium, he brushed them off.

He was unyielding, tedious, and selfish, though not entirely unin-
teresting; and though he may not have been an enthusiastic lover,
he passed, and he was reliable. At times, he could even be endearing. For instance, once he'd brought one a bunch of wildflowers,
and a cold lobster and salmon plate for another. A surprise. Also, if
the women, because his lovers were mostly women, suffered palpitations because of some light automobile accident, and he called
them in the morning, he sounded genuinely concerned. He rarely
paid a visit, though, because there was no reason to. Poor lovers,
they lay in bed in their darkened rooms moaning, or if they were
not moaning, they were anxious, their voices frail and thin. They
would have liked to snuggle up to my father's reassuring presence
like little girls, sheepishly, carefully, in order to avoid exciting either party unduly, while my father piped into the receiver like a
sister of charity. Wherever he was—wherever!—eight times out
of ten, he thought of my mother. He thought of her a lot. If he
spotted my mother on the crowded street, he went in pursuit like
a hyperactive adolescent. Then they would board the bus. Would
you like to take the wheel, dear?, because they pretended that
they were driving. My mother's proximity made my father tremble, his lips and his breast, too. He felt a painful numbness and, as
if counting his rosaries, he kept whispering my mother's name to
himself. When he waited for my mother, then, too: trembling,
numbness, whispering—imagination helped to pass the time. For
example, he pictured that something had happened to her. A military convoy's crashed into her and he, my father, is stuck with the
kids. Well, never mind. After all, he *could* sacrifice himself. He *will*
sacrifice himself. He will devote his life to sacrificing himself. Or
would that be pushing it? He might become bitter, and the children would suffer the consequences. Fine. He won't give up a
thing, but he'll take care of them just the same (Boy, will he take
care of them!, as you see, this hypothetical tragedy has not blunted
his sense of humor). But let's be practical. He'd clearly have to hire

someone, a sort of housekeeper. A housekeeper . . . Too finicky. Back to square one. If only the kids had been with her in the car. A head-on collision. Political scandal. The Interior Minister trying to clear himself. Meanwhile, he (my father) would go on struggling a while longer with nothing. When he imagines this, worked out in detail, it turns out that it's the same struggle as now, a struggle with everything. That's the moment when my mother usually shows up. But time and time again, it is too late. His knees are weak, like putty. If they didn't take a bus ride, they'd go someplace for ice cream. They'd sit in the sun, loud in conversation, and they'd order one portion with two spoons, like children. They'd treat the old waiter, who was as brown as a Gypsy or a Black Christ, like an accomplice, no, no, the other way around, not two portions with one spoon, but . . . and no chocolate, my mother doesn't like chocolate. People looked over their shoulder. They skipped from topic to topic as they chatted—what a nice feeling of satiety—about anything, about everything, the independence movements in India and that nice waitress they found in Switzerland, the arms trade, and my mother's yellow shirtdress. My mother was nuts. She wore colorful dresses. Her latest friend was a bona fide tailor, a men's tailor, and though not for free, still, he made her all sorts of things at an appreciable discount. He was trying out new styles on her, as it were. My mother got ice cream on her dress. She and my father had a good laugh over this, too, especially the stains—about what sort of stains they were—with a decidedly rowdy undertone. When he was with his lovers, my father spoke mostly about problems with the children, theirs and his own, he was annoyed, the beanbag, they can't find it, and did she get her (one specific) period. Halfheartedly, he exchanged views with them on their respective mothers-in-law who, despite their advanced age, had become unreliable and childish, and were prone to libido attacks whose subject was the husband or the son-in-law who, as we know, are not *terribly* exciting characters. There was also mention of the underhanded shenanigans of the double-dealing brothers-in-law with respect to the compensation coupons. On the other hand, when my father looked at my mother, his eyes turned into bleary cow eyes with a sugary-sweet solemnity in them as if (each time) he was seeing my mother for the first time, something my mother could not abide. She lashed out at him mercilessly. She didn't make fun of him, but she laughed—though not at my father; her laughter was independent of him, you might say—but it was this *independent* that appeared to annihilate him. Except, he was not annihilated. He kept staring at my mother's strong, pearly-white teeth. What strong teeth. The two of them created a stir wherever they went. My father's face beamed like Moses' own after his little chat with the Lord. He should have covered it with a kerchief, too. The gentleman's tailor could have made him one. Also, there were the trembling knees and the endless waiting, never to be satisfied, all of which evidenced a precarious sense of imbalance. We're not children anymore, my father kept saying. But it didn't help. Then he tried to imagine all sorts of distasteful things about my mother, hoping that these images would chase away the hysterical images of his reveries. For instance—and this was a classic—my mother sitting on the john, or better yet, in a rural outhouse in the heat, the stink, the flies, the flapping, cut-up squares of newspaper smeared with excrement, the plunging sound of the excrement, or something he'd overheard the other day, that basically there's no effective cure against eczema, but if anything helps, it's your own urine, you have to urinate on the surface in question. He liked to imagine in lively detail my mother as she struggles to effectuate it, botching it up, placing her arm between her legs, close to the source, but she urinates over everything, and then she cups her hand, knowing full well that pouring her urine back on herself would not be easy. But this didn't help either. As they ate the ice cream, she (my mother) kept pawing my father distractedly, which usually took the form of her placing her strong, substantial palm on my father's thigh (there was no brushing *that* off), thus stirring sweet reveries in them both. For his part, my father placed his hand on the curve of my mother's shoulder. He did not move, and yet it was a stroke, a so-called zero-motion stroke. My father felt that he was the strongest man in the whole wide world. The waiter is going to die, my mother said, and she thought, a husband, what a nice, comfortable proposition.

●　　●　　●　　●　　●

69. When was it? When his spurs broke? No, it was later. The thought had occurred to him many times before, but only in passing, the way a thought would occur to you or me. My father, too, felt that there is a difference between a slice of bread and a thought. He felt that bread is more substantial. It was only when his horse reared itself up by the stream, his boot slipping out of the stirrup, and he was surrounded, only then. Ant flies swarmed all over him in his dreams, and then. A group of children attacked him, and with the wild, silent slashing of his sword he cleaved the head of one of the boys in two, and slowly tipping out, like a watermelon, the two halves of the scalp parted, and then. He butted in on the king, who, surprised but collected, smiled, and then. He suffered a hysterical confession fit, but couldn't find a priest, and even Archbishop Pázmány refused to see him, and he kneeled by a bush called Mordechai and solemnly recited the Ten Commandments, one after the other, finding a little something in each as the bush trembled in the breeze, and then. After prolonged pleading and threats, decked out as humility, a certain someone satisfied a certain by no means ordinary request of his, and then. That's when he was suddenly gripped by fear. Fear had him by the throat. Or the stomach. And the lungs and the heart, too, as if something were tugging, churning and shaking his insides.

Wheezing, he found it increasingly difficult to breathe. He suffered a humiliating defeat in battle. The ants gnawed his flesh down to the bone. The dead child had his revenge. The Court declared him persona non grata. The bush caught fire and burned with frenzied tongues of flame. That's when my father was flooded by the cold, clear feeling of sin and fear and trembling, and dark waves of nausea flooded over him—the feeling that something irrevocable had happened by virtue of the simple fact that he was alive. That his life was wreaking havoc with his life (and maybe life in general). Better make use of these fragment moments of fear, my father thought, and take stock. Waste no time. How should one live? For the glory of God. What is permissible and what is not? Risking his salvation is not permissible. And what is his salvation if not the love of his life (my mother)? If anything should happen to him, what would become of her? In short, he must not die. The only moral solution is eternal life, the "not dying." Banally not dying. What a shame.

70. My father, a black knight, is standing in his black coat of mail in front of an infernal castle. The walls are black, the looming bastions ruby red. In front of the gates, columns of sizzling white fire soar toward the sky. He (my father) steps gingerly over them, crosses the castle yard, and goes up the stairs. One by one, the rooms open their doors to him. The sound of his footstep melts away against the stone blocks of the walls. The place is as silent as the grave. At last he enters a round room in a tower. Above the door a red snail is carved into the stone. He can feel the centuries-old thickness of the walls. The room has no window and no light is burning, yet the room is suffused with an uncanny, shadeless radiance. Two young maids, one a brunette, the other a blonde, are seated around a table, and also a woman. Though they bear no resemblance to one another, they are clearly a woman and her two daughters. On the table in front of the brunette, a heap of long,

gleaming horseshoe nails. She takes them in her fingers one by one, carefully examines their tip, then stabs the blonde with them, her cheeks, her limbs, her breasts. The blonde does not respond, no sound passes her lips. Then the brunette pushes back the blonde's skirt and my father sees that her thighs and tortured lower body are one gaping, bloody wound. These soundless motions are so slow, you'd think a secret contraption had arrested the march of time. The woman seated across from the girls does not speak, she does not move. Like the holy pictures of the Virgin in remote rural hamlets, over her chest she is wearing a big red heart cut out of paper. My father sees with horror that as a response to each prick of the nail, this heart blanches. He knows he cannot take any more, and flees. As he retreats, the doors, secured fast by iron bolts, fly past him. At this point he realizes that behind each door, from the tip of the tower to the bowels of the cellar, people are being tortured everywhere without end, tortures that no one will ever hear about. I entered the secret fortress of pain, my father says, and the very first thing that met my eye was too much for me to bear.

71. At one time, in 1621 to be exact, the Austrians, whatever that means, occupied Heidelberg. My father, who was running the Vatican at the time, Uncle Jocó Varga the milk farm, and Dad the Vatican, taking advantage of, how shall I put it, his Austrian *connections,* immediately dispatched two Papal cavalry battalions with the intended aim of pilfering the great library of Heidelberg. And pilfer it they did. Who would have thought that the Vatican's treasures are stolen treasures, too, not just the Soviet Union's, though, come to think of it, in the end, the Soviet Union collapsed. My father nodded, or broke into a sweat, or broke out laughing, or shrugged, or launched into a profuse disclaimer.

72. At the age of twelve, my father came up with a life plan. He would be a good master to his subjects. Despite the changed cir-

cumstances, he would try to ensure a secure livelihood and a foreseeable promotion for them, and would in general do everything in his power to effectuate what the unwritten laws of his family demanded without any *wenn und aber*, German in the original, without thinking, as it were, like a studious schoolboy. His personal aims would involve the following: to find a relationship between love as one of the so-called imperatives, the essence of Christ's teachings, and the state of the world. This in turn would involve finding an answer to the following subsidiary problems and/or questions: Why did God create the world? Why did He need to? Does God need anything? Aren't perfection and omnipotence the same as inertness? And if not, why not? What is the prime mover? And what does it move? Why did the Lord share His power with Lucifer? Or did He? Why did Lucifer rebel? (All whys refer to the structure of the world, why is the world such that Lucifer, et cetera.) Why does free will inevitably lead to what is bad, or even terrible? Why is it presumably free will that leads there? Why is it free will that is the dark abyss that leads there, and not God? It's not God who leads us into war, infanticide, and so on. Or . . . ? Why didn't the Lord create a better mankind for Himself? What's the good, where's the business, the inevitability? Why are we made to kill our gods? It'd be bad enough if we should happen to be the kind to cook a child's favorite bunny rabbit in boiling hot water. The distance between the bunny rabbit and the Lord is infinite, so the situation, too, is infinitely worse. Why? Blood, sweat, and tears, with rare, brief instances of brightness, this is our history. Why? What has happened to love? And why? This is what my father wrote in his notebook at the age of twelve, then began his hopelessly long search for said notebook.

73. My father cared only for music, and Miklós Zrínyi for literature, so they decided to team up and—based on a third-party idea!—write a musical, maybe a Szörényi-Bródy. Everybody assumed

they were at war, the "bastion of the Western world" against the "Turkish Scourge" and the like, whereas they were preparing for the show. My father set up a cavalry regiment at his own expense, that was the chorus, the bass on the right, et cetera. One winter, they won victory after victory. The Turks couldn't make heads or tails of it. They knew that Zrínyi was a brilliant military commander and respected my father, too—but what they were up to now was impossible to follow! No wonder. Everything happened according to the dramaturgy of a musical.

74. Once upon a time, when my father rode into the town of Eperjes in disgrace, the people lined both sides of the road, because they wanted to see my father, and they also wanted to see his horse Challenger. Many people stood way up front, or to put it another way, in the first row. But even more people stood in the second, third, and fourth rows, and what went on beyond the fourth row, well, that had precious little in common with your or my idea of what a row should be. And so, in order to catch a fleeting glimpse of my father, many people had to raise themselves on their toes, and (on top of everything else) they craned their necks like so many *précieux,* and with such vehemence, extending them with so much recklessness, that after my father rode past them in the evening twilight, they stayed stretched out like that for the rest of their lives. Because of this, if fate should bring a man with a long neck your way, you must not make fun of him or stare with your jaw dropped open, for that man is surely the grandson or grandson of the grandson of a man who, driven by a singular yearning, a long since vanished sentiment you and I can no longer find in our hearts, wanted to catch a glimpse of my father.

75. The boy was the prince of Karlovac or whatnot, a likable, sensitive youth, an unripe fruit, as wine experts would say, with a great deal of potential. In any case, he made Lipizzaner studs an item.

He was sitting next to my father, with the King across the table, and diagonally across, the Queen. They were talking it over: How should they settle the compensation? What form should the payment take? What should they do about the horses (my father was wheeling and dealing with the Muraközis at the time, good strong, useful horses), and what with the prisoners, particularly, what should be the fate of the leftover stock of prisoners after the exchange, and should the horses be included, and if so, what should be the rate of exchange? Or, should they be destroyed, and in what manner—by the rope, the gun, the sword? There was a lot to mull over. Who was to do it? Each his own? Or should they call in impartial executioners? A tedious business-type discussion, when my father cast his eyes on the no-longer-young yet extremely pleasant Queen. Nothing special, there was nothing in that glance, but it wasn't nothing that was in it either; his eyes happened to wander in that direction, quite by chance, you might say; without a doubt, a man was looking at a woman, but that was all. At which the King, a Hohenzollmeier, who caught the glimpse, pushed back the throne with an ear-splitting din, and sprang to his feet. My father who, thanks to his upbringing, knew perfectly well that a subject does not sit in the presence of a standing king, did likewise, and they ended up *face-to-face,* the King staring at him, panting. What's the matter with you? Got ants in your pants? But my father was in no position to allow a single word to pass his lips, especially not in the form of a question. Meanwhile, the servants pushed the throne back under the King, who sat down. As did my father, who shot a questioning glance at the Prince of Karlovac, who lowered his sweeping ebony black eyelashes and buried himself in his fresh beard. He (my father) didn't dare look at the Queen. It hadn't worked before either. They're sitting quietly at the table now. Monday, Tuesday, March, April, March again. The horses, the leftovers, become old jades, the prisoners die of their own accord, the young prince's beard is gray, my mother's waist, too, is grown majestic, and though not dramatically, her blood pressure goes up and down. Only the King has not changed. A king is always a king, and that goes double for my father's glance. It's majestic, and that's all there is to it.

76. My father was the bishop. Stranger things have been known to happen. Once a deputation of serfs went to petition him: the crop was poor, could he release them from the tithe? My father didn't want to. He gets a tenth even when the crop is plentiful, so what the fuck do they want? Why don't they work harder instead of squeezing the state's or the bishopric's or—in this instance, in con- creto—my father's dug dry? Still, he liked a good joke, so he said, who among you got the most brains? The village magistrate stepped up to him. That'd be me! If you can answer one question, I'll release you from the tithe. How many hairs have you got on your head? The village magistrate scratched his head. It'd be nine on the outside, I guess, 'cause if I had ten, Your Excellency woulda taken that tenth a long time since. Not bad, my father said with a wry smile, but did not release him from the tithe. This was part of the joke, this funny business, this historical jest, because a clever sentence is one thing, and a sack of wheat another. Which reminds me. When Joseph II stopped at the bishopric in Eger, he was as a matter of course my father's guest. They couldn't abide each other, but since they had to cooperate, they did. My father laid it on thick, surrounding the Emperor with great pomp, and giving a series of magnificent suppers in his honor. But for some reason, it was never dinners. For what we are about to receive, may the Lord make us truly grateful. Either he ate too much or he was in a contentious mood (or both), be that as it may, Joseph II spoke thus: Bishop, you are the descendant of the Apostles, except the Apostles did not live in such luxury, get my drift? The camel and the eye of the needle. *Kapisch?* My father swallowed hard (he was eating). Mum's the word. But the following day, after my

91

father's faithful but chagrined servant, Thomas, announced that the noonday meal was being served, my father led the Emperor into a small room, a sort of a cell, where the only other company was a priest belonging to the Court. The table was set with clay dishes, wooden knives and wooden forks. The meal consisted of three simple courses. The Emperor, who liked his stomach more than the Hungarians (or the Austrians, I might add!), waited a long time to see what fine foods would come after this strange appetizer he assumed was the antipasto. But in vain, because they didn't bring so much as an empty plate. The Emperor could not hide his dissatisfaction. Bishop! What sort of joke is this? It is no joke, Your Majesty, my father said solemnly and a bit moodily. Yesterday, Count, *here my father's name followed,* was Your Majesty's host, today the Bishop of Eger, the poor and unworthy successor to the Apostles. What was there to do? But to interject, news of my father's erudition had reached distant lands, and when a young man from home visited the famous German professor Detlef Groebner, he was just leafing through one (or another?) of my father's books. Is, *here my father's name followed,* still alive? Yes. But he's constantly drunk. Well, why can't someone who isn't drunk constantly write books like this?, that decent fellow Detlef asked, chagrined. Joseph II liked rummaging through my father's pocket. Though emperor, Joseph II was no aristocrat. He was more than an aristocrat, and he was less than an aristocrat. Which is why he lost out in the end—he was not in his place. The lyceum of Eger, which was commissioned by my father, won the admiration even of this "uncrowned king." *Quanta costa?* It's paid for, Your Majesty, said, *here my father's name follows.* (It is common knowledge that my father destroyed all documents pertaining to the cost of this admirably equipped, first-class girls' school, so that it should never get out how much, *quanta,* this institution of learning had cost him.) The Emperor felt like picking a quarrel with the pontiff. This lyceum is so nice and big. Perfectly suited for a barracks, he said with a wolfish smile. (Which seems like a remarkably tasteless comment, considering that it had been his mother who, on the advice of Archbishop Ferenc Barkóczy, who suspected that the intention of the plan for a lyceum was to establish a national seat of learning vis-à-vis the universities of Vienna and Nagyszombat, denied Eger the rank of university; whereupon my father took the full expense of the entire construction for the consistorium or collegiate church upon himself, immediately fired the younger Gerl, who had solid connections to the Viennese Court and who was Barkóczy's man, and commissioned the dependable Jakab Fellner who was no Borromini, not even a Pilgram—my father and said Pilgram having once admired the beauty of Rome together, my father the promising student of the Collegium Germanico-Hungaricum and Pilgram a young architecture student—but he was a reliable, conscientious professional, a man who could be counted on. The fact that my father wrote his name with an *sz* in the Hungarian manner in order to set himself apart from the aulistic, royalist branches of the family seemed to confirm Barkóczy's suspicion though, and as my mother wittily and nastily remarked, the *sz* may not be aulistic, but it's got a lot going for it just the same.) It was built by the count and not the bishop, Your Majesty, my father said with a glint in his eye. His will stipulated that should the lyceum be stripped of its original function as an institution of learning, it should revert back to the, *here my father's name followed,* family. Item: when they entered the church, the Emperor (and King) Joseph took off his hat, while my father, who up till then had humbly followed the monarch with his hat in hand, now placed his biretta on his own. Your Majesty, he said softly, a touch of threat, a touch of pride, in this place, I am the monarch. Item: the Emperor is studying our coat of arms. He is having his little fun again. What might that animal be on there? he asks my father. A griffin, Your Highness. And can you tell me, old friend, where's them birds come from? The same place as the two-headed eagles, my father said, playing his hand, then steered the Emperor into the confessional. The Emperor confessed that he did not believe in God, at least, not in the personal, Church-mediated version. Don't even mention the Church, my son, my father said, warding off any possible excuses by the Emperor. As for atheism, don't rely on it. Atheism has its bad days, too. The day will come when you too will plead with your Lord and God on bended knees. Is that a threat, Bishop? What an idea, my father said, waving it off. At which the Emperor waved, too, I'll be dead before that can happen. A short pause followed. Then, with an inimitable, tender and sagacious gesture, my father took hold of the Emperor's wrist, gingerly, with two fingers, soft, and sad, like an old family heirloom, a monstrance, the work of the goldsmith János Szilassy from Lőcse, 1752, enamelled scenes from the lives of the Virgin Mary and Christ, gilt silver, 77.5 cm. high, and with a nasty, primitive smile moved the Emperor's hand from his thigh to the Emperor's. My father shook his head. There's still the deathbed in case you need to reconsider and relent. Item: My father could not abide Germans. During his Transdanubian travels in a small town, early one morning, he woke to some noise. What's happened?, he asked his manservant. Nothing, Your Excellency, just a German itinerant youth who hanged himself on a tree. If only every tree would bear the same fruit, my father sighed, quoting the famous saying of the Greek philosopher and misanthrope, Timon. Later the Hungarian Nazis took him to the camp at Sopronkőhida along with the politician Bajczy-Zsilinszky and the actor Pál Jávor, who suffered from inflammation of the gums.

77. The ornamental goblet with the nautilus shell (Germany, second half of the seventeenth century), silver-gilt, chased, molded, finely chiseled, got loosened. My father doctored the great Nürnberg goldsmith Hans Petzolt's handiwork, removed (carefully) the alle-

gorical figure of Wisdom from the top, and from the bottom the figure, in relief, of Triton riding atop a dolphin. Then he put the priceless mother-of-pearl shell, which makes up the body of the goblet, to the same use as the truck drivers do their key rings when they stop for a short respite. Like Alexander the Great, he'd take afternoon naps with the mother-of-pearl shell in his hand (Alexander the Great used an ivory ball), and as soon as he fell asleep, the shell would fall out of his hand, he'd be startled out of his sleep and would resume work. He had to piddle with the plastic belt buckles, paid piecemeal by a private entrepreneur, because he could not be lawfully employed, even though he hadn't *done* anything in '56, though he did *think* it, as far as that goes, which in a revolution is too little, and after a revolution, it is too much.

78. Though you couldn't tell by looking at him, my father was a veritable Gargantua. He was scrawny, blond, frail, and wore spectacles, but he could fart as he walked, keeping time. Right, fart, left, fart. This is how he marched practically all through Europe with the king of Naples and the dubious Metternich, enveloped throughout by this sweetish, pungent, soporific fart smell. A real proli. My father, the rebellion of the masses. The rebellion happened de facto when being overconfident in his above-mentioned talent and reckless, too, once he shit in his pants. He pulled everything in, he contracted his sphincter muscles in vain, too late. The shit was already slithering down his thighs. This country stinks, my father commented. Those around him, his followers, nodded. My father gave the battle cry: Let's go free Táncsics and fight for the Commune! Naturally, he did not budge. Given the circumstances, it would have been fatal.

79. There was a slight hitch. Though by then Napoleon had had it, my father concluded peace with him too eagerly, whereas the endgame called for extreme caution and ruthlessness. Metternich,

95

of course, was beaming with satisfaction, and no wonder: if their plan should go awry, my father would have to bear the brunt of the blame, while if they succeed, he and his pigeon breast would be first in line with respect to the proper placement of the medals. But drawing up peace treaties is no greased lightning. It's a long and painstaking process that takes inner equilibrium and strength of vision. Any one day on its own is of no consequence. It may pass in triumph, but that doesn't count for much. Only the end result will tell us what counts and what does not. A day acquires meaning only after it is over, and not *there* and *then*. There and then there is only the doing, plus the visible effort. My father, however, was so overeager, he was concluding peace with such gung-ho eagerness, you'd think he'd be finished by Sunday. And it was now Wednesday afternoon. In the morning, as he crossed the palace yard on the way to his office, he'd spot himself in the mirrored glass panes. He'd look, he'd see. And he'd think—knowing full well that this was an exaggeration—I feel like I'm twenty-five, as bright as the sun, and the future before me. He nodded at his mirror image, and his high-spirited mirror image nodded back at him. As a matter of fact, he really was twenty-five. Speaking of the future: in order to prevent Napoleon's son from making anything of himself, to make him a laughingstock in a way that he wouldn't notice until it was too late, laying the foundations for a peaceful future thereby, my father & co. came up with a plan. They'd offer the kid a piddling ducal title. Instead of Herzog von Mödling, my father's congenial idea which, *mutatis mutandis,* is like the Prince of Lower Bronx, Metternich chose his own, less ingenious Herzog von Reichstadt, the crux of which was that there was no Reichstadt. But regardless of his name, the little guy did not present a problem.

80. My father had an elaborate take on things. *On the one hand,* he was concerned about the sanctity of the confessional in face of the newly proposed police law. According to this law, they could

conceal bugs in confessionals. Metternich's confidant and spokes-person did not deny that in theory the installation of tapping de-vices in confessionals could not be ruled out—a small army of tiny funnels in the shape of bluebells would direct the voices of the penitent to the appropriate place—since at this point (it is now Thursday, ten-thirty a.m.) the bill does not contain provisions for special compensations. My father made an official announcement. In order to protect the secrecy of the confessional, every priest is willing to go to the outer limits. But in order to get the informa-tion, so was the secret police. (Oy!) *On the other hand,* in-depth re-search on the "domestication," if not of bugs in general, yet of cockroaches, these stubborn creatures that cannot be cleared out of Hungarian homes, were being conducted in my father's lab, of all places. Due to the multitude of uses they can be put to, these bugs, my father explained, must be kept in the forefront of robotic research. Thanks to cockroaches fitted out with mini-cameras, within a few short years it would be possible to look for people buried under the ruins of houses that have collapsed as a result of an earthquake, and they could also be put to good use for spying, since they can slip in anywhere under the threshold. They could even crawl into the confessional! The five-year "cockroach robo-tization program," which involves the implantation of minute mi-croprocessors and cameras into the backs of the cockroaches through surgical means after the extraction of the insects' feelers, whereby they could be directed with the application of electronic impulses, was launched this month (March). The electronic load, which weighs 2.8 grams and is twice their body weight, would not weigh down the cockroaches, because bugs are strong and can support a mass twenty times their own weight. In my case, this would come to 1,670 kilograms, my father smiled humbly, as if in-deed he were a bug himself. But then just to be on the safe side, they switched to the stronger and larger, i.e., more corpulent American roaches for purposes of experimentation, though even in their case it often happens that when they hear the order, Turn right and advance five centimeters!, they suddenly leap to the left. (Praised be the Lord!)

81. *How are you?* My father could say this quicker than anybody. He was always the first to say how are you, provided the occasion called for it, and he saw his chance. Thanks to this skill, he was made ambassador to England, and he held this post for thirty years. But he lost favor with Metternich. Though Metternich was familiar with my father's reliability, intelligence, objectivity, and above all, his intimate familiarity with local English customs, he could not forget the former brouhaha over the sanctity of the confessional. The English were so thoroughly the first in everything and everywhere at the time, that this time, they didn't mind coming in second. *Coming in second,* they grinned, the way only the English know how, with a mixture of a cute adolescent and a dangerous madman. The island country had my father to thank for this "second," and they were duly grateful.

82. My father made my mother's acquaintance in London by going up to her and, after briefly clearing his throat, saying to her (my mother), *Lesson number one. I am a man. You are a woman.* Like that.

83. My mother, who idolized the elderly Haydn, gave him not only a golden coach with six horses outfitted with velvet harnesses, but raised his salary, too. Subordination, discipline, social standing and a sense of obligation were now a thing of the past between them. The world-famous musician enjoyed such profound respect now that he'd been to London, that once, when my father cut in during an orchestral rehearsal, Haydn said, My apologies, Your Highness, but I give the orders around here! My father left without further ado, or without taking offense. When, with the confidence and natural attraction of one great heart toward another,

my mother took my father's genitals in her mouth, she gagged with deference and awe. Her face was radiant with joy, and she felt as much profound, passionate love toward my father as never before. She'd put up a long fight. She didn't want to. Didn't feel like it. While for his part, my father felt like nothing but this. It started out as a sort of dalliance. My father is a huge prick, but he had principles. I'm not about to sleep with just anyone. Still, a little titillation never hurt anybody. According to my mother, this is some sort of Catholic sleight of hand, whereby you both get it, and you don't. But he found his match in her, because my mother took the opposite approach, first the fireworks and the winning lottery ticket, and only then the . . . she refused to say the word. For a long time, they teased each other, testing their wills, mutually humiliating each other, until my father gave in, threw in the towel, and copulated with the girl of lowly birth, but a sensitive heart. The first time caught my father off guard. My mother's puttering about was unexpectedly solemn, the way she pulled off my father's pants, painstakingly, sober-minded, as if it was required of her. The socks, too, she rolled down with solemnity, meticulously placing them inside the shoes, as if reinstating some sort of invisible order. It was in this vein that she bent over my father's groin. Like Mapplethorpe, my father thought. He took the phallus seriously—the phallus as character actor, not a clown or an ironic understatement (my father had spent years as ambassador to England). On the contrary, despite all the solemnity due to the occasion, my mother thought it was amusing that the part should represent the whole. A representative entrusted in full, this is how my loving mother called this fragment of my father. My father did not understand, but he was in no position to ask questions. (Once my mother asked—a bad joke—isn't it unhealthy? On the contrary, my father grinned. It's not easy, women and the truth in equal measure. It's healthy. Practically medicinal. Ask the Ministry of Health. It's rich in vitamins. The answer was aloof, but not off-putting. Never mind, my mother nodded into my father.) My mother treated my father's prick with respect and good cheer. She felt that she was swallowing their future, as well as their life together, and she did so with awe and ceremony, and with cannibalistic eagerness. As for my father, thanks to this complex hymn, he suddenly understood what a man's body was about. My mother's passion awakened my father to his body as the body of a man. He felt a new sense of calm, this time devoid of any superciliousness. *I am a man, you are a woman.* Tired, my mother turned on her side and fell fast asleep. She was as heavy as a sack. She snored softly. My father watched her, and he felt happy. He thought he understood something. He stroked my mother's shoulder, the nape of her neck, and from time to time, he kissed her. He was empty, full of my mother, and vice versa. The horizon was bathed in topaz rays of light. Meanwhile, Master Haydn, who outwardly was always smiling a sedate, cheerful smile, was wracked inside by secret struggles and agonies. He was dissatisfied with himself and doubted the judiciousness of the world's assessment of his person. He felt apprehensive that the bright glory, his fame and great wealth was his without his fully having deserved it! My mother's letter threw this into high relief. Written in the spring, she comments that Haydn had said to her, I would like to compose something that would make my name immortal. Absurd! One hundred symphonies, nearly eighty string quartets and other masterpieces, and then these words! What would make his reputation permanent he wanted to write only *after this!* Ridiculous.

84. *You could be my son*, the woman (my mother) said to my father, who took this to mean that he could be my mother's little sun, let's head for the house of the rising sun!, and with a grin that promised much, but one thing indubitably (as if offering himself up on a silver tray, my mother said disapprovingly), he pulled down the shades. My mother was frightened. Lookie here, Irén,

she said to herself by way of encouragement, you'd better rephrase yourself, girl! And lo and behold, she reshuffled the focus of the sentence to mean explicitly, *I could be your mother.* The wind taken out of his sails, my father curled his mouth—and from that day on, even though some mad and secret hope continued tugging at him, he understood that his life was nothing but a tragic fairground farce written by women with godlike powers—and he pulled up the shades. (Tugging at them like a fucking coward, my mother said.) Which is how my father and my mother met.

85. $M$y father was learning English. Taking pains over it. Once, for instance, instead of saying *how are you*, or even more to the point, *the pen is on the table,* he confidently and elaborately launched into a sentence about the structure and nature of European culture with special regard to the nostalgic character of the present, specifically, that we prefer what is passing or what is past, something that, in a certain sense, no longer exists; but, and this was meant to be the crux of his point, the—how should he put it—the *bite,* or to put it another way, the *wound* or *pain* of his assertion, that this is not a question of choice, and it is not a question of decision, on the contrary, it is the immediate result of the *shape* of this culture; in short, when he offered this up for debate in his— he believed—best newly acquired English, though he was aware of an element of uncertainty and poverty with respect to conjugation, word order and word choice, still, he was surprised that his partner in the conversation, a bald, gorgeous hunk of a Turk in chains, a strong, handsome specimen dazzling as the sun, a real man, whatever this word may or may not mean, answered with a wide—and considering his miserable situation—with a friendly, amicable smile, okay, okay, we'll play Ping-Pong after lunch, if that's what you want. *My father has the ball.* Had my father taken anything seriously, he'd have burst into tears.

• • •

86. According to some people, my father carries his brains, or intellect, *down there*. Some people go ahead and point to their groin, at the *down there*. No matter how refined the person may be, this gesture, accompanied by nervous laughter, is always repulsive, filthy, disgusting, enough to make you puke. The titter, which never fails, is a sign of envy and awe, an approbation of sorts, while the comment itself is meant to be reproachful and belittling to the extreme, i.e., that my father cannot be trusted, what *moral insanity,* running after his prick, his prick ruling the roost. If only that were true, my father sighs like a bad actor in the only major role in his life, and touches the *down there.* A heavenly gesture.

87. My father's life was mapped out for him in advance. The plan was not particularly inspired, but it opened up pleasant prospects. What could go wrong when he had a fucking big entail? But my father had a plan of his own, one that was realized with such fury that it didn't even have to take the historical circumstances into account, though the menu was plentiful, Versailles, Szálasi, Russian occupation, 1956. No lack of excitement. At the heart of his plan was the fact that he did not like greasy mutton. He had a special kind imported from the Near East that collects fat in its tail; in the process, it becomes as large as a ball. When baked, it is a true delicacy. Now then: in order that these dumb creatures of God should not have to pull this grease ball behind them like their entrails, he (my father) concocted a small two-wheeled cart for them. This is what kept him busy his whole life; this is what we would observe as he'd sit on the porch or out on the pasture, or by the bank of a ditch, or under a tree, fashioning these small sheep carts. They were even named after him. A species of hazelnut, nobody knows why, and these. The goats wandered all over the estate, you just had to find which parts of Transdanubia were marked, or grooved, by the parallel wheel tracks, and that was all ours. Of course, expropriation is expropriation. And parallel lines

are parallel lines, my father said. My father remained a landowner throughout his life, not a great landowner with land, but one who owns the country, or its grooves, at any rate, its parallel lines. Parallel lines, my mother said with a dismissive wave of the hand as soon as they'd made each other's acquaintance. They don't count. They never meet. Except somewhere out there, in the infinite, a goat winked back at her one day.

88. Even while watching the flock, my father kept sketching sheep in the sand. Nobody taught him, he knew it innately, as if it had been stamped into his hand. When Cimabue got wind of this gift of my father's, he was impressed and asked him (my father) to come work for him. My father said he'd love to, provided his father did not object. He didn't. Unlike Michelangelo's father, who beat Michelangelo to a pulp when he caught him doing it (sketching). He considered painting, and art in general, as "inferior," below the dignity of the family. (There is something to be said for that.) Another similarity between my father and Michelangelo is that he, like the latter, was wedded to his art, with the paintings being the offspring. My father would daub into the middle of the night and when my mother threw a gentle glance of reproach his way to the effect that tomorrow is another day and he might consider retiring, he shouted, *Oh che dolce cosa è questa prospettiva!,* which, however, was spread abroad as "how sweet a lover perspective is," to wit, that *prospettiva (la!)* keeps the artist from the conjugal bed. (There is something to be said for that, too. On Pope Sixtus IV's sepulchral monument, Pollaiuolo, represented perspective in the shape of a woman.)

89. My father kissed a man in earnest just once (thus far), on one occasion. It was not quite a real kiss, but much more than a manly kiss. This is what happened. My father had a friend, a writer, i.e., a friend who was a writer. My father liked his work, though their

views differed significantly. The writer was a skeptical observer, a passionate and resigned stock taker, and it never occurred to him to change the world. He considered it an erroneous *ars poetica*, ridiculous, vain (with respect to himself). My father was just the opposite. He was incapable of accepting the world for what it is. He castigated the politicians for their selfishness, and the people for their cowardice. Life shirkers!, he said, and that you can't leave your life to others, meaning that you can leave it, as far as that goes, but why should you? My father loved life from the vantage point of death. He went about his business relentlessly in keeping with an outmoded humanism; at least, this is how people saw it. He taught mathematics to Gypsy children, he had unwed mothers learn the Mendeleyev periodic table, and held dancing classes for mentally handicapped boys (both beginners and advanced). My father's constitution was heroic. Just like a Union insider out to find grace, his friend laughed. According to my father, in spite of everything, in spite of the scandal that is the twentieth century, there is nothing to prevent love and goodness from ruling the world, not even human nature, though admittedly, what we've got is only a narrow cross section. But he's starting out from those he knows, that's his point of departure, and not those he'd read about. Needless to say, he knows ignoble characters, too. Still, he will not relinquish his contention, which rests on an emotional basis, as it were. Emotions are ill suited for creating systems, my father's friend said, disheartened, whereas that's what we're talking about. It was no comfort to him that he was right; being right is one thing, truth quite another. Life's not worth a fig without love, my father whooped merrily. (They'd been into their cups all afternoon. Not for any reason in particular; it was just one of those afternoons.) The writer laughed. Love is dangerous. Don't play with fire. My father waved him off. Computers! The foundation stones of a new culture! The demise of the word! The end of history as we know it! That's all you people can say, as if everything were dispensable. Well, could you dispense with *this*? He leaned across the table, took the writer's hand in his own, and stroked it. The writer laughed again, and nodded. Sentiments are always immediate, they're always of the present, my father insisted. But not a force to move a nation, the writer said with a dismissive wave. Oh, yes, they are! Besides, who cares about nations? You and me, if we don't want new barbaric hordes marching down our garden path. My father: You can't go around niggling and nitpicking like this. You gotta have faith, and that's all there is to it! Is that so?, the writer said, raising his brow, spoiling for a fight. He was on home ground. My father raised himself in his seat, and so did his friend. My father had an intimation of the emptiness at which the writer was aiming; no, no, the myth must be taken seriously! Seriously and ironically, the writer said. Now it was my father's turn to feel disheartened. The writer shrugged. He was thinking he should apologize. All right. Name one thing in the world we can regard without irony. God. What God? God. The writer waved him off. It's not me who is being ironic. It's His situation that's ironic. God who art not, help us! What's this if not irony? Existential irony. My father had no liking for this sort of talk. It was here, at this point, that my father leaned forward and planted a lingering kiss on his friend's lips, a warm, wet, throbbing kiss. It was the first time in his life that he'd kissed a man like that. Begad, it felt good. At which, red as a lobster and sober, his friend said, There was hardly any irony in that. And now, I must go.

90. My father's opinion about mankind (according to his friend) is that mankind is good. Ha-ha, my father's friend says, who mentions this as a piece of absurdity, even though he keeps bringing it up in company with something like pride and good cheer, as if to say, see what a beautiful human being I have for a friend? My father, my father's friend's friend, listens and grins. But once he whispered in his friend's ear (who quite rightly considers man a

bloody savage or, when he's had a bit too much to drink, he says that yes, my father is quite right, people are good, except they don't know it) that when I say that mankind is good, I am not talking about mankind, but about the manner in which I am talking about mankind. At which my father's friend leaned across the table and planted a lingering kiss on my father's lips, a warm, wet, throbbing kiss, something that he'd never done before, needless to say. Which is how my father and my mother met.

91.　It is far better that God should have granted my father the option of sinning than if He had prevented it, because He could have prevented it only by treating my father as if he were a rock or a stone, bringing the weight of His implacable might to bear down upon him. But in that case, my father would not know or praise His name. He'd be too confident. Not knowing the face of sin, he'd think he was as spotless as the Lord. Consequently, it is incomparably better that God should have allowed my father the possibility of sinning than if He'd have prevented it, because sin (my father's), in the face of the Lord, is as chaff; though it be great, the Lord can and does triumph over it for His sake, for His eternal glory, without having harmed my father into the bargain. Of course (need we say), God could not have changed what He'd foreordained in order to keep my father free of sin without harming His eternal truths, because, in that case, my father could not have sung His praises with all his heart, which is the primary and sole purpose of Creation.

●　　●　　●　　●　　●

92. My father was a monster. My mother, ditto. Monsters from morning to night, from night until morning, willy-nilly, from reflex, culture, character, and pure chance. But they were monsters, all the same. Sometimes they gave a dinner or went to the theater or organized pleasurable trips up into the Vértes Mountains, just to relieve the monotony of their horrible deeds. But in actual fact, they were like the characters you see in American B movies. Though they are impossible to watch, they are, sociologically and anthropomorphically speaking, accurate (my parents).

93. Late Tuesday night, the fifty-six-year-old pump operator of the MOL gas station situated on Kőalja Road in Ózd scared off her attackers, two masked fathers of mine who demanded at gunpoint that she hand over the day's receipts. The intrepid pump operator cried for help—Help! Help!—and my two fathers decamped, i.e., fled the scene. Which is how my mother met my father who, for his part, later didn't remember a thing. He chose not to remember, not even the cost of the 95 octane unleaded gasoline.

94. The course of a family's life is subject to a variety of happenstances, the pulsating currents of history plus personal factors, once one branch, then another being in the ascendant. Unexpect-

edly (?), the oldest son dies a hero's death, while the one next in line for the succession—but never mind. For instance, in my family, the gramophone proved to be the decisive factor. My father was passionately fond of gramophones (after they were invented). There were three children in the family, all boys, my father in the middle, but he inherited everything. How could this have happened? My father couldn't get his fill of the new *revolving,* this turning round and round, and in order to make it more . . . more tangible, he ingeniously stuck feathers into the plate of the gramophone and watched it with his older brother (the heir apparent to the estate) until their heads whirled. Later, they became active participants in the revolving; they used the feather contraption as a sort of masturbation device (my father's very first invention!) by cleverly positioning their pricks between the feathers which, as they turned, tickled (their pricks). This invention was noteworthy in two respects: physically, because of its splendid automatism and unfailing reliability, and morally, because it did not count as masturbation, because you (my father and his older brother) weren't using your (their) hands! Which brought a great inner relief (the formula "Forgive me, Father, for I have committed an unnatural act," so much a part of Sunday confession, was petty and depressing), and this in turn affected the body, adding to the enjoyment. (Oh, those sweet pleasures, innocent of the responsibility toward a second party, just a respectful bow of the head to Nature, with no holds barred.) In which case, what was the problem? The problem was that one day this revolving nipped a bit of skin off the eldest boy's purse, and that was that! As for my father's younger brother, who was still too young (he was supposed to inherit the fish ponds and forests around Mór), he was watching his older brothers from behind a curtain, and what he saw—the black record album, the revolving bird feathers, and the rigid rigidity rearing between them—put so much fear in his heart that he never wanted to have anything to do with this rigidity, ever again, as long as he lived. Which is how my father became the sole in-heritor and the main branch, not to mention the pleasure inher-ent in all that revolving.

95. His taste buds! My father had lost all he had, not to mention the estates, the fish ponds, the forests stretching up to Mór, the houses, the palaces, the stocks and bonds ("I have securities, too, but they're advance security, and the sum by which the collat-eral security could be redeemed brings more profit than if I were to . . ."), and he lost his homeland, too, into the bargain. Or maybe just his country. (In keeping with family tradition, he car-ried his homeland in his heart. "I have no home anymore, just a roof over my head and a bed . . . More importantly—or if there's such a thing as tragedy, then more tragically—I have lost my soli-darity with Hungarian society. Who is there to sympathize with? The dishonest bourgeoisie? The greedy and brutally selfish peas-antry? The uneducated working class? . . . As for my own class, there's no class anymore, just a couple of individuals, as far as I'm concerned. I have come to know its loathsome characteristics, and it horrifies me. I no longer feel solidarity with Hungarian so-ciety, and this is the worst thing that could have happened to me. And now that they're up in arms because they're losing the ground from under their feet, or their positions, or they're com-plaining about the fate of Kassa and Nagyvárad, again, I feel no real sympathy. They were blind, avaricious, deaf, greedy and ruthless in their desires. Well, they got what they were after. I serve my native language, but I no longer feel solidarity with the society that speaks this language.") He lost my mother, who got fed up with my father's escapades, he lost us who, alarmed, drifted along with our mother, but amid this drabness alternating with drabness, he did not lose his lust for life, namely, his love of mak-ing fine distinctions in taste. The taste buds! The dictatorship of the proletariat had no effect on my father's taste buds. My father

gobbled up the world. Once—when was it? in 1952? or 1953?—somebody brought him a bag of piglet tails to make something from them, if he could. He could. It became known as the renowned ragout à la Brasov. Ragout à la Brasov was first served up by my father in the early fifties. Everybody thinks it's some sort of ancient Magyar dish. Ancient, but like this! He invented pike perch à la Dorozsma, too! Actually, it'd been invented before, but it didn't have a name. And then my father took out the map of Hungary, Close your eyes!, he told his eldest son (the others hadn't happened yet!), and point! He pointed. Dorozsma! Even as he was forcibly resettled in the countryside, he soon came up with the idea of opening a small tavern. The women's toilet was in the children's room. If anybody found a fish bone, they got a free bottle of champagne, but nobody found any. You should've seen the crowds! Andy's, that was the name of the tavern. But it wasn't like people could eat whatever they fancied, but nice and easy like, my father talked them into it. *Stören,* to meddle, which became "störening," that my father's at it, he's "störening" them again. The waiters liked him, but laughed behind his back. Look, the old man's störening again!

96. Truffle soufflé, that's how my father died. It was poisoned. His friends and admirers had known him as a man who enjoyed a lighthearted debate and who was well off without God. As a result, he regarded man not as a creature of God, but a machine. His *liebling,* the favorite part of the machine, was the head. Philosophy, irony, esthetics! He contended that the brain is the wellspring not only of the intellect, but of our dreams and pleasures, too; in short, that nature has endowed us with the capacity for happiness; in short—and my father was happy that his line of reasoning led to this particular conclusion—*Carpe diem!* The guiding principle of his life, his motto, was the playful, disrespectful ver-

110

sion of love's commandment: Love whatever and whoever you want, just as long as you love! (In Vienna: *Liebt, wen oder was Ihr wollt, ab er liebt!*) As my father was fond of saying, man is born ignorant but, if he is wise, he dies a skeptic.

97. $M$y father, he'd been gone a long time, with only the sausage he used to make remaining after him. Dry, richly spiced—he had a brilliant seasoned concoction of his own, good enough to be patented, a so-called peasant sausage. Mouthwatering. It hung in the pantry, with the breezes blowing through it. My father loved meat more than anything. He had gout. He loved it even more than he loved gold. Whenever I eat meat, I feel that I'm somebody. When I take a bite—because you gotta bite into meat, you gotta have a good set of teeth—I know I've made something of myself. I know that I'm alive. That I've got a life of my own. Seaweed or corn won't do the trick. He went broke overnight. In the evening, he was still a golden boy zipping around town in a Sports Volvo à la Simon Templar, visiting the Canary Bar with a different woman on his arm every time, including my mother. He'd been supporting the entire family since he'd turned fifteen, because my grandfather refused to lift a finger and hadn't done a thing since then. He'd put himself out of commission, and decided to spend his time in the back room with the drapes drawn, reading. He spent the whole day reading. On Saturday he called for my father, armchair and whiskey, and behind closed doors and with the light turned out, he had him present the accounts. He was not allowed to sit down. My father was standing up, my grandfather was sitting down. He sat in his armchair, with his book in his lap. He never used a bookmarker. He would not stand for it. *A person knows where he's at.* He'd pull the bookmarkers like weed from between the pages of a book. He knew where something could be found, and in which edition, from thirty, fifty years

ago. Where's Nemecsek's fatal bath, page *x,* upper-left-hand corner. Toward the end of his life, he began reading his favorite books again, something about William the Silent or William of Orange? Or is that the same thing? Standing by the door, my father asked, how many times have you read it, Sir? Three. Once because I felt like it, once because I understood it, and now to take my leave of it. My grandfather reread all the books that were important to him in order to take his leave of them. (Not all, because that would have taken a whole new lifetime, the end of which he'd have had to set aside once again for rereading.) In short, my father was the provider and my grandfather a *versager,* a good-for-nothing, but his unimpeachable authority over the family went unchallenged. He held the world in contempt—*for those people?!*—lumping my father in with the rest of "those people." When my father announced an important visitor my grandfather should have received in the interest of the family, Grandfather asked while continuing to read, does he speak Hungarian? And if the visitor did not, he just said, too bad, and sent my father from the room. The old man was a prick, but a *somebody,* in the evening a rich man, in the morning a beggar (my father), because they started importing a polyester-based textile that became all the rage. People went wild over that stuff. It was just a passing fashion frenzy. It didn't make it past the summer, if that. But by then my father had nothing left to his name but his debts, and he was reduced to collecting seaweed, for instance. He could make a really tasty dish from lard, flour, water, and strong spices. That's when he came up with his famous spiced "baste." Then the family's gums began to bleed and their teeth got loose, and the doctor said, scurvy. And then all of a sudden my father became a rich man, in the evening scurvy, in the morning gout, great big slices of beef over charcoal, *azado,* constantly basting and bathing in his famous spiced pickling sauce, plus mustard. One year eight thousand, the next year eight hundred thousand. As for the sausage, it is better bitten off than sliced. A strong grip, and hum. Or break some off. It's good like that, too.

98. Day in and day out, my father stuffs himself with a vengeance. He eats like a pig, because he mustn't drop below ninety kilos. The extra weight doesn't look bad on him, except he wheezes. He never told anybody before where, because it would be a shameful admission, but the Nazis implanted a gauge which, in the eventuality that my father should drop below ninety kilos, would explode, bang!!! Stuff yourself, Jew, he was told, because *in there* everyone was skinny, the ribs and everything, and then they (the Jews) complained, even if only in a muted whisper, asking if it couldn't be just a little bit more, a little something, not much, but still, cabbage leaves, maybe; no problem, they said, and ever since, there's nothing but this stuffing.

99. Forty summers later, my father compensated for his—let's call it infirmity of purpose—during Arrow Cross times. He trained his (pure-bred) puli to run about the apartment, searching as if it'd gone berserk, whenever he shouted Nazi! (my father, to the puli), while the guests, should there be any, Jews and non-Jews alike, laughed and pointed at the dog, and sometimes at one another, then always, without exception, applauded, except for my mother, who looks down on my father, the puli, and the guests (Jews and non-Jews) in equal measure.

100. My father was picking clover, fifty-six thousand holds. He had to do it, it was about to rain, and that's why he joined in late, kicking three goals by the middle of the second inning. Then he asked to be replaced. Sorry, boys, gotta go, you know, the clover.

101. Hamburg muscatel was my father's favorite. In horses the Lipizzaner, in wine, Hamburg muscatel. Come, come, Mati dear, don't

talk nonsense. How can it be your favorite wine when there's no such thing. Muscatel from Hamburg. The very idea! Muscatel in a Hanseatic town! Meanwhile, my father started retching like a dog at a country wedding, kicking up a row and taunting, saying that it's Hamburg muscatel he'd just been imbibing in excess. We, in the adjoining room, were trembling with fear. Well? Do you still doubt my words, you . . . *Thomas!*, my father roared triumphantly. To say that my mother doubted, no, that wouldn't be quite true.

102. The Parmesan, sardines, olives (beans and oil), from Ignaz and Cristoph Spöttl, the sour cabbage from Joseph Haderlein, the ale from Karl Lieffner, the kitchen utensils from Kerschek and Kubitsek of Temesvár, the Havana cigars from Hess and Sons, the cheek-pieces and trappings from Antal Molnár, the two new *federblatts* for the yellow carriage from János Matics. The stable boy Gyóni's cap for Majk from József Veszeli, and likewise, the three blue jockey caps and spectacles from Simon Waldstein, optician and technician for the imperial and royal Court, not to mention certified royal treasurer, which titles he bore also in the service of the German emperor, the Italian and Spanish kings and the Prince of Wales. Three wooden tubs from József Púla, petroleum jelly from Just and Comp., the net to catch hawks, who knows, and likewise the tatofinum (?) grease for the carriages. This is where my father ordered them. He conducted a scrupulous discussion with his chef, Maître Baldauf, every morning. As Hume said, we're so used to the sun coming up every morning, it is bound to come up again. It was in a similar vein of presumptive certainty that my father consulted with his man every morning. They told each other what they would like—to eat and to cook. Then they told each other about all the things that frustrated their plans, because there's no coriander, for one thing, or my father doesn't feel like kidneys with onions, or Russian troops had just

been spotted near the manor house, raping anything—cats, women, welted top boots. Having dismissed the chef, my father would then prepare the daily schedule, so he could pass it on— have someone pass it on—to my mother. Not a single day passed without the following item on the agenda: personal encounter. Which is how my father and my mother met. The chocolate was dispatched by Pietro Rinaldi from Vienna, and at times by the imperial supplier Sala.

103. It goes to show. My father, my grandfather's son, lord inheritor of Csákvár, was banished from the castle while still a babe because a soothsayer, the soothsayer of the village, told my grandfather at harvest time that the child slated to be born to him (my father) would be *bound* to be his murderer, and my grandfather loved life, he loved it generally, and his own specifically, so he had my father bundled out to the Vértes Mountains. But he was saved and was brought up at the court of a count at the mining towns of Ajka and Inota, known for its power plant, because he was mistakenly assumed to be lord inheritor of Ajka and Inota. Then one day the soothsayer surprised my father by saying he should leave his home, otherwise, he—and here came that word again—would be *bound,* unwittingly and inevitably, to murder his father and cohabit with his mother. Oh, lordie lord! My father took this *bound* seriously, and left the home he thought was his home and the father and mother he thought were his father and mother. Just before the mountain town of Bakonylép, at the place where three roads meet, he ran into Grandfather whom, in the wrangle over the right of way, he (my father) made short shrift of. Insolent old man! Having reached Csákvár, he cleverly solved an acute problem plaguing the community (the sewer system, or did he cut a clear path through the maize of public social security dues?), and the grateful people elected him count, and he won Grandmother's hand into the bargain. (Who was about

the same age as Gitta is now.) They lived in peace, honor and dignity, he had two sons and two daughters by his mother (unbeknownst to him, though on photographs the resemblance is marked, the foreheads, the curve of the nose). Anyway, next thing you know, the pestilence breaks out for no apparent reason, so the people of Csákvár turn to a soothsayer once again, who sends a message to the effect that they must find and punish Grandfather Lajos's murderer. My father threw himself into the detective work like a pro, and step by step, with admirable skill, it (everything: his father's thingamajig, his mother's whatnot) came to light. Grandmother hanged herself, and my father struck out his eyes. He chose eternal darkness, and packed off to where he was eternal lord: the far from uncommendable sewage system and *modus vivendi* re. the public dues remained, and the soothsayer's prophecies were fulfilled.

104. My father contends that the increase of entropy is contingent upon the sinfulness of mankind. The decline of the West and the repeated stock market crashes are the axiomatic outcome of the second law of thermodynamics. Now, if a happy family becomes unhappy, entropy increases, *cf.* the first sentence of *Anna Karenina!*

105. The counter legend goes like this: Christ. At the local train stop on Batthyányi Square, Jesus Christ approached my father, his words garbled, his gaze misty, a fresh red wound on the wing of his nose, a sour stink issuing from his heavy overcoat. Tired yet respectful, he asked him for some change. Ain't got none, my father said, pulling a wry face, because he had only a thousand-forint note on him. My good man, said Jesus Christ, taking my father's hand in his. Alarmed, Father drew it back, trembling at the lightness and silken softness of it. Fuck off!, he said, pushing him away, beat it! And the Son of God answered, From this day

forth, you are the one who shall fuck off, and may you have no peace neither night nor day. And so it came to pass. My father wandered from one local stop to the next, from one country to the next, but found no peace, not even *requies aeterna,* the peace that comes with death. In His divine anger, God bereft him even of that. Wherever my father passes now, he brings calamity. (The rivers overflow their bounds, the sheep get the staggers, et cetera.) In the end, my father found himself in the predicament of the Jews. The anti-Semitic overtones need no comment.

106. At the local train stop on Batthyányi Square my father, whose words were garbled, whose gaze was misty, a fresh red wound on the wing of his nose, a sour stink issuing from his heavy overcoat, stepped up to Jesus Christ, and tired yet respectful, asked him for change. Haven't got none, Christ said, pulling a wry face, because he had only a thousand-forint note on him. My good man, my father said, taking Christ's hand (God's right) in his. Alarmed, he drew it back, trembling at the lightness and silken softness of it. Fuck off!, said the Son of God pushing him away, beat it! May you have no peace neither night nor day. And so it came to pass. My father wandered from one local stop to the next, from one country to the next, but like a wandering Jew, found no peace. Even the rivers overflow their bounds, and the sheep get the staggers. Suffering. There's no getting around it.

107. Man is a creature of suffering. Every creature of suffering is a threat to society. My father does not pose a threat to society. My father is not a creature of suffering. (!) My father is not a man. Excuse me?

108. With an appeal to the American (USA) code of law, my father initiated a civil suit against God because of the great drought. The

wheat was parched, et cetera. He won his suit on the first round, because the respondent didn't show. On the second round . . .

109. My mother owned a Singer sewing machine. It was stacked up and elaborate, like a cathedral. On this machine, my mother made stars of David out of yellow silk duvet covers for my father and my father's son, one bigger, one smaller, for the law had stipulated that in case of mixed marriages, a male child must be considered a member of his father's church, a girl child her mother's. There they stood in front of my mother, my father and my father's son, drawing themselves up to their full height as if they were being fitted for a new suit, and she, with pins between her teeth, trying to find the best place for the stars on the lapels of their coats. Whether my father had plucked up his courage and—in his son's interest—decided to ignore the official decree, or whether thanks to his conversion to Christianity he'd found a loophole in the law, we shall never know. Be that as it may, the yellow star that looked so much like a puffball or dandelion lay in the drawer of the sewing machine in the company of colored threads, rags and buttons for a long time afterward, but except for that one occasion, the "dress rehearsal," they, my father and my father's son, never wore it again. Suffering. It is so unseemly.

110. Had my father been the mad tyrant he's sometimes made out to be, a narrow-sighted asshole, a shallow nonentity, rendered human, if at all, only by his suffering, it is not likely that in his tender years—the lion's claws showing!—my father's eldest son would have bothered to think up "a good morning wish for the dearest of all fathers" (*Morgenglückwüsche* in Latin) on every day of the week. Good and beautiful and plenteous, let this be Monday. The first rays of the rising sun, may they put a spring in your gait. May Jehovah, who abounds in good deeds, watch over your plenteous good health. This is how the day began, day after day. Yet my

father was just a father, a mad tyrant, a narrow-sighted asshole, a shallow nonentity. Only his sufferings rendered him worthy of mention, poor dear.

111.  My father never meant to cause suffering, not in the slightest. He went to great lengths to avoid it. He lied, he dissembled, he paid through the nose, he loved his neighbor as himself, he sacrificed his lunchtime—in short, everything, really. This horror and dread of suffering caused immeasurable suffering all around.

112.  My father wanted to be inevitable, fated and preordained from the beginning of time. His every word, gesture, action, sin, act and omission thereof, every gulp of wine (weak, table) that he drank, everything . . . , but never mind. In short, even part of his output reveals the unrelenting, desperate effort with which he (my father) attempted to deny his own contingency.

113.  (Views of my father weeping.) An aristocrat was riding down the street. He ran over my father. The place and time can be determined with precision. But the point is, it was my father's fault. Preoccupied with his thoughts, he was just turning a sentence over in his head. It wasn't even a sentence yet, just a jumble of words, a stage for a sentence, an *Ich-Erzähler,* a first-person narrative. He was oblivious to everything around him, except for these words. He was just about to shift them around when bang!, the open BMW convertible butted him, as it were, from the side. My father fell face forward, and the car rolled over him before it could stop. His head crashed with a thud. He remained like that, quietly leaning his head against the asphalt. He would not move. Meanwhile, socialism continued on the march. The chauffeur, a young man with sunglasses and an unpleasant, ingratiating smile, his face a jumble of apprehension and annoyance, leaned over my father. Who still would not move. But seeing the apprehension and

ignoring the annoyance, my father tried to comfort the young man from there, on the ground, embracing (more like clawing) the asphalt like a pillow, saying, don't worry, it's an open-and-shut case, there's a guilty party and the guilty party is him, my father, not partially or basically, but completely and exclusively because, as they say—because that's how they say it, don't they?—he stepped off the sidewalk within braking distance. He takes full responsibility. He does not always participate in the struggle for survival. Some people may find it peculiar, but he does not wish to change. On the other hand, his present situation *could* definitely use a change. He's perfectly aware that it is not *comme il faut* like this, in front of the wheels, what he means is under them. He'd get up if only he could, but he can't. He can't move. What's more, though he wouldn't think of offending the pleasant young man and his charming companion, it's the furthest thing from his mind, he doesn't even want to. He feels that he's found his place at last, this is what he feels, when and where can be determined with precision. Now, when the exchange rate of the dollar is so scandalously unpredictable and the daffodils have begun to open on the green lawn across the way, he feels that he'd *arrived,* as if his existence and essence had united into one at long last, that this is his place, where he is now, this is his home, the platform from where he could *talk,* and not like the present century, muttering to himself, because theoretically it is possible to talk about subjects of common interest from down there. In short, on this platform, or stage, he could be the *Ich-Erzähler,* the narrator of his own story, and that's the way it is. So please don't touch him. He doesn't feel like moving. And though he's sorry about the inconvenience, he'd like to stay like this from now on, with his face pressed against the warm, dusty asphalt. And so it was. My mother sat rigidly in the BMW, looking straight ahead at no one in particular, though there were plenty of people around.

·   ·   ·

114. The world's first garage is in Ladenburg, near Mannheim. It was built by the Benzes to house automobiles. Once a week Bertha Benz, the legendary Bertha, drove into Heidelberg to buy gasoline at the local pharmacy. My father.

115. My father felt under the weather. Tipsy. Gloomy. Why bother brushing his teeth, et cetera. Dark, heavy clouds, dry, passed behind his brow. Little likelihood of rain, a lively north wind, gusty in places, the temperature will drop slightly, with 15 to 20° in the early afternoon. Stockholm cloudy, 11°C. Athens windy, 25°C. Berlin cloudy, 16°C. My mother doesn't know who she is living with (Strindberg). He never removed his hat (my father). This is how he became known in town as the mad hatter. Him and Whistling George on Váci utca. They were building the Metro, capable of transporting large crowds swiftly underground, thereby relieving surface traffic. Walking past the guards at the Astoria station, my father descended to have a chat with the workers. A frustrated artist, family affairs and traditions forced him into the school for agriculture, cows, et cetera, his thesis: "Crop Rotation—Solution and Temptation." He could talk in rhymed couplets at the drop of a hat. Nobody noticed. He talked like this with the caisson workers too. (A caisson worker doesn't count, et cetera.) The Metro, unlike my father, is still in service, transporting people daily to work and elsewhere—the movies, soccer games, garden restaurants, pharmacies. Its time has come, my father said, pointing to the dark, damp, bunker that was the tunnel. As they listened to "the guy with the hat" in the half-light, the workers went about their work. This, too, is a building. And buildings, gentlemen, are held together by two things. Technology is one. How we place stone upon stone. If you will recall, anno Domini we had the Gothic. New arches, buttressed. Everything began stretching upward, the half circles disappeared. A church was no longer just big, against which a man stood as a

speck of dust. It aspired to the sky. And even in his essence as a mere speck of dust, man raised his eyes up to his Lord. Up to his God. In short, gentlemen, this is the other thing. The stones are one, this freedom inside the other. Can you feel that awesome span, gentlemen, that awesome coincidence of the material and the spiritual? Well? . . . The fact that technology should reach the same place as the spiritual *at the same time?!* Or, could it be that wherever the spirit is, that's the *place*, if you know what I mean . . . All right, gentlemen, I accept your answer, which is a question. But in that case, kindly tell me where the spirit dwells today? I see only what you see: this brilliant piece of reinforced concrete. Stone remains upon stone. This is what I see. And now, gentlemen, *au revoir*. I must be off to my rooms. It's time I brushed my teeth.

116. After a long, long time, my father—God only knows why—decided to court my mother. (Flowers, champagne, fellatio. Excuse me, the other way around, cunnilingus.) But by the time he'd come back with the champagne glasses, et cetera, my mother was deep in conversation with someone else—a breathtakingly beautiful young girl, slender even as she sat, creole, with two big yet elegant rings in her ears, her hair brushed back like this, flat (the way my father's would be at the time of his death), thus displaying the spectacular shape of the head. My mother had never seen anything so strikingly beautiful before. Nature's shape perfected! Glancing to the side, she spotted my father, and surreptitiously waved to him. The gesture told him to leave her alone; or, even worse, it was a wave of a stranger, as if the two weren't even acquainted. My father was so surprised, his jaw dropped. My mother continued to smile and chat. She was working. The young girl hung on her every word. Shall I tell you something, dear?, my mother said, taking the girl's hand, it would have been simply *awful* if I saw you here, and I didn't do *something*. Awful!

But you did, the girl said. Yes, my mother said, and kissed the palm of her hand. They walked past my father as if he were a waiter. My father heard my mother say, You, my dear, are your own explanation. My mother did not look, but gestured behind her back with her hand. The gesture told my father to leave them alone; or, even worse, it was a wave of a stranger, as if the two (my father and my mother) weren't even acquainted. Which left him alone with the problem of the champagne, et cetera.

117.　She's a nice lady, my father said, and stuck to it for the rest of his life. Which is how he and my mother met.

118.　My mother liked to pretend that she didn't have a husband (namely, my father), or children. She liked to travel, to explore with an easy heart. Once it was the hidden terrains of Mali, another time, Hispania. Jenő Baradlay offered to accompany her, whatever that may mean. My father grew suspicious. You are going away with this Baradlay. Fine. But swear! My mother raised one brow, something she'd learned from my father. Swear that if, *a:* you eat lobster, or any other crustacean of choice, *b:* if you eat putty (?), or *c:* are drinking, swilling, sipping sangria, you will feel bound to think of me. That chomping Jenő Baradlay will fade before you—He does not chomp! (my mother)—and I will appear before the mind's eye, big as life, a holographic form, in color, and in the most flattering light. My mother said nothing. But I wouldn't like you to think I'm unreasonable. If it's fish, you do what you want!, my father continued, though obviously you're going to be eating a lot of fish. I know how much you like fish. My mother still said nothing. And that goes for rice, too! My mother looked questioningly at my father. What about paella? My old man responded with a lukewarm nod. Naturally, certain types of paella are unthinkable without *gambas.* Fine. I swear. My father howled like a dog. Later, when radiant and chocolate brown after two glorious weeks my mother flounced out of young Baradlay's lap, who, for his part, acted like a gentleman throughout, his only fault being his natural melancholy, and she clung to my father's neck like a monkey or a hyperactive adolescent, my father first brushed her off, then kneeled in front of her. Never go so far away from me, ever again, he pleaded. Not even to Érd or Piliswhatnot. I want you here with me all the time. At my beck and call. I want you waiting, waiting for me, like a fireman for a fire. I want you hanging around the key ring, and when I whistle, I want you to say, in English, *I love you*. Neither more, nor less. Whistle, *I love you*. That's not so hard to remember, is it?!

119. On Christmas Eve, my father took out his shotgun again. He wanted to go to Mecsér and gun down my mother. Luckily, he was abruptly wracked by a coughing fit so severe, spouting so much (red) blood, that he collapsed and had to be hauled back to bed.

120. Having missed the last bus, my mother from Balassagyarmat hitched a ride home with a minivan near the railway station at Dejtár. My three fathers sat in the vehicle, with two falling on her without preamble. They tore off her dress and tried to wrestle her down. But my mother kicked and hit them. She even bit the hand of one of her assailants, my father. At last, having had enough of the pugnacious "wildcat," my fathers threw my mother out, flinging her clothes after her. The police headquarters in Balassagyarmat is presently conducting an investigation for attempted rape against unknown offenders (my fathers).

121. My old man has taken on a superhuman challenge, deciding to do twenty-three thousand kilometers on a bike in 115 days, in the decimal system, mind you, straight across the North and South American continents. He hopes the trek, which will begin in

Patagonia and end in Alaska, will call the world's attention to people suffering from sclerosis multiplex (SM). The old man's really something, pure multiplex! The race gun will go off on the Ides of March in the city of Ushuaia in Argentina, the Earth's southernmost tip. My father feels that the effort he is going to expend in order to complete his trek successfully is going to benefit SM victims directly. Of course, he hasn't been sitting at home twiddling his thumbs up till now either. He's done the Australian desert on a mountain bike. (Which is where he met my mother, by the foot of the famous mountain.) He's been preparing for the upcoming trek for some time. The team that will follow my father in two dilapidated microbuses will include a Dutch doctor (who happens to be a bicycle repairman) and a reporter (who has two left hands). My father will attempt the trek on a combination race and mountain bike. He's taking with him only two extra wheels and twenty tires. As far as unforeseen mishaps go, one can't prepare for them, he says. He fears the same things he fears at home, Nevada rattlesnakes, Alaskan wolves, and bears. At his rest stops, he is planning to participate in mass sport events organized by the local SM clubs. He would also like to organize some small–field (soccer) event, but anything will do. He'll even run if he must. Those interested can follow my father's trek on the Internet (www.alba.hu/eea).

122. My father had been planning a trip to Australia for years. He wanted to see for himself, he said, that he will not fall off the globe. There's so much hearsay. Naturally, this is not the real reason he went. My father fell in love again. He saw a color postcard of Australia, a great uninhabited wasteland awash in purple. It was love at first sight. From that moment on, he could think of nothing else. He could not get this purple wasteland, this tourist's dream of emptiness ("a land of sharp contrasts and wild beauty"), out of his mind. Whatever he loved, or better still, whatever he

was attached to, whatever weighed on him like some sweet burden, he could discover none of this, nothing, on the photograph. Nothing. That's love. Which is how my father and my mother met (once).

123. For several days my father had been seeing a girl, always in the same place and at the same time. For several days he'd been meaning to approach her. She was so . . . (Australian?) in every way. But he didn't dare. He was anxious. He didn't want to offend her. He was scared, and oh, the butterflies in his stomach! Finally, on the seventh day, my father pulled himself together. At first, the girl listened warily to my father, her head bobbed to the side. Then she heard him out, and her expression gradually turned friendly, but without trespassing the limits of social etiquette, which my father was just then in the process of trespassing. Needless to say, everything happened as it has to happen when a heart spills over with unbounded yearning. So much red tape!, my father broke out with annoyance, and met my mother, so much red . . . !

124. My mother has teeth like a horse. At first, this gave my father— who made overtures (to my mother) if not with outright indifference, then with reserved courtesy—the wrong impression. But later, that admirable mixture of brains and beauty, maturity and pubescence, anarchy and moral fiber, swept my father off his feet. You are a milestone on the highway of the female sex, my father said (pretty loud). With my mother being nearby, he behaved like a drunk. You should have seen it! This was no light inebriation, but something much more serious, more manly, untainted by hesitation. This was intoxication in earnest, intoxication without a trace of the usual trepidation, nothing but that glorious lightness of being addressed to the whole of Creation, an inspired flightiness before the final leap. But that's not quite right. It lacked direction, and yet was more substantial. It had no aim, and no

purpose, perhaps this is the best way of describing it. It helps if you know that my father is an alcoholic, only then can you fully appreciate the nature of this ethereal ecstasy. Which is how my father and my horse-toothed mother met.

125. My mother missed my father very much, the one who happened to be away on matters of state (Lola). I can wait, my mother wrote my father, I could even manage it as I squat. My father imagined it. My carriage pole stands ready, my father wrote my mother. My mother imagined it. Time's wingèd chariot was hurrying near.

126. My father was not a revolutionary, just a great soul searching for the meaning of life, specifically, the meaning of his life, and even more specifically, the nature of freedom. He got fed up, and dismantled the country's largest red star sitting atop the Houses of Parliament. This was no easy feat. The symbol, three meters in diameter and weighing half a ton—and let's not go into speculation whether a symbol can be this heavy—is now resting hacked to pieces in a warehouse of the National Museum in Mátyásföld. For thirty-nine years, the huge star shone atop the Parliament dome, and let's not go into for whose benefit— for us all. Though it was removed from the dome for a short time in 1957, this was done only to doctor the damage inflicted upon it by the revolution—sorry, the antirevolution. But the damage was the same. With a saw at the ready, my father began to dismantle the star on January 31, 1990. The fragments and my father's instructions for reassembling the star, a true masterpiece of its kind, were put in boxes and are now gathering dust in a museum warehouse. My father would have liked to place the hulking relic on permanent display, but it would have cost an arm and a leg to put back together again. In short, the red star is neither red now, nor a star, but might still cost us. Consequently, my old man put on display the old, two-and-a-half-meter-wide

coat of arms of the People's Republic that had graced the former Party Headquarters. After all, two and a half meters are better than nothing. My father also made plans for a Kádár exhibition, but let's not go into that.

127.    He was old, stooped, and parchment yellow. He was said to be a hero. He had scalp disease and stank to high heaven. His hands were swollen from cutting rock. He was building the Danube channel, and he survived only because someone, a sympathizer (my mother), (stealthily) sneaked him a spoon of cod liver oil every day. Theoretically, he was pitiful, *de facto* he was repulsive: my father.

128.    Since he had to provide for his family, and the political situation, too, was relatively stable, my father decided to breed eunuchs. Though he had two doctorates (in law and political science, with an eye to the management of his estates), and though he spoke English, French and German—he first worked on road repairs, then laying parquet floors, and finally, making plastic belt buckles or whatnot. And now, eunuchs. Breeding eunuchs calls for a lot of attention, empathy, and expertise. It begins with the choice of stock, because it is not enough to recruit exceptionally well-cut youths (a pun, ha–ha!), you must also figure out what to do with them, their cut, what should happen to them, and how to put their beauty to the best use. The requisite operation, too, can be dangerous, though in the case of prepubescent surgery the chances of recovery are good. There are several schools of thinking on this matter (castrati, spadones, thlibiae). Generally, my father had only the testicles excised (with very young boys, he had them crushed and also the genital glands triturated). Stopping the bleeding is essential. After the procedure, my father took the arms of his little protégés and walked up and down the room with them

for two to three hours. This was crucial. In the summer, it was customary to bury the delinquents in sand up to the neck until the wound healed. No water for three days. All of which was the source of much suffering—the thirst, the traumatic fever, the absence of urination (they got bloated with urine), and when, under my father's supervision, they pulled out the metal needle, as if they were tapping a barrel, the urine, held back for days, came spurting out like a fountain, or if it did not, that was a sure sign that the urinary tract was inflamed, blocked, and the patient was as good as dead, but let's not paint the devil on the wall. When this happened, my father's loss was immense, and not only money wise and emotion wise; it damaged his good name, though everyone agreed that a certain amount of loss was to be reckoned with. But those who survived and became objects of lust (*Lustobjekt*), made father an appreciable profit. Not bad for a day's work, he used to say. Most of the boys were satisfied with their new lives. Being youthful and severe, they shared the current view that the road to purity is lined by the paralyzing quagmire of womanhood; while others were later sorry because, for instance, their passion had not abated entirely. But it was as good as crying over spilled milk. (Sorry about that.) Anyway, they hated my father, and if later in life their paths crossed, they deceitfully promised him all sorts of things—power, influence—and talked him into moving with his family into the palace, where they'd made it to head eunuch, a brilliant career. My father took the bait. Not suspecting that he was the object of revenge, he moved to the palace with his loved ones (my mother was delighted, she'd been wanting a palace for some time). But he soon realized that he was entirely at the mercy—how shall we put it—of his former pupils. They forced my father to castrate his four handsome sons, then they forced the sons to castrate their (my) father. Grimaldi, Farinelli, Nicolini, my father piped, trying to put a good face on things. (Shark!, shark!)

129

But he didn't know what lay just around the corner, what sort of quagmire.

129.  Her voice verging on the hysterical, the resident teacher of a girls school in Ajka reported to the duty officer at the local police station that an armed man had accosted two of her students that evening. The police soon took my father, a local resident on whom they also found a loaded Jaguar-type popgun, into custody. How did this happen? Out on the street one evening, with gun in hand, my father stepped up to my mother and her girlfriend, wanting to force them into committing unmentionable acts (i.e., just one, one per head). My mother managed to effectuate her escape, but my father grabbed her friend by the arm and without further ado, confessed his love for her, saying he'd been head over heels for her for some time [sic!], and if she won't be his, he'll have to shoot her. The girl broke into a run, and my father, left high and dry, stood on the roadside with his loaded gun and unfulfilled passion. He was soon caught, because my mother remembered him in vivid detail and provided a remarkably accurate description. My father doesn't understand, even though he'd been sentenced for indecent assault before. But now he was being accused of infringing on someone's personal freedom. I just followed my natural instinct, he said when questioned, I just wanted to fuck, and if something should go wrong, shoot to kill. But only as a last resort. Besides, although they ran away, it was more like prancing, which takes some of the responsibility off me, doesn't it? I can't understand the conduct of the authorities in this case. They kept hitting me as if they were surprised. I consider this excessive, though admittedly, there are different ways of looking at the same thing. The Ten Commandments, for instance. Do not kill, for instance. Of course, some people have God to do the killing for them. I'm not saying it's easier, just that it's different. Somebody's got to do the dirty work.

130

. . .

130.  The detectives of the antiterrorism department of Scotland Yard interrogated my father about the Markov affair in Sophia. Georgi Markov, who emigrated in 1969 and was working for the BBC World Service, was strolling along Waterloo Bridge when, according to the reenactment, my father accidentally (ha-ha, that's a good one, accidentally!) stuck him with a concealed weapon. The poisoned dart ejected from my father's umbrella was discovered in the gentleman's shinbone (who was a member of the opposition) four days after his death. Because of the situation at the time, the investigation came to an impasse. Not so now! According to the reopened files, my father, who was third secretary at the Foreign Affairs office back then, was sent to England in September 1978, shortly before Markov's death, on a forged diplomatic passport. Then after the murder, the humble diplomat (my father) was appointed ambassador to Stockholm. My father doesn't understand, because—and this goes without saying—he'd never been sentenced for anything (any violent crimes) before. Annoyed, he turned the *Sunday Times* reporter away, saying it's "none of their damned business" whether Scotland Yard interrogated him or not. Besides, he's "surrounded by wolves." I consider this excessive, though admittedly, there are different ways of looking at the same thing. The Ten Commandments, for instance. Do not kill, for instance. Of course, some people have God to do the killing for them. He even kills the firstborn of every dumb beast. Somebody's got to do the dirty work.

131.  My father and the Good Lord were fast friends. Once he (my father) was in trouble. Like a real man, he tried to pull himself out of the dark pit that had become his life by the hair, but he got nowhere. Then the thing somehow righted itself. Meanwhile, time marched on. (What is a God without Man? The absolute

131

form of absolute boredom. What is a Man without God? Pure madness in the form of innocence.) Suddenly, he thought of his friend. Lord, you were always with me, and I knew this, and I looked behind me, and I saw the traces of our feet, two pairs. And now, or just before, when I was in dire straits, or am, I don't know, why are you not with me? I looked behind me, and saw only one pair of feet. That's right, Son. Because I was carrying you in my lap.

132.   In the eighteenth century my father did away with religion, in the nineteenth century he did away with God, in the twentieth century, he did away with man.

·   ·   ·   ·   ·

133.  There had been profound silence for some time, though the world continued to pound in the human heart. And then, Turkish riders hiding behind their colorful costumes sneaked up to the manor. First, they occupied it by subterfuge, then they massacred the people of the manor down to the last man. The blood flowed in rivulets. Brains splattered against the whitewashed walls. Vultures fed on the intestines of dead children. My mother counted the dead putrefying in the sun. She stammered as she did so. The world was pounding, pounding. (At this time, if not earlier, my father should have realized that he should go to the devil with his cradled and cosseted ego, his finely chiseled, painstakingly, and immaculately refined self, because it no longer counted for anything, it had ceased to be, because space is not empty, and the world, which we fill up with games of our own choosing, is not empty, but full—full of pain. And I am not referring to unhappiness, *giaour dog,* the Turk said as he was about to stab my father, but then he didn't, as if the world were empty, which we fill up— with our little games.) My mother continued to count the dead putrefying in the sun, stammering—in Turkish.

134.  The news came: the pagan hordes are plundering Gimesallya, Kara Mustapha has attacked the peacefully grazing Magyars, this

was their custom, and ours to bear it. Vienna insisted that we put up with it to an extent, in the interest of peace, but this time, we didn't. We sorely needed a taste of success. And my father said to my brother László: Choose your men and go forth, fight with the pagan hordes. I will stand on top of the hill of Vezekény with the rod of the Land in mine hand. So my brother László did as my father had said to him, and fought with the pagan hordes and Count Forgách, the captain general of Érsekújvár, and also General Pál Serényi went up to the top of the hill with him. And it came to pass that when my father held up his hand, then my brother prevailed, and when he let down his hand, the pagan hordes prevailed. But my father's hands were heavy, and they took a stone, and put *it* under him, and he sat thereon, and Forgách and Serényi stayed up his hands, the one on the one side, and the other on the other side, and his hands were steady until the going down of the sun. This is how my brothers prevailed over the armed pagan hordes. Still, it remains by way of addendum, for the sake of the whole horrible and banal truth, that Serényi dropped my father's hand three times, and Forgách once. The first time, sitting atop his horse Challenger that he hath promised unto me, my brother László lost his life, as he followed, *here my father's name followed,* milord János and Marci, his manservant, and also around twenty riders besides. Having been forced into a wide, muddy stream, the horse did trip up with him, but he continued the fight on foot, and did slaughter two of the Turks, until at last, languishing from his several wounds, he did lay down his life. As is shown on the helmet and breastplate in the Museum of Military History (Heeresgeschichtliche Museum) in Vienna, he received one slash of the sword on the head, and one bullet that ripped a piece out of the hem of his breastplate and entered his body. The latter probably caused his death. Count Ferenc fell next, and a Turk beheaded him. Tamás received several gunshot wounds, while Gáspár's body was covered with a dozen sword cuts. The shocking debt of blood that fate had ruthlessly exacted from one family on a single day and within the span of an hour stirred the conscience of the nation and all of Christian Europe. Counts Mansfeld and Puchheim delivered the Emperor's condolences, while the papal nuncio brought the Pope's words of comfort and benediction. There was also a touching funeral at Nagyszombat.

135. After they'd killed my father, the authorities that were by all odds responsible for the so-called abuse of authority sent a telegram to the family. But for some reason, they sent it not to my mother, but my father's son, who at the time was a toddler and could not read. This is what the telegram said: We have killed your father. It was a regrettable blunder on our part. We apologize. My mother read it, looked up, then read it again. They could have furnished the details, she said.

136. The papers say that my father's life, not to mention his death, was so adventurous, it'd make a great book. He was killed brutally Tuesday at noon. The perpetrator of the horrible crime, name of no consequence, is a twenty-four-year-old car mechanic and resident. My parents' marriage had gone on the rocks the last couple of years, and my thirty-three-year-old mother moved in with the car mechanic, though he didn't even own a car. But because of her four young children (that's us, except years ago), she decided to go back to my father, but she continued to screw Attila (the car mechanic) on the sly. The two hatched the plan. My mother sent word to the mechanic that they'd be going to Tihany for the day, where they need to see a real estate agent around noon. And so it was. After the real estate agent left, satisfied with a job well done, and my mother went to the store for sour cream (for the pumpkin soup), the car mechanic sneaked into the house, and with a heavy hammer which, for all practical purposes, was heavy, perpetrated the plan, which was a cold-blooded crime. The fact that this was

not a very nice thing for my mother to do is proven by the fact that she was taken into custody as an accessory before the fact to the crime, which sounds like a lot of hogwash. That scumbag—not my father, but her lover—pleaded guilty, along with the 120 thousand forints that my father withdrew from the Savings Bank in Füred that morning, before his death. There's much that could be told of my father's life besides the gruesome details of his death—photojournalist, graphic artist, Hungarian-Swedish dictionary (abridged), and poetry. His East Asian collection is valued at millions of forints. 100 Ft. is approximately 1 DM, so you can imagine. My father's rate of exchange.

137.  The viaduct built in 1938, the last year before the war, which has since become the symbol of the town, has been the means of suicide for 250 people to date. Forty meters of free fall! The last two were practically children. They plunged to their death holding hands. They were in love. The girl, my mother, was fifteen years old, the boy, my father, eighteen. They were students from the same school. Good students, too, my mother open and inquisitive, my father timid and introverted. What's more puzzling is that instead of forbidding their love, my grandparents encouraged it. Their families, too, were stable and financially secure (especially my father's, of course). Why? Why? Why? This is what my father's schoolmate carved into his desk three times. Why? But neither the teachers nor the psychologists had the answer. The town was in mourning, the student body was in shock. Nevertheless, during the weekend, at the request of the students, the school held its annual alma mater celebrations all the same. The motto of the celebrations was: Life goes on! Which is how my parents met, i.e., which is how my father and my mother met.

138.  My father grew up in the town of Veszprém. Why? Your guess is as good as mine. Anyway, the word "viaduct" rubbed him the

wrong way. When they said to him, viaduct, the shit flooded his brain and he lashed out. (My father grew up in Debrecen. Why? Your guess is as good as mine. Anyway, the words "nine-hole bridge" rubbed him the wrong way. When they said to him nine-hole bridge, the shit flooded his brain and he lashed out.) (My father, Berlin, Reichstag, he lashed out.) (My father, Vienna, Heldenplatz, he lashed out.) (My father, New York, skyscraper, he lashed out.) (My father, Budapest, November 7 Square, he lashed out.) (My father, Athens, *logariazmo parakalo*, he lashed out.) (My father, Bethlehem, manger, he lashed out.) (My father.) (He lashed out.) ( . . . )

139. Every Easter since 1962, in the settlement of San Pedro de Cutud, north of Manila, they've been crucifying my volunteer fathers in front of the watchful eyes of the faithful, journalists, and curious crowds. My fathers (believers and nonbelievers alike), who hope to atone for their sins or plead for the recovery of their ailing parents in this manner, have the palms of their hands and feet carefully disinfected and pierced with three-inch-long nails through the dorsum and the base of the toes. My father hangs on the cross for two to ten minutes. The leaders of the Philippine Church have repeatedly raised their voice in protest against this rite. *Big deal.*

140. He didn't have to die this way. My father could have died a thousand different deaths. We could even bring politics into the picture. After all, why would someone with two doctorates become a pump operator in Zala, if not under the yoke of the Communists? (This would be true even if we were to split hairs about the time.) It happened way after 1989 (or before 1945), past midnight, at the peat quarry, in the town of Ötréte. The oil stove caught fire in a trailer at plant G-2. The fire startled my pump-operator father awake, who grabbed the burning stove and threw it into the lake

by the trailer. So far so good (except for the burning stove and the turn my father's life had taken). But in his haste, my father was also set on fire. He applied the same procedure to his person as the stove, jumped into the lake, and drowned. He drowned because he did not take into account the fact that the whole includes all of its parts. In short, the fire in the stove subsided, and the stove sank to the bottom of the lake. My father's fire also subsided, and he, too, sank to the bottom of the lake. The Nagykanizsa fire brigade fished his body out of the lake on Saturday afternoon.

141. Schrödinger has locked my father inside a thick-walled box. This is the situation: besides my father, the box also contains a piece of radium that has a 50 percent chance of emitting a tiny fission particle within the hour, and a 50 percent chance that it will not. If the particle is emitted, an apparatus inside the box will detect it, open a valve, and flood the box with cyanogen, which will kill my father (mourned by his wife, i.e., widow, four sons, five daughters-in-law, a growing number of grandchildren, as well as countless admirers of both sexes). Schrödinger's question is as follows: Just before we disassemble the box to ascertain whether my father is alive or dead, what can we say? Does it contain a living father or a dead one? The answer is as follows: At that particular moment, we cannot say that my father is alive, and we cannot say that he is dead. If we must say something, the most we can say is that my father is either alive, or he is dead, i.e., that there is a 50 percent probability that he is alive, and a 50 percent probability that he is dead. This is all we can say. Naturally, if we open the box, we can assess whether my father is alive or dead. In the first case, we can say with 100 percent certainty that he is alive, and in the second, we can say with 100 percent certainty that he is dead. But then the following question arises: If, after opening the box, we find that my father, Benő Bárci, is dead, can we say that my father's state of being dead was objectively real before we opened

the box? If we had not opened the box, then after an hour there would have been a 50 percent probability of my father living the good life inside. At any rate, for every observer, the box as a system would have functioned like a box in which there was a 50 percent probability of a living father, my father. Is it possible that the observation itself, the observation of the son, could kill (could have killed) my father, or unequivocally restored him to life from the 50 percent state of death, if we happen to end up with that result? This is why it is forbidden to touch one's father. Who wants to be his father's murderer, even if the probability of it occurring is only 50 percent? Poor Schrödinger. He suggested that we put the box out to a place where three roads meet. He wouldn't like to do it personally, though, as his legs hurt, with some sort of inflammation on his feet, and his ankles are swollen, too.

142. At this juncture, my father merely offered the comment that regretfully, we are all Schrödinger's cats, and from time to time a well-meaning, love-oriented, bearded, curious old man reaches out from behind the clouds where, in my father's words, the sky is always blue. He opens the box, which is cat and cyanogen and radium and detector in one (I'm saying "and," my father says, only as a joke, because I'm talking), and cheerfully asks, How are you, son. And we tell him. With a certain probability. So said my father.

143. Inheritance. It passes from father to son, as long as there's a father, as long as there's a son. *A Manual for Sons*, n.d., n.a., translated from the German by Peter Scatterpatter. Treasure trove and inventory. Some of my fathers are mad, stalking up and down the boulevards, shouting. Avoid them, or embrace them, or tell them your deepest thoughts, *secco yedno*, they have deaf ears. If, on the other hand, they are simply barking, go up to them, say you're sorry. If the barking ceases, this does not mean they forgive you or

understand you, it only means they are experiencing erotic thoughts of abominable luster. Permit them to slobber for a space, then strike them sharply in the nape with the blade of your hand. Say you're sorry again. It won't get through to them because their brains are mush, a moth-eaten rag, that's what their brains are like, but listening to them, your body will assume an attitude that conveys, in every country of the world, sorrow—this language they can understand. And then the food, the feeding. Always carry bits of leftover meat in your pockets. First hold the meat in front of their eyes, meat, so that they can see what it is, meat, and then point to their mouths, so that they know that it's for them, the meat is for them. If they don't open their mouths at this point, throw the meat in between barks. If the meat does not get all the way into the mouth but gets stuck in their nose or glasses, strike them again in the nape with the blade of your hand, this often causes the mouth to pop open, and *voilà,* in it goes. But possibly nothing may work out in the way I have described; in this eventuality, you can do not much for mad fathers, my mad fathers. If they cry aloud, *"Stomp it, emptor!,"* then you must attempt to figure out the code. If they cry aloud, *"The fiends have killed your horse!,"* note down in your notebook the frequency with which the words "the" and "your" occur in his tirade. If they cry aloud, *"The cat's in its cassock and flitter-te-hee moreso stomp it!,"* remember that they have already asked you once to "stomp it" and that this must refer to something you are doing. So stomp it. ♦ The true and the not-true. No father ever knowingly teaches what is not true. In a cloud of unknowing, then, my father proceeds with his instruction. Remember son. Tough meat should be hammered well between two stones before it is placed on the fire, and should be combed with a hair comb and brushed with a hairbrush (beforehand). But iron lungs or cyclotrons are also useful for the purpose. (My handsome uncle died in an iron lung in 1954; Grandmother would still be crying if only she hadn't died, too.)

Nails, boiled for three hours, give off a rusty liquid that, when combined with oxtail soup, is useful for warding off tuberculosis or attracting native women. Do not forget to hug the native women immediately. Lose yourself in their gigantic haunches, close your eyes, open your mouth, *sheri, sheri* (according to my father). Savages are easily satisfied with cheap beads in the following colors: dull white, dark blue, and vermillion red. Expensive beads are often spurned by them. Nonsavages should be given cheap books in the following colors: dead white, brown, and seaweed. Books that in both subject matter as well as texture praise the seas are much sought after. When Satan appears to you in the shape of Satan, try not to act surprised. Then get down to hard bargaining. If he likes neither the beads nor the books (despite the subject matter and the texture), offer him a bottle of cold, cheap beer. That should do the trick. Fathers teach much that is of value. Much that is not. ◆ My fathers in some countries are like spools of thread. (Scram, filthy cats!) In others, they're like clay pots or glass jars. Sometimes, my father is like reading, in a newspaper, a long account of a film you have already seen and liked immensely, but do not wish to see again, or read about in the papers, this is what my father is like. Some fathers are triangular. Some fathers, if you ask them for the time of day, spit silver ducats. Some fathers piss either perfume or medicinal alcohol. I have fathers who have made themselves over into convincing replicas of beautiful sea animals, and some into convincing replicas of people they hated as children. I have fathers that are goats, some are milk, some teach Spanish in cloisters, one does not, and one is capable of attacking world economic problems and killing them, but he is biding his time. I have fathers who strut but most do not, unless possibly at home; some ape horses, though most of them do not, except in the eighteenth century. I have fathers who fall off their horse, though most of them do not. I have some who, after falling off the horse, shoot the horse, though most of them do not. I have fathers who fear horses but most fear women instead. I have fathers who masturbate because they fear women, some fathers sleep with hired women because they fear women who are free. Some of my fathers never sleep at all, but are endlessly awake, staring at their futures, which are behind them. ♦ The leaping father is as rare as a white owl, but white owls exist, except, they're rare. There's no public hall, baroque *salle,* socialist prefab in which you won't find two two many leaping fathers of mine. The best idea is to chain heavy-duty truck tires to them, this will slow them down, they will take stock of their lives, and that will do them a world of good. It was in 1969 or 1970 that my father got into the habit of going out to the People's Park, where he leaped about pushing away from himself a brown leather object with the circumference (more or less) of one foot. Oh dear, my father's son nodded, a sin, that's a sin of some sort. There was also a dipping net, my father tried to scoop up his sin with it. A hopeless undertaking. There's something deflating, something dreary about this fiasco. This leaping about is disheartening, it's marked by the loss of heart. Maybe because my father's legs do not reach the ground? ♦ The best way to approach a father is from behind. Thus if he chooses to hurl his javelin at you, if he feels an irresistible urge to pierce your heart, he'll have to twist his body around, which will give you time to run, to make reservations for a flight to another country. To Rukmini, there are no fathers there. In that country virgin corn goddesses become impregnated through the long, wet Rukminian winter in ways not known to us to produce offspring. Not a bad place, Rukmini. But what's that over yonder? A javelin? Javelin marks everywhere, everything wounded in a hundred places. Still, it is still best from behind. ♦ I had one concrete father, children by the bushel, and he sold every one of them to the bone factory (probably a glue factory). The bone factory will not accept angry or sulking children, therefore my father was, to his children, the kindest and most amiable father imaginable. He endeared himself to his sons by feeding them huge amounts of calcium candy and the milk of minks, told them interesting and funny stories, and led them each day in their bone-building exercises. "Tall sons," he said, "are best." Once a year the bone factory sent a little blue van to the house. ♦ The names of the fathers. Fathers are named: A'albiel, Aariel, Aaron, Aba, etc. ♦ Every one of my fathers has a voice, and each voice has a *terribilità* of its own. The sound of a father's voice is various: like film burning, like marble being pulled screaming from the face of the quarry (in the early morning), like the clash of paper clips by night, lime seething in a lime pit, or the morbid screech of the bat. The voice of a father can shatter your glasses. When not robed in the father role, fathers may be so-called hendentenors, but they can also be good-for-nothings, or farmers, like the poet Berzsenyi, or tinsmiths, racing drivers, fist fighters, or salesmen. Most are salesmen. Many of my fathers did not wish, especially, to be fathers, the thing came upon them, seized them, by accident, or by someone else's careful design, or by simple clumsiness on someone's part. Nevertheless this class of father—the inadvertent—is often among the most tactful, light-handed, and beautiful of fathers (I wonder why). If a father of mine has littered twelve or twenty-seven times, it is well to give him a curious look—this father does not loathe himself enough. This father frequently wears a blue wool watch cap, on stormy nights, to remind himself of a manly past—landing at Normandy (1944), marching into Prague (1968). Many of my fathers are blameless in all ways, and these fathers are either sacred relics people are touched with to heal incurable illnesses, et cetera, or texts to be studied, generation after generation, to determine how this idiosyncrasy may be maximized. Text fathers are generally bound in blue. The father's voice is an instrument of the most terrible pertinaciousness. ♦ My fathers are like blocks of marble—giant cubes, highly polished, with veins and seams, placed squarely in your path. They cannot be climbed over, neither can they be slithered past. They are the "past," and very likely the slither. If you attempt to go around one father, next thing you know, you will find that another has mysteriously appeared athwart the trail. Or maybe it is the same one, moving with the speed of paternity. Look closely at the color and texture. Do they resemble a slice of rare roast beef? Your very father's complexion! Besides the marble, there's also the fanged father. If you can get your lariat around one of his fangs, and quickly wrap the other end of it several times around your saddle horn, and if your horse is a trained roping horse and knows what to do, how to plant his front feet and then back up with small nervous steps, keeping the lariat taut, then you have a chance. There's a thirty-two-centimeter fang in the whaling museum in Tata, mistakenly labeled as the tusk of a walrus. Even a half-wit can see it's a father fang. And the half-wit is happy that he's never met up with this particular father of mine. ◆ If your (my) father's name is Francis, Joseph or Mátyás, run, make yourself scarce, get thee to a nunnery, or flee into the woods. For these names are the names of kings, and your (my) father Francis, Joseph or Mátyás, will not be a king, but will retain, in hidden places in his body, the memory of kingship. And there is no one more blackhearted and surly (depressing) than an ex-king. Fathers so named consider their homes to be the royal palace at Visegrád, and their kith and kin courtiers, to be elevated or depressed in rank according to the lightest whinges of their own mental weather. And one can never know for sure if one is "up" or "down" at a particular moment; one is a feather, floating, one has no place to stand. In short, if it's Francis, Joseph, Mátyás, Rudolf, István, Géza, head for the woods before the mighty yataghan leaps from its scabbard. (My sympathies, Mother!) The proper attitude toward such fathers of mine is that of the toad, lickspittle, smellfeast, sponger, and Judas. When you cannot escape to the trees, genuflect, and stay down there, on one knee and bowed head and clasped hands, until dawn. By this time he will probably have gotten as drunk as a rolling fart, and you may creep away and seek your bed (if it has not been taken away from under you) or, if you are hungry, approach the table and see what has been left there, unless the ever-efficient cook has covered everything with clear plastic and put it away. In that case, you may suck your thumb. ♦ Color is important. My bay-colored fathers can be trusted, especially those with a mahogany hue. They can be gainfully employed: (1) in solving the Gypsy problem, (2) as catchers of red-hot rivets when you are building a bridge, (3) in organizing the wiretapping of assistant bishops, and (4) for carrying one corner of an eighteen-meter-square mirror through the city's streets. Dun-colored fathers tend to shy at obstacles, and therefore you do not want a father of this color, because life, in one sense, is nothing but obstacles, and his continual shying will reduce your nerves to grease. The liver-chestnut-colored fathers have a reputation for decency and good sense; if God commands them to take out their knife and slice through your neck with it, they will probably say, "No, thanks." The dusty-chestnut father will start sharpening the knife. The light-chestnut father will ask for another opinion. The standard-chestnut father will look the other way. Sorrel-colored fathers are easily excitable and are employed most often where a crowd, or mob, is wanted, as for coronations, lynchings, and the like. In bungled assassinations, the assassin will frequently be a blond-sorrel father of mine who forgot to take the lens cap off his telescopic sight. Red roan-colored fathers of mine are much noted for bawdiness, and this should be encouraged, for bawdiness is a sacrament that does not, usually, result in fatherhood; it is its own reward. Spots, paints, pintos, piebalds, and Appaloosas have a sweet dignity that proceeds from their inferiority, and excellent sense of smell. The color of a father is not an absolute guide to the character and conduct of that father but tends to be a self-fulfilling prophecy, because when a father of mine sees what color he is, he may keep pace with his

145

destiny. ♦ Fathers and dandling. If one of my fathers fathers daughters, then our lives are eased. Daughters are for dandling, and are often dandled up until their seventeenth or eighteenth year. The hazard here, which must be faced, is that my father will conceivably take it into his head to sleep with his beautiful daughter, who is after all *his* in a way that even his wife is not, in a way that even his most delicious mistress is not. Some of my fathers just say, "Publish and be damned!" and go ahead and sleep with their new and amazing sexual daughters, and accept what pangs accumulate afterward, the result of their haste. Most of my fathers, though, are not like this. Most are sufficiently disciplined in this regard, by mental straps, so that the question never arises. But should my sister sit in my father's lap, who is to say what's what, where the fool-blooded woman begins and where the blood of your blood? But in most cases, the taboo is observed, and additional strictures imposed, such as "Mari, I will beat the shit out of you, if ever I catch that filthy Hans-Sebastian Lottermoser, German in the original, lay a hand upon your bare, white, new breast!" Or, with a gesture pointing into the future: "Here, Mari, here is your blue fifty-gallon drum of baby-killing foam, with your initials stamped on it in a darker blue, see? there on the top?" But the important thing about daughter-fathers is that, as fathers, they don't count. Fathers of daughters see themselves as *hors concours,* and this is a great relief. They tend, therefore, to take a milder, gentler hand re. the prerogatives of fatherhood. It can even happen that my father is the one who is dandled. Even this can happen. ♦ From time to time, my father twists my tongue. ♦ The pertinent literature on the subject speaks of twenty-two kinds of fathers (my fathers), of which only nineteen are important. My drugged father is not important. My lion-like father (rare) is not important. My Holy Father is not important, for our purposes. The one falling through the air, he's important. My father is falling through the air, what am I to do? We don't

146

know what you mean by father, why don't you cut down on your bicycling? The falling father's hair, the wind throws it in every direction. His cheeks are flaps almost touching his ears. My father's sons have taken to wearing slices of raw bacon in their caps, and speaking out against the interest rates. After all he has done for them! My falling fathers hope to stop the falling by redoubling their efforts, really put their backs into it, this time. They are important because they embody the "work ethic," which is a dumb one. The "fear ethic" should be substituted, as soon as possible. ◆ My fathers get lost in a variety of ways, sitting, standing, in fifties-type cloth caps, borsalino hats, undershirts, breeches, loose hip shirts. Often they will wander away from home and lose themselves. Melt into thin air. Often they will remain at home but still be "lost," locked away in an upper room, or in a workshop, or in the contemplation of beauty, or in the contemplation of a secret life. War, as is well known, is a reliable place for disappearing. (My uncle, my father's brother, was lost in a war, too. Disappeared. He who disappears is expected back for a long time. We're not taken in by news of his death, but after a time, we come to terms with it all the same. He hasn't died, but after a while we stop thinking of him as if he were alive. He's alive, except he's not coming back anymore. Last spotted in the vicinity of the internment camp at Bicske. He had a rucksack, and he was laughing.) Armed with these clues, then, we can place an advertisement in the newspaper: *Lost, one thoroughbred father, somewhat worse for wear, 184 (182) cm., armed with his faithful Smith & Wesson .38. Answers to the call, "You ancient, trembling poplar, you!" Reward negotiable.* Having completed this futile exercise, we might be inclined to ask the only relevant question, do we really want to find him? What if, when he's found, he speaks to us in the same tone he used before he lost himself? Will he again place nails in our mother, as before? Also, he's still got his spear. Or javelin. Or whatever. And suppose it flies around the dinner table like before? In short, under what conditions do you wish to live? Yes, he "nervously twiddles the stem of his wineglass." Do you wish to watch him do so for another quarter of a century? Let him go off to Borneo. Or Celebes, that'll do as well. He will also nervously twiddle the stem of, et cetera, but the natives will consider it a novelty, and he will not be brave enough to make a scene, throwing the roast through the mirror, thrusting a belch big as an opened umbrella into the middle of the birthday dinner. Beating you, either with a wet, knotted rawhide or with an ordinary belt. Ignore that empty chair at the head of the table. Give thanks. ♦ When rescuing a father, regardless of the reason you think for a moment that you are the father and he is not. For a moment. This is the only moment in your life when you will feel this way. ♦ Then there's my father's prick. My father's prick is the official, socially accepted name for my father's penis. A magical member. In the quiescent state—and this is nothing to be ashamed of, it's a fact—they are small, almost shriveled, and easily concealed in bathing suits or ordinary trousers. Actually they are not anything that you would want to show anyone unless expressly called upon to do so, even though they are metaphors of nature and resemble the bolete mushroom or the common snail. The magic, at these times, resides in other parts of my father (the tips of the toes, the forehead). What if— because this eventuality cannot be ruled out—a child, usually a bold six-year-old daughter, will request permission to see it? This request should be granted, once. But only in the early morning, and not when an early-morning erection is present. Let her touch it (lightly, of course), but briefly. It is not advisable to arouse her curiosity! (She's just learning to read and write.) Be matter-of-fact, kind. No need for theatrics (drama)! Pretend, for the moment, that it is as mundane as a big toe. Cover it calmly, without unseemly haste. Keep in mind: touching, not holding! About sons you must use your own judgment. It is injudicious (as well as un-necessary) to terrify them. You have many other ways of accomplishing that. Semi-erect fatherhood brings up a fascinating question of philosophical inquiry: Aristotle considered it a state of imperfection, its effect on the history of European sculpture (mutilations, et cetera), are well known. We consider it a basic rule: the standing member belongs to who and/or whatever made it stand up. My father's prick is superior in every respect to the non-paternal prick, not because of the size when erect, or weight, or any other considerations of that sort but because of a metaphysical "responsibility." This is true even for poor, bad, or insane fathers. African artifacts (Mali!) reflect this special situation. Pre-Columbian artifacts, for the most part, do not. Or rarely. ◆ The names of the fathers: Badgal, Balberith, Böll, etc. ◆ My father's son knew a father of mine who was landlord of the bear gardens in southern Csongrád. He (my father) was known to be a principled man and never, never, never ate any of his children no matter how dire the state of his purse. Yet the children, one by one, disappeared. ◆ We have seen that the key idea, in fatherhood, its root, is "responsibility." My fathers are responsible for ensuring that the sky, that proverbial celestial harmony, should not cave in on us, and also that the solid earth should not turn into a yielding pit beneath us. The responsibility of the father is chiefly that his child not die, should have food to sustain it, and heavy blankets to protect it from the chill, cutting air. My father is steadfast and valorous. This is what my fathers are like (except in the case of child abusers or thieves of children or managers of child labor or sick, unholy sexual ghouls). The child grows like weed, good work, Joe, the kid's budding on the family tree, has a good job selling thermocouples, and a girlfriend, whom you like, and has impregnated her to the point that she will doubtless have a new child, soon. And is not in jail. And is not a junkie. But have you noticed the slight curl at the end of Joe Jr.'s lips, when he looks at you? It means that he didn't want you to name him Joe Jr. for one thing, and for two other things it means that he has a sawed-off shotgun in his left pant leg, and a baling hook in his right pant leg, and is ready to kill you with either one of them, given the opportunity. My father is taken aback. "I changed your diapers for you, little snot!" A mistake. First, it is not true (mothers change nine diapers out of ten), and secondly, it instantly reminds Joe Jr. of what he is mad about. He is mad about being small when you were big, even your shadow greater than him, but no, that's not it, he is mad about being helpless when you were powerful, but no, not that either, he is mad about being contingent when you were necessary, not quite it, he is insane because when he loved you, you didn't notice. You didn't notice. ◆ When a father of mine dies, his fatherhood is returned to the All-Father, who is the sum of all of my dead fathers taken together. (This is not a definition of the All-Father, only one aspect of his being.) The fatherhood is returned to the All-Father, first because that is where it belongs and secondly in order that it may be denied to you. Transfers of power of this kind are marked with appropriate ceremonies; top hats are burned. Fatherless now, you (who?) must deal with the memory of a father. Yes-ing and no-ing, yes no yes no, keep my father's son in a quandary. At what point and where does he become himself? At no point and nowhere, wholly, you are always partly him. My father's last attempt on my life. ◆ The killing of fathers is contrary to law and custom. Also, it proves, unnecessarily and in retrospect, that the father's every fluted accusation against you was correct. ("Shame on you, you . . . patricide, you!") It is all right to feel this hot emotion, but not to act upon it. Nor is it necessary. It is not necessary to slay your father, time, that faithful servant, will slay him for you. Your true task lies elsewhere. You must become your father, but a paler, weaker version of him. If he played soccer, you play water polo. If he spoke three languages, speak two (or one). If he was a general with the lancers, you should be a sergeant. If he was 184 (182) cm. tall, you should be 178. . . . If he studied math, you should study math and physics. Practice being a father of mine, study the inventory. And don't forget: law and custom, and time.

144. My father, the dead father. A borrowed idea, dead. Oh, Donald! Let's go, my father's oldest son says to him, and they walk to the cemetery. A light drizzle, real graveyard weather, hundreds and hundreds of people standing round the hole holding black umbrellas. Well, this is it. What do you mean, this is it?, the dead father asks. This. This large excavation? Yes. My sister looks away. My father and his son are standing by the side of the excavation. Farther off, bulldozers. What is to be built here? Nothing. What a long pit. Long enough, I think. My father looks again at the hole. Oh. I see. I think I see . . . And these people? Who told them to come? They wished to pay their last respects. Wreaths, music, grieving crowds. No fleece? No nice woollies? My sister lifts her skirt. Quite golden, my father says. Quite ample. That's it? All there is, my sister says. Unfortunately. But this much. This where life lives. A pretty problem. As mine as yours. I'm sorry. Quite golden, my father says. Quite ample. He moves to touch it. No, my father's son says. No, my sister says. I'm not even to touch it? No. After all this long and arduous and if I may say so rather ill-managed journey? Not to touch it? What am I to do? You are to get into the hole. You want to bury me live? You're not alive, remember? I don't want to lie down in the hole. Few do. The rain, it's drizzling. My sister is standing by the grave, with hands hiking up her skirt. Just once to place my hand on it? asks the dead father. Last request? Denied, my father's son says. Unseemly. I have the Order of the Golden Fleece! my father shouts. My dear, my dearest, my sister says, lie down in the dark hole. Will it hurt? Yes it will. But I'll come and hold your hand. That's all? That's the end? Yes. But I'll come and hold your hand. Okay . . . Did I do it well? Marvelously well, Daddy dear. I will never see it done better. Thank you. Thank you very much. And

then my father's son places his hand on the fleece, outside the skirt. Climb, my sister says. I'll hold your hand. It is lovely, my father says, I am covered with admiration. And soon, with good black earth, my sister says. Sad necessary . . . Oh to be alive, for one moment more . . . That we can arrange, my father's son says. My father stretches his great length in the hole. A perfect fit. I'm in it now, he shouts from below. What a voice, my father's son says, I wonder how he does it. Hole, pit, but I'm inside. My sister is holding a hand. One moment more, my father said . . . Bulldozers.

145. My father, a trembling poplar, with just one thing on his mind, his last will and testament. Otherwise, he sits outside in the sun. When the shadow catches up with him, he yelps. Someone moves him back in the sun. When the urge to make a will gets the better of him, a wild untamed fire flares in his eye (or is he just playing? adding fuel to the fire?), and he orders my sister to him, or my brother, or my father's eldest son, and begins to dictate. My four thousand volumes of cabalistic literature. Cycladic figures to the number of 118. My gouges. The straight gouge, short bent gouge, long bent gouge, V gouge, U gouge, 5/32" gouge, 3/8" gouge. Four skew chisels. My box at the opera. My Bennie Motel records. My Thonet rocking chair. The regiment. To whom will you leave the regiment? Parade it. Make it do the rounds, like Singer his sewing machine. Have regimental dinners. Fold and unfold the colors. Defend frontiers. Tamás Esze and what have you. Remember? Border duty. March them to Belgrade against the Turk. They have hundreds of uses. On the other hand, mercenaries are costly, the fodder and the TV, too. If it's cheap you want, buy a Trabant. All right, okay, let us table the question for the time being. There are lots of other things. Let us lump it together under "incidentals." Do you want Regina? Never having met the lady, put a question mark at the end. There are no ques-

tion marks in a will, that's the beauty of it! No question marks! No question marks! Get me? Get me? Get me? Father, please don't cry.

146. What is it? Read it, Father. It is a will. Whose? We, my siblings and I, the blood of my father from the blood of my father, thought it best to take the precaution with respect to death. A step. There are too many surprises waiting at the end of the road. But I don't want to make a will, I don't want to think about the end of the road. No one wants to make a will, Father, nobody wants to. Still, it is only to be expected, Father, and we, my siblings and I, thought that you should expect it too, and that you, in your wisdom, should also take this step. Oh, sure. My wisdom, Father said. Infinite. Unmatched. Still, I don't want to make a will. But prudence and wisdom are two of your strongest suits, Father. Dash my suits. I'll not do it. It is not yet time. You know, Father, time's time . . . That too will have its time, except . . . Of course it's entirely up to you, Father. If you, Father, wish to leave your affairs in rotten mishmashy cluttersome disarray . . . I'm too young. I want my condom. As for you, my children, go to the devil!

•   •   •   •   •

147. As far as my father's son remembers his father, everything worked for him (my father) according to some sort of distorted, disjointed logic. My father's son was seven years old when my father admitted himself to a Young Pioneer camp as an artist, and he "went along." Once he was sitting in the deserted dining room, eating borscht, my father across from him, in "ah ain't drunk" condition, watching him eat. Suddenly he extended a hand, his fingers curved back like a snail. Then the snail (my father) straightened itself out and thumbed him on the nose. First his head whirled, then the tears came. His tears fell into the huge plate of red borscht in front of him. The cook sitting next to them screeched, Can't you leave the child alone, you drunken pig! You're crazy as a hoot, you know that?! As always, my father's son took my father's side, You don't understand, ma'am, my father is a good man, he's just having his little fun! The cook wiped away a tear, then left the room and brought the boy some cake, sugar candy and two glasses of mixed fruit compote. He continued eating. After a while, my father spoke up again, Well, son, how ya like them sweets? In his view and the view of the age in which he lived, the problematics of "a child's tears" could be easily solved. In the scale of rebellion, a mixed fruit compote clearly weighed more in the balance than a tear. My father's son has long

154

since forgotten the taste of the sugar candy that melted so easily in his mouth, and he's long since forgotten the angel food cake soaked in the fruit compote. He remembers the whole thing only in broad outlines, and only through certain associations. But he can still recall the red borscht, big as a trough, the transparent, hot tears falling into it, the dull pain on the top of his head, and the timid self-reproach: Why? What did I do?—because he must have done something, otherwise he wouldn't have gotten that sledge-hammer blow . . . The compote did not answer him, but at least it diverted his attention. He found the answer only years later, and now, through the far reaches of time—the worthy son of a worthy father!—my father's son stretches out his hand toward him (my father) and with his fingers like steel springs, thumbs him on the nose. And my father's eye falls into the borscht, his brain fizzles out through the sockets of his eyes. With a child-like gesture, my father rubs the back of his hand against the gaping black hole, and blinded, begins to cry. My father's eye: an infinite cul-de-sac.

148. On the other hand, for eighteen years, a father of mine who was by all accounts a White Russian, accused my mother of cheating on him. Though he never told her about it, he suffered a thousand secret torments. After eighteen years of untold agony, he called my mother to account, who told him with an honesty that was in every way convincing that his suspicion was unfounded. At which my father ran into the adjoining room and shot himself. He couldn't bear the thought that he had suffered so long for nothing.

149. My father pursued the truth because, as he was fond of saying, it is deucedly difficult to tell a lie when you don't know it (the truth). (Was he thinking of Horthy, or sitting in his cell in Sopronkőhida under the Hungarian Nazis, the Germans, or the Communists, I wonder?). His relationship to a sentence, to stating something, was closer than most individuals'. Speaking requires a

155

bit of (extra) exertion, a sentence a bit of extra self-assertion. (Possibly self-deception, too, but let's not go into that.) "In every respect," my father was "larger than life." When he was born, he weighed thirteen pounds. According to the Lord, solitude is a bad thing. All of us have a sentence that we become familiar with through the course of our lives. This is what my father came to know, this bad, and he fought against it all his days. He did not lead an austere life. His life was not austere in the least. He was a Freemason, a member of the elite *Zur gekrönte Hoffnung* cell founded by Emperor Frances, whose friend and companion he was on their midnight escapades—the popular Quin-Quin of Viennese society. Mozart wrote his famous Freemason requiem for him (according to Köchel Op. 477), and the hero of *Der Rosenkavalier*, too, took him as its model. But he was diligent in his study of the Holy Scriptures, gleaning from them what best suited his nature. He made an inventory of the causes of sadness—for, as opposed to joy, which is bound up with salvation and the presence of God, sadness is the bitter fruit of sin, and it separates us from the Lord. How long, Lord?, my father cried. (Some people consider the anthropomorphic conception of God humiliating, humiliating with respect to God, and man, too. My father is not one of these people.) How long wilt Thou hide Thy face from me? How long shall I take counsel in my soul, having sorrow in my heart daily? How long shall mine enemy be exalted over me? Not to worry. My father had plenty of enemies, but they did not exalt, for at this point in time, two glorious generations of the family found themselves heaped one on top of the other, barring the road—willy-nilly, one might say with tact—from just about everyone else. Wherever you turned, you were bound to run up against them. The father and the uncle were steadfast pro-Habsburg Labanc, Pálffy's men. My grandfather married from this camp, taking to wife the "wasp-waisted Szidónia Pálffy," who gave birth to twelve children, including my father. After Onkel

156

József was elected Lord Chief Justice, he presided over the National Assembly in the absence of the gravely ill Pálffy, and though suits cut in the German fashion were in vogue just then, he wore his Hungarian ceremonial costume to Parliament. The Queen liked him, but when she confided to him that the German lords did not sympathize with the Hungarians—The stink of the anti-Habsburg, Kuruc canons are still in their nostrils, Count!, our relative screwed up his nose as he listened—and that she, the Queen, is forced to make her decisions without consulting the Hungarians, József spoke in all honesty as follows: The centuries have indeed justified your mistrust, Your Majesty. I shall refrain from furnishing the details. Still, the hand that rules the realm must not waver. The antipathy in question is not directed against the Queen. (Just the Empress, but hush.) National aspirations are based on ancient laws, and the Hungarian lords have sworn eternal allegiance to them, but they never honored them. And when the old pro-Habsburg Labanc said this, the Queen broke into tears, and complained about her hapless situation. This transpired in Bratislava on July 17. There was also milord Antal who became the faithful field marshal of Prince Rákóczi until the latter's death, this during the anti-Habsburg wars, as a result of which his fortune passed on to his two brothers. This, however, did not come between them. They had great affection for each other. My father was the youngest member of the new glorious generation (his brothers: Miklós, the ambassador to St. Petersburg, and Károly, the bishop of Eger, after whom the Ho-Chi-Minh high school received its name). He was exceptionally bright, with the best European education. He was blessed with impeccable taste and good looks. (His portrait hangs in the Portrait Gallery of the National Museum.) He was a lord of great wealth besides. By the age of twenty, he was Lord Lieutenant of Moson County, by twenty-six, Imperial and Royal Chamberlain. Still, sadness is man's faithful companion. We feed on the bread of tears. Theoretically, the situation is clear-cut: behind man's infinite sorrow there lurks sin as its real and effectual cause. The Scriptures point to the Redeemer as the cure: If sorrow springs from sin, then joy is the offspring of salvation. My father did not see this quite so clearly; he held the somewhat more profane, stoical view that attempts to avoid sadness, knowing full well that fear of the Lord rejoices the heart, and fills it with ecstasy and elation—and a long life. This—that life, life's length—is a joy unto itself, this is what my father came to know. He worked a great deal. The eighteenth century was the century of construction. He was responsible for the family's most beautiful palace at Cseklész, and the reconstruction of the former Hungarian Chancellery in Bankgasse (the most stately embassy building in Vienna) is also attached to his name. In the meantime, as the leading figure of the famed Brotherhood of Cavaliers, he went bed hopping—not infrequently with his namesake, the Emperor. (Hopping from bed to bed was one way of spending the eighteenth century.) Maria Theresa's disposition was serious, and so she was nettled; she didn't like idleness. My father was not unserious either, but the serious and the unserious coexisted within him, each alternatively gaining ascendance over the other, and though this ascendance may have had a design, it was anything but predictable. My father was idle with a vengeance. This does not mean that he *wanted* to be idle, just free. He let his idleness run its course—all of this being spurred on by his global fight against sadness. A heavy heart is the source of sorrow, but a clever man will pay it back, the Scriptures say. My father, it seems, out of one bed and into another, was busy with this payment all his life. (I might mention as a point of curiosity that it was a decree of his that domesticated the institution of the pawn shop here in Hungary, based on the French model.) Regardless of the path the previous night may have taken, by nine in the morning, he was always in the presence of his Empress. Maria Theresa studied her man, whose eyes, especially the corners, spoke volumes about the night before. She said my father's name, severe, unpleasant, as if she were calling him up to the blackboard, Kovács! Sulking, my father bowed his head. What's that you say?! his Empress and Queen said. Have I no right to demand of my subjects that they address me in full, grammatically correct sentences? Basically, she liked my father, specifically, his talent. She could not resist his talent. But she disdained irresponsibility. My father grinned at the Empress. Yes, Your Majesty, you have every right to demand it! In fact, you must! The moment people start muttering in front of Your Majesty's throne, the faulty conjugations, subordinate clauses hanging loose upon the main clause like a bad hinge, if you'll excuse the expression, the moment that the Wienerwald wind flaps hither and thither, the moment that silence or discerning speech is replaced by chattering nonsense, in short, when the presence of Your Majesty, the glance of your eye does not mobilize the inner strength needed to create a sentence, then . . . Desist, Count, unless you wish to be like my son. No, of course not, my father said with a charming bow. This happened after the birth of my father's eldest son. My father did not wish to be like him, his eldest son, either. The birth of his children reduced him in size. Every new person related to him, or who would be related to him, was yet another occasion for sadness. He attempted severity with his children (if you spoil your son, his acts will fill you with horror, and if you treat him like a friend, he will be a disappointment unto you; do not be endearing with him, lest you regret it, and you'll end up holding the short end of the stick); he tried— cutting off the detours—hope, hoping (when a father dies, it's as if he hadn't died, for he leaves behind his own likeness); he tried attempting peace (a heart that is wise and prudent knows not despair), but the bottom line was that he'd have liked to have nothing to do with anyone, save for my mother and—and let's not beat about the bush—he succeeded. The decisive year came with his appointment as *Direktor des Hofspektakels,* the lord and master

159

of the Burgtheater—which effectively meant that he was free to supply the usual yearly deficit "from his own pocket." An expensive honor, indeed! *O, unser lieber Quin-Quin!* So the goat's to get the cabbage after all?, whispered the Viennese salons. The north wind occasions rain, the whispering tongue an angry face. My father avoided angry faces. He much preferred laughter. Also, from time to time, he tasted the cabbages that had been entrusted to his care. Power attracts. Literally. He was still laughing when his good fortune brought him together with Antonia Nikoletta Richard. Antonia Nikoletta laughed, too. A woman with an easy laugh. She did nothing of note, but her heart, her intellect and her physique were laden with attributes that attracted this Hungarian man to her, and in this respect, my father was, first and foremost, Hungarian. My mother was not a woman out of Hamlet, her world no mystery, her heart an open book. She wore it on her sleeve. As an actress she was mediocre, frivolous, irresistible. (She was a staunch royalist and an exceedingly Catholic woman, but news of her beheading—that having apprehended her and putting her head at bay, the passionate anti-Habsburg Imre Thököly had beheaded her—is a bunch of lies. After Thököly's very logical fall, my mother enjoyed the best of health for many years, her good cheer never wavering, and as for her appetite, though she would not eat a whole St. Martin's Day goose all by herself, she'd finish off a duck in one sitting. Notwithstanding, Thököly could have been of use to his nation, my father said maliciously in his dotage, but it seems he was of use only to the poetaster Kálmán Thaly— who, let it be said, added extra zap to the popular dreams of a greater Hungary.) In the persons of my father and my mother, two irresponsibilities met. People hoped that these two would unite into one new seriousness. But this was not to be. Still, they were seriously taken aback. When they realized that they had, how shall I put it, found each other, they got really scared. It scared them that they'd found someone they did not have to fear.

Seeing how well rounded Nature was—because they became rounded out once they'd found their other half—shook them to the core. Their love for each other taught them to respect the world around them. At the time, my father had thirty-seven years behind him. He'd dogged out a place for himself in the world, and this place was bright and spacious. High. Irresponsibility is not fragmented, it is not satisfied with fragments. It embraces every-thing and respects nothing, yet is rarely radical. It is not a storm that rips the trees of life out by the roots after we'd been nursing them with such earnestness day in and day out. It is even-keeled and gentle, like a light autumn rain (Paris), the morning fog or April sunshine, which gives little warmth, yet brings tears to our eyes—and through the veil of tears we hardly see the above-mentioned trees; we either crash into them, or we do not see them at all. Irresponsibility is pleasing. It is well balanced. (Or is only my father's such? After all, irresponsibility is not even-keeled, and it is not as tough as concrete but is feather-light, its conse-quences unforeseeable—the hotbed of a lack of balance.) Even during his reckless wanderings, my father did not forget his high office, nor did he abandon his most personal ambitions. He did not believe that the way to the good was through the bad. He did not believe in difficulties, in pain. He did not believe that a palm grows best under strain. He believed only in joy and good cheer. *Es muss immer Spass dabei sein!*—if it ain't got no joy to it, it ain't worth a bag a beans! Needless to say, he did not believe in God ei-ther. The Good Lord seemed far too morose for his taste. My father did not consider the world a vale of tears. He realized that from the vantage point of his privileged position, it would be pretty darn difficult to do so, that his view of things was bound up with his person, and that his assertion (or its opposite) said more about him than about the assertion itself (or its opposite). His view of the world was personal, he knew. What else could it be? And is it not possible that the Lord has created him expressly in order to embody this *personal*? He's perfectly aware that it is easier for a camel to pass through the eye of a needle than for a rich man to enter into the kingdom of God, but he does not think that a moderately rich man or a poor man would have it any easier. As for the camel, train him properly! He even saw life's meaningless-ness and cruelty as something cheerful. If called upon, he'd have taken the side of Creation in the face of the Creator himself. A nonbeliever was speaking the language of religion. Of course, it was not God my father rejected, but sin. An irresponsible man cannot believe in deadly sin. He is incapable of assuming of him-self that he would be capable of hurting his God in this manner—this in contrast to God, who is very much capable of postulating such a thing. It appears that God would gladly harangue man about sin day in and day out, if only we'd let Him. As if there were no other subject to be broached, save for this clammy-cold shivering fear of sin. But isn't this the only fundamental difference between you and me?, cries the Lord indignantly. Of this, my father understood only the only, and launched into a praise of Creation. The Lord felt it incumbent upon Him to stress the dif-ference; He did not consider this some sort of Jewish nitpicking. After all, that was a given, the similarity in their countenances *hin oder her,* neither here nor there, German in the original. He'd have liked to remind my father that there's such a thing as being unpre-tentious, but he was not pretentious, and that was the crux of the problem. He happened to respect hierarchy, and he said so, espe-cially since he held pride of place in it. In which case, it's no big deal, grumbled the Lord. Who said it was, my father retorted, his patience at an ebb. That assumption again, as if what comes easily were of lesser value than blood, sweat, and tears! It's as if I were to say, Lord, that it's no big deal being God when man, if you'll ex-cuse me, is omnipotent. *You* should try living on a pension, or as a schoolteacher, if you don't mind my saying so. . . . Almighty God! It is to you I owe my life and my fate. You must not expect me to be ungrateful. I fly on wingèd feet because my fate will let me, and in the direction my inner self prompts. My father knew that he was not at liberty to indulge his inclinations to the full, though he could indulge himself sufficiently, and since he knew this, he allowed himself even more indulgences. He knew what was all right to do and what was not, and in such cases, it is generally all right to do what one should not. My mother is a commoner, and it is not right to marry a commoner. No sweat. We will request, against a prearranged sum, the emigré French nobleman of a certain age, a certain de Durville, to kindly marry the actress in question, then proceed to die, and in this manner, on July 6 we rush our mistress, now called Baronesse de Durville, to the altar. My father's calculations were (naturally) right on; society does not insist on its principles as long as its style is not meddled with, as long as the "delinquent" is able to come up with the right packaging. Even the cabbies on the streets of Vienna knew perfectly well that Miss Richard (*a.k.a.* my mother) is neither a genuine Durville, nor a genuine baroness, only the pecuniary background of the sham marriage was genuine, a fact of which the whole town was also perfectly aware; still, hiding their defective teeth behind their fans, even the proverbially mean-spirited ladies of the Viennese salons teetered appreciatively about that nice Quin-Quin's (*a.k.a.* my father's) latest brilliant machinations. My father's growing influence—first Court Chancellor, in '64 Grand Master of the Knighthood of the Order of St. Stephen, in '65 Hungarian Royal Chief Chamberlain, in '71 Knight of the Golden Fleece, in '73 Lord Steward of the Household, and in '83 Viceroy of Croatia, which after all is the third highest public office in the land—was even sufficient to polish Durville's son from his first marriage into a real baron. Talent is always superabundant, an exaggeration, an excess by its very nature. There is no need portioning it out; it is the lack of talent that needs portioning and nurturing, like the light of our eyes; we must not portion it out irresponsibly; we

must save it for a better (worse, rainy) day. We need not economize on what is good, my father said, we should economize on
what is bad. Even the wealthiest man must give his spendthriftness
free rein. Marriage did not alter my father's main drift. We know
that upon his visit to Vienna, his French nephew, Valentin Ladislas, notes in his diary with not a little surprise that his uncle is
without a doubt faithful to the former actress, his wife. That little
fraulein knows something, Vienna said nastily. And as a matter of
fact she (my mother) did. Those were not unsettled times, and
they were not stormy, with each passing year bringing its share of
sorrow. It wasn't like they'd hardly gotten over one hardship,
when the next was already hard upon them. On the contrary, they
laid their heads on their pillows without a care in the world, secure in the knowledge of what tomorrow would bring. In each
other they discovered the outward joy that life had bereft them of.
They were brought closer to each other not by ceaseless sorrow
and calamity heaped on calamity; this is not what opened the
floodgates of their hearts. The more inclement their fate, the
wilder the raging storm, the more they gravitated toward each
other—no, this is not how it was. They were drawn to each other
in spite of it. If it is true that once upon a time man and woman
were one, and that we have all lost our other half, then my father
can be said to have found his. My mother's physical and spiritual
good cheer would not have sufficed to bring this about; even the
irresponsibility would not have sufficed (for it has many directions, irresponsible in what direction, that is the question). My
mother's knowledge consisted in the following: she stood square
behind my father in his fight against God. In the fight against sin.
Simply put, my mother did away with sin (to be understood from
the direction of my father, which goes without saying). But my
mother taking God's place, this is not how it was, or my mother,
like some sort of bunker (or skirt) becoming my father's safe
haven, a place where my father could hide, and because he's feel-

ing good there, body and soul, that's where he'd like to stay, ignoring the world outside, it wasn't like that either. My mother did not shelter my father from the outside world. She created a separate world, a world that is not contingent, day in and day out, on the continuous, threatening presence of sin, nor the fear of sinning. Its pallor. Its staleness. As soon as my mother appeared on my father's stage, my father could stop fearing that God might forsake him. My mother was a great actress on this stage, one of the greatest. My father got up early. He liked to see to the official papers and his correspondence before breakfast, while my mother liked to luxuriate in bed till noon, because she was indolent. She certainly satisfied all the conditions of indolence. She would sleep twelve hours at a stretch for a song. Accordingly, my father's life began each day with his casting a glance at my sleeping mother, and then he would turn to the Lord: See, Lord, I told you so! Cheerful as you can be. My father is a good example of a so-called cheerful father of mine.

150. The fortress built atop a steep dolomite cliff has stood in the service of the family since 1622. It was a castle the Turk could never occupy. The summit affords a handsome view of the myriad quaint serfs' villages. On a clear day, and with a sharp eye, you can see as far as Sopron. It is known for its 142-meter deep, so-called Turkish well. My father, who was known as a man with a penchant for experimentation, threw my mother into the well, and measured the time—after it was invented, with a stopwatch, the masterpiece of the watchmaker Victor Paillard, and before that, he simply counted, one, two, three, keeping in rhythm until the splash, with relative precision. He took $g$ to be nine-eight-one. Which is how my mother met my father.

151. On June 22 of the year, practically on the vernal equinox, my father grabbed the servant maid Janka Motta, my mother, and

raped her. In the course of copulating with her, he bit off her ear, the tip of her nose, and a piece from her breast and her labia. (To cut mother into pieces and preserve her in salt, for this he had no time.) When he was apprehended forty-eight hours later, he couldn't remember anything, and thought they must be joking. (Okay, show me her ear. Or the tip of her nose!) Not so my mother, who remembered everything perfectly. She remembered (it all) for the rest of her days. Those who know my father insist that he is of sound mind. In which case, what happened to him? Intellectual capacities do not necessarily preclude the momentary loss of a sound mind. Drink, too, can help one sink to the level of a lowly beast—though, come to think of it, could such a thing happen in the animal kingdom? Yes, it could. After they multiply, amoebae eat their partners, and so do the praying mantis, the scorpion, the spider, and also the female crab. Even the otherwise peaceful cricket eats its partner in the process of mating. In the process?! In the process. The cricket?! The cricket. Still, isn't the example of the unicellulars and the arthropods a bit too too remote? After all, regardless of what we may think of him, he, my father, is neither a unicellular nor an arthropod, if you don't mind my saying so. Less drastic forms of orality during copulation can also be spotted among vertebrates—and my father is definitely a vertebrate—the kissing ritual among fish, for instance, the rattling jingle of birds, and also the love bites and licking among mammals. The experts say that love and hunger unite in a woman's breast. Love and hunger: my father. The ear, the tip of the nose, the breast, the labia: my mother. This is how they met, one the other.

152.  My father, the man without qualities, slept with his older sister. Fuck it/him/her.

153.  My father growled at my mother, lookee here, love, take it easy (names changed by the publisher), I'm not interested, if it's eighty

kilos it's eighty kilos, and my father brought up the prospect of a not-too-distant deadline, yet practically speaking generous, a last point in time, a last point, there are ways today, programs, fruit cures, it's used against cancer, if it's of any use against cancer at all, the Jane Fonda method, he doesn't care, or something hefty, drastic, surgery, they should cut that extra fat out of my mother, he doesn't care about the details, honest to God, just do something with yourself!, also, there's these pills. She could resort to them, for all he cares, as long as she doesn't grow a mustache from all that hormone shit. Fuck. It's gonna cost an arm and a leg, but no problem, he'll dish it out, the problem is that my mother is as fat as a pig, and he's not interested in this inflated bag, this balloon, this shapeless superfluity and effusion, in short and once again, because he's not selling a pig in a poke, my mother either pulls her act together, or else he, my father, has had it with her as a man. He's through, he's not gonna navigate his own prick around a huge white hunk a meat when they're between the covers, and if, and he assumes this is the case, my mother wants to keep up the status quo, well, he's passing the ball, he's not impatient, just determined, and she mustn't think he's barking her down. He's not barking her down. Barking somebody down is entirely different. This is the intellectual exchange of two mature minds, reflections on life, their common future, that's the way to take it, and not get all hot and bothered under the collar because of the unusual nature of certain expressions. He's the way he is and there's no need to make a mountain out of a molehill. Not to mention tears. That'd really be idiotic. My mother was hurt by what my father said because, for one thing, she knew she could not effectuate serious changes to her body, and for another—and this was at the heart of the matter—she was surprised, because although she didn't like every single one of her eighty kilos either, it was a relatively new situation—to use my father's expression, "like a pig"— that brought her back to her body again. She enjoyed herself

167

more, her body, and my father's, too, and she couldn't believe that my father didn't feel any of this. But in that case, what is she to do? What the fuck? Whiskey and fucking on the sly, i.e., finding new paths to sensuality, plus a bit of numbness, maybe that. And so it was. But it did my mother in because although she enjoyed it—the enjoyment gave her wings, she was a brilliant drunk, and she always made her always incredibly young lovers happy, still, it did not agree with her makeup. Only my father agreed with her makeup till death did them part, except as we know, he got bogged down with those eighty kilos.

154. My father was overtaken by death, which almost always comes too soon, when my mother's happiness re. my father was at its height, i.e., she had reached the most beautiful—till then the most beautiful—stage of her life. The sorrow that's death's sorrow weighed so heavily upon my mother's heart that she could not part with my father, my father's body, and spent not only the last night with him under the covers, but the night after the last, this is how they were united for the last time. Yet my mother's pain would not subside even in this ecstasy beyond its time, only after her death, it subsided then, possibly.

155. My mother was waiting at the bus stop. She was cheerful. The rain was pouring. It, too, was cheerful. People were scampering for shelter. Only my mother remained standing cheerfully at the bus stop. Her face, which she held up to the rain like a half-wit, wore a seraphic smile. My father crashed the brake and rolled down the big 1950s-type Csepel truck's window, yo! yo! the way you call to a snoring man, and with the familiar light, beckoning gesture of his index finger, he motioned to her to come over. I haven't seen such a happy beckoning gesture since, my mother said, that was itself and also its own parody, a crude male gesture and its own apology, too, if a halfhearted one, as if to say: kindly

take me seriously. Hop in, muffins! Fuck off, my mother barked. My father slammed the door and stepped on the gas pedal. Which is how they met. (My father was so ecstatic from having spotted my mother, he crashed into the bus in front of him, though only lightly. The vehicles were not damaged. My father and the bus driver had a good laugh: a prince from Africa (Mali) who received his Ph.D. in Szeged, stuck. Stuck in Hungary. The following day my father's head ached. He felt vertiginous. He couldn't find his place in the world. He'd dislocated a vertebra, which hurt for the rest of his life, without affording relief. His head became an aching head. It ached and ached.)

156. My father, no, my mother, kept nagging my father. Do you love me? My father loved my mother, so he said he loved her. But my mother would not believe him, or if she did, she pretended she didn't, and—this was the nagging—she kept asking my father for assurances. Will he, for instance, love her till May 5, this being April 25, and is he positive? My father took his appointment book out of his pocket.

157. Every single morning, in winter and in summer, in wind and in rain, my father would go up to the window, and with his nail, amid nerve-wracking squeaks, he'd write I ♥, and here my mother's name followed. But my mother was so damned lazy, she slept so late—and she snored, too, like a pig on the turf—or was not sleeping any longer, just luxuriating in bed, that by the time she opened her eyes, the writing was gone. Which is how they met.

158. This is how my mother and my father met (draft of a letter addressed to Hungarian Radio): Sir: In last night's program, you said a certain word twice within a context that is of no consequence here. Guadalayara. What sonority! If I could only hear it again. Guadalayara. Dear Sir! You can't imagine what a word like

Guadalayara means in a bleakness of national proportions such as ours. In last night's program you said it twice, or better still, sneaked it in—sneaked it into the broadcast—and my life. Could I hear it again, please? My father never answered the letter.

159. My father, who marched into town with Prince Paskievich's troops, was quartered in my mother's house, which was one of the handsomest residences around. My mother told us that the count (my father) placed his tall shako hat in the window so the people in the street could see who was staying there and not harass the inhabitants. My five-year-old mother felt a superstitious attraction toward the shako. My father once caught her as she was stroking it and handed it to her. Let her play with it, if she felt like it. In 1912, a picture was taken of my mother. On the picture she's sitting in a wicker chair, gazing into the camera. She is wearing mourning clothes and a somber black mourning necklace almost reaching down to her knees. She is not smiling, but she is not grave either, she is looking out from under the preposterously large cylindrical headgear composed of soft, black cloth with equanimity, like one who wishes to cast a last searching glance at the world where she's been sojourning for some time. Her eldest son later said he'd have given years of his life if by some miracle he could have seen my mother as a five-year-old running into the room where the Russian officers, whom she did not fear, were eating lunch, wearing frilled white undies reaching to the ground, and on her head my father's (the count's) shako.

160. Gym class had to be canceled because Aunt Ica felt dizzy. She wasn't feeling well, and Uncle Feri had to lead her out of the gym. My father's son got home earlier than expected. He didn't have a key to the garden gate but he didn't ring the bell. He could get in without it. A bit of fastening, wedging, et cetera. He was about to open the door when an animal scream issued from within. In his

170

fright, my father's son screamed along. Verging on the inarticulate, beyond "the bounds of civility," the scream from inside recalled the sound of soccer games; the character of the voice did not give away whether anyone had kicked a goal, or was it the fucking referee again? My father was sitting in front of his typewriter screaming at the top of his lungs: I love you. My mother, my father's son assumed. As for Aunt Ica, she was pregnant, as it later turned out, and Uncle Feri took over her classes. (Later, the two gym teachers tied the knot. The wedding was held in the gym. During the ceremony, class 8A presented phys ed exercises. My father, as it turned out later still, called Aunt Ica Mrs. Ferenc, after her husband. My dear, my very dear Mrs. Ferenc.)

161. Being bosom buddies with Vasarely no, Wesselényi, my father received permission to go around Budapest, no, back then still Pest-Buda, in a rowboat. Anywhere at all! (Due to the sudden melting of the snow and the resulting ice jam, the swollen Danube threatened the city with a flood, then made good on its threat in 1838.) During the Reform Age, my father tried appealing to the young ladies with this boating privilege, my mother especially, who had a thing for floods to begin with. What will have its way will have its way, et cetera. They were just rowing in the direction of the Franciscan Church in Pest. Ignác Horváth, professor of engineering, was lecturing his students from a "hydrometric station" built from pontoon boats. The fish swimming in the floodwater looked up. My mother and my father looked down. (My mother had not been officially introduced to my father, and so it was awkward when mutual friends from the nearby Kárpátia Restaurant shouted, We didn't know you were introduced! We're not, my mother said. My father continued rowing.)

162. We children could hear it in our room. You think it's that simple, all you have to say is you love me, and then I . . . I . . . I have

no right to say anything? Is that what you think? Yes, that's what I think, my father said. My mother started screaming, Get out! Go back home! Go wherever you want! Don't you hear? Bogyi and I will take care of it. And take your briefcase with you! Everyone was dead when my father's eldest son found a piece of paper, on it a sentence (like the draft of a letter): The only thing I would like to forget is that I said it's simple. My father's and my mother's handwriting looked so much alike at the end. It's not at all unusual, they say.

163. How was it? The war was over, the country had sung itself to sleep. There was no longer need for hushabies. Or, on the contrary, was nothing over yet and did everything still matter? Do you love me? (You love me?) Yes, I love your eyes, I love your knees, I love your ass, I love your hair, I love your tits. Does that mean you love all of me? Yes. And how about you? I love your forehead and I love your thighs and I love your balls and I love your shoulders and I love your lips. Does that mean you love all of me? Yes. Which is how they met: my father, my mother, the part, and the whole.

164. My father was waiting for Louis of Baden. They'd made plans for a glorious triumph over the heathen hordes. My father was a gifted soldier, while Türkenlouis, a.k.a. Louie the Turk was who he was; in keeping with family tradition, my father was born a soldier, and became the commander of the troops thanks to his talent; but the man from Baden was a born commander. It was raining, cold, somber, you'd think it was November, whereas it was June 2. My father bided his time reading (what?) in his tent, or strolling through nearby Eszék; in short, he was chasing after solitude and profundity, society and colorful shallowness all at once. And yet, like Tonio Kröger, he felt that life was passing him by. Still, this feeling rarely caught up with him, and when he was

with my mother, never. He gave the young newcomer from Baden, who washed his shoulder-length, curly locks only twice a year, a fervent hug. Tut-tut, the latter grumbled upon receipt of this unexpected display of emotionality, like an old man, a faithful old watch dog, tut-tut. At last!, my father shouted. He couldn't take his eyes off the handsome youth. You know, old boy, I can't do without women! Or men. I need someone. Someone concrete. Louie of Baden listened to his friend with sympathy and impatience, and from then on, he ordered a girl from the village every night. Now why didn't I think of that?! What? The girls? No, I thought of the girls, it's the ordering I didn't think of! Louie couldn't understand why my father, who was a great lord, sometimes acted like a provincial butcher shop, like a nobody. But that's just it. My father was a great lord and a nobody, that was his specialty. Besides, he liked complex relationships. Sending for girls was too easy. It simplified things. Still, he had a grand old time with the village maidens, a grand old time every time, until the glorious triumph. Then he turned somber. (Louis of Baden had no admiration for my father's so-called feminine traits, he insisted on the traditional view of manhood, i.e., and for instance, prudence + screwing anything in skirts.)

165. Who was my father? A puppy, six of one, half a dozen of the other. He was that he was, he is that he is, he will be that he will be. A great lord. Still, his wife left him (one fine day). Or did he throw her out? A handsome woman, attractive, engaging. Just possibly a tad sleepy-like inside. Be that as it may, there was my father, as solitary as my little finger, orphaned, unpartnered and alone, for the past two hours at least. It was around noon (lunch at the tolling of the bell), so he called my mother on the phone, who was also said to be attractive and engaging. Could they have lunch? Without further ado (not waiting for the appetizer, even), my father gave an open, honest assessment of the situation, the so-

lution to which he (my father) thought he had found in her (my mother), and without so much as a how-de-do, without waiting to catch his breath, he launched into a detailed account of the future material circumstances of my future mother (my future mother's future material circumstances), pocket money, the use of the coach and four, tram tickets, separate vacations every other month (negotiable!); jewels, concretely, some for everyday use only, some as a gift; concretely, the minimum number of nights to be spent together per month, the so-called conjugal minimum, plus money for clothes. My father got all hot under the collar. Love. It must be love. My mother sent him up the devil's arse. Which is how they met.

166. My father announced that he wouldn't want my mother if she were the only woman on earth. But my father didn't think this through; after all, only is everything, and he (my father) wanted every woman he could get.

167. A young girl spoke *into* my father's phone, a mystery, because it was a so-called in-house phone reserved for finance officers, et cetera. The girl asked for her friend from Kosovo. Fine, my father said by way of a joke, I'll see if he's in. I'm sorry, young lady, there's no one here from Kosovo. How beautifully my father speaks English, *indeed*, and the like. Indeed, he'd been serving his king (emperor) for forty years as ambassador to London. He could navigate through the maze of verb tenses like Puskás among the defense: with ease. Like a eunuch in a harem: with equanimity. Like a small water bug on the water's surface: with serenity; like a ballerina, with effortless ease. What for any other Hungarian is an unnavigable quagmire is for him a chance to show off. Where is he from? From here. Who lives in the apartment? Just him. Oh. Actually, not finding her friend from Kosovo is hardly a tragedy. She can't abide southern irresponsibility anyway, and what a

lovely chat they're having, the two of them, spontaneous, and how old is he? Sixty-five. (He was three days short of forty-three.) Oh, what a pity, because in that case, he could be her grandfather. A wounded animal, my father cried out: So what? How many grandfathers have you got?! Which is how my father and my mother met.

168. As soon as my father saw my mother and her schoolmates pitching pennies in the Museum Garden, he fell head over heels for her (my mother), right then and there (on the spot). Love coursed through his veins, limb by limb. He started shivering, and a hot flash ran through him, as if he were thirty years older, and a woman. He had no idea who she was, he didn't know her name, nor her family, nor her place of residence. He followed her to the student dining room. Having entered the courtyard between the back gate of the Kárpátia Restaurant and the editorial offices of the Catholic *Új Ember,* my mother turned around and gave my father the once-over. Who'd become deeply solitary in following her. Nakedly obvious. She waited for him to catch up, then addressed him as follows: What are you staring at? Haven't you seen white folk before? Stop following me! My father presented her with the facts of the case, and told her that she mustn't draw the wrong conclusion. My mother responded to him in the following vein: Don't get your hopes up. I'm not about to bring shame on myself. What you want is not what you are about to get. So forget it. I just want to look. That's all I want. Oh. That's all right then, my mother said, ascertaining the facts of the case. Still, will you tell me, fair maiden, are you a freeman or a serf? A serf. What is your name? Chalwa. Who is your lord and master? God, my mother said. You shall know what lies in the seventh heaven quicker than the answer to your question. Forsake what cannot be. Tell me, fair maiden, where and when can I see you again? At the same time and place every Friday, where you saw me today.

They were facing each other. Suddenly, there was no more to be said, but then my mother asked who should go first, You want to, or should I? You go first, my father said, and may God be with you. My mother walked toward the bridge and glanced back to see if my father was following her, so my father did not. But he tried following her with his eye, then he ran up to the church and made inquiries, but he'd lost track of her. Ever since, my father stands in the Museum Garden every Friday, waiting at the appointed time—for nothing. Either the earth has swallowed her up, or the sun has melted her away, but I never saw her again. An intense fire burns in my heart, more intense than burning coke.

169. When asked who his favorite fiction heroine was—an easy question—my father put my mother's name down without a second thought. But the jury, the editors, literary opinion and the up-and-coming bourgeoisie, Party Headquarters, the cathedral chapter of Eger and the Viennese Court, plus my mother, did not accept this as a possible answer. Which is how they met—on paper.

170. My father is a gifted, cynical man who sold his soul to the Communists for peanuts. He was so scared of them he couldn't sleep, and if he did, he was startled out of his sleep by his own terrified screams. He was drenched in sweat. The neighbors kept reporting him to the police. The militia came to the house and warned him, stop the screaming, it's bad for the cityscape. Which terrified him even more. In his mounting terror, he developed a method. In the soft version, he clapped a hand to his mouth simultaneously with the screaming. His hand slapped over his mouth like a spring or a trap. But the sound filtered through just the same, and the scream turned into a horrible whining or wailing that—need we add—did nothing to pacify the neighbors. Later, he learned to puke, and the puke physically blocked the path of the scream-

ing—that wee rattle that comes from choking that is more like a gulp or the clearing of the throat. Which made it his private affair. He'd seduced my mother, a simple village girl, who was constantly worrying about when my father would grow tired of her. His private affair. Et cetera. Et cetera. You're certainly good at telling tales, except you digress, my father said. *You* digress, my mother said in her defense. Never mind, it's all interesting. Soap bubbles . . . Soap bubbles. Soap bubbles? Soap bubbles. This great big colorful life. My mother could never forget the laugh with which my father said this. Transfigured. This laugh, we might say, was transfigured. Transfigured laughter. At the same time, he always spoke like a schoolteacher, as he'd done now. My mother discussed this with her friend Rita (or Petra?). No problem, Rita said. It's like *The Thousand and One Arabian Nights*. As long as you keep telling him stories, he won't leave you. My mother flushed with joy. Suddenly, it was night. (If this is true, his goose is cooked, my mother thought. Should the stock of stories start depleting, I'll simply embroider them, but that won't be necessary, because life . . . oh, yes, life, as long as it goes on, is inexhaustible.)

171. Being a man, my father uses thirty-nine (different) muscles when he kisses. For the time being, let's not consider whether it's Emperor Leopold or János Kádár. It's the amount of work that matters. He burns 150 calories doing it. Providing he is not in love. If he is: Good Lord!

172. Two days after my mother gave my father the boot (or was it my father giving the boot to my mother?) because it wasn't working out, or, it was working by fits and starts, my mother suggested that they not throw out the baby with the bathwater (little did she know how right she was). They shouldn't break it off entirely, she suggested, i.e., they shouldn't date anymore, just make love, which shocked my father, who regarded my mother's openness as

licentiousness rather than daring. But my mother didn't want to lose my father, no matter what. It was all a misunderstanding, she supposed. They're expecting too much of each other. Or too little. In any case, they're doing something wrong. Messing it up. This "all or nothing," she felt, was not fated. If they could only get rid of the awkwardness. But since the physical contact, this whole love gymnastics is practically *neunkomaneun,* almost perfect (German in the original), it could give them a handle on things. At first my father agreed. But later he was ashamed that he'd been separated from his prick in this shameful manner, and the shame also caught up with my mother—that's why the boot—because there was a slight hitch. For the first time in her life, she was with child. She found that she was *in the family way,* or in a state of grace, as they say. She ran into her father in front of the lab door, because that's how chance works. He had a grease ball excised from behind the ear, and truly puzzled, he asked his daughter, my mother, what she was doing in the hospital in front of the lab when she was such a healthy young maiden. A healthy young maiden, Grandfather said bursting with pride, veritably hurling it in his daughter's face, here's the truth, you might as well face it, you're a healthy young maiden! My mother flashed her most ingratiating smile. I lost my *maiden* head, Daddy dear. Oh, what a scatterbrain you are, her father said. My mother had finished in the lab by then, so she kissed her father, Peter piper picked a peck of pickled peppers, she whispered in his ear, and ran off, as cheerful and light as if she were a healthy young maiden indeed. Grandfather grinned with satisfaction. The young doctor, whom her friend had recommended to my mother because her family had full confidence in him, greeted my mother gruffly, because she was smoking like a chimney, a factory chimney. If you don't change your ways, young lady, this is the last time you see me. *The last time.* Doctors play this wise old-man game as if they were in on everything, as if our problem was their problem, thereby justifying their harsh tone. But later, he did very well by my mother. He said that my mother was lucky, because he'd practically—*practically*—never seen such a *young* embryo before. Nothing's developed yet, he said. My mother said brusquely that perhaps he shouldn't go into detail about what the baby, who is—*practically*—not there *now*, would have next week. Which just went to show that behind her apparent calm, she (my mother) was apprehensive all the same. The doctor warned her about the area hospital to which she was assigned. A slaughterhouse, he said. But he knows someone in Gödöllő. My mother didn't want to involve my father in this thing, if it's over and done with, it's over and done with. But then, as chance would have it, she told him anyway because they accidentally ran into each other, and it would have been unnatural not to tell him. My father got scared. So scared, he pretended he was happy and said he'd take full responsibility and was willing to change his life to suit the altered circumstances. He went even further. He put himself at my mother's disposal, and accompanied her to Gödöllő. My father was at the wheel. Afterward, it hurt a bit, but my mother was given something to contract the uterus. Also, she was kept under observation until the afternoon. Then, finding everything in order, she was released. They let the doctor who accompanied them out at a taxi stand. My father offered to drive him home, but he nodded and said he thinks they should spend some time alone. This, however, is not how *they* felt. My father did go up to my mother's place for a cup of tea, but afterward he left. At this juncture, we could make a joke about how adventurously it began, the life of my father's eldest son. Or, what would be an even better joke, who is who in the story. But because not everything can go smoothly, that day, on the way home, my father's clutch got stuck. Also, my mother's cervical orifice became ulcerated. This, too, is part of the day's summary, an addendum that took some of the fun away.

•  •  •

173. Cheerful and devil-may-care, this was my father as a young man. He loved wine, women, and song. As the fourth son and his parents' sixth child, he didn't have much money, but he didn't mind, as long as he got what he wanted—wine, women, and song. Also, if he didn't get it, that was okay with him, too. He spent his life in idleness. He let things (what? what things?) take their course. Grandfather Dénes gave his children a strict upbringing—through proxies, of course. For twenty-five years he was County Judge of Kolozs, and it was from the height of these twenty-five years, this certainty and infinity, that he regarded the world around him, including his unfortunate offspring. His severity, however, was restricted to pecuniary considerations. In their discussion of ethics, or so it is said, the Catholics have come, over time, to focus exclusively on the Sixth Commandment; they have come to restrict their ethics to this. And so, pecuniary considerations were also the pith and substance of the tiresome paternal discontent, the subdued offendedness that took the form of grumbling. Yet my father cared not a jot for money. He didn't want to be a rich man. He wanted nothing but to have a good time. It was less, even, than wanting, because when an obstacle—such as lack of money—presented itself along the path to a good time, my father, instead of sweeping the obstacle aside or resorting to some ruse, shrugged, stopped in his tracks, or stopped in his tracks and shrugged, and did an about-face. In short, Grandfather had to stand and watch my father conform to, or obey, his every pecuniary restriction, or nitpicking, but not by satisfying said restriction, but by thumbing his nose both at said restrictions, *and* the money. Thumbing his nose at the former, he easily despaired of the latter, and he did so with no trace of pain. And yet pain, the pain of the sons, is a comfort to fathers. In this respect, too, my father was an exception. He found no comfort in the pain of my father's eldest son. It did not excite him. It left him cold. Never was there a moment in my father's son's life when my father found

him of the slightest interest. He was not being selfish: he was equally disinterested in himself. (My father's son's cup was brimming over with gratitude when the seemingly obligatory paternal snarls were not forthcoming. But the indifference hurt, all the same. He resorted to the most hopeless and fatuous, though widespread tactic: he tried to be friends with his father. Don't. Ever. Making friends with your father? Forget it. A big mistake. Difficult. Neither a friend, nor that rigid, irritable, cold-shouldering, didactic detachment. It is difficult.) Because he stopped in his tracks, my father did not take the straight and narrow. His lies were not premeditated deceptions; he simply took the path of least resistance. All of which was apparent even in his gait, and also his features, especially the eyes; everything just a bit off. Being devil-may-care is not necessarily endearing. It implies a lack of prioritization and therefore, balance. It is unreliable. The only reason it does not cause any more damage is because it also implies a weakness. My father met my mother when he was young. She (my mother) was a soubrette by the name of Róza Tótpataki, this at the theater of Kolozsvár. My mother suited my father's purposes perfectly. But my father did not suit my mother's purposes perfectly. She wanted to get married, especially later, when in due course, their affair had taken a very real shape in the form of two offspring. A weak character, a real shit, my father played for time and kept asking for a postponement "till next Whitsuntide," saying that my grandfather, meaning the family, meaning the gentlefolk of Kolozsvár, to which we must add the conservative Transylvanians, disapproved of my mother, Mama Róza (with the Transylvanians disapproving the most of all). My father's family is but a small branch of the copious, far-reaching, *here my father's name follows,* tree. It is not dwarfed or old and scraggy, it is not even insignificant, just of local interest. Local interest is nothing to scoff at, especially locally; it is also familiar, transparent, measurable, tangible. It is of this world. The power and authority of the thicker branches of the family tree is irreproachable and magnificent, because you can't see its origins. This impressive greatness does not come from the sky—though there were enthusiastic family-tree researches tending in this direction—nor from Vienna, as the ill-disposed tongues would have it. It is not from somewhere, it just *is,* and not thanks to Grace. Being Catholic or pro-Habsburg Labanc will not suffice (just try it!). It is part of nature, and thus needs no excuses or explanations. It just is (was). Eminence such as this can be highly tolerant of itself. It need not be circumspect, nor is it in need of proving its legitimacy. It need not concern itself with itself; it suffices that it concern itself with its concerns and affairs, all of which serve to strengthen its prestige. Which is only natural. He who is rich is the richest. Eminence such as this cannot be destroyed, because it could be destroyed only along with the world, in which case, there is nothing to be done. To kick up a storm or protect against it would not only be ridiculous, but superfluous as well. My county judge grandfather, Dénes, was sitting securely on that certain branch, comfortably, pridefully, calmly, watching my father's, his youngest son's, insecurities, restlessness and weakness, with disapproval. When it was spread abroad—because a thing like this gets spread abroad—that the soubrette, my mother, was with child, my older brother, supposedly from my father, my grandfather decided to look her up. In person. You can always see eye to eye with a woman, he said. There's a remedy for everything. He was a handsome man, *eine Sünde wert,* as the elderly female members of the family used to say, like accomplices, with a blush, as if they'd tasted already of that certain *Sünde.* He was the proud owner of hundreds of waistcoats. Just like prestige, one waistcoat engenders another, and Christmas and other holidays a flood of waistcoats, an avalanche of waistcoats, and my grandfather was pleased with each and every one—if they suited his taste, i.e., his mood, then that's why, and if they didn't, his spirit soared with the discovery, oh, what a variety of tastes there are in the world! He wore these, too. He wore incredibly tasteless waistcoats, causing a sensation (and many a suppressed smile) all over town. He knew who had given him each one, and each one had a name, just like a dog or a horse. The "fringed piece" or "Jancsi" was from his father, John IV. (Once, his enthusiasm getting the better of him, when staving off the election of deputy lord lieutenant János Horváth of Kocs—this when great-grandfather was lord lieutenant of Veszprém—he infuriated the electorate so badly that they, namely, the noble gentlemen of Szentgál, threatening to beat the living daylights out of him, broke down the door of the county hall assembly room. Physical violence was avoided only because my great-grandfather, accompanied by his faithful master of the hunt, whose name has not been preserved by ingrate family memory, had quickly taken off for a side door. With the rebellious voters at his heels, he made for the rest room; but just as he reached the door, they caught up with him and tore off one sleeve of his beautiful fur-lined *mente* coat, at which juncture the master of the hunt (his master of the hunt) brandished his knife before them and, pushing my great-grandfather through the door, put a sharp end to the chase. Years after the event—as my great-grandfather stood in for the Master of the Horse at the coronation National Assembly in Bratislava—he had himself painted at the Emperor's special request on horseback (there are several xylograph copies extant), shown wearing a waistcoat made from the torn *mente,* the fringed one, alias Jancsi.) He received a black waistcoat from his Aunt Terézia when she was forced to marry Lajos Révay, and a crimson one when she became a widow. ("I am not happy, János, dear, but I know how to bear my burden . . . But where to? . . . This happy crimson color, from now on, it's part of . . . the world . . . the family . . .") He received a white one from his Aunt Bora, with innumerable small dovetailing crosses (as if it were herringbone), after which his only son's nanny—or so the lore would have it—

proceeded to drop him from the castle window at Szentdemeter, this upon the instigation of Zsófia Gyulaffy. He received the "little sooty" from his Aunt Antónia, who met her death when she snuffed out a candle in a most unfortunate manner, with the flames catching her headdress and garments, burning parts of her body so badly, that her demise was indeed most agonizing. Her portrait hangs in Bratislava, with our relative István. "Maria Theresa" he received from his mother, a heavy, purple velvet piece surrounded by such an aggressive, cloying cloud of sweat, that my grandfather wore it only in a crowd (elections, processions). (So, in the beginning, my great-grandfather's mother's parents were Protestants, but the father converted to Catholicism, and in order to convert his daughter, who was betrothed to Sámuel Teleki, the future chancellor, with the approval of Queen Maria Theresa, had her torn from her mother's arms, who was protesting—*and* adamantly Protestant—this in Örményes, by military might, and she was dragged to Vienna, where she solemnly converted to Catholicism under the eyes of the Court. Her nuptials, as well as her future education, were overseen by Countess Mihály Michna, the Lady in Waiting, under full command of the Queen. It was thanks to her concern that the family came into possession of a chest containing clothing ornamented with the imperial arms, as well as a gilt coach with seating pillows covered in red velvet.) The brothers, too, paid their waistcoat dues. The "belted" is from Alajos-Fidelis. (As standard-bearer in the Alvinczy regiment, he took part in the siege of the castle of Cuneo. He volunteered for the assault, received a shot in the shoulder, and was taken by the enemy. He recovered while he was a prisoner in the castle, and was released after it surrendered. Later, he often talked about how they assuaged the hunger in their stomachs by tightening their belts.) László, who kept away from women all his life, lived a life of chastity, and enriched the valuable collection of coins started by his father with several equally

valuable additions. Enjoying Metternich's confidence, and entrusted with the secret imperial archives, he came up with a fascinating bit of documentation that discusses, in great detail and
from an exceedingly particular point of view, the conditions of
the Hungarian Partium region (copy in the library of Oszlop). In
short: the waistcoat is the handiwork of the tailor (Singer) be-
spoke by Metternich, a black and yellow silk vestment, which
bears the name: "Metternich." Item: one of the handsomest
pieces, colorful, with flowers, as if it were from San Francisco,
*make love not war,* is from my grandfather's nephew Károly who, in
his melancholy—the result of an incurable spine disease—took a
gun to his head. The "Prussian" is from György, the foster son of
the above-mentioned Károly who, as second lieutenant in the
12th Haller Hussar regiment, took part in the anti-Prussian war.
When the first division of his regiment attacked the infantry on
July 3, his horse was shot from under him. Leaping on the horse
offered to him by Hussar private Joachim Bódi, with the latter
following on foot, he managed to effectuate a most fortunate escape at a moment when they seemed completely bereft of hope.
On his waistcoat, or chest, the following badges of honor were
given pride of place: the Russian Order of St. Anne, 3rd Class, the
Prussian Order of the Crown, 3rd Class, the Order of St.
Wladimir, 4th Class, the small cross of the Legion d'Honneur and
the Officers Cross of the Order of Takowa. But to return to the
brothers and finishing with the list, the "Liszt" is from Mihály,
who nurtured a passion for geology and music, and with several
others, did aid the infamous musician with respect to his studies
in Vienna. There was, however, a waistcoat whose origins are
shrouded in mystery, the "silver": like a heavy coat of mail, the
witness of heroic battles, a small, indolent animal with silvery
scales, an accidental survivor, *old* animal, it came by mail, sender
unknown, not to his home, but to his office. The soft little package was tied round with a huge crimson ribbon. The thing was

unattractive and garish. There was something unrefined about it, maybe in the red, but more so in the incomprehensible *offness* of the whole. Nothing, not even a letter was attached to the package, unless we regard the glaring imprint of a pair of rouged lips at the "heart" of the waistcoat as such. Which could never afterward be removed. Grandmother Cecília Haller was a firm and insistent lady, but not when it came to Grandfather. They avoided each other, but she wanted to throw the silver waistcoat out without a second thought. Interesting. It is also interesting that Grandfather—who cared nothing for objects and even less for fashion (for fifty years he wore whatever Józsi, the *leibdiener,* gave him of a morning, and after him, his son Józsi, without a word of complaint)—now put his foot down and vetoed the disposal, insisting on the mysterious silver piece. My grandmother managed to prevent him from wearing it, which is a dubious achievement, for in this way the waistcoat became unique, special, different, dangerous, the waistcoat that for some reason "is not being worn." Now, on his visit to my mother Róza Tótpataki, Grandfather wished to wear it. To everyone's surprise, Grandmother did not object. No one in the house knew that she'd already been to see my mother. Grandmother was considered a tough woman, without feelings. She had feelings, she just didn't wear them on her sleeve. But she acted according to them. True, she respected Grandfather, she didn't love him, but she adored her son, practically the only thing in the world she cared for. Her one and only concern was whether my father needed money, fever medicine, rest and recreation, ski boots, or Wiener schnitzel (from pork). Poor man— meaning, my father—if he only knew! She spoiled him so he didn't even notice! She never interfered directly (with him), but when he took it into his head to drink (my father; then gradually his whole body, his neck, his collarbone, chest, belly, loins, thighs, his shaky knees and unreliable ankles), she felt she had to do something. So she went to see the little soubrette. My grand-

186

mother did not look like a woman of means; she dressed with inimitable (intrepid) bad taste; on her the sinfully expensive clothes, screaming in anguish from each other's proximity, found a safe haven of sorts. After the defeat of the revolution she wore only black, but this didn't improve the situation. Black cotton stockings, heavy flannel skirt, shirt, gray or white, plus the black raincoat on which the graying, even bright yellow stripes, were in the act of fading. Nothing showed of the family glitter, neither the small branch, nor the big. With all her aristocratic ancestry, my grandmother was not an aristocrat but a cap-à-pied plebeian— though possibly her deportment and persistence, the scope of her thinking, "impersonal selflessness, selfish impersonality" were rooted in the former after all. She did not give Mother notice of her visit, she just showed up. She knocked, entered, glanced at the maid who shrank away in mute terror. She did not step away, she was swept with the tide, my mother was rocking herself in the wicker rocking chair in the spacious inner room, in front of the window, studying her part. Needless to say, she could tell at a glance that her lover's mother had entered the room. She did not budge, she delivered the trustworthy old *Klopstock* a bit louder, *Messias wurde geboren.* Grandmother stopped under the interior arch and watched the swinging, swaying and muttering young woman. My mother was beautiful, movie star beautiful. It was impossible to tell what was real and what was not, but the beauty she displayed seemed authentic enough. Grandmother did not trust this hide-and-seek beauty—that's why she was standing un-der the arch. She watched the other woman at length, but felt nothing for her, not even jealousy. She cared only for her son, only he mattered. The woman did not. Yet she'd come to ask her for something. My mother was still acting as if her salvation depended on poor old *Klopstock,* as if nothing else existed but this outdated German text. There would have been something to it, if only she were really studying her lines. She misunderstood my grandmother who, as if she were going into the foray, with two gigantic leaps, like some sort of tiger, was at my mother's side, the ubiquitous black raincoat, like the Bolshevik banners in the Bolshevik films later on, flapping behind. She, pretending fright, looked up. Who is it, what is it? Like a child, Grandmother squatted by her side, took her hand, and stroked it. O (or oh?), my mother announced, from the middle of Act Two (the middle act) is my guess, from total darkness, we don't remember anymore what we're doing in the theater, who pushed us in here, into this heavy brightness, from the dark, and we don't know yet why, how, under what circumstances we will depart from here, if indeed we depart. You are a wise woman! My mother pulls her hand away. Her only sincere gesture the entire afternoon. Not that! Grandmother took her hand again. Though she'd have done anything for her son, she couldn't pretend. She found it difficult to speak. She spoke reluctantly, as if asked to recite her lessons. You misunderstand me, young lady. My husband will come, save that for him. I am only saying that you know my son needs you, I am only saying, asking—she's not finding it difficult to say—don't leave him. She's stroking her hand eagerly (my grandmother my mother's). Each likes the other's hand, the skin; finer than they'd have thought. Please don't leave my son. He is a weak man but not a bad man. Don't leave him, dear. As if she were being strangled, my mother was shaking with laughter; great, forceful, cosmic laughter, like Captain Köpenicki at the end of *Captain Köpenicki*. *Unmöglich,* my mother muttered, like him, *unmöglich.* But the actress had long-distance plans. Refused to be on familiar terms with her (my mother with my grandmother). She saw that Grandmother was wise—you are a wise woman—in short, she's got to be circumspect in her lies. Your Excellency misunderstands me. Just the other way around, I want to hold on to Géza. Didn't he mention it? I want him to marry me. Marry me, Count, or go to the devil! But he doesn't want to go to the devil. My grandmother's countenance turned hard, so my mother continued thus: The devil take it, Countess. I'm not talking about marriage, that'll take care of itself, one way or the other. You, dear, just don't leave him. You want me to be his lover, his concubine, his moll? my mother said indignantly in place of my grandmother. I will not go into that, if you don't mind. I have never been anybody's lover, and by all odds, nor shall I ever be. (According to ill-disposed tongues, the number of nights my grandmother spent with Grandfather equals the number of the children born to them.) The devil take it! What are you getting at, Countess?! Your grandchild is here in my belly! It's moving! Do you want the poor innocents to be illegitimate? Grandmother shrugged, she couldn't care less about the grandchildren, and because she knew that her son didn't give a damn about legitimacy or social advancement, she knew that her son's happiness was not contingent upon Kolozsvár's approval. What they think doesn't count. She didn't give a damn for any of this. A mother's love turned her into an anarchist, this was my mother's ill luck. (And so it came to pass: my father's children were born illegitimate, and it was not my father but his older brother Kálmán, who dedicated the rest of his life to righting the lives of the poor orphans. You see, in the meanwhile, my father passed away. Uncle Kálmán was made of sterner stuff than my father. On the occasion of the first assault on Nagyszeben—the Bem campaign, Mátyás Hussars—a cannonball tore off his right elbow. His arm was amputated on the battlefield, and the overhasty surgery had to be repeated at Marosvásárhely. Afterward, he painted excellent landscapes with his right hand, and with the same hand wrote studies on history and geography while his wife, Paulin Bethlen—who was very Bethlen, three out of four grandparents being Bethlen—was better than an amateur poet. My father came under my mother's spell through Uncle Kálmán, who was the intendant of the local theater. Uncle Kálmán did not like my mother because he did not like problems, and Mother was a problem, and it was even a greater problem that the children would have to bear the stamp of illegitimacy, because all the documents at the time listed them as such. They could not be army officers, et cetera, for instance. This is why he didn't like my father either, who just laughed off the encouragements to wed, and tried to pull the wool over Uncle Kálmán's eyes, too, with the Whitsuntide excuse; nor was he able to achieve the extension of the title of count to include the orphans. But Francis Joseph made them legitimate, *per gratia Principis*, then he made them noblemen, *allerhöche Gnadenakt*, giving them the name, *here my father's name followed*, of Kisiklód, because Uncle had signed Kisiklód over to them. In all of Hungarian history this is the only gift of nobility that didn't come with a coat of arms. He wanted to give them the Hofmarschallam, the family coat of arms, with the so-called "bar sinister," a black slash going diagonally from left to right, which in the imperial heraldry is the sign of illegitimate origin, but Uncle Kálmán refused.) Tell me. Why are you so dissatisfied? My grandmother was readying herself to leave, she saw on my mother that my mother was not going to leave my father, and this was enough for her. She also saw that this would kill my mother, but she didn't care. Don't be dissatisfied, she said stroking the young woman's hand. See, Géza is never dissatisfied. In her anger, my mother almost cried out, but then flopped back in the rocking chair, leaned back leisurely, closed her eyes, and whispered maliciously, Mama, dear, would you help me read my lines? The thorn in my grandfather's side was not my mother being an actress, which was only the result, but her family, or lack thereof. Where are they?, he asked. My mother stood in the world alone. How was one to know anything about her? A person's *got* a family, and that's that. He didn't quite know what he wanted from my mother. To go with the silver waistcoat, the one he never wore, he chose a walking stick with a silver handle. It doesn't make one look old, yet calls attention to one's years. It commands respect.

(The walking stick had once belonged to our ancestor Dániel, who served Rákóczi, poorly, as an anti-Habsburg, Kuruc lieutenant general; he was a meek and tight-lipped man, legendary for his slow wit, whom Bercsényi initially supported, but subsequently called him the Quaffer, this with cruel witticism, because during the grueling campaigns he fell ill, and liked to look into his cups. At times, his illness (?) made him so weak, he had to direct his troops from a cart, mostly atrociously. In his letters from the baths at Pöstyén and Stubnya, he described himself as a man whose body is a wreck and who is unhealthy besides. He was suffering from gout ("my joints did swell like loaves"), plus he walked with a limp—thus the walking stick!). My mother stuck to *Klopstock,* since it had worked once before. Now she was playing the countess from Act One. Grandfather lapped it up. They drank tea, ate cake, throwing in a disapproving word or two about my father, my grandfather had a grand old time. In parting, he bent over my mother's hand. Can I count on you, Róza, dear? My mother backed off, had she misconstrued the old gentleman, and he's much more sly than he's giving himself out to be? Naturally, dear Count, she said, and with a quick, forceful movement, pushed the back of her hand closer, thereby veritably pushing Grandfather's gums up his nose, as far up as possible. There was no coercing my father. It didn't do my mother any good, and it didn't do Grandfather any good. Whether it did Grandmother any good we'd have to know if my father was happy. He was cheerful, a fine example of the so-called cheerful father. But he never married my mother. Or almost never. He was on his deathbed when Uncle Kálmán "called for a priest and Róza Tótpataki." The priest first married my parents, then gave my father the last rites, but my mother didn't wait to see it.

174. My father was still considered young, eighteenth century?, no, past that, though still young, early nineteenth century. Be that as it

may, there he lay naked in bed, grinning, gobbling up the morning sunshine streaming through the bedroom window with both
cheeks, you might say. A Narcissus, he studied himself, with especial attention to his manhood, as it went about its early-morning
awakening ritual, and which, independently of him (my father),
was rearing itself on its own, as it were. What are you looking at?,
my mother barked. Why are you so darn occupied with yourself?!
With . . . with . . . with . . . myself?!, my father yelped, grabbing
his waking member by the scruff of the neck. Whose is it, anyway? Who am I keeping it for? Well?! My mother listened to my
father's lies with satisfaction. Meanwhile, Vörösmarty launched
into his great epic, and Goethe, too, was scribbling something in
his notes.

175. One of my grandfathers, the maternal, was in the employ of my
other grandfather, as the steward of his estate, or whatnot. Even as
a child, my father had looked wide-eyed at my mother, below
whose yellow tulip-printed skirt there dangled a pair of dancing
legs. My grandmother, the paternal, did not approve of what she
saw, not because she looked down her nose on it, but, on the contrary, because she wanted to protect my mother from my father,
whom she knew like the back of her hand. (Not that she thought
the two families were well matched, or anything.) We're up high.
Mountain herd with mountain herd. (Variation: puli with puli,
greyhound with greyhound.) She wanted to cure my mother of
my father by ordering her out to the yard and showing her how
the tomcat was mating with the pussy cat, because the tomcat was
mating with the pussy cat. My mother wanted to get away, but
Her Excellency detained her until the stormy love scene had
blown over. That's what men want, Mária Rickl said, so beware.
Your mother started the same way. Without us—for at this point
she reverted to the royal we—don't you dare so much as speak to
a man. And don't forget what you just saw. You want to lie in the

dust belly down, like an animal? Because that's where love will lead you. My mother had no wish to lie in the dust belly down, like an animal. Still, the thought of where love would lead her, this she couldn't get out of her mind, and she continued to dangle her legs for my father's benefit. (Grandmother: a flesh-enchanted harlot.)

176. It goes without saying. My father had many faces, one with a mustache, one with a double chin, one like a Cumanian, et cetera. Kept changing them through three acts. He met my mother, who made a very good impression on him, and the affection seemed mutual. But in all the changings of the self, my father forgot which of his faces he had put on for her. Awkward. Finally, he stood before my mother, and he showed her every one of his faces, like a criminal, one after the other. The one with the mustache, the one with the double chin, the one like a Cumanian, et cetera. But my mother did not recognize him. Which is how they met: my mother and my father.

177. As chance would have it, my parents' wedding day fell on the day (and night) that the Communists arrested one of their top men, László Rajk. Rajk was carved of hardwood, so to speak. On the inside, his body had a superabundance of supporting elements (beech, oak, ash, walnut, et cetera) as opposed to simple conveyors, like veins. Before the war, when Horthy's men had tried to beat out of him what on such occasions they usually want to beat out of people, and in the most brutal manner imaginable, not a word passed his lips. But as a result, when during the show trial that bears his name a word or two did pass his lips (he made a full confession), some of his comrades paradoxically saw this as proof of his guilt, even though no one in his right mind could have taken the accusations against him seriously. There had to be something there if this cap-à-pied Communist was willing to break his

193

silence! In short, Rajk's best qualities proved to be his ruin. This intellectual–logical–ethical–esthetic bag of fleas is the mainspring of every society in which social principles (et cetera) are held in higher esteem that human beings. Only in a tavern are human beings of value. The wedding banquet started off with consommé made from a cube, Japanese pearls in cups, followed by Brittany sturgeon from the Danube; the newlyweds were also served venison in tasty wine sauce with parboiled vegetables, fattened pullet with noodles on a spit, mixed French compote, lucky dough rolls with ice cream flowers and cookies, also cheese, fruit, espresso; with lunch there was also beer on tap, white wine from Pannonhalma, red Château Hungarian wine, and Louis François Transsylvania champagne.

178. During the wedding banquet, my father kept turning to my mother, and without further preamble said: Gida Hódossy sends her love. Or: Alajos Degré sends his felicitations. After which, he fell silent again, or talked about other things, nor did my mother ask any questions.

•    •    •    •    •

179. No man on earth was more ill suited to marriage than my father. He had no illusions about himself. He knew that he was not cut out to be a faithful husband, that temptation got the better of him every time. One year before his nuptials, he still described himself as a man who felt like another woman every day, and every day he'd have liked to marry another girl. In the back of a heavy bound notebook is his diary, and in it, recorded in an exquisite hand (mostly in red ink, with minute flower motifs decorating the indiscreet revelations), appear the names of those he was most smitten with. The ladies were further classified with secret signs. These include crosses, also something like a *beta*; there's also a slanted and crossed out *v*, a *p*, a *c*, with a dot in the middle. Only two are supplied with an explanation. The *U* with a dot in the middle means she hasn't interested him in some time, and two dots with the same placement means *"Auch nicht,"* neither does she. The explanation for the frequent changes in the form of the hand is provided in nearly illegible small print: Copied by my friend Géza Stenczinger; copied by my sister Ilon, my sister Gizella, my sister Margit, my friend Lajos Gréf. To make a long story short, as a young man my father was in love with the follow- ing women: Mariska Kovács, Róza Bruckner, Ilona Balogh, Veronka Szabó, Mari Fazekas, Milly Schwarzenberg, Irma Fucks,

Ilka Guttmann, Margit Csanak, Piroska Csanády, Mariska Kálmánchey, Terka Gáll, Natália Drahota (later added next to her name: I don't want her anymore!), Laura Guttmann, Janka Zagyva, Margit Csanády, Ilonka Csanak, Mariska Nánássy, Ilka Makó, Paula Zucker, Ella Varga, Ilonka Csanády, Zsófia Löwenberg, Éva Thököly, Magduska Szabó, Róza Nánássy, Zsuzsika Piránszky, Irén Filotás (who gave him a ring, which he accepted without batting an eye, then gave it to his sister Margit), Erzsi Nánássy, Teréz Hubay, Erzsike Riedl, Piroska Sesztina, Erzsike Beke, Ilka Vojnovics, Irma Göltl, Irma Segenweiss, Gabriella Lux, Paula Otte, Róza and Ida Brunner, Erzsike Sóvágó, and Ilona Sesztina. The list does not include unregistered casual acquaintances from Pallag, Nagyhegyes, Vienna and Graz ("When the cow jumps over the moon, that's when I'll want her, ha-ha-ha."), whose numbers must also have been impressive.

180. My mother is a wise woman. She knows a great deal about my father. But she doesn't know everything. For instance, she doesn't know that on the plains of Pallag, Nagyhegyes and Haláp, everywhere where the, *here my father's name follows,* family have estates, in every spot where a young thing was willing to satisfy my father's hopelessly unquenchable passion, no haystack has remained unturned. Also, she (my mother) doesn't see that my father, who keeps changing his ideal, but is also in need of a *real* physical relationship, is in the grip of something too great even for her hands to curb and guide in another direction, and that the Jekyll who sings along with his younger sisters to the strains of the family's Bechstein piano is not identical with Hyde who will sleep with anyone willing to oblige, and who, for the sake of a stolen hour resonant with love's passion, will break every oath and forget every given word. He can't help it. He forgets.

. . .

181. When my mother chanced upon my father's secret notebook, the one with the heavy binding full of poems written to strange women, tea for two and two for tea, I love you and you love me, et cetera, she took a pencil, EBERHARD FABER 1207 2.5=HB, sharpened it, and corrected the spelling mistakes. (Later, between a poem addressed to Ilka Guttmann and Margit Csanak, she wrote their own marriage's death sentence: Washing, October 28. Sheets three, tablecloths eight, napkins eight, pillowcases seven, sheets for quilted coverlets three, towels six, women's shirts twenty-one, men's shirts twenty-two, undies eleven, petticoats sixteen, handkerchiefs sixteen, socks fourteen, boot rags eight, dust cloths three, plate rags three, six patterned facecloths and two serviettes, underpants seven.)

182. If we are to approach my father from Maria Theresa (and in the eighteenth century, from where else?), we must first make mention of my paternal uncle, whom the Empress showered with the most precious jewel of her most especial attention, and who was later to come into not a little conflict with the emperor son of the Empress. His petition of May 8 against the Emperor's attempt at Germanization remained fruitless; what's more, it brought on his head the severe admonition of the Highest Office in the land. My uncle, however, was not one to succumb without a fight, regardless of the heights from which the "whim" originated, especially where it concerned Hungary. The French ambassador, most probably Durfort, writes: An enlightened intellect, a just mind, who in his office of thorns enjoys the trust of his nation, yet is not sufficiently subservient to the will of the Empress; wherefore he doth hazard his Office, not to mention the enhancement of his influence. Still, family tradition has it that when the Order of St. Stephen was founded, the idea having originated with him, and he became Chancellor of the Order, the Queen called him for an

audience. Uncle gave a self-assured bow of the head. He knew his queen. What's that you say?!, Her Majesty yelped. Have I no right to demand that my subjects address me in full, grammatically correct sentences? Never mind. I shall accept your silence as a grammatically correct sentence. And having said that, she pinned her own cross on the breast of her favorite, *here my father's and my uncle's name follows,* with her own two hands, with the proviso that should any of his descendants become worthy of this order, they should wear this particular cross, and no other. (The statement, after the fact, in the 52nd issue of the Sunday weekly *Vasárnapi Újság,* to wit that this order was worn by First Chamberlain Károly, won't hold water, because, as everyone knows, he wore the small cross of the Order of St. Stephen, and not this.) Maria Theresa was getting just a tad fed up with the family. My father, who passed away without issue after he suffered a stroke in his coach on Himmelpfortgasse in Vienna before he could take his leave of his younger sister Countess Ferenc Fekete, got thoroughly entangled with the eighteenth century. The thing—need we add—began with the eighteenth century getting thoroughly entangled with the country, first and foremost, its customs. Until then, Hungary had been progressively nurturing its language under the Latin influence, and had set up Latin and biblical morals—which it considered practically one and the same thing—as the sole models worthy of emulation. Hand in hand with a certain concomitant view of the world, these had become part and parcel of Hungarian culture. But in the eighteenth century, Hungary came into contact—and not just sporadic contact, mind you—with modern language, culture and morals. And since this contact, or tangoing, went hand in hand with the weakening and deterioration of national culture and biblical morals, which the country equated with the nation, it is not to be wondered at that this circumstance should have been regarded as a blight on the nation, one that undermined the nation's inner strength, and placed it at the mercy of those hoping for its downfall. My father did not agree with this notion. Ill at ease, he tried to keep his balance at the crossroads of the old and the new. He was loath to identify himself with the weak, squandering, unethical people at Court, whom the contemporary pasquins and their satirical poems (the best and most original parts of the literature of the times) pitted against the old, swarthy, thrifty, valiant and honorable Magyars. If truth be told, and we might as well tell it, despite all the zealous attempts, modern culture and the Hungarian national spirit are still at odds. Granted, the new cultural trends have made a certain headway, but they have not been able to bring about a unified national culture as of yet. Though this manner of pitting the old against the new with recourse to such false reasoning saddened my father, it is incontrovertible that the old, rough-hewn but solid morals came to be supplanted, in dress as well as in the deportment of life, by morals characteristic of the overrefined aristocracy, who had long since lost their ethical bearings. At the same time, instances such as my father's stymied the new trends, just as they failed to recruit supporters for intercourse with foreign lands. My father began his brilliant career at the embassy in Paris, where he initiated a highly expensive affair with a duchess from Nassau, an affair that the husband did not mind in the least, but when my father, giving ample proof of his greed, turned his (sensual) attention to the duke's mistress into the bargain, the doubly cuckolded husband cried for blood, which, via a duel, he got, not much, just enough to wash his honor clean. But being a worried mother, Grandmother Duchess Susanna Lubomirska immediately ordered my unruly father home in no uncertain terms, giving added weight to her wishes by freezing his generous allowance, whereupon my father returned home, to the sincere regret of the Duke of Nassau, who was "bereft [thereby] of the young Franci," and had to make good his wife's astronomical bills once again. At home, Grandmother Lubo, who was, one might say, naïve in conjugal matters, took it into her head to bring my father to heel through marriage, and found him a wife, the fifteen-year-old Nesti (Ernestine), the stunning daughter of a great Austrian family, whom my father married, and who was not known for her analytical gifts (*tochis*-brain, *tochis*-brain!). On the way home from the altar till death do them part, seeing the beaming faces of his mother and bride, and joining them in that beaming, he cheerfully confessed to his mother that he'd brought a souvenir back with him from Paris, a touch of syphilis. Oh . . . The Duchess Lubomirska waited for the blessing in the domestic chapel, then outraged, called off the wedding night, and had her brand-new daughter-in-law join her in her own bed, saying, "no chickabiddy meat until he's cured." For a while my father bided his time around the house, but when it became evident that his recovery would drag on, he packed his bags and absconded to Paris. Feudal life is not a hotbed of unimpeachable ethics, it never is. Lord and serf, especially in matters of sensuality, are of necessity each other's corrupters. Where the mutual and equal respect for life and honor is missing, there is no other escape—either you keep busy and aspire to lofty principles instead of ephemeral pleasures, or you resort to strict religious and moral instruction that will brook no ifs, ands, or buts. My father was governed by great chaos. Though he was not devoid of the respect due to life and ethics, he aspired toward lofty principles and ephemeral pleasures at one and the same time. And all this, need we add, against the background of the strictest religious and moral instruction. The devil take it! Who the ( . . . ) can figure this thing out? No class is as corrupt or susceptible to corruption as the aristocracy when it disregards its political duties. Maria Theresa did not have an easy time with my ungovernable father. The queen and woman, whose rule in so many respects marked the beginning of a new era, was the staunch and untiring champion of the old ways, in matters of religion, as well as ethics. In this she was the ally and, with all the weight of her authority, the motor behind national consciousness, which, in cases such as the one we are presently holding under investigation, does not judge lightly. And yet, despite the Empress's exemplary life—it is a lie that the Hungarian guards, with their big, black tools, from behind, while Her Majesty's waving to her faithful subjects below, this is a great big lie—and her legendary severity, the Viennese Court was hardly better under her rule than before. She had to yield in face of the ruling conditions ("Every lady of style has a lonely room, or boudoir, where her well-mannered husband will not enter, and where only her lover of the moment may intrude upon her privacy"), and she had to yield in face of her own marriage. (To such an extent, that despite her well-known jealousy, she would receive the chosen ladies of the imperial grace in the best company, the fat Canale, the Sardinian ambassador's wife, née Countess Pálffy, who distinguished herself by her constant presence at the gaming table, and later, Duchess Auersperg. I do not mind the lovely Duchess, she writes her beloved daughter in Paris, only God knows how sincerely. At her husband's death, she speaks from the heart even vis-à-vis her rival: We have both lost much, Duchess.) She limited herself to the scandalous events. Tradition was more persuasive than the call of the new. The Empress had a penchant for sticking her nose in other people's private affairs, which led to the establishment of the so-called *Keuschheitscomission,* or modesty board. Nothing must be indifferent to a married woman. This was the principle the Empress espoused. In the case of the peasant maidens of Upper Austria, she brought up the prospect of "changing the stuffed corsets and lengthening their short skirts." She issued an edict regulating who could wear what sorts of jewels, depending on her station, and forbade the use of rouge even for her ladies-in-waiting, which backfired, embittering and bringing suspicion down on those ladies whose color was rosy by nature. The modesty board took measures not only against those with reproachable morals (my father!), but would force their way into the family sanctum on mere suspicion or in case of denunciation, and like in all instances where the rough and uninitiated hands of intrusive forces pluck the most delicate strings of human relations, the board became the cause of more problems than it would have been capable of solving. They forced their way into my father's family sanctum, too, though as we have seen, he did his darndest to ensure that the place where they were in the process of forcing themselves could hardly be called a sanctum of any kind. The board members were especially eager to prevent abductions, but they abducted my mother! How could this have happened? My mother lived as a real *virgo intacta* at home in the countryside, under the watchful eyes of her severe mother-in-law, while my father lived his own life, ignoring his so-called conjugal duty. My mother got a crush on a dashing young Schulenburg count, and one morning she woke—by then there could be no talk of this *intacta*—to . . . oh, dear. Being unfamiliar with the ways of the world, the young couple decided to flee, which was a real stupid thing to do, because having your little fun on the sly was perfectly acceptable, even back then, but running away from the conjugal bed whenever the fancy took you was definitely not. My mother donned a beautiful green velvet men's garment (we know this from the recently discovered warrant of apprehension), and posing as two young men of standing, she and her lover took off in a coach and four and a Schulenburg footman, and headed posthaste for the Swiss border. When he heard the news, my father didn't bat an eye; if anything, he felt sorry for my mother for their having become entangled in each other's lives in this way. Maria Theresa, however, was up in a huff. She didn't care in the least that she was going to be protecting my father's (nonexistent) honor; with her, it was all a matter of principle, even if not quite as resolutely as with her son. She sent word to Prince Thurn-Taxis, the imperial Postmaster General, that should the fugitives attempt to change horses at any post station, he should have them apprehended. The Habsburgs are dependable bureaucrats. The princely Postmaster General delegated the matter to the office of postmaster Count Lillien ("Apprehend them! Forthwith!"), along with a description of the one in a green suit which, alas, by all accounts came from my grandmother, who'd been responsible for raising my mother's station at Court. Yet they loved each other, and my mother, though she was too young and immature to understand what was happening to her, knew how to handle my grandmother. Had she a life of her own, my mother would have found a common de-nominator with the people in it. (My father had too much of it, this Schulenburg not enough!) My mother was a plaything, and she had bad luck with the players. It is, however, more likely that we are all pawns in a game, the one that they happen to be playing with us at any one time, the game that *can* be played with us. In short, this particular game, and no other, was the one that could be played with my mother; this, in short, was her fate. Except, she was so young and so innocent, so much like a child and so much like a plaything that, willy-nilly, everyone took their turn playing with her. (My father's son would have liked to play with her too, oh, someone to play with, a mother who can be played with! His head spins when he thinks about it. He doesn't think about it.) The game is not frivolous, not in the least, yet is accompanied by a constant temptation toward frivolity. If our king is caught in the net of fierce rooks and pawns, it would be a mistake to underesti-mate the weight and seriousness of the situation. It is just a game—no player would ever say this, or even think it. Yet, as our above-mentioned stalwart hero, up to his neck in sticky blood, awaits the last blow, after which the country will fall prey to the Never-Never Landers, this "after which" differs, after all, from the drama of a chessboard. How? The frivolity of the game comes from there being a variety of games. The match can be played again and again. The game ends, and this end brings hope, and the temptation of knowing that there's hope, that hope is guaranteed, this is the frivolity, the irresponsibility. They played with my mother, too, with the same sort of irresponsibility. This is how her parents played with her, sending her to my father and washing their hands of her, and Schulenburg, too, who then also washed his hands. They did not realize that while they were concentrating on pawns C2–G6, my mother was galloping, out of breath, at the head of a lancer division in heavy fog, i.e., she had only one game to play, her game, and the others did not take this into account. Even Hans Georg Nettelhof could, did, and dare place my lovely young mother on his own chessboard, a Nettelhof!, the young Schulenburg's *leibdiener*—in short, someone who wasn't on the same chessboard, much less in the same galaxy, as my mother. A manservant is as good as his service. He exists only in terms of his service. The fourth generation of the Nettelhofs were serving at the Schulenburgs at the time, the oldest male progeny always being given the name of Hans Georg—a gracious present and inheritance from the count's family, as it were. The old Count's grandfather was called by this name, and it was he who had permitted his upright manservant to baptize his son with it. The chief hunting dog, too, was always given the same name (Clio). The Nettelhofs were quiet, reliable, with a good head on their shoulders. They were as helpful around the kitchen as around the coaches or, in the case of domestic service, inside the palace halls. Still, people asked why they were allowed inside. At meals, Hans Georg's father, the old Hans Georg, served at the table, and he did so gracefully, unobtrusively, and with finesse—unobtrusively, for centuries. But no, that's not true. If there were new guests at the table, which was often the case both during lunch and dinnertime, and the guests, quite innocently, laid eyes on the Hans Georg just then in line to serve, they'd let out a little scream. The women put their hands up to shade their eyes, while the men made a shocked, if discreet, grimace. They'd never seen anything so unsightly before. And this was passed on, like the name, from father to son—the sons and daughters resembled one another only in this incredible loathsomeness. It was this shocking loathsomeness that they had in common. The hair was either thick and wavy, or straight and limp, like discarded silver foil (just an example). Some were obese and some were skinny, some had hooked noses and some button noses; there were low brows and wide brows, brunettes and blondes alternating with each other. Though new women and new blood would sometimes mingle in their veins (every Jack will have his Jill), the alarming vehemence of their loathsomeness remained constant. Ugly. We don't like to say this about anyone. An ugly face. But only the face and the head. The bodies, the Nettelhof bodies were strong. Well built. The men preserved the sprightliness of youth, if not the compactness of their boyish proportions, while the women had something splendid about them, in the pride of their bearing, in their dignity and lack of presumption or, to put it another way, they had Germanic abundance, strong yet lithe hips, waists that reminded people of the curves of the nearby slopes. Still, the body could not compensate for the outrage of the head. There's no escaping ugliness this easily, as there is no escaping beauty, either—it will have its way. But you can take to your heels. Ugliness, like beauty, changes your life. True ugliness is complete. Ugly, but with a noble soul, or a heart of gold—no such thing. Ugly, but ugly—that, yes. There's no escaping it. Or if there is, then we're up against a stand-in for ugliness, mere poetic fancy. Cyrano de Bergerac. An elegant metaphor. The repository of all sorts of beauty. Ugliness is all inclusive. It is everything. The Nettelhof faces had this everything: the bony chill and the constant bluish shiver on the wings of the nose and the cheeks. Simply put, Joseph Haydn, but uglier, and with a superabundance of fat. Adam's apple and chin. Even the eyes are fat! Fleshy, watery, red. Enough to make you puke. And the tumescences on the back of the neck, swelling with yellow pus. The hair greasy, flaky with dandruff. Enough to make you puke. You'd like to avoid looking. You'd like to be someplace else. You'd like to be someone else, in some other world, where an outrage such as this could not happen to begin with. Too late. You're not someone else, you are who you are, and it is not enough. Ugliness is a mirror. It shows you your own deformities. And right away, you want to puke. Beauty presents us with the same picture, except then you don't want to, or can't, puke. Beauty is a matter of mutual agreement, and though it is not the case that taking themselves (who else?) as the point of reference for the phenomena of nature the Nettelhofs saw everyone else as ugly, but were not bothered themselves by this *thing,* because for them this thing did not exist; no, this is not the case. It's just that what did exist, because something has to exist—and we all have a natural instinct for beauty, and simplicity and dignity are not mutually exclusive—that did not turn their stomachs. It did not disadvantage them, and so they did not concern themselves with it; if anything, they were free to consider themselves as so many Cyrano de Bergeracs. The Schulenburgs didn't mind them. They'd grown accustomed to them (or else, they're blind, some people snickered). They even enjoyed the discomfiture of their guests; what's more, this became the signature of their home, its coat of arms ("That's not ugly, that's a Nettelhof"). There's not much to be said of the young Count (though he cuckolded my father, don't forget). His less-than-distinguished good and bad qualities lived within him in a harmony of sorts, and the course of his life flowed in a well-regulated riverbed. The Hans Georg who was next in line to be Hans Georg was the first Nettelhof who hated his body. Whenever he saw himself, he was disgusted. An anti-Narcissus, he ruffled up the water's surface when taking the horses to drink, and would not go near the duck pond. The pimples appeared even before he reached pubescence. These were the first concrete objects of his hatred, these countless little pus wells

206

(though here, disgust went hand in hand with a modicum of pride, that all this inexhaustibility came from within. Under a different set of circumstances, this is how he would have come to understand infinitude). They were the home base of his hatred, which then pointed the way. The pimples led to the skin, as if the skin were at fault—he actually looked!, looked to find the culprit!; he hated his face, the most personal part of him, separately, followed by his hair, to which he was a stranger, and yet was not, a head of hair always disheveled, knotty, uncombed, yet weak, fragile, an unpleasant bush or turf, a turpitude, a wet rag, oppressive, distasteful and dry, and the dryness led to the scalp, the red, blotchy, scabious patches of the scalp, which caused a constant itch. Self-hatred knows no bounds. There is no sating it by recourse to some pleasing body part. It is naïve to wish for deliverance from a pretty pair of lips, firm thighs, or the occasional, though unquestionable, gleam in the eye. The Nettelhof body did nothing to gainsay this loathing. On the contrary. The loathing was passed on from Nettelhof body to Nettelhof body: loathing for the mother, contempt for the father, a shudder of disgust for a brother or a sister. Next in line came the villagers. Then the castle, including its present owner. Whenever he looked at him, it was all he could do to suppress his nausea. He was not afraid of ugliness, but did not like throwing up, so he walked around with lowered eyes which, erroneously, the gentlemen took as a sign of humility. The genie had been let out of the bottle. When a stranger showed up in the village, an itinerant student or mason, or he, Hans Georg, while he was out riding to nearby Neustadt—he was allowed the privilege of riding—spotted someone there, or on the way there, anyone, a priest, a soldier, a gentleman, a child at play, a servant girl on the way to the market, anyone: instantly, he hated them. Next he imagined Vienna, Linz and Prague and Augsburg, and he imagined people populating the street and the squares and sitting behind the windows, men, women, short and tall, fat and lean: and he hated them, too. He hated the possible. He loathed all warm-blooded creatures. He felt the warmth, the rhythmic surging of the blood as it throbbed in unison with his own, and that . . . that turned his stomach! In short: horses, cows, goats, dogs (he wasn't so sure about pigs; pigs were so obviously created for loathing, that at first he suspected that they were God's little practical joke), then chickens, ducks, swallows, and birds in general—here, the light panting, the slight wheezing, made up for the current of blood, the throbbing. When, through the mediation of the fly, he next progressed from birds to fish, he extended his realm to fauna in general, with snails, fleas and anteaters thrown in for good measure. It wasn't until he reached the plants, yes, it was at this point that the gist of this thing came to light. He did not hate dry twigs, nor autumnal foliage. And then, when his grandmother died, who danced beautifully even in extreme old age, her bearing tall, regal, dignified, as if this dignity was the instrument of revenge on the hardness that was her life (for her life consisted of nothing but this hardness)— and whom Hans Georg hated more, possibly, than anybody else, especially this "revengeful regal bearing"—when she passed away, the loathing suddenly stopped. Hans Georg, in short, hated everything. Countries, cities, mountains, lakes, famous men. He hated the world. All of it. He hated Creation, and held Creation and the Creator responsible for his plight. There was just one thing he did not hate, he veritably longed for it, conceiving of it as a pause or cesura in Creation: death. Logic would have us conclude that we are faced with a mass murderer, except the young Nettelhof was weak. He lacked the determination. But my mother brought the player, the gamester, the gaming spirit, out of him, too. With the capable, sly guidance of this manservant, who outwitted the inspectors, the young couple managed to flee as far as Görr. In the back of beyond, Görr consisted of three or four houses and the inn called Zum Görr which, like in an old Fernandel movie, lay on the border, with one half in Switzerland, the other in Austria. Count Schulenburg would have liked to travel on to the safety of a safe haven, but his manservant spoke up, he deigning to speak, The Countess's condition, he said. Nesti glanced gratefully at the eyesore—who, when last they changed horses, had already notified the authorities. He hated the Count and the Countess separately, but together like this, oh, how much more he hated them! And when he thought that inside the Countess's body, an object of loathing in and of itself, rosy and panting and throbbing and all afire, sweet-smelling and hot, that inside this body there was another no less repulsive, *growing* body, his passions grew as tempestuous as any revolutionary's (passions such as this lead to peasant uprisings and rebellions against earthly and celestial powers). But though his passion was great, his vision was limited, and his revolutionary fervor, aimed at Creation, satisfied itself with this unfortunate pair of young lovers. Nettelhof was life's little joke on them. He made sure that Nesti should retire for the night on the Swiss side, and the Count on the Austrian side. The latter would have liked to sleep together with the former, my mother, but the manservant interrupted once again, Her condition, Count, her condition. Yes. Of course. Having descended on the inn, the Austrian soldiers apprehended Schulenburg. My mother, however, they could not touch. She wept in silence. Nettelhof watched her in secret. He was elated, and would have loved to kick her in the belly, but he lacked the courage. Schulenburg was put under arrest, and with all their money and my mother's jewels apprehended, he was thrown into a Viennese prison, where he was soon released with the mediation of my generous-hearted father. But how could it be, Maria Theresa asked shocked, that you, *here my father's name followed,* are asking for pardon for the man who, et cetera?! *Gewiss Majestät,* my father was supposed to have answered, *er hat mich doch von der Babage befreit,* in short, that he had taken the . . . package?, burden?, baggage? off his shoulder. Also, it was my father, and not that shit Schulenburg family, who financed my mother's stay in Switzerland. Deep down, my father was a good man. My mother was fool enough to return to her parents, who immediately passed the poor thing off on a convent in Graz, where she lived the rest of her life, if you can call that living. Not so my father, who, as ambassador to Naples, had a high time of it amid the lovely and willing ladies. A married man without a wife: an ideal state of being. Priggish Admiral Nelson and the lovely Mrs. Hamilton were among his company. When Napoleon's troops were marching toward Naples, Nelson thought it best to pack the royal family off to Sicily. According to contemporary newspaper accounts, my father was with them on the battleship, and they came into such a raging storm on the way, that all extra weight had to be flung overboard. This is how my father's son's inheritance, the silver from the Tata entail, along with my father's Roman Age statue and coin collection, ended up at the bottom of the Mediterranean. The English papers also mentioned that when the storm was at its worse, my alarmed father even threw his golden snuff box into the sea (after giving the naked enamel portrait of his mistress of the moment a dramatic kiss). Later, the Hamiltons accompanied the Queen back to Austria, and they went on an excursion to Kismarton to hear Haydn, who performed his famous Nelson piece for the occasion, and the Admiral presented him with his golden pocket watch. Haydn raised the watch to his ear, his famous ear, and grinned like a half-wit, It's ticking!, he was supposed to have said. The gentlemen smiled graciously. Then my father was appointed ambassador to Paris, but wishing to take his leave of his younger sister, he died on the way. A pity. The rumor-mongering Viennese christened my father's child—whom family chronicles mention as having died at a young age—Schulenházy. In actual fact, though, he died without issue at the age of fifty-three, and was a cavalry colonel. The colonel lived a lonely life and could not abide anyone save for the old manservant by his side, which gave cause for rumors of a certain kind. This manservant and the officiating priest were the only mourners standing by the coffin. When Hans Georg Nettelhof looked down into the grave, he felt a deep sense of satisfaction. He did not even pretend to pray.

183. My father was bullish on quantum mechanics. My mother flew into a rage. Her cheeks were on fire. She lost weight, she gained weight, she slammed doors. After studying the manner in which English playboys tie their shawls, my father took to wearing colorful silk neckties. He spent hours in front of the mirror; he hadn't spent this much time in front of the mirror in all his life. He asked for a clean shirt, socks, and underpants every day. He hadn't been so particular in this department either, before; he even bought new boxer shorts. He kept vexing my mother about the ironing. My mother made a face. You're overdoing it. My father kissed her reverently on the forehead. They could neither talk nor listen together. My father came to the realization that as opposed to Newtonian physics, quantum mechanics does not preclude the possibility that the desk standing in our room (with my father's typewriter, the Hermes Baby) might at some point rise into the air without the application of outside force. The placement of every single elemental particle of the desk is determined by chance, and so it is theoretically possible that at any one moment in time, each is coincidentally at the same higher spot, as a result of which, well, wouldn't you know, the desk rises into the air. Furthermore, by the same token, i.e., with the same energy, the desk could turn into a griffin at the drop of a hat, or Einstein; it could rearrange itself into Einstein's reincarnation, provided—and here my father gave a charming smile, like a young chaplain who had, thanks to his oratorical skills, just supplied the youngest members of his congregation, barely younger than himself,

incontrovertible proof of the existence of God—provided it contains a sufficient number of elemental particles. Or you. The table changing into me, is that it?! You're a congenital idiot. A reject of Creation. The chaplain was not shocked by Satan's tongue. Yet in theory, my dear, nothing stands in the way. The laws of statistics do not stand in the way either, just make it highly unlikely. The probability that this desk will suddenly rise into the air is much smaller than the probability of a monkey composing the *Odyssey* while it is randomly banging down on the keys of a typewriter. My mother leaped over to the Hermes Baby, tore the sheet of paper out of it, inserted another, rasping, with the copy paper, and began banging on the keys. The tears were streaking down her cheeks. My father threw a furtive glance at his watch. My mother finished typing, stood up, playfully began to imitate a monkey, hanging her arms down to the ground, swaying to and fro, scratching her head, grinning. My father gave an impatient wave of the arm, as at a child. At which my mother plunged at my father, Eat it, she screamed, eat it, damn you, or I'm going to stuff it down your throat!, and proceeded to stuff the paper with the typing into his mouth. They were panting. My father took the paper ball from his mouth, unfolded it, read it. *Tell me, Muse, about the man of many turns, who many / Ways wandered when he had sacked Troy's holy citadel.* He shrugged. Two lines, that's no proof. Proof is the last thing my mother wanted; she just couldn't take any more of the Catholic drill.

184. To my mother's profound regret, but there was no helping it, my father has a dual nature, sometimes he acts like a particle, sometimes like a wave. The latter was proven by a certain Thomas Young back in Napoleonic times. Though a physician, he was fascinated by my father's fascinating nature. He cut two parallel slits in a nontranslucent umbrella, rather close together, lowered my father over the slits, then gathered him up on a second umbrella

once he'd passed through the slits. They laughed a lot. Two grown men. *A duke or a mangy dog? Well?* Anyway, my father showed typical interference signs, a fact that could not be put down to fatigue, innate melancholy, or even Napoleon's growing appetite. The ultimate question, one that my mother had been asking for some time, reared its ugly head: Where is my father when we cannot detect him in the form of particles? Still, though the question may beg for an answer, it is pure nonsense. We'd like to talk about such a place, but there is no such place, there is no such *where*. Naturally, we are not positing that my father is nowhere, because if we see him, or better yet, if my mother sees him—because, after all, she's the one most closely involved—in a tavern, on the battlefield, or in bed, then that's where he is, drinking his schnapps, getting into his cups, going under the influence, tanking up, etc. But if she can't see him, then it's no use, her making a scene. It's pointless to shrivel up into a ball from jealousy, to become so small, you could step on her. It's no use brimming over with hatred, claiming that my father is ruining her life, and that overall, his conduct is reprehensible, re-pre-hen-sible, do you understand, son? A man, a father, with four children as beautiful as the four of you, has a responsibility toward his family. To the four of you, son. He is responsible for you. Where is he hanging out this time, you tell me. He was kneeling here, no, here, and he swore on the Bible, his mother's life, the future of the nation, that he'd stop and never do it again. He begged for my forgiveness, and what did I do fool that I am? I forgave him, son, because your father is not just anybody, I've always said so, he's an exceptional person, a first-class intellect, except he's a weak shit of a man, son, and that's the truth. A weak piece of shit. Don't be angry, that's the way it is. But this is the last straw! He's got to make up his mind, a duke or a mangy dog, wave or particle, because I can't take it anymore and I don't want to either, I've had it, son. This was the last drop. I'll offer him my hand one last time, but if he doesn't avail himself of the opportunity, I'm calling it a day. Let him draw his own conclusions. But it's no use, it's pointless, my mother carrying on like this; there is nothing to ask, for who can say where my father might be when he's nowhere, and not because he's good at hiding. The information is not insufficient, it is not forthcoming. My mother spent the best part of her life searching for the hidden parameters. I'm going to let those parameters out of the bag yet, she kept saying. But now we know that this was *theoretically* impossible. Needless to say, my father is a real gentleman. If they ask him, is he a particle, he nods cheerfully, and crashes into something, like a cannonball. If, however, certain people would rather see him as a wave, he playfully snaps his ankles together, and breaking into a song, produces interference waves. *My father depends on the question.* What is he like? He is the way he is. (He's like the rabbi in the joke. You're right, son. You're right, too, son. But Rabbi, how can you agree with two such diametrically opposed views? You're right, too, son.) In short, the state of my father is in a constant state of flux. The last word is not said, because there is no last word. When my father died, his dying words were, *Mehr particles*. Or waves. Which doesn't surprise me one bit.

185. I'm not saying it happened every day, but two or three times a month, my father woke up in the morning with the name of some woman on his lips. Startled out of her sleep, my mother propped herself up on her pillows (she always used four or five pillows, small, large, hard, soft, with and without slipcovers; she'd have been unhappy with anything less), and watched my father's lips, who (my father), in that pleasant state halfway between sleep and awakening, was just whispering to himself (and my mother, which goes without saying), Lucy (*cf.,* Lucy in the sky with diamonds), Suzie (*cf.,* wake up little Suzie, wake up, with the An-

drews sisters thrown in for good measure). My mother memorized the name, Lucy, Suzie, the Andrews sisters, jumped out of bed from my father's side, who was still at it, and got into her clothes, repeating the names between clenched teeth, just to be on the safe side, Lucy, et cetera, and marched off to district police headquarters with her ID under her belt. After 1956, one of her schoolmates, Viola (Aunt Viola to us), was put in charge of people's IDs, and changed my mother's name whenever she asked her to—Lucy, Suzie, the Andrews sisters, et cetera. Aunt Viola did not see eye to eye with my mother on this, but did as she (my mother) asked. And then, one early May morning, my father said the fatal word, Waltraud. My mother: propping up, pillows, clothes, marching off. She looked down her nose on this name. How could you sink so low, Mati dear? But next thing, she stood in front of her friend. Waltraud. What did you say?, the policewoman asked, because she didn't like this Waltraud. Afraid she'd be made a laughingstock, and the socialist authorities couldn't afford it. At which juncture my mother thought of something, possibly for the first time. The GDR! They have lots of Waltrauds there! At the time, the authorities were afraid of East Germany, and so was Aunt Viola, so she gave her consent. On the other hand (because of her fear), her relationship with my mother went sour. Good-bye, favoritism! What could she do, my mother told my father what was what. They're in trouble. My father understood, and from that day on he stopped whispering the names of women as he woke up in bed. Still, he had to wake up somehow, which from then on took the form of a chilling, bloodcurdling scream, a terrified yelp. Every single day. My mother leaped on top from between her pillows and kept kissing him and coddling him until he (my father) calmed down. We didn't have an alarm clock in those days, but were never late to school. Except once. My father wrote out the excuse. A nosebleed, he wrote. Or a headache? Or a passing fainting fit? It was always one of these three: nosebleed, headache, passing fainting fit.

186.   My father would have thrown my mother out a long time ago, his nerves were so badly frayed by the way my mother spoke— form and content—how she could never end a conversation properly, but why, *but whyyyyy,* she'd whine again and again, but honey, *whyyyyy,* why, meow, like a cat. My father couldn't abide the honey either, the recurring grammatical mistakes, like a foreigner, for God's sake, mixing up "would" and "should." His nerves were set on edge so badly by the way my mother moved, the way she hyper-moved, scurrying after the bus like a teenager, the neighbors, the mailman, the watchman, oh, dear sir, sweet sir, she'd shout; in short, she was overeager, unpredictable and vehement, as if it were eternal spring. And the way she caught you off guard, *surprise!,* the way she'd show up with a panda bear or a bill of sale, and if anyone put their hand over my father's eye on the street, guess who?, yes, happy, bursting with enthusiasm, you got it, that, too, was my mother. His nerves were rattled so badly by my mother's way of thinking, the way she disdained logic and rationality, not to mention her inability to negate statements such as "diamonds are a girl's best friend." What's worse, this objective, this challenge, left her cold. She couldn't care less. What diamonds? What girls? What friend? And oh, the profusion of shrugs and the meows that followed, *whyyyyy, whyyyyy meeeee,* meow. His nerves were wearing thin from my mother's lovemaking, too, her—or as my father felt—being too eager to touch his groin, her impatience to undo his belt, her tugging at it like the fresh wind, or as if it were eternal spring. My father didn't like it when, in her eagerness, my mother would bite his lips (though the taste of blood was titillating). He didn't like it when she called his dick munchkins, as if I were your son, my father complained, so what's it to be, my mother asked mischievously, what should I call you?,

216

windstorm? typhoon? Well . . . windstorm, maybe, my father said softly, though he couldn't quite figure out how they'd slipped into this meteorological line of reasoning. If, within the above-mentioned connection, a munchkins should pass my mother's lips all the same, my father raised his index finger (for one), at which my mother corrected herself obligingly: windstorm. Also, he didn't like the cotton between my mother's legs (because of cystitis). Sometimes it would stick out in the back like the bushy little tail that waitresses dressed as bunnies wear. Furthermore, he loved the act of lovemaking, but it upset him that regardless of windstorms and regardless of typhoons, he'd have to use his finger on her each and every time to achieve orgasm. This made my father feel insecure, not so much, but still. In short, he'd have thrown my mother out ages ago, he'd have relaxed his grip if . . . if my mother had not resembled, so sweetly and disarmingly, my father's youngest brother (blond, fragile and bespectacled), his wiry hair as it flapped in the spring breezes like so much affirmation of happiness, the bony physique, concretely, the collarbones, the narrow shoulders, the shoulder blades (wings!), the golden-haired belly, the mischievous glance, the indefinable greenish color of the eyes, the entire disposition as such! Maddening! In short, my father was head over heels in love with my mother until his brother, on the way home from Naples, during the charge of the Paddington light brigade, died on the battlefield. But then it all came to an end, the frayed nerves were frayed for good. It's all over between us, my father shouted at my mother. My mother acquiesced, for she entertained a great fondness for my father's youngest brother herself.

187. My father resorted to the use of logic to prove—my father's thesis, 1931—that within any given system, it is impossible to deduce all the truths that can be formulated within that system. Surely, one or two, my mother muttered under her breath. Enraged, my

father screamed, what are you talking about?! Pure logic. Not only has it never been unequivocally defined, it can't be. Period. He huffed and puffed. If you will tell me what you mean by logic, I will tell you a game in which this logic will put us on thin ice. Get me? My mother gave an almost imperceptible shrug. If we bring logic into the game, we are all bound to lose, is that it? You and me, both. Whereas if we were to play according to a different rationale, we could win. You and me, both. That's your problem, my mother nodded, you think life is a game. My father raised himself up haughtily. Yes. Precisely. In the best case scenario. Then he lowered his head. But I understand that this comes as a shock to you, dear, he said. Many, many years must pass, I see, before you will own up to your theoretical limitations. My mother flushed scarlet. You know, Mati dear, that goes double for insolence.

188. Social psychologists—theory + practice—have known for a long time that some roughnecking or unpleasant altercation is often indispensable if we are to attain to mutual trust and intimacy. My father, too, started trusting Little John only after they'd come to fisticuffs. At first, my mother acted willingly on this theory. She beat my father to a pulp, but after a while she got bored and she stroked my father's cheek, Mati, dear, let's not fight for the short time that's left to us. Do you mind? I'd rather do without the intimacy. But by then, my father could concentrate on only one thing at a time, namely, the conditions for achieving harmony, so he slugged my mother without further ado, *cf., The Taming of the Shrew*. Petruchio won the bet, did he not? . . . My mother's nose was bleeding.

189. My father was about to strike my mother, something that—need we add—was nothing out of the ordinary, but then he just shook her instead (presumably like Christ the shoemaker), and stormed out to the kitchen. He paced up and down, huffing and puffing,

abusing my mother under his breath, who (my mother) had just made a general comment regarding the sadness she felt with respect to her life. (Not a reproach or accusation, just the realization of complete failure, which is reproach and accusation.) My father ripped open the refrigerator door: three milks, one in a bottle, two in plastic bags. He slammed the bottle to the floor, the milk squirting all over the place. In the meantime he was already tearing at the plastic bag with his teeth, forcing the milk out, which squirted in his face, fuck! He fucked it down and trampled it underfoot along with the third bag. The kitchen was awash in the squeaking milk. He took the honey from the cupboard, one tube and one bottle. The bottle—as a matter of custom, we might say—bang!, to the floor, and meanwhile he was forcing the liquid gold from the tube. Drip and stick everywhere. It'd have been good, had my mother sneaked quietly, cautiously out to the kitchen, and watched him rage for a while, whirling round, shirt-tail hanging out of his pants, everything about him tentative, his gestures, his grimaces, his sentiments, and then she, too, could have joined him, trampling into the new, sweet terrain that was the kitchen, into the guck, and she could have embraced him, whispering, you, you . . . you land of milk and honey! Instead, my father stormed into the living room, pulled my mother off the sofa—she was huddled there, torn between tears and dry eyes—and as he shoved her toward the kitchen, he shouted, You are going off to the land flowing with milk and honey, but I will not go up in the midst of thee, for thou art a stiff-necked people, lest I consume thee in the way!

190. My mother talked incomparably more about galley slaves, the king's counselor, King Béla IV or the captain, than about my father. She gave us information about him only reluctantly, and what she said was terribly bizarre. For instance, sometimes she'd say he was a landowner, while at others she'd claim he was noth-

ing, or a clerk at the Ganz Machine Works in Pest. Then there was the one about him being top dog at the public swimming pool, which is the one we liked best.

191. Once, quite by chance (this was not the same chance as in the case of the Rajk trial), my mother found out how much my father was making. (She met a colleague of my father's from the AgroBank on the promenade, who kept craning his neck like a bird, as if he were on the make. My mother asked how he was making out, which he misunderstood. Not as much as your husband, eighty-two crowns or pengős or Rhenus forints less.) In the evening, after they'd put the kids to bed, my mother confronted her husband (my father). Will he kindly tell her how come they're living so well? She expected that my father would be taken off guard. But he wasn't. He smiled, as he always did, and said, loans. Loans?!, my mother cried out, aghast. Who exactly do you owe? Everyone. My mother was so shocked she couldn't question him (my father) any further, but by then my father had launched into it, and what he said was so breathtaking and beautiful in its absurdity, that she found herself unarmed, incapable of turning her weapon upon her adversary. I wanted you (my mother) to have a new start in life. I wanted to make amends for the humiliation of your curtailed youth. I love you, and I wanted you to be happy. To have something to be happy about every single day. I wanted you to live the tale. And didn't you? Weren't you happy? How could you?!, my mother cried, Good Lord, how could you! Who lent you money in this world, where credit is not given, even where credit is due? I told you. Everyone, said the face as it turned to her, the face she thought she knew, but which she never really did to his dying day (nor, for that matter, did anyone else). My mother nodded, she was not surprised. How could anyone deny this face anything? What about the food?, she pressed on. My sisters sent it from the village, my father said, and his voice fal-

tered for the first time. Took the food out of their own mouths. In her mind's eye, my mother could see once again the silent misses with whom she'd never exchanged more than a word or two. She stood up, took an exercise book from Béla Junior's schoolbag, and asked her husband (my father) to dictate how much he owes, and to whom. From now on we will live like other poor people. We will pay everything back piecemeal. If I ever find you asking anyone for a loan, I will divorce you. The child—your child—is on the way. Is this how you want to start him off in life? Are you angry?, my father asked, not remorseful but smiling, as if his wife (my mother) had somehow amused him. She seemed so implacable and serious. Do you think I have deceived you? Again, the question was absurd, because he had indeed deceived her, but not the way people usually deceive other people. She did not lose but gain by the deception. This line of reasoning was difficult to follow. Were you angry?, my mother's son asked my mother many years later. They were both smoking. She (my mother) was sipping her coffee. She shook her head. Then they, the sharers of great secrets, gazed into each other's eyes for a long time, my father's wife, and my father's son. Of course not. How could anyone be angry with him? Ever?

192. The king of Sweden sent ambassadors to Wallenstein, and so my father was gone all weekend, a waste of time. On Monday, eagerly, he came running home to my mother—around, when was it?, one-thousand-six-hundred-and-something. He'd hardly thrown his skis off, as they say, when, smiling like the cat that swallowed the canary, trying to make light of it, he launched into a tirade about how the problem is that he can't decide, though possibly it could and should be decided, whether he loves my mother, or is in love with her, because he'd taken the loving so much for granted up till now, which is nothing to scoff at, of course, because love isn't the sediment at the bottom of a relation-

ship when passion fades, no, that's not how it happens, but lately he'd caught himself heaving such heavy sighs, in Prague, too, the other day, the Swedish delegates were gabbing on and on, nobody paid attention, of course, they didn't either, besides, Wallenstein's lost all restraint, he thinks he's the emperor, which is practically the case, but for a Habsburg, this *practically* is enough, he'll dig his heels into this *practically,* and that's what this Wallenstein doesn't realize, that time is on the side of the Emperor, time is always on the side of the emperor, and all the while, his heart ached for my mother, it was a combination of a tingling sensation and pain, and he had trouble breathing, he had to take deep breaths, he was wheezing, in which case, they're probably up against a case of being head over heels in love (with my mother). Or asthma, my mother retorted dryly, which my father—the dryly—did not notice, and burst out laughing from the guts, ha-ha-ha, like a child. But my mother, who was not angry, went on, objectively stating the facts of the case, you're just saying this, she said, and this time my father heard, because you had plenty of time to contrive it, you must've been working on these sentences ever since Bratislava, shit, my father thought, indeed, and since Bratislava, indeed, and you polished them, my mother went on, and now you're saying them because you don't want to waste them. Whereupon the following things happened to my father, in order of appearance: (1) his feelings were hurt, (2) he lost his good cheer, and (3) he felt the tingling sensation and pain round the heart again, and the quickening intake of breath, stupid cunt!, he screamed, fuming, if it's not asthma, then what is it?! But he immediately understood that he was just saying this. My mother was shaken with tearless sobs. She was crying for herself and she was crying for this sweet, irresponsible man, to whom she could not get any closer, nor did she want to, possibly.

•　　•　　•

193. One morning my father woke up and realized he was scared stiff (terrified, et cetera). He'd hardly come to, guck in the corners of his eyes, his neck sore, his body weighed down by a thin coat of early-morning sweat, something he'd experienced often of late. He had no idea what scared him (terrified him, et cetera). But it was inside him like never before. He didn't bother making a list of his so-called sins. Besides, they were not something he'd have wanted trumpeted abroad. He was a mediocre sinner. Was this what had scared him so? Would he rather be a saint or a true sinner? Easier said than done. He was simply scared of losing my mother, and then . . . and then he'd have nothing left, because by my father's own admission, my mother was the only person my father considered real. Not his parents, his father, his mother, nor his children, his sons, or any one, his friends, his girlfriends, et cetera, no one, save for my mother. What about Archbishop Pázmány? My father waved it off. And King Leopold? My father waved that off as well. The Turks? Wave. The land of Transylvania? Wave. The old Count? Wave. Your lovers? Excuse me? And: wave! What're you waving for? O, noble father of mine, the source and origin of my life, from whom, much like in a good narrative, everything of substance springs, tell me, what art thou waving for? He's waving because he feels that save for my mother, everyone is a creature of his imagination, a lowly subject of the universe he'd created out of his own words. But were he to lose my mother, he'd lose his words, too, because the other shore of his words are reliant on *this* shore, too, they need something that's not them, though it's not the words themselves he's concerned about, their loss would merely be indicative of the fact that in that case he'd have nothing left, truly nothing, and though he, the prince of nothing, has learned to get his bearings in this nothingness, he knows his way around, with special reference (tasteless as it may be) to the land reform plus nationalization, he's not con-

223

cerned with these, or barely, he's gotten used to it, he'll be the prince of everything all the same, as he was fond of saying, the change of the names of the owners in the Land Office do not ruffle his feathers, and he means it, when viewed from the perspective of the centuries, it is *tangibly* all right; as far as his person is concerned, at any rate, this everything-nothing *thing,* by which, i.e., the all right, he's merely trying to say that as far as he's concerned, all this is not a metaphor, not an intellectual or psychological loophole, but everyday practice, a feeling, his life. On the other hand . . . on the other hand, were he to lose my mother, he'd be homeless for real, plunged from the everything into the nothing *in earnest,* much like that schlemiel of an Oedipus, and he's fully aware, of course, that in that case *that certain* catharsis would follow, but he doesn't want it, it's my mother he wants. Catharsis. Who the fuck needs it. Whereupon he did wander into the wilderness, and did fast for forty days and forty nights, and when they ended, he afterward hungered. And the devil said unto him, If thou be the Son of God, command this stone that it be made bread. And my father obeyed and transformed the stone into fine rye bread with sesame seeds. And the devil taketh him into the holy city and set him on a pinnacle of the temple, and my father nodded and cast himself down, for it is written. They also went to the top of Budapest's Gellért Hill so that if thou therefore wilt worship me, et cetera. My father felt that they were putting his haughtiness to the test, and this got his goat; always the same old song, him being aristocratic and whatnot, and he humbly did fall to his knees and did worship the devil, at which he did depart from him, and lo, angels came and ministered unto him. Without anything having changed, gradually, step by step, from one morning to the next, did he in this manner forget his fear.

194. Let's be friends, my father said to my mother. Up yours, my mother said, and gave him the finger. Which is how they met.

(He snatched my pussy from its context, she said, even though she was already a grandmother.)

195. My father had a beard hanging from his chin as long as a Russian patriarch's or any prophets. Nobody, but my father, yes, he really was a prophet in his own country; they respected and appreciated him, even awarded him an honorary doctorate. Years later, one of his students confessed to him than years before she'd been head over heels in love with him. Heels?!, my dad said chagrined, why didn't you say so, you little fool? We could've had a good lay! My father, my mother.

196. At times my father behaves like a king whom the union is itching to vote out of office, if only it could. At times he pesters his puny little realm from his tall armchair in front of the TV, at other times he's like a man without a home and without a name, a man who is not even *there*, offender and offended all rolled into one. Yet he is also perfection in the flesh, and consequently, he sees nothing but fault all around, obtuseness and stupidity, spitefulness and helplessness, obesity of the mind. It'd be a veritable blessing if only the old man were to learn to say what he thinks. Wear his heart on his sleeve. If, for instance, he were willing to admit that at times he's afraid, and if he'd stop wanting to fuck everybody on the fly . . . If at times a quiet, soft caress, a touch, or a gentle lullaby were enough to satisfy him. Sometimes he wants to please so badly, it becomes impossible to tell who wants the pleasing. Sometimes he feels pangs of conscience because of his opponent's missed orgasm. Sometimes, while studying my mother's intricate and enigmatic lap, he's overwhelmed by a feeling of inferiority (a prick is so predictable sometimes, so languid and trivial). Sometimes he laughs off the responsibility he should be feeling with respect to missed orgasms. ("I owe you two orgasms. I'll see that you get them. But afterward, you and I are no longer an item.") Sometimes he'd like

to slip between the covers two or three times a day, while at other times it doesn't occur to him for weeks on end, and he doesn't get the hint either. At times—indeed, more and more—he gives thanks to Almighty God that He made him a man with a dick and balls (granted that one hangs lower than the other), and is willing to give himself over to it more and more, to give himself over to the wisdom, the wisdom of his prick, asking for its opinion with respect to dangerous places, about the where, and whether he should take private English lessons *(How do you do?)*. My father is (one) intricate mechanism.

197. You are about to become a father, my mother said to my father. What about your husband? *Ein Theoretiker*, my mother didn't even bother to shrug.

198. My father announced that he wanted to live without care, the way the angels live without care, who (said angels) do not work, but praise the Lord the livelong day. So he took off somewhere (the desert, most probably), to sing the praises of the Lord. But hardly a week had passed, and he was back. He knocked on the door. Before she opened up, my mother asked, Who might you be, stranger? It is I, your brethren, *here my father's name followed*. My mother wasn't too keen on this brethren stuff, this snake in the grass slithering in. If push came to shove, she'd rather see my father drunk. She answered thus: *here my father's name followed*, is no longer among the living. He has turned into (has become) an angel. But it's me, my father pleaded. But my mother would not open the door for him. She tortured him until the break of day. Then she relented and opened up, saying: If you are a man, you must earn your bread, embrace, and—and here she put a hand to her groin. A foot rag, my father threw himself at my mother's feet and said: Can you forgive me?

·  ·  ·

199.   My father, no, my mother, grew old.

200.   Ten years ago, when he was in the prime of life, my father made his eldest son promise to tell him should he discover signs of senility in him. The boy promised with an easy heart. And now that my father has just hurt him profoundly for the third time with his boorish prima donna callousness, he knows that he will never tell him. It is not possible. When it is time to tell, it is not possible, It is possible only when it is not yet time to tell.

201.   He's grown old (my father). He's also shriveled up. He's shorter by now than his smallest, i.e., shortest son, even though he is still taller than his tallest daughter. He doesn't shave as often as he should, and his chin is covered with a rash, the sort of small boils at the sight of which people say, he's eating with too good an appetite. Which isn't true (i.e., that he's always eating with too good an appetite). He has a new girlfriend, who has recently taken an interest in mathematics. She's developed an appetite for it. She keeps sending my father to the library to bring something on Banach spaces, because her hip hurts. Sometimes she'd like to turn to my father's son for professional advice, but for some reason she won't, or she's afraid to. So she sends my father to him. He laboriously fishes a slip of paper out of his pocket or someplace else, his ancient, worn, briefcase with the flap, for instance. He can hardly find it. He reads what he needs to know from there—orthogonal lines, and the like. My mother used to make lists like this for us years ago: five rolls, the way they now wrote inverse matrix down for him. My father has to take the answer back. He makes notes, but tries to remember most of what he's told. He doesn't get any of it, that's obvious. But his memory failing him like this, this is something new. Even as he reaches the garden gate he keeps repeating what he'd just heard with a smile. At times, he looks at his eldest son, to see if he's got it right. If he

227

can't manage (some complex continuity criteria), he weeps. My father weeps.

202.   My father has grown old and also shriveled up. But that's not the point. The point is that what he says is not intelligible, unless it's marmalade. But that's not the point. The point is that one day he started speaking in complete sentences, subject, verb, object, something he'd never done in his life. He always threw words at people, interesting as they may have been, and in an ingenious order. But that's not the point. The point is that he's become as brittle as a little bird. He is no longer 83.5 kilos, or 80, or 60, but 52, dressed and with his shoes and glasses on. His face is smaller, too, so he has grown a beard, a so-called Kossuth beard, in order to make up for the loss, because he knows that his face is too small. He sees that everything is in order, except that he is getting progressively smaller. Only his vanity has lost nothing of its grandeur, thank God, because in that case he (my father) wouldn't have grown a beard. But that's not the point. The point is that my mother saw right away that she was now dealing with a weak old man, that her time had come, and she took revenge. She now keeps nagging him, kicking away the stick that my father lets drop (he's been walking with a stick lately). She serves him cold soup, pretending it's hot. Oh, dear, my father smiles, I can't even feel the hot soup anymore. Since he's grown a beard, his shortcomings gladden her (my mother's) heart. It gladdens her to spot them, and it gladdens her to point them out. She feels she has finally come into her own. She humiliates and reviles him in public, and when they have guests for lunch, she describes in minute and embarrassing detail his betrayal of her through the years, his style of life which, seen from a distance, may seem heroic, easygoing and colorful, but from up close it is petty and pointless, a sly and ugly masquerade. She does this in order to justify her present cold-heartedness and intransigent hardness, while my father smiles, just

like with the soup, gently prodding my mother, can't she remember? When she was in college, he used to cook for her. He was so much in love with her. Couldn't she write this to his credit? Couldn't this mitigate her judgment? First, you never cooked for me, ever. Second, when you did, it tasted like shit. And third, whether you cooked or not, who cares, it's too late, it doesn't count. And with a slight flick of her elbow, she knocks my father's glasses off the table, firstly so that he shouldn't be able to see, or as my mother put it, so he'd have to "play blind mouse," secondly, so that sooner or later someone should step on them (the glasses), and thirdly, to help pass the time. Hopefully, the afternoon will take care of itself. (P.S. During the last couple of days, my father's been wanting to listen to Wagner. My mother puts Schubert on for him. Schubert!)

203. My father doesn't count. He took part in the Austrian-Sard war and died one year before my mother, the renowned beauty Contessa Rossi who, if the truth be told, hated country life every bit as much as the muddy roads of the Bakony Mountains, and sorely missed Viennese music. She kept busy for a while by giving birth to the requisite number of children (eight pieces), and organized the local Gypsies into a chamber orchestra. Since the Gypsies of the Bakony Mountains could not read music, she played the melodies for them on the piano, which they would then play to perfection. She was also a first-rate composer. This came to light quite by accident, because she left a will saying that all her compositions must be destroyed after her death (all her "scribbled notes," she said), a wish of hers that was honored, of course. On the other hand, my mother neglected to consider, because she was no longer in a position to consider, that the score of the music she wrote for her own funeral would survive. It was as if she were speaking, as if she were addressing us, thus achieving the most that can possibly be achieved at a funeral—we thought of the deceased instead of

our own sorrow. The score may be seen at the National-bibliothek's Music Collection in Vienna. In short, my mother hated Réde, and when she became an old woman, she gave up all things Hungarian, including my father, and bought herself a villa in Hietzing. A young, *here my father's name follows,* countess was also living in the neighborhood at the time. Being with child, she advertised in the paper for a nanny, rather snobbishly giving her address as Gräfin, *here my father's name follows,* Hietzing. One day a servant tells my mother that a crazy woman's come to see her. She says she's a nanny, and she's here because of the ad. Let her in. They brought in the nanny who said she was a nanny, and who was inordinately surprised to see my mother, who was past seventy. In a strong Viennese dialect she asked whether the countess was my mother: *sans die Gräfin?* In accordance with the truth, my mother said she was. *Na ta schau her, und sie kriegens a Kind? In dem Alter!* A child? At your age? *Wos ti Herschaften nit fertigbringen!* The high and mighty will do anything. Soon it was all over town that at the age of seventy-five, my mother was with child. (My father's eldest son won't say "me," he just points silently at himself.)

204. My father was a great clown. He held forth, he raised his eyes and hands to heaven, as if aping and burlesquing a davening Jew. Oh, the grandeur, the invention, the ardor with which we hold forth on our failures and bunglings (missing the ball in soccer), which seem to have inscribed themselves indelibly in our memories. Oh, how feeble, foolish and belabored our attempts to capture the fleeting moments of beauty, solace and hope in barren words! My mother smelled a rat. She couldn't figure out what this wildly gesticulating man (my father) was up to. Yet she also thought it possible that he wasn't up to anything. Anything, anything is possible! Still, what is he getting at with this impertinent oversimplification of the problem? I can't recall, he said gingerly, a single instance in all of world literature that has perfect happiness

for its subject. On the other hand, I could count the passages about suffering, frustration, and disappointment ad infinitum, for they are as boundless as the ocean. At this point my father fell silent, while my mother fell to thinking. After lengthy reflection she finally recalled, however tentatively, a passage from *The Divine Comedy* (not the last four lines!), and also the scene from *The Charterhouse of Parma,* when Fabrice looks out of his cell. Lean proof, indeed! They'd been together for many years. At times my father would have liked to say everything, at times nothing. Now, after protracted silence, he spoke up. The thing I cannot reconcile myself to is not death, but the circumstance that we allow ourselves to be terrorized by the apparent bleakness of existence. You'd think we were born only to die. And all the time, the glorious moments that we experience nonetheless, whether they are immoral, dangerous and transient, like the plague, we hardly enjoy at all. From which my mother understood that the day before, my father had been diagnosed with advanced cancer of the bladder. So she didn't take offense at the comment about joy, though obviously, it applied to her person, too (by way of reproach). We're leaping headfirst into the Saran Wrap of life—my mother gave a nervous cough—trampolining from death to death. And all the time, we're hardly aware of anything, except for the fear and trembling. Still, what I feel most keenly now is not the fear of death, but that *other,* the suddenly emerging fear of the things I had neglected to do, and the neglect cannot be remedied. It is too late. The pain won't make room for the joy. I was standing in front of Giorgione's *Reclining Venus* this afternoon, the one Titian had to finish when Giorgione died of the plague. And I felt a profound sense of melancholy because I will never be able to enjoy this wondrous thing of beauty again without pain, which is my new, constant companion. My father looked at my mother as if she were a stranger. But he addressed his words to her. What memories or hopes, what intuitions of the past or of the future,

231

are greater than pain? My mother looked at my father as if he were a stranger. But she put her arms around him, as if she were inviting him to dance. She leaned close to my father's cancer and whispered: It is often the moments that seem inconsequential— here my father raised his brow in a typical gesture—even commonplace, memories that we remember only vaguely, if at all, that are the source of our strength and encouragement. Neither one looked at the other. They did not speak. It was good, being in Szováta, my mother said softly. Good. When we danced in the park. And also under the trees, my father whispered. They began a dance, slowly, awkwardly. It was good, you stroking my big belly when I was with child. Still, don't forget the bad. To make it real. Write it down on a piece of paper. Draw a line down the middle, the good to the left, the bad to the right. You'll see more clearly that way. The first time with you was bad, because we had to rush and the key got stuck in the lock. Besides, I didn't feel like it. Giving birth was bad [that's me!], the abortion was bad, the blood was bad . . . Now you're leaving out the good. It's bad that my mother drives me crazy, but it's good that I could sleep with her when my father was off somewhere. It was bad listening to them make love, and bad when they were having a fight. The sweet jelly rolls were good, and the helium balloon my father got me was good. Receiving Holy Communion was good, the wafer, white and cool, was good, and it was bad, because I dropped it. The swooning in church was good, the incense, confession, and singing in the choir, bad. When Tóth junior kissed me for the first time, it was good, and it was bad when he copped a feel, though later it was good again. And it was good, Cartouche is good, *often the same thing that is bad is also good. Being with you, for instance, and the haricot bean soup.* The two-week Student Council seminar was good, and it was good when once I reached inside the pocket of your trousers in company. The juice and vodka at Tóth junior's is good, and when on the beach once a man hooked a finger inside my bikini, that too was good, and bad, too, because the rubber band was tight. It is bad when a stale odor escapes from under the blanket in the morning, and it was good by the Balaton, when there were all those dead eels, and also good sliding down the rail. It was bad kicking my mother in the ankle, but the hip circle in gym was good . . . They continued the dance, though without moving, my mother holding my father tight, who got back every joyful and hopeful moment of his life thereby, moments that, though they had faded in his memory, were still potent enough to make him happy, a voice, his dead father's voice, a gray detail of a gray, monochrome Váli canvas, the scratches on the bottom of the silver cigarette case (he'd never told anyone where the scratches came from, and now he never will), the heady green of the early-morning woods on July 23, 1956, that *certain* manuscript, that certain operetta tune from *Three Little Maidens,* that certain day, the first day of our heroic revolution, when someone asked, where is life? In the room, the street, the fields, or . . . And then he smoothed his palm over her skirt, the crane's nest at Csobánka, as Russian trucks drove down Main Street, the photograph of a cliff, some discovery, some piece of silliness, some piece of seriousness, words, smells, of a dog's urine from the backyard, from 1947, of black coal, from 1938, and paprika from the stairwell, from 1956. A divine experience and an attack of the gout, simultaneously. That middling yet memorable night at Carnegie Hall, and the day when he wasn't even nineteen and was reading Dante's *Divine Comedy* in a stuffy attic room for the first time, in Chicago (or Valparaiso?), and that five-minute woman under the tree whom he never saw again, but been carrying her inside him ever since. My father got everything back between my mother's arms. Everything. By now my mother, too, felt tired. She lowered her head and was lost in her reveries. Then, with disarming, girlish shyness she whispered in my father's ear, who'd been dead a couple of minutes by then, that Jeanne Moreau's smile, her smile is something you shall never have, my darling.

205. When my father's son told my father that my mother had died, he raised his right hand to his lips as if he'd burned them, or as if he'd said something he didn't mean to and instantly regretted it. He dropped his left hand and with palm turned out, pressed it awkwardly to his side, like someone who has suffered a stroke, and said nothing. He just stood in the kitchen door at the spot where they ran into each other, and never again picked up the sentence he'd begun, meant to find out whether his son would like some of the lemon-flavored cookies that he'd just brought from Eger where he'd gone shopping when the telegram arrived from the hospital.

206. Wilhelm II had no liking for my father, and my father had no liking for Wilhelm II (though at the time neither could have had the least inkling either of Hitler or the camp at Sopronkőhida). Their conversation was neither sincere nor open; the tension appeared in what was not said, or in their curtailed sentences. For instance, I am not competent in the matter, Your Majesty, my father said. Actually (?) King Charles took pleasure in his prime minister's intransigence. (The German emperor arrived at Laxenburg on July 6. My father had to introduce himself. He showed up at the palace. He was received standing up. The Emperor demanded an explanation in no uncertain terms for why Kramař had been awarded clemency. My father's answer: [a] It's Austria's internal affair, [b] if the reasons for the clemency are important for military reasons, Prime Minister Seidler might supply the relevant information. This answer was not well received. You are not well oriented in questions of military policy, it seems. In-

234

deed, *Euere Majestät,* the Western front is, practically speaking, a black hole as far as I'm concerned. Are you aware that in France, an *x* number of horses die of horse plague? This is the first I've heard of it, Your Majesty. Alas, in the fall of '14, Joffre used requisitioned taxicabs. (Extremely sharply:) Will you kindly remember, do you know what decision I was faced with in the General Staff? I can't imagine, Your Majesty. I had to choose. Should we take in Calais and Paris? This is what he said, word for word. May the realization pose no greater difficulty than the choice, Your Majesty. The German emperor regarded my father at length, then said: *Genug, danke.* By the way, according to my father, in *The Tragedy of Europe,* Bartlett provides a false account of this audience. At the formal dinner that night, everyone pinned on their German medals as a matter of course. But not my father. The *Eiserne Krone Orden Klasse I* meant for him "had been forgotten on the Emperor's desk." Bárczy, his secretary, quickly got him one, but when my father whispered that he didn't *have* a medal, Bárczy didn't know if he could wear his own Order of the Second Class. My father assured him that he could, and a couple of weeks later, he, too, received the Order of the Second Class through the Viennese consulate, without an accompanying note. During his term as Prime Minister, he was not invited to Germany.) When my father left the Burg, he was in a bad mood, and walked along the Graben in that spirit; Germans, Communists, war—the world was in turmoil. And then suddenly, at twenty-three hours thirty-six minutes, as if he were having a mystical experience, he felt that he's not a person to whom everything will be happening here, and to whom everything has already happened, he's not a person, just an eye. He watched the banal, bustling crowds on the Graben innocent of what was to come—king, emperor, deterioration, competence. A bridge should be erected over the gaping schism between the thinkers and the nonthinkers, he thought. And also that he should pull the thinkers from off the pedestal of their aloof superiority, thus bringing them in touch with the people of the street. It was in this regard that my father had made a commendable effort.

207. It may have been the creamed corn that was to blame, or the pickled fish, or the shame, or the blues, European power relations, or possibly the changeable weather. Be that as it may, my father got the runs, and he kept having to go out. He ran to the jakes by the hour. Fortunately, the negotiations did not have to be postponed. My father's clever personal secretary—a gifted peasant youth from Zala—scheduled the speeches so that my father could disappear repeatedly without the merit of the negotiations suffering thereby. My father sat asquat on the new, English-style "cuckstool." No one was going to knock. The historical corridors were empty. Everyone was crowded inside at the negotiations led by him (expertly, it must be admitted). It may have been the creamed corn, or the pickled fish, or the shame, or the blues, European power relations, or possibly the changeable weather that was to blame (or the grilled mutton kidneys which gave his palate a fine tang of faintly scented urine), but there was a horrendous stink. From what? My father's presence? What he was up to? The shit, that's what was giving off the stink, the feces. Furnishing the details would not avail us. Still, we must add that the shit came bursting from my father along with the gases in such a manner that it would have been impossible to say which was pushing the other before it. In any case, it was a "difficult birth," but afterward he sat over the results, i.e., the stink, with satisfaction. He was breathing deeply, with ache and enjoyment, veritably inhaling himself. The gap between himself and the world had been removed, and he now felt he was *Ich-Erzähler*. He was skeptical about the English contraption—if you're not careful how you pull the thin chain, the excrement disappears (forever) without you having had a look, which brings with it a sense of anxiety com-

bined with disgust as if they'd stolen it, as if a part of us had gone, incomprehensibly, just as it is incomprehensible what we've just spent our time doing. This is what makes us feel not a little ill at ease. For this reason, and because there didn't seem to be anybody around to be tactful with, he didn't flush the toilet. The stink might even get absorbed in his garments; he thought maliciously. He laughed out loud. He might even be doing a service to the Monarchy. ("As long as the chain is swaying, the seat is warm.") But when he opened the door, it was being opened simultaneously from the other side. A surprise. Oh, my father gasped as he ran into the ambassador from the Vatican. Your Excellency, they said of each other in chorus, and smiled broadly. The man from the Vatican was a man of the world, and cultured besides. His ideas were often unrestrained, pleasantly unsuited to Rome, though sometimes verging on a bluff, because they were unfounded and rambling. On the other hand, they were always on a grand scale. His countenance, the roughness of his skin and its ruddiness, which did nothing to disclaim a love of drink, along with his bushy brows, reminded one of a sailor rather than a refined diplomat. An insatiable curiosity for all things fired his soul. If he came upon something his eyes sparkled and an expectant smile appeared on his lips. My dear friend, my father said, trying to detour the Italian by putting his arm through his, my impression is that your comment on my speech was more like a question than a response. The ambassador nodded enthusiastically, *si, si, si,* but would not budge. In his arrogance, my father hadn't even opened the small window. Well, yes, yes, my father said, playing for time, but this way, the answer comes before the question . . . Couldn't this have been done in a more down-to-earth manner, more in line with custom, as it were, first the question, and then the answer? Provided there is one? Will you please release me, the ambassador shouted, pulling his arm from my father's. This—his regained freedom—seemed to calm him. Naturally, he said. Except it's the answer that led me to the question. If there were no answer, how could you have a question? Then, with a smile and Christian (Catholic) forbearance, he walked into the loo. My father shrugged and crossed himself, though not in that order.

208. My mother was bursting at the seams with *joie de vivre,* and the sun, too, was shining, the hillside bright and radiant. My mother made a sweeping gesture. If you love me passionately, all of this shall be yours. But this is not what she said. What she said was: isn't the weather lovely. I wouldn't go quite that far, my father said, looking around him.

209. When it comes to sounding a retreat, my father is the best. Ingenious, free. It is not true that he is cynical and an adherent of relativity. Your father is shallow, no wonder he's free, this is not true. When he was ordered to clear the rabble from the square in front of Parliament, he promptly told his men to take up their firing positions, and they (need we add) aimed their guns at the crowd. It was fall. In the deadly silence that followed, my father drew his sword, shouting at the top of his lungs: Comrades! The crowd saw red. (My father realized he'd made a mistake. He didn't make a greater mistake than anyone else of his quality would be expected to make, except he was quicker to remedy it.) Ladies and Gentlemen. Watzlawick. (?) I have my orders to fire at the rabble. However, since I see a number of good decent citizens among you, I request that they kindly leave the square, so that I may be sure of shooting only the rabble. The people went for it, and in a matter of minutes, the square stood deserted. What happened, and what was the psychological gist behind my father's ingenious solution? Obviously, my father was facing a threatening crowd. (Why him? A good question.) The essence of his orders was to pit animosity against animosity, i.e., add fuel to the fire, and because my father's men had arms, while the crowd—possibly the rabble (for we must

keep this, too, in mind)—did not, it seemed the logical thing to do. In a wider context, however, the resultant change would not be a change at all. Just the opposite! Though this particular square might be emptied of people, other squares would become crowded in turn. In short, due to the appearance of a new empty square, the probability of empty squares would increase; i.e., had I more fathers, or the same father replicated in multiple numbers, and he were called out to all the squares that needed to be cleared of crowds, one of my fathers would bring the other into a difficult pass, and in the end it would be my father who'd draw the short end of the stick, and it is possible that the rabble—because by now it would certainly be a rabble, the pox on them for putting my daddy in such dire straits!—would draw and quarter him. But my father pulled the situation out of its immediate context, and reformulated it so as to make it acceptable to all parties concerned. My father's solution is typically quasi-rational. Logic based on hostility would never lead to this solution. If it's a tooth for a tooth, and the tooth is not yours, then why not a tooth for a tooth? (On the other hand, if it's your tooth . . . It's the ellipsis my father took advantage of.) His training could not have led him to the solution either, though its sagacious nature is not to be questioned. Possibly, the idea, which came to him like a revelation, may have occurred to him during the moment of meditative self-absorption as he drew out his sword. Put up your sword, and whack! Needless to say, he couldn't have acted like this in every situation, he could have never become an officer had he done so. Still, he found many opportunities for sounding a retreat. Retreating from a comfortable and convenient trap is a daring and dangerous undertaking. But it is your only chance, especially in a difficult and deeply rooted match. My father's family was not ashamed of abandoning the construction of the cathedral in Siena. My father was all for it. If Florence has one, we need one too, he insisted. In fact, it's got to be on a grander scale, if possible. So they had the wall that lay farthest away built first, so that Florentines would stand in disbelief of my father's future church. But the money ran out, my father put down his tools, and never gave the cathedral a second thought. Later, when a complete, if not enormous cathedral—but with zebra stripes—was built using the side aisle of the originally planned cathedral—thinking of God this time, and not the people of Florence (under the direction of the Florentine master builder Renato Pasta and his wife, by the way)—they decided not to pull down the huge, awkward freestanding wall. On the contrary. My father and his family were proud of "the most bombastic spatial symbol of the frustration of man's plans." They were not ashamed, because they did not fall into the "too much invested to quit" trap—something my father was not able to do with regard to the dam at Nagymaros. It was pulled down as if it were never there. The only problem is that it was there. Even my father can sound a retreat only where he'd made his entry.

210. My father: a horse has four legs, and it still trips up. In the same way, the Danube has two banks, but they shot the Jews into it just the same.

211. My mother tells me that my father is being tried. Your father, as you know, was one of the Milice big shots in the Vichy government. Between Rákóczi, Rodosto, and Paris, et cetera, the family got frenchified. It's no secret that in '47–'48 he (my father) was hiding out in various monasteries, which is how he got arrested, while he was in hiding. He was sentenced to death in absentia on two counts. These sentences are no longer valid, partly because they've done away with death sentences, and partly because a good part of the pertinent crimes fell under the statute of limitations. France distinguishes between war crimes (e.g., the torture and execution of prisoners), and crimes against humanity (e.g., racist crimes). The former expire after thirty years, the latter

never. The first count of indictment against my father is the execution of seven hostages. The story is as follows. On orders from London, the resistance assassinated, or, to use my mother's expression, "did away with" the minister of propaganda of the Vichy government. This was in the spring or summer of 1944. Initially, the Germans were said to have demanded the execution of one hundred hostages, which in the end my father bartered down to eight. These eight were thrown into one cell. The selection was not what you'd call equitable, because seven of the eight were Jewish, whereas Herriot was not shot by the Jewish resistance, but the French resistance as such. Then one early morning my father and a *milicien* opened the cell door, and led the hostages to the execution. However, while still in the building, my father looked at one of them (this eighth belonged to the top leadership of the resistance, which was no secret), and sent him back to his cell. Seven is less than eight, your idiotic father reasoned, that's why he learned mathematics. For that! Your poor, idiotic father. *(Poor!)* The others were shot, the eighth was spared, and had just testified. He said that he knew right away, without the shadow of a doubt, that his life was spared because he's not a Jew, while the hostages who were shot were (Jews). As soon as he finished testifying—and no one could deny what he'd said, neither your father, nor his defense attorney—the public prosecutor saw his chance. Incontrovertible proof that he (my father) had committed a crime against humanity. Do you follow me, son? Your father's sparing someone's life, that's what indicted him. He committed a crime against humanity because he managed not to get one person shot. If he'd had all eight of them shot, he would have never been indicted. I will leave you to ponder the abyss that opens up at this point, she (my mother) said, taking me in her arms.

212. My father was given an award for his painting entitled *Buchenwald*. At first everyone was outraged—my father subtitled the

painting *Happiness*—then they gave him the award. Does he feel, the reporters asked, that they've made amends? Forty years ago they dragged him off to Buchenwald, and now they're giving him an award, putting him up in a five-star hotel, and dining him in exclusive restaurants. My father smiles. His gold tooth sparkles like an old Russian babushka's. I don't see the connection between the two things, he says courteously, reflectively, a bit languidly. I have received this award because I'm a painter. But I was taken away because I'm a Jew. Applause. My father makes a slight grimace. Of course, had I been a painter even back then . . . (Like this, with the "even.") Loud applause. Now he's pretending that he's deep in thought, my mother whispers. My father is pretending that he's deep in thought. Then, as if bringing some mischief into the light of day he adds: though as far as that goes, I'm still a Jew. Silence followed by thunderous applause that stifles the silence. My mother hates it when my father sums up the essence of things so well. She hates it when my father's sentences "sit." Since when does the essence sit?! Look, she whispers to her friend sitting next to her, and points at my father's legs, showing, showing from under the table, look how thick his ankles are, poor dear. Full of water. Just look what they've done to him.

213. They dragged my daddy off to Mauthausen where, along with everyone else, they killed him. When he returned, he weighed forty kilos. He cried a lot, and his skin, which had turned a repulsive gray, was covered with festering sores that took forever to heal. He became taciturn, trusting neither the living nor the dead, nor the stones, nor the River Danube. Then in 1945, when barely eighteen, he joined the Communist Party, because he wanted to break the silence. But this didn't work out either, and he got involved in some shady affairs and was locked up, but then around

'56, he was released, and then everything was back to normal, sometimes for better, sometimes for worse.

214. My father holds (with hardly any reservations) that life is a miracle because (according to my father) the natural, normal and obvious thing is to die in Auschwitz. You're dragged off, and you die: everything is in order, it is in order *there*; everything proceeds according to plan, if there is a plan, or if there is no plan, then everything proceeds by common consent (some slight resistance in order). It is not natural or normal, in short, it is a miracle, if you do not die in Auschwitz. The miracle isn't supposed to mean or imply that the probability of this occurring is small, whereas the probability of this occurring is small. It can be put down to a number of things: chance, accident, so-called luck *(mazel)*, or the erratic and nonspecific hysteria of the will to live. It is, further, not natural, it is not normal, and therefore a miracle, never going to Auschwitz at all (i.e., dying someplace other than Auschwitz, or not dying). Which is a frequent occurrence, and therefore misleading. The nature of the world as miraculous: this is problematic. But I am not saying, my father said, that if the world were normal *without* faults, it would be easier, harder, or just the way it is, miraculous.

215. In A. my father became a bad person. He survived A., but he became a bad person. He hates the entire world—men, women, animals, plants, and also raw mineral deposits. He'll do you a bad turn if he can. He spreads gossip about people, pitting them against one another. Sometimes entire nations. His influence is appreciable at Court because of this A. In short, he is highly destructive. For instance, he'll stretch a nylon fishing wire across the bedroom, and when my mother trips over it, he makes sure the blame falls on my father's son. Let's posit that my father—and

never mind now whether from natural or unnatural causes—dies (*ganz egal*). Let's posit, furthermore, that all the people who were in any way related and/or connected to my father, those who in spite of everything loved him, and also those who, having been hurt by him, hated him, dies. What then? Will A. then cease to be? Or, in our fear, my father dictates irritably—who is perfectly aware of the essence of A., though he disregards its concrete up-shot with respect to his own person—will there always be those who *know*, who will not forget, who will remember till the end of time? Is this what the world is all about? This "end of time"?

216.   My father's tutor, who was brought in from Nagyszombat, was a strict man with a fondness for method and order. Above all, he was disciplined, a consequence of his chief character trait, suffer-ing. He made no bones about it in front of my father. He'd always been a pariah. He'd known nothing but persecution and enmity, and regardless of what he was thinking, his thoughts were consid-ered heretical. He'd always stood on the other side. The sidelines. The side of death. Which is only natural. Here is the man, my father thought, who has made the world whole, complete and real. And who was my father? He was the world. Not worldliness, but the thing that this wandering Jew had made whole. The pres-ent, practically by definition, is unending misery. Still, my father felt at home in the world. He did not hoodwink himself. Con-trary to his tutor, he considered this homeliness as natural and its opposite strange and curious. Having said that, though, my father, too, stood alone, in opposition, and against. On the side. The side of life. It was in this way that he became the man who made the world whole, complete, and real. And that's not the end of it. The question, though there is no one to ask it (*Hegel ist gestorben*) is: what is the nature of the world? Is God our Father or a dangerous madman who'd possibly committed suicide a long, long time ago? That is the question. If it is not true that my father and the tutor

from Nagyszombat together make up the world, then it is not true because their experience of the world is incidental and personal. In which case, it comes down to this: the one had *pech,* the other *mazel.* That's all there is to it. One was favored by fortune, the other smitten by it. One was not loved by his mother, and while he was still inside, she kept scraping his fontanel with a knitting needle, while the other was kissed crispy pink. Which is as nothing: one whines, the other grumbles—both are kitsch.

217. The double-talk didn't work. My father saw through him, his son. There was a desperation in his voice signaling that he'd survived "the years of persecution" only physically, that from time to time he's startled awake by his own nightmares, and he can still hear the fall of the guillotine over his head. Just the other day, too, the faulty ignition of an automobile made him jump out of his skin. He thought the sound came from an assassin's gun. Besides, he's feeling empty, burned out, and alone. More and more often he feels tempted to escape his sufferings and the ungrateful world by putting a bullet through his head. For the fraction of a second, my father's son felt the stirrings of a long-forgotten hope. But in that case, if you're being unjustly persecuted, why are you still hiding? It is time you faced your judges! He, his son, would gladly follow him on this path, he'd gladly offer his full support. He'd be with him day and night. *Daddy!* After a short pause, a sharp, metallic voice: There are no judges, just people bent on revenge!

218. My father was the spitting image of Princess Diana (until he opened his mouth). Because of this, the British royal family hired him (i.e., they hired a private firm, and the private firm hired my father) as a double, which meant that from time to time, he had to stand in for the princess at various functions. He has just resigned from the flattering post. Being Princess Diana drove me nuts. It made me sick. He sympathized so much with the princess

he was asked to imitate that he began to suffer from the same depression, had the same marital problems, and even had a bout with bulimia, like the princess at one time. His marriage, too, was on the rocks because my mother could not accommodate herself to my father's double life. Did he also stand in for Di during her well-publicized affairs? And now, see what's happened . . . A double's fate.

219.   Who (my father!) is an alcoholic? An alcoholic is not one who drinks to excess, but one who can't stop drinking. What do the statistics say? In a class with twenty-five students, on the average three come from families who are alcoholics. In any random group of young people, every eighth or tenth has at least one parent who is an alcoholic. In any given city, problems with alcoholism mark every tenth home. My father lived in one such home. What does Jesus Christ have to say about this (to my father)? (1) You're not alone. I am with you, et cetera. Plus the statistics. (2) The problem is that you're incapable of solving your problems, and you're incapable of sweeping them under the rug, because they're bigger than you are. And so is the rug. But I am greater (taller, also wider, i.e., more weighty) above all things, including your problems. Rest in my bosom. (3) Change. This is scary and involves a certain amount of risk, but don't forget, et cetera. (4) I'm waiting for your nod of agreement so that I may be the source of your strength and assistance. (5) I love you, I accept you the way you are. My love is not contingent upon your actions, which are slop and abomination, but on what you are, for I have created you in my image. I bless you now and forever. (6) In which case, *chin-chin,* in the name of God!

220.   In the beginning, for in the beginning was the beginning, my father drank two glasses of Zubrovka, because he knew (knows) from experience that mankind has yet to invent a better breakfast

potion. In short, a glass of Zubrovka. Later, on Pushkin (formerly, *here my father's name follows*) Street, he had another glass, but this time it was not Zubrovka, but coriander vodka. A friend of my father's insists that coriander vodka is an inhuman drink because while it renders the limbs strong, it weakens the spirit. It had the opposite effect on my father (strong spirit, weak limbs), though that too is inhuman. Accordingly, he proceeded to drain, then and there, two mugs of cheap beer and a bottle of Moldavian white wine, the latter as a chaser. He also remembered having guzzled two glasses of Jägerwodka on Chekhov Street. To this day, from the Eastern Railway Station to the town of Nyíregyháza, people are drinking my father's famous mixed cocktails. The Balsam of Canaan ("little skunk" to the simple folk) is a grayish-black-colored liquid, it is medium strong, with an intensive aroma. But no, it's more than an aroma, it's a veritable anthem. "Even if we drink vodka from the bottle, on its own, it won't have any effect, discounting the spiritual torment and chaos. The mixture of vodka and eau de cologne has a certain amount of whimsy to its credit, but even that is missing the pathos. Not so a glass of Balsam of Canaan! It has whimsy, intelligence, pathos. It will even bring on a certain metaphysical experience. Still, which component of the Balsam do we value most? You got it. The methyl alcohol, whereas methyl alcohol, the object of our enthusiasm, has no en-thusiasm in it whatsoever. What then, do we prize in it so much? The water, of course. Plus the poisonous vapor it emits. In order to make this unwholesome brew more potent, we might wish to spruce it up with a bit more aroma. This is why we like to add a 1–2–1 ratio of brown beer to the methyl alcohol—Ostankino or Senator are recommended. Another option is pure varnish. I don't wish to go into the manner of purifying varnish, anyone can tell you how it's done. No one in the land knows how the great poet Petöfi came to meet his death, but anyone can tell you how to purify varnish." In short, 1 dl. methyl alcohol, 2 dl. brown beer,

1 dl. pure varnish. The Smell of Genf: 1 dl. White lilacs, ½ dl. foot spray for sweaty feet, 2 dl. cheap beer, 1 ½ dl. varnish containing alcohol. Komsomol Maiden's Tears: 15 gr. lavender, 15 gr. verbena, 30 gr. Woodland Spice aftershave, 2 gr. nail polish, 1 ½ dl. mouthwash, 1 ½ dl. lemonade; the mixture should then be stirred for twenty minutes with the addition of woodbine, though some people swear that in case of an emergency, devil's guts make a fine substitute for woodbine—a false and evil contention. Bitch's Entrails: 1 dl. cheap beer, 0.30 dl. Szadkó and Wealthy Guest shampoo, 0.7 dl. rubbing alcohol for dandruff, 0.25 dl. brake fluid, 0.08 dl. Minute Glue, 20 gr. bug spray; mix and let stand for one week on top of tobacco leaves suitable for cigars. After just two glasses of this cocktail a person will become so etherealized anyone can walk up to him and spit in his face for an hour and a half without his moving a muscle.

221. Regularly, of his own volition, with discipline and relish, my father took into himself a liquid (orally) produced by the fermentation of fresh grape juice containing methyl alcohol, glycerin, acids, sugars, nitrogen products, tanning, color- and odor-enhancing materials, enzymes, essential vitamins, as well as ash constituents (potassium, iron, etc.). Though it did not contain sugar, he took into himself with equal perseverance a certain something that, though it contained no sugar, it did contain at least 40 percent so-called alcohol, as well as a negligible amount of so-called trace materials. Though reluctantly, and without approving of it, he'd also accept a cheaper version of the same brew, made with the addition of essence. Synthetic compounds, disgusting! There's another, for which my father uses 17 to 19 kg. malt per 1 hectoliter of liquid. Once these were absorbed in my father's stomach and entered the bloodstream, they began to affect my father's central nervous system and reduced the inhibitions in the old man's gray matter. My father's gift of observation was noticeably

diminished (spider? black widow?), his gift for association turned shallow (Tom, Dick, & Harry, Harry, Tom & dick), his memory (Who the fuck are you, you little prick?) and learning ability ( ... ) took a nosedive, his judgment became unreliable, not to mention the flagging of his self-criticism and restraint, and euphoria, i.e., a sense of unsubstantiated elation, would set in for a period of time. Freed of its inhibitions, the excessive excitation of my father's mainspring took the form of talking too loud and speechifying, singing, wrestling (playfully, or so it seemed), engaging in competition games (what's the capital of Brazilia?). Which was also accompanied by a faltering tongue, a reeling walk, plus his ingenious double vision, not to mention trying to fit the key into the key hole. Then, as the overexcitement subsided, my father's breathing slowed down. He exhibited signs of fatigue and drowsiness. He lay down or, as my mother put it, the pig is snoring in his pen (or: the poor pig is snoring in his pen). Over time, my father developed a Pavlovian reflex, a bridge between his yearning and alcohol. But whether he should step on said bridge was no longer up to my father to decide. There was also a change in the ratio of the dose needed for simple relief, and the dose needed to achieve euphoria. Initially, this was 1 mug to 6 mugs, then 3 to 5, then 4 to 4, and finally, 5 to 3, i.e., euphoria with all its concomitants (key, key whole), and with no relief in sight. Needless to say, my father knew nothing about this bridge, and he'd never heard of that darned Pavlicheck either, and so, he held himself in contempt along with us, because he thought that it was a matter of the will. He thought that this was the challenge, and that he'd failed. But you can't live in contempt of yourself all your life. This, of course, gave rise to the game of hide-and-seek—hiding stuff in the vinegar bottle, the thermos bottle, the linen closet, under the bed, inside the toilet tank. Then, after the blood alcohol level dropped, there came the sweating, the restlessness, the oversensitivity (not just about the Jews!), weakness, the runs, sleep disturbances, pronounced trembling (the tremors), plus a whole slew of psycho-somatic whatnots. The hallucinations fed mainly on the images of colorless, nippy little things: small animals, the classical mouse, not infrequently albino, insects, cats, lions, cords, wires, water sprays. My father showed a marked preference for the mice, after which he'd sleep like a log. The house was as silent as the grave. "My Child. Though the Father be ever so brilliant in intellect, as a human being he leaves much to be desired . . ." "How often did I plead with him, please relent. Think of your responsibilities. Not that odious tavern. Anyone with a name like yours and with four sons such as yours must not stain his character so. Poor Father. I feel so sorry for him. And also for myself."

222. On the first time-plane my father took to telling the child in question that he'd made him/her do it, he didn't mean to, except the child in question is so *sweet* that he was disarmed, but if he/she tells, if he/she tells anybody, then my mother and Granny—for whom the child in question has a special fondness—will surely be angry, get real upset, and for all he knows, might even give the child in question to the Gypsies, or, what is even more likely, if he/she squeals, then he, my father, will wander off and then they, the family, will go hungry, and will have to sell the house at a discount. At such times, the child in question usually has no choice but to commit suicide, but fortunately, he/she is pulled out of the water in time. On the second time-plane the child in question entertains strong doubts that my father has sufficient strength to apologize (et cetera), so the child in question shouldn't have to carry the odious burden on his/her own. Hate him! Despise him! Take revenge!, he/she cries, but by then my father is (was) dead. Besides, I'd probably have felt sorry for him all over again. A piece of shit. If you feel sorry for a piece of shit like him, you can't hate him sufficiently. Whether the shit hits the fan or the fan hits the shit, it comes to the same thing. My mother took my father's side.

In her eyes, the he/she in question was (basically) a cheap little whore, and since he/she got my father all worked up, the least he/she could do is calm him down. My mother had no time-plane.

223.  Having surveyed the multitude of choices, the Swiss *Kinderschutzbund* endeavored to work out a set of criteria. According to these, it is considered odious if (1) my father appears in the buff in front of the child in question; if (2) my father strips in front of the child in question, especially if they are as alone as my finger (especially the middle finger); if (3) my father brings up the topic of his genitals; if (4) my father plays Peeping Tom re. the child in question: undressing, bathing, sitting on the loo; (5) French kiss; (6) manipulative touching (obvious where); if (7) my father talks the child in question into touching his (my father's) penis; if (8) my father masturbates in front of the child in question and the other way around; if (9) my father thinks it's high time that my sister— the child in question—finally learned to do something my mother does, too, even if not the way and not as often as he, the head of the family, has every right to expect, but that's why my little sister is around. It's her turn now, which is no reason for my mother to carry on like a stupid jealous goose, and so he pushes my sister's head down to his fly, who is alarmed and would like to straighten up, but it's not possible (it wasn't possible), and who afterward throws up (*Du bist doch mein Vater!*), and also runs a fever and skips school the next day, where in religion class they are just learning about the life of the angelic doctor St. Thomas Aquinas, and in math class, Euclidean axioms; if (10) my father penetrates the vagina and/or the rectum (of the child in question), either with the application of the finger, the prick, or a foreign object; and finally, (11) if he just rubs it against him/her. Like all people whose lives and thoughts are based on moral principles (Christian Hungary), my father—who out of the 280 thousand abuses (of which

twenty thousand were performed on minors) has only 75 percent of the cases weighing on his conscience (the other 25 percent being performed on brothers and sisters, an uncle, an aunt (!), friends of the parents, et cetera (e.g., the researcher of the history of the Royal Society)—agrees with the association's views as set down in points 5 to 11, but disagrees with the first four points, which he says were dragged in by the hair. Are we to return to the former times of prudery? Is my wife to fall, swooning, into an armchair if her child, my son, should discover her in a nightgown? Not likely, says my father, putting the dot on the *i*.

224. My father won't talk. He shudders and won't talk. He's running scared. The fact that he's in trouble is indicated by a number of mute signs, which we tend to ignore far too often, alas. Signs indicative of my father's shame and ignominy may be: the compulsive washing of his person. When, feeling that he is unclean, he compulsively washes, showers, and bathes himself. Also, when he wears clothes that have long since gone out of fashion (wide breeches), in order to hide his feminine curves. A general lack of contact with others, and panic provoked by contact with members of the opposite sex. Refusing to undress in the locker room before gym class. Peeing in bed. Stealing (my father). Wandering off into the wild blue yonder. Threatening suicide. The shame and the fear kills the words. Attentiveness sparks hope. The buttocks, trampled sore, are obviously in a separate category. Though his thighs (my father's) are as sturdy as Rákóczi's oak, the abomination throbs and throbs.

225. My father's favorite delicacy is tongue of whale. He likes it even more than he likes kidneys. He and his friends surround the whale and pinch it, at which the whale rolls over on its back from the pain, opens its mouth, *ah-ah-ah-ah*, and my father and his friends pull out the tongue. If they succeed, my father is happy. He's in

seventh heaven. If only the whale didn't die as a consequence (the whale dies as a consequence). But oh, he didn't mean it! It pains him more than he can say! Also, he and his friends have a thing for young seals. They catch a whole bunch of them—it's not a pleasant sight because young seals cry—and this is really interesting, they start playing ball with them in the water in order to stimulate the young seals' blood circulation, because they (the young seals) are more tasty that way. My father likes to live the good life. But once—this was sometime after Christ—they caught too many young seals, and one was left over. They'd stuffed themselves silly, and nobody wanted it. (My father was a gourmet and a gourmand rolled into one.) Then my father prompted and guided the young seal out to shore, back to its mother, who was in seventh heaven. She was prepared for anything, except for this.

226. My father was a good human being. There are only two categories: the good and the bad. Hitler, for instance, is (was) bad, and my father good. But luck also played a part in this, because after he'd decided to shoot himself through the mouth, but only after he'd shot my father's two sons first, and he'd checked his gun, finished with the preparations and came into our room and stepped up to my brother, he was so angelic in his beauty, his beauty was so radiant, a blond angel, a black diamond, that terrified, my father fled the scene in order to effectuate the second half of his plan (i.e., a third, if we take into account the number of shots). Though who knows? The shots, the unfired shots, might have had no effect on the good.

227. What gives? To put it bluntly, my father is molesting my father's son. He calls it love. He molests him, sees that he's molesting him, so he must love him. My father's son, on the other hand, considers my father's molestation of him molestation (even if at times he sees that my father is mixing the molesting with the loving). My

father will not relent, and insists that my father's son love him—in his, the boy's—best interest. If not, he's got to be forced into it—in his, the boy's—best interest. Who sees the molesting in the molesting more and more for what it is, which results in his being molested all the more, all in the name of love. What can he do? My father's son attempts to conceal what he knows, and he also attempts to conceal that he has anything to conceal. At which my father speaketh thus: Insincerity is a bad thing. If you lie, I will punish you in your own best interest. As a result of which my father's son recognizes that he gets punished most of all when he considers my father's molestation of him as molestation, and he conceals that this is what he's doing, that there is something he's concealing. And so, my father's son conceals everything from himself, he does not step inside himself. At which my father takes the next step. He's of the opinion that stooped shoulders and a lowered head are clear indications of stupor, stupidity, and cowardice, and so he's come up with a variety of devices to doctor it. The *bridge* is radical in its very simplicity. Intended to strengthen the neck and back muscles, the bridge entails the use of two chairs, placed at body distance from each other, so that the body should be stretched straight by being supported at the heels and the back of the neck. In order that my father's son should not go about with a distended, overproud chest, my father has developed a *deflated-chest gismo,* by far the most revolting gadget ever invented, which obstructs the chest so that the lack of air contorts the whole body. The *shoulder fetter,* outfitted with metal springs, serves to pull back the shoulders. The *straightener* aids the proper seating posture. It was made of an iron crossbar that my father has fixed to the writing bench, and the horizontal of the crossbar presses so hard against the collarbone and shoulder blades that you quickly stop protesting and take up the required heroic posture. The *vertical support column* prevents young people from throwing one leg over the other, which is to be avoided not only because it checks the blood circulation, but also because of other, one might say delicate, reasons. The *strap equipped with a ringed shoulder stay* gets you to stay in the proper sleeping posture, thereby preventing your irresponsible, amorous rolling to the side. My father is happy when the consciousness elicited by the pain turns into the ennobling force of habit—granted that at times a certain inflexibility is made inevitable thereby. To these have been added washing in cold water (including wintertime) and the brutal interdiction on self-abuse, irrespective of the seasons, alas. In this way has my father's pedagogical daemon attempted to stay in equilibrium in the malleable flow of time.

228. I'm going to tear you to shreds, like a fish! It was not the beating, but the anger and self-disgust (because he was so scared of my father, and had humiliated himself in front of him like this) that kept him (my father's son) awake, silently weeping, like fish in water. ("I never knew the meaning of fear until I came to know him. He was the first human being who instilled a terror in me that, I think, has never let up. Not even when I became a grown man, and he old. He brought fear into my heart even then, especially the way he looked at me with that rigid, yellow glance of his. That look paralyzed me. I can see it, even now . . .") During the last years of his life, my father made several attempts—which, being sniffy and standoffish, did not suit his nature. Nevertheless, he made the attempts. But my father's son did not respond. This thing was greater than him. He could not swallow the anger. There was too much of it. And also, he lacked generosity of heart, he's sorry to say.

229. Where was it? And when? In Naples, or what have you, as ambassador. Where he gobbled up all the soft, sweet and succulent— no, not the women, the figs. And in the meantime, he took notes (my father). He'd been taking notes for a long time by then, about

the old count (his father). Memories and stuff. (The monumental-
ity of the material far surpassed his memory and intellectual capacities.) Every blessed day. It felt good, being with him like this.
Then, having returned in accordance with his father's wishes, he
brought him, what was it?, a silver snuff box or German marks,
under the counter, so to speak. In short, he had been given a
chore to do and he did it. The heralds were faster, though, and he
hadn't even unpacked when his father paid him a visit. They
hadn't seen each other for years. They embraced. He's shriveled
up, his face, his body, he is no longer taller than I am, my father
thought. The snuff box?, Grandfather said, freeing himself of the
embrace. My father handed it to him. His father took it. Then
saying he's got something to take care of (at the pharmacy), he left
with his entourage. Ninety-seven seconds, my father said glancing
at his watch (Bréguet-Sapin), this is how much time his father had
given him. He thought of his notes, of the "every blessed day,"
and the feeling of gratitude brought color to his cheeks. Still, we
have come a step closer to the truth, it seems to me, to make both
of us feel a bit more at ease, and to make our lives, and our deaths,
too, possibly easier to bear.

230. My father kept mucking about, should he or shouldn't he, until
they dragged him off. They dragged everyone off, my father's son,
too, and my mother, too, but then they pointed the women in
another direction, and packed us in cattle cars. My father was
scared to death. He'd get scared at the drop of a hat. He couldn't
help it, that's just the way he was. When the train stopped, raving
soldiers, or persons who looked like soldiers, would always break
into the cars and always carry one person off. Always. And always, just one. They didn't make a big deal out of choosing, they
didn't make a scene, but the person in question could always feel
when it was going to be his turn. After a while, this is what was on
their minds twenty-four hours a day—life, death, that minute jolt

as the train came to a halt. No wonder they became highly sensitive. When we stopped once again and my father could feel it was his turn, he broke into a sweat, a repeated tremor, a veritable spasm ran through his hands and over his eyelids. His stomach churned and heaved. He was ill (he upchucked). Then, with a sudden, savage gesture, he kicked my father's son out of the wagon, landing him at the feet of the uniformed men, who then dragged him off. At this, at long last, he (my father) felt a sense of relief. He lived to a ripe old age. If anyone mentioned his eldest son, he'd say: My son, my sweet, sweet son.

231.   He was a harmless old fart. No. A cheerful old gentleman, sweet and understanding, attentive, weak. No. He was dead. The day before his funeral, we made an inventory of his sins in order to fortify ourselves, one might say. Not the harmlessness, not the weakness, nor death itself blunted the scorn and outrage of his children, which flared up once again now that they were compiling the inventory, even if one or another paternal outrage was no more, really, than an innocent prank, some silly piece of nonsense, a bit of tomfoolery. They remembered, they snarled. The desertion of the dying grandfather. He didn't even attend the funeral. (He'd spread the rumor that the city had been bombed, and that's why.) A mad dash for the bomb shelter during an air raid, plus the outrageous abandonment of my mother and her ailing children ("he's running across Church Square, hunched like an old man, at the age of thirty. I can see it even now. Oh, how often I saw it!"), followed by a string of cowardly excuses. Going hunting on the day my father's son was born, and visiting my mother in the hospital only days later. My mother was not just offended, and not just shamefaced in front of the other women; she'd come to realize that she'd miscalculated, having attached false hopes to the coming of the infant. Even though the children reminded him and even offered to help, neither for Teachers' Day nor Mother's

Day ("she's no mother of mine"), nor for Christmas, did he ever buy a gift for my mother, ever. He didn't ever greet or congratulate her. He held custom in disdain. Sprawled out on the sofa, he watched my mother work, and then, as if he had no hands of his own, ordered her around, making her bring him stuff from the table. And also the gruff barking down of our mother. Why can't she stop pestering him *at last,* when my mother was just trying to put my father's bookkeeping in order, to the extent that it was at all possible. Hour-long phone calls to the meat people (Butchers' Syndicate), et cetera, but she still needed two pieces of information from my father. His gravely ill mother, who asked after him every day, his sick friends, he wouldn't visit any of them, but was filled with rage when this happened to him (a runny nose). When people called, we had to say he's not available, he's busy, and then he, changing his mind, would grab the phone, leaving us with our lies. If we called him away from the tavern that was next door to school because an animal was taken ill, he had people say he's not there (I'm not here, we heard him say from the back), but kicked up a storm if he found out that we took the dog that'd been run over, let's say, to another veterinarian. Methodically, one by one, he tore up my father's son's star photos. Though he never read anything, he took the books we got for Christmas away from us for days (Kostolányi, *Kornél Esti*), and if it was a mystery, he'd tell us who'd done it. (The butler.) He knew perfectly well that my father's son loved cats, so he set his dogs on stray cats and let the dogs tear them apart in front of his son's eyes. When he was drunk, he bawled out the butcher's apprentices in the yard so loudly that for days afterward, we'd have to hide from the neighbors, until one of them would say, "we know what the Doctor's like, he didn't mean it." The tavern keepers kept asking for my mother to take my father home, because his drunken brawl was scaring away their customers. When we were forcibly resettled, and we lived in cramped quarters, he kept bringing home dogs even though he knew perfectly well he wouldn't walk or feed them, and then he would threaten to sell the ones we liked best, and the only reason he didn't do it is because we talked the buyers out of it behind his back. Though she pleaded with him not to do it, he sold my mother's horse to the stock yard of Jarolimek's Viennese slaughterhouse for horses in Budapest, and though Mommy cried over it repeatedly, he thought it was great fun. He never gave his children any toys (or even a hoot), but would regularly set the two older ones against the youngest, who then shook the bars of his playpen like one possessed, his hair drenched in sweat. When once in a great while my mother fell ill, he kept her on her toes from dawn to dusk, telling her to fetch a pail of water, then tumble after, et cetera. Knowing that my father's son is sensitive to smells and the smell of boiled bone turns his stomach even worse than Campbell's chicken soup, he cooked the deer antlers he'd brought home from a hunt when we were sitting at the table, then watched his son's suffering with contempt. When he took them for a walk and the dogs had to pee, he wouldn't stop, and they had to "do it" in midmotion, because "it is their duty to accommodate themselves to their master." He lied and told our schoolmates that we're not home. He threatened and bullied our mother in front of us. Strident midnight whispers, weeping, clapping of feet, slamming of doors, kicking, furniture tumbling (it wasn't just our imagination; the marble top of the night table, which was cracked to begin with, was split in two the next day). Toddling into the middle of the "scene" in a dreamy daze at the age of four (thereby saving my mother)—in short, without understanding, yet knowing everything. Consequently, it was also my father's fault that the first loves, my father's son's first loves, came to an untimely end. He kept hovering around the loosened baby teeth, trying to catch us off guard with a mixture of threats and pleading that sounded ridiculous even back then, trust me, trust me, don't be afraid, Daddy won't hurt you, he just wants to have a look, to see if it's *wobbling*—and if in fact it was, we'd hide it with our tongues, because my father's given word meant nothing. He kept scaring us, saying our mother would not come back because they locked her in the bell tower of the church ("there she is, swinging on the ding-dong bell!"). When mother had an operation, he took the pot of hot water off the stove just once, and even then, he cursed under his breath. He slapped his hunting dog until it spit blood ("pussy-footing two-timer!"). He gave my father's fifteen-year-old son the good advice to take pictures of kulaks on their deathbeds, and the grieving family would put in an order. This from a man who never worked long enough in all his life to earn the price of a camera! He always lived as he liked, but did his darned best to take the wind out of my mother's sails, so that after a time my mother suffered pangs of conscience for every second she spent away from home. He forced me down on the sofa next to him. When my mother burst out that she can't take it anymore, she can't and she won't, he threatened to shoot everybody first (i.e., before the divorce), and then beat them to an inch of their lives, or beat them to an inch of their lives, and then shoot them. Making people cry, then ingeniously prolonging the tears, especially if they were members of the family. When he exhausted the ways of tormenting my mother, when, try as he might, he could not get her to break her bell jar of silence, he started picking on the dogs, anything, as long as he could inflict pain. He even held a gun on us. His wild and savage outbursts were followed by a phase of exhaustion and weakness, and then he'd order us to his bed and made us listen to him tell us what a good man he is, and how he'd give the shirt off his back for us, except we've been turned against him. Then, drowsy with self-pity and weeping softly, he'd drift off to sleep, et cetera.

232. At times the hopeful heir to a fabulous fortune, at times its lord and (to use a jocular expression) its captive, and at other times still,

260

just the opposite, struggling with destitution and as helpless as a man plunging from a great height—we're a busy family, a bunch of do-it-yourselfers—my father was immersed in so-called real life. He never felt compelled to reflect on his own ("I haven't got the time"). He did not keep a diary. He did not commit the current of his life to paper (how much current per how much paper?, this did not concern him), while what little correspondence of a private nature survives deals mainly with public or pecuniary matters. Every comment about my father is based on thin fact and a heavy slathering of intuition. He could make a good example of a so-called sad father of mine. He was a quiet man who wouldn't hurt a fly. He lacked the savageness and drama of depression, and he lacked the more sedate variety of the greatness and beauty of melancholy. Yet to say that he was out of sorts would not suffice. Besides, he wasn't. For instance, he'd laugh a lot. Sadness was a part of him like some shadow. (In short, the sun was always shining.) He took up a career in the military and became captain of the 52nd Infantry Regiment of the Grand Duke of Baden. His career was guaranteed; the world was padded with the family pillows. One fine day, however—on the nineteenth of May—in the town of Gainfarn in Lower Austria, he led my mother, a burgess by the name of Luise Ross, to the altar, because "as a consequence of the lees of the Freemasons, who were losing their influence by then, along with the Jacobins, who were just rearing their heads and, last but not least, the French Revolution," the aristocracy had taken to marrying women of common birth, which the family would either accept, or not. In accordance with the stringent custom of the time, it was incumbent upon my father to resign from the military, and so he resigned from the military. It never occurred to him to stand up to his family; he *came* to be opposed when he found that he'd become an embarrassment. He did not marry my mother out of defiance, and he was not swept along by blind passion to a place where he would not have wanted to be if sober. He fell in love, and married her. Marriage is like faith, he used to say. It works only if it has joy for a companion. Still, it can work in hundreds of ways. It can be made to work through self-interest, by the application of discipline, or it can be the means of diverting one's attention, it can be your daily chore, like early-morning mass. It can work and be thrown into gear for its own sake. But its real countenance, its authentic self becomes visible only if there is joy. Faith in God is joyful, he used to say. My father was not a weak-willed man, but he was not strong of will either. He did not know how to want, which is another bag of fleas. He lacked ambition, which was not to the family's liking. They considered him idle and slothful. The family did not realize that the ambition was within it, and not in its individual members. They would clamp down on a lack of personal commitment and ambition with a cool, tough hand, thereby bolstering their own impersonal ambition. His family's indignation surprised my father, but he was not indignant in return—in which case the Uncle Déneses and Aunt Josefas would have backed off fully satisfied. He merely withdrew. He disappeared from the scene, and moved into a small villa in Vienna's Theresienfeld, just like any ordinary Viennese citizen. (Second child, Csesznek branch: no big shakes financially.) My older brother Gyula would often stand with my father at the window of the small salon that afforded a view of the hilly vineyards, where the Riesling was too sour. Gyula was allowed to stand on a chair, pseudo-Empire with yew inlay (which was first covered with a narrow strip of cloth, it even had a name, Gyula rag), which brought them to the same height; they didn't talk, they watched the perfectly aligned rows of vine—beauty and industry. They rested their hands on the nape of the other, two men, and from time to time, with a gentle stirring of the thumb, they would stroke each other. At such times even my mother who, six years after my father died, married Jeromos Airoldi, would not dare disturb them. On March 2, Gyula ran a fever. It happened to be a Saturday, and my mother had gone to visit her younger sister (another person of bourgeois descent) for the weekend to Wienerneustadt, along with my older sister Myra. My father had given the servants the weekend off, said servants consisting of one cook and one maid. My father would keep getting involved in long, supposedly friendly chats with the domestic servants; he was afraid that the profound disregard he would have liked to let loose on them might show, but my father, in this particular case the Count, lacked the nerve. It's the nerve that was missing from the man who *naturally* wouldn't have given them a second thought. So my father was glad when the servants got the day off, because only then could he really be on his own, and he liked being on his own. In this sense, my mother was much more consistently an aristocrat. You were born into the wrong family, she used to say to my father, laughing. My father was in the library, reading, a favorite pastime of his. He loved English novels, especially *Pride and Prejudice,* and imagined he was Mr. Bennet, Mr. Bennet's wry wisdom, his unambitious intelligence, was close to his own heart. He felt that Mr. Bennet, too, was a sad human being. Gyula was given permission to read *along with* my father, i.e., at a distance from him, in the other half of the room, and in imitation of his father's posture, he was leafing through a history book with colored etchings. King Louis II dead in the River Csele, for instance. And the best of all, Frederick Barbarossa surveying his troops. At which point, the fever came like a flood. My brother Gyula began to shake, his brow burning up, his lips chapped. Daddy, he whispered. What?, my father yelped. Mr. Bennet was especially particular about one thing: being left in peace with his books. He didn't see and he didn't sense the danger. Go on, read. Only when the child tumbled off the chair did he look up from his book. He didn't know what was happening. Gyula gave a thump, then lay inert. First my father rang for the servants, only then did he spring to his feet. The child was lying on the carpet like a small, still animal rolled up into an incredibly small ball. This disproportionate smallness was death itself, for a moment he thought his son was dead. He shook his head. He had a facile view of the world, about order, about what is possible, and what is not. Our mothers, our fathers, yes, that's in order, it's difficult, but such is life. But a child . . . If only the servants were in the house. Or my mother. He lifted the child up in his arms. He could tell that he was alive. He watched over him the whole night, wrapped a wet rag round his wrists and ankles. By morning, the child was dead. My father could not suffer the tragedy. The following day he died, as they say, of a broken heart. He died as he had lived, he pined away. The father's heart had broken over the death of the son, this on March 5, the thirty-second year of his life. Sad.

233. My father played Satan, the Good Lord himself, in two parts, sixty minutes each with a fifteen-minute intermission, and in keeping with the custom of the times, in a decrepit old machine shop (as if the GDR had gotten into every pore), bread with onion rounds, a spritzer, but the entrance fee surprisingly steep unless you knew someone who would take you in for free. (You did.) The Good Lord was tired, fatigued, resigned (faith substitute!). He didn't trust Himself, He was like a top manager who always succeeds, yet feels it's not enough. My father, on the other hand, was in his element, his eyes sparkling with irony and wit. His teeth, his whole being sparkled. He was handsome, as handsome as a Spaniard. The fourth row was occupied by Spaniards. They didn't understand a word, but they waxed enthusiastic. They understood everything. Being Spanish, it's fabulous. The Good Lord's apprehension, that my father might chase Him out of the seventh heaven, too, was justified. He'd already chased Him out of the first six: when one heaven was saturated with sin, one of the seven deadly, and let's not go into whose fault it was, the

Good Lord immediately got cold feet and climbed one higher, or backed off, into another, cleaner one. The Good Lord didn't stand a chance against my father, whose eros (at the time) was on the rise. It filled up the stage, whereas we're talking about an amateur. But my father was hungry, while the Good Lord, by definition, was sated; my father was ambitious, full of yearning, he elbowed his way, while the Lord, like the Kádár regime: "Oh, let's hope the status quo remains the status quo!" No wonder. Eternal life has no way to slip but down. As the argument got nastier, the Lord accused my father of putting his filthy feet in everywhere (*Dreckfuss*), et cetera. He gave him a piece of His mind. My father shrugged, the Lord, as always, was right, and that's the truth, he'd put his filthy feet in it, *yes*. From the truth, i.e., from the revelation of His own self, and due to His nature and present state of indifference, the Lord calmed down, while my father, being more playful by nature, felt that this thing was trivial, and it bored him. He was also bored by what looked like his sure victory, this doing the Lord out of every one of the heavens. And my father saw that it was good—and that was too much for him. A gentleman does not bet on a sure thing, he said to the Lord, and became unhinged. It was a roaring success, though the audience consisted mostly of friends and acquaintances: the created world, plus the Spaniards in the fourth row.

234. After my father became unhinged, he thought that the scratching he'd been hearing inside the wall, which until then he thought had come from a stranger, was a personal message from God. People think he's crazy because he'd come closer to the truth infinitely more—*cf.* the scratching—than they, who have had no share in divine revelation, either because they keep cats for pets, or for some other reason. He's capable of sensing the emanations from the divine nervous system, while others are not. It's as simple as that. My father stands in the light like a shaman, dressed in women's

clothes, so that the feminine within should also be given its due. We have nothing to talk about, he said with flamboyant satisfaction, I am like Hamlet's mother. When his son asks, does she see anything there, the woman says, no, nothing. But I see everything that's there. But how does she know that what she sees is everything, that she's seeing everything that's there? The difference is me. (To make this thing clear: if we add my father to anything, we end up with everything. If we add him to nothing, ditto.)

235.  When my father became unhinged, God appeared on our threshold. Howdy folks! He became a presence not only in our daily prayers, My first thoughts of Thee, et cetera, but also in our feelings and five senses, our thoughts and our deeds. Everything turned its countenance toward the Lord. (When my father died, this ceased.) He had a hotline to God, a constant, cosmic rendezvous. A flirtation. A miracle. But it ruined his health. There wasn't a pea-size spot left on his body that didn't suffer the consequences. Every muscle ached. Everything hurt. According to my father, going nuts—though it was after he'd gone nuts that he said this—is less like an illness than a language, or speech. In short, that his condition, too, is best understood as a means of communication. In the case of illness, we speak of illness, of causes, treatments and cures, whereas they just don't understand what I am saying. Have you thought how peculiar it would be, not to say amusing, if someone were to speak French, and just because we've never heard French spoken before, we were to call for a doctor? The person in question would say, *bonjour petit poutain,* whereupon I'd attempt to comfort him, suggesting a cold water cure, diverting his thoughts to life eternal. The sentence destined to prescribe the desirable way for us to conduct ourselves, should it not contain, rather, the words "learn" and "meaning"? In his madness, my father saw himself as a person who posed a danger to God. God, who is in trouble. This is how

he called his adversary. In God's fight against my father, God was on his side, this is what my father knew.

236. And the appearance of the glory of my father was like devouring fire on the top of the mount in the eyes of his sons.

237. Is my father capable of creating a boulder so large that he himself could not raise it?

238. Why must my father be a noun? Why not a verb—the most active and dynamic of all? Hasn't the naming of my father as a noun been an act of annihilating that dynamic verb? And isn't the verb a hundred (a hundred and ten) times more rainbow-like and personal than a mere static noun? The anthropomorphic conceptions and symbols for my father may be intended to convey personality, but they fail to convey existence as life, that my father is a living be-ing. If there were such a verb, my father could be the thing in which we exist, move, in which we participate, creating our own verb. My father once answered a question saying, I am that I am. Much has been said of this self-definition, that, for instance, my father did not wish to make his name an easy prey, the expression *pater absconditus* also came up, the father who conceals himself, and also, that the answer reflects back on the questioner, i.e., that he should be satisfied with what he gets, accept his limits, and do as my father says. There could, however, be an interpretation that would start with us conceiving of the verb "to be" with relation to my father in the future tense. In which case, my father's words would be as follows: I am that I will affirm myself to be. In short, the question, who is my father, is open. Time and time again, my father will affirm himself.

● ● ● ● ●

239. My father and three surviving snapshots. On the first he is standing tall in boots with spurs and a Magyar ceremonial costume, one arm placed proudly on the hip, smiling out at us. On the second, his wedding picture, he is wearing a pin-check suit, his blond muttonchops sheared into a fashionable wedge, his wide cravat secured with a pin. He is wearing a small round hat with a narrow brim, a bird's feather stuck inside it. He is twenty-two years old, and almost as prepossessing as his father. He is radiantly strong, sober, handsome. Anyone who sees the third picture, on which he is barely forty, will find it hard to believe that he is seeing the same man. If my twenty-two-year-old father reminded the viewer of his handsome father, my forty-year-old father will remind him of another face—my grandmother's, whose features were hewn in the rough. This picture is sad not because it shows the passing of youth, but because it confronts us with the fact that the courage, too, is gone. The man looking into the camera is defeated, broken, bereft of hope, grown old before his time. This face knows that there is no help and no escape, that life is drawing to a close, and that he has accomplished nothing. My twenty-two-year-old father—you can tell just by looking at him—is the type who by all odds likes to write poems. The forty-year-old face is that of a man who has even lost his taste for books. His terrible life and terrible

mother and terrible wife of the terrible fate (Mommy) have sapped his strength, and there is no miracle in the world that could make his hunched back straight again. (The cause of my father's death: "depletion of the life force and a stroke.")

240. My family was on friendly terms with the Kosztolányi family. My grandfather conducted the autopsy on poor Géza Csáth, Kosztolányi's cousin. The mother's side of the family hails from Austria and Sátoraljaújhely. Their opinion of the young Kossuth, who was studying there at the time, was devastating. There is a family legend about a sunken barge on the Danube. Only my great-grandfather knew that its nail shipment was noncorrosive. That's how he opened his hardware store. They were also into wine making. It was my grandfather on this side of the family who taught my father's son to collect butterflies and to use a fretsaw. Once in the Zebegény woods the cyanide bottle used to hold the butterflies was lost. Much ado. My grandfather converted to Catholicism on death row, while he was minister of finance. At the age of twenty-six, my mother became a widow with two children. Before the war, she went out in hat and gloves. In devastated postwar Budapest she was an occasional street porter with a rickety baby carriage. She is seventy-eight years old today. She promised she'd give the New York Lehman collection a good look from upstairs, because it's so dear to my father's son's heart, but only its 1990 version, because unfortunately, they've reorganized it since then. My sister emigrated to Salzburg. We opened a bottle of champagne for the farewell dinner. She became a Benedictine nun. Now she's moved back home, and founded and built a convent near Kaposvár. My wife is a Ph.D. and a blonde. My father used to ski in Switzerland. He owned a motorcycle. He was a good dancer, and he loved Wagner. He died in the Soviet Union.

• • •

269

241. My father's son was still a child when he heard that my father once fell from the fourth floor. How did it happen? He was a twenty-year-old college student, and just before Easter vacation, he visited his relatives who lived in one of the old apartment houses along the Pest side of the Danube embankment. His girl cousins saw him to the stairs. He was standing on the topmost step on the fourth floor. The stairs, which had been deteriorating for a century, reached the outer limit of their endurance just then, and began to plunge downward. One of the girls, who was standing on the landing, reached out a hand. He (my father) didn't take it. He crashed along with the collapsed stairs floor by floor, and a couple of seconds later, lay unconscious on top of a wardrobe in a ground-floor chamber, among bottles of preserves. We, children, were flabbergasted when we heard the story. We probably would not have even believed it, had he not shown us the piece of chipped-off marble that got caught inside his coat pocket as he was falling, and the blue silk La Vallière cravat that was still rough to the touch from congealed blood. He survived because, guided by the instinct for survival, he grabbed hold of the balustrade that was tumbling along with him. On the other hand, its iron mountings cut his body up pretty badly. The heavy scars on his thighs and chest were visible even in old age. This is how the man who was later to become my father escaped death. When my father's son was born, my mother was seventeen years old, my father twenty-four. He (my father) surrounded my father's son like some black forest. His stature and strength were awesome. When he slammed the door behind him, the house shook to its foundation. A stir of his angry eyebrow, and your heart skipped a beat. Even his small pillow smelled of cigars. My father's son watched him sitting under the lamp, studying the chessboard. Tried to guess what he was thinking about him. Or them. Mostly, he (my father) said nothing. The sense of mystery surrounding his person grew with the years. He spent his time puttering about in

270

his studio among his test tubes and chemicals. He drilled and carved. He handymanned. He made our toys himself. He gave us Leyden bottles, wax records, fox tails, dancing elderpith puppets. He was a poor man. He gave us nature to play with. Summer and winter, he was up by five. He held his favorite cats in his arm and talked to them. Then he sat down to his piano and his reveries until it was time to take us to school. He liked Beethoven most of all. My father's son first heard Beethoven's sonatas in his sleep. When he woke up he felt a joyful buzz around the heart, but didn't know why. He'd studied in Berlin, with Helmholtz. At one time he'd written learned treatises, and in his youth, his name appeared in literary announcements. He turned to the natural sciences due to a *crise de coeur.* He fled to the countryside, too, in order to preserve his peace of mind. He was known as a man who liked a good time, but not in excess. A man who could turn a pun. One Christmas he surprised my father's son with a small theater whose wooden frame he trimmed with his own two hands, whose trapdoors he fretsawed himself, and whose props and puppets he pasted together personally. He even threw in a play he'd written in strange, convoluted rhymes. As a child, my father's son tried repeatedly—awkwardly, timidly—to get closer to him (my father). He shunned it every time. Sidestepped it. He couldn't tolerate confessions, sentimentality, emotionality. He looked down a bit on my father's son, and must have considered him a bad clown of sorts. Even as a grown man, he could love him (my father) only from a distance, by caring for him. Later on, the icon and manly ideal of my childhood stood before my father's son, broken, shriveled, gray. He glanced at him from under his lids. Offered his hand, as he always did. But my father's son would not take it. He pressed him to his bosom, showering his hands and face with kisses. Meanwhile—held against his shoulder—he turned his head away, because his tears were flowing and his lips got distorted with mute sobs. It was the first time in his life he dared embrace and kiss him, because he felt that he'd become an old man (my father). He wasn't his father anymore, but his child, in need of his protection. Later, one winter afternoon, my father's son received a cable asking him to come home because my father had suffered another attack. He was sitting on the sofa fully clothed. The hair on his broad forehead was disheveled. He appeared restless. No, overheated. As if he had a light case of champagne euphoria. He was excited as he spoke. After a while, he even recognized my father's son. Thank you for coming, he said. He made a superhuman effort to control himself. He chose his words carefully, to hide the truth. Except, it kept slipping out. He took the man who had given him life in his arm, and put him to bed. Thank you, he said. He generally said thank you for everything. He died like a gentleman. It took three days. On the last day, he lost consciousness. Then his old, strong voice returned, booming with the solitude of his childhood years. In his hallucinations he lectured and explained things to his students. X plus Y, he said, don't you see, an equation with two unknowns, and he kept pointing at something. He kept his eyes closed. In the afternoon, my younger brother, a doctor, gave him a camphor shot. He came to. He opened his incredible eyes and looked around, possibly searching for his place in the world which he was about to leave. He was as hesitant and innocent as a baby who, having newly come into the world, tries to find its bearings. He looked closely at my father's son, who was sitting on a chair by his bedside. He took his cold hand in his. Oh, son, he said at last. My poor son. What a curious coat. And he fixed his eye on the sleeves. It's got letters on it . . .

242. It happened like this. My mother was twenty-four, the ink was still fresh on her teacher's certificate, and my father twenty years her senior, and they fell passionately in love, but that's when the second Jewish law was passed, and it pertained to my father's wife,

and those bastards would have willingly separated them if they could, but as he was a good man, divorce was out of the question. My mother wouldn't have wanted it either. He'd just decided to start divorce proceedings after the siege of Budapest was over when his wife, poor woman, lost her mind and ended up in an asylum, in and out, then in again, so it was again out of the question. This went on for forty-six years. Forty-six! From time to time my mother would weep, but all in all she was reconciled to her fate. She was happy that she'd found the love of her life. Her only regret was that she had to do without the blessing of the Church. Meanwhile, at one point, they didn't see or speak to each other for eight years, because there was this silicate engineer, a fine old gentleman, and he was in love with my mother. It was hopeless, but when he fell ill, he asked Mommy to marry him, so the nice inner-city apartment wouldn't go to waste. And while he was alive, because he wasn't as ill as he seemed and thought he was, my mother would not see my father. This was a matter of honor with her. Meanwhile, the crazy woman also died, so in the end it was just the two of them, and that nice inner-city apartment. But by then they couldn't move in together, because my father had become a helpless invalid—hospital, treatments, paralysis, intravenous feeding. When he died, my mother felt that her life too had come to an end. It was hard. She could hardly bear it. She was heavy with pain. But the pain wove its spider's net round the happiness, the happiness of her life. Needless to say, my father never told my mother, he never even hinted that his wife lost her mind over my mother. It's a good thing he didn't tell her, because this would have been too much for her to bear. As for my father, in whom everything thus united, like rivers with the ocean, he thought (when he was alive) that surely, there must be someone, someone who doesn't tell him everything either, so that he, too, should be able to bear it somehow.

•  •  •

243. My father was a self-centered prick, but he could be nice, too, and definitely amusing, and in certain circles, prepossessing. Also, dangerous. For instance, he'd unexpectedly butt his opponent in the head. His alley-cat ways were mixed with the reflexes of a clever, intelligent person with a modicum of erudition thrown in. Nouveau riche bad taste was more my mother's province, though my father enjoyed her superficial airs. He told tasteless stories about the old days in a revolting manner, though not without some style, about whom they took turns screwing in company, and whom they made my uncle suck on a certain street corner, where the gas station used to be, like the woman from the pharmacy who is seventy years old now, seventy!, and no teeth either anymore, get it?!, no teeth! Perfect! Anymore! They taught their only child, a boy, that life is a battlefield, the stronger dog gets the bitch, so he might as well be the stronger dog, use his bare strength if need be, strike out, spring a trap, and so on, if need be, with brains and cunning, if need be, tell on people, lie, dissemble, organize a secret society for poleaxing the boy next door, then pledge eternal alliance and brotherhood with him behind their backs, and so on. If nobody got in his way, or he thought nobody had, my father was a first-class, pleasant sort of man. He was kind, definitely amusing, even ironic, if unintentionally, but just so. Strange. When he was ironic, it was always just so. He knew how to have a good time. He'd get people together, and he'd be the life of the party. He sang and he danced, and if he had too much to drink, his aggression didn't get worse (except with my mother. He beat the money out of her, because my mother's money was a major bone of contention. She was a rational bookkeeper, and farseeing). He'd fan the flames of the partying, if anything. He possessed what nowadays has become a rarity, the ability to enjoy himself. My father was what they used to call a true pal. Needless to say, he played soccer. He cheated unscrupulously, and he didn't mind describing at length how he'd cheated. He always set up the

teams so that his would be the stronger. Afterward he'd humiliate the losing team with no holds barred. Trampled their dignity into the dust. Made fun of them. Abased them. Brooked no opposition. If he was losing, he automatically turned on his own teammates, yelling and savagely pitching into them, mixing actual fact with overwhelming prejudice. In forty years of soccer, not once did he say I'm sorry. Not once was anything his fault. He denied the stars out of the very heavens. In his own way, he respected just one thing: the game. He had a discerning knowledge of it. He drove himself relentlessly. He ran fast enough for three (unless his feelings were hurt), and though he'd never played in a proper club, just out on the meadow, the beach, amateur fields, he had a profound familiarity with the essence of the game. He had eyes for the field, as they say. His balls had eyes. He took advantage of his extraordinary sense of rhythm, both when he kicked a header, and when he got the ball away from another player. With his long, matchstick legs, he pinched and lifted the ball away from the other players with ease. He kicked most of his goals with his head (à la Pali Orosz). If it hadn't been for him, the soccer group would have fallen apart long since. Just like in a dictatorship, after a while the players got used to the humiliation. Through the years, each attempted a rebellion or two, but—this was part of the nature of the thing—finding himself without a backup, he'd back up himself, and make himself scarce. But this happened in just one or two cases anyway. They learned to accommodate themselves to my father. This game was his, it was his Sunday morning. Everyone else was partly a guest, a stranger, and they knew it and stopped striking out against my father's whims. They understood that it was pointless, as pointless as grumbling in wintertime that it's cold, and in summertime, that it's hot. In mid-February—winter, cold!—my father discovered what he called a small knot on his back, an inch or so above the rump bone. He waved it off. Fat deposit. It tingled, it prickled unpleasantly, it throbbed. In short, there was something about this knot my father could not put his finger on. The knot was there, and it made its presence felt. I must have strained myself lifting something. Or the snow shoveling. The pain came out of the blue, treacherously, from one minute to the next. My father bent double with the pain. He walked lopsided, and within a week, he'd turned meek, his aggressiveness a thing of the past. My mother sobbed and begged him to shout at her again, call her pudding head, et cetera. You're like a stranger! The stranger looked at my mother without batting an eye. That look was like a child mature before its time, dim-witted, helpless. Three tumors, spreading like a spider's web. They'd reached the bone, too. The operation lasted twelve hours. They even removed some of the bone. They cut an $8 \times 5 \times 3$ centimeter hole in my father. The whole thing, it didn't last more than three weeks. At last my father put an interdiction on visitors. Everybody got offended. His sons, his wife, his friends. The women. (By the way, the Sunday mornings continued, except nobody cared anymore who won. When he won, and he almost always won, my father was happy the whole afternoon. This is what's missing, this happiness. It is gone forever.)

244. This pitching of my father to and fro between nothing and everything, you'd think he was doing it on purpose, I swear. Let's take a morning as an example. It is May, the light trickles onto the terrace, the light is warm, the marble floor cold, there they are, my father, his girlfriend (my mother), and his friend, enjoying the day's sleepy satisfaction. My father knows *nothing* about the difference between sour cream and kefir. He asks my mother, who explains in minute detail, with a detour into the problematics of buttermilk, cottage cheese, and heavy cream. Plus yogurt. Now Dad knows *everything*; but then he thinks hypophysis, that he's got it mixed up, he's got it in there somewhere between hypothesis and sweetbread. He asks his friend who, just like my mother, ex-

plains in minute detail. So now he's got it. Along with a buttered roll with jam. He's got that, too. It wasn't even ten yet, and he had *everything*. Yet he had *nothing*, because in the early morning Mommy sneaked out of her room, and my father's friend sneaked out of his. Yet it was he who'd brought him the news that he (my father) had been appointed sole imperial purveyor to the army. So now, *everything* depended on him, including the Moscow campaign. But later, he had *nothing* left. But then Mommy came back to us. It took nerves of steel, this pitching back and forth, I can tell you that!

245. My father had a voice like Fats Domino. Or Tamás Somló. His voice came directly from the angels, and he used it for singing. It wasn't even singing, but more like a rasp and a warble. He was always very strict. According to my maternal aunt, he didn't even love us, his sons and his daughter, because he had five children to support on fifty holds of land so barren, even the acacia would hardly grow on it, and there is no making friends where there is nothing but the sweat of your brow. He taught himself to play the violin of his own volition, but my grandmother smashed the violin across her knee, Go, till the soil, boy, she said. She wasn't angry, she just smashed it because the soil needed tilling. Later my father built himself a cither, hid himself in the dark, and played the cither without sound. He played it in the dark, without a sound. If you hummed a melody for him, he played it back to you faultlessly. An ear like Mozart, people said. My grandmother was a handsome Slovak woman. She took the milk, the sour cream, eggs, everything: kefir, buttermilk, cottage cheese, heavy cream, even yogurt, into town, to the Jewish druggist, for instance. And my father is from the druggist, that's where he got his gift for music. He's dead now (my father), but when his children hear the blues over the radio, they always think of him. When his youngest son was in the army, he got a cable saying his father's dead, he'd

better get his ass on home. (Permission granted, but if he's not dead, you'll have the devil to pay!) What is it, Mother? If you ask me, Son, he's not dead. What happened is this. My father suffered a stroke, he was taken into town to the hospital, and from there down to the morgue, because he was like a dead man, gray, still, quiet. They laid him in a sort of cassock, wrapped in a sheet. This was on Saturday. My mother goes to visit him, fruit compote and custard, no good, they tell her, what custard?, he's in the morgue, but my mother went down there anyway, seeing how she'd come all this way, forty kilometers, in a carriage. She didn't dare touch my father, but looked, walked around him; if you ask me, he's not dead—but that was on Saturday, there was no one to talk to, she went home, and we ate the custard, because custard spoils quickly. But by Monday my father got hungry, and the hunger woke him. He looked around, shit, what's this, fuck, a dead man on my right, a dead man on my left! He sat up. The cleaning lady was just coming through the door and passed out (the cleaning lady). My father lived for another ten years, but he couldn't sing anymore. We had to bathe him, because in the meantime, my mother had died. When my father fell in love with the woman next door, my mother looked on with a jaundiced eye. I could've had a sweet-smelling, educated lover, but didn't, while just look at your father rolling in the hay next door. But he didn't roll. He was just in love. Though no longer a spring chicken (cock), he was in love. One of my father's sons worked at the post office, climbing his way up the ladder to success, and when my father came in his bare feet and wide peasant pants, he pulled the curtain to close off his work station. (He was ashamed of him.) My father came home and cried. Yet he was as tough as the surrounding alkali flats. Though we got home at two in the morning because we celebrated the winning team (8 to 1), we needed to be up by four to do the mowing. He didn't care about anything, except this need. But his favorite child, the one at the post office, rebelled, We're not getting up! We'll get up at five-thirty. You treat us like . . . like slaves bound hand and foot. They stood squaring each other off, then my father bowed his head and left the room. Now then, son, he asked quietly—we were eating our midday meal under a tree and the distant church bell was ringing—we're alone now. Tell me, what's a slave bound hand and foot? I don't get it. There were about another forty holds of land left at a great distance, useless, sandy, bad soil. It yielded nothing, just sucked the life out of you. The Land of Nazareth is what my father called it. Was it because it was as far away as you or me from the Holy Land, or because of the Jewish leaser, or for some other reason, the Father, the Son, the Holy Ghost, nobody knows. Or if they do, they won't say. As he lay alone and helpless, we loved him (my father). That's when we learned we loved him. He even turned on Jani with a knife. Don't give me that garbage, Father, when you and that woman next door, et cetera. But the following day, my father apologized to him. He apologized to his own son. If you educate your sons, people on the farmstead said to him, you make enemies of them. But my father knew what it's like when a man's got the capabilities but he's forced to lead a different life. Playing the cither in the dark, without making a sound. He knew. People would ask him to sing, at weddings. He did, but he took his time. Let them talk him into it. He waited till his sons filled their bellies. We were still growing. On the way home, my mother says, bursting with pride, what you said back there, Dad, that wasn't right. My father takes her arm. He is pleased with himself. No, it sure wasn't, he says. But it was good all the same, he says. Yes, it was good, my mother says.

246. Blank, *name of no consequence,* was a faithful servant of the family. My father loved him very much. Many years later, he and my mother went to see him (time travel). The old man spent the day cleaning, cooking, preparing my father's favorite, sweetbreads in

mustard sauce. The conversation proceeded in fits and starts, but everyone's countenance beamed ceremoniously. It proceeded in fits and starts because, for one thing, my mother doesn't speak Hungarian, and my father had to act as interpreter. I'm bored out of my wits, Mati dear, my mother said, let's get the hell out of here. Meanwhile, she continued to smile stiffly, as if she were saying, what a nice place you have, dear, *name is of no consequence.* It may have been the euphoria of the sweetbread or the fatigue or interpreter's reflex that was to blame, but my father switched from German to Hungarian, and with the consistent social tone in the air said, I'm bored too, sweetheart. I'll tell the old fart we have to be off and make a beeline for the door. It was too late. There was nothing to be done. There is nothing to be done. The old servant had waited thirty, no, not that many, twenty-five years at most for this evening. It was not a bad evening. What a terrible *faux pas!* What a terrible *faux pas!* Don't worry, Your Excellency. It's my fault. I didn't realize how much time had passed. Please forgive me. I have gotten on in years. Yes, we have all gotten on in years. Time does not play favorites. We are all the same in front of the throne of time, my dear, *name of no consequence.* May I ask, Your Excellency, if the sweetbread was to your liking? The sweetbread, son, was excellent. Faultless. Impeccable.

247. He went into hiding. Like the proverbial outlaw, the *begyár,* my father went into hiding. First the wild Bakony Mountains, then the marshes, then over the Adriatic, with his entire fortune in a sack between his teeth. While in hiding, he picked up the name Hausmeister Riedel, Hansjürgen. As Hausmeister and concierge, he rented bicycles and TV sets to the tenants at reasonable rates. All goes well until the remote control goes bust. He can't resign himself to the fact that fixing the remote is more expensive than the TV set itself, though the former is appreciably smaller. This gets his goat. One of the tenants, an engineer who couldn't un-

derstand this intimate relationship between sentiment and geo-metry, asked, if it were even smaller, would his goat be gotten even more? My father left him without an answer. But the next time the tenant locked himself out of his apartment with the key inside turned halfway and no way of wangling it free and he called, scared and worried, asking for help, my father let him plead into the answering machine and didn't show up until the morning (with the engineer and his family in a hotel). When he did, he opened the door in a jiffy. But first he asked the engineer to turn his back. Why? I have my little secrets, my father said, smiling like a hyena. Knowledge is power, he added sweetly. (Once the engineer commented that in a certain sense a concierge is the same as a stool pigeon. My father nodded enthusiastically. Yes, indeed! He snoops. And gets you into hot water! Yes! The engineer shifted in place uncomfortably.) My father was basically a bad human being, a miserable louse, but basically, this never came to light, there wasn't time. If he helped, it was always with bad grace. But he helped. He'd been afraid of having to go into hiding, because he felt at home in his homeland. He didn't want to give up this prerogative of his. But after a while, he got to like being an alien. Being uprooted. The beauty of not belonging. The opportunities offered by a vacuum. What would it be like if he were in hiding like this forever? He fixed the engineer's heating without a word of complaint, but he left one of the cut-off valves open. The radiator was hot. It sizzled. Like the fires of hell. Into that lovely, pink, budding month of May.

248. According to my father, if you're a Detlev, you're either gay or a Catholic. (Not like the Jews, who have hooked noses and are generally called Kohn or Sternheim.) The Catholics are pale, like unrisen bread, and reddish-blond. As counterfeit as real pearls. Even their eyes are off. Pigheaded and debauched. Pray and pee in bed. Their parish priest (priestie) sits in the confessional behind

a curtain, waiting for the girls, screwing them on the sly. You can tell a Catholic girl by the knee socks she wears. They have to light candles all the time. Catholics are idolaters. Martin Luther threw his inkwell at Satan. Satan is Catholic. Catholics are afraid of sin and the tortures of hell. But first there's the cleansing fire. On the other hand, their rosaries have no roses in them. They love the Virgin Mary and also Jesus, who has a heart of gold (baroque). They keep kneeling during their rites, then they ring a bell, and the parish priest (priestie) sprinkles holy water all around. On Friday, meat and bologna are out. But eggs and fish are in. By the evening meal the parish priest is drunk. He drinks enough for everyone. At a baptism, he draws a cross on the newborn's brow with spittle. Their churches stink with incense. The choir members are the most pious of all. Their Christmas manger, though, is nicer than the Protestants'. On the other hand, we can drink wine with the Sacrament, and our church songs are nicer, too, especially Martin Luther's (*Eine feste Burg* and *Ein haupt voll Blut und Wunden*). So now you know everything; about the blacks, who stink and are gay, and old women, who carry poisoned candy in their handbags, and also the rat whose throat I just bit in two, the blood still dripping from between my lips. But more of that later.

249. A man, Robert Bly, told my father the story of a man who went in search of the father who had deserted them, his mother and himself, when he was a child. Everything that the man knew about his father, everything he thought about him and hated in him, too, had taken root in him through the agency of his mother. For years he looked and looked, and then when he was in his midthirties, he found himself on his father's doorstep. He rang the bell, and while the door was being opened (the key rattled in the lock), he wondered what his father would say. Maybe it would be, go, leave me in peace! He was scared and nervous. The old man recognized his son, who told him the purpose of his visit, specifi-

cally, that he would like to get to know his father, face-to-face. He would like to form an image of him, of who and what he is, and who and what he is not, because he does not wish to see his father through his mother's eyes anymore. The old man looked at his son and said, in that case, I can now die in peace. Why are you telling me this, my father asked Robert Bly. There's no why with a story, Robert Bly snapped impatiently.

250. Knocking over a glass or dropping a knife at the table, that's uncouth! The (so-called) mopping up of our sauce with a bit of bread, slathering, gauche! Slurping, chomping: slathering! Uncouth, gauche and slather—these words embodied, for my father, the modernity he hated with all his heart. It is no way to behave, he kept saying. None of you know how to behave. I can't take you anywhere. You're so uncouth, the lot of you, that if you were in a restaurant in England, they would chuck you out right away. He had a very high opinion of England. He thought it was the most civilized place in the world. There is only one (1) civilized country in the world. He used to comment over lunch on the people he had met during the day, the people he could not avoid meeting. He thought everyone a fool. A fool or a half-wit. He seemed a proper half-wit to me, he would say, criticizing some new acquaintance of his. As well as the "half-wits" there were the "yahoos." To my father, a yahoo was anyone who had gauche, awkward and bashful manners, anyone who wore the wrong clothes, who didn't know how to climb mountains or who was ignorant of foreign languages. Every action or expression of ours that he considered out of place (!) he would define as "yahooish." Sow a yahoo, reap a cockle! The gamut of yahooishness was wide: town shoes on mountain walks, striking up a conversation on a train or in the street with a fellow traveler or a passerby, talking out of the window to the neighbors, taking off one's shoes in the sitting room and warming your feet at the door of the stove, com-

plaining on mountain hikes of thirst or tiredness or sore feet, and altogether, complaining on a hike, or taking greasy cooked food on hikes and napkins to wipe your fingers. A mountain will not stand for such things! Permitted: fontina cheese (triangular, processed), jam, pears and hard-boiled eggs, tea without sugar. The tea was prepared by my father, in the open. He would bow his head frowningly over the spirit stove and shield the flame from the wind with the flaps of his jacket of rust-colored tweed that he wore all the time. The stuffing was hanging out, and it was singed around the pockets. It was also yahooish to shield one's head from the sun with a kerchief or straw hat, or to keep off the rain with a waterproof hood, or to knot a scarf around your neck; protection dear to my mother, which she would try, on the morning of the hike, to slip into the rucksack for us and herself, and which my father, if he got his hands on them, would angrily throw out again. My mother wasn't too keen on mountain hikes. The treat that the devil gives his children, she used to say, and she always did her best to stay at home, especially when it came to eating out of doors, because, like the lord and master of her home, she also liked to read the newspaper after lunch and to doze indoors on the sofa. The mountain climbing began the night before. My father assembled, and had us assemble, the appurtenances, then kneel on the ground and grease everyone's boots with whale oil. He thought he was the only one who knew how to grease boots with whale oil. Then he would go to his room to read, but would appear in the doorway from time to time, frowning suspiciously, checking on what we were up to, and complain to my mother about our maid Natalina, Your precious Natalina!, he would say, heedless of the fact that Natalina, in the kitchen, could hear every word he said. Which she did, but she wasn't the least offended by it, and when my mother offered an embarrassed apology, she waved it off, oh, the Doctor's got so much on his mind! The smell of leather in the coach made her stomach turn, and she threw up all over it a number of times. Once, to everyone's surprise, instead of imbecile, my father said, Poor, sweet Natalina.

251. When anxious and stressed, and consequently in a great hurry, my father opened his truly amazing impregnable umbrella, a gift from Pious XII for his birthday, English, a so-called family model, numbered and made by Smith and Hodges, of jacaranda wood, and started off in the pouring rain with hurried strides, a faceless woman my father had never seen before caught up with him, slipped under the umbrella, and berated him in no uncertain terms. Does my father not think it selfish to start off in the dark like that? Does he not think it behooves him as a Christian to share this incredibly ugly umbrella with his fellow men (women)? Does he not think that in a situation such as the present, it would be only proper and salutary were he to look around him, and help the poor and the downtrodden? In other words, her? No, he does not think so. And does he not think about the tears of the orphans and the widows in the ravaged villages? No, he does not think about them either. They walked on in the pouring rain in silence. My father tried to be helpful, but he was awkward, and so they both got drenched to the bone. When the woman turned the corner into a small street where my father, too, was about to turn, he (my father) commented, what a coincidence, the two of them living on the same street. Silence. Possibly, even the same house. Silence. Or the same apartment. Silence. Excuse me for asking. But you're not my wife, are you? The unpleasant woman gave a weary laugh. My father stopped. He'd reached home. He raised the umbrella slightly, releasing the woman, who continued on her way, from under the Smith and Hodges. Good night, my father said, but softly, so the woman shouldn't hear. But the woman answered all the same. My father held on to the umbrella, the family

model, with both hands. From under and inside, it was very like the sky. My father shook his head. No, no, no. My father, my mother.

252. My father had a thing for jacaranda wood, a costly, reddish-brown, heavy wood for furniture that comes from South America. Before his life went on the bend (like wheat? wheat from Bánkút, for instance? early-maturing with straight stalks?), he was a passionate student of jacaranda wood. He corresponded with a factory in Chicago as well as master carpenter Richard Swenson from London, who was known as "Dream of Palisander." He had incredible stationery, sheets and envelopes with a dreamy letter-head in intaglio print and a gorgeous watermark representing jacaranda wood. Compared to it my father's stationery, his en-velopes . . . well, you'd think the Russian had come in already). Where did the name come from? For all we know, possibly every solitary piece of jacaranda wood dreams of Master Richard han-dling it. It is hard to tell. With the English you never can tell, and it is pointless to challenge them. They insist hysterically on the passing of time, which they call tradition. As we can ascertain from the letter of Imre Janák's daughter, Imre Janák was a former social-ist electrician from Pesterzsébet who after the war, during so-called coalition times, made it to Parliament as a representative. A new nation, new people. Then he was thrown into jail. One can-not say that the tortures of the Ávó were pleasant, though Imre Janák was small-fry, a routine victim of the Communists. But a beating is a beating, bleeding in the ears is bleeding in the ears, and fear is fear. But that was as nothing compared to the suffer-ing caused by his cell mates. The substance of his suffering con-sisted of them—my father, a Catholic prelate, and a Calvinist preacher—talking, arguing, year in and year out, about the same thing, nonstop. Since Uncle Imre was anticlerical and a social democrat, he felt a pronounced antipathy, first and foremost, for

Catholics and the aristocracy. To him, my father was anathema. Even twenty years later he'd fly into a rage and accuse the Ávó (Uncle Imre) of the rarefied villainy, by no means foreign to the organization's nature, of putting him in the same cell with my father and the clergy on purpose, just to drive him insane! Yet basically, and in conformity with his temperament, my father couldn't be bothered with who belonged to which church. He did not think that one path to salvation was any straighter than another (he was, indeed, much more prone to worry himself sick over whether there was a path at all, or whether all the paths we take are really paths). But as fate would have it, he was a Papist, and he threw himself into his Papism, and would never miss a chance to make minute, stinging remarks against his Christian brethren. The Calvinist preacher from Bihar County discovered that there was a place by the name of Bihar in India, and came up with a plan to obtain jacaranda wood for the damaged local altar from the Indian Bihar, because the Indians, he reasoned, would wax emotional over the identity in the names, and that would do the trick. At which juncture my father put in, don't you worry about that inlay, Your Reverence. I have a reliable man in London, and that will do the trick. Before His Reverence could express his stiff-necked appreciation (begging being "a great humiliation," et cetera), the canon, to the extent that the size of the cell made it possible, of course, pulled my father *aside*. In my opinion, your generous offer was ill-advised, and certainly overhasty, Your Excellency. A Hungarian nobleman and a Catholic should not make offerings to a Calvinist church. My father fell to thinking, or pretended he fell to thinking. You could never be sure with him; there was—perhaps this is the best way of putting it—there was a sort of remoteness in his makeup to begin with; he stood once removed from himself, and he stood once removed from his life. He hemmed and hawed and acknowledged the judiciousness of the reprimand. But what am I to do? I've given my word. Once it's given, it's given. From then on until their release in 1956, they kept dissecting this "affair," cutting it to the bone, seeing if there wasn't some way to smooth over the dissenting contrariety between the two principles, going at it several times a day, sometimes with primary reference to Luther, sometimes the jacaranda wood. The old social democrat listened to this shallow, ingenious debate with mounting bitterness. He couldn't quite shake off the unpleasant, nagging feeling that Mátyás Rákosi may have been right after all to put the bourgeois behind bars. The days that made up these debates and the words he heard were so alien to him, my father's playful line of reasoning, the pious severity of the prelate, the insistent inferiority of the priest, he was so far removed from them in his thinking, and from the whole thing—he became so thoroughly destitute in that cell once more, that he would have liked to howl, he would have liked to knock my father's spectacles from off his nose (four and a half and five diopters strong, respectively), bite the well padded Catholic hand, and kick the lean Calvinist buttocks. He was boiling over with rage. But from then on, he too had his daily chore, trying to reconcile the irreconcilable—the sense of justice that came partly from classical social democracy and partly from his natural temperament, something that was at once elemental and painful, and the sweet, irresponsible feeling that accompanied his plan of revenge. The most important thing in prison is to make time pass. The worst feeling is if you're locked up, and one day passes after the other, while time does not pass. Imre Janák knew this. And though even years later he liked to recall his old injuries, deep within himself, he was grateful to his cell mates. When the wires had deteriorated inside the walls of my father's son's home— the house is short-circuited, the family laughed—they called him to do the electrical repairs. He and my father hugged. Who at the time was in a pitiful condition—the bends, his brain burst apart, also his heart and his life—but hopefully it didn't show. He tried to keep it under wraps (my mother especially!). The electrician did a great job, his fee was reasonable, he even gave us a bill, though at the time there was no practical advantage to it, there being no appreciable value added tax to speak of. Social democracy, too, was in a bad way. But there was nothing the electrician could do about that.

253. Just for the sake of argument, my father is not being persecuted, and he (1) knows it, but never mind, so much water under the bridge. If he continues not to be persecuted, and he (2) does not know it, i.e., he thinks he's being persecuted whereas he is not being persecuted, let's face it, that's paranoia. On the other hand, if my father is being persecuted, and he (3) is fully aware of the fact, then my father's name is Victim. A noble profession. But if he *is* being persecuted and (4) he doesn't know it, well, there's no Hungarian word for it. It is too bad that there's no word for it.

254. My father's name came about as the admixture of a personal lifestyle, historical and cultural tradition, origin and helplessness where the words "murder" and "seignorial harem" (*seraglio*) meet. Every time I say it, every time I get a chance to say it, out loud, with a din, with a shrill, strident, trumpet-tongued, sonorous, stentorian, straining, rasping, trilling, dissonant, soft, slow, piano, hoarse, wine-drenched, grating, screaming, shouting, howling, wailing, bellowing, whimpering, squealing, screeching, yelping, scheming, malicious, resentful, rancorous, savage, humming, stammering, whispering in the wind, mumbling, murmuring, muttering, with hatred, resentment, animosity, aversion, antipathy, disgust, loathing, nausea, fear, dread, repulsion, alarm, terror, horror, blind panic, rudely, crudely, softly, gently, meekly, tamely, indulgently, heartily, lovingly, tactfully, courteously, discreetly, if I get a chance to say his name, I am happy. I will say his name: Mordechai. I am happy.

•   •   •

255. When he was a little boy, my father's eldest son often heard the neighbors and relatives, especially his aunt—my mother's older sister—and also her son, who was barely four years older than him (but at that age it makes for a substantial difference), that my father is a reputable buffalo pianist. A reputable buffalo pianist. At this point, the person saying this generally laughed or winked, and often a playful argument would spring up about whether my father—as a buffalo pianist, of course—was indeed reputable, or merely noteworthy. My father's eldest son grew up in the uncertain knowledge that my father is a reputable, and in any case, a noteworthy buffalo pianist, but he didn't know if he should be proud of it, or ashamed of it. The mud that buffaloes turn up with their legs, and which then dries into a disgusting sea of lumps, that's the buffalo piano, Oskar P. said the other day. But what does that have to do with my father? As usual, Oskar P. suppressed a smile, and as always when he started to talk about words—and he talked about words often (and beautifully so)—joy and a facile, though tangible pride mixed with a sense of decorum appeared on his countenance. When he got drunk, your father would come home on all fours the back way through the fields, where the buffalo roam. Nobody was as good at it as your father. Enthusiastic, masterful, substantial. Neither Gould, nor Zoltán Kocsis. Not even János Rolla. And he doesn't even play the piano! You should be proud of your father, son. And so it came to pass, his son was proud of him.

256. The earth animal is a great big blubbering animal that sleeps. Who sleeps. Sleeps real deep, but is highly sensitive to the smell of humans. If he smells the smell of humans, he thrashes out in that direction, yet his eyes remain closed. Or better yet, he'll roll over next to the human smell and with a strong, colossal gesture enchain or fetter the person emitting the human smell. But his body

and biology and his nervous system is so constituted that the nice human warmth will put him to sleep again instantly, instantly and peacefully, and then the person emitting the human smell can proceed to free himself, like Houdini. Which is no easy task because the earth animal is a great big animal and weighs on top of the poor little human child with his great weight. But the poor child heroically frees himself every time, and that makes him happy. This was the earth animal game. It was played every Sunday morning when there were still Sunday mornings.

257. Here's a joke. My father's sitting in the coach box atop the coach. It is raining and the wind is up. It is not a tempest, just a common, unpleasant evening, a drab Wednesday. My father is shivering from the damp cold. The water is dripping from the rim of his coachman's hat—drip, drip—hesitant like a man bent on suicide before taking the fatal leap. The gilt door of the Officers' Club opens, and my father's youthful master comes staggering out. He is pale, and his white scarf shines up at the moon. My father leaps down. The young man is keeling over. My father grabs him not a moment too soon. In order to keep his balance, he's got to kneel into the puddle and the mud. He is holding his master in his arms like a child, who can't decide if he should fall asleep right then and there ("like lightning"), or give the coachman a dressing down. Weary, he decides upon the latter, while the former catches up with him. My father rises from off his knees and watches the raindrops pelt the boy's face. They could be taken for tears. All right, my angel, here we go, he says endearingly, and gently bundles him inside the carriage. He lays him on the seat, arranges his limbs, rounding them to make room for the legs, and covers him with the English blanket bought from Paris (part of Great-grandmother Roisin's dowry). Then he goes to sit in the coach box again. It is cold. He gently flicks his whip at the horses, giddyap,

my angels, giddyap. How is it, my father considers up in the coach box, that my father is a count, and my son is a count, only I am a coachman?

258. In 1917, in short, just in time, because that's when everything ended so that new everythings could begin, the Virgin (hand-in-hand with Mary) appeared to my father at Felsőgalla and imparted three secrets to him, the last of which was to have been made public in 1960. However, because of Vatican intervention, and in order not to hurt János Kádár's feelings, the third secret was never divulged, thereby saving the world from the prophetic vision of the demise of the Soviet colonial empire. The first secret gave warning of the foreseeable visit by all sinners to hell, with autobiographical overtones. The second prophesied the reforms in Russia. In order to stop the rumors about the distress signals that lay hidden inside the third secret (the end of the world in 2000, et cetera), the Vatican felt it incumbent upon itself to send a message through Bishop Ratzinger to my father last October, saying that the secret had lost its relevance. What's more, it doesn't even exist. My father had a hard time figuring this out—though he figured out that if he could figure it out, things would be easier for him. Except, he had a hard time figuring it out. But then this Ratzinger, a smart and a clever fellow, explained it to him.

259. In Romania, they erected copies of my father. I'd be hard put to say why the choice fell on my father though, as a matter of fact and statistically speaking, aristocrats are just a wee bit less nationalistic and anti-Semitic than the common folk, not because they're any hootin' superior to them, or more level-headed, possibly even more circumspect, that's not why, but because said circles never interfered with their own, the serf was a serf, regardless of whether he was a Hungarian or a Romanian; as for the Jews, they had no commerce with them, because for a long time they didn't

have to think about money, you could be wealthy without it. The basic idea was that inside each thingamajig that was built with an eye to my father's scale, at the point where the imaginary vertical line connecting the top with the base and which marks the upper third of the body, there are exceptionally beneficial energies being emitted. Made to a scale of ten to one, the version at Piteş has preserved my father's ratios, who served as the model, to perfection. The sewage water waiting to be cleaned circulates through a 1,300-meter-long network of sewers. The innumerable "miracles" begin here: though the sewers are uncovered, there are no unpleasant odors of any kind inside my father. On the contrary, those who work here swear that from time to time—for reasons no one can explain—they can smell newly mowed hay. You should see my mother making faces! The staff swear—cross my heart and hope to die!—that since they've been working there, their health has noticeably improved, social spending has doubled, and so has the GDP. There hasn't been a single instance of illness in ten years, and they'd even drawn closer to Europe. The visitors uniformly attest—here, again, my mother may be said to be the sole exception—that when entering my father, they feel euphoric and see everything through a pink haze. Shit, Dad, old boy, you're incredible! Those working in the intersection of the previously mentioned imaginary vertical line marking the upper third of said line have placed comfortable armchairs there for the benefit of those who'd like to tank up. Mice, rats, even flies and mosquitoes keep clear away from him. His interior (my father's) gives advance warning of earthquakes. Hours before the last Romanian earthquake, my father's breath became ionized to such an extent that it fluoresced in the dark. Scientists say that when placed at the "intersection," a used razor blade will self-sharpen, foodstuffs will not spoil, used oil will be renewed, gasoline octanes will go up, and women will get their periods on time. Despite tangible evidence, no one takes the merits of the case seriously. This is my father's fate—as if he could not catch up with his life. It has even occurred to him that possibly this cannot *is* his life. Yes, yes, yes: no.

260. XXX. Whether this is your first time on my father or you've been here before, welcome to this long-suffering, passionate terrain. We, his sons, are always happy to welcome new guests. We have a long history of entertaining strangers. My father is beautiful, and those who look him up regularly will agree with us as they marvel at the gentle slope of his brow, his refined fifteenth-century thoughts, or simply hope to refresh body and soul in this idyllic place. During the last century, the geographer Elek Fényes wrote of my father, "A beloved homeland to the people, for it is blessed and pleasant, and according to the folk, the most beautiful in the country." Our opinion has not altered to this day. Still, throughout the centuries, my father was never an isolated island of the region, but along with the surroundings—let's call them people, lords, serfs and lumpen proletariat—he formed an organic economic and cultural unit. We heartily recommend him to all those who do not know (did not know, could not know) him, as well as those who are well acquainted with his natural, physical and intellectual qualities. Nor must we forget those who are forever in transit. Perhaps they too will discover some small fatherly particular, the steadfast, mischievous glint of the eye, the tobacco-stain tint of the teeth, the boyish constancy of the hips, the varicose veins on the back of the legs, the pleasing roughness of the neck, its ruffian brownishness, one might say, or the noble quaintness of some of his expressions, balanced, on the double, by an everpresent, universal irony. And then there's his silence, his— one might say enigmatic silence—something that might overcome the indifference and fear hidden behind their boredom. My daddy, too, sends his love, *XXX* + 1 snapshot of the mayor (P.O.D.).

·  ·  ·

261. My father delivered his address (it wasn't a funeral oration, but more like a commendation, or his appreciation of a commendation, or a dinner speech, so that the price of the dinner—150 place settings, after all—could be deducted from his taxes) in a so-called foreign language, speaking the words and sentences of this foreign language into the microphone, letter- and inflection-perfect, but where those for whom this foreign language was not foreign (either because it was their native tongue or for some other reason), and they could have let their attention lag, my father shifted into high gear, and where they were as one, he took his time, leisurely, whereby new words and new sentences came to being in a new language without a name. Those who were listening to him—150 place settings or eighty mourning handkerchiefs, after all—could tell that my father was speaking in that certain foreign language, but didn't have the vaguest idea of what he was saying, about whom, and what, and why, and how; they could make out only two words of the entire speech, "my father" and also, "thank you very much," but this, according to my father, is enough, regardless of the views of his audience.

262. In his nervous excitement, my father let out a poop in front of Catherine, the Czarina of all the Russians. The wise czarina nodded: an honest sound at last.

263. Before my father delivered his soul back to his Maker who, some contend, is even greater than dukes and monarchs, he was as deaf as they come. Deaf as a cannonball. *Nomen est omen*, this is how it went: he was just reading one afternoon while his valet, who was the same age as himself, was busying himself around him, when the munitions factory in nearby Wienerneustadt blew up. All the windows of the castle at Pottendorf were shattered, the entire noble structure was shaking, like the pork in aspic made in Miskolc.

Meanwhile, a whole slew of housewives, chefs and hobby chefs ascertained that the pork in aspic is shaking like the castle at Pottendorf. Should they have been more sparing of the curcuma?, they wondered. My father raised his head from his newspaper, threw a glance at his faithful servant, in all the world possibly this was the face that he saw most often, and irritated, he said, You were always a faithful servant of mine, and oh, for how many years, for an eternity, is that not so? But I forbid you to fart in my presence! It is typical of this sort of story as well as the lives of the people, that the answer remains a mystery. A valet does not speak. A duke speaks. Also, fathers *will not* speak. This, too, is typical.

264. My father is a good example of a so-called really dumb father of mine. I mean it. He was known far and wide for his good heart (second-born sons are good-hearted), his sweet disposition, and also for never being on time. Being on time is the privilege of kings, he shrugged. When the king of Italy was here on a visit and my father received an invitation to the big Hungarian royal banquet, the governor's aide-de-camp called him up and begged him to be on time, just this once. Since we lived at a good distance from the royal palace ("whose tenant at the moment is a sailor"), it must've been eight hundred meters, at least, and the invitation was for twelve-thirty, my father decided that rather than leaving the poor aide-de-camp with peptic ulcers, he's going to be on time. He ordered his driver to show up in front of the house with the brilliantly shining white car precisely at noon. The passersby, who were studying their own reflections in this unusual mirror with awe, scooted off when my father appeared at the gate, all got up. The church bells just began to toll. He walked through the gate; then, at an instant, he stepped into something not quite modest in size, a big lump of a trap, an eyeful, if you will. It would have taken an expert to ascertain what kind of dog could have produced this. And it wasn't that he stepped into it; it was more

like he tripped over it. But when you're a duke or a count, and you're off to a royal banquet, and the automobile, too, is waiting, the big Daimler, you're not thinking. It is inconceivable that you might step in shit, that you will step in shit, that—to take it one step further—there is such a thing as shit. My father, however, was courageous enough to accept this truth in all its obvious and unpredictable complexity. Furthermore, he knew from experience that you don't go to the royal palace for lunch in shoes reeking of dog shit. So, as quickly as he'd come out, he now turned around and went back in for a change of shoes. Though it wasn't him who'd shit on the sidewalk, the blushing driver removed the "unimaginable" article with a small shovel, plunging it on the other side of the automobile. He then resumed his position by the vehicle, waiting at attention for his lordship my father to show. A quarter of an hour later, there he was, in immaculately clean shoes. This time, he was careful. As we have seen, one's place in the feudal pyramid is ensured even if one's acknowledgment of reality is limited. Still, "contrary to the opinion of the *Stammgastes* of the Japanese Café," not every aristocrat is a moron; my father took no risks and walked around the car, and before the terrified driver, grown just a tit sluggish by the weight of centuries of service, could open his lips to speak, once again—innocent as the day is long—he stepped into it. The driver was not irritated, he was not ashamed, and he certainly did not gloat: he burst into tears. His tears flowed like rivulets. My father—still smiling—returned to the house once again for yet another pair of shoes. All told, he was just fifteen minutes late, if that. This is when the aide-de-camp had his big moment. Your Excellency, he said leaning close to my father—and while the driver had just now whimpered, he giggled—to be perfectly honest, the invitation was for one p.m. I hope you will forgive me, he said, shooting a triumphant glance at my dad. You'd think they'd managed to get out of the war with the Germans, or something. Oh, said my father after a while in summary of what he'd just heard, in that case, not only am I not late, I'm actually early! He laughed at the aide-de-camp. The young man felt a numbness around the heart, a vertiginous whirl of sweetness mixed with bitterness, the kind he'd never felt before, nor would he feel ever again, in all his living days. For one instant, this at approximately twelve forty-seven p.m., the aide-de-camp was a happy man.

265.  My father is a good example of a so-called wide-span father of mine. His span extends from Szigliget to London. In London he was as deaf as a cannonball. He owned a beautiful silver ear trumpet, but he was too vain to use it, as a result of which not only was he shouting when he spoke, but so was the person who had something to say to him, including the Queen, who on June 23 gave a ball in his honor in Buckingham Palace. The old gentleman felt at home in his beloved England. He was acquainted with everyone and greeted long-seen acquaintances right and left with a wide smile and a booming voice. How are you? How are you? A pleasure to see you again. I thought you were long since dead! The Queen said to Lord D'Israeli: It is such a pleasure for me to see this man. He made my childhood so pleasant and colorful. If only he didn't shout like that! I have so much to say to him, but damn it, everyone would hear! At Szigliget, on the other hand, my father wandered around the village wearing old, comfortable, not infrequently stained hunting clothes, as was his custom. Once a peasant landowner, a stranger, suffered a broken carriage wheel on the outskirts of the village. A forester-type happened to come by, and offered to help. The two of them were working, and when the work was done, the peasant patted the forester on the shoulder and stuck a shining pengő in his palm. The latter thanked him and put the coin securely away, then said a courteous good-bye. To quench his thirst, the farmer stopped at the inn. He told the story

for all to hear. The inn fell very quiet. Then old man Franci Reiter spoke up: You gave him a pengő, friend? I did indeed, friend, said the stranger with pride. The men nodded, a pengő, that's good money. And do you know, friend, who the forester-type was? The stranger shrugged. Who?

266. (They found a suitable clearing and, gun in hand, the two parties positioned themselves about thirty paces' distance from each other in keeping with the custom of fighting a duel that many Hungarian writers, and practically every Hungarian writer of aristocratic origin, have described in detail.) I had an argument with a stranger, Father. It was nothing, really. I slapped him, and then he killed me in a duel near Kalugano. Please forgive me, my father wrote my grandfather in his last letter.

267. My father, the promising youth. The night before the fatal duel he set down the rules for the so-called group theory. He knew he was going to die, and he wanted to pass his intellectual abundance down to humanity. He wrote through the night. He didn't think about my mother, he didn't think about his father. He laid down the rules, that is all he could think about, the laying down. No wonder that the following day, tired, his face covered with bristle, he practically leaned into the bullet that was flying at him, and which pierced his heart, light and rapturous from the night be-fore. A beautiful death, one of the most beautiful deaths in the history of mankind (my father's).

268. I'd be hard put to say when it happened, but it happened in time; *tie-break,* to use my father's expression, before the tie-break (at Zadar). My father's mother, my grandmother, the widow, *here my father's name follows,* spoke thus: Come to my bosom, boy! He came. Go on and play, boy! He went, he played. Come 'n' eat, boy! He

came, n' he ate. Go on, do your lessons, boy! He went, he did his lessons. Come, you've been called up, boy! He came. Go on to the war, boy! He went. My boy ascended to heaven. He ascended.

269. When the liberating Russian troops—the barbarians, as the residents of the palace called them among themselves—stormed the palace, everyone fled for their lives, except for my father. If my Heavenly Father doesn't bother about me, what's the use of living? Having said that, he then walked across the Russian camp, and the Russians did not see him. Lo and behold, my father said, I am alive. I must do as the other people have done, and flee. And that's what he did. At which point a young Russian soldier spotted the fleeing man, got scared, and aimed. You don't have to aim with precision when using a machine gun, just close enough. Then he fired.

270. Thinking will get you far, my father thought, but not far enough. Not everywhere. Take this war, for instance. He started thinking about it (my father). Like a child. Or a schoolboy. They're prone to thinking about the nature of the world, instead of what they are going to do in gym class. And dead serious, he came to the conclusion—one that humanity clearly and spectacularly does not share with him—that as a Christian, you cannot make war. It's either Christian, or war. It is simply not reconcilable with loving your neighbor, because . . . because he's not buying it, there's a small loophole, namely, instead of hating the enemy, hating only his sins and abominable deeds (it is sin that turns contention to hate). A man who is being shot at is being hated. You can't go around shooting someone in the name of love, now, can you? Which leaves hatred, and he considers this hatred ridiculous. He refuses to hate on principle, worse comes to worse, only because he is fallible. So far so good. Let's not consider anyone our enemy, not even he whose enemies we are. This is a solution of sorts,

though obviously, it reduces one's chances of survival. And that's not all, because in the name of brotherly love we must show solidarity toward those who are being mowed down by those who, in keeping with the above, we do not wish to hate. It could even be, furthermore, that there is only one (concrete) path to solidarity: war. He's not saying that whoever lives by the sword dies by the sword, because there's a sentence for everything. Peace is not of this world, this too is a sentence. Aggression is the natural state of man, this, too. In short, as a Christian he must draw his sword, i.e., hate, something that, as a Christian, he cannot condone. Regardless of how he looks at it, it is simply not acceptable. Okay, there's a sentence for this, too, that life is full of contradiction. But to this extent, and this concretely? He's thinking that there's nothing more to think about; on the other hand, something must be done, he can always think about what he's done afterward. Which is not only fraught with danger, but is also alien to him (my father). To hell with humanity, he cried in his helplessness, and humanity went, and he went with it, because he knew he was no better than the rest, he's no closer than anyone else to a solution, it's just that he likes to look at things from all perspectives. Also, it worked so far, because if he couldn't come to a decision, then that was the decision. But now it won't do. This looking at things, this on the one hand and on the other hand, it's just not human, it seems. It's human to join up with your horde, and you can join up with a clear conscience only if you believe that that's where the truth lies, or at least, that it's destined and cannot be otherwise. We embrace the truth so we won't have to spit ourselves in the face. I've got no perspective, I'm just gazing ahead, gazing at the horror. There is nothing but the horror. In a war you can't say I. The intellectual level of a secretary from East Germany, that's where I'm at.

271. My father happened to be working on the manuscript he would never finish when a bunch of soldiers came looking for Germans.

They were young, practically children. They burst in with a great to-do, shouting, rushing around, and we had no way of knowing whether they were raging mad or simply making a wild time of it. My father, who speaks Russian even though he denies it, barely looked up from the manuscript, bade the officers welcome, and told them to make themselves at home, though personally he would rather not insist on it as he was, in fact, quite busy, as they could see. Working on a sort of novel. In short, *he's writing* a novel. That's right, a *roman*. Indeed? The boy in charge turned bright red and began ranting and raving about how, while they had been up to their knees in blood, mowing down the enemy— and heaven knows, it was no picnic—my father was sitting there arrogantly, no, brazenly, scribbling. And with that the boy grabbed the pile of manuscript pages and hurled it into the fire. It burned. My father let out a roar and gave the downy-chinned sol- dier a slap in the face. Then there was silence, fragile, bare. The boy headed for the door as if it were all over, but then turned back in a flash and motioned with his head, as if to say, come with me. When my father went up to him, he said softly, almost pleasantly, like someone determined to be polite, "We are going to shoot you." Just then a Hungarian officer burst in—*must have turned coat or something* and cheeky as they come—and asked what was going on. Well, naturally, my father was scared, but fear loosened his tongue, and gave him the courage to light into the officer. Who do you think you are, anyway? Who do you think you are, fool- ing with life and death, giving it, taking it? What makes you think you can do anything you like? Who is to stop us? God, for one. There is no God. Satan then. The officer laughed. If there's no God, there's no Satan. Fine. Have it your way. Maybe there is no God, and there is no Satan, there is nothing, there is nothing just you and your companions, you are the only ones that exist on this earth, you and no one else. Fine. But in that case, kindly take note that you are nothing but a bunch of filthy pigs, and may you be cursed for all time! The soldiers were bored, not so much with my father as this whole thing. They were tired, they cursed, and they left. My father sobbed, whereas generally, he loved such scenes. My mother was inside the wardrobe, trembling, afraid of being raped. The smell of mothballs still turns her stomach.

272. Words can get you drunk. Words can turn you into a wild animal. That's how, for instance, nationalism works. Not him, he'd never fall for a cheap trick like that. It's out of the question. He'd never hate anyone or be prejudiced against them just because they live on the other side of the tracks, so to speak. My mother smiled indulgently. Come, now, dear. Are you saying that you're an *übermensch*? No, not that, my father replied with wounded pride, just a *mensch,* yes, a *mensch* by all means, don't you agree? My mother shrugged. But from then on! From then on, my father stopped being the magical and awesome man that he was, and my mother considered him Hungarian in every respect, and herself an . . . er (Outlander). All the problems, strains and tribulations that life had brought their way (bringing up the children, the Rákosi regime, her period), she treated as a Hungarian- . . . (Outlander) conflict. Even back in Asia, you Magyars were no better than you should be!, she'd say to my father accusingly. Or: Your beloved, highfalutin' Kossuth! My father didn't quite understand what was going on. It perplexed him. He hemmed and hawed. Still, after a while, he began to take the Asians under his wing, *just a tit,* and even went so far as to say that he is no Kossuth fan himself, but still, he (Kossuth) can't be written off that easily. My mother screamed. Typical! You Magyars are always like this. Bumptious, arrogant! High-horsing it! But sweetheart! Don't you sweetheart me! We . . . ders (Outlanders) have known this for centuries, and have suffered more than enough under the yoke! What idiotic talk is this?, my father growled, wrinkling his beaten, Magyar brow, then retorted with something condescending about my mother's way

303

of thinking, and because by then my mother had been saying for over a month how she's an . . . (Outlander) heart and soul, the comment clearly targeted . . . er (Outlander) thinking. My mother sprang at my father and dug her nails into that Magyar monkey face of his. What did you say?! Are you trying to humiliate us, us and our ancestors, who'd been part of the civilized world when you were still softening Heidegger under the saddle?! Thus my mother, with a bitter laugh. You stupid . . . (Outlander) goose, my father, who was appreciably washed out by now said, and struck my mother across the face. Magyar brute! Barbarian! What did you say?! Pow! Bitch! My father got into the spirit of the thing. At first he'd strike my mother methodically, and on purpose, then later, only when he was in the mood. For instance, they'd be sitting at the kitchen table, panting, enjoying the peace that comes from exhaustion, as if it were over, when my father, without thinking, with a backhand, like a child, struck Mommy, Loudmouth . . . ! (Outlander!), he growled. My mother's nose and lips were bleeding, the skin on her forehead was split open. She wiped her face and heaved a heavy sigh. Lovingly, she looked at the man sitting across from her. So then. The experiment is now finished, she said. You see, you *can* get drunk on words, you dear, darling—and she held a mischievous pause—Magyar! Well, what this . . . (Outlander) cunt got from my father is something I'd rather not even think about.

273. At the gathering that was more than a function but less than a soirée held in celebration of his birthday, my father lavished his attention not on his best friend, who gave the keynote speech, but on a woman, a so-called stranger. She was at least 180 centimeters tall, and her blond hair reached all the way down to her behind, or her behind reached up to her hair. My father had found a long, light strand of hair on the inside of his lapel, and he offered it to the woman, like some silver bagatelle, or nothing. The woman,

this 180-centimeter-tall block of sensuality, was about to accept the nothing (*Blow Up*) with a friendly smile, but when she touched the hair, she shuddered with disgust. Willingness and repulsion vied with each other on her face and her body. She had no way of knowing that my father thought the strand of hair belonged to her, and he was now trying to give it back, as if in reference to some nonexistent mutual past. Though she might have been repulsed even so. Meanwhile, the keynote speaker was just going on about my father's meticulous manner of buying shoes, and demonstrated how my father goes about checking the upper skin, the lower skin, the middle skin, checking them centimeter by centimeter, followed by the fit, the flexibility, sitting, standing, lying down, walking, strolling, running, jogging, standing in place, as if growing roots; the guests laughed impatiently. My father's friend spoke well, but too long. Surprisingly, my father's response was addressed only to the shoes; objectively, he merely said that that pair of shoes was a pair of shoes even after twenty years. His friend's feelings were hurt. He shrugged, then they embraced. I feel safe when I'm with you, his friend whispered. My father hugged him again. The (approximately) 180-centimeter-tall woman had completely slipped his mind. Next morning, he'd have liked to bang his head against the wall. When it was his friend's fortieth birthday, this on March 9, they were in hiding in the vicinity of Stuttgart, fleeing, as my father said later out of abstracted self-pity, from everyone, meaning from themselves, which amounts to the same thing, two men in a tunnel. There was a full moon, they were sitting by the riverbank on the outskirts of a German village, somewhere in the vicinity of Schwäbisch Gmünd, and my father's friend, just then turned forty, chatted as if they were in someone's sitting room (in that continually self-important, object-independent, speaker-dependent ostentatious and perfidiously ironic social way of his); he gave an impromptu dissertation about women's fashion in Berlin; it was his contention that said women dress with frankness, they do not hide anything under wraps, the wraps is missing both from their vocabulary and their lives, what is is what they show you, and what they show you is what is. Clear enough, my father said. Not in the least, old boy, for instance, a French woman will show you what is beautiful. If her legs are beautiful, she will show them, if her legs are not beautiful, she will show her skirt, which is beautiful. Honesty is typically a German way of looking at things, moral, while this, the skirted, the French, is esthetic. What is is beautiful. Clear enough, my father said. The birthday boy laughed, waved him off. Just then they heard the sound of guns, practically within arm's reach, though they'd taken a thorough survey of the area before, they thought it was just the two of them, that it's just the two of them sitting there, in a strange land, under the starry sky. They should have seen a falling star, too, but didn't, besides, falling stars left my father cold, *dirty stars*, that's how he felt about them. My father's friend was frightened. He was not a coward, but he felt now that he was going to die. Don't be silly, said my father with a dismissive wave, and stubbed out his cigarette, no use being lit-up targets. Oh, said the other. Warm blood trickled on the back of my father's hand. You know, old man, his friend wheezed without altering his former sociable tone, I could never rid myself of the suspicion that the aim of Creation is not ethical in nature, it can't be, it can't be ethical, I could never, and panting, he took a great intake of breath, get rid of the thought, ever; in short, I did not conduct myself like the Lord in the case of the first pair of humans, though admittedly, we did not conduct our affairs from identical platforms. Clear enough. The man's head fell on my father's arm. Even today, he feels that light touch on his arm, that thud from the ninth of March.

274. My father is just like Piero della Francesca's father: metaphorical.

* * *

275. Ivan Toporishkin, pseudonym, my father, is ordering for every-one at the table when the waiter says, unexpectedly, I don't rec-ommend it. They all stare at him. I don't recommend it, the waiter says again, then looks everyone in the eye in turn, includ-ing Ivan Toporishkin, my father, pseudonym. Pseudonym, Ivan Toporishkin, my father, points again at dish #3012, and says, I want it. I don't recommend it, the waiter attempts for the third time, then writes it down, #3012, and heads for the kitchen. The guests, including Ivan Toporishkin, my father, burst out laughing. They laugh so hard, their foreheads touch the linen napkins that are placed standing up on their plates. The maître d' is called. I don't recommend it!, my father, Ivan Toporishkin, the pseudo-nym, says convulsed with laughter, and their foreheads touch the napkins once again. Impudence, the maître d' says. The food fi-nally comes anyway. They wave the waiter over, then dismiss him. The waiter brings the food, including #3012, to the table. I do not recommend #3012, my father, Ivan pseudonym Topor-ishkin says, lays down his knife and fork, and reaches for the nap-kin. They call the maître d', while the waiter resumes his duties. Time and time again, stories such as this give my father renewed courage (or to put it another way: fleeting moments of happiness).

276. My father got as fat as a pig. Why? Because he stuffed himself like a pig, that's why. He liked to eat. He also kept a so-called midnight kitchen, so that if His Excellency's august whim (my father's) should so dictate, he should be able to eat wild boar stew at three in the morning, or *saltimbocca alla romana*. He got so fat, the chairs had to be fortified with iron cross bars, and a semicircle had to be cut out of the table (louie katorze, you'd think it was plywood) to accommodate his belly. My father was a passionate reader. Read-ing was his life. But due to the above-mentioned obesity, his fin-gers turned into sausages. My father had to hire a so-called page turner, a young boy who turned the pages for him with great tact

and a good sense of rhythm. Consequently, my father was reading as if he were playing music. After the war, this was one of the most serious charges brought up against him, namely, that in the person of the page turner he was supposed to have humiliated the Hungarian people. The so-called page turner sobbed, I'll never have a count like him, ever again. Indeed. Of course, no-body bothered to ask him what he'd been reading. New political powers are not interested in lists.

277. My gigantic father, the giant, was sitting peacefully in front of his giant hut one evening. It is a sight to behold, the giant, my father, said after an hour had passed. I will go now, and lock and double lock all the doors of my giant hut with the great big ancient key that my grandfather had bequeathed me when I was just a babe in arms. At this point, my father fell silent. Then he said, but why? Why must I do this? For what reason? By reason of the dwarfs who again and again help themselves to what is ours under cover of the night. Mere bagatelles, they call it. Houses, friends, moun-tains. The Star of Even-Morn.

278. Just like any former chief of staff, my father could have been a night watchman several times over, but he wasn't. Never, at any time in his life, was my father a night watchman, anywhere. The man on the night shift was always late because he had a whimsical girlfriend who kept him on his toes, held out hopes of a surprise rendezvous, or ordered him to her, then sent him away to arrange the urgent inspection of her car, and that's why he was late. Is it, could it be true, he asked my father, panting from the rush, that Gauss had taken measurements to prove the existence of non-Euclidean geometry? My father started gathering up his things. He wasn't the least upset about the other's slight delay. He had as much time on his hands as any count. No. It's not true. I know personally of at least two independent studies that prove without a

shadow of a doubt that what we're up against here is a rumor spread by Sartorius von Waltershausen, who was a geologist and Gauss's bosom buddy. Dawn was on the horizon. They shook hands. A cosmic conjunctivitis had settled over the city. Or eyes red with tears.

279. The Shah of Persia gave my grandfather a talking parrot. The parrot spoke German fluently, though far from perfectly (*der-die-das* endings), certainly not well enough to be granted an intermediate-level state certificate. His colors were fabulous. Due to my father's negligence, the cat ate this parrot. In his helpless rage, my father hanged the cat. My grandfather ordered him into his presence. My father offered an apology and declared that he would willingly and stoically bear the just and impending consequences of his father's severity. Stand up, you wild and rash child, and make sure I do not see you again today. We will discuss this thing properly in the morning. My father voluntarily shut himself in his room and spent the night examining his conscience. He was afraid of the Lord, and he was afraid of his father. He was full of fear and trembling. The next morning, the family gathered for prayer in front of the profligate son's door, shutting him out, as it were, from their circle. Then they had breakfast together. No further punishment was meted out or announced, it had already come to pass. Grandfather, too, just said, Eat, child, and do not despair. Or to put it another way, my grandfather settled inside my father like a veritable *Über-Ich*. And so it goes, generation after generation, since the end of the fifteenth century. My younger brother breeds dogs. My younger sister screws around with the Shah's grandson. As for my father's eldest son—God only knows.

280. Provided we take his small weaknesses tactfully in stride, my father can be generous and playful. For some inscrutable reason, he's against dirty nails, and when certain people who shall remain

nameless shove their food around on their plate during a meal, he will not stand for it. For the love of God, he shouts when this happens, not with the thumb, and he makes a grimace to show his distaste. If you must shove it around, use the tip of your nose or your big toe! Anything, except that horrid thumb! It is mostly whims and eccentricities of this sort that make up his dislikes. Also, we have to keep quiet between nine in the morning and noon because Daddy's working, and we have to lie low between four and five in the afternoon, because he's taking a nap. To go into his study while he is pursuing his mysterious labors would amount to sacrilege of the worst kind. None of his children ever considered doing anything remotely like it. Even the smallest little mistake can get his goat (my father). It is a terrible thing to be out of favor with him, even though (or because) he doesn't like to express his disapproval in harsh words. His silence carries more weight than his lectures ever could. On the other hand, it is not easy trying to guess what he'll take objection to, what he'll jump at. My mother gives my father's sons a tongue-lashing when she sees they're up to their usual tricks—the childish dipping into the grownup jam, staining the freshly ironed sailor's shirt with ink, like pigs. My father has been known to ignore such obvious atrocities. And yet, he'll get his dander up at the most innocent mistakes. A father's authority is an awesome and unpredictable thing.

281. A great guy, a charming nineteenth-century fellow, you'd think he was Krúdy's bosom buddy; past his prime, dissipated from drink, like hamburger, that's what his flesh is like, his cheeks flaccid, his hair thinning, he's even taken to dyeing it, and his teeth are not what you'd call healthy either. Also, don't be taken in by this nineteenth-century stuff; it's no synonym for gentleman. At times an embarrassment, stinking and vulgar, my father is adorable, a charmer, a prodigious piece of shit. (The way he'll say at a party to a woman he'd never seen before, I'd like to f..k you,

dear, the way he comes out and says it, it is so beautiful, virginal, sweet and joyful, you'd think a host of angels were flying around the room—and terrible, too, for the same reason. The woman he's just addressed regards him with mute admiration or, if she *really* doesn't want anything from him, she laughs and gives a merry shrug. As he gets into his cup, he becomes progressively useless, but even though an embarrassment, he remains lovable. Have we slept together yet, you and I? When he asks he is not being provocative, he is not being obscene; the question clearly weighs heavily on his mind, about how it was, if it was.) My father is in the details. ("Your mother . . . she'd beat me if I didn't sleep with her.")

282. My father is a great cook. He composes dishes with his tongue. Others hear the music just by reading from the score, he tastes the food from just reading the recipe. (His inventions are not only generous in scope and radical, but in the traditional sense of the word, tasty. He thumbs his nose at tradition. This is his way of improving on it.) My grandfather refuses to eat his cooking. Who cooked today? This is his first question when he comes home. Our son, Grandmother says proudly. At which he turns on his heels, walks out the door, and heads for the inn across the way, where the food is inedible. My father shrugs it off with a laugh. He and his mother eat alone. The food is delicious, Grandmother says, stroking his hand. My father pulls it away. I know.

283. When my mother became part of my father's family—as my father never became part of my mother's family; it never came up, it was not even a remote possibility—my father's paternal uncle, Uncle Pityu, the reigning dukes, plus my father's younger sister, the Mother Superior of the Sisterhood of the Virgin Mary, ordered my mother, the young teacher in the yellow cotton dress, to appear before them. They wished to impress upon her who she

was (going to be) living with (my father), because my mother was clearly not aware, she *could not* have been aware, what a precious jewel in the history of the nation she'd married. A universal genius. Morality in the flesh. The apple of Miklós Zrínyi's eye. The victor of Eszék. The lord lieutenant in perpetuity of Sopron. An inheritable ducal title, and the right to marry within the royal family. At times my mother laughed, at other times she nodded gravely. Fuck you. She listened to these gloomy people looming over her and showed that she understood. She couldn't figure out why they were so afraid of her, but she made my father, the victor of Eszék, pay dearly for it. Then, as time passed, she came to see the light.

284. The average height of Icelanders, my father had read, is 182 centimeters, i.e., the probability of someone in Iceland being 172 centimeters or 192 centimeters tall is equal. When I stood on line for bread in Kolozsvár (or at Kolozsvár), I could see to the front of the line over the heads of the people. What would be the situation with me in Reykjavik? I'm not getting up today, he calmly announced to my mother, I'm not getting on line for bread today. Unperturbed, my mother continued packing. This time she didn't say what she'd used to say before, you're 193 centimeters, dear, with the probability of 1.

285. As a young man, a man thinks that he's gotten over my father. He doesn't write him off, but accepts the status quo, or hopes to turn a new leaf someday, or doesn't even hope anymore, seeing what he's like: he's the way he is (my father). But when a person is in his forties, he suddenly finds himself wondering who this man is. Father-hunger. Father-definition hunger. Naming-your-father hunger. Again and again, a person's eyes fill with tears. Father-son dance till death do you part. Before he died (my father), my father's son went to the late-night kitchen in search of the com-

mon ground of feelings and sentiments. He leaned down to my
father, who was sitting there like a king (and was incapable of
looking in the eye the fiasco that was his life). He wanted to offer
him a helping hand and to hold him close, but my father did not
reciprocate. He'd been paralyzed by the offense he'd suffered.
The role of my father was being played by the legendary József
Timár.

286. One afternoon my father, my father, who was handsome and
weak of character, came out of his room, stepped up to his eldest
son, planted a kiss on his forehead and said, I'm proud of you, son.
I had such a beautiful dream about you. I'm proud of you.

287. My father—it was chilly, a bad autumn, in the bathroom a
clammy fog, and in the pantry the lifeless, yellow leaves, ankle-
deep—slipped into his eldest son's four-poster bed, tickling and
stroking (the boy, not the bed). Planting kisses on his neck and
chest. Looking for proof of God inside the boy, except it hurt (the
boy). It hurts! My father laughed it off, and whispered in his ear
that it was high time for him (the boy) to learn what a real man is
like and what a man does, because if he doesn't learn, he'll never
be able to find himself a real man or woman but remain a withered virgin like—*mutatis mutandis*—Aunt Mia. A dry stalk. My
father's son stopped resisting. Besides, it wasn't so bad or strange,
actually, because my father wasn't as vehement now as a moment
before. But then he grabbed his hand and placed it over his penis,
which was big and hard. My father's son was terrified. He
couldn't move, especially not *there*. But my father held his wrist in
a vice. Stroke it, he said severely. And also, if he refuses (the boy),
he doesn't really love him (the father). As for it being big, it having gotten big and hard, that is only natural. It is a sign of brotherly love. Not to mention the fact that it is only right and proper
that he should be the one to show him, and not someone else, a

stranger. The family should remain within the family. My father said these words hurriedly, excitedly, whispering and kissing them into his son's neck, the nape of his neck, his cheeks, his lips, as he pressed the above-mentioned hand to the above-mentioned penis. His breathing quickened. He began sighing and panting as if he were ill. When he'd suffered a heart attack, Uncle Theo huffed and puffed and sweated in the same way, but before he died, he didn't, he got a shot, and the doc massaged him with both hands. Remembering this, my father's son quickly turned on the light and was about to call my mother, but my father stopped him cold, where do you think you're going, child of the Turkish wine and roses? This thing is just between you and me. Just the two of us. Get my drift?! And especially, not your mother. Jealous goose that she is, she wouldn't accept that it's not her turn this time. Besides of which, she wouldn't believe a word you say. He was trembling from fear, and he was crying (my father's son). Later, when he heard the panting, he was glad because he knew that it (everything, i.e., my father) was nearing the end. The first time, he vomited. Then he ran a fever and had to skip school the following day. They were just learning about the angelic doctor, St. Thomas Aquinas.

288.  Who is my father to me? A friend. A great man ("with whom I was nearly identical"). A. P. Chekhov (et cetera). A sparrow (my father is thrashing about by his son's shoes as they cross the square, following in tow, not flying away). A woman he'd seen for an instant only when they placed the tin lid on top, then led her away. The crucified lions of Carthage. David Copperfield with a sign around his neck: Beware! The boy bites! An eighteen-month-old child who froze to death in a windowless prefab apartment in 1985, while his parents were out doing the town. Irina T., who was apprehended on her way back from church, because she was supposed to have been praying for Stalin's death. A new peasant

by the name of Latzi Pál who has a maimed nose, and so he talks softly inside his nose (". . . Ih'm goin' to towhn, fohr the bahrbehr to wash ohff the bloohd, and he sahys, there's noh pious man to help me, so now they cohme to stahre"). The man with the tortured face made of plaster, lying under glass at Pompeii (covered with dust). The poet Mihály Csokonai hiding inside his mother's wardrobe in eighteenth-century Debrecen, daydreaming. Czar Nicholas I, who defined God as the last link in the service chain. A doctor who advises Chaadaiev against "bad thoughts." The Protestant preacher who, after he was set free, kept his hand round his neck till the day he died (the prelate Szelepcsényi had hit it with a sledgehammer). The painter who speaks thus: "God, who hath set fire to the wheat fields of thine enemies with foxes of the burning tails." Little Suzie on the beach in her bikini. The eternally silent extra in a silent film. An interrogator from the fifties, a "beater," by now endowed with a certain perverse charm, a lifeguard. Simplicissimus after he'd been uglified by the smallpox, and his hair too had fallen out. Richard Wagner during a performance of *Nathan the Wise* as he holds forth on the best way of burning the Jews (all of them). A bus driver who curses the passersby under his breath. The daughter of Scianus, whom the executioner, because it was forbidden to kill virgins, first raped under the scaffold. Mozart's aunt, reading Wolfgang's own entries from his diary: "I stayed home with a funnel up my ass so I could shit, it was unpleasant with that funnel up my ass . . ." (et cetera). A so-called modern youth (". . . a motherfucking bitch, that's what this fucking job is, and I fucking don't fucking like it . . ."). A dog (sold as a Scottish terrier, but it turned out it wasn't Scottish) standing in the garden every morning, looking up at the red star atop Parliament . . . weeping. The gravedigger from *Hamlet*, except he says things that aren't at all what we expect. Et cetera. My father.

• • •

315

289. The young professor's field of research was the development of European self-awareness in the eighteenth century. His mother was dying. He called her every day, but she couldn't get more than three sentences out, put together. And even then, what sentences!, the professor said to his father with a sigh. Up until then they hardly spoke to each other, except in greeting. Now they discussed the woman's condition every day. My father couldn't believe the young man's levelheadedness which, however, was not offensive (to whom?!, for whom?!), not even distant, merely—as a consequence—novel. Of course, he hardly knew him (my father's son). Instead of the usual greeting, one day the professor said, She died. In his confusion or pain, he said it in English, *she died*. My father was fumbling with the key in the lock when the professor opened the door to him, *she died* . . . They stood silently facing each other. The professor was handsome, but now his expression was barren, empty. Their eyes locked for a long time, as in a movie. Forgetting that his mother had been dead for seventeen years, my father felt as if he'd just learned of her death. Needless to say, tears flooded his eyes. After a while, the professor's, too. For a moment, my father didn't know where he was. They smiled at each other from behind their tears. No one in the world, not my mother, not his parents, brothers and sisters, not his children, friends or girlfriends, not even the black woman from Amsterdam's red-light district, were ever so close to my father, ever. There was nothing they could do about this fact, and so they didn't.

290. My father owned a so-called bachelor's pad. We might even go so far as to call it a palacette. At first he meant to give it to the Duchess Maintenau, but took it back when she grabbed the hand (or some other part of the anatomy) that was being offered and bit it, thereby humiliating and betraying my father, whereupon he bequeathed it to an African courtesan whom he'd pulled out of a

certain window in Amsterdam. But then he ran scared, not from her, but himself—the self he discovered in the black woman—and there were other tenants as well, solutions that promised to be more than temporary. Why? The answer lies not in my father's unbridled and restless and inconstant nature, but in the attraction, which he disregarded for years, that bound him to the said bachelor's pad. The need to possess it. Indeed, the moment that he kicked out the last of the women, an English journalist with four children, he and the apartment found each other, on the intellectual, physical, spiritual and personal level, too. The generous proportions of the rooms. Ye that enter here leave all despair behind! Though not quite in this shallow yet witty manner. Space is drama. It is rich and desolate. Empty. And melancholy, too. But always, participatory, creative (active, constructive). It is constantly in motion. It creates the illusion and makes you trust that you and the apartment have something in common. That the above-mentioned, the drama, the richness, et cetera, are within your domain. You set foot in the apartment, and right away, you are talented. Your thoughts, too, come into line with this state of being, they center around it. This is not the temple of art, and you are not consecrated. This thing is more untamed than that, it is more hysterical, substantial, self-centered. If you are not on your guard, it will swallow you whole. My father! When my father donated his fabulous collection of paintings to the nation—more from necessity than simple patriotism—he also had to part with this little palace. It was a sad parting. Since they had been hidden by the years, for years he had not thought about the countless objects he'd amassed through those years. Since everything was in its place, he did not notice it. But now this *place* had ceased to be, and nothing remained but the amassing, from the folk-style plates to the Megyik drawings, from the silver cigarette case from Augsburg to the small stand for mixing champagne. There was a prospective buyer, a company, one lump sum, but after some hesitation, my father would not sell. But to pack on his own—that was out of the question! And so the duchess, the African courtesan, and even the English journalist showed up to help with the packing. For a number of reasons, the mood was not what you'd call jovial. My father had to clear out of the apartment by March 28 (correction: May 5), and it didn't occur to him until the last moment that this was the anniversary of his father's death. Is this moving out my gift to him, or his gift to me? The African courtesan, who'd have long since abandoned her profession, though she remained a courtesan all the same, a wise old lady, a grandmother, gave my father a look of contempt, but also satisfaction, like after they'd made love, and said: Or maybe it's no gift. Which is how they met.

291. The Hungarians—and my father is a Hungarian—are like the Norwegians. By February they long for light and warmth, and dread the cold (they live in dread of it), and they recite mournful hymns. Nothing but cold and snow and death, for instance, while they steep themselves in melancholy. In February, my father will not speak. On the other hand, by March, when the first light of spring arrives, which is salmon-colored and feeble, he smiles mischievously, like the cat that swallowed the canary. There's no more snow, he shouts triumphantly, there is nothing, but death!

292. The fact that my father's son, as opposed to his friend Zipper, had a father, my father, earned him people's special respect, as if he had owned a parrot or a St. Bernard. He was always showing his father off. His father had bought him this, forbidden him that, or that my father wanted to speak to the teacher, to arrange a tutor. The picture of my father that took shape was disagreeable, but at the same time, a serviceable spirit. From time to time Zipper met him, and my father, in his inattentiveness, talked to him as if he were his son. Do up your collar, the wind's round to the north-

west and you could get a sore throat. Or: Show me that hand of yours; you've hurt yourself. We'll go across to the chemist and have something put on it. Or: Can you swim yet? A young fellow must be able to swim. Then he had to return his father, just as he had to return his *Swiss Family Robinson*. Every so often, they would walk around, all three. My father was much preoccupied with time (that fucking time). He had a timepiece that was justifiably referred to as a chronometer. It was a big gold watch with a lid. The dial was painted in lilac enamel, the black Roman numerals were trimmed with gold, and a clear, silvery bell would strike the hour and its quarters. It could as easily be used by a blind man as by a man who can see. He must, of course, reckon the minutes himself, my father added wittily. He laughed. Added minutes! It has already gone for forty years, day and night, and has never yet been to a watchmaker. I acquired it in Monte Carlo under highly unusual circumstances. My father's son and Zipper exchanged a look. Highly unusual circumstances! He was a man like any other, with a round black hat and a stick with an ivory handle, but there, in Monte Carlo, this particular father of mine had an unusual circumstance . . . My father ate onions when he had a headache, put spiders' webs on open wounds and trod water to cure gout.

293. What is a day in July like in Stockholm (Sweden)? A day in July in Stockholm (Sweden), according to my father: in the morning winter, at noon spring, in the afternoon summer, the country (Sweden) is transformed, the women (my mother, et cetera) divest themselves of their clothes.

294. My father's son was not being particularly contemptuous just then, he was just joking, really, about what?, that the bland cake must have been dietetic, and as such could have served no other purpose than that my father (who was on a strict diet) should eat it, et cetera, lightly, inconsequentially. My father was old and

weak. He ate and smiled. He whispered into one of his grandchildren's ear, in one ear, out the other. My father's son jumped at it, sweetly, What? the cake? Outraged, my father jumped to his feet, the chair toppled over, he swept the cake from before him, whipped cream and chocolate all over the place, and with his face distorted, he started berating my father's son, You!, he panted, you!, you scoundrel! My father's son did not rise to his own defense. He stood in place and tried to tell himself that he had no idea what was the matter, I don't know what's the matter, I don't know. Sobbing, the old man continued beating him. This happened just the other day.

•　•　•　•　•

295.  Neither a duke nor a count, and only moderately well-off, my father was the greatest lord his son had ever seen. Toward the end of the war, the family went into hiding for a time, ultimately from itself, effectively from the Russians and the Germans, which, when all is said and done, looked as if they were trying to flee the earth for the limitless moon or the Star of Even-Morn. They found themselves in Southern Burgenland where, self-assured, as if it were the most natural thing in the world, my father entered the first peasant house we came to, where they were just getting ready for their midday meal, the man at the table, his wife at the stove. Instead of a greeting, my father said in subdued military notes, *Welche Regiment?* The peasant jumped to his feet, pressed his hands to his side, raised his chin, pinned his eyes somewhere above my father's head on no-man's-land, *melge gehorsamst, Kaiser-jäger Mödling,* the Imperial Riflemen's Regiment, Sir, Mödling, Sir! My father nodded, walked over to the table, his host quickly pulled his own chair out of the way, pardon, pardon, it's still warm from my behind, and pulled over another one. My father sat down. He ate alone. Meanwhile, the two families, the peasant's and my father's, waited, and in their hearts there lurked (lay ensconced) the same two feelings: hatred and respect.

•   •   •

296. They had a song, my mother whispered sadly, her mournful tone standing in such sharp contrast to her words that her voice keeps coming back to me. Gizi stood on the table, dancing among the glasses, my father clapped and sang, Oh, Amanda, oh, why toil in a bordello, oh, when you don't need the dough? What was that?, my father asked, charmed out of his pants. Yes, my mother faltered. *Here my father's name follows,* kept slapping his knees and couldn't catch his breath from laughing, anyone who has ever seen my Aunt Amanda, always in black, with a ragged bird's head on her hat, a gift from Queen Zita, and similar to her own, carrying mysterious odds and ends in her crocheted net handbag, could associate anything with her, except for this: that she's a whore. And what did she say?, my father asked, screaming with laughter. Was there a scandal? Speak up! I shouldn't have told you this either. Everything, you make fun of everything. When this happened, Gizi would sing her reply. She sang, I toil in the bordello, oh, because I sorely need the dough! That's not funny. My father was reeling with laughter. (For the love of God, my mother said at another time, why can't you understand? Why? They were having their little fun.)

297. The high point of my father's career as an amateur photographer came when he bought himself a camera with a self-timer. Being the man with the camera, he'd been left out of the family portraits, only his shadow would slip onto one or another of the pictures. He was hoping that with the help of the self-timer he'd be in the picture, too, at last. But it was easier said than done. The self-timer worked with a glycerin pump which, as we know, is highly sensitive to heat. So then: my father fixed the camera on the tripod, positioned us, my mother and younger brothers, so he could join us, he pressed the self-timer, then ran over. Joyously expectant, the family glared into the lens. Birdsong. A light breeze stirring the leaves. An ant climbs up one of my father's son's legs. The

camera keeps mum. My brother cries because a mosquito gets in his eye. In the midst of the tortured waiting my mother asks, is it not conceivable that in the midst of the tortured waiting they might have let the all-important *click* past their ears? My father's son's body is about to atomize from the persistent itching. Birdsong. A light breeze stirring the leaves. My father, too, loses his patience, makes for the camera, but as soon as he does so, the camera goes *click*. Later, the picture shows only Daddy, minus the family. On the second attempt, the preparations for which are no less ceremonious, my father's son is overcome with uncontrollable laughter and so they do not hear the *click* and stand still for what seems like ages, but for what? The third and fourth attempts at bringing my father's family and my father into one frame as a natural, informal unity, are equally dismal failures. There was no telling when it's going to be *click,* always, like a bolt out of the blue. During the fifth attempt, the family discovered that the family was standing on top of an anthill. Birdsong. A light breeze stirring the leaves. Meanwhile, the self-timer gets overheated and is so fast, my father has to make for us with a wild bounding leap each time. After a while, there's no reaching the family before the *click,* click interruptus. Later, the developed snapshots showed the family in a grotesque entangled heap that'd put the Laocoon group to shame. These were not family portraits, but images of chaos. Whereupon my father turned to landscape photography once again; only my father's son was worse off, because my father could never succeed in showing and recording his real face on a picture. I'm out of focus.

298. My father is two or three times more ethical than the national average which, considering the present state of the nation, the decades of atheist contagion, is nothing to write home about. However, this is where we live, these are our points of reference, and two or three is two or three. For instance, he had the worst

kind of opinion of Emile Zola (he placed the emphasis on the first syllable, Zoh-la). He saw red when anyone mentioned *La Curée*. But after his death (not Zola's, not the abbé's, but my father's alas!), it turned out that he'd fathered a male child, on the sly as it were, by a girl from Sudetenland, with whose family we are still on friendly footing, though obviously, not in keeping with my father's intentions. But when he sat down by the piano, despite these two or three times, he kept singing lascivious songs, *A Virgin's Prayer* and *I Dream of a Young Man in the Reserves* (my father). Also, there was the *Aygerlaynder haltay tzoozaymen (Egerländer haltet zusammen)* as well.

299. Okay. From time to time, like a pig, smashing things, that's how drunk my father got, the brute surfacing in him, gaining the physical upper hand. A father can be very upper, and we could've been hurt. But the daddy, the Pater, the pater familias, this was never in him; he lacked this sort of authority, nor did he aspire to it. The decisions were made by my mother. My father had to ask her for money—for cappuccino—and in revenge, my mother kept the answer dangling, will she?, won't she?, paying sadism with sadism. People know the birthdays of their children. He didn't. Though to be sure, that included his own. He couldn't believe it when his eldest son turned thirty, he's thirty?, he could've just as well been twenty. Or forty. He didn't have the foggiest notion about anything, which occasioned much amusement. He earned respect as a renowned, exceptional hunter. When Baron Rothschild returned from Paris, he asked my father to accompany him on his chamois hunt, and if there were problems with the racehorses in Vienna, they sent for my father—these things we enjoyed. He did well, neglecting his practice. He'd have devoted himself to his profession only as a final resort. He put the minds of the peasants at rest. Put your mind at rest. All you gotta do is bandage it, or starve it *properly*. Don't fret, it'll be all right. No need for a vet. He didn't

keep any records, because, what for? And when he helped, he wouldn't take money. He told them to come to the pub. You can bring a couple of eggs, if you must. My mother was left to pay the bills. We were impressed. The rest of the family generally feathered their nest. We generally lived in poverty. We thought that everything was interesting, even pleasant. My father didn't give a hoot about discipline or duty. He was the inspector. He lay in bed till noon. The butchers knew this. We had to say he's on the way, he'd left a long time ago. We went to his room, pulled the quilt off him, urging him to get up, the consignment from Vienna had arrived. At first, this was embarrassing. When the phone rang, we had to say he's not in, but on a whim, he'd grab the phone away from us. This sort of thing was terrible, and we laughed. He could be really mean, there's a list, a flood of childish complaints that one never forgets. Once he tore up the star photos. He set fire to the matchbox collection. It's ridiculous, bringing this up at the age of forty-something, but still. During an air raid, he always beat us to the bomb shelter. Also, when he finished the seventh grade, my younger brother Julianus had to take a make-up exam in Latin, he broke his hand, he couldn't take notes throughout the year, and he asked our old man to help, because he knew Latin well and not just kitchen Latin, but he (our old man) wouldn't. And when my brother came home from the make-up exam, my father locked the two of them in the adult room, and began thrashing him with the dog whip like a madman, and we banged our fist on the door, which just made things worse; it was a real stupid thing to do. Because of the black and blue marks, my brother went around in long-sleeved shirts for weeks and wouldn't go to the pool either. In short, we saw that our father is unpredictable; in short, we considered this, too, like a natural catastrophe. When I was a child, the indignation went hand in hand with a sort of leniency on our part. I don't know how it is, but this "guilty—not guilty" was never strictly gauged. My father did not become a Nazi, whereas veterinarians are prone to becoming Nazis (biology, genetics). Possibly, he was saved by his innate—one might say guilty, even criminal—leanings. And most of all, by his capacity for good old style *schlump*.

300. My father's fathering was limited to Sundays. He promised he'd be there by three. Promptly at three, my father's sons looked out the window. The VW was standing in front of the house. He was in a hurry. He was impatient. But he never argued, never even said, Well, well, what's keeping you? After four minutes he just started up the car and rolled ten meters. Another four minutes, another ten meters. Finally, his children caught up, Good day, sir. My father gave a nod, Good day. Where to? To the castle of Spornheim, my father said. The Counts of Spornheim were your ancestors, part of the family tree; John the Second, Count Spornheim-Kreuznach, was the father of Walrab von Koppenstein, whose mother was the wife of a ministerial officer, whose sons, since she had no rank, could only be barons; this is the castle we're visiting today. He also mentioned a bunch of dates, and spun the threads of family relationships all the way to the present. My father's sons, on the other hand, had something entirely different on their mind, namely, who would get to sit next to my father, and who in the back. The fight for the front seat, which included the application of brute force, quick thinking and lack of character, was on until my father roared, That's enough of that!; this roar was the tip of the iceberg, and afterward, there was silence. Anyone who'd heard that silence will never forget it, ever: memories of my father.

301. In the seventies it sometimes happened that my father's eldest son would spot my father walking down Váci utca, looking at the shop windows (my father). Briefcase, glasses, white shirt. Just looking. Had come from work. Liked strolling down Váci utca.

The truth is that when his son saw him, he didn't always go over to him. He didn't always greet him. What did he feel when he saw him? Wasn't he happy? He (my father's son) wasn't living with him (my father) anymore. Their meetings were few and far between. He should have been happy to see him. Yet sometimes he would go over to him. When he did, they'd spend a few minutes chatting about inconsequential things—like when we run into a former teacher of ours, of whom we can say nothing good or bad, he was nice to us, and understanding, let's say, and he wasn't a bad teacher basically. But not good either. (There is only one important question: Can we, in the course of our lives, learn to love anyone here on Earth? Can we learn to love our parents, our children, our wives, our neighbors, our friends? Our former teachers?)

302. My father was different from other fathers. He wasn't at all like them, and his children soon caught on, they were no dummies. Other fathers eat breakfast with their family. They shop and go to the office or the factory. But not this one. He issues out of his room around noon. A sacred sanctum. Visits by invitation only. And an invitation was forthcoming only if the Magician (this is how we called him) felt like reading to us—and he felt like reading to us only when he had time, once in a blue moon, "after tea." He read very well. He read Andersen tales, and Hauff, and the Brothers Grimm. Later he also read us what he, whatchamacallit, wrote up. At least, now we knew what he was up to in the morning. His children were impressed. Thought it was real cool, my father being so diligent. Nobody made him, he didn't have a boss, and still! He had to write, or if not write, then think all the time, you could tell. This is why he was constantly absentminded, preoccupied, inconsiderate. He needed peace and quiet to think and write. He lost his temper only when this peace was shattered, otherwise never. He didn't mind the bad marks, and he didn't

327

mind our laziness or lack of manners or lies until my mother snitched on us, though she did it only as a last resort, and thus, seldom. My father's authority was mighty with us, and my mother's, which she'd throw into the fray time and again, did not lag far behind. Her irate disposition and hot temper was an inheritance from her father. (My maternal grandfather died in 1942 of pneumonia, because at the time, it was still a fatal illness.)

303. My father: brings home sugar candy, buys pencils, places in drawers, projects, covers, says, files with deerskin, withdraws early in coarse overcoats, token-punishes, brings in on time in cold overcoats, retrieves, goes out, sits, does, says, recalls, endears, compares, sits down, turns on, listens, lowers, stands up, turns on, sits down, watches, sews, gives to drink, warns, upbraids, compares, makes a mental note, underlines, inscribes, reevaluates, crosses out, reads, reevaluates once more, lends an ear, listens, inscribes, erases, borrows, inserts, closes, ponders, laughs, quotes, laughs, takes, comes in, hands out, hands out, puts down, throws, puts down, comes out with it, worries, buries, ponders, forgets, raises a pencil, puts down, writes down, speaks, keeps mum, speaks, speaks, steps out, stands out, turns out.

304. My father? Handsome, tall, distinguished, very proper, punctual, methodical, not very broad-minded or artistic, a practicing Catholic but no bigot. My mother, on the other hand, was extremely vivacious, sensitive, imaginative, lazy, indolent, nervous, almost too nervous, riddled with complexes, phobias, illusions. (The Károlyi family had numerous mental diseases. When I stayed with my grandmother in the country I was almost frightened out of my wits: the large, low house was divided into two parts, one inhabited by my grandmother, the other by her son, my mother's brother, an incurable lunatic who paced the empty rooms at night, trying to overcome his terror by strange monologues that gradu-

ally turned into curious chants and ended in inhuman screams. That lasted all night. The atmosphere was pervaded by insanity.) In those days, there was a quantity of servants, the French governess looked after the children and my mother simply gave orders to the cook, the maid, or the gardener. But that didn't stop her saying that she had "the whole household on her hands," that work was "ennobling," that the garden at the Roman Baths "is all my own work," and "fortunately *I* have a practical mind." "In my spare moments I like to read Spencer and Fichte," she would say in all sincerity, although the works of these philosophers occupied the lower shelves of the library, their uncut pages gleaming. She had nothing but admiration for everything she was not. Her ideal was the mother with intangible (Catholic) principles who concentrated on her duties and sacrificed herself for her family. She identified herself with what she admired with a truly remarkable naïveté. We, her children, rapidly discovered the best way to torment and tease her. The key was denial. We simply had to say, systematically, the opposite of whatever she might say. In the meantime, my sister and I especially became masters at it. My mother only needed to say, "the sun is shining" for us to reply in amazement: "What? Go on with you! It's raining." "You've got a mania for saying silly things!" she would answer indignantly, whereupon one of us would continue in a conciliatory manner, "Let's say that it isn't raining, but that it might rain!" And after a moment's thought one of us would add, "Let's say that it isn't raining, but that if it started to rain it would be raining, is that not so?" We pursued this standoffish ironic game with her for years. She loved us very much.

305.  My father's straight blond hair, the color of wheat, reached down to his waist, it patted his buttocks in response to his sprightly steps, like the Vietnamese women, except theirs is black. This was to him what his hat was to Joseph II, his cigar to Churchill, his glasses to John Lennon: an emblem. On the other hand, the house

was invariably pervaded with a stink like when they're burning the bristle off a pig (formerly with straw, now with a gas burner), because my father did not cut his hair or have it cut, he burned it. This, too, just like the length, he got from the women of Vietnam. Burning is healthy because it doesn't crush the strands, and the hair can breathe freely! Breathing is important for the hair! Setting fire to flies, the form of animal torture widespread among children, produces the same smell. When my brothers and I first burned a fly (during our forced resettlement), we looked at each other in surprise and cried, Daddy!

306. My father had a reputation for being a colossal prick, in the graphic and worst sense of the word. They also said he smells like ammonia and he's got abscesses under his armpits, fungus between his toes. His secretaries laughed at him behind his back. He kept asking one of them to his weekend house, timber, Czech, i.e., Czechoslovak import, but she either let it pass, or couldn't believe her ears. Finally, she asked straight out what my father had in mind. My father had in mind a good screw, i.e., that it was high time he screwed her, a straightforward answer to a straightforward question, why not put together what we've got, et cetera. But in that case what am I doing here, the secretary asked, because, I forgot to mention, by then they were at the weekend house, my father, the secretary, and her four-year-old son. Guess, my father said, placing a hand on the woman's behind. They were not on a first name basis yet. For chrissakes, will you relax! The woman did not pull my father's hand away, but she still couldn't figure out what was going on, so she started playing with her son, turning her attention to the child, who seemed surprisingly adept at a variety of parlor games. My father even commented, by way of a joke, fine, he who laughs last. When it was happening in German, he said, *ärgere dich nicht,* old boy. Still, he was reluctant to join in

330

the game; for one thing, with the exception of Monopoly, he didn't like parlor games, for another, that's not why he was there. He got his hand in motion. The other two chose colors, while he imagined what would come after, which seemed more unavoidable than exciting, zipper, oh-la-la, the works, panting, yearning, wide as the seas, loneliness and so on, but just then he caught the boy's searching (protective) glance, because although he was no genius (my father), he recalled that certain Dostoyevsky sentence with the child, and understood that this is why the woman had brought the boy along. Still, he did not remove his hand. Which is what the woman understood. The little boy had the best average. Then my father decided to put on the "aging male" record, Hungaroton, bakelite, about how lonely he is—how lonely?—in the bosom of his family. His wife cares only for the children, he's got no one to talk to at home, just television, his only human contact, though he can't get the Duna channel, besides, dear Annamária, after thirty years of marriage, the bodies don't talk to each other either anymore, we *nicht sprechen*, though he's never made a secret of the fact that the call of the body, even now, when he's on the way out, instead of in, a call to arms, Annamária!, because he's still young inside, not a youth, but he's still ready for action, within limits, of course, and with the utmost discretion, need he add, but that's no problem, this small house is right by the suburban railway, they wouldn't have to show up together. He's had an extra key made, here it is, she's just got to make sure to put it in the other way around than usual. This will cause a problem later, because they will get used to it, and the novel will become habitual, in short, this other way around will be nothing but a nuisance, but that's in the future. The other thing to remember is that on holidays the last train leaves at nine-thirty, that's important, he's even written it down for her, here, here it is, with the key. I've got a good feeling about this, my father said, stroking the

331

silent little boy's hair. Or, when it happened in German, he said, *ich habe ein gutes, ein gutes Gefüh.*

307. My father changed. My changed father shows his feelings, his ups and downs, he's not ashamed, he's not hiding inside his shell anymore. He doesn't hide affairs of the heart. He is genuine, open, warmhearted, obliging. He is no longer a control freak. He is thinking in terms of relationships between equals based on an equitable exchange of views, for instance, with regards to sharing the housework with my mother. Who, for her part, is less than one and a half meters tall. My father considers this humiliating, which is only natural. His cultural and social standing demand a minimum of a 158 centimeters. Impertinence, he screams, and he asks my mother in a genuine, open, warmhearted and obliging manner, would she mind growing a little, for God's sake, it's the least she could do. However, my mother did not grow, and so could not forgive him.

308. After the war, when he was with the police for a short time, my father bought a white horse, Eugene. He didn't mean to. He spent the day drinking with a friend in the tavern, and when he'd gotten as drunk as a rolling fart, he palmed it off on him, a bony, scraggy, old draught horse, and so decrepit, it had to be shot the next day. He shot him in the head with his service gun in Dolyna, in the back of our kitchen garden, not far from the Murányi house. No matter how hard he yanked the halter, the horse would go no farther, it stopped and bowed its head in defeat. Later on, this horse became a symbol, because my mother kept bringing it up as incontrovertible proof of my father's squandering and gullibility.

309. When my mother and my father were apart, my father could think of nothing but my mother. The more out of reach my

mother was, the more she filled my father's loving heart. My mother's absence conjured up images of her a thousand times more potent than her presence. At which point my father realized that without my mother he is nothing, a life cripple, a dead man in his own life. He realized how much he had my mother to thank for. Thank you. He realized, grasped, understood and accepted the elemental necessity that it's the two of them, together, et cetera. My father saw life at its best as some sort of give and take, proximity and distance, being near, being far, being, being. Except, my mother never left my father's side. She wouldn't budge. She felt that my father was joined to her by some sort of elemental necessity. She felt that even at the price of her sacrificing herself, she must stay within body distance. Literally. My father clearly relies on the body, following its call. Its advice above all. At times she feels she is being held in check by the two of them, my father and my father's body. At times, they seem to trap her, the way he starts begging, humbly, on the verge of tears, would my mother satisfy certain by no means natural requests of his, which then she, my mother—even if with a slight initial reluctance—satisfies, but it's no use, because from then on my father will ride that slight reluctance like a hobbyhorse. It is all he will talk about. Reluctance as betrayal, defeat, humiliation. Why can't my mother understand that it's important to him, an elemental necessity, for which he'd have given anything at that particular moment—all he possessed, his life, his salvation. Yes, he'd have even risked his salvation. But my mother hesitated. Why? It's incredible! She should have done it out of pure self-interest, if for no other reason. In short, why didn't her, my mother's body, *tell* her to do it? But my mother's body never told her to do anything. She told her body what to do. She felt that her life belonged to my father. She was sacrificing it for his sake, it's just that my father didn't realize, he hadn't grasped it, hadn't understood, hadn't made it his own. It hadn't penetrated yet. Besides of which, where's the gratitude? My father's absence filled up the universe. This is what my father called gratitude.

310. My father's, my mother's and my father's, or my mother's lover, Tomi, was an annoying fag who couldn't curb his tongue. He rambled on like a smart-ass schoolboy or a New York egghead, at times about the foundations of culture, at others about money, concretely, about a concrete inheritance, or about the waiter's cute (!) shirt, this when they had dinner together. Flies (*diptera*) came. Nervous, squeamish, disgusted, Tomi shooed them away. At this point a fly, *name of no consequence*, alighted on my mother. It was resting on her upper arm, close to the mysterious recesses of the armpit. What do you think, dear, Tomi asked turning to my mother sweet as sugar candy. Could it be—and he pointed to the fly that was, indeed, throbbing with satisfaction—is it conceivable that this is due to your feminine effluviums? My mother was aghast at such impertinence. My father, too, felt that this was over the top. And because the couple—in unison, as it were—fell silent, and only the flies were still buzzing, Tomi was left to fend for himself. A cold shiver. Then he burst out laughing, unexpectedly, oh, he whooped, you can't get a merry fart out of a sad ass, I guess, and with that—but never mind.

311. There was this Tomi once, whom my father loved with all his heart. After their first night together (i.e., between the covers), my father said, in a voice theoretically shaking with rage, practically with irritation, but in any case, held in check by his own ridiculousness, I don't care how big. It can have a hole in it for all I care. Or it can be short. But I insist that we draw up a contract stipulating my right to my own blanket! Without my own blanket I will never, do you hear me?, never sleep with you again. This hurt Tomi's feelings. But why didn't you say . . . Ha! Besides, you keep pushing me over to the side of the bed. You kept forcing me

into a twenty-two, do you hear me, a twenty-two-centimeter-wide stretch. Besides, why twenty-two, I ask you. Is it some sort of literary thing with you? Catch 22, or something? Tomi turned his eyes to heaven. Thank God I'm not your wife. Oh, if only you knew, little prick, the infinite remove that separates you from that eventuality, my father thought with sudden animosity. (He must have had a bad conscience.) This happened exactly twenty-two years ago, ha-ha!

312. My father would blush till his dying day. This drove my mother up the wall. Hypocrite! But she was wrong. My father loved to laugh. When he could think of no more to say, or when there was nothing more to be said, he'd laugh, like a teenager, in place of a shrug or an apology. Sometimes, this sudden easy laugh would supplant a whole line of reasoning. The Union needed a snapshot, everyone stood on line, like at the company doctor. Please don't laugh, the young insouciant photographer said, whereupon my father broke out laughing. He couldn't help himself. And he blushed, too. The young woman waited. Concentrate! Look into the lens! No one's ever said that to me before, my father said sweetly. The young woman waited. Having been shamed, my father looked into the lens, searching for the woman's face behind the camera. Where are you, you little bitch, he said to himself, working himself into a state. I'll concentrate until you beg for mercy! I'll concentrate you to bits, stupid goose, I'll concentrate you into atoms! I'll concentrate right through you! I'll concentrate you into the dust! We're ready, the young woman announced. Tired by now, she appeared from behind the camera. My father lowered his eyes. Hypocrite, she said. And like that.

313. One fine, serene, sunny day my mother admitted to penis envy. Which is how she and my father met. In the meantime, my mother would not stop using the stationary bike. Did you know

that ten kilometers of steady bicycling, by which I mean that I'm drenched in sweat, is the equivalent of approximately 150 calories? No, my father said, then after chewing it over, he asked how much they were, those 150 calories? One yogurt. I see. One yogurt. And so, when the next time my mother started wiggling on the bike, it was my father's turn to be envious, and envious, he said, The yogurt is on its way—short pause—down. The yogurt is on its way—pause—down. From this pause, or the way, or the down, on who knows, my mother's spirits would soar every time. Neither could abide yogurt, and this formed a bond between them (and their mutual envy).

314. My mother (they say) fell in love with her future husband, a charming Persian philologist who was her professor at Budapest University (international exchange program), and from one day to the next, from Tuesday to Wednesday, not even waiting for the weekend, she left my father. So far so good. He (my father) understood that it was reasonable for a woman to seek, how should he put it, security, stability, and what have you. But he could not understand that everything was now over between them. He couldn't understand the over and the everything, that over meant over, and everything meant everything. When years later he ran into my mother at a reception, his heart beat faster, and he tried to catch my mother's eye, but couldn't find it. He couldn't contain himself anymore, and approached my mother from behind, touching her shoulder, by way of a sign, as it were. This simple, nothing of a gesture was bursting at the seams with intimacy. Annoyed, my mother whipped her head around, like a horse when the driver pulls on the bit. Hello, my father said gentle and happy, the flood of memories bringing a blush to his cheeks. My mother acknowledged the greeting with a curt nod, then turned back to the company. With barely a touch of contempt, with barely a touch of annoyance and disgust, as if she hardly realized who this

piece of unpleasantness, this piece of tactlessness was, she shook my daddy off. My daddy couldn't believe his eyes. He grumbled. He waxed indignant. If it's over, it's over. Fine. But the past! He'd have liked to strike my mother, and he'd have liked not to pain her. Is this, then, what the end is like? This nothing. Is this all that's left once it's over? Could it be that outside of everything they shared, there is nothing at all? Nothing? This did not suit my father's constitution, because he never wanted to end anything, ever. Correction. To end it, yes, sometimes. But not to call it quits. This was his way of challenging mortality. For want of anything better, he now thought of their lovemaking, mischievously, her thighs on fire, her lips trembling, she beside herself, gulping for air, as if she were about to drown . . . From time to time she lowers her lids, and he strokes her belly and her groin, he strokes it and massages it, as if trying to grasp on the outside the thing that is inside; as if emerging from under water. Never in all his life did my father feel as comfortably secure in his manhood as he did with her (my mother). When he was old he said, Your mother's existence is not susceptible to proof. But I am honor bound to believe in it.

315. His heart skipped a beat, that's how scared he was (my father). They were playing Twenty Questions, and my mother was advancing on him like a knife through butter, just a step away from the answer, when my father took matters into his own hands. Damn it, he roared, isn't it bad enough, you're prettier than me, you're smarter than me, and oh, I nearly forgot, you're stronger, too (when they wrestled, my mother could easily wrap the old man up into a bundle, folding his leg back to his ear, I'll have you eat your glasses, little cobra, et cetera). And now you want to prove that you're even . . . Forgetting the game, my mother started giggling, No, don't, don't do that! You're doing it on purpose! Yes, yes, but I'm in trouble, my father said, playacting. In

337

short, your thighs, those noble columns of marble! . . . Stop! Don't!, Mommy screamed with delight, as if she were being tickled, Don't! I can't think when I'm bubbling over with love! It's about time, you stupid goose, my father said—to himself.

316. My father was napping on his deathbed. They'd brought in the thick, heavy candles, towers as wide as a thigh, a present from the bishopric, in this particular instance, a natural and thoughtful gesture from a relative. Everything was outfitted in purple, pure silk and broadcloth with gold thread. It is details such as these that impart a certain *je ne sais quoi* to history. My father's mind was rambling once again, his soul crying out for salvation. The end of his life's journey was hurrying near. He was at death's door. He rambled on, as if chanting, ye lovely lavenders and roses, hollyhocks, big and small, ye proud gladiolas, curly crested basils, ye tender violas, Death hath many doors, so take care, ye lovely flowers! Then he asked his son to wake him at a certain hour. The boy promised. He adored my father. When the time came, he softly sneaked into the room, and because of the candles and the deathbed, for a fleeting moment he thought he was Death, Messeur Death. Then he gently shook his father awake. At which, like the wild and frothy crest of an ocean wave, my father crashed out from under the covers and gave his son a horrendous slap. Though he'd heard about it, he'd have never believed that the thing could be true—in his pain, my father's son saw stars, one after the other, the Big Dipper, the Evening Star, and so on, and so forth. Ten years later—where was my father by then!—he asked, Why? Sorry, old boy, my father laughed, but you woke me with such pleasure, such brazen impunity. My father's son understood what my father was getting at. He could no longer remember the pleasure, but he could not rule it out. Messeur Death, is that it?!, Pow!, a resounding slap, bells in the ears.

• • •

317. My father fell silent. His father had sauntered out of time. It hasn't been a week, and it's very hard. He'd "practiced" so much, he thought he was prepared. My father loved his father very much. He needed him to be around, even if at a distance. He needed to know that he's there, even if their chats over the phone were puerile, to say the least. Even their personal meetings required long silences and not a bit of ingenuity. At first my father was put out because 70 percent to 75 percent of their conversations involved his father describing to him, in meticulous detail and with obvious relish and involvement—which you could never, ever, and I mean ever, experience any other time—the forthcoming repairs in his girlfriend's apartment, especially the fortes of repairing the bathroom, the foreseeable (!) unreliability of the repairmen, which will manifest itself, above all, in the perfidious handling of the planometer, if the Gräfin didn't have her wits about her, if she didn't know a trick or two herself—well, well!—and didn't know that they place their little finger under it (the masons, under the planometer), but the Gräfin will simply lift her little finger, and they will bow their heads in shame. My father tried various subjects, politics, foreign and domestic, finance, culture, literature, et cetera: seeing how they could not broach anything personal, either about him, or about him, still, he'd have liked to take advantage of his father's ascerbic intellect and exceptional knowledge, bringing it into play, thereby sneaking back in through the window what they'd flung so dispassionately out the door. But it didn't work. *He bored his father to such an extent, it made him blush.* And then unexpectedly, like a new paragraph, he saw, he discovered his father as a unique, nonrecurring object, a body, a unique cellular construct, a *nie da gewesen,* a unique product of Creation, a miracle of which there is simply *no other,* anywhere, neither on Earth, nor the Moon, not even in heaven. And he began studying his father methodically, from the top of his head to the tip of his toes, detail by detail, one by one, the strands of hair

separately, the fine body hairs separately, then the overall effect, the hair on the head, the hair on the body, comparing them to previous pictures, photographs, mental images: then came the perusal of the relationship of the individual elements to one another, the gestures, the facial expressions by the thousands, and more and more irresistibly, the memories, the childhood memories, the railroad station, the country fair, the merry-go-round, "the jawbone twitching," and thus a huge number of images stood at his father's disposal. Furthermore, he did not study him only when they met, but sometimes also on the sly as he stood in the March sun, tired, faint, like the light itself, or as he conducted a whispered telephone conversation with the Gräfin, an orange-colored plastic sports bag in his hand which suited him even in its preposterousness; he looked and looked and could not get his fill of him; he discovered something new about him every time, the shaving, for instance, or simply the background was different, and that made him think of something different, and this made the difference in what lay before his eyes: his father. My mother was in the throes of the green-eyed monster. She flew off the handle. She screeched. She screamed. She clawed. But my father was interested only in his father. He sat at his feet and watched him. He calculated the time. If he had about thirty years left, because he'd definitely need thirty years, his father would be 108 years old. Just enough for a fleeting glance. Or not. How did I pass the time till now, I wonder? And he rejoiced in his father once again who, for his part, was finding all this just a tad too much. He complained to his children about my father. Your brother has a screw loose. Did you know?

318. My grandfather died. My father panicked. He felt that the countdown was on, ten, nine, eight or one million and ten, one million and nine. It's all the same. The numbers were chipping away. Apropos chipping—he'd read a definition somewhere

about the infinite: that there's a huge rock the size of Gellért Hill, and a little bird alights on it every one hundred or one thousand years and ever so lightly touches its beak to the rock, and when the rock wears away, that would be like a second compared to eternity, and though it was clear that this was nothing like eternity, just a great, a very great deal, still, he thought he understood what infinity was: something horribly *different*—and the fact that time has always been chipping away, seven, six, does not make things easier. He was alone now. The next in line. He understood that it would be arrogant of him to make fun of time, because time will catch up with mockery, too, and will suddenly "taste of metal, like a silver teaspoon after the first steel bridge." He had a dream that he was his father. He discovered it when he called his father, and his father didn't answer. Of course! He's him, he's Daddy, he's him! And now . . . It hasn't been a week, and it's very hard. For one thing, this panic. For another, he loved him very much. Et cetera. My time is running out, Grandfather had said to my father last summer. But when it happens, it's different. When my father learned that my grandfather was gravely ill, he went to him right away, but by the time he got there, his father couldn't talk anymore, but my father stayed by his side for a whole week all the same. He sat there, watching his father, watching his cells. My grandfather wrote on a piece of paper: "Time has turned your eyes so fragile and porcelain-blue. And don't you go telling me it's due to biological aging. Your mother commented on this thing, too, that you can't say anything to Miklós anymore, especially not about his work. His eyes are so fragile." My father became a mature grownup, a sort of intellectual manqué. Not what you'd call a successful life. But you've got to keep up appearances, everybody does, even after the deep-seated, secure knowledge that they will stay young and immortal forever is a thing of the past. And so he founded a company, Tatr GmbH. He's got a small but enthusiastic team, three freshly hatched engineer eggs, which he's trying to develop into an even larger enthusiastic team, though he knows deep down that the larger the team, the less enthusiastic it becomes. Still, there's always hope.

319. Son, my father's father said to my father, let's have a little chat. What about? My grandfather gave a merry shrug. Whereupon my father shrugged with the same "plopping" motion of the shoulders—oh, the inheritance?—except, he was irritable. He wanted out of the tête-à-tête, and said he's busy. He was fifteen. At that age you're always busy. His father was small and weak by then. Handsome, sedate, dignified, weak. He was sitting in the garden. The size of a pear. The wasps were knocking about. Twenty years later, when she was suffering a belated memory fit, my grandmother, a whore past her prime, a common slut from Dunavarsány who'd given up her trade by then, threw her arms around my father—possibly for the first time in her life. Wasn't it touching and beautiful back then, twenty years ago, when your father asked you to have a little chat. He came to me with the news. Our son was here, and we talked for an hour. For a whole hour! I was happy, too, and for once, it didn't cost him. You made your father very happy. Your father died happy. Thank you, son.

320. She died: my mother, giving birth to my father's son. My father was sitting on the side of the bed, sobbing. She died! She died! So now you took this, too, from me! You took it from me! He brandished his fist toward heaven, then he brandished his fist at his wife. And his wife said, But the child lives! My father shrugged. Is the child yours? My father shrugged. His wife shook him with both hands. Is the child yours? Yes. Are you sure? My father nodded. Swear! He swore. Then his wife said, I will bring him up. He's already got two brothers. They died in a ski accident. They, my father's wife, and my two brothers. My father couldn't bear to live without something concrete, so he hastily married a young

342

thing, French. Seven months later she left him for a coffee merchant, a certain Baldassare Cucculi, who had a blond beard and an Alfa Romeo, the latter bought on the installment plan, plus a wife and four children in Torino. He died: five years later, my father died in a plane crash. Mother.

321. He hasn't got much left, they wrote, so my father's son hastened to see his father in the countryside, to see him for the last time. This must have been in August. They were sitting in the garden, looking at Nocsak Valley sprawled at their feet. My father was in the old "basket" chair with a blanket thrown over his knee. His pale, hoary hand, which was covered with a web of thick, blue, bulging veins, was fumbling the whole time with a piece of wicker or what have you, that had gotten free of the arm. He was clearly taking his son for one of his younger brothers or a friend of his youth, because he kept saying, do you remember when . . . but everything he was referring to happened before the boy was born. And then my father stopped spinning his yarns and turned to my father's eldest son (directly). It is not right that you never sent us any of your books. My father's son felt profoundly shamed. Needless to say, he hadn't sent the books on purpose, his way of taking childish revenge, if you will, because they just hindered them being written, if anything. He should have been more generous, of course, and above all, he shouldn't have mucked about, mixing his father into his revenge. Anyway, that's how he feels now, he thought. And the last picture, beyond the personal: the next day my father's son left. At the breakfast table or while he was packing, he couldn't help notice that my father wasn't there. Insisting that a guest should be given every consideration—he'd forgotten again that it was his son—the old man sauntered out to the front of the estate to say his farewell from there. The three hundred or four hundred meters took him half an hour. When his son reached the spot with his suitcases, my father was leaning on his

cane by the tall fir tree, the one he'd planted forty years before, and next to the old, barely legible sign: PRIVATE PROPERTY. NO TRESPASSING. His white hair fluttered in the breeze. He followed my father's son's retreating figure with an attentive gaze as the latter worked his way down into the valley.

322. ( . . . ) My father's son knew my father and he knew him not. My father was his father, and yet a stranger in the night. He didn't know what my father was really thinking, he knew nothing about his dreams, his hopes, his feelings. He ate at my father's table for eighteen years, obeyed his orders and served him, reluctantly, just as my father served others reluctantly. But who my father was, he (my father's son) still doesn't know. He doesn't know what his relationship to my mother was like, did he love her, did he not, or was he merely serving her, too, because my mother had the upper hand. He doesn't know what he thought of his sons, whom he greeted with a short grunt even after they'd been gone for a long time, ah, so you're back. When the end came, he was lying next to my mother, each in their own bed. They were sharing deathbeds, both of them ill, waiting for death. My father wanted to pass on before my mother. He insisted on it. Categorically. You cannot go until I am gone. Kindly wait your turn! For the first time in her life, in her death, my mother obeyed him. For the last time in his life, in this exceptional situation, my father had his way. (With a little help from the Heavenly Referee.) His stomach perforated, he died before my mother, and when his stomach perforated, he said this sentence: So then, it has come to pass. *(So, und jetzt ist es aus.)* This time, it was no false alarm.

323. My father's son became a successful, celebrated movie star, and as such, visited my father repeatedly in order to squeeze some acknowledgment and tenderness out of him, at least once. Long pause. I've just made a new movie, Dad. Is that so? The, *here the ti-*

*tle of the wildly successful film followed*. Oh. Pause. Did you see it? Uhum. Did you like it? Uhum. Pause. This was one of their longer conversations. Then my father asked for his beer and a shot of whiskey (?) for a chaser, my father's son slipped some money into his pocket, got into his chauffeur-driven limousine, and shuffled off to Buffalo. Years later he was told that his father saw the film with his drinking pals from the tavern, and when his son got knocked out in a scene, he buried his face in his hands, and when toward the end of the scene he was close to winning, he sprang up and hollered. Go for it, son, go for it! When he saw the ketchup, my father covered his face. But when his son was brought home from school covered in real blood, my father was standing on the other side of the street, angry and annoyed. See what comes of horsing around outside? He should have said go for it, son, go for it back then, too, but didn't. He was exceedingly proud of his son, they say. Well, it'd be too late, patting me on the shoulder now. Besides of which, he's dead.

324. (Getting to know my father: Bess, the orphan, is at the center of the story. She had to make do without parents all her life . . . Rodrigo is dead set against Ricardo giving the family jewels to Paula. Elena tells Julio that she's not in love with Ricardo anymore. Nice, who enters the room just when Rodrigo and Ligia are kissing, thanks her foster father for taking her out of the orphanage and bringing her up. Rica finds a young pullet. The young pullet is sick. Her name is Meryll. It soon turns out that Schober is keeping them illegally. Selina is planning to run away with Anthony. A woman comes to Richard's office. She is Meryll, Armstrong's first wife . . . Peter has a bad conscience because of Alex's spontaneous abortion. When he finds out that the girl wasn't even pregnant, he's filled with rage and crosses Jordan . . . Raul refuses to forgive Brittany. Ashley finishes her videotape in which she tells Abby that Victor is her biological father. Leo reels

at Vanessa's stunning revelation that Trey is his brother. Nikolas believes Luke is holding Laura prisoner, until Lucky makes him see that their mother is irrational. Truth or consequences. Reality TV. Criminal court. Red slippers. Men on women. The dance of yearning. The Peeping Tom. The sleeping tiger. Oprah. Lofty living. My tomato's got eighteen holes (brief stories of golf). The waning of the spotted hyena. Sex and the city. Four tanks and a dog. The Addams family. A gruesome twosome. Bleak house. Sunset beach. Eurosport.) A couple of years before his death, my father got hooked on television. He was a changed man. We couldn't recognize him.

325. I'm sorry about your father. Sentences like this make you cringe, even if they're sincere (the sentences). What's there to say? That there'll be some joy and laughter at the end of the road? The acceptance of the absence of order? But that's my father's story already, who'd been lying in the hospital since April, this in the unyielding, merciless vintage year of 1923, his arms and legs paralyzed by a stroke. He's touchy, he smart-asses and manipulates; he introduces his girlfriend to us, whose existence he'd been keeping under wraps for years; much ado, he introduces her to us, watching for our reactions (primitive); he trusts no one and keeps the keys hiding, playing us off against each other with respect to our inheritance, not that there's anything to inherit, but he tries just the same. How is it? Do you have to spend years preparing for this role of the wheelchair tyrant, or does it just happen? We shave him, and he lectures us, berating the world and his own condition, keeping his distance, but not without a touch of humor—and a certain furious and proud dignity. Oh, God, this very-much-us family arrogance, it boggles the mind! Every one of his children has inherited this need for dignity, plus this proud disdain. Shit!

· · ·

326. Granted that my father made fun of people who insisted that there's a world (there exists a world) independent of man, so-called reality, ergo he (as a social and linguistic construct) and science, too, are a form of faith *(Glaubensystem!)*, still he hanged the world chock-full of passionately named names and words, with the passionate referring to the hanging, yet he made no such fine distinctions when it came to crying, whether it was sobbing or sniveling, wailing or whimpering, whining or whinging, howling or shrieking, blubbering or bawling, squalling or boo-hooing—he made no distinction between spilled milk, a birdbath and a flood of tears; instead, there was crying and there was almost crying (the latter when everything is together, tearful eyes, screwed-up face, but the "thing" will not happen and is swallowed back down). He laid out a simple legal-size sheet and started counting it on there, because after he'd come home from several days in jail, where God only knows what happened, he kept crying. The counting was a sort of defense, obviously. I may cry from weakness, but not cowardice. I cry in order to keep the world's pain in equilibrium—this is the motto he jotted down on the piece of paper. Not being able to distinguish between crying at night and crying in his sleep—these he did not count. His daytime record was twenty-one, sixteen full and five half cries. (Both my father's hands were bandaged, so his eldest son—a small boy at the time, practically a babe in arms (given the above, clearly not my father's!)—drew the notches for him, four and then a fifth across, the way it's usually done. At times he asked, is that a full or a half? And—depending on the social and linguistic construct—my father would say, half, full.)

327. My father fell head over heels in love with Slovenia. My mother grumbled. My father—in keeping with the new situation, i.e., being prejudiced in its favor—made Slovenia the measure of all things. My mother shrugged. She had her suspicions, but by then even her suspicions bored her; down the years she'd come to

suspect—and this was highly unpleasant—that her suspicions regarding my father had less to do with him than with her, and this is what came to bore her. My father, on the other hand, was never bored by anything, this is what made him come out on top every time. For instance, early September?, he'd ask early into a meal, early September, isn't that when they start burning corn husks in the valleys of Slovenia?, and he'd glance at my mother as if he'd just stopped the Turkish onslaught singlehandedly at Belgrade. My mother kept silent. She had her hands full handing out the paper napkins. We always had pretty napkins, so pretty that some of our guests wouldn't wipe their lips with them. Our parents said nothing, and they said nothing when, in response, we'd smirk after wiping our lips on the Dürer reproductions. Our father blew on a napkin, which fluttered to the floor like an obese butterfly. Whereupon my father: Okay. And what's to be done in case of an icy north wind off the Adriatic? My mother couldn't believe her ears. In case of an icy north wind? Off the Adriatic?!, she kept repeating, fail-safe and irrefutable proof that my father was nuts. And let me tell you something else. The sun was streaming in the kitchen window. Raise your hand, sweetheart. Like one bewitched, my mother would often (i.e., always, her entire life) obey my father's every whim. (Needless to say, the old man never caught on.) Do you see the shadow of your hand? I do. In Solvenian it is called *shenka*. Shenka. Can you remember that? Yes. Shenka. And now, kindly stand. Good. Now walk past me. See that shadow there? Yes. Shenka. That's just it! It's not shenka, but *tenya*. If a shadow is cast by a woman, and you are a woman, and the woman is moving, and you are moving, then it's *tenya*. Admirable! Only the English, English verbs, are capable of something similar, addressing the puppeteer before five o'clock tea, in a humiliating manner, by the use of the substantive. See?! They've got a separate word for a moving feminine shadow! Tenya, that's your shadow when we go to Slovenia and the sun is shining . . . Understand?! Isn't that delightful? Will you kindly evidence some delight? This word, I brought it back especially for you from Slovenia. Can't you be happy? (Needless to say, my mother was happy, except she didn't know it, while my father, he didn't see it.) It was around this time that he started promising my mother the Lipizzaner. That he'd buy a real Lipizzaner for her. They're real horses, Spanische Reitschule + stagecoach + warhorse. They embrace all of human activity: play, work, war. The Neapolitan horses, they were like this, too. My father was trying to network his way to Archduke Karl, Regent of Carinthia, Styria, Istria and Trieste, who gave his name to Karlovac, but in vain, the Lipizzaner never came. My father talked about it constantly, he even put some of the food money aside for hay, et cetera. But how will they share the horse? For instance, Monday, Wednesday and Friday are his, Tuesday, Thursday and Saturday are my mother's. How about Sunday?, my mother asked, jumping at the chance. On Sunday we'll go half and half, my father said cheerfully. Will you kindly stop flaunting your stuff?, my mother said sharply. My father looked genuinely surprised. Why?

328. It was Easter, and Monday, but you'd think it was summer. Still, while one tree was covered in verdure, the branches of the other were reaching toward the Patou-blue sky naked, barren. Foolish April! Soon, one of my father's brothers disappeared in the war, another died in the great polio epidemic, while the third was so far away, it was as if he didn't exist at all. This was the last time they were together like this, because soon, one of them would disappear in the war, et cetera. They were sitting under the walnut tree, the bark shimmering in the light, as if it had been resurrected. They were playing chamber music, piano and the clarinet. My father was watching his brothers' faces—on them, too, the play of light, plus the joy of satisfaction. How my father hated it when they were using art in this way, how he hated this self-satisfied wallowing. Had he known, though something like this

can't be known, that they were sitting together like this for the last time, he might have been a bit more tolerant of this cloying Bach-playing, or the expression on his face might have resembled his brothers' more. He attempted to make up for this for long years afterward. But whenever he thought of his brothers, the feelings of their last time together would reappear—and with it the annoyed disdain, plus the impatience.

329. My father can't remember his father's body. List your father's body! At such times he listens like a deaf fish. Whereas it's vital. Still, he remembers some important fragments, a bath he thinks, and grandfather's floating testicles. And my grandfather's business was thus: As a true man, my grandfather lived an irreproachable life among his contemporaries and he walked with God. Then he planted the vine, because he gave himself to working the soil, and so on and so forth. To make a long story short, he got stinking drunk, couldn't stand the clothes on his back, and throwing them off, he went to the kitchen, lay down on the floor, and pressed his face against the cold marble. (Actually, just pressed sandstone, but at a third of the price.) That's good, he panted. My father had two brothers, the three forefathers, the three branches, the beginning. My father, who kept eating himself sick and snacking as if he had diabetes, he loved pizza, instant Chinese soup and wild spinach turned in oil, and so kept going in and out of the kitchen the whole day, saw the nakedness of his father, and told his two brethren without. The two went backward into the kitchen and covered grandfather's nakedness. Hussar's pelisse. And grandfather awoke from his wine, and knew what his youngest son, my father, had done unto him, and he said, Cursed be my youngest son, a servant of servants shall he be unto his brethren. And that became his name thereof. My grandfather and grandmother, while my father and his brothers were small, in short, they didn't bother with nudity, and brought rigorous rules to bear only when it

turned out that my Aunt Daisy (name to be changed), she, no, that's not it, the neighbors invited guests for my Aunt Daisy, a barbecue or whatnot, where she talked about what she'd seen in the parental home with respect to nudity.

330. According to experts, my father made his first appearance in the early twenties. My father's curly locks, parted in the middle, hide a brow of medium height; the wide ridge of the nose, which is straight and level, joins the root of the nose without curving, and from there, the gently drawn, thinning eyebrows arch toward the outer corners of the eyes. His glance is open, and his eyes, brownish in color, gaze steadfastly at the observer (my father's eldest son). The wings of the nose are thin, the tip of the nose regular. The Mercury hollow just below the medium-thick lower lip highlights a slightly convex, almost narrow chin. The glimmer of a smile on the oval face imparts a friendly appearance. The brownish hat adorned with ostrich feathers and round pearls that sits perched aslant on top of his head, the whitish-silver drop earrings, the string of pearls encircling the thin neck, as well as the armband wrought of gold crosses seen glistening on the right wrist, leads experts to conclude that my father (or his double) must have belonged to a family of some note.

331. On an oil painting that does not surpass a middling eighteenth-century Alt, and whose every attribute cries out for aquarelle, my father is smiling slyly at a woman. He is looking at her, the painter, and the Viennese Court simultaneously, which is not flattering. Meanwhile, he is leaning his head to the side, on the woman, as it were, which makes his chin hang loose, like a careless cravat, which is not flattering either. My father looks like a lascivious rabbi cut loose from his roots just before converting to Catholicism, and all the time, his expression suggests the dubious knowledge that "this isn't going to do him much good either"—and as

for the helpmate of his new career, the Imperial House, it too is headed for trouble in a big way.

332. When my father (age and physique of no consequence) dressed his father (age and physique of no consequence) in black, putting a black, ankle-length cashmere dressing-gown over the ash-gray night attire to make the general appearance appear all black, and pulled a wide-brimmed black hat over his head in order to hide as much of the face as possible, and propped him up on a forty-centimeter-tall black plinth in his bare feet, to let the stalls see the feet, and with the reluctant yet overeager help of his inexperienced but cunning assistant (age and physique of no consequence) moved his limbs about as if he were an object or an animal, trying various gestures and lights on him, as if applying the final touches to a final scene, with special attention to the humiliation, It's perfect!, my father shouted gleefully, the helplessness, It's gonna make an impact!, my father shouted gleefully, the hopelessness, trying to place these in the limelight (the same spot where his father stood); irritated, my father kept the cunning assistant on her toes, why this and why that, do it this way, do it that way, get going, asking her for a light, he never asked, but ordered her around with or without recourse to words and lashed her with his tongue when, for instance, she suggested that they place a mouth flip in my father's father's mouth, Too obvious!, he shouted irritably, Belaboring the obvious!, besides, he's due at a caucus, he had to finish positioning his father in time, they had the hat removed, on his father's head just a few tufts of hair lying lifeless, my father studied the bare skull dubiously, Needs whitening!, he ordered, the hands, which my father called paws, claws!, paws!, he laughed, Unless he clench his fists, the assistant offered, He mustn't!, my father snapped, first they withdrew the hands from the pants pockets, then raised them, joined, to the chest, then they downed the head a shade more, forward and down, or as my father said, just a jot

lower, they added to the nudity, his father shivering, He's shivering, the assistant said, my father said nothing, they rolled up the ash-gray pajama legs to the kneecaps, the kneecaps also needed whitening, they checked the lighting again, the greenhorn's suggestion that his father (my father's father) might raise his head an instant my father dismissed gruffly, Raise his head?! In this world?!, he rolled his eyes, A catastrophe!, but then surveyed the scene with satisfaction, Terrific!, he enthused, He'll have them on their feet!, he raved—and after all this had happened, because what had happened could happen, and what can happen is again and again a possibility, amid the storm of applause my father's father raised his head and fixed the audience, and then the applause faltered, died, and after prolonged silence the lights too faded out, as if nothing had happened, ever.

333. My father—a drunken pig in Winesburg—made his eldest son swear that should the situation call for it, he would finish his book (my father's). He hasn't started the book yet, but he's worked on it a lot, slaved over it, except this ceaseless politico-religious claptrap with Kollonics has drained him of energy, and though he's fighting the fight, Kollonics is unbeatable, a Catholic bureaucrat who is a prince primate into the bargain, a man like that is immortal, a man like that would . . . all right, maybe not scare, but make the Good Lord Himself sound a retreat. The basic premise behind the book is as simple, as plain as a bootjack. Unless you're careful, it can easily slip your mind. The central idea, the pith and substance, is that everyone in the world, down to the last man (woman and child) is Jesus Christ, and everyone is crucified. This is what he's bent on making clear, and his son mustn't forget it, regardless of what the future holds. He'd better not go and forget it. Is that clear?

334. (In line with contemporary fashion, in black and white.) When asked what the pith and substance of the thing is, it's heart, in short, how one could sum up this "what's it all about," this life-fiasco, despair and desperation, this present and future (impending) catastrophe, this undermined life from which (correction) they have stolen even the possibility of tragedy ("Oh, the thieves are after me, oh, they're about to pass by me!"), this trivial ballroom dance of suffering, this small-time carnival, without giving it a second thought, my father cheerfully said, Green women wrestling in a blue room.

335. Why? What on . . . ? My father hides (correction: writes), he writes in order to and with the intent of and so as to effectuate certain relationships, to erect a bridge between the heavenly lights and the taste of death. That's why, this.

336. Why? Pursuant to the heroic death of my father's older brother László, "the handsome count," and three of his cousins in that paltry battle at Vezekény, all the, *here my father's name follows,* falling like chaff, the responsibility for the family suddenly lighted upon the shoulders of my sixteen-year-old father; by nature reflective, a sedate child with a fondness for books, the repeated initiator and

participant of a variety of amateur theatricals held in the castle yard under wide, colorful canopies, he liked to sing and recite, and at night to study the firmaments through the telescope, and had intended, from the very first, that while others, i.e., his older brother, were away fighting for the triumph of the good, it being the natural consequence of their power and greatness, he would work for the good in a gentler manner, it being the natural consequence of the lack of power and greatness; he further intended to seize every advantage and opportunity inherent in having no power, and to apprehend the beauty of creation through the intellect and compose music, celestial harmonies, and above all, he would write, he would write prayers to the Immaculate Bride of the Lord, the all-merciful, and romances for the people—in short, he found himself now in his older brother's place in all respects and became, by default, a great lord, a very great lord, who never knew what it is like to open a door with his own two hands . . . The other explanation for why my father never became a writer, a poet, may be sought in my father's weak stomach. My father decided that he would become a great writer. He placed an empty sheet of paper in front of himself on his writing desk, the pen on his right, the inkwell on his left. This is how Thomas Mann did it. A page a day. It's the way great writers do it. But nothing came to mind. Then he remembered that Mann smoked cigars. He ran down to the corner and bought a very cheap, very poor quality cigar. He sat down in front of the sheet of paper again, and for the first time in his life, lit up. He smoked and smoked, down to the Buddenbrooks' stump. There's no seasickness that could have vied with my father's condition. Joseph Conrad, my father thought, but it was too late. Years later my father thought once again that he'd become a great writer, a poet. Having enrolled in college, he was just studying Sainte-Beuve in depth (whose father had died before S.B. was born). He read until his eyes were red. He was reeling with fatigue. Next he took Raymond Chandler as his ideal, who staggers into his office after a hard day's work, sits down by his desk with his trusted medicinal whiskey by his side, but just then a long-legged blonde comes into the room and makes him an offer he can't refuse. So my father went and guzzled my grandfather's jealously guarded whiskey collection (all told, one forty-year-old Old No. 7 Jack Daniel's) on an empty stomach, and thus came to hate literature with a passion. If writing is this nauseating abhorrence, this alienation turned upon itself which is chaotically itself and yet is as objective, real, and substantial as this early-morning's vomit, then he'd rather not. If it's like that, he'd rather not open a door with his own two hands. He'd rather be made palatine.

337. My father asked his children to give a sentence about their father. Specifically, if they had to give a sentence (word, story), what would it be? It's important to him, it'd bear with importance, but they mustn't make a big deal out of it, meaning, they mustn't think about the responsibility. Let him, my father, worry about that. After all, what's a father for? They (his children) can even lie if it's easier for them, though it won't be, he should know. But it makes no difference, it's him who will have to turn them all—the truths and the falsehoods—into the truth. His children said nothing. They couldn't figure out what he was talking about. He (my father) tried to help. For instance, if he should die. If I died, what would you say then? Too bad.

338. My father says: Did you love me? He says: For once in my life I wanted to enjoy myself like other people, but it didn't happen. He says: Whatever I may have said, Father, I am sorry. He says: When I think who came before and who came after, it's not that bad! (Horthy; before him Béla Kun, after him, Szálasi.) He says: When they're pumping you, it makes a hell of a difference which side of the Browning you're on. (He was drunk.) He says: We have seen

every country in Europe and all their capitals. (He was quoting Grandmother.) He says: "At such times a man either takes to drink or fathers a child." "It'd been better if you had taken to drink." (Who says that to whom?) He says: I do not wish to break my earthly binds. He says: Do not despise me! Do not despise me! He says: I am not about to explain to you why, despite our losing the country to the Turk in 1562 at Mohács, life is beautiful. He says: I have not yet tired of my search for God. (He said dead-tired.) He says: We have no tragedy inside. At times this is modern, at times anachronistic. At times this is inspired, at times superficial. He says: The country was repeatedly fighting for its independence, while we (the family) were repeatedly talking about freedom. He says: I will now go pee, just to nettle you! He says: My typewriter repairman has died. What is to become of me now? He says: Stop messing with my hand, I'm not dying. (He said in the hour of his death.) My father.

339. Let's proceed step by step, though it's all a big jumble, which is not surprising. When my father's father died, it took my father by surprise. Well, I'll be!, he said, and he kept whipping his head right and left like a birdie that's been punched in the nose, whereas he shouldn't have, everything was fine, except for the fact that it happened. My grandfather was of a certain age (seventy-nine, the same age as his mother and father when they died), while my father was at the age when a man (if ever) is strong (a veritable golden fleece inside, et cetera). You couldn't complain about the manner of his death either. The old gentleman finished his midday meal, heard the land steward's report (he didn't make the decisions anymore, but he wanted to know what it is he is not deciding about), then—a recent habit—he lay down for a short afternoon nap and—basically—he woke up to find he'd died. He was about to go downstairs for his afternoon snack, took one step, and collapsed. The doctor—a gifted peasant boy whose

357

studies in Amsterdam were financed by the family—said that death was instantaneous and he didn't suffer. He couldn't remember when he'd seen such serenity on a dead man's face before. Later, when my mother died, the surprise was not forthcoming; he (my father) just looked chagrined, like when he's displeased with us, his sons, what're you up to?, and he screwed up his face in an impatient sort of way, as if he'd bitten into a lemon (lime). When he died, there wasn't even that—no surprise, no screwed-up face. We could also launch into my father's son's facial expressions, punch in the nose, lemon (lime). (By the way, my father died just like Grandfather. He woke up from a nap, took one step, and collapsed. You can see where his heels slipped on the linoleum from under him. I might also add that every (blessed) day, at exactly a quarter to four, because that's when it happened, the Lord sends down one of His angels who mucks about a bit with the traces, so they shouldn't disappear. He places his heel where my father's had been, crash!, bang!, and he slips, imitating his (my father's) death. They (the angels) take pretty hard falls. It's always another one coming, because they hate this job. Some even cry. Crash, bang, slip, cry.)

340. My father made repeated attempts not to believe in God, and to some extent (*comme ci, comme ça*) he succeeded. He went about it in the following manner: My father says that it is clear, it is as clear as day, that man needs God. The psychology—if not the logic, that frightful Pascalian, namely, that man is better off with what is than what is not—specifically, the need for someone to turn to with our petition, and if, as usual, our petition goes unheeded, then at least we have someone to blame, and also, our humility needs a target; in short, we need a Father who—and here we must really put three dots . . . (well, wouldn't you know, the Trinity, my father giggled)—in short, for all these reasons, in lieu of humanity, as it were, which, in its best interest and having suc-

358

cumbed to blackmail, believes in God (the atheists, the growing number of those who are indifferent, the seemingly relentless secularization of the world did not pull the wool over his eye, a short-term *Zeitgeist*, that's all, the narcosis of the life force, et cetera), he, my father, wanted to and *willed* not to believe in God, in the interest of human dignity, as it were. And then once, when instead of clasping his hands in a prayer of thanksgiving he gave a superior shrug of the shoulder—probability calculation, he hissed between his teeth—he realized that he'd been had. God had played a trick on him. Clasp or shrug, it's all the same. He thought he was swimming against the tide, but the water is flowing in both directions, simultaneously upstream and downstream, or maybe there's no water at all, or there is, but it's not flowing, and we are all standing around in the puddle, or maybe there's water, and it's flowing, but nobody's swimming, just rolling along with the current, like a drowned man; he, the rebellious nonbeliever believed that he was scaling the vertiginous heights of disbelief, whereas he was just strutting about in the cloak of disbelief, striding up and down, prancing about in the colorful garbs of disbelief, and he's no better than those who, out of self-interest, lick ass. He was behaving just like them, except in reverse—in short, the same way; he was also dancing as God was calling the tune, except for him, it was a different tune. The question is not whether God exists or not, but what the nature of this Supreme Being, about whose existence we are uncertain, is like (that's good, my father laughed, He is the one that is, then zap!, maybe He's not. But what can you expect of an outfit where the Chosen People don't recognize the Messiah? Clearly, *here* that's the way things work. Clever, I'll hand Him that!) In short, what the world is like. His world is just like theirs. The absence of God takes on the shape of God. But no. His standpoint is even more ridiculous, for he happens to be defending the so-called dignity of so-called mankind in the face of God; it so happens that the safeguarding of man's dignity serves the glory of our so-called God. A cul-de-sac, and he marched right into it. A bum ride, my father said and then, with a cold heart and renewed arrogance, he kneeled. All right, Jahveh. In that case, have mercy on me. My father: again and again.

341. My father—to use the words regurgitated by the cast of a so-called techno-party of universal proportions forty years later—let the sun shine in. That's how he woke up every morning, with this shine. If only there were a God at times like this, how good, simple and natural it would feel to thank Him. My father considered the sunshine direct proof of God's existence, the considering proof of Satan's existence, and his yearning as romantic proof of his own existence.

342. Since they both drove a hard bargain, my father could not come to terms with the Lord. My father applied for easier terms. This was after 1956, when life became easier. But it was this easier that made it possible for him to gain an overview of the whole, which became harder by becoming easier—in short, the moral support of "it's very hard" had been taken away, while the Good Lord was operating with ingenious Leibniz postulates (the best of all possible, et cetera), and this went on and on until my father opted for madness. Some sort of tremens (delirium), I think it was. Love and pus are united in the Lord, and everything happens on a voluntary basis. Princess Bowjolay whispered into my daddy's ear. Go to Madeira. Go. Blue and white, as my father had painted it in his imagination. The Mamselle asks, Do you see pink mice? He does indeed. And right away, swoosh, they scamper across the room, friendly, impressive-size animals, tame, as if they'd been tamed. And the day before yesterday, she actually told my father to count the cups in the cupboard. My father is counting. Five. There should be a set of twelve. One or two might be in the sink.

No, just one. Can't you count? As a matter of fact, once he counted five, once seven, one, two, three—facts have a calming effect on me, he says as he regards his fingers. Aha!, my father shouts, but the princess does not respond to so-called interjections. Aha! She's squatting in my father's left ear, the one that's partly deaf. Lately, also the right. Which means that there must be a little man inside. They meet when my old man is not looking (he's sleeping). Bowjolay seems cranky lately. But where do they meet? The nose pharynx area. That's how a person (my father) gets to be disgraced. Who then looks up his doctor, who is the topmost expert in that particular part of the body. He looks cheerful and is an adherent of the Swedish cure. *Skol,* he says. Did I not ask you to stop using cotton? Will you kindly pull that wad out of your ear? Fresh air, he adds. Fresh air. Back home, the little cunt starts whispering again, grumbling because of the doctor. I gotta get married, I'm with child. You and the doc can't do this to me, my father says aghast, but *pas de* answer. Love and pus.

343. The guests were everywhere, in all our rooms and terraces. The servants were having a grand old time in the kitchen, while the French governess, Mamselle Titez, who was in charge of my three-year-old father, was drinking sherry in her room. My father was wandering around the building. He unintentionally opened the bathroom door on a distant niece of my grandfather, who was just rising from the seat, and was about to pull up her panties. Everything of substance on level with my father's head. The little boy sees the magic triangle, can't get his eyes off it. The woman, too, is frozen in place. Then the child's (my father's) face lights up with the joyful, satisfied grin of recognition: Mama!, he shouts at the triangle. The woman—a perennial spinster, sour, Dame of the Star Cross Order and Lady-In-Waiting to Empress and/or Queen Elizabeth of illustrious memory, recipient of the special second-

361

class medal of the Red Cross, burst into bitter tears. She is sobbing her heart out in the baroque jakes. The little boy (my father) grimaces, then makes a quick retreat.

344. Noun plus verb, this is not from God. There is nothing in nature to substantiate it. It is an arbitrary feature of language. For instance, if to run is a verb because it is an action and lasts a short time, then why isn't fist (or working class) a verb? And if man and house are nouns, because they are long-lasting, stable events, or things, then why isn't living or growing a noun? Somebody should have a talk with language. Couldn't it deal the cards differently. By way of an aside, he (my father) mentions in passing that in Hopi everything that flies, with the exception—and this is beautiful—of birds, is indicated by *one* noun. Surprising, isn't it? On the other hand, an Eskimo is surprised to learn that we have only one word for snow when, for instance, what has morning snow to do with afternoon snow? (As we know, precious little.) When I was at boarding school, we were always having to go to confession. After we'd confessed ourselves silly and we had no sins left, but we had to say something just the same, we said we stole some snow. Father, I have sinned, I stole some snow. We didn't realize how terrible it was that we had nothing to confess, that there is no sin, only the state of sin. Sin is a noun.

345. Whenever a big fish swam into sight, my father and the others behaved in an intriguing manner. As an historical class they'd had it, but still, intriguing is intriguing. They had no way of knowing if the big fish had a mind to gobble them up or not, though being educated boys, they were familiar with the saying that the big fish eats the little fish. Except, they had to be sure. The simple solution would have been to blow a retreat whenever they spotted a big fish. But in that case, their lives would have been nothing but this retreating—though, truth to tell, they were close enough to it to

begin with—and they would have had practically no time to spare for other important life functions. (Love, literature, God, fatherland, family, or when he was young, soccer, and later the defense of the homeland. The defense of the homeland in constant flight . . . How? By doing a quick about-face, like the Huns, for instance, and shooting arrows at the big fish? But in water this brings up certain logistical problems.) The other, fatalistic solution, the "let's wait and see what it wants," would have been too dangerous. Besides, they would have fallen into the sin of too much optimism. My father and the others did the following (as a consequence): a small group went to meet the big fish. They advanced a couple of centimeters, stopped, then another couple of centimeters, and so on. When they were close enough for the big fish to swallow them up if it felt like it, but didn't, they swam back to the others and resumed their daily activities with (relative) equanimity (love, literature, God, homeland, family, or when he (my father) was young, soccer, followed by the defense of the homeland). But if the big fish caught one of the reconnaissance party, my father, for instance, the reconnaissance party would rush like mad to sound the alarm—stop the love, literature, God, et cetera. The dilemma my father and the others were facing was as follows: one or two individuals of the reconnaissance party can chuck the whole thing and turn back. The one to turn back, my father, for instance, would be safe personally, but if everyone were to think likewise and turn back, then they all might fall victim, including my deserting father and his progeny. On the other hand, if the other members of the reconnaissance party do not chuck the whole thing and do not turn back, everyone of the remaining group, my father included, might (in the given situation) find themselves in an even more perilous pass than in the previous case, because the chances of his falling victim are increased should the big fish, God forbid, happen to be a father eater. (The situation is identical in every respect to the problem of public grazing grounds.) The facts—*um so schlächter für die Tatsachen,* so much the worse for the facts—indicate that in my father's group cooperation seems to hold sway—which is surprising, and definitely goes against the view Hungarians have of themselves, that there's nothing but contention, internecine fighting, spitefulness, and lack of cooperation. (I'm not saying this, it's the so-called other side!) The question thus became how my father and the others should elaborate the spirit of cooperation. If someone casts a stone at you, pay him back with bread—would this be it? But when my father was hit with a stone in the middle of the forehead, pow!, he was out cold. Besides, the bakery was closed for the day. To come up with a solution, the German ethologist Manfred Milinski designed a clever experiment. He placed my father in a rectangular aquarium, who (my father) was swimming at one end (breaststroke). He placed another aquarium at the farther end of the first aquarium with a big fish inside. My father's partner—indeed, best friend—was simulated by placing a mirror along the longer side of the aquarium. When he took off toward the big fish to reconnoiter, my father had no idea that his friend was his own mirror image. In short, he was initially cooperative. Because of the mirror, his friend went along (naturally). So far the experiment is a model of the situation in which the partner cooperates. However, if they moved the mirror by 45 degrees (which they did), my father could not help but notice that his friend was leaving him in the lurch. At this point, my father also sounded a retreat. It turned out that my father and co. were following the so-called tit-for-tat strategy that a Yankee social psychologist, Anatol Rapoport, had come up with. It's real simple. You make your opening move with the best of intentions, you cooperate. But your next move will depend on your friend's (or generally, a friend's) next move. Tit for tat. There are exceptions: Despite his friend's betrayal, my father would at times go to reconnoiter the big fish on his own. Yes: my father was motivated by the spirit of brotherhood and forgiveness. My father is a good man. Another interesting version is when my father is the big fish. It's a lot more comfortable, you don't have to tire your gray matter out so much, re. John Neumann and the game theory; the tiny little what have yous sweating their ass with all the intellectual rock-rolling, while my father, when he got hungry, and hunger isn't something you gotta think about, humm! It also happened that he wasn't even hungry, just humm! Loved the glimmer of fear in their eyes. He later came to his own defense by saying that he thought *he* was the true Magyar, but this was not accepted because just then those who were fleeing were considered true Magyars. Angry as hell, my father next gobbled up the independent Court, humm!, but he never regained his former good cheer. Pázmány, too, kept thwarting him. Also, he had to fill out some questionnaires, which he hated with a passion, besides of which it surpassed his intellectual capacities.

346. In order to become the hero of an anecdote, you gotta be likable. Or not. My father belonged to the second group. He inspired fear. He was arrogant. Distant. Aloof. Tall. But not lanky. Lean, but not gaunt. The elegantly curved figure, leisurely way of dressing (light shoes, soft jackets, not fashionable but expensive stuffs), were in line with his moderate, yet dangerous, and by all odds unpleasant, irony. He's got a heart of gold, my mother kept saying, except he doesn't show it. Shooting cows on Tuesday. Signature. This was the sum and substance of a friendly invitation to a hunt. When Uncle Nicky, the head of the family, died, being the unquestionable authority on the matter, they asked my father to deliver the eulogy. The anecdote begins when my father supposedly takes the carriage from Csákvár to the cemetery at Pottendorf only because he'd calculated that he'd be able to put up on the family estate all the way, and also change horses. (We know that he had a more-or-less justified reputation for thrift. When he was Prime Minister and he had to go see the king in Vienna, he

traveled second class. It takes me to the same place, he said. How true.) The funeral fell on a tempestuous day in February—the winters were still cold back then, the little *el niño* left at home in the manger—and my father who, like a well-prepared tourist, spoke fluent Latin, decided that since half of the mourners were partly Austrian and half partly Hungarian, he was not going to speak twice, but would deliver just one (piece) of eulogy, in Latin. If anyone doesn't understand, that's his problem. My father had, to put it bluntly, a mother of mine, my mother, in Vienna, a short little brunette, French, always in avant-garde hats and high lace-ups, a nice woman, smart, with a pleasant grasp of the arts, natural mannerisms, and always twenty years my father's junior, and the widow of our relative. (A thorough study of her thighs offers a spectacular rebuttal of the "matchstick" rumor.) This mother of mine wanted of my father only as much as he wanted, but that much she insisted on. Except, it's not easy, knowing what my father wants. He wanted it and he didn't want it, sometimes the one, sometimes the other. My father accepted the world for what it was, and since he was a great lord, the world tried to please him. This is what gave the appearance that it was he, my father, who was making the decisions, wanting, yearning. What would you say to my coming to the funeral? I have an official invitation. I could visit you in Pottendorf. A great idea, my father says without much enthusiasm. I could check to see if you're properly put up. Don't worry. I'm not. Don't worry, I won't stay the night. I have a round-trip ticket. It's been a long time. Annoyed, my father keeps mum. He can't get used to this new gadget, the telephone. Foolish Count! That's true, my father nods. Foolish, foolish, foolish! All those *oo*'s touch my father to the quick. (See? Every sentence, even the most straightforward, is metaphorical: they were speaking in French, *fou, fou, fou*. In which case, it was all those *ou*'s. There's always some letter or sound.) My father met my mother ten years ago, right after the war, at a soirée hosted by my father's cousin, the young Schwarzenberg duke. My father was engaged in political discussions with his substantially Austrian relatives, in a light royalist tone. He was worried about the country. He'd gotten used to being responsible for what was happening to the nation. He did not trust Horthy, and he did not trust the Germans. It bodes no good, he said, in French, naturally, which imparted a sharp tone of irony to the sentence, when they humiliate a country this deeply (Hungary). They switched languages depending on how it felt best to say something. Depending on the subject. (My father's son is dismayed whenever language is used merely as a means of communication. He does not mean to pit practicality against Hungarian tradition in which tradition (Hungarian) language is a strong fortress, a refuge, a shrine and a sacrament, that's too much for him. On the other hand, if he can't sense the awe and cornucopia of riches that belonging to one language involves, that's not enough, because it is precisely as a thinking being that the individual—yes, he's going to say it—belongs to just one language.) When the monarchy collapsed, the threads had to be picked up again, and naturally, the question posed itself, who was going to do it (pick up the threads)? What is Austria without the Habsburgs, i.e., something *that small,* can it still be Austria? This uncertainty also meant freedom. Hungary felt only the loss of its territories, that two-thirds of it was gone, and no one thought, including my father, that after four hundred years, the country had become independent at long last. They forgot. From time to time my father glanced at my mother, who lived (had lived) in a scandalous marriage with our relative, old Trauttmansdorff. People said all sorts of things. (My father said that he'd met few people as likable as he. The old man had just reduced his wife's nightgown, the wars in the Balkans, and the idea of space as conceived of by modern physics, to a common denominator. He repeated his sentences *sotto voce,* and his mouth was always full of saliva.) My father's eyes were, how shall I put it, uncurbed. His eyes were beautiful, and beauty is strength, and strength affects us, whether we like it or not. This is why beauty is constantly in motion. There was laughter in his eyes, even jubilation. Anyone who glanced into that pair of eyes felt that this was everything, this defined everything. This was the law. In short, resistance is possible, but beware of the consequences. My father had something jupiterian in him. He could even be majestic, exhibiting a twentieth-century version of majesty that cohorts with the quotidian. But then, how else could the king of the gods act, when there is neither king, nor god? The jupiterian starts and ends with itself. It makes itself the measure of all things, because it considers itself all things. My father was in love with love, as the saying goes. Women came in second. Is it love he wanted, but not the person who "went" with it? Of course not. He may not have wanted this "wanting" either. Still, he held the body in great respect, his own, and others', too. He did not divide people into body and soul. He saw the body as the manifestation of our humanity or, better yet, its emblem. Trade sign. Business card. Don't we spend most of our time in it? Don't we talk to it, day after day? What about? Death, naturally. What constitutes the story of the body if not the story of decline, decay, and dissolution? Where else does this path lead, if not down, down into death. This is how my father saw it. It is not our intellect, nor our thoughts, not even the soul, but the body that reminds us of death and mortality, because it is *us* who are dying, slowly, spectacularly. The body is a faithful and honest companion who sounds the alarm every time, my father thought, that we are dust and unto dust shall we return. My father looked for and found what is human in death. He was not afraid of death (before his death), nor did he make friends with it; he welcomed it like some problematic and not-too-pleasant gift. He (my father) found so much delight in everything that is, he did not differentiate between good and bad, he never felt the urge. He exulted in everything, and he exulted in death, too, though admittedly, in this case, the word of the body did not concur; the body could not very well regard its own passing as a good thing. This is what led to the melancholy, the passing melancholy. Possibly, this jupiterian meant no more and no less than that my father was able to present and feel the throbbing of his body and the vertigo of his loins as something personal. In the meantime, my father forgot about the short brunette. He forgot his own glance. He was not one of the great, celebrated seducers. They know the importance of detail. They know that seduction is concrete. My father didn't care a fig about that. But that's not true. Sometimes he cared, and sometimes he didn't. Sometimes he cared about one thing, sometimes another. For instance, he was never reluctant to engage in petty tasks of a political nature. He retired from big-time politics after the war. Seeing the vulgarity and inevitability of the consolidation that followed the Communist putsch, he lost heart, then later he was put in charge of the petty, objective, daily work of the Parliamentary Finance Committee. What should the future of the country be like?, people asked. But all my father would say was, 2 percent and tax exemption, and the like. He made the decision to retire during that certain Schwarzenberg soirée. Gentlemen, my father said with an enigmatic smile, for the others had no way of knowing that his announcement related not only to that evening but the next ten years, Gentlemen, with your permission, I shall retire. His room was in the east wing, toward the corridor named after Duke Eugene. He knew the way well. He turned into the various hallways without thinking. He had but a few steps to descend when he heard his name, *here my father's name followed*. My father turned. My mother! She'd been following him! My father grinned. Jupiter was elated. Come, my father said hoarsely. I can't, not this fast. Oh, well, in that case . . . My father shrugged. My mother nodded gravely, still, something, maybe a little something. Fine, my father said with a renewed grin, and leaned against the wall. Jupiter was as happy as a child with his present. You

Catholics, my mother said—and the touch of sadness (for it was with a touch of sadness that she got up off her knees) disappeared from her eyes—you like hiding behind other people, and you don't see that there's no one there, just you. It is amusing, seeing you playing hide-and-seek. My father shrugged. Who? This was ten years ago, but the grin is still there, and the serene knowledge and the light sadness is still there, too. The constant yearning. And gradually, in the meanwhile, everyone had to prove his pure Aryan origins stretching back at least four, yes, four grandparents. There was at the time in the House a count who went by the name of Fidél Pálffy, who was known for being a whopping idiot, and as you'd expect from a whopping idiot, he idolized Hitler. My father couldn't stand the smell of him. Once in the corridors of the House, when in his characteristic palsy-walsy manner lacking all sense of distance he asked my father how he was faring, my father smoothed a hand over his careworn brow. These are difficult times, my friend. I had an ancestor by the name of Salamon, I'm called Móric, while my wife's got a problem with two of her grandparents. Hearing this, the young bullock ran gleefully with the news to anyone willing to listen. He knew it all along, he'd suspected as much, he felt it in his bones, and now here it was, in *schwarz und weiss:* he's Jewish! Everyone in Parliament laughed the whole day (they thought they had time), until someone (the kind-hearted Laci Berényi) explained to this nitwit that my father had taken him for a ride (made an ass of him), insofar as my father's family trace their origins back to the Salamon clan, and Móric is Móric, and the problem with two of my mother's grandparents is that there aren't any, they don't exist, because her mother and father being first cousins, there was only one set of grandparents. This is when Pálffy said with his impeccable logic, Fine, fine, but where there's smoke, there's fire. To give him his due, in the end he was right. Another version of this story is that when my father returned from being held prisoner of war by the Americans, he received assistance from the American Joint Distribution Committee, or applied for it. Anyway, be that as it may, he's standing on line, the Committee people are looking through his papers, Móric, fine, mother's name Schwarzenberg, fine, but tell us friend Móric, how did you manage to get such a beautiful name, *here my father's name followed.* The hide-and-seek my mother mentioned also lasted, a hide-and-seek embedded in yearning, as a result of which my parents got entangled in rather childish conversations. They acted like two teenagers. A good thing we're ridiculous, and not tragic. We don't even have to talk. You could just laugh at me with that cosmic grin of yours and press me against the wall, that's all it takes. Not too difficult, is it? No, it's not too difficult, my father said uncertainly. It's difficult with you, Count. My father felt a great surge of pride. You're flattering me. My mother made a grimace. No. It is difficult. Really. I never know when I should be afraid of you. Always. But I'm just joking. Joke or no joke, Count. If that's how it is, then that's how it is. This is what Your Excellency doesn't seem to realize. You'd like me to be afraid of you, because when I'm afraid—and in this you are quite right—I am prone to behave properly. The way you'd like me to behave. The way you expect me to behave. Now it was my father's turn to make a face. He didn't like people complaining. But my mother would not desist. You like your comfort, Count. You're satisfied only when I don't present a problem, when I don't have a headache, and plunge from one orgasm into the next (or the other way around, my father intervened; shut up, my mother yelped), and don't leave my wristwatch under your pillow. Though if all goes well, you're a good lover. You're impossible. I see you don't believe me. My father screwed up his face again. See?, my mother shouted. You should see yourself in a mirror now! You'd see how impossible you are! You shrink and turn petty-minded. Shrink, like a shirt hung out to dry! My goodness, what similes. I'm glad you didn't say underpants. Have you any idea what you're like at

371

times like this? Like a mouse! A mouse?! Me? A *maus*, to be perfectly honest. Your nose becomes pointed, and so on. If anyone
had asked him what sort of animal he'd have liked to be, my father
would have had a hard time coming up with the answer. Lion,
bear—that's too much. But a mouse? A *maus*?! I am a grown
woman, Count. I will go wherever I want to. If I want to go to
Pottendorf, I will go to Pottendorf. Kindly stop treating me like a
child! As you wish. And don't you dare be offended, my mother
said brimming over with love. I'm not letting you off that easily.
Be that as it may, my father held his nearly forty-five-minute-long
eulogy in his very best Latin, while the mourners had to listen
with uncovered heads in the stormy weather. The following day
half of the *Gotha Almanac* were in hospital with the glanders,
pneumonia and pleurisy, plus rheumatic fever (!). Everyone kept
asking why my father wanted to wipe out the Austro-Hungarian
aristocracy? He is a good example of a so-called father of mine.

347. When my mother was exquisitely young and beautiful and
wanted to sleep with my father all the time, who was also exquisitely young and beautiful and wanted to sleep with my mother a
great deal, she called my father on the phone all the time, who
was working at the Bank for Commerce, in winter, over the
frozen Danube on foot, like old King Mátyás. He was in charge of
foreign correspondence, because he was the only one left who
could still speak so-called foreign languages, the old staff having
been kicked out because they were supposed to be enemies of the
regime, which happened to be true. My father was also an enemy
of the regime, but he thought it only right that they should be
hiring young talent. But to kick someone out just because he talks
with an aristocratic lisp is ridiculous, unless we're talking about radio announcers. But we're not talking about radio announcers,
and he told them as much. It didn't matter to him anymore. His
knowledge wouldn't save him, while his name was like the yellow

star (except not as lethal): you could know everything right off, provided there were rules about what that everything was. My mother chirped on, you could hear it through the ear piece at the other end. My father hinted that they might be bugged. Fuel to the fire. Let them, she cooed, at least they'll have something to enjoy in this little revolution of theirs. Not that little, my father growled. My mother disdained the Communists. What a lot they are! Not so my father. He'd have liked to feel sorry for them, but they were far too dangerous and harmful, so he was angry with them instead. Good and angry. Morons! They go and make every historical mistake imaginable! And they're even proud of the new ones. Hopeless. Say something intimate, my mother pleaded. My father loved it when my mother purred like a cat, but this *thing* over the phone, this got his balls. Lemme alone, he grunted. But there was no hurting my mother's feelings at such times. She pleaded, she begged unashamedly, just one word, my darling an-gel, just one intimate word, something *sweet,* you, you darling . . . whose ass is better than Stalin and Rákosi put together! My father imagined it. I don't know. After all, Joe is a sturdy lad, he said, playing it coy. Plus hoping they weren't being bugged. My mother adored my father's ass. She was proud of it. She'd have liked to show it off if she could, like a racehorse. A little some-thing intimate, she cooed once again. My father got bored. Inti-mate, he said. My mother gave a disappointed yelp. They were overplaying their scene, and some little bitterness came creeping in—from where? to where? My father glanced at his watch. He had fallen behind with everything, the translations, the reports on the translations to his superior, plus the promises promised to the secretary—and with a gorgeous, deep, throaty, excited whisper he whispered into the phone, fifteen hours, twenty-seven minutes, thirty seconds. The other end fell silent. What, what did you say?, my mother gasped, blushing with joy. My father repeated, chang-ing his confession to thirty-three seconds. Oh, you!, my mother shouted, and slammed the phone down. She was elated. This worked beautifully for quite some time, even in the early sixties, when Khrushchev became my father's chief competition in the backside department, eighteen hours, eleven minutes, thirteen seconds (overtime?), and my mother was moist up to her ears. Then from one day to the next it stopped, though except for this stopping, that day was not special in any way. It wasn't even said, or if it was, it was in vain, twenty-three hours, eighteen minutes, fifty seconds, nothing happened, nothing, just the time passing: badly.

348. In the late forties and early fifties, my father organized a number of conspiracies at the university (mostly just anti-ideological and not against the state, simply in the name of sanity) and the liberal-oriented People's College, which had been partly disrupted by the state by then. (He did not participate in these conspiracies formally, but he helped where he could, willingly contributing his assistance, intellect, erudition and acquaintances.) Then he went and told the secret police about these conspiracies. Shit!

349. Once, every single time, the work supervisor would interrupt my father with elaborate deference, if you don't mind, Doctor, sir, Lord in Perpetuity of Csákvár, Count of Majk and Várgesztes, Your Excellency, but . . . My father called from atop the threshing machine for the tenth time, just call me Otto. Which just increased the embarrassment. What Otto? ◆ He (my father) reinstituted the village band, but on one occasion he was reluctant to start rehearsal, because the bassoon player hadn't arrived yet. You people have no respect for time, you think that in a proletarian dictatorship time has no value?! Chagrined, he kept checking his watch. At long last the unfortunate musician showed up, and mumbled an apology. Only then would my father raise his baton. Let us start, Gentlemen. *A Little Night Music.* (I might add that

Mozart did not use any wind instrument, least of all the bassoon.) ♦ Another man who arrived late (later) arrived in a Workers Guard uniform. Perturbed, my father asked, are we at war, sweetheart? ♦ In matters of interpretation he (my father) was inflexible. What are you playing there?!, my father snapped at one of the musicians who was plodding along with his solo. He's playing it the way it is written. And what's written? Ad lib. As you like. My father raised his eyebrows, as *who* likes? ♦ György (George) Mendelssohn-Bartholdy, my father's friend from the Vox Record Company, was my father's right hand. One day a man showed up from county headquarters, and this uninformed comrade asked my father's name. He told him. Oh, sure, nodded the man from the county. And I suppose the comrade sitting next to you is Haydn?! No, said my father calmly, the comrade is Mendelssohn-Bartholdy. ♦ The parish priest turned to the fire chief. Excuse me, but what does your score say, what have you got in this bar, B or B flat? My father flew into a rage. If you have a question, Father, why don't you ask me? After all, it's my piece. (They were rehearsing the Second Symphony.) Because you never listen when I ask you anything. My father called to the so-called *concertmeister*, What did he say? ♦ Nobody knows where he got it, but my father came to the conclusion that the sperm was poisoned (whose?). ♦ My father converted to Catholicism. Their houses of worship, the music, the colors are so beautiful. The whole liturgical show. And what discipline! Besides, God, Mozart, Beethoven and Schubert are also Catholic, so it's gotta have something going for it. ♦ What happened in Jerusalem? My father, who'd been attending a dinner, wanted to go back to his hotel. He tried hailing a cab, taxi!, taxi!, he shouted, but there wasn't a single cab anywhere. On the other hand, people from the nearby houses called down to him to shut up. My father went back to his friends. There's not a single cab anywhere, he announced at the door, beaten, just Jews. ♦ My father saw a gentlewoman home, then proceeded to seduce her. The woman would have liked to get out of it, but she couldn't, as my father was in third gear. Tell me, Maestro, the victim asked, practically gagging, I've been meaning to ask you for some time. What is the tempo of the beginning of Mozart's symphony in G flat? My father immediately freed himself of his own embrace and went to the piano. Okay, listen to this!

350. My mother kept counting us, my father's eldest son and my brothers and sister, like ducklings, whether we're all there . . . One-two-three-four, and five, and she pointed at our father, but she never said five out loud. One, two, three, four, pause. Oh, dear, sweet pause . . . !

351. My father. My mother lived her married life with my father. Death. Death, which is always unexpected and unjust, claimed my father when their life with my mother had reached golden heights and they were surrounded all around by beauty and joy. In her black, passionate sorrow, my mother slipped under the mourning shroud next to my father, this is how they were united for the last time on the night of the wake. After my father was gone for good, the pain never left my mother, or she never left it, until she died (my mother)—maybe.

352. Something tells me, my father said after wracking his brain long and fruitlessly, that the most sacred thing of all is the thing we do not recall.

353. My father had a vision. It was about time. The Turks were still in charge of the country, but Emperor Leopold was determined. For some time there had been nothing but the day to day tasks of the nation to see to, weekday followed upon weekday; my father could look neither ahead, nor behind [I was writing this at twenty past three in the afternoon, my father could look neither ahead

nor behind, be-hind, I had just written the "hind" when I was called to the phone. My father had died today, the fifth of May, at a quarter to three. What follows from this? Possibly just this: that when year after year, day after day, many times a day, someone writes down the word "father," all sorts of wonderful and terrible things happen to him; *this* here is an alien body, but I don't care. I put the phone down, ( . . . ), sat down again, and continued the sentence], only in front of his feet; in short, the ruthless shuffling for position that characterizes peacetime and the end of any century had begun, and he'd personally taken an active part in it. (For instance, laying his hands on the estates from the purges in Northern Hungary and the Wesselényi conspiracy's "discontents." Some people even say that he himself was involved in the conspiracy, which also had to be compensated for at Court). He was approaching fifty, up to here in what we call life, but which has neither direction nor fullness, just finitude. But even the heroism that comes with the finitude was deprived him; being submerged in it, he didn't recognize it. And as he rode along the River Vág at the head of his splendid troops, blues and yellows flashing in the valley, he suddenly had a vision—no, not that he *isn't,* that he does not exist, because this thought was not new to him, and being too literary, it didn't lead anywhere, even though he dutifully tried to experience that, for instance, someone is just dreaming him, or that he's an imitation, a clone, in which case this is a Socratic, or at least a Platonic idea, the shadow on the wall of the cave. No, this wasn't it. What he came to realize there, in the purple light of the Star of Even-Morn, is that he is not a person (an individual), but a glance. Looking. In other words, it is the other way around, more or less—no, *exactly* more or less. He guarantees others' existence by looking at them (my father). In short, he casts the light on the person who then appears on the wall of the cave in the form of a shadow. In short. He is not a person, but a pair of eyes, a glance. He experienced this as a relief from a burden, as if his life had gained meaning by virtue of the fact that he need not think about himself anymore, just the thing he sees. He refrained from asking questions pertaining to his life not because he'd come up with this elegant solution, but because he was cowardly, too busy, and besides. Hegel. Let him worry about final questions. Besides, the answers come even without the questions, like now. The River Vág roared on, unperturbed. I'll fabricate the questions from the answers, my father chuckled, and looked up at the cloudy sky. Then the news came that Thököly's father, the great anti-Habsburg Kuruc, had died. It's not easy, requisitioning under such circumstances.

354. The places, the hips and waterfalls, the events and persons in this book are real. They accord, or correspond, to reality. For instance, my father's steed really did slip in the mud of the August gully. My father's son invented nothing, and each time that his old habits as a novelist led him to invent something, he at once called imagination to his aid—for instance, that my father is carried on his back by his own animal, or steed, and that this steed is his nature, specific to the individual, and so anyone who wishes to learn about my father should look not at the cut of his clothes or try to catch his habitual gestures, but should make a study of his secret steed instead—and right away he felt (my father's son) that what he'd written like this, he must chuck out. Even the names (my father) are real. Feeling such a profound intolerance for any invention as he did in writing this book, he was unable to change the real names which seemed to him inseparable from these real people. It is possible that one or two of them will be displeased to find themselves in this way with their first names and surnames in a book, but there is nothing my father's son can do about that. He wrote only what he remembered, and there will be readers who, thinking of this book as a factual account, will discover 1,001 inadequacies. Though the author dealt with real life, he thinks it

ought to be read as a novel; in other words, without asking either more or less of it than a novel can give (everything). To this we should add that there are also many things that he remembered but had omitted to write about, including many that concern him personally. He did not feel inclined to talk about himself. In short, he wrote—though not necessarily *down*—the story of my father's family, not his own. He should also add that the idea of writing a book of stories about the people surrounding him had come to him at a tender age. He showed the introduction to my father, who liked it very much (my father). This is in part that book; but only in part, because the memory is finite and unreliable, and because books drawn from real life are often no more than feeble glimpses and fragments of the things we have seen and heard.

355. My father's son does not want to write about my father. He doesn't feel like it. He'd like to keep my father, my father's person, at a certain remove from this circus. This much, he feels, he owes him. My father was the best father in the world, the best he could ever imagine, then and now, because my father, as the possessive pronominal indicates, is his, he is a father of his, and this "his" is irrevocable and unique. Furthermore, not only does he not want to, he can't. The words keep slipping out of his grasp. Or possibly, the thing that is my father, his essence, keeps slipping out of the grasp of the competence of his words. And all the while, there isn't a single word that goes untouched by this "his." Mine.

356. My father's eldest son is a sort of prodigal son. Though he's got a good head on his shoulders and a pleasing face, he couldn't find a place for himself in the world. He wandered around, he drank, he whored, he lived a life of dissolution. He was cut off from the inheritance, too, but that's just by way of an aside. My father (on the other hand) is profoundly religious and strict, a veritable patriarch who leads an industrious life. He knows what is good and what is

bad and lives accordingly, relentlessly measuring everyone by his own high standards (my mother, et cetera). The prodigal son having passed on (having returned to his Maker), my father grieved with all his heart, the way it is right and proper, but he was also (somewhat) relieved. His son having been a burden to him all his life, his son's shame was also his, his son's miscarriages, too, were also his. An open wound. Now at the open grave, this wound was beginning to heal. Interrupting the service, which she's discussed previously with the Reverend Father, my sister asked to speak. My father bowed his head with annoyance. Of the finest cut, et cetera, as if of marble. You're happy to be a human being, just looking at him. Swallowing her tears, my sister told the gathering that fifteen years earlier, her brother had placed a piece of writing in her care for safekeeping, with the injunction that she was not to show it to anyone. She was now going to read it. And basically, she read a prayer, despite the faint, sobbing voice, a text that was profoundly evocative, disturbing, powerful, brimming over with personal emotion without being obtrusively intimate, relying on the familiar words and expressions of psalms and prayers, and yet . . . And yet it was his prayer, but we could have all prayed it. The person calling from the depths (to You, Lord) must have been very close to him (the Lord) just then. He was begging for mercy, he implored, he made solemn promises, et cetera. He did not change his life, he drank, he whored, he lived off of workmen's compensation, plus his brothers and sister, in secret, because my father frowned on it. Taking himself as the frame of reference, he considered weakness as the most heinous of sins. My sister finished. Her face was soaked in tears. A lump of earth rolled down into the grave. My father looked around. My brethren. My beloved son. You lived by my side for fifty years, and yet I never knew you. I thought you were a different man. Now I ask in this place, before all those gathered here, will you forgive me, son? Forgive me, forgive me, forgive me. He had to be led away from the grave. He was now mourning his son in earnest, and not from above, but from the depths, darkly, retching, from the guts. This is when my father became my father. In the twenty-fourth hour, one might say.

357. The tall bishop's miter of pine marten (on it a medal, and rearing up from it an egret feather), the cloth cloak, the pants with leather foot rags, and also a pair of handsome fine linen foot rags, and the rosary made of small, cherry-size bone beads were laid at the ready. Mother of God, help us. My father's earthly existence was nearing its end. His aspect was altered by illness. He was ashen and he shrank in size, the skin on him sagging like borrowed clothes (no, not borrowed: inherited from a big brother; except my father did not have a big brother; he had always been the eldest, the majoresco, the lord of the manor: a stranger), but there was no telling whether he was suffering, and if so, to what extent. The fact that "at such times" the extent is impossible to gauge, well, this never entered (enters) the mourning family's mind. He didn't seem to suffer. (He scorned and disdained suffering all his life.) If anything, he seemed impatient. He'd have liked this thing to be resolved. Or let him live forever. But in that case, make it snappy—though in that case, he'd have plenty of time for everything, he could be dying day in and day out, but let's not go into that; or else, *finito!*. but then, *aus!* Something like that. Clearly, my father had no respect for death (the incorrect mediator of suffering); he considered it intrusive, as if he were being molested by ticket inspectors on the tram (on the same line!, again!); in short the meddling of office, something, in short, that one can survive (my father too held an office, he was the palatine), but still, it's extremely annoying. For her part, my mother—this is all that remained of her love— wished to take advantage of what were surely their last remaining moments together, to talk my father into repenting and turning to his God. For one thing, God does not exist. For another, even if

He did, He wouldn't be mine. This pompous, childish dialectic—my mother decided to ignore it. Calm down, Mati dear, and listen to me. Look at yourself in the mirror. Who would you fight like this, my dear, in this wretched, withered condition? Well? Shut your mouth, silly woman. My father waved a hand. Forgive me. You were always a silly woman. Why wouldn't you be silly on my deathbed. I beg you to forgive me. Like someone about to offer something that's in short supply, some rarity, from under the counter, my mother lowered her voice, mysteriously, if heaven is empty, you're just making yourself ridiculous in your old age with this ranting and raving, and if our Heavenly Father's throne is up there—hearing the "up there" my father gave a loud grunt, weighing whether he should swallow back down or spit out "his prey, this trembling golden vermin," and it was this momentary hesitation that made my mother lose her cool, what do you want, you pitiful speck of dust, you piece of mediocrity, you nobody, and she began shaking my father, like a piece of rag. She had to be pulled off him by force. My father enjoyed the scandal. A pity it hurt. You're clumsy. You always were. In the kitchen you're meticulous, but as you come near me, you're all thumbs. Even your tongue is all thumbs! How is it? Just now, God was the no-body, and that's why I was supposed to be ridiculous, and next I'm the nobody, or as you like to put it with your parvenu witticism, because you think it's plebeian, a grod-for-nothing, that I'm a good-for-nothing, and that's why I am ridiculous. Tell me, dear, don't you think that's ridiculous? My father was speaking in earnest now, but my mother saw her chance again, oh, oh, how unsavory our purity!, how aggressive our meekness!, how pompous our humility!, how cruel our mercy!, how frail our strength when we glance into the mirror that is Christ! What do you want from me, Irén, my father asked, suppressing his rage. It was his turn now to fly off the handle, because with him, it was the baroque that did the trick. My mother promptly switched tones, and lightly, cynically, barely noticeably, though both he and she noticed, parodying my father, trivializing, basically, the Pascalian line of reasoning—holding the cosmic, terrifying tenants of the ridiculous up to ridicule—trying to make my father see the light, offering my old man's Voltairean spirit a chance to blow a retreat (retreat as the only form of victory) by reminding him that in this game with zero odds?, or not with zero odds?, the believer's chances are better than the nonbeliever's, and consequently . . . If there was one thing that nettled my father even more than the baroque, that was the instance when stupidity appeared in the guise of wisdom. He was raging. He was not about to comment on God, especially not under the present circumstances. His (i.e., the Lord's) kingdom come, His will be done, but as for him (i.e., my father)—and at this juncture his rage turned the profound Einsteinean joke inside out—he, my father, is no gambler! Neither is he an Engelbert Humperdink, he's not about to pull the quasi postrabbits served up perfidiously for his benefit, out of his top hat—pardon, his fifties felt beret. He was screaming. Then silence. The moment of truth, my mother hissed between her teeth maliciously. Clearly, she must have thought that my father would soon come face-to-face with that monstrosity, the everything or the nothing that dictionaries call by the name of death, and that this monstrosity, she, my mother, would soon see spreading over my father's countenance. Instead, a golden light spread over my father's countenance, pure America, celestial harmonies, his features relaxed, his lips turned up in a beauteous smile of forgiveness. My father had arrived. (When they changed the sheets they discovered that what had happened to him then is what happens to people who are hanged. This was my father's last gesture, his last shout, his last trump vis-á-vis transience. Plus my mother.)

358. Due to the application of chemicals, my father, like anyone else in a similar situation, lost his hair, not all of it, but almost. Yes, like

that, combed down, that's it, that's what he looked like (appeared like). Never, never in all his life was his hair so nice and serene. Nice, serene, majestic, and helpless.

359. My father was administered two kinds of infusions, one yellow and one red. When it was the red, he painted his toenails red, like a gentlewoman who'd seen better days, applied a thin coat of rouge, put on a red necktie and red underpants, and while he still had it, he painted a red tinge into his hair. When yellow, then yellow. I gotta prepare myself for the great chemical gathering, don't I?! It *is* a gathering, after all, is it not? A meeting, a rendezvous, inside. (There's this chief physician, the cock of the hill, nothing but hierarchy, no sense of humor, like a wooden toilet seat, and he tells my dad, who is like a skeleton, bald, one kidney missing, half of his hipbone resected, to remove his shirt. My dad puckers his lips, snaps his fingers and says, softly: With feeling or without? Excuse me? The doc doesn't know what hit him. His entourage is shaking with suppressed laughter.) He called the yellow lemonade, and the red tomato juice; come, my lovely, come, my precious, he said endearingly to the poison, and it came as long as it was being sent. In the throes of the green-eyed monster, my mother gritted her teeth.

360. Before he died, my father went soft in the head. His eldest son stood him in the tub every day and scrubbed the day's feces off him. The smell of paternal excrement is unlike anything else. My father's son didn't think he could stand it. My father, Knight of the Golden Fleece, bosom pal of Emperor Charles V, something or other of some Rudolf or other, a student of Metternich, and for a glorious moment, which then passed irrevocably, the spiritual heir to Miklós Zrínyi, would sometimes demur. He didn't want to undress for his son. Was it modesty? Could it have been modesty in his condition? Poor man, how sad. Ever since my mother left my

father's son a gift by dying in his arms, he's been just a bit less terrified of death (my father's son). Before, everything came out of
my mother, too, when they turned her on her side, but it was different, it was runny. Her intellect, too, was intact to the end, she
was almost ninety, and the retreating, rosy-red tongue fluttered
gently in the half-opened mouth for some time. Then he bent
over her (the son, over my mother), and wept over her for a long
time afterward. For hours afterward he could feel the warmth of
her former existence on the sheet beneath her. (Sometimes this
memory fades, sometimes he's much more terrified that he'll end
up sharing his father's fate—the unending dance of the images he
carries of them. How, how will he endure it?)

361. After his twenty-first birthday, my father's son decided to appoint
a guardian for him. They were sitting at the table. My father's son
had finished making all the necessary arrangements. My father was
sitting next to him, he was crumbling the cottage cheese on the
plate in front of him with a spoon. My mother was in the kitchen,
she'd been taken into his confidence, an ally!, you could hear the
clanking of the dishes. Father, my father's son began as my father
raised his eyes from the cottage cheese and glanced at him over his
glasses, Father, I have something to . . . what I mean is . . . there
are things whose significance is far inferior to what we are prone
to think in an awkward moment of surprise, when we are taken
unawares . . . , what I mean is, in short, the point being . . . I have
something to . . . an announcement . . . in short, I have something to say to you. Up to this point my father listened in silence,
but now he bowed his head over the plate of cottage cheese, with
only his wide forehead bulging with veins showing, and it seemed
he understood the situation, or himself. Something. He turned
toward the light. That's just dandy, he said. You want to appoint a
guardian for me, and he sprang to his feet, knocking over a chair in
the process, and slammed the ball of his hand on the table with

such force that the tabletop started shaking and the bowl of cottage cheese was dancing, never!, he roared, never!, over my dead body! He towered over his son like a giant, in a rage of fury, behind the table, in front of the window, where at this moment a dove flew past with an olive branch in its beak. My father removed his hand from the tabletop, which was still shaking. My mother was standing in the door. My father's son had heard her let out a cry in the kitchen. He'd heard the dishes being broken. In her fright she'd dropped the porcelain tray, retied her apron, the dishcloth on her arm, her hand held away from her body. She knew this would happen. She'd warned my father's son. Dad, he now shouted at him, come to your senses! A home? Who is talking about a home? How could you think such a thing about your wife, the woman who loves you, and your son, your own flesh and blood? What we, Mother and I and the boys, want is just to take certain measures, a step, which calls for understanding and fellow feeling on your part, and which is for your own good. After all, honored father of mine, and we might as well be aboveboard about this, some of your, how shall I put it, eccentric habits, which I wouldn't for the world call negative, *au contraire,* they are lovable, if anything, as you yourself are well aware; still these habits of yours are impossible to reconcile with family life and a state of normalcy. We, your beloved wife and I, have therefore made inquiries and have lighted upon a residence eminently suited to you. A health cure in the countryside. Regular meals. Fresh air. After a long life diligently spent in the service of your family, which has understandably worn your nerves to tatters, you sorely deserve a bit of rest. Meanwhile, my father had walked over to the window, his hands playing with the drapes, his fingers sunk between the folds. He appeared calm. My father's son heaved a sigh of relief, and unobtrusively slid the piece of paper from which he'd been reading his speech into his pants pocket. My father whirled around. No, he roared, never! He pushed the table aside, and with a mighty leap, he fell on my father's son so unexpectedly, that my father's son couldn't even begin to resist. With one hand he grabbed his neck, holding it so tightly wedged, that my father's son turned blue as he struggled for air, and his eyes were popping out of their sockets, while with the other he (my father) got hold of my mother who (my mother), near fainting with fear, stood paralyzed. He then pressed their heads together and looked into their eyes, first my mother's, then my father's son's. Hans Christoph, he said. Hedvig. Don't blame yourselves. The tears were streaming down his face. My father's son and his (my father's) wife helped him to the sofa. My father's son picked him up, my mother lovingly covered him. Mati, dear, she said tearfully, is there anything you want? My father wanted to be left alone. He wanted to think everything over once again. He asked for understanding and forgiveness. He was an old man, it'd only been a couple of weeks since they'd cele- brated his sixtieth birthday. My mother was deeply touched by my father's tears. Mother, my father's son cried in the kitchen, taking her (my mother's) hand in his, do you think I don't have feelings of my own? Do you think your son is a monster?

362. You don't need to stand at attention in front of death anymore, you don't need to follow its orders on the double, uncondition- ally, Howdy do!, death says cheerfully and is about to embrace us, but grumpy and sleepy, we wave him off, *not now!*—and it's time for the all-powerful shots, intravenous feeding, oxygen tents, iron lungs, heart massages. It'd been a week by then. From time to time, my father seemed to be in need of exercise. He asked for Paul Gerhardt's book of psalms, his eldest son took it to him, and in the evening, without familiarity with the Bible or psalms, he'd read to him. On these evenings, between the jaws of death, a new understanding was born between them. Up till then, a certain de- tachment and timid deference, and distrust, too, surely, with a bit of fear thrown in for good measure, had served as the mainstay of

their love for each other. During my father's last days, the mullion that had stood between father and son was quietly and unceremoniously stepped over. In the small, stark and barren room—on the wall a crude landscape and the obligatory Crucifix—in this confined world, between the four whitewashed walls where the moans of the woman next door dying of cancer came filtering through—in this room there was no space for anything but the truth. Truth is called dread, and it is called pain, and it is called death. This truth was mightier than any moral or ethical consideration, and in one of my father's lucid moments, this might have made my father's eldest son turn to him with these words: It is time you died. He understood (my father), gave a nod, and with half-paralyzed tongue whispered, I believe. The following day he refused to have his shots. Enough. Howdy do!

363. His body smell embarrassed my father. He felt embarrassed by the smell of feces. When the young male nurse slipped the bedpan under him, he sent us out into the corridor. Afterward the smell, his smell, floated about the room, which he tried to veil with eau de cologne spray. He asked us to open the window. He screwed up his nose to show his aversion. Then, confused and scandalized, shook his head: Disgusting. What a stink. It's enough to turn your . . . The smell that my father's son remembers of my father, which he took with him—writing about a father's death?!, eager-beaver prose peddler, have you no shame?!—is a mixture of disinfected hospital air and the eau de cologne with which my mother rubbed my father's brow and neck several times a day. *Le père pue!*

364. In the bathroom, the broken-down gas heater is heating the water with a shrill rumble. It is rusty, just a hairsbreadth from destruction. My father accidentally knocks his son's toothbrush off the shelf. He is standing on the plank floor, naked in front of his son. His son is scrubbing his back. On the wall, chips of flaking paint.

Paint in little, flaky pieces. Twisting pipes. Gas pipe, stove pipe. Between my father's legs, a small pipe (tube) with two branches and a cork. It is hanging out of the genitals in place of the genitals. We get everything wet. *Death on all fronts. No babies for me!*

365. My father had a number of elaborate takes on his own death. He imagined it in a variety of ways—in bed, among the pillows, during the Charge of the Light Brigade, in the service of his country, also while the referee calls a penalty kick, right after finishing his appetizer of *coquilles St. Jacques,* in his sleep, on Wednesday, in the nominative case, in the sixteenth century, the seventeenth century, the eighteenth century, the nineteenth century, in 1956, in a hat, in a boat, in 1991, and on Wednesday once again. But he was even more concerned about his funeral. Large funeral, small funeral, medium-size funeral; music, silence, speeches, quiet. A minor mannerist-style cult of the dead, at Nagyszombat. But wherein the time doth come upon us for the funeral, we did take up the body *die* twentieth *martii,* the crowd being multitudinous, both his brethren and also the strangers, from the chapel at Sentér did we proceed to have him transferred onto the carts each of which hath previously been covered to the very ground with fine red cloth. Also the cart horses, all, so that the cloths of the funeral, they were all red, and also the banners. There be also twelve cavalries. Milord Bottyáni two, Milord Nádasdi two, Pápa and Devecser two, Gyarmat, Léva and other outposts three each. Milord Erdődi one, one made up of the servants of the lords and strangers one, two troops of domestic servants, and the black troop from the Court. And also besides these horses in fine getup, lead horses with trappings, garbed equestrians, and many other garbs besides, and also the people untold in number. All of which did easily surpass five thousand men in number. On that day we did proceed to Farkashídja, and the subsequent day to Nagyszombat. Then he died (my father); not like that. (The person who'd been his secret

389

lover since 1944 said to my father, Don't expect me to attend your funeral! You don't mean that! I most certainly do. Just wait and see. You can't do this to me! Do you want a scene? A scandal? After the fact?!)

366. Basically, my father went and killed himself. He said that when he reaches a hundred, he's going to kill himself. And then he closed his lips, and nothing in, nothing out. We couldn't pry it open, though we tried long and hard, even with a chisel, we tried forcing a tube through, but that didn't work either. His eyes remained cheerful, though. Except, the point is, he wasn't even a hundred. His death was futile! Futile!

367. Mother had as much blood pouring out of her as a Hajnóczy novella, then they did a D & C on her, stuffed her full of cotton, etc. My father was running so scared, he forgot who he was. I keep thinking of your cunt, he said in his loftiest style. Lemme alone!, my mother yelped at him, irritated. But dear, this is important, otherwise we might be inclined to think that there's nothing but a bleeding wound between your legs . . . I know, I know, my mother snapped, whereas *you* think it's heaven! That's right, my father nodded with pride, that's what it is, heaven. In that case, kindly keep in mind that from now on heaven's got some blood on it, and the little angels are not sitting on fluffy white clouds singing praises to the Almighty, but—and she started screeching—cotton, sterile cotton! But there was no scaring my father off by then. He'd painted the little putti on the canvas of his imagination, as well as soft, gentle, snow-white cotton, by the ton! I'll wait, he grinned, and then I'm going to pitch into you like the farmer's boy into the hay. My mother gave a listless nod, sure, like the farmer's boy into the hay. But things turned out otherwise. Her body let her down (my mother). She started bleeding again—where does all the blood come from?, o, beloved

mother of mine, where?—and she was taken back to the hospital. She became weaker by the day. My father sat by her bedside, and held her hand. They did not talk about heaven, there wasn't much to say. My mother made her peace with what seemed to be her fate, while my father was upset, often on the verge of tears. My mother laid her hand on my father's thigh—her last gesture—slowly worked it up and smoothed her palm over my father's fly. Heaven and earth fell silent. Then in her new, throaty voice, my mother whispered, hay-pitching postponed. Maybe next time.

368. Parentheses. The moment we knocked on our father's door, not waiting, like at other times, to hear his grumbling, or yelp, which at times gave us permission to enter, at other times denied it, still at others acquiesced, *humm!,* we entered his room to announce the news of his father's, our grandfather's death, just received over the phone. He was just writing the sentence that my father could look neither ahead, nor behind. Be-hind, he was just rounding the *d* when we knocked, and with ill humor he was just about to give us a dressing down for not waiting, as we were supposed to, for his permission, but then he caught the look on our faces and saw that something was wrong, or would be, in short, that some-thing is wrong, but naturally, what is or will be, in short, what was, he couldn't possibly imagine. Close parentheses.

369. They made fun of my father and called him Red. He had no eyes and no ears and no hair. The red, too, was just for the fun of it. He couldn't talk, because he had no lips. He had no nose, no hands, no feet, no belly, no back, no backbone, no intestines. Shit, he had nothing. In which case, what's this all about? But let's not go into that.

370. Zeus loved his old friend, my father and raised him up and set him among the stars as the constellation Sagittarius. Here, in the

Zodiac, now above, now below the horizon, he assists in the guiding of our destinies, though in these times few living mortals will cast their eyes respectfully toward Heaven, and fewer still sit as students to the stars.

371. And yet: someone spotted my father ambling along, practically dragging himself along behind himself. He's bent, like a straightened-out saxophone. Not bad, just slow, his deportment is slow. He lowers his head to avoid banging it into the heavenly spheres.

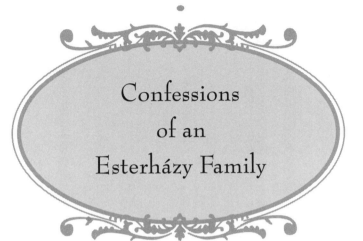

## BOOK TWO

Confessions
of an
Esterházy Family

*"The characters of this adventurous biography are creatures of the imagination. They are authentic only within the context of this book. They are not living characters, nor were they ever."*

# CHAPTER ONE

### 1.

"I don't know how to put this, Your Excellency, but the Communists are here." Old man Menyhért Tóth, Uncle Menyus to us, didn't so much say this as breathed it, or better yet, nodded it, as if hoping that if he didn't say it, quite, it wouldn't quite be true. What he saw, though, put more fear, even, in his heart, for it was something he had never seen before—fear on his mistress's countenance. (Fear and Communists, everything here begins with them, and will end with them too, it seems.)

### 2.

Grandmother was twenty-three at the time, a young woman, a newlywed. It is hard for me to imagine, even though it is not difficult for me to recognize her on the yellowed photographs. I can see my father's face in hers; the two of them (the three of them, because my aunt, my father's sister, included), they look like caricatures of one another. The *self-same* improbable forehead, a spacious, open terrain, a landscape worthy of the loftiest description, the wrinkles like furrows; the same curved, one might say hooked nose—it is a matter of taste, education, and political climate, whether we think of it as a Roman profile or a Jewish one—and the same perpetual squint, the persistent and enigmatic laughter in the eyes.

Still, though I identify this generally badly dressed young woman ("Your grandmother dressed with intrepid bad taste; on her, the sinfully expensive clothes, screaming in anguish from one another's proximity, found a safe haven of sorts"), whom I see on the formal, traditionally posed family portraits or, on the contrary, on awkward, fortuitous "snapshots," at times in the company of her younger sisters, each artfully framed by a window, holding a bouquet of wildflowers, lovely, budding young women!, at times in the company of her children and her husband, on the front stairs of the palace, as the real if not titular head of the family, at times by the side of my handsome grandfather, emphatically a second player, at times literally (an ingenious photograph!) in the shadow of her mother-in-law, the indomitable Princess Schwarzenberg, still at other times with a rake, her sleeves rolled up, swarthy as a man, surrounded by awestruck, frightened peasants—it is all in vain, for I see an unfamiliar relative, a familiar stranger, a perplexing cousin of sorts who, judging by the backdrop, is living sixty years earlier than she should be. I can't imagine my grandmother except as an old woman. Even older than that. Not all grandmothers are like this, but mine is (was). At any rate, that's how I see her.

An old woman all her life and—though she is never alone on the photographs, never!—always on her own. Companionless, though not lonely. No one *suits* her, neither child nor grownup, neither man nor woman. She didn't *need* anyone by her side, and if there was someone there, it seemed coincidental, like when it's raining, whereas it could just as easily be a sunny day.

# 3.

Later on, I entertained the same thoughts about my father, that
there are people who don't need other people; I, for one, am not
like that, but he—for one—is. I was mistaken. Still, on almost
every picture there's that easy *otherness,* Kraus and Sons, Tata,
Bildstelle Wachtl, Wien, Lerner Photo-Report Bureau, Ofotért
State Photo Studio, knickerbockers and more knickerbockers,
Prince de Galles pattern, an organ pipe, he's standing next to his
brothers and sisters in spectacles ordered from Simon Waldstein,
as if he were a world apart, with nothing to tie him either to his
childhood, or the war, and afterward, to anything whatsoever, a
new, unfamiliar country. He's got nothing except us. Truly nothing. The count of nothing.

# 4.

On the photograph he's smoking, the joint hanging loosely from
the corner of his lips like in those French films (black and white),
the ubiquitous Worker, every muscle of his face expressive of
laughter, only his eyes a bit off, bleary, as if he'd had too much to
drink, though possibly he's just young, unfamiliarly young, in
threadbare work clothes, a much-worn, soiled pullover, the background indistinct, he may be leaning against an adobe wall, making a cocky Churchill gesture for the sake of the camera. Could
this mean that regardless of what may come to pass—which afterward did—we're invincible? On his head, playfully cocked to one
side like a military helmet, a white-plated chamber pot. A potty, a
potty.

## 5.

Provided that my grandmother was the type of person who had no need of anybody else, it follows that she had no need of my father either. What I mean is, she needed him, he being her first-born—a family of our standing can't do without a firstborn, a boy, that goes without saying. I know of course, I know perfectly well that in every family someone is always first to be born. But not every family goes around numbering them. Firstborn, and a boy, that was my father. But there didn't seem to be much demand for him *personally.* Or so it appears. But when Menyus Tóth, the *doyen* of the domestic household servants, entered the white salon, presumably no one worried about this, neither my grandmother, nor my father, and as for me, well, neither did I. As for Menyhért Tóth, who's asking?

## 6.

The white salon received its name from the white Roisin furniture that Grandmother Roisin, Great-great-grandmother Roisin to me, my grandfather's grandmother (no: one down, my grandfather's grandfather's mother, my ancestress Marie Françoise Isabelle de Baudry, Marquise de Roisin and a legendary beauty, this just for the sake of the record; without these details life is so banal!) had brought with her from Paris. She was the confidante of Marie-Thérèse de France, the "Orphan of the Temple," daughter of King Louis XVI and granddaughter of Maria Theresa. In 1796, at the age of sixteen, the princess was let out of captivity, and until her marriage lived in Vienna under the protection of Grandmother Roisin's aunt, the high stewardess Countess Chanclos.

This is where they befriended each other. (We had a chinoiserie-patterned something at home, God only knows what to call it, a sort of *secrètaire*, a small bureau with drawers. Once I saw something like it at the court of the Spanish king and shouted, I know that piece!, which baffled them. Our parents called it the *shanclo*. This gave us much occasion for laughter, what a stupid name, but we called it a *shanclo*, too. We were not allowed to touch it. Needless to say, we did when no one was looking. We played blind man. We closed our eyes and stroked it, feeling the images in the round, a Chinese landscape, pagoda, trees, birds, and the wide, yellow mountings on the sides. They were made of brass. Or gold. We opted for gold.)

Roisin grandmother's father—and I'd rather not split hairs just now over how we are related, we just are—was put to death along with the royal family. He left a silken scarf behind that his daughter brought to this "dark, desolate, barbaric land," on it a brownish stain that his descendants insisted was blood. A scarf from the scaffold. *Liberté, égalité, fraternité*. Though in all the confusion, we may have been on the other side. Everybody running around like a chicken without its head. Succeeding generations kept the scarf on the wall of the domestic chapel, a relic, which my grandmother, of all people, took objection to on strict, Catholic grounds. Strangely enough, it was her father-in-law, who was no less clerical in his convictions—I seem to remember that he was the founder of the Christian People's Party—anyway, it was he who would not hear of it, opting instead for the inviolability of tradition. French rationalism and *nonchalance*: this too played a part in my great-grandfather's tenacity.

I inherited a white rococo buffet, too. A dream. And having said that, I haven't said half. What I mean is, it's at times like this that the brutality inherent in beauty reveals itself. The way it wreaks havoc with things. First and foremost, a beautiful object is not harmonious, but powerful. A buffet like this bursts a modern home apart at the seams. In order to accommodate a buffet like this, you need to build different houses, you need to live different lives. My buffet speaks about this otherness like an unsolicited Rilke, even though I tried packing the top full of books, magazines, sandwiches and, conversely, I cleared everything off, allowing the Carrara marble top to gleam. Surreptitiously, I may have even sneaked a silver candlestick on it. To no avail. On the other hand, in my father's house which, as far as its spaces are concerned, is like my own, the situation is fundamentally different. He has a corner display cabinet from the same series, a piece no less spectacular, but it behaves, it doesn't get out of hand, like mine. I think I know why. My father's eyes, his glance, puts the white monster where it belongs—in the past, and in the personal.

My glance is not like that. I can look like that only with my eyes closed.

## 7.

This great-great-grandfather of mine was a wise and gifted man ("*bewies vile Verstädnis und einen rightigen und klaren Blick sowohl für Menschen als auch Dinge*," his mother's friend, Ludovike Thürheim, writes), who was supposed to have said that in the mirror he sees himself as a dwarf, but in company, he feels a head taller than anybody else. (In one place my grandfather writes that he's 60 (!) percent taller than his dearly departed father, but I've made some calculations, so I can't underwrite this family legend with anything like a clear conscience. On the contrary (he writes), he feels just the opposite; he feels 60 percent taller and thus happier in the company of those who in matters of culture, erudition, power of discernment and humor eclipse him, for only in this manner can the knowledge and spirit of strangers improve our own, something the great Horace himself had considered a good thing. Poor grandfather, I reflected, there couldn't have been many people to his liking. Stupidity was not his strong point (*"Dummheit ist nicht meine Stärke"*). But he knew this too and so added another sentence: For lack of society of this ilk, the quiet reading room of a good library is a heartily welcome substitute. A heartily welcome substitute—clearly, grandfather made every effort to keep his innate arrogance in check.)

As the ambassador to the Vatican, this small, enigmatic man was responsible for negotiating the new concordance between Austria and the Holy See, which apparently was considered a major political tour de force. Possibly this is why Francis Joseph was supposed to have offered him the foreign affairs portfolio, but being introverted by nature, he would not take it. It was as a minister without portfolio that he became the *éminence grise* behind the throne, the gray eminence of foreign affairs in the years preceding the Austro-Hungarian Compromise. At the time Austria's affairs were in the hands of the "government of generals" who were itching to start a war somewhere, anywhere. Concurrently, Bismarck was fishing for an excuse to go to war with Austria, which, *cf.* the above, the generals were more than willing to supply. God knows why, but they simply could not see eye to eye on Schleswig-Holstein. Which led to Königgrätz, popularly known as Hradec Králové, a massacre that ended with Prussian victory, whereupon the generals had it spread round that it was my wise, short-statured great-great-grandfather who had made them do it (twisted their arm), because his Catholic bigotry could not abide a Protestant Prussia. What can I say. Still, this was over the top.

He almost never set pen to paper and communicated with the foreign ministry via messengers. He took pains, we might say, to destroy every shred of evidence that could have exonerated him. (With slight exaggeration, he hardly wrote anything more than twice in his life: a diary at the age of twenty when he, along with his mother and two older sisters, were guests of Charles X and they took an excursion to Trianon when it was nothing more than a pretty palace, etc., but the diary was destroyed in 1944–45; and also, there was the heated, intriguing correspondence with his friend, the Prince of Reichstandt, Napoleon's son, the eaglet whom Metternich kept on a short leash—*L'aiglon,* as Rostand calls him in his play. It was my great-great-grandfather who'd kept body and soul together for him.)

The smear-mongering may have worked in part because he ended his life at a mental clinic in Pirna, near Dresden. These gentlemen, the smear-mongers, wrote all sorts of things in their memoirs. For instance, that he set his palace at Csákvár on fire, and before he was confined to a mental institution, he beat his wife. Ridiculous! Still, for lack of written evidence, it was difficult to silence the "storytellers."

Besides, he did set fire to it. He set fire to the drapes. He tipped over the burning candle with his elbow, the one that his valet, the grandfather of the above-mentioned Menyus Tóth ("In your grandfather's palace the names of the dogs and menservants never varied, so he wouldn't have to learn new names all the time!"), regularly set out for the express purpose of lighting His Excellency's after-dinner cigar, delivered to him on the last Thursday of every third month by Fischer & Sonnenberg from the establishment of H.J. Hoess & Sons. (Neatly filed, we still have the bills—a bill with value-added tax from the last century as an object of art!) (For as I have read in László Berényi's indispensable work, *The Definitive History of the Match,* gentlemen were loath to light their cigars with the foul-smelling, sulfurous matches available to them at the time.) As for the wife-beating: for one thing, let him throw the first stone, et cetera, et cetera, and for another, anyone who had ever laid eyes on Maria-Polixena (Xéna to the family), Princess von Lobkovitz, who far surpassed her lawfully wedded husband in height as well as width (here the 60 percent applies!), laughed such rumors off. But then, not everyone had laid eyes on her.

As for his mental disorder, today we'd call it chronic depression. ("Depressed? How can a God-fearing man be depressed?" "Hold your tongue!") My grandfather was deeply troubled by the bum wrap history had given his own grandfather, providing as it did an entirely false picture of his endeavors while ignoring his merits and achievements, attributed to other people. During his Vienna years, he spent a lot of time in various libraries and came up with ample evidence which, alas, he was no longer in a position—plus the time was not right—to put in the public domain. He found Xéna's letter, in which she wrote her sister that "Königgrätz was a disaster, but it is even more disastrous that they are now blaming Móric Miklós for it, whereas, my dearest Louise, he was the only one to raise his voice against the war. Furthermore . . ." Later, my grandfather found this "furthermore," too, in the Crown Council records . . . Francis Joseph told Great-great-grandfather that Napoleon III had applied the most pressure on him to go to war. He's holding a gun to my head, the Emperor said. To which my great-great-grandfather replied, We can't go to war with the Germans because that would result in an immediate uprising in Italy, and we're in no position to wage war on two fronts . . . Are you quite certain, Your Majesty, that that gun is loaded?

That's the truth.

Was *odi profanum vulgus* his motto? I don't know. But I'm willing to bet it was.

His favorite saying was handed down in the family from father to son: *oui, entendu mais pas écouté*, heard, but not attended to. It sounds a lot better in French, which is why the family said it in French. Always in the language that'll do it most justice! Well, I put a stop to that, *ich don't sprechen.*

# 8.

When Menyus Tóth entered the Roisin salon to announce that the Communists had arrived, Father gave Grandmother's belly a horrendous kick. Not to worry: from inside.

The kicking of an expectant mother's belly by her infant son from inside, that's legitimate kitsch: the belly—what's more, a bulging belly!; the cards stirring, in a version with more *finesse,* the winning card tumbles to the floor; touched to the quick, the paternal hand throbs in unison—there's no cheap anecdote that won't do the trick. On the other hand, and in the spirit of the Fourth Commandment, it is of course to be frowned upon.

I frown upon it too, personally. True, I have hardly hit anyone in all my life. I could count the number of times I've done it on one hand. It'd hardly take more fingers than the usual five. Even if I were to add those I'd have liked to hit, and not just theoretically, like I'm going to do a fast *csárdás* on Big Huszár, or give Brezhnev a punch in the nose, but when overtaken with rage and humiliation, from which only one path seems to lead, when the muscles are strained to the breaking point—even then the number isn't much greater. And, needless to say, I was never even close to hitting my mother or father. Well, yes, my father once. But that was ages ago. Besides, he was smashed out of his skull, so it's like it wasn't him at all. No. It's not like that. When I slapped him—but no, it wasn't a slap, it was worse, it was kicking, a rough-and-tumble header, et cetera—a stop frame, in high focus, like in a film, we stared each other down: let's not beat about the bush, that was him and that was me. I was right, and that confused me. It confused me.

## 9.

The customs and opportunities for a good fight evidence an admirable variety through the ages. Grandfather related to me how, when he studied at Oxford (read for his exams there), the Duke of Kent invited him to dinner. Since there was no one in the palace when he got there, no one except for the servants that is, he asked for a horse and went riding to pass the time. He reached a hedgerow at the same time as another rider, so much so, that they collided. The other rider, a young man the same age as my grandfather, shouted a number of imprecations at him, then asked him to dismount.

"Naturally, sir. What is it you want?"

"I want to fight, sir, that's what I want," and he fell on Grandfather with his riding crop. The latter was somewhat taken aback at the island country's unconventional choice of weapons, but did his best to accommodate himself to the circumstances and peculiarities of the unfamiliar playing field, and conscientiously gave the stranger back the thrashing he'd received. Later that night at dinner they met again. The Duke of Kent gave him a friendly nod.

"My honored friend. I think we have met before."

"Possibly," Grandfather said in confirmation of his cordial host's surmise.

The story cannot be translocated to the Continent.

## 10.

Grandfather told his stories as if he were dictating. As if his teeth were being pulled. And yet, without a break. He pruned the fruit trees, at times the roses, and told his stories. Knee britches, cardigan, bill cap, pruning shears. The pruning had to be finished by the first hallelujah. As if I weren't there. As if he were talking to himself. But for the sake of the record. As if he were ashamed. He felt it "out of place" to talk about himself, so he merely hinted at the stories, bringing them up as if they were common knowledge (could or should be common knowledge). Such and such a thing transpired. As if he'd taken an oath to be as sparing of his words as humanly possible. He'd have much preferred to avoid the use of the first-person singular altogether, regardless of the consequences. No skin off his back.

Maybe it's because I was his first grandson, but he never told his stories to anyone else, not Grandmother, nor Father, not his other grandchildren, just his grandson, just me.

He loves England, the English people, the English language. He'd spent his formative years there (that's where he "got to know the world"). He loved the awesome, re- and reelaborated, strict order of their traditions. It's no small feat being strict and skeptical at the same time. Yet it's this contradiction that makes for good husbandry. It's easier in English, he kept saying.

I was, he said, present on the crowded, poorly lit gallery in October 1899 when the aged Joe Chamberlain placed President Krüger's letter on the table of the House, inaugurating the bloody Boer War thereby. I shook hands with Cecil Rhodes, the billionaire founder of Rhodesia. Many thought he was the brains behind the war. He gave me a dedicated photograph. Since I was a good rider, in that pitch of war fever, I volunteered for the university team. When my foreign citizenship came to light, they left me high and dry in Southampton. Not all my friends who were shipped out made it back.

Also, he was a frequent guest at Blenheim, near Oxford, at the palace of the dukes of Marlborough, gifted to the first duke, Victor von Höchstädt, a colleague of Eugene of Savoy, by a grateful nation in 1704. It came to pass that William II came to visit his grandmother, Queen Victoria. The M's invited him to a pheasant and rabbit hunt. A couple of us "senior" Oxford students, Grandfather said, were the beaters and couldn't get enough of the sight of the guests, the coach and fours and sixes, the lantern festoons hanging from the trees, the rows of brightly lit rooms. How was I to know that in twenty years' time—as a government official of relatively high standing—I'd be meeting him as an enemy of England.

I was also a guest of the dukes of Devonshire in their opulent seventeenth-century baroque mansion at Chatsworth. In the domestic theater, an incredible number of fabulous artworks and amateur theatricals. Though I'd been around, I haven't seen such wealth since. As Lord Huntington, my host was present in the political arena. His elderly wife was a passionate bridge player. They called her *Ponte vecchio* behind her back. (Not long ago, as grateful as ever, the State reclaimed the mansion in lieu of inheritance taxes.)

From a window on St. James's Street I saw Queen Victoria's cortège. It put an end to an age. Later, the sarcophagus of Francis Joseph would put an end to another.


11.


The first joke of my life has to do with Queen Victoria. My father told it. Everyone had a good laugh. I laughed too, though I didn't understand it, because I didn't know what a joke was. I knew that this was a joke only because they said that this here is a joke. In which case, is it true, or not, and what makes it interesting? The fact that it happened, or the fact that the world is constructed in such a way that it could happen *because* it's interesting? Or is my father interesting? But I didn't ask. I laughed. I heard it many times afterward, too. My father loved telling it, it was always a success, as if it were to his credit that the thing happened, or that the world is constructed in the way it's constructed. The joke puts Queen Victoria in the center who, being well advanced in years, could no longer control every little quiver of her physiology; once, during a formal reception, a certain sound issued from her abdominal region. Pardon me, offered the French ambassador, bowing low in the stink and the silence. Soon afterward, the old, royal physiology made itself heard once again, followed by the chivalrous *mille pardons* again. Meanwhile, the German ambassador got a jaundiced eye, these scapegrace French, a ladle in every soup, but he'd beat him at his own game. And so, when the Throne of all the Brits gave off another popping sound, the German ambassador sprang to his feet, snapped his ankles together, and loud enough for all the assembled company to hear the generous German offer, announced, "Your Majesty! In the name of the Great German Empire, this and the next five farts I take upon myself!"

My father may have said it in German, because it works better in German, *das und die nächste fünf übernnehme ich im Namen des grossen deutschen Reiches.* Because it came from the heart, my father was good at making fun of those *piefke* Germans.

## 12.

At Blenheim my grandfather made the acquaintance of a stout young man. His mother, Lady Randolph, was friends with our family. They used to drink beer together. He was an astute, cynical youth. He smoked an incredible number of cigars; the smoke ate itself into Grandfather's tweed jackets. They enjoyed each other's company. They studied each other. They felt very distant yet very close, and this fascinated them both. Fascination is the basis of friendship. One day the Hungarian ambassador offered

Grandfather the cautious remark that he might possibly limit his appearances with the young man in fashionable locales, inasmuch as it could lead to a drastic reduction in the number of invitations, especially in the case of the duke of Marlborough, who considered the young man as something of a black sheep. But before my grandfather could be forced into making a decision, the problem resolved itself. The young man was sent to South Africa as the war correspondent for the *Morning Post*. Later the world learned to respect the unruly, overindulgent lord as Winston Churchill.

A small, unlikely story, as if I were reading it in a book of fairy tales. My grandfather owned the complete edition of *The Thousand and One Arabian Nights*, a real rarity. He brought it from London. The translation was by Sir Richard Francis Burton, whom—Grandfather was always quick to add—the booksellers knew as Captain Burton. Sometimes he read out loud from it. The fact that I didn't know English was no impediment. Obviously, it never occurred to him.

It was during these Churchillian times that Grandfather took a trip with his father to the New World to visit the widow of our relative Miksa for the Easter holidays, this Miksa—first bid!—being possibly the first cousin of my great-grandfather and an avid *sportsman*; he founded the Magyar Athletic Club, the MAC, then invented a gauge or whatever that could count steps—long-distance runners, he said, can't do without them. As a young man, he became secretary of the embassy in a place called Washington, which was considered an exotic locale at the time. (The list that he got from the Ministry of the Exterior indicating those he could safely socialize included 3, i.e., three, names.)

This relative, Miksa, was for all practical purposes a firstborn son (his older brother, poor thing, was mentally retarded; back then, they called lots of things retardation, whereas it is possible that he was simply dyslexic), but having fallen head over heels in love with the ravishing and witty Sarah Virginia Carrol, widow of General Griffin, he disqualified himself. (I'm referring to the inheritance, of course.) And to add insult to injury, Aunt Sally was not only from common stock, a *mésalliance* (I like misalliances; my mother, for example, was one; she descended from a long line of misalliances), but a Methodist Protestant to boot. You can imagine. Also, this transpired just when the Counts of Frakno (us!) were, for a short time, wealthier than the dukes.

This came about, it seems, because on February 16, 1833, at Prosnitz, the older brother of my short-statured great-great-grandfather, the eldest son of Franciska Roisin, led Marie Gräfin von Plettenberg-Wittern zu Mietingen, one of the wealthiest heiresses in Europe at the time, to the altar. They fell in love, or whatnot. Being the last scion of the wealthiest branch of her family, she came well equipped: Mietingen in Württemberg, Davensberg in Westfalia, also the estates in Nordkirchen, Meinkövel, Seeholz, Lacke, Buxfort, Grothaus, Alrot and Hanselberg, with four palaces, of which at least two are included in all the art history books, three in the standard editions—all in all, a territory as large as a third of the kingdom of Württenberg, with the entailed property of Tata thrown in for good measure. The German estates also came with several smallish towns and a number of villages with thriving industries. Certain calculations put the income per hold from said estates at eight times that of Hungary. According to other calculations it was fourteen.

This is the eight or fourteen times that Aunt Sally had torpedoed, but it was worth it. She enchanted all who knew her. The entire family. (Which did nothing, need I say, to alter the order of inheritance). My great-grandfather and grandfather were among those enchanted. "A matron very like eternal spring," my grandfather says with trembling lips—which, considering his aloof and unresponsive nature, was tantamount to enchantment. It was during this Easter visit that Aunt Sally said certain words to the two men, one fifteen, the other forty years her junior, which over time became legendary in the family: *"Nicola, Maurice, kiss me here!,"* while with her index finger—but at this juncture there are several variations in currency about where the matron, likened to eternal spring, may have pointed.

Fascinating, the way an inheritance such as this rolls hither and thither like a huge ball (balloon), pressing (oppressing) everyone and everything with its weight, while it is diverted this way and that by deaths, loves, infertilities, contractual agreements. An inheritance is dreamlike, unexpected even when it is secure, an open-and-shut case. The weighty Plettenberg inheritance flies through the air with the greatest of ease, like the man on the flying trapeze. In short, the older brother disqualifies himself through sheer happiness; his good younger brother, also a preeminent sportsman and horse fanatic, a "Sport-Nickerl," the first foreigner in the Jockey Club of London, a European-champion gentleman rider, a member of the circle of the Queen Elizabeth Riders and rumored to be on intimate terms with the Queen herself ("Not true, not true, not true"; also, "Aunt Liz didn't evidence a liking for the bald-headed hermit because of the horses, but *in spite* of them"—revolting!) could, and did, enjoy the fabulous fortune for twelve years, deceasement without a wife, the ball is passed back one, uncle, the firstborn of the Hungarian Honvéd colonel from 1848, three years' enjoyment, then the youngest brother comes on the scene, or would, had not the former left a sloppy last will and testament behind, but did, whereby, taking the whole of the incredible riches with her, the widow slipped through the eye of the needle that had thus presented itself, even if with more difficulty, perhaps, than a camel, but lock, stock, and barrel, finally selling the beautiful Nordkirchen to the dukes of Aarenberg. The grandson who did not inherit all this—i.e., this was the all he did not inherit—has the same name as me, which is one of the reasons I told you the story. He comes highly recommended. I follow the course of his life with special attention. When we first met, he showed me his passport—a pretty mixed bag of fleas. My mother gave me this name because as far as she knew, no one else in the family had it. I resented her mistake. My multiplication confused me. There it was, my name, me, with the likeness of a stranger. Shoo! Shoo!, I would have liked to say, Away! Away! On the other hand, I have no other relative who is as close to me as he (me). He lives in Belgium. To make a long story short, he belongs to the Szigliget branch of the family. A man to be reckoned with, he loves to eat. He knows how. Could I have inherited this from him?

## 13.

From the point of view of *"all that wasn't,"* ours, mine, is a good branch. Had I lived at any time during the past four hundred years, I would have never had to put, or have someone else put, more than five people out of the way at any one time in order to have it all. Including, naturally, whoever happened to be my father at the time.

## 14.

The shameful Dreyfus affair also fell to my grandfather's youth. We had plenty of embarrassment because of the notorious Major Walsin, who played a regrettable part in it all. To this day, in certain countries (France, Norway) our name is mentioned almost exclusively in connection with this trial.

When I first heard about the dastardly Esterházy major or captain or whatnot, I just shrugged. Ours is a big family, you'll find all sorts, extra large, winged, tanga, royalists, democrats, patriots, traitors, mostly pro-Habsburg Labanc loyalists, though also some anti-Habsburg Kuruc patriots, each according to his heart. It's only natural, I concluded.

But I was wrong. All it took was some inquiries addressed to the family, a bit of reading, and I saw clear as day: every Esterházy is cap à pied a man of eminence. Each and every one. (Women, too, in rare instances. But the real *esterházy europaeus* is preeminently a male, worse comes to worse, a hermaphrodite.) Also— and this just for the sake of argument—were one of us to turn out to be less then preeminent, then—sooner or later—it would inevitably surface that the individual in question is not a real Esterházy.

Just like the truth, we depend on the details. I will thus furnish the details. Marianna, the younger sister of the celebrated French Valentin Ladislas, my small-statured great-great grandfather's grandfather's grandfather's older brother, whose name was Antal, and who faithfully followed Prince Rákóczi into exile in Rodosto, was born on October 9, 1741. Calling this a problem would not be warranted. I wouldn't even call it a problem that about twenty-one years later, an uncle past the first blush of youth, a certain Jean André César, Marquis de Ginestus, began an affair with his half-orphaned relative, from sheer boredom, probably, and said affair bore fruit.

"Oh me, oh my, what a nasty bloating!" the indisposed little Marianna's mother cried out, but the uncle, a man of the world, reassured her and posthaste sent for his own physician, Dr. Valsin, who came up with a diagnosis of dropsy, and animated by a suggestion from his employer, promptly offered to accompany his (new) patient to a bath for a cure that was sure to bring relief.

We have no reliable information on what they meant by relief. But in any case, with the passage of a certain number of months, Marianna brought a baby boy into the world who was entered into the records at Vallerangue as Jean-Marie Auguste Valsin, then she returned to her mother in Vigan, who was delighted, indeed, about that nasty bloating having disappeared.

"That nasty bloating has disappeared," said she.

"Yes, *maman,*" her daughter said with equanimity.

But that's not the point. The point is that it soon got around that the newborn was the adopted son of Dr. Valsin. So as we can clearly illustrate, it was the grandson of the faux-bastard son of this Valsin who was the incriminated Dreyfus bloke.

So far so good. Life went on its merry way. The fact that the French Revolution broke out wasn't a problem either; on the contrary, it was the high point and shining glory of history. In the process, they guillotined the royal family, alas, while my Aunt Marianna, who was on good terms with said family, was taken to the Temple. Again, no problem, just an inconvenience. (By the way, when a son was born to her older brother, Louis XVI sent the following letter: *I was very pleased to learn that a little Hussar was born in the Marais and that mother and child are well. I beg that the father accept my heartfelt good wishes. A tenant of Versailles.*)

But to return to the problem. It started when, night having descended, the prison having turned quiet, a member of the guard who was insufficiently fired by revolutionary fervor slipped a piece of paper into the hand of the lady Marianna. She'd been in prison for months, but her hands had not been roughened by labor. The paper said, *Madame, do not fret, I shall set you free.* This was the problem, this goodness, because who do you think her liberator was? No other than her own illegitimate, misbegotten son, the bastard, whom we thought we had paid good riddance to just now. Afterward, on September 22, in front of the Nîmes registrar, M. Fouquet, the grateful mother acknowledged this (good-hearted) Valsin as her natural son and adopted him, whereupon he took the name of Valsin (Walsin) Esterházy.

Well, that's how it happened. In short, the ignoble lieutenant is an Esterházy, but just barely, *un peu*; by the same token, anyone

416

could be, you, or me. Needless to say, we lost no time is suing him for usurpation of our name. However, the French Court only stripped him of his title of count (*kleine Fische, gute Fische*), but in the spirit of the Napoleonic Code, allowed him to use our name. A constitutional state. The family was up in arms. According to my grandfather's notes, "though it cost us several thousand francs, he finally relinquished our name, documents in the N. (National) Archives."

Typical. The collective family lore, or disposition on this thing, is trying to excuse even this intruder insofar as it agrees with the opinion of certain (celebrated!) French Academics who insist that this valsinized Esterházy is as much a victim of the intrigues of the traitors in the highest echelons of the French Ministry of Defense as Dreyfus himself. They contend that his superiors forced him to bear witness against Dreyfus, so that afterward, leaving him in the soup, they should force him into voluntary exile in England.

In short, Walsin. Not a jot of Esterházy. I will question him, announced my implacable grandfather, but then didn't.


# 15.


The same thing happens to me that happens to all those who decide to study their family tree. I realize how little I know about my ancestors. But then we always know little about them, just the little that we know, and no more. There is little that we can know about them, and this is independent of the family and the availability of documents. All that any of us can discover, time and time again, is that our grandfather was a stern-looking, dignified old gentleman with a goatee, and virtuous, *cf.* his seven children.

Another thing. It's not like we simply call up the past, strolling inside it at leisure, taking an objective survey, it's not like that, because the present is always too aggressive, it plunges into the troubled waters of the past in order to fish out what alone can be of use to it. Maybe I don't remember the past very well, and simply gobble it up in order to feed what I am today.

To live is to fabricate a past for ourselves. (Saying courtesy of my grandfather.)

## 16.

Which reminds me, incidentally and in retrospect, that a Diesbach–Belleroch (count), who is related to the wife of my Belgian contingent, writes in her work on the life of Catherine the Great that pursuant to the French Revolution the refugees veritably flooded the Court at St. Petersburg, where through intriguing against each other and fabricating horrendous lies, they attempted to obtain pecuniary favors. Among them was the above-mentioned Valentin Ladislas, poor Marianna's brother, the ambassador to the Russian Court of the French royal family in exile, who was present at the audience with his son (whom a couple of years before a "tenant of Versailles" greeted with such gallantry) in order to express their gratitude for little Valentin Philippe's appointment as honorary lieutenant of the Imperial Guard (which brought a small stipend with it). As the child lowered himself on one knee for the ritual kiss of the hand, in his excitement he let pass some wind, whereupon the Czarina commented with a sigh:

"Ah, my lords, an honest word at last!"

This by way of an addendum to the Dreyfus affair.

## 17.

Thanks to my father's perfectly timed kick, Grandmother assumed that Menyus Tóth was saying that the Communists were in her belly. That's why the look of alarm. Besides, how did her servant know? ("These people always know everything.") Grandmother always knew her duty, and expected the same of others. That's why she appeared to be on her own—because she belonged not to people, but to her duty. The other thing that set her apart from other human beings I've known was her steadfast belief in God. She believed in Him the way only those who lived centuries before us knew how. How do I know this? I don't.

## 18.

Once I received a phone call from a madman who started telling me that the Kádár regime got inside his mother's belly, but I mustn't think he's mad because he's telling me this.

"I wouldn't dream of it!"

He sounded pretty convincing. It had occurred to me, too, that a dictatorship must surely transform the body, too—we end up growing two noses, or webs between our fingers. Actually, it wasn't inside his mother, but his father. His father's guts. That's why he joined the police. To fight for the regime that ruined him, because his father had sacrificed himself. And for what? For nothing. Because to join the police is a sacrifice, isn't that right, and I don't mean the traffic police, if you get my drift. I said I did. He thought he was talking to my father, not to a child.

"Why are you telling me this?"

Swearing like a stevedore, he slammed down the phone.

# 19.

In short, my grandmother first thought of the Lord, because she always thought of Him first, then she thought of her duty. Which at the moment was kicking up a storm inside her.

"Have you gone mad?! Menyus?!" When grandmother was angry, there was no knowing whether she was asking a question or making a statement. "Who are where?!"

Being reluctant to let the horrible word pass his lips yet again, the faithful manservant merely waved an arm behind him, making faces into the bargain. Grandmother nodded.

"You really are mad. A pity."

The faithful manservant continued to shake his head feverishly. He appeared chagrined, as if he were playing a game of Twenty Questions with his mistress, and she couldn't catch on. Still, the information was so preposterous, Grandmother believed it without a second thought. Even if poor Tóth's gone mad, he can't have gone *that* mad. There are things that cannot be imagined, even if we let go the hand of reason. *The hand of reason,* I heard this a lot afterward.

She walked over to the wide rear window, which afforded a view of the park stretching into the distance in front of the palace (or the back, there were various schools of thought on the subject contending with one another), for a while meandering in place in front of the huge, unpleasant neoclassical building, then taking a French leave and leisurely disappearing among the peaks of the Vértes. The true mistress of the palace was not my grandmother, but her mother-in-law, the "old Excellency," whom I got to meet later on, when we were forcibly resettled. That's where she died. For weeks before her death, she lay in bed, motionless. She had only one gesture left to her—if she had to yawn, she put her hand up to her lips. This one gesture lasted until her death, the universal bane of humanity.

My father's birth—because he's going to be born even though right now he's kicking around inside helplessly like a crypto-Communist—brought Grandmother her independence when the family moved to the palace at Majk, originally intended for a hunting lodge.

Grandmother was short on kindness. This made what was tough in her even tougher; her requests sounded like orders, though her orders never sounded like commands. On the other hand, her consistency made her actions predictable, reliable. This, coupled with her natural inclination to help others, would at times take on the appearance of kindness, just the same.

Speaking of appearances, though both her parents were Károlyis ("Your grandmother is impeccably Károlyi"), there was nothing aristocratic about her to the eye; also, apropos shortness, she was short on the need for pleasure. (She complied with the Victorian advice about lovemaking to "close your eyes and think of England" with remarkable ease.) She cared not a jot for beauty, she cared not a jot for what was on her plate, she had no contact with the world of the senses. My grandmother didn't even have a body, except when she bore children.

"Have you ever been in labor, Menyus?"

Menyus turned red. He loved my grandmother very much, even though he couldn't have known at the time that his mistress's second child, my father's younger brother, would be given the same name as his. Love is not the right word; he wouldn't presume to love her; let's just say that he respected her emotionally.

"Because I'm about to."

"No, you're not, Your Excellency, you're not going into labor at this time."

"Then what would you say I'm doing?!"

"Talking to me." He turned red again. "I'm sorry, but you

421

mustn't go into labor now. The timing is off." He gestured behind him once again, but this time with his head, like when they're pulling the bit on a horse. Grandmother gave an impatient wave of the hand.

"What have you got against the Communists?"

"*Me,* Your Excellency?" said the abashed valet. He wanted to say that they're not talking about him now, but he didn't, because no one ever talked about him. I wouldn't be surprised if at the bottom of her heart my grandmother were a Communist. One thing is for sure; in every sphere of life, she strove for equality. But no, this may be misleading like this. My grandmother was no revolutionary, she was a lady of rank. But she judged everyone by the same standard. She probably didn't think that life determines consciousness. Of course, if it does, she couldn't have thought this to begin with.

"Menyus," Grandmother said, thereby putting an end to this highly irregular chat, "go get the carriage harnessed. I need to make the express to Tata. And stop that ridiculous pointing. As for you, son," she said severely for the benefit of my infant father, "you will have to wait." Actually, she said what Faust said in the moment of his joy, to wit, tarry, my son, tarry, it is far better for you inside. Then, pushing her bulging belly before her, she made her way out of the salon we called the Roisin.

## 20.

My father did as he was told and stayed put inside the agreeable darkness for another week or so. The last peaceful week of his life. His last week of freedom. He waited until they declared the glorious Republic of Councils.

His life began with more complications than our family had a right to expect. A new Esterházy life slips into this world as effortlessly as if everything, everyone had been waiting just for this, as if there had been a void in nature, a vacuum, a lack, a deficit, a no waiting for a yes, a wound—a light scrape—which, just like a new shoot, appears as if from the heavens, softly, without pain, healed. Order is restored. The serfs leap about by the light of their bonfires, while inside the palace, palaces, glasses of cut-crystal click against one another; priestly hands, chaplains' hands and bishops' hands, are clasped in a prayer of thanksgiving.

The way new films are advertised at the movies: Coming soon! Coming soon! Coming soon! How much attention, attentiveness, labor, planning preceded the new arrival! They were concerned for the newcomer, and they were concerned for themselves; midwives, barber-surgeons, nannies, priest and, last but not least, solicitors crowded around the event in droves. Except this time, the droves were missing.

My father, as I have often heard and read in the family records (for it was a recurrent motif of epic proportions), was the first Esterházy in centuries to have come into the world without rank and means. Without rank and means, the family kept repeating, proud as peacocks, but proud all the same. See? We even managed *this*! Not only have we got more rank and means than we know what to do with, one of us even managed the opposite. Of course, they said this only *afterward*; they thought back on these few official Soviet Council days as a joke that's had its day, a historical scherzo. They had no idea at the time how easily one can get used to such jokes, how well we'd fare without rank and means, that my father was simply the first of a long line. His rumpled layette marked the end, the end of the aforementioned centuries, except no one knew it at the time. The finality of the last moment is seen for what it is only from the vantage point of the moment after the last and, therefore by definition, too late.

## 21.

The new century, which made its appearance in the guise of so-cialist principles and liberalism (or as one of us put it at the time, alas, this whole Jewish *virschaft*), was not welcomed by the family with overwhelming enthusiasm. You're either a staunch Catholic royalist conservative, or overwhelming enthusiasm. These princi-ples, the old Count announced, either had in mind a nation of in-dividuals without faults and weaknesses, or a nation made up of automatons who, provided they're well oiled, programmed, will do the work assigned to them without thinking. But these theo-ries are not for human consumption.

Collective family lore does not reach its spiritual heights through the recollection of revolutions, its visual angle narrows—petty-mindedly, we ignore the point of view of our murderers; of what was aristocratic, only the squeamishness remains, plus a pinch of self-conceit, plus presumption tinged with fear—this the intriguing voice of the aunts.

## 22.

The dictator of our community was a certain Gyula Halnek, the foreman of a construction brigade, whose family had lived on our estates for generations, and died in our service. My great-grand-father dismissed only his father from my great-grandfather's service, though because he would not stop drinking. When the revolution broke out, this foreman stood at the head of the socialist party cell of Csákvár, which had been recruited from a bunch of work dodgers and braggarts of both sexes. This socialist wolf pack lost no time in launching an attack on "the Count" and "the Priest."

Though Halnek's character and style of life were to be condemned (said Great-grandfather, shocked at himself for having remembered Halnek's name), I must say (said he), that Halnek was a first-rate agitator. He went around the village smiling enigmatically:

"The Count better watch himself. He hasn't heard the last of us yet."

Halnek knew that a government relying on the will of the masses must take the old proverb *panem et circenses* to heart, so he assembled a brass band which, on major occasions, played the "Marseillaise" full blast, possibly even with as much conviction as it could muster, but painfully, hopelessly off-key.

More than a week before the event that was to come more than a week later, my great-grandfather was informed that by way of punishing him, one might say, the socialist party cell had voted in a red-flag protest march accompanied by the brass band. The red flag took Great-grandfather by surprise.

"Am I to understand that Halnek has turned his back on Socialist principles in favor of Communist principles?"

"We wouldn't know about that, Your Excellency."

My great-grandfather, in my great-grandfather's own words, made those men of his who were Party members promise to join the march, pacing themselves so that there should be someone in each line in order to prevent any possible excesses. But he wasn't worried. He'd seen enough workers' marches ("In order to satisfy my curiosity, I marched with the crowd in a number of towns"); he had a high regard for the iron discipline which ensured that there would be no infringement of the regulations—provided that that's what the leaders had in mind. But now my great-grandfather was told that Halnek was intending to lead the march into the palace yard, and hold a people's rally there.

That hit closer to home.

# 23.

"My relationship to the people of Csákvár was no run-of-the-mill relationship, to say the least. Most people see a mysterious something in the lord and his manor which, independent of my person, is supposed to be the cause of all things good and bad that transpire at Csákvár. Should someone be short of money, he asks for a low-interest loan from the retirement fund; should misfortune strike or a fire break out, people turn to the manor for bricks and other construction materials; should someone suffer from an incurable disease, they turn to the lord for aid—time and time again I had the impression that when someone dies, I'm held responsible for that, too!, a dubious honor, as if I were immortal! I think they think I am. I will have to disappoint you, good people! The kissing of the hand was also still in currency. But when 'his benevolent lordship' decided—whether in keeping with the modern way of thinking or from fear of infectious disease, plus the running noses in wintertime—to discourage the kissing of his hand, right away they said, 'He's too proud. He won't even let us kiss his hand!' Only much later, during the Commune of 1919, did friend and foe alike stop calling me Your Lordship and my estate a domain. But when, by the grace of God plus the innate good sense of the people, Communism was overthrown on August 2, the most bloodthirsty insiders were among the first to kiss my hand, cowards that they were. In the village, the palace and its lord were taboo. I can't express it in words, but even under the Communists, for instance, I often heard my indignant gatekeepers and hunters report that so and so is a Communist because he had the audacity to whistle or yell while on the palace grounds. Needless to say, I never brought up the whistling with anyone. But the idea that anybody would want to effect entry into the palace without

426

permission seemed so extraordinary and ridiculous, that on that particular morning, some people laughed in disbelief. 'Have you heard? Halnek wants to march into the palace yard!' As if they were saying that he wanted to fly, or that he's the Pope."

24.

After my great-grandfather decided that they would rather be cudgeled to death in their own home than anywhere else, they waited with equanimity for things to take their course. For the sake of appearances, Great-grandfather had servants stationed by the doors, and he took some money and assorted valuables to himself, recommending that the rest of the family do the same, in case they must flee the palace. They were expecting luncheon guests, my great-grandfather's sister-in-law, Countess Eleonora Lamberg, and our immediate neighbor, Count Fülöp Merán. There being no political agitation on their estates, they were surprised at the local goings-on.

"I had no idea a revolution was in progress!" the Countess laughed. My grandmother looked out the window. From time to time she had to, so she wouldn't have to see people. Afterward, she confessed these weaknesses of hers to the priest.

Since my great-grandfather was in the habit of taking a sleeping cure out on the terrace after lunch—a habit he refused to break—he took leave of the company, saying he hoped they would continue to enjoy themselves. He also requested that they abide by the cautionary measures he'd put into effect, which were based on sangfroid, self-possession, and forbearance. He leaned back in his chaise lounge, brought from Kolozsvár, and slipped inside his comfortable foot sack. He couldn't see anything from his terrace, but he could clearly make out that characteristic rumble, that undifferentiated drone that crowds make and which onstage—as far as Great-grandfather knew—was imitated by the extras standing in for the crowd by repeating the words "rhabarbah, rhabarbah." I think that for my great-grandfather, this is what the revolution meant, this rhabarbah.

## 25.

"They stuck the red flag on the uppermost step of the staircase from where Fendrich, excuse me, Comrade Fendrich, who made his living as a logger, carpenter and master mason, opened the rally. To the right and left of Gyula Halnek, two henchmen stood at attention. The perseverance with which these two bodyguards stood their officially appointed ground, even in the cruelest cold, during rallies held out in the open, at meetings that often dragged on for hours, filled one and all with awe. As I see it, the unruffled stoical perseverance of these two strong men did more for this whole Jewish *virschaft* than all the words that they (and us!) thought were so important.

The sum and substance of Halnek's speech was the division of my estates. The motion was unanimously passed amid frenzied shouting. I won't pretend I liked it.

Conservative parties always make the same fundamental mistake. They refuse to acknowledge the legitimacy of the need for land reform. In Parliament, their fight against radical liberal and social aspirations exhausts itself in unyielding protest. Spinal sclerosis! The priest from Környe sent so-called prescribed exercises. (Ever since Uncle Miksa, people think we're a sporting family.) Luckily, they can't see up on the terrace. The parish priest is a strange sort, I wouldn't like to lock horns with him. But his prescription may work—proof positive that a man with the wrong ideas can still do good. His penmanship is admirable, his use of the quill imparts rhythm and dynamism to his calligraphy. I must do the exercises slowly, he writes, at least three times each with breaks in between, which comes to fifteen minutes in all.

Rhabarbah, rhabarbah.

During his address, there were frequent angry outcries against myself and the Esterházy family, who had been bleeding the people dry for centuries, but enough is enough—which, to non-socialist ears, mine included, seemed to be in utterly bad taste.

Then came the rope affair, right on schedule. It was always brought up against me at such rallies, I am told.

Though I'd been handing out kindling wood to the needy, a custom I took over from my late lamented father, within the bounds of reason, of course, stealing wood took on unprecedented proportions in the village. Also, they were not satisfied with plundering the woods. Besides collecting dry twigs in the castle park, they broke off branches and young saplings. Is it any wonder if at times I ran out of patience and with a show of determination sent the culprits scurrying from the grounds? (Some people even bragged, 'The Count sent me running *personally*!') Under the circumstances, I had every right to do so, de facto, because I had been victimized, and de jure, because it came to my attention that they were trafficking with the wood they stole from me. Driven by mutual envy, some people actually approached my wife to complain that it was becoming impossible to pay [sic!] the price [sic!] of the stolen kindling, because they were asking two crowns for an apron full. As a result, when subsequently an old woman wanted to tie some kindling wood round with a rope, I took it away from her, led her up to the palace gate, then went home with the rope. The rope was not my property, I admit. But it is an out-and-out lie that I gave the woman a sound thrashing with it, also that the woman wasn't even old, and that I, so to speak, cosseted her into the bargain. This too is a malicious lie. Anyone familiar with my age, character, biography, my views on the family as well as my commitment to my Church (during my

great trials and tribulations they mockingly said I danced attendance on the clergy) will know how ridiculous this is, and that it
reflects on itself and those that spread it abroad, rather than on me.

In short, this 'Esterházy rope,' which came up at most of their
rallies, grew into uncontested proof of my aristocratic callousness,
avarice, and arrogance. At such times vigorous interjections were
to be heard. For instance, that the rope should be used to string
me up by the feet, so my lovely blue blood could circulate back
and forth, which I took as a healthy manifestation of folk humor.
Meanwhile, the old woman attended all the rallies, loudly clamoring to be heard, saying how she'd become the victim of my
despotic whimsy. In short, they were now bringing up this rope
under my very windows. It was not pleasant, having to listen to
their abuse in front of my servants, especially because one of my
domestics, who had been in my service for above thirty years,
greeted the red flag with malicious glee. Human gratitude is no
Rock of Gibraltar.

My family and guests, including my expectant daughter-in-
law, watched this shameful comedy, this shabby parade of human
baseness and weakness, from behind closed windows as if from an
incognito theater box. I am almost certain that Halnek must have
been very much surprised that we ignored him so completely. After all, the show had been put on for my benefit. I was supposed to
tremble and come to terms with his importance. Alas, I had to attend to my sleeping cure."

## 26.

"The coach is ready, Your Excellency. Also, here's a change of
clothing." After a short pause he added, "from my wife."

"What?! Why?!"

This snapping of questions must have been a family trait.

When he watched us play soccer and we passed the ball on the foul, my father would shout, *Who to? Where to? Why?*—the worst thing about a bad pass. Like the Good Lord talking to us from up above, who to? where? why? Come to think of it, these are the only questions. Plus one more. When we explained something to Father to convince him (bring him round), he'd lower his head slightly, push his glasses down the bridge of his nose and looking at us over the rim, gently, soft, helplessly soft, not the least bit snappy he'd say, *Is that so.* It was a question, but he wasn't asking. In retrospect it also occurs to me how stylized this gesture was, a game, the gesture of a gesture, for my father is (was) shortsighted, it's shortsighted people who need their glasses to see at a distance. To predicate that through this gesture he was indirectly saying, My sons, you see how close you are to me, would be excessive.

"You might want to change your clothes, ma'am. We don't want to create a stir."

"Why complicate matters, Menyus?!" said Grandmother with a wave of the hand, for she truly and utterly lacked guile. Her thinking was not on familiar terms with ulterior motives. She always walked the straight and narrow. If I were in a joking mood, I might even say that she took the straight and narrow even forty years on, when she repeatedly went into Oroszlány—and I know from experience what it means to walk the straight and narrow on the bumpy road to town.

She waved a hand and made for the yard. The rally had just ended outside, the last revolutionary slogans had been proclaimed, when the crowd started singing the National Anthem. At which Grandmother repeated the first phrase along with them, "God bless the Magyar!" loud and clear and charged at the crowd. Which separated like the Red Sea. No one else in the family could have gotten away with it. My father, possibly, but when his time came, there was a different sort of crowd. Or do crowds never change? Besides, in a certain sense the crowd opened up for my father even back then; after all, he was in there, inside Grand-mother's darkness. Halnek pretended he didn't see.

Neither did my grandfather who, until my father was born, i.e., until he laid eyes on him, disapproved of his daughter-in-law's ill-considered action. On the other hand, to his "inordinate surprise," he did hear the National Anthem. Was the singing of the Anthem on this particular occasion a naïve misapprehension of the Comrades, who had not yet been sufficiently fused into a unified international mass, or was it an antidemonstration aimed at Halnek? He decided that he could not decide.


## 27.

"We have orders from Pest, Your Excellency, to liquidate you."

"I see. Anything else?"

"Kindly withdraw yourself outta the way, sir."

"You want me to go into hiding?! You want me to hide in my own country, my own home?!"

"Yes. No. No, of course not. Except maybe for a little bit, just while we go over the premises . . . maybe back in the wood-shed . . . where Your Excellency could go on with your reading."

(Break.)

"A thousand pardons for the inconvenience, Your Excellency, we're off."

"As you wish."


## 28.

To call our apartment at the foot of the Castle in Budapest a palace or a palacette would be a gross exaggeration, naïve, vainglorious, though it was spacious enough to catch the eye—if the times are right, anything can catch the eye, not only fifty thousand holds, but fifty holds, it's clearly a question of the eye and the catching; and so, the rooms on the ground floor, which had served as Great-grandfather's living quarters, were requisitioned without fail and given to a so-called working-class dentist, and my grandfather and his family had to make do with the three or four rooms upstairs. This too is a question of the eye, this making do.

As soon as Grandmother entered the apartment, she went into labor, and as soon as she went into labor, the large pendulum clock in the living room stopped, even though Grandfather had hoisted the chain (the weight hanging from the chain) on Tuesday, and under normal circumstances, it should have worked for two or three weeks. It was eerie. The weight stood at the upper third of the chain, it wouldn't budge, it wouldn't lower itself another jot. My grandfather concluded that in some mysterious manner and for some mysterious reason one of the small chain links must have gotten stuck crosswise and the cogwheel couldn't catch it. Mr. Schatz—Olivér Thomas V. Schatz, as he liked to be called—the watchmaker from Brasov whom Grandfather called Saturday afternoon (he looked after our clocks in the city; he must have lived near us; he was always there in the blink of an eye, as if all day, all month, nay! all year he were waiting only for us to call him); anyway, he said he'd never seen anything like it, that even when examined through his magnifying glass, the link is faultless and the phenomenon does not adhere to the basic laws of physics; since the weight itself, and the weight of the chain pulls the chain downward and keeps the chain taut over the cogwheel, someone or something had to lift it for a second so the loop could turn sideways like that. The cogwheel, though, was in perfect condition. The position of the linchpin, the catch were faultless as well.

Suspicion is like an inheritance. It gets diverted. But this time there was no one to divert it to, unless Grandfather—the key to the glass door was in his vest pocket!—but to imagine that it could have been him . . . Some things defy the imagination. Mr. Schatz, who was putting his lenses, his magnifying lenses, back inside their black case lined with dark purple velvet and inscribed in gold letters with 1706-1856 LEIPZIG, muttered as he did so, "Sometimes one tends toward the awkward conclusion that an army of mischievous sprites are taking us for fools."

Grandfather watched the proceedings with suspicion. Mr. Schatz said that in his opinion the clock needed to be kept under surveillance for a while and asked permission to check it for the next five days, Sunday included, if possible, every afternoon at the same time—at which point it was his turn to shoot a suspicious glance at Grandfather—between two-thirty and a quarter to three. Grandfather nodded, tantamount to giving his assent, then saw to it that Grandmother was taken to the maternity hospital in R. Street.

## 29.

Which is where I was born. For some unfathomable reason even in 1950 it was considered an elegant, gentrified place, although by then there was no elegance, nor gentry. Still, swallows return to the same place, they say, even though *that* swallow is not *this* swallow . . .

Be that as it may, my father forgot to bring in the layette and the baby clothes. He sailed into the room with his big, unwieldy briefcase ("big-bellied, gleaming, greasy, like an expectant bitch"). It was inseparable from him. I saw him with it for decades afterward, the badge of his profession.

"Where are the baby things?" Mother asked in alarm.

"What things?"

"The things to take Péter home."

"Oh. It went clear out of my head."

We were still living up on the hill then, by then and still, an hour and a half there, an hour and a half back. In desperation, Father suggested that they wrap me in one of Mother's dresses. "We'll put him in the briefcase. It might raise some eyebrows, but no matter. We'll dress him up suitably when we get home."

Mother was beside herself with fury. I'd never seen her so angry.

"Have you gone mad? A baby? In a briefcase? Is this why I brought him into the world? Get out of my sight! Go home! Go wherever you want! Bogyi and I will think of something. And take your briefcase with you! Just get it out of my sight!"

Ever since, I have regarded this cruise-ship size, unwieldy briefcase as my real layette, my crib. It is where I got my start—or nearly. It got a lot of loving from me intended for my father; I stroked the leather, which was turning darker with time, darker, shinier, I loosened the belt with which the briefcase embraced itself, as it were, and like a caring mother her infant's ears, cleaned out its convoluted, dusty grooves—just so long as no one was looking.


30.


"Tell me," Grandfather said to Mr. Schatz, who was on the point of leaving, addressing him possibly for the first time (in words), "it's a professional question, after all. Are we headed for a new reckoning of time, or what?"

Mr. Schatz, who pretended he didn't quite catch Grandfather's drift, answered him all the same.

"It's not the time that has stopped, but the clock," he said, then took his leave. But he was prevented from checking the clock

435

ever again because that evening, Grandfather was put under arrest. He was dragged from his bed in the middle of the night. He was reading the *Spectator*, his favorite.

What can I say. Grandfather was born to be arrested. Everything about him was suspicious, too perfect, as if he'd been the original model of the aristocrat—refined features, elegant gestures, old-world self-assurance, culture, erudition, arrogance; Grandfather was not merely himself, he was "everything," a bygone world, the quintessence of gentrified rascalry and a fairy world; in any case, it would have been difficult to look down on him from below, and so, as the century progressed, again and again they'd arrest him without a second thought, before he could ever get a word in edgewise. But if he did, that just made things worse.

When he directed his cold, centuries-old gaze on a person, the person in question turned to stone.


31.


We even learned about this in school. Every time we went on a field trip, they showed us the stones. We had this intensely Communist vice principal, Mrs. Váradi, who practiced the class struggle on the two of us, my younger brother and me.

And also, my mother. Except she couldn't, because my mother wasn't afraid of her. What I mean is, she was afraid, all right, because everybody was afraid, but you couldn't scare her anymore. By the sixties she'd depleted her stock. Only after we were grown up did she fall prey to fear again. She drove us up the wall, though it hardly mattered by then, as if my mother's life as an old woman didn't belong to her, as if it were appended to her. Nothing was happening to her anymore, it seemed to me. The sad part of it was she probably felt the same.

Class outing, Bakony-Vértes-Gerencse, palace yard.

"Another appalling example of feudalism," Mrs. Váradi declared, indignantly pointing at the stones.

"Your grandpa must've been quite a guy," my classmates whispered.

"Yeh."

My classmates and I didn't feel particularly appalled. Besides, they were fed up with me, because Mrs. Váradi kept bringing me up, what I mean is, my name (though—and for this I was grateful to her—she never once looked at me). A stroll in the Vértes Mountains and my name, they were inseparable. Besides, nobody believed that for miles around, everything was ours, which seemed to be the gist of Mrs. Váradi's say. Nobody. Only Mrs. Váradi got her indignant proletarian dander up.

Whenever we reached yet another hunting lodge, the boys shrugged, that's yours, too, I bet, and I said, you betcha, whose do you think it is, Tyereskova's, and then, screaming with laughter, we gave the finger—to no one in particular.


## 32.


Mrs. Váradi put fear in the hearts of one and all, parents and teachers alike. We knew that a teacher was an official person of sorts, but Mrs. Váradi was also government, as if she'd been personally delegated by János Kádár, or better yet, Béla Kun—in short, she was a true-to-type Communist, something that wasn't quite real for me. Or if it was, I thought of it as the equivalent of terror, nausea, and deviousness in the flesh, something not worth my while thinking about. A human being is not a Communist, a Communist is not a human being. A Communist is not like us. He's a common criminal, a contemptible traitor. There's no need to preoccupy ourselves with him, or if we must, only because he's preoccupied with us. He wants to stamp us out like a mad dog, or a rat, or a flea.

I'm not saying I learned this at home. I figured it out for myself. There's nothing to think about. They're traitors. My father kept mum, while my mother's infrequent remarks did nothing to alter my perception.

Since everybody hated Mrs. Váradi, I concluded that everybody shared my view of Communists versus human beings. Naturally, this was not the case. But since I considered this as self-evident as "two plus two makes four," it seemed easier, what I mean is, it seemed the obvious thing to do to make the facts fit the theory. There was Józsi Bór's dad, for instance, who was a decent man and still called himself a Communist, though he scorned those Communists we saw around us. This was an exercise in primitive Communism, but of course, I didn't know that. I didn't think it worthwhile to familiarize myself with the thing I was rejecting out of hand. No, I wasn't rejecting it, I retched it back up. You rammed it down my throat? Well, I will vomit it back up! In this manner, I had effectively solved the problem of one of the major experiments in twentieth-century philosophy. Poor Sartre, had he known. . . .

The vice-principal comrade made pronouncements otherwise confined to the newspapers. Other people said similar things, but you had the feeling they were saying it under duress. There was Mr. Helmeczi, for one. We liked him a lot. The old school. They knew the value of literature. They held it in regard. When he read Ady's poems, he had tears in his eyes. When he said stuff like raw naturalism is unworthy of the working class, he winked, working class, wink!, though only when he had too much drink in him. And even when he didn't, because this eventuality could not be ruled out, theoretically, at least, he'd start snorting, soh . . . soh . . . soh . . . , snorting like a pig, soh . . . soh . . . socialism, ha-ha-ha. Our poor country, we thought. Aunt Márta, our physics teacher, looked like a silver granny, the embodiment of the Hungarian middle class, now a thing of the past, an elegant, refined elderly lady with a reliable intelligence, high intelligence, something I hadn't encountered before, either/or (I wasn't really thinking about the middle class, unless it was the boys in Class B, I was just thinking that Aunt Márta's like a relative, on my mother's side). Anyway, she practically doubled up with pain when she said these sentences, and she turned black, and not just her face, as if she were in mourning, and it hurt.

We felt sorry for her, but we didn't share her pain. These were not real sentences.

Mrs. Váradi's, that was another bag of beans. Which means we had every reason to fear them. Had we known what a dictatorship was, these sentences would have shown us the face of dictatorship. As it is, though, they seemed empty, devoid of meaning. But they threatened us all the same. She flung these word-demons, these weighty balloons into our faces and waited to see if we'd so much as stir, and if we did, she swooped down and dragged us to the principal's office.

But the principal, Aunt Sári, was a decent sort and did her best to protect us. She was strict, but she hid her strictness behind her strictness. If she handed us a written reprimand, our mother would veritably praise us for it.


33.


It was scorching hot on that field trip to the Vértes. We could hardly keep our eyes open. The air burned our throats. I remember the grass, yellow, parched, as if it were August, or Bulgaria. Behind a drooping bush, barefoot, in Silesia-cloth pants, Bárány and I stood to one side of the clearing after soccer, taking a leak.

In those days we'd just switched from peeing to taking a leak—

a side effect of soccer—pumping ship. Or is the difference no more than I say tomayto and you say tomahto? Salting. Everything was steaming, me, him, the ground, the piss. I felt a sudden urge to unite these separate steamings, I needed to feel the heat from below, from above, and not just the heat of the soil, but my own heat, the piss, the sizzle of my piss. I shifted my foot forward, raised it, turned it in like a ballet dancer, and aimed the hose in my hand at it. A thrill ran through me as if I'd united with the soil, while somehow turning back into myself, too. A pungent smell hit my nostrils. Bárány was so surprised that it practically broke, his stream was practically broken in midsteam; plainly speaking, he pissed on himself. We laughed.

Then he shifted his foot as well.

And then, as if by accident or some misunderstanding, timidly, carefully, we stopped laughing. We aimed at each other's foot. As if our feet were rooted to the ground we did not move because we couldn't, as awed, surprised at ourselves, we watched the yellow streams crisscrossing each other. It's so nice. Hot. And smarts, too, a little! As if we were bathing in soda water. Or champagne. I knew about champagne by then. As if we were Nofertete or Nosferatu, or whatever, Cleopatra!, but she bathed in ass's milk. In short, I felt what was happening to us was something sublime, grand, as if the urine were made of gold, steaming-hot gold, the new source of our august, majestic existence.

Bárány was a big, uncouth fellow, a blockhead. He failed twice in a row before he was kicked down to our class, but by then he was playing for the front team of the Gasworks. Dumb as an ox, but his heart was in the right place. He was now aiming his cock with so much delicacy, discretion, and guarded sagacity, with such chaste affection, he surprised me. (His cock had refined him. . . . ) I had nothing in common with him, not even soccer; since he was a pro, he couldn't play on our class team, the boys from B torpedoed it. Which I didn't really mind. Yet when we played together, like now on the clearing, he chivalrously held himself in check, throwing not his strength but his knowledge of the game into the fray.

He was a real moron otherwise.

Once he was supposed to have told Mrs. Váradi he'd find her a man.

"Brother! The size of 'em tits! And alone, day in and day out! Day in and day out, nothin' but the Party! Keeps mucking with us instead. It ain't right!"

He presented his offer to the dreaded teacher so sweetly, in-geniously, you'd have thought it was his eagerness to help that was motivating him, that here was someone thinking that a fellow hu-man being—now this is something that would have never entered my mind—was in dire need of help, and he meant to oblige. Mrs. Váradi lurched forward to slap him, but Bárány held her down. Or so they say. He could throw a small ball the farthest, seventy-two meters. I got as far as twenty-eight meters, but I wasn't disap-pointed. Mrs. Váradi ran from the classroom in tears. Now this I don't believe, Mrs. Váradi didn't know how to cry. The tits, though, are a fact—a fact is a fact, especially if the tits are sizeable. But Bárány got off because his Workers' Militia father came in and smoothed things over, even though he hadn't seen Bárány in ten years. Bárány lived with his mother, who attended all of his games even out in the countryside and practice games too, she got her-self drunk as a skunk, and Bárány had to drag her home, which he did without a word of complaint.

We leaned shoulder to shoulder and crossed each other like that. When we ran dry, simultaneously, almost, that too was like some sort of mutual tact. I turned slightly toward him, he toward me, and we touched our members as if they were giving each other a kiss. A quick kiss in passing. A friendly handshake. It was obviously important to me that I think of my cock as a person or creature independent of me, someone I could sympathize with, though I wouldn't bet my bottom . . . my bottom dollar on it. I can't take responsibility for it, at least, not fully, unless like someone who happens to be in the same company with me, unless like that.

Bárány didn't make such a capital case out of it.

"You got a nice bunny on ya," he said. He talked to me as if I were a girl. Nice. A sign of respect.


## 34.


My grandfather's grandfather, the short one, Francis Joseph's faithful subject, was on good terms with the latter's brother, the ill-fated Emperor Maximilian—Miksa, let's call him Miksa—who let Napoleon III talk him into accepting the Mexican throne, but then the French deserted him and he held out heroically and was shot in the head, this in 1867, the year of the Austro-Hungarian Compromise. But first my great-great-grandfather visited him, and though neither Esterházy stew—nor Pushkin Street, the former Esterházy Street—were named in his honor, he had a prodigious appetite. Still, Mexico got the better of him. Not the local specialties; my great-great-grandfather was an intrepid culinary adventurer; he didn't mind blasted corn or roasted caterpillar, the taste and texture reminding him of our crackling, thereby building a joyful—because there was something joyous in this surprising similarity—bridge between far-flung continents. Could it have been the manner of cooking? The Central American idea of hygiene? Or the unaccustomed stomach bacteria? Were the good old reliable Hungarian stomach bacteria not up to par? Be that as it may, from the second day on, he couldn't eat a bite. He lost five kilos. Five! (Which, unlike in these dieting, weakling, catharsis-free times, counted for a veritable tragedy in the last century. In days of yore, a Hungarian (man) did not lose weight!)

On the first day of his arrival, an elaborate banquet was held in his honor. In the afternoon he attended Empress Charlotte's famous *Montagempfang*, or Monday salon. In the evening he sat next to the "little Coburg" (as her sharp-tongued sister-in-law, our Queen Elizabeth, called her). At a certain inevitable point in the course of the evening, he had to relieve himself. Servants in fancy uniforms showed him the way. The place where he was led surprised Great-great-grandfather no end, even though it was beautifully appointed, everything Spanish baroque, golden doorknobs, faience bowls, arched ceiling, palms. At first he didn't understand what was what. It was the first time he'd seen or experienced a public lavatory firsthand. He was about to turn indignantly on his heels, but the call of nature would brook no delay.

Which wasn't all. A young boy stood by the pissoir, a mestizo, let's say, holding a fine linen towel. (It is heartwarming, and as such only natural, that they have a word for all possible combinations. What "snow" is for the Norwegians, "mischung" is for the Mexicans. There's a table made up of sixteen squares, on each of the sixteen squares there are three figures, a man and a woman and the fruit of their loins, a child. A mestizo is the child of a Spanish man and an Indian woman, a castico is the son of a mestizo, a mulatto is the offspring of a Spanish woman and a morisco, there's also chino, lobo, gibaro, who is the child of a lobo man and a chino woman, and albarazado, who is the child of a mulatto woman and a gibaro man and the father of a cambujo, who is the father of a sanbaigo. In the square before the last, at the offspring of a Tente Eu El Aire and a mulatto woman, the unknown compiler of the table runs out of words, as it were, and writes: *Noteendiendo*, i.e., I don't understand you . . . )

The visiting relative was not particularly embarrassed by the presence of the boy, to look through servants, that didn't even amount to arrogance. However, when he finished urinating and came to the delicate problematics of the last drops (any man who says he's found a satisfactory solution is lying, only novelists make up such things, specifically, female novelists), the boy, almost a child—though the dark, gleaming, bronze color of his skin made him seem older—stepped up to him, which confused the great white lord, and before he could protest, with an inimitably light, silken gesture, he wiped clean the ancient branch.

"Muchas gracias," the ancient branch said gratefully. He then looked deep into the dark, round pair of eyes.

## 35.

I could've said moochoes garcias to Bárány too, but instead urged him to get a move on. I saw Mrs. Váradi through the bushes. To my surprise, I didn't tell Bárány.

"All right, already, we're goin'," Bárány piped with a grin, giving his rod a little shake all the same. This offended me as if he'd shaken off my touch—an exaggeration. After dinner Mrs. Váradi wanted to see me, but I got off. She didn't bring up the urination, just told me to stop being destructive, draw in my horns.

Me: "What do you mean, ma'am?" She: "You know perfectly well, what I mean." Me: "No I don't, Aunt Teri, I really don't, cross my heart and hope to die."

That was the first time I called her Aunt Teri. None of the boys in class ever called her that, just the girls. We were too proud.

Bárány's information about Mrs. Váradi living without a man turned out to be correct. She lived with her son, a twenty-five-year-old but with the brain of a two-year-old; he wet himself, messed up his pants; Mrs. Váradi looked after him by herself. She always rushed home. She put her son even before the Young Communist League. But how were we supposed to know that; and even if we had, we wouldn't have believed it. We feared and hated her too much to give it credence.

# 36.

"On March 24, at four-thirty in the afternoon, my daughter Mia and I were about to sit down to our tea—abomination!—made from a substitute. My wife and daughter Valentine were visiting the neighbors. Visibly shaken, my manservant announced that Halnek had broken into the palace at the head of armed gendarmes and people's vigilantes, and demanded I be brought into his presence.

Demanded. The last time anyone demanded anything of me, it was the King and Emperor, though formally, even that was a request. And also, years ago, the children the donkey cart. Móric stood resolutely in front of me and with the even-tempered severity that became his trademark later in Parliament, he addressed me as follows: Father. My brother Alajos and I demand that you make good on your long-standing promissory note with regard to the donkey cart.

My first thought was that the vigilantes were going to arrest me.

Arrogant, challenging, armed with mannlichers and guns, the gendarmes surrounded me. Halnek drew a telegram from his pocket which he proceeded to read out loud to me in stentorian tones, to wit, that People's Commissar Lukács had directed County Deputy Velinczky to seize the artworks from the palace at Csákvár, this on the pain of death, and that the local directorate should act on his orders without delay. All their decrees ended with a death sentence, a threat on par with the dizzying heights of their fines.

So it was going to be an inventory, not incarceration, I thought, much relieved. No time to lose. My daughter Mia and I exchanged a quick touch in lieu of a glance, and I said that due to

445

the precarious state of my health, my daughter would lead the delegation around for me.

'What delegation?' Halnek's live-in girlfriend snapped, who, with her loose (!) red hair, a shapeless man's coat flung over her shoulder and provocative cleavage inappropriate to the time of day, made such a vulgar impression that my brave little daughter blushed inordinately and answered for me with lowered head that *they* were the said delegation, were they not?

I could hardly suppress a chuckle. No matter how terrible the moment, there is always humor in the world, except you won't always find someone to do it justice. But it's there. In the meantime, the room filled up with as choice an assortment of dubious characters of both sexes, male, female, from Csákvár as you could hope to see, one part in an official capacity, the rest drawn there by malice and curiosity, hoping to be present at the seizure of the palace and the subsequent 'dethronement.'

My daughter led this horde out through one of the doors. When the last of the comrades were gone, I hurried to my wife's apartments through another door, summoned her personal maid, quickly relating what had happened (all the while not being able to shake off the absurd thought that I'm in a Marivaux farce), and asked for the keys to the chests in which my wife kept her valuables.

Paralyzed with fear, she stood there gaping as if Halnek and his gang had already turned the world upside down, and the down was up and the up was down. That was after all the purpose of their little game, and not what the Jew Sterk's son said, that there's no up or down, when of course there is! In short, as if I were the valet and she the lady's maid, and her mistress were watching, or rather, waiting, waiting to see if I got what I was after. I looked at her, the first time since she'd been in my employ. How interesting! She lowered her head the same way as my daughter Mia had done a moment ago. Outrageous. After all, I'm an old man!

446

As the comradely footsteps approached from the hall, we looked for the key in great haste, and at long last the chests opened up and some of the valuables found a safe haven in my wide breeches as I attempted to slip them through my belt so they could get lodged at the knees, where the breeches were cut tight. I loosened my belt and also two buttons up front, and lowered the pieces individually down into the cavern thus created which, being cold, tickled the part of my thighs left naked as they descended. Later I also spotted a number of light scratches made by the spangles, medals, and earrings as they plunged and slid downward, for I threw them in haphazardly, grabbing them in a precipitate manner. Then what do I see, but the maid, who is no longer standing with her head lowered but is looking in earnest, staring, staring at me, my hand and my open breeches.

'Close your eyes!' I scolded her rudely, which I later regretted, but she didn't.

'Turn away then!' I said, as chagrined and impatient as before, for I did not know how long my ingenious daughter could keep those men at bay. But the maid would still not turn her head away.

'All right, then make yourself useful!,' and having said that, I directed the dumbfounded maid who, according to my experience with servants to date, had been acting in a way that could not but surprise me, to the mouth of the cave. An extraordinary afternoon! And so was the evening ahead.

I quickly threw a shawl over the maid's shoulder to hide the chest with the jewels containing the most valuable pieces, and directed her through a flush door out into the garden, telling her to secrete the chest in a certain place, then return to me on the double. This came about without any prying eyes noticing. In the meantime, Mia conducted, and had others conduct, a veritable museum tour of her and her siblings' apartments, engaged herself in jocular banter with the Communists, even that certain vulgar wench, stretching the procedure to its outer limits in order to give me time. I had barely returned to my room, my heart pounding and body exhausted by the great danger and the surprise, when the delegation entered with my daughter at its head. I put myself at my guests' disposal.

Besides Halnek, the other principal character was a bath supervisor and corn cutter from a bathing establishment in Budapest and Ostende. I was tempted to offer him a job. The females in my family were victimized by these treacherous protrusions, and if there is one thing I admire, it's expertise. However, I said nothing, for I had reason to fear that my request might be misconstrued. The records were kept by a retired security guard from Pest, a heavy breather and wheezer and nonstop drooler, whose saliva kept dripping, at times on himself, at times on the paper, at times atomized into mist. Whenever in the interest of speeding and simplifying the proceeding I offered a suggestion in the best of faith, he always cut in with the same thing:

'I know this better than you. When they inventoried the Ernst Museum I was on guard duty, and I'm proceeding in the same way as the teachers.'

Consequently, my books, for example, were entered in the inventory as such: '129 Italian books (one big art book and historical lexicon), so many centimeters high.' Instead of Voltaire, they wrote Moltke. I said nothing; if it's good enough for the teachers, it's good enough for me.

Next came the chapel, which these rascals entered without removing their hats. Halnek and the corn cutter got in front of me, at which I delayed genuflecting, for it might have looked as if I were kneeling to them, but then, a feeling of shame having overpowered me, I kneeled anyway, knowing full well who I was truly kneeling to. Even an old man has his vanity.

The shirt, sword and medals of my son Alajos, who fell in the war, are displayed in a glass cabinet next to the altar. Some of the armed men who'd been to the front regarded it with reverence. But not Halnek.

'We're not putting these in the inventory, Comrade. It's of no value or interest to anyone.'

This little episode brought home to me the infinite danger of Communism, its destructive drive and energy, indeed, its very nature (for it couldn't act otherwise even if it tried). The fact that they're sitting sprawled out in my *fauteuils* is merely inconvenient. But they will leave. In the worst-case scenario, they will put a bullet through my head. Also highly inconvenient. But eternal life, it's not at this palace. They turn people's heads with prurient intrigues and wreak havoc with the country. Inconvenient, to be sure. The country is strong—even when weak, it is strong—it will survive. But that dismissive wave of the hand at Alajos's objects of reverence was horrifying beyond all things. May God forgive me, but that gesture was so powerful, it could have been His, the Lord's own gesture, the Creator in the act of annihilation.

A heroic death? No such thing.

Reverence? No such thing.

My son? No such thing.

We're not putting him in the inventory. Ergo, he does not exist. There is no past, no history, no nation, no tradition. The Communists are the present, the brutal *now*. The feeling of contempt, of which I always had plenty for these comrades, was now mixed with the unpleasant and repugnant experience of doubt and uncertainly.

In this manner did room follow upon room. Halnek pulled open the drawers, searching every nook and cranny like a hunting dog, and he kept inquiring after the 'art.'

'Art! Art!' he yelped. I showed him my paintings and the portraits hanging on the walls. The works of various masters down the centuries.

'Nobody's interested in your family portraits,' he snapped. My antique furniture didn't satisfy him either. 'The Soviet government wants us to secure the art. An Esterházy . . . an Esterházy must know what art is and where it can be found.'

'As far as that goes,' I said between my teeth, 'I *am* an Esterházy, yes.' "

## 37.

Mihály, the son of Palatine Pál, was said to be the most Esterházy of us all. The fact is that Pál took to wife Orsika, the daughter of István Esterházy and Erzsébet Thurzó, who was the child of the offspring of his father's and his mother's first marriage. Accordingly, his father-in-law was his half brother on his father's side, and his mother-in-law was his half sister on his mother's side and consequently—*minimo calculo*—said Mihály's maternal great-grandfather, paternal grandfathers, maternal grandfather, father and even his mother were Esterházy. (There's a divinity that shapes our ends, plus a special providence in the fall of a sparrow—not to mention the wheel coming round full circle.) He was the one who launched the construction of the palace of Fertőd in the boggy marshlands in the neighborhood of Süttör. He also played the clavichord.

## 38.

" 'You haven't heard the last of us yet,' Halnek shot back, also between his teeth, as if neither of us wanted the other to hear. I didn't care for this similarity.

When we reached my wife's apartments and I showed the delegation the Chinese, Japanese, Saxon and other collections of porcelain, that seemed to satisfy him more or less; and since I sang the praises of two valuable Chinese vases that were in the study, and since we now happened to be in a lady's room, he dictated the following to the clerk, who by then had dribbled saliva all through the palace:

'Two ladies' vases of porcelain!'

We subsequently took over this classification, using the phrase without any visible sign of sarcasm; some of us even used it at face value.

In the meantime the rest of the crooks stood around, legs outspread, something I couldn't have done even had I wanted to, *cf.* the miscellaneous valuables inside by pants. Even so, there was a certain stiffness to be observed in my gait, which the comrades must surely have put down to arrogance. This is how legends are born, via a pair of stuffed golf pants. Especially one, a small-size scepter tip-tapping whose origin family lore traced back to King Mátyás, endangered my knee, the handiwork of an anonymous master from Nürnberg, one of my ancestors having won it from that certain good fellow Estván Illésházy.

However, all must come to an end, this tragicomedy included. Faint with fatigue, we went our separate ways, though Halnek did not miss his chance to announce that I am responsible for the inventoried items, which are now 'in public domain.'

'As you wish,' I muttered. 'Ever since I can remember I have had responsibilities, always, and so had my father, and my father's father before him, and so does my son, and my son's son will have responsibilities, too. It is part of the package. If there is one thing we have plenty of, it is responsibility. You might want to put that in your inventory as well. But only tomorrow.'

In the evening an emissary came in seçret from Pest with the good news that my daughter-in-law had given birth to a baby boy. Poor little Mátyás! The first Esterházy for centuries to have come into the world without rank or means!"

My father waited until the establishment of social justice before he came into the world. A decree was issued that day: a Red Army is to be set up; ordinance no. 4 of the Cabinet Council replaces the old law courts with a Revolutionary Tribunal that may be joined by any—any!—worker, and ordinance no. 5 provides for bringing scaremongers to justice. The tribunals are to do their work by summary proceedings, and their sentences cannot be appealed, no redress can be sought. Death sentences were to be brought unanimously and carried out immediately. From the twenty-fourth of the month, Soviet People's Commissar for Foreign Affairs Chicherin and Béla Kun exchanged telegrams daily—Béla, have I got a *borscht* recipe for you! Stop!—and so it was on this day, too.

And the large pendulum clock in the living room stopped—though, according to Mr. Schatz, time itself did not—and my grandfather, who was born to be arrested, was promptly arrested. In the afternoon my father almost came into the world, but then didn't, and my grandfather came home, mission unaccomplished. His son hadn't even been born, and already a disappointment! At two p.m. he stuck his head (or the top of his head) out into the world, a world of shadows, actually, because the moment that the *thing* could have taken its start and slimy with blood he could have had a better look around (or are babies like kittens, their eyes closed?), the light went out, which we can safely put down to the Republic of Councils, and my grandmother screamed, because she thought they were dead. Or dying.

The electricity (not from the screaming) came back on again, at which the nurse, a certain Györgyi Kárász (later Aunt Gyuri to us), screamed because my father had unusually thick hair for a newborn, which in this swift off-and-on flash of the light radiated a silvery hue. Or, to put it another way, it was a wiry-haired gray old man blinking at this Györgyi Kárász from between my grandmother's thighs.

"A shaman!" she screamed, and fell hopelessly in love with my father. (Later she went to clean house and cook for my other grandmother. For a while she even lived there. She was from Transylvania. Sometimes she managed to get her hands on halvah, which we couldn't abide. But it's a real *delicacy,* she'd say, and shake her head in disbelief. Poor thing. Once my younger brother and I tripped her up. It's not that we objected to her being in love with our father, but that she should be in love at her age. We made it look like an accident. Good work, my younger brother said, throwing a sober glance my way, for he was a great fan of our mother. When our parents questioned us, we denied everything. Mother's eyes had a strange glint to them.)

In short, various white folk were screaming and screeching, at which my father temporarily withdrew himself.


## 40.


Back in the dark, my father turns to the Lord.

"What was that?"

"The world, what else?"

"That screeching?"

"I told you."

Also, my father should stop complaining. It's beautiful when women scream. It's one of the most beautiful things in the world. He'll see for himself one day. These frightened, animal screams.

"That didn't sound too convincing, Lord."

This shying away, this leapfrogging back and forth into the world, this is the line I continued, though I wasn't born twice, like my father, I was born dead.

I was blue, I was born blue, I weighed in at five kilos. Five thousand twenty-three grams, the same number of grams as my father. What is this if not a miracle? It's a miracle, no doubt, but what kind of miracle? What does it mean? It's some sort of equivalence, after all, five thousand twenty-three equivalencies. I was born dead. They plunged me into hot water, then cold. This is how they saved me. It took a couple of minutes. My grandmother, who'd come up to Pest, cried. (For the first time in her life, I think. And the last. And in mine, too, come to think of it.) I was too big, I had to work very hard to slip out, which exhausted me. Not bad for a start. I heard that at such times you lose a lot of neurons. I always thought that this was fatal. Just imagine how intelligent I'd be if only those neurons weren't missing! (Grandfather, who knew everything about the family, who's who, titles, ranks, appointments, honors, branches, offshoots, in order to avoid possible future inaccuracies, wrote an obituary for every newborn in the family; the telegram with the joyful tidings came from somewhere in Pápa, Kismarton, Vienna, Paris, Cseklész, let us rejoice, the babe is born!—whereupon Grandfather chewed on his pipe, nodded, then with the telegram in hand, sat down at his desk and began to pen the innocent newborn's obituary. An archangel with sword in hand. We are but dust. He wrote mine too, posthaste.)

My father's hopes, as yet in the womb, were naturally high. But there was no pretentiousness involved. (Honestly. My father was unpretentious all his life, I never once heard him brag, he never pushed any of his personal gifts into the foreground. Possibly only his solitude was immodest, it alone bordered on arrogance.) Afterward, de facto, events took an unexpected turn. The problem, if there was a problem, was not that his life turned out differently, but that history repeatedly crowded him out of his own life, as if an actor were receiving his instructions from another play, from the logic of another play. There's this bombastic director, his breath reeking of halitosis, pushing my father toward the rear left exit . . . My father is playing in a serious royal drama, while he's being instructed from the direction of a light music-hall cabaret. Or the other way around. And he's being swept along with the tide, what else is there for him to do?

## 42.

So then, Grandfather was thumbing through the *Spectator*—England suited his mental habit and sharp intellect best—when a small but boisterous gang of so-called Lenin boys burst into the room. Who had the key? and how?, a simple question, but we'll never know—and announced that Grandfather was under arrest.

He put down the magazine and nodded, because he ascertained the facts of the case, then he asked why, because he always asked, sometimes silently, sometimes out loud, sometimes of others. (My father's "who to? where to? why?" must have been an offshoot of this.) There was also the icy stare, but it didn't work this time. These impudent Lenin boys had no intention of turning to stone. They didn't give a hoot about my grandfather—possibly a first in the life of the family, not to mention the nation. Fear, yes, hate, yes, but not giving a hoot?! Not giving a hoot about him?! These people don't know who I am, Grandfather realized with a start. If it mattered they'd know. But it doesn't. That's the nice thing about a revolution. It forges ahead, not realizing it should be afraid, and so it isn't, which in itself is fearful. Somebody's got to be afraid, always, and since *they're* not afraid, I am. A new order, a new hierarchy. A people's commissar is not afraid of the king. They don't stand related. They haven't been introduced. This is why the king is afraid (provided he is still among the living), because as far as he knows, he stands related to everyone. In this particular case, everyone is his subject.

Grandfather got dressed. Slowly, commodiously. Then they took him to the transit prison, and from there to Kőbánya.

In the early morning of the third day after his arrest (the third day: an accidental Christian coincidence), several automobiles stopped in front of our house once again, and a bunch of Lenin boys ("this terror horde") showed up again, this time to requisition, on their own initiative, Grandfather's belongings, "Papa's (sic!) in the can anyhow, he ain't be missin' nothing."

This is what they said: Papa.

Which makes you think. In the family, everyone called their father Papa, my grandfather, my father, me and also my brother and sister. In the immediate family circle—and strictly within the four walls—the endearing Papi was also in vogue. Toward the world we were a little bit—but just a bit—ashamed of our sentimentality. (When my father's big molar fell out—it started wobbling, he showed us, laughing, as if it were a stunt and he proud of the wobbling, nudging it with his tongue from behind, as if he were playing puppet theater, horror of horrors, the royal throne tottering, but the crown definitely, we implored him to stop and desist, the badly hidden royalist sentiments coming to the fore, but he just laughed, and in our childish severity, we didn't so much disapprove of this lack of seriousness, this uncalled-for frivolity, as (if the truth be told) condemn it. It was then that our sister, who was always the least sentimental of us all, said with a deadpan expression, *pulppaperpapi.*)

# 43.

When we were young, we addressed our parents in the formal mode, Papi, if you please, Mami, if you please. But overdoing the respect with linguistics was generally not acceptable. It's for servants, our mother informed us, not arrogantly, just by way of explanation, matter-of-factly, her purpose purely didactic. She called an armchair *fauteuil*, pronunciation impeccable, a menu a *carte de jour*, and the nasal *en* at the end of *souterrain* warbled in her throat as majestically as if the moldy, dark hole where we lived back then had been a splendid ballroom.

Mother was in charge of our education. It was she who made the rules and nursed hopes—and consequently, disappointments, too—for us, ain't, gonna ("Communism is a bad influence on you!"). Our father never had such concerns. His attention to our upbringing was inattentive, to say the least. When relatives or guests asked about us, he smiled broadly and replied, growing like weeds, at which they nodded appreciatively. Our father was busy day and night with his little diamonds in the rough, meaning us. *Mir gesagt.*

We stopped using the formal mode of address in high school, though not entirely, as it could never turn into real familiarity. We heard ourselves use the informal as if it were a joke, as if our parents, exceptionally, again and again, had given us permission for the fun of it. Along with the use of the familiar, and despite our mother's vehement protests (*contra linqua non est piss*), we called them Mutter and Vater, though not quite the way it was commonly used, the way the bartender, let's say, would inquire, how 'bout another shot, Vater old man but . . . , I don't know, more respectfully?, or as if it had more in common with the German original? We felt the subjective character of these words keenly,

constantly, yes, as if we were using them as first names, Vater, Mátyás, Luke and John, bless the bed that I lie on. It's a lot simpler in
German. Whether a man or a woman, a palatine or a lady-in-
waiting, whether two or two hundred years old, if the person in
question is a relative, we use the familiar form of address with
them. But who is a relative? We didn't hold much commerce
with our own class, and we didn't hold it with our father—who
couldn't care less with a vengeance—at the helm. Still, who is related and in what way—the thing was known all the same.

There was an unintended, living-breathing family image. A
family can be described, just like a city, Chain Bridge, Watertown,
town hall, police station, Danube. Just like a landscape. But can
you describe a landscape? Is there such a thing as a description of a
landscape? Can the world be described? And can it be read? By
family we basically mean the patriarch. It's a reflex. Father, the
law, et cetera. But it turns out that it is especially the et ceteras that
make a family, the extended family, the clan, for the notion of the
latter depends not on parent-child or sibling-to-sibling relationships, intense and deep, yet *finite,* but rather on the countless
convolutions of branches and offshoots—black sheep on the horizon!—of nieces and nephews, cousins and stepparents, uncles and
aunts which, in keeping with the clichés, at times threaten to en-
snare us, while at other times we swing back and forth on them,
reaching dizzying heights.

The bigger a family, the better it knows itself.

I found slips of paper in the unlikeliest of places, up in Grandmother's attic and among the pages of a Stendhal novel, slips torn
hastily and at random from some notebook, and also at times an
*intent* piece of paper folded in four, with intricate family-tree der-
ivations—and not just in a woman's hand or a shaky old hand, i.e.,
written by way of compensation for something, but rather, as a
sort of exercise, the way you might give a horse a run now and
then, giddyap!, because you must not forget, or else, like an ongo-

458

ing game, a sort of brain gym, a quiz, let's see, now, how are we related to the viceroy of Altamira? ("We're always related through the Lichtensteins." —Father.)

Mother, too, left behind such slips of paper on which someone is "derived." With her, it was probably the need to prove to herself that she could navigate her way around the family maze—slips of paper and notebooks, the left-behind traces of what we generally call a woman's life. These exertions, these notebooks were commenced, then broken off in midstream. One contained the biographies and list of works of the Italian Renaissance—*re-né-sanse* masters, Mother droned, another contained attempt at learning a language, fragmented and nipped in the bud: *à gauche* = to the left, which is then transformed into a diary, a baby diary from 1950. A literary tour de force, as if I had written it: *My sweet little mommy is very clumsy, but she's trying very hard. She'll get into the swing of things, except, oh, I hope she's not going to drop me in the tub. Oops, she dropped me in the tub.*

And then, oh, in back of another small, tattered notebook, between the lines, among the list of the daily expenses, very, very personal entries. My eyes are dazed (I am blinded). With incredibly minuscule letters, but with Mother's dynamic loops, so no one could decipher them, so that their very existence should be cast in doubt, being possibly nothing more than the light scratch of the tip of the pen, not even writing, just ink, dates, exclamation marks, dot-dot-dots, abbreviations. You can tell that the hand is reluctant to write what it is writing, yet what some final resolve, desperation and perverse hope, unrelenting and merciless, is forcing on her all the same. Or revenge. So that she shouldn't forget.

In short, the act of addressing someone presupposed a brief climb up the family tree, after which came the *Du* or *Sie*, though the climbing generally brought those in question so close that the climb back down almost invariably resulted in a *Du;* the purely

459

theoretical possibility of a family relationship is in itself considered a family relationship. (Unlike an inheritance. You can't solve an inheritance with a *Du*.)


## 44.


Aunt Mia and Grandmother did not use the familiar form of address with the requisitioners, who acted as if they were one of the family regardless. It's not easy distinguishing requisitioners from relatives. They drop by whenever they feel like. We may be glad to see them, or not, but we put our best foot forward, just in case. It's in our best interest. Well, well, new family, Grandmother and Aunt Mia said as they looked at the intruders. (I just realized that it can't have been the third day. They couldn't have let Grandmother out of the maternity hospital on the third day. But never mind.)

That was the beginning of the concrete looting of my father's layette. Otherwise, they were polite, they laughed at the ladies' jokes, and like a real gentleman, one of them even asked Aunt Mia to go for a stroll along the promenade. The nerve! The other one helped them hide some things from the "comrades" (and thus, from himself). Why? One of God's little mysteries. A woman's fear generally fans the fire, aggravates brutality, but Grandmother and Aunt Mia were more dumbfounded than frightened. They didn't know that they were up against brutality. As they said later, all they saw was a lack of military good breeding.

Grandfather knew all about the lack of military good breeding—sawing the gate of a manor house in two, forcing the expectant lady of the manor to hand over her valuables, putting a bullet through the head of the husband without a second thought who, startled out of his sleep, comes running into the room in his nightclothes, and also his young son, and then the mother, she with two bullets, but by some miracle she survives, and by some miracle brings her baby into the world, who'd been hit by a bullet while still in the womb—and so, when he entered the room unawares, having just come from prison healthy and unharmed, though infested with lice and in sore need of a bath, he knew that they were in big trouble.

And so they were. Except, trouble is not rational. The brigands could have used their guns, but they laughed instead.

"Out already, Papa?" guffawed one of them and smiled, a clear indication, even in retrospect, that they were taking no chances. Still, they showed no embarrassment, they grabbed whatever they could lay their hands on (Grandfather watched in silence: this was fear in the flesh, this silence), loaded their booty into their cars, and made off.

## 45.

Speeding car, airplane. Béla Kun, for example, fled the country by plane. In the afternoon—at about five, an airplane rose above the Soviet headquarters in the Hotel Hungária, crossed the Danube and, passing the palace on top of the Várhegy, banked steeply toward the Gardens. The pilot of the aircraft was none other than the People's Commissar himself. He flew low, barely twenty meters above ground. His face could be clearly seen. He was pale and unshaven as usual. He grinned at the citizens below, and even waved a mischievous, naughty, mocking good-bye to some of them. His pockets were stuffed with fine chocolates and jewels, the precious stones belonging to countesses, baronesses, gracious, philanthropic ladies, chalices from churches, and many other treasures besides. Heavy gold chains dangled from his arms.

As the airplane began to climb and was just disappearing from sight, among the distant clouds, one of these chains happened to fall down into the dead-center of Vérmező, where it was found by an elderly gentleman, a long-established resident of the Krisztina area, an excise clerk who worked on Trinity Square in the Castle, a faithful man of my great-grandfather by the name of Károly József Patz. And since a medal bearing the coat of arms of our family, the lion-griffin with a sword in one paw and—no, not a hoe, but three roses in the other—was hanging from the chain this decent fellow, Patz, surrendered to my great-grandfather and later my grandmother gave it to my mother as a wedding present. It, plus the story. Mother never wore it.

"Now, now, Mati, dear, you don't expect me to wear it after a murderer." According to my father, on this basis you could never wear old jewelry, just about every piece of jewelry is steeped in blood.

"But at least they weren't Communists," Mother retorted.

A nice piece. It's mine now.

## 46.

Aunt Mia disappeared for the day. Grandfather's family in Pest assumed she was at Csákvár, Great-grandfather's family at Csákvár assumed she was in Pest. Where she was nobody knows. She arrived at Grandmother's like always, around noon, in accord with the schedule of the Tata express.

She rang the bell. The maid opened the door.

"Good morning, Mia Countess. I hope you had a pleasant trip."

"Indeed," Aunt Mia nodded. But she didn't budge, just stood still by the door. The maid picked up her bag and headed upstairs. Aunt Mia remained standing by the door.

"Is something the matter, Countess?" the frightened maid asked as she turned around.

"Nothing's the matter, dear, just help me in."

Now it was the maid's turn to stand still. She couldn't figure out what the Countess wanted from her.

"Are you still there?" the Countess asked. Frightened, the maid dropped the traveling case. "Ah, you are. Well, then, help me in. Take my arm as if I were drunk, and help me up the stairs."

But she wasn't drunk, she was blind. She'd gone blind. There were no visible traces of violence in her eyes, the area around her eyes, or her face, my father said. He heard it from Grandmother. When arm in arm with the chambermaid they entered the upstairs room, by way of greeting, Grandmother raised my father.

"What an appetite, do you see?" She nursed him herself, which was considered a rarity at the time. Her sister-in-law turned toward the source of the sound.

"I've seen it before," she said softly. Grandmother was about to take offense when she saw that something was amiss. She saw the black glasses which from then on Mia, like the publicity-shy Greta Garbo, would wear for the rest of her life, even at night. We spied on her once, she wore them even at night. But then—as a token of respect to my father?—she took off her glasses for the first and also for the last time, and for the first and also for the last time, a certain sentence passed her lips.

"I am blind."

She didn't say she'd gone blind, or been blinded, she said she was blind. As if she were saying her name. She wouldn't let a doctor look at her, she refused to talk about how it had happened. Strangely enough, neither her older brother nor her father could get her to submit to a medical examination. What is strange about this is that they should accept it, accept that Aunt Mia was suddenly stronger than they. Aunt Mia knew something they did not, something that they didn't know, something they were reluctant or too cowardly to learn.

We knew we mustn't, but my sister asked anyway.

"Aunt Mia, what made you blind?" Our aunt pretended she didn't hear. "Are you just blind, if you please, Aunt Mia, ma'am, or deaf, too?" Aunt Mia let fly a right cross, slapping my sister squarely on the face.

"How many times must I tell you to eschew vulgarities?"

## 47.

"I conducted a bizarre, though far-from-unenlightening conversation with the revolutionary Károly Sterk. The somewhat irregular, incomplete, hasty inventory of the palace left me with hefty problems that soon reared their ugly heads. One evening around ten-thirty, my manservant came running to my room. Halnek and Sterk had forced their way into the palace and posted guards at all the entrances. No one was to go in or out. In order to calm my fears I told myself that this show of force was aimed at the 'as yet unfound' valuables. (I didn't tell the family about the 'secret of the breeches,' only Vilma, the lady's maid knew, but she never let on.)

We proceeded to bed and had a good night's sleep. This too is an Esterházy trait. The night is for sleeping. Ergo, at night, we sleep. The next morning I was at prayers in the domestic chapel when they called me away and said they would take another inventory. Also, all the rooms containing books would be sealed off.

'The Comrades are not afraid of books, I hope?' at which Sterk smiled sarcastically, but to give him his due—formally, at any rate—this was the most discourteous of his actions.

'The manner in which you say the word "Comrade" boggles the mind, Count. Nothing stands to justify the revolution better!' he later commented reflectively, as if to himself.

Comrade Sterk intrigued me. He was the son of a Jew from

Csákvár with whom, when I was fire chief—good Lord, I was everything, why not fire chief?—and he the association cashier, we were on better footing. It's been said that one shouldn't speak of Jews as such unless the Jews expressly ask, seeing how there are all kinds (as such), this and that, and if that's the case, I should say he's like this, and if he's like that, then that he's like that.

I wish to take issue with this, because on this basis I shouldn't even say Italian or Prussian. And though undoubtedly Tuscany had never seen a Prussian more *précieuse,* over-scrupulous and dull than Comte Costacurta, just as there can be no question about my distant cousin in Berlin, Freiherr von Landsberg, being an eccentric good-for-nothing braggart, who with his Italian character traits is more Italian than anyone from Naples to Venice; still, is it not justified? Is it not expedient to talk of Italians and Prussians, especially with reference to the clichés that, after all, undoubtedly point to the basic differences that exist between Naples and Berlin?

Sterk came in a uniform, without insignia of office, nothing but the Socialist hammer for decoration. As first lieutenant, he spent the war 'at a proper distance,' and after the outbreak of the revolution, everyone knew that he was the real *spiritus rector* behind Halnek, but in the true Jewish manner, he pushed Halnek into the foreground, and when the latter found himself short of funds, either official or private, Sterk would help him out.

I kept an eye on Sterk, but Sterk also kept an eye on me. I entered into diplomatic negotiations with him. The outcome was that I could continue to use the rooms that held the books, but they would drape blankets over the bookcases, and seal them.

'The dictatorship of the proletariat is so complex!' I laughed, but Sterk did not. I 'championed' this seal idea hoping that once these conditions ceased, I would have saved my library. I am often motivated by the principle of preservation. I might even call it my guiding principle. Indeed, this keeping, uniting, surviving, preserving for posterity may justifiably be called our family philosophy. Some people disdain it as far too worldly. They equate it with the drive for material enhancement. They suspect ulterior motives, selfishness, vulgarity. Yet mine is a radical view of the world. It also requires discipline. He who regards discipline as petty and cowardly, he who sees it as a civil servant mentality instead of the enthusiasm it entails, the curbed passions, the greatness of civilized man, is petty and cowardly himself.

We spent long, bitter weeks in these draped rooms, but I could not touch the books, because a supervising 'authority' checked every day to ascertain that the seals were unharmed! There were no newspapers, the postal service was irregular, most of the Budapest newspapers had folded, the ones from Vienna came sporadically, which left nothing but the Communist press. Nothing but brazen lies.

It became painfully clear that the Communists had usurped the language. The inventory too started with Halnek and his men ordering the palace servants, including the gardening staff, to assemble—and assemble they did. A couple of weeks earlier, they'd have asked *me* or—so be it—ordered me to call my people together. But now the tables were turned. Sterk knew it, and Halnek felt it, which was as good as knowing. A person always knows when the tables are turned. There's no such thing as having the tables turned in your favor, and you not knowing. Like I'm king, but I think I'm a short order cook at Swatsky's. That's not possible.

On Revolutionary Council orders they started carting the paintings and statues out of the chapel. Everything that was preserving superstition—in short, religious feeling—among the people, to be liquidated. I happened to mention to Sterk that this is why the Communists won't last, they've declared war on God. I spoke relatively openly with him. I had nothing to lose, just as I had nothing to gain by dissembling. In the long run Sterk and his comrades were doomed to fail. In the short run I had already lost all I had. Which left me my curiosity (and to some extent, the fear of death).

'It's chutzpah!' the Jew shouted jubilantly, at which I heard myself reply, 'Indeed.'

'What do you mean, Your Excellency? Gall and guts are everything. The whole world's got it'—and he pirouetted on his heels like a prima ballerina—'or, looking at it another way'—and this time he raised his index finger like a pedant—'that's all there is, the whole world!' Then with a chuckle he added, 'The whole world, Your Excellency! And that's just the tip of the iceberg!'

The Communists always talk about the whole, never about the details; they help themselves to the details. Everything that could be moved, the paintings, the porcelain collection, the antique clocks and art objects they hoarded into two big rooms. Their eyes filled with tears, our old servants carried all the beautiful, valuable things from our rooms, things that along with us they'd always regarded as inviolate. Even certain members of the Workers' Council who pretended that they were Communists offered the honest but whispered apology:

'We must do something despicable now, sir!'

'Must?' I asked sarcastically.

'Must,' one of the men nodded in all seriousness. He was worn out, serious, hostile. Still, as I stood in front of those objects hoarded together so callously and flung into a pile like a ton of bricks, fused, ceasing to be individual objects because their history had ceased, because they had been torn out of their own time and space and context, and having been regurgitated, or belched back up, were now made to lie in their new place—in short, for the first time I saw what it was that could be repugnant about abundance when abundance is not dazzling riches but this nauseating puke pile in the middle of my palace. For a moment I thought I understood these Reds: they must have always seen it this way, taken out of its context, always, because they were not familiar with the context to begin with.

Sterk sealed the bookcases one by one, while I stood around as if to help. Like a bad butler. He said he'd been a confirmed Communist for fifteen years. I said I'd been a confirmed Catholic for 350 years.

'Universal,' I said. Touché! He nodded enthusiastically:

'Yes, yes, of course.' Then he laid my mind at rest. I wouldn't have to pay taxes anymore. But my mind was not laid at rest. (I wonder why?). Also that they'd 'communize' the palace and use it for nobler purposes. And in the meanwhile, he made me understand without so many words that were I to trespass any of his prohibitions, a revolutionary tribunal would make short shrift of me.

'Are you threatening me, Sterk?'

He pretended not to hear. Our discourse was resting on thin ice. Our mutual courtesy was in need of beauty treatment. I didn't mention anything about my aversion toward the Jews, knowing full well that they don't like being differentiated in this way, while they differentiate themselves very much. They have the same attitude toward mankind that the Székelys of Eastern Transylvania have toward Hungarians. When asked if he's a Hungarian, a Székely nods, which is more of a yes than a no, then adds, 'even better.'

There were many examples of this self-differentiation in evidence now. The insane squandering of money was outdone only by the *virschaft* of favoritism which attempted to impart power, affluence and prosperity to the most disreputable Jewish elements. If a Catholic was put somewhere, the entire swarm of 'people's commissars' from all rungs of the ladder flung themselves on him to bring him down and replace him with one of their own (*von ünsere Leit!*). To understand the uncivilized, ill-mannered insolence and cruelty these parvenus evidenced in face of the former owners, you'd have had to see the loud, who-if-not-me busy-bodying of the Jews in public places.

The Jews were terrified of the peasants. Since Trotsky and Lenin had bad experiences with the communization of peasant holdings, they wouldn't touch estates under a hundred holds. But the large estates didn't change much either, because the coopera-tives retained the old frameworks, only the 'beneficiaries' changed, of course. No big deal. They stole it from me, and now the Jews and the renters of the cooperative have become the large landown-ers. The difference is that now I had to go out to the manor on foot, and my former clerks with my horses, throwing a friendly greeting my way as they rode past me on their way on some offi-cial errand. From peasant to aristocrat, it is but a step. The question is, what sort of man will take that step . . .

I see no reason whatsoever why I shouldn't be anti-Semitic, which involves a certain prejudice, obviously, namely, that I don't like Jews. On the other hand, should I meet an amiable, decent sort among them—and who could be so narrow-minded as to deny the existence of such individuals—I promptly reconsider my views. I'd be foolish not to do so. I do not like financiers. On the other hand, I am not offended if someone does not like aristocrats. On the other hand—as if the world were made up of nothing but 'other hands'—the common people are full of silly prejudice which their new 'leaders' cleverly turn to their own advantage. For instance, there was no convincing Halnek's girlfriend that my daughter's room is really my daughter's room. It wasn't aristocratic enough for her.

'Gentlefolk sleep on lace sheets. I know because I used to serve in genteel households!' In that case, madame, my household is not a genteel household. But I didn't say a word. In my family, no one ever slept on lace sheets, though admittedly there might be such 'families' and such 'ladies,' too.

469

Having brought these prejudices into the light, our conversation took a different turn.

'Is it not possible, Count, that you are the victim of false prejudices yourself,' Sterk asked, throwing a painful glance my way. 'Is it not possible that I am not a filthy Jew,' he added, panting and spitting all over the place, just like that certain corn cutter, 'not a blood-sucking leech on the healthy body of Christianity, but a human being, Károly Sterk, a thirty-one-year-old, good-intentioned Hungarian able and willing to improve things, the Jew Károly Sterk, if I may be so bold, a Jew of Jewish origin and Hungarian, *nu,* with faulty emphases, raised word ends, impossible nasals, an arrogantly hooked nose, is it not possible that I am merely I?, not distinguished, like you, Count, and I won't say I don't envy you, not filthy rich, like you, Count, and I won't say I don't want to change this, not aloof and elegant, Count, and I won't say my own body and sanguine temperament do not pain me. Still, is it not possible, I beg, that I am just a man all the same, just as you, Count, are nothing but a man in Yahweh's eyes . . . a man . . . a man . . .'

An uneasy silence followed. I took an involuntary step back. He looked at me the way a man does not look at another man, the way it is not done between two men so far removed from each other. Or is this the distance he was talking about? He must have felt the awkwardness of our situation, too, because he turned away and looked out the window at the park.

This is what I don't like about these Jews, this sentimental fear of death. You'd think they were forever on the way to the slaughter, where dastardly Catholic butchers are waiting for them. (I ask only in passing whether history didn't start the other way around. Whose hands are bathed in the blood of our Lord Jesus Christ? Sterk would probably say it's not *his* 'business.') Meanwhile, in certain areas of modern 'art,' is it not them who, making good use of their possibly not unlucrative over-sensitivity, whipping up all this hysteria? Harping on the undeniable pogroms of the past, don't they, at the mere mention of the word 'Jew,' foreshadow their own dire fate?

As for the concrete, hysterical Jew fears that pertain to the present, to this century, like an advance or credit (typical Jewish thinking!), these must be rejected out of hand, and qualified, too. I would call them unfair, and am not far from the truth when I say that their aims are ignoble. To talk about pogroms, or even to suggest such a thing in this day and age, is simply a lie. This is the twentieth century! Anyone who presupposes something like this in this century is either a crook or a madman! A century in which ideas and religions coexist side by side in a friendship formerly inconceivable. Let us just think of the bloody religious wars of past centuries and the generosity of the present day, which has gone so far that there is no idea today or, what is worse, the lack of one, that can be challenged without consequences. If I were to make a joke with reference to my family and history as such, I might even say that if the Protestants have nothing to fear, then the Jews have nothing to fear either. Nothing.

There's something else I don't like about Jews. Their constant mocking and ridicule, that characteristic part of their thinking that makes them parody things around them. They parody everything without a second thought. What am I to think when I see this otherwise self-collected man beside himself, panting with excess of emotion, his eyes glistening with tears, saying to me that he is a man! Does he think I don't know, *un homme!,* that this is what Goethe said to Napoleon by way of defiant introduction?! In which case, what am I to think of these tears? I know perfectly well that this is not merely impertinence. After all, he is not simply suggesting that I am not Napoleon, a thing to which I had never aspired, but also that he is not Goethe, or only to the extent that I am Napoleon, but in that case, what does it all mean? What is the meaning of this leapfrogging? Is he not suggesting, perhaps, that everything is small, insignificant, that the grand, the noble—simply put, the big—does not exist? And does this not derive, by its very nature, from the denial of Christ, and does it not result, willy-nilly, in trampling everything under foot? And is it not the bounden duty of a man of my convictions to take up arms against this bias with every means at my disposal?

Still, the uncertainty, the wavering that led me to ascertain the tears in the Jew Sterk's eye put me in an awkward situation all the same. For one thing, I couldn't help but see that they were real tears and no show. For another, I couldn't help but notice that they're part and parcel of that certain Goethe paraphrase and cannot be severed from it—emotional depth and buffoonery. I must reconcile these—something that one would think cannot be done. This is why I kept silent and was struck dumb, feeling I was in a world foreign to me and in which I cannot find my bearings. Whereas I'd experienced the world as a place where you can always find your bearings—though at this juncture modesty checks me from furnishing the proof—that, in fact, the world has been created, it is made, so that I can find by bearings in it.

'Are you referring to Yahweh, the Creator? I was under the impression that the world was created by the Communists.'

Having calmed down, he pirouetted back from the window, answering my question with a laugh:

'No, no, we wouldn't think of taking the responsibility off the shoulders of Heaven . . . We're simply creating it anew . . .'—and he turned pensive once again. 'If I were a believer, I would make God my business. But since I am not, I make myself my business . . . I am a Jew, but I do not believe in God. I do not even believe in Jewish tradition. Neither did my father. But he passed it down to me. I am a nonbeliever, but I will pass it down to my own sons in turn.'

His eyes misted over once again, and once again I regarded him with a sort of involuntary respect. This faith without faith made me reflect. Where would I be, I thought, without God? What could I do? Nothing! Nothing! For me God is not a theoretical construct, but life itself!

'Does your lack of faith not scare you?' I asked softly. He understood what I was saying, I saw. I was saying something I had never said to anyone before, not even myself—namely, that I am afraid of a lack of faith, and most of all, I am afraid of my own lack of faith, but am also afraid of his, the lack of faith is contagious. I am afraid of it, I stand in terror of it. Contemptible. Hideous.

His tearful eyes were laughing now.

'*Hauptsach, her Herrgot isch gsond!*'—As long as God is healthy, flinging it at me like a present of sorts, this unique and very questionable lightness of his, and I was exceptionally grateful. God is hale and hardy! Whereupon I lost no time in sharing with him my thoughts on Communism as the sinister proconsul of the moment.

'You have a sharp mind, Count. And you're most observant!' I could have done without such praise. But then, as if to continue his previous thought, he added, 'When we have stopped wanting anything and our ambitions and aspirations have evaporated like the mist, we turn into our own observers, our own audience. A rare show indeed!'

'But there's no present without the past and the future. The past is the precondition for the present.' He was curious, and so he waited curiously for me to continue. 'Unless we negate time!'

'No, no, we're not negating it, we're re-creating it! A new time, a new time reckoning!' At which it was my turn to make a gesture of dismissal.

'Imagine an oak without time! An oak without rings! What would it be if not an empty, putrefying mockery?' The Jew Sterk grinned. I'd walked right into his trap.

'Oh, yes, indeed, Count, you took the words right out of my mouth. Empty! Putrefying! Mockery!' His grin mingled with kindness, then turned into a smile, the smile of a timid adolescent. 'Still, I wouldn't assume that Your Excellency is a Communist.'

'Indeed not,' I answered sternly, though—fate giving me the finger—when I learned that without papers from the local authorities plus a Socialist Party membership I.D. you couldn't take the train, and also that in the shops up in Pest they served 'comrades' only, I instructed my staff to have me and my family registered as members of the local Socialist party. If it's a piece of paper that makes a comrade a comrade, and only a comrade is a human being, who am I to object? What could the Party leaders do? Certainly, they weren't overjoyed when they guessed my motives. (Later, when the Commune failed and there was no danger anymore and my peers returned from their self-imposed exile, they criticized me haughtily to the last man for having obtained train tickets in this manner and at such a price, this without the slightest familiarity with conditions at the time. Yet we took this step without anyone demanding that we betray our convictions. Nor did we, ever.)

Theoretically, they could have called me comrade. The world had stood on its head! The Communists even make a joke of themselves. The present! The present! Just as journalism is the literature of the moment, the Communists are the aristocrats of the moment. Except, you can't be an aristocrat for a moment, for a moment you can only be a Communist! Self-definition as self-contradiction leads to parody. Instead of value, the parody of value! And just as the newspaper-dictated world takes the place of the real world, in the same manner, parody becomes of the essence, it becomes everything, while the sacred reality that has been ripped open by the knife of parody and has been brazenly turned inside out disappears from the scene.

'Brazenly!' Did I see what I thought I saw? Did Sterk shrug his shoulder? Did he—humbly—shrug his shoulder? 'Sterk, you and your pals have merely turned the world on its head. You did not transform it. You made up and down change places. What was up is now down—and I refused to point at myself!—and what was down, is now up. But, as I sincerely hope, others will come, who will once again . . .'

'Are you threatening me, Your Excellency?'

'By no means. Let me finish the sentence. Who will once again set the world on its feet. If you don't mind me saying so, the people couldn't care less whether Miklós Móric Esterházy or Károly Sterk is the up. It's just that they've grown used to me. Also, I've gotten the hang of it, more or less.'

'As far as we're concerned, there's no up and down. We've made short shrift of it. That's the whole idea behind the revolution.'

'Short shrift, indeed. We can only hope.' Sterk looked disdainfully at me, as if to say, he's caught me red-handed, I can't wait to lord it over others once again. 'You are mistaken, Sterk. Where persecution won't let up, the moment always comes when the victims turn just as base and contemptible as their persecutors.'

There was nothing more to be said. The limits to our candor had been reached. Still, I mentioned once again that they had declared war not only on those who were up, but on the Lord as well, and that will be their downfall.

'Just think. Napoleon couldn't even manage Moscow!' I found myself shouting with such vehemence, I surprised myself.

'Are you saying. Count, that the Kingdom of Heaven is colder, even, than Moscow? The assumption does not lack logic. The realm of eternal ice, where the Lord is the ice queen!'

'I beg you, sir! Too much! Desist! Must you make a joke out of everything?'

'*Pardonnez moi*, Count. In my own humble way, I was merely trying to point out the symmetry whereby hell, where eternal fire rages, appears to be warmer than desirable, while upstairs, it would seem to be much colder. See, Count? This is why we

Communists have chosen the earth. It is centrally located. There's no above and no below. Everything is right here, Count. Both heaven and hell. Everything.' He rushed his words as if someone were at his heels. His eyes had an ingratiating gleam. I knew him well enough by then to realize he was thinking of something. These Jews are like young eager beavers, like so many gifted, eager-beaver schoolboys. They always volunteer the answer. It'd kill them if just once they'd have to be clever *in silence,* inside, and for themselves. Now I was his audience. 'My place,' he said self-importantly, 'my country, just like the Mystics', is the void that precedes God!'

He looked at me expectantly, but kept sealing the blankets all the while. I was holding up the corners for him.

'You speak well, Sterk, but you speak false. No, no, your country is not the void, though this has occurred to me, too. I see your nihilism, your chaoticism. No. But as I come to know you and the others better, I see that your home is the seal, the stamp, the official I.D., the cultural index'—the proletarian dictatorship evidenced a keen interest toward the arts, with the usual nonsense and clumsiness; the deification of culture, hand in hand with its annihilation; the so-called cultural index was invented expressly for this, never has anything so ridiculous appeared in history before. A people's commissar classified the arts into various classes and categories, which classes, just as in the strictest bureaucracies, were matched with various categories of remuneration—'No, Sterk, it is not the case that you have seen fit to put man in God's place, which would amount to blasphemy, but could not be denied its share of courage, of rebellion. Luciferian, but courageous. Nor is it the case that you have blown hierarchy sky high. You have merely occupied it.'

Meanwhile, we continued sealing the bookcases. 'The truth is that you have put bureaucracy in the center of things, and this is where the naïveté of Communism lies, its ill-conceived modernity, but also its formidable aspect, for in this short span of time bureaucracy has made its awesome strength quite evident, whereby it has acknowledged neither God nor man, as the saying goes. Some sort of mechanical god is sitting perched atop the throne of history, like the dwarf inside Farkas Kempelen's mysterious chess machine whom no one knows and whom no one can influence, but events take their appointed course, and not even in the face of logic, which would itself be logical, but at random. Though sometimes it's checkmate . . .'

I fell silent. For a moment I couldn't decide if I should continue, but I continued.

'Bureaucracy will be the deity of the twentieth century. This much you have achieved, Sterk, and it's no small feat. And I am incapable of seeing to the end where all of this will lead in all its necessary repercussions. Nor do I doubt that you and the rest must feel the same way.'

'The difference being,' the Jew Sterk said with infinite sadness in his voice, 'that we couldn't care less.'

'My dear Sterk, your Communist theories are doubtless the best of all possible theories. Certainly, they are commendable socialist theories. You have been spreading them around for decades in the hope of a new Golden Age. But now, when you and the others were good enough to put them into effect . . . Just look at these sheets over the bookcases, how unavailing, how comical.' Sterk made no answer. As for me, I continued talking. There wasn't much else I could do. 'These brilliant decrees are nonsense to begin with, or will prove to have been nonsense, because they have accomplished the exact opposite of the ideals and aims you and yours were pleased to run off about at the mouth.'

Sterk still made no answer. He was taking me seriously, I felt, and I respected him for it, most especially because I couldn't feel the same way about him. Or only in part. After the fall of the Commune he came to see me, but getting the better of myself, I would not admit him into my presence. They said in the village that he'd fled to Vienna, then to Moscow, then back to Vienna, where he died under mysterious circumstances. Some of the news I received mentioned suicide. Others simple, accidental extinction! 'The apportionment of the homes of the bourgeoisie, as you say, among the indigent proletariat? *Bon*. But no, not *bon*, because the bourgeoisie worked for it. But never mind. The horrible result: filthy, unhealthy mass housing. The transformation of castles into sanatoriums with the stroke of the pen, does it not sound noble? And anything that opposes it, is it not egoism of inhuman proportions? Ridiculous superficialities, Sterk, ridiculous, if you don't mind my saying so!'

How strange. I heard myself yelling. My servants were carrying things in and out—my servants, on their orders. Next I shared with him my views on objects taken out of their context, and I did not conceal my dismay upon seeing the *heap* of art objects and valuables, at the sight of this centuries-old dunghill, which they had always seen as such, ignoring their context, without which all this is merely a shapeless, nauseating dump pile. I consider this dementation barbaric, but I didn't say so to the Jew Sterk. Instead I said:

'Admittedly, this batch of things brought together in this place is an unpleasant sight. A dinner is one thing, if you don't mind my saying so. But gorging yourself is quite another, if you follow me, Sterk.'

'Of course, Your Excellency. Nonetheless, the presence of hunger adds a certain *nuance* to your line of thought.'

'Excuse me?'

'If a person is hungry. That's what I'm saying. Because in that case, it's not easy differentiating between dining and gorging oneself. A gourmet looks down on hunger, I know. He is right! The very idea of eating for any other reason than for the taste! The very idea of owning something for any other reason than beauty!

Still, when hunger and satiety are squared off against each other, the needs of the former do not congeal on the esthetic. A slice of larded bread, Count, has, as you put it, no context.' I would have liked to cut in, but he wouldn't let me. 'If there is nothing but the larded bread, if that is the whole world, if there is nothing but the painful emptiness in the stomach, if that is all there is inside, and the larded bread outside . . . Is this not the same thing as saying that outside is the starry sky, while inside, if you follow me, moral principles?'

That incredible, impertinent frivolity again! I don't like Jews. Take this dramatic, plebeian oration. I am just about to accommodate myself to it, and then this unpleasant cabaret twist at the end! Kant as a *boulevardier*.

'Hunger is not to be taken lightly,' Sterk added cheerfully.

'I don't know what to say,' I said wryly—a recurring experience during the "glorious 133 days" of the Commune, this inability to comment on things. I came into conversational (!) contact with those of my fellow men who were normally separated from me by veritable oceans. The oceans had now run dry. In many a travelogue they describe in colorful detail how the caravan, dropping from exhaustion, drags itself over the desert, scorched and barren from the rays of the sun, and how the memory of a cool drink once enjoyed now comes uninvited to the parched travelers, multiplying their present torture a thousandfold. Similarly, our own days drag on, interminably, intolerably, slowly, slowly.

With reference to my limited experience of hunger, I commented:

'Perhaps I won't make a good Communist after all.'

'Indeed, Count, I think not.' He seemed disappointed. I had a hunch that he had been expecting something more from me with respect to this.

The absurdity was even more alarming than the atrocity. I find it alarming when I don't understand a person or a thing *at all*. For

I cannot assume that the person in question does not understand himself either, whereas this approach might, at times, be easier to deal with. I am convinced that absurdity comes from faith without God. If we remove the infinite from the horizon, the eye falters.

'Your Communism is like that faltering eye.'

'Does not the danger lie in the looking? The eye as it gallops along and falters! Is not the blind man the most placid of all observers?'

'I am tired of your paradoxes!'

'I am tired of your logic! And also, is not our Christian attitude that of the blind man who pins his glance on the infinite and empty horizon?'

'Are you being impertinent?'

'Not in the least, Your Excellency.'

I believed him.

Then I reverted once again to the absurdity, for my antipathy toward Bolshevism originated less with the fact that I had lost my fortune, or my horror of bloodshed, than from witnessing the spectacle of savagery, the lack of culture and the *almost intangible* stupidity that manifested itself in the way these bastards implemented Marxist principles.

'The almost intangible stupidity . . .'—Sterk chewed and tasted the words in his mouth, but not like one who is hungry, not in his previously mentioned wild helplessness. On the contrary, he masticated it like a connoisseur, enjoying it at his leisure—'almost, almost intangible, that's the beauty of it, the almost intangible stupidity . . . Yes, indeed, stupidity is not to be taken lightly.'

Hunger is not to be taken lightly, and stupidity is not to be taken lightly; the revolutionary Sterk, it seems, is bent on not being taken lightly. In any case, he must think a lot more about his reputation than my family ever did. It is an unfair ideology.

'Custom, Your Excellency, and your family knows a lot about

this,'—Sterk turned crimson as he spoke—'is not without a certain remove from ideals. There is always some sloth and intellectual laziness involved. The word "stupidity" probably expresses it well, though doubtlessly, it does leave the question of responsibility out of the deal. Just think, Count, of the long—I might even say vicissitudinous—history of the glorious Holy See.'

'Are you comparing the Church to the Soviet system?'

'Of course not. Though I might point out that in both cases we are dealing with an institution built, operated, and taken advantage of by men.' Panting, he drew a deep breath, then showed his hand: 'The regrettable excesses of the individual cannot be blamed on the whole.'

Oh, how often would we hear this in the upheavals to follow! When we asked so-called sober socialists whether such repugnant excesses were part of their teachings, which were supposed to serve the good of all, at best this is what they'd say: the regrettable excesses of the individual cannot be blamed on the whole.'

'Amazing, the way you can comfort yourselves with adjectives and *bon mots*!'

'Is not the Ten Commandments a similar collection of *bon mots,* Your Excellency? Do not kill. I like that! Two thousand years of Christianity, two thousand years of war! Do not kill! Ingenious to the extreme, is it not? And we haven't touched upon the other nine yet!'

'Stop! You and yours have replaced reflection with wit, truth and justice with *machbarkeit*. Truth is what you can get away with. And whatever you can get away with is truth. This is how the pursuit of pleasure comes to replace love. Whatever exists automatically wins your support. This is not how Jesus spoke, Sterk.'

'Jesus can't help us, Your Excellency. He couldn't even help himself. Jesus plays on your playing field, not ours.'

'Don't talk like that.'

'Excuse me.' He smiled ever so lightly, and I don't know why, but I smiled a little too.

And then, all of a sudden, we had no more to say to each other. The words got stuck in our throats. As far as our conversation was concerned, we did not dine, but gorge ourselves, I admit. We became sated without, however, finding peace within—more like doubt and uncertainty, that's what we were trying to stifle with our silence.

Suddenly, we turned to the big window facing the park at one and the same time, as if we'd rehearsed it beforehand. Spring raged rampant in the park, the thick-foliated branches touching, twilight slowly falling, a brownish-gray half-light descending, leaving only the vibrant green patches of the trees and the purplish-pink glimmer at the bottom of the sky.

'Evening Star outside, Evening Star inside,' giggled Sterk, for he was referring to the legend according to which our family was supposed to have received its name indirectly, and through a number of linguistic translocutions, from the Evening Star. And also the Morning Star. The Star of Even-Morn.

'Born Morgenstern.' Now it was my turn to giggle, for I was referring to the fact that the *stern* visible on the western sky after nightfall and on the eastern sky before dawn, was once thought to be two separate planets, Morning Star, Evening Star.

Gradually it turned pitch dark. For a long time we stood in front of the window wrapped in silence until they asked us, as if we were children, what we were up to in the window niche."

## 48.

The legend goes back to the thirteenth century, its main character that certain Miklós of the Salamon clan, thanks to whom the straight line of descent can be demonstrated in various documents—we have the papers!—and about whom the said documents tell us nothing whatsoever, because they do not mention him. They mention only his son László as his son, *filius Nocolai de cognatione Salamon*. A father who exists only through his son. According to the legend, on certain evenings the Fairy (?) of Csallóköz visited my forefather's garden in order to bathe in the tub put out expressly for her. When the Evening Star became visible in the sky she began to divest herself of her clothes, and it was supposed to be my forefather's office to announce to the fairy that she can start, the star's here, the sweet little evening star.

When the old man died, the fairy sent a scribe, his name was István, who, to the accompaniment of his lute, sang the song which for a long time afterward was considered the family's own, secret hymn; a powerful plea that speaks of namelessness, of all things, the longing for namelessness, when it would have seemed that a name is everything. An itinerant chorus sang the death song, they say.

*Beloved name Evening Star*
*flee from me flee from me*
*a naked man needs not*
*such heavenly sweet company*

*The sky, it has lost its name*
*the earth it has lost its name*
*a naked man needs not*
*anything so fair*

*Everything has lost its name*
*names are free now, free to flee*
*my beloved Evening Star*
*go join your celestial company.*

# 49.

Even after her mishap—this was the official name, mishap, we were forbidden to call it anything else—Aunt Mia continued to carry the news back and forth between the palace and Pest, whereby she met not one, but two members of the Red Guard on the train.

We now had two members of the Red Guard (hooked, lock stock and barrel) of our very own.

One was the son of a servant of long standing in my great-grandfather's employ who ended up sailing on socialist waters because he was a metal worker, but he did so without forgetting the "*à la longue*" relationship between our two families, and so offered to help Aunt Mia. The two young men whose "innocent souls" were permeated through and through by the new current teachings, delineated the bright future for the benefit of the Countess in glowing colors, not forgetting to mention how splendidly and without a care in the world the young lady's father would live—never mind that the young lady's father had been living splendidly and without a care in the world up till then; he'd even receive a life annuity, they said, the state would take care of him. It would even see to his fortune.

My great-grandfather noted down these novel ideas of the new regime, appending an *i* here and there: irresponsible. Childish, irresponsible: *i*.

Later, too, the two youths helped us repeatedly. In many a perilous moment did they come forward as the responsible guardians of the family's safety, for often the new, irresponsible motifs made the moment dangerous, indeed. Thus, we might as well add the letter *d: d*!

Since the outbreak of the revolution, the state telephone was available only to official persons. Still, it rang.

"Hello! This is the Red Guard!" As if he'd touched a serpent, Great-grandfather dropped the receiver.

"Hello! This is Esterházy!" he shot back. One here, one there, or the other way around: who there?, who here?, double, redouble, I call your bluff, reshuffle!

The Red Guardsman told Great-grandfather that some relatives were due at the station in the afternoon, and would need a carriage. A couple of hours later the caravan arrived, and consequent upon the consent of a number of comrades, "the little proletarian Mátyás," the embodiment of much hope and joy, made his ceremonious entry into the place that would no longer be called his paternal inheritance.

Heine writes that his crib teetered at the turn of the eighteenth and nineteenth century. My father's crib also teetered, quite dramatically. Thousand-year-old Hungary was on the brink of collapse.

## 50.

The family council was soon convened, not because of the collapse, though, but because it was time to flee, there being a strong probability that my darling little, barely cooing Daddy would be taken hostage.

Actually, it was more like a quick tête-à-tête. A bona fide family council is a well-defined legal and family institution. The first to call "my senior milords" together was Palatine Miklós, a long, long time ago, desiring that the family gather together like this once every year; if there is anything to discuss, to discuss it, if there isn't, "to pass the time in tribal love." In his last will and testament he provides meticulously and on a grand scale, but with an eye to the minutest detail, for the tangible as well as the intangible effects, always keeping fairness and concord in mind, giving advice and a free hand, when he writes: "Should any questions arise about those things put down herein in this, my Testament, my descendants may not involve themselves in any suit whatsoever, nor must they carry my Testament from place to place, but have six elders from among themselves gather to determine this thing."

Among German aristocrats most families have a permanent council, as well as so-called regularly appointed *Familien* days. In our family this was not the custom. We were called together *ad hoc*. Needless to say, the members of the council served without remuneration; if their business involved much work and time, it was the custom to show our gratitude to the members who were not related by blood with a present (gold cigarette case, cuff links).

Family councils that were called together de facto were rare. It was the family council of our branch, the counts of Frakno, who decided to petition the ruler so that the estates confiscated from the anti-Habsburg Kuruc field marshal Antal (Pápa-Ugod-Devecser-Cseklész) should not pass into a stranger's possession, but that the ruler should make a gift of it to the two surviving brothers. (He did.) Presided over by Primate Imre, it was again the fam. coun. that brought a decision re. the inheritance of the wife and daughters of Prince Mihály, who died young, his wife being the Italian Anna Margherita Tizzone Biandrata, Marchesa de Sata. The family council even prescribed how many horses the marchesa's carriage could have, and how much space would be allotted them in the stables of the palace in Vienna, and where they could keep the firewood made available for their use. Our family is anything, if not thorough!

In keeping with the spirit of the Palatine's testament, anyone who turns to the courts to appeal the family decision automatically loses his right of inheritance. (My father, too, liked to say that one does not bring a suit. Suits just fatten the purses of the lawyers. I didn't even know what he was talking about. Bringing suit? It sounded like something out of an old novel.) Also in line with the tribal love of this last will and testament, every Esterházy became heir presumptive of the palatine's estates, this in a predetermined order, provided his own branch of the family died out. (For your information: in case of the extinction of the dukes, the oldest male scion of the oldest branch of the counts of Frakno— yoo-hoo! here I am!—receives the inheritance, followed by the eldest male scion of the next-oldest branch. The next in line, were the counts of Frakno to become extinct, would have been the branches from Csesznek, followed by the Zólyom branch, with the same conditions.)

This is why the consent of *all* the Esterházys was required when Francis Joseph permitted that in the interest of paying off the debts (and especially the interests), a certain amount of lands from the entailed estate administered by a sequestrator could be sold off. After lengthy deliberation and leaving the original rules of inheritance intact, the heads of all the branches of the family agreed to the sale.

It was also a family council that started a suit against that certain Walsin of the Dreyfus affair, to prohibit him from the use of the family name and title.

Grandfather was a member, and also the head, of several family councils. Being a count is a demanding job.


51.


The family council was to be held in the Knights' Hall at the castle of Lánzsér. For its duration Count Miklós ordered special chairs to be placed around the huge oak table. The chair legs were sawn off to accommodate the members of the council in such a way so that their eyes and cheeks should be on a level, serving as a reminder that they are conferring and should confer as equals, that they should conduct themselves according to that obligation, and also with autonomy.

52.

The joy and idyllic good cheer subsequent upon the arrival of the infant did not last. Being informed that they were out searching for him (and in those days such searches boded no good), my grandfather, who despite his youthful age was already a defeated prime minister, chose himself a safer haven.

To make matters worse, Great-grandfather Károlyi had set up the antirevolutionary government at Arad, taking over the presidency when it was moved to Szeged. We learned all about it in school. Mrs. Váradi was screeching like a stuck owl.

"The Christian, ultraconservative, antirevolutionary forces!"

His photograph stood next to Grandmother's bed on the nighttable, in a place of distinction. An ultraconservative, antirevolutionary force. I studied him closely. He bore a strong resemblance to Grandmother's younger sister. From the look of him I couldn't help but conclude that it's not such a tragedy to be a Christian, ultraconservative, antirevolutionary force if one happens to be such. Of course, Mrs. Váradi didn't have a photograph.

My great-grandfather's and grandfather's photographs stood side by side. In life too there was uncommon harmony between the two men. They were bound together not only by this Christian, ultraconservative, but also by that unobtrusive, gentlemanly, Hungarian lack of ambition which, given all the esteem to begin with, is no big deal, nobody said it was!—and of which Great-grandfather adopted a pleasant metaphysical variety, while Grandfather a sharper, mocking version. As far as they were concerned, Mihály Károlyi was, first and foremost, too loud. He wanted something, and that was suspicious. Later, in the early forties, both out-of-service prime ministers by then, they exchanged letters like you wouldn't believe. Sparing, that's the right word, such sparing letters have probably never been written (in Hungarian) before or since. The two aged gentlemen were sitting in their respective palaces hundreds of kilometers from each other, watching their throats being cut. No, that's not what they were watching, they were watching the world, the whole world, that's what they were used to watching. *Dear Móric, the more I think about it, the more convinced I am that with regard to the proper course of procedure Kállay and not Bethlen is correct. Hitler's speech of yesterday only confirmed this for me. Cordial regards, Gy. Dear Father-in-Law, thanks for the nineteenth. I fully understand and share your doubts. M.*

I could have studied the frames at my grandmother's for hours on end. They were so improbably intricate and beautiful, they were made with so much care and devotion, I'd never seen the likes of them before. I'd always thought that the beauty and sense of proportion that manifested itself again and again in everything my mother did was due to her personal eccentricity, that my mother was for some reason trying to push herself in the foreground in this way; that as a mother and housewife, her taste and refinement were given no space, because this space was designed for a beast of burden, and she was a perfect beast of burden until the day she died.

I did not think that her refinement, which manifested itself in objects, pointed beyond her person. I did not think that there could be a world where it mattered how a piece of paper is folded, how something is pasted on, or mounted, and that, in short, the world, the world created by man, has esthetics. I thought that only my mother had esthetics, that the beautiful is not something that *is,* it is something that she created. You can't find it in a shop, and you can't order it, not even through a private merchant.

On the other hand, there they were on Grandmother's table, in all their glory, these fine objects, stood up this way, and mounted that way, and some were even stamped, Kellér & Sons, Tata, or Angerer Hof-Photograph. In short, that there exists a world from which these originate. This was a major discovery for me, just like the Western cars later on, namely, that there is a world where hundreds of people work for years only and exclusively on the arch or curve of the tail lights. That this could be important. That there might be more to the world than a cosmic shrug—the curve of the tail lights?! what's the difference? as long as they work!

When the news about his father-in-law reached his ears, my grandfather suspended his comfortable exile in the countryside, and returned to the palace to effectuate his family's escape, for should Béla Kun manage to arrest and take the daughter and grandson of his major enemy hostage, he'd have a trump in hand.

The war council convened, and everyone in turn (except my father) had his say. They were intent, and they made intent faces, but no use. They could not take this fleeing game seriously. It seemed so incredible and improbable that they should be outlaws in their own country, that they were just making believe now too that they were in dire straits and needed to flee without delay, in such real, great, dire straits, that one grows vertiginous with fear and the need to act, one's very being shrivels up, and one is on the verge of a nervous stomach and a fainting spell.

I don't think the family had ever been in such a pass before.

# 53.

1652, the twenty-sixth day of the month of the birth of the Blessed Virgin.

The glorious history, hardly begun, was nearly nipped in the bud. A hairsbreadth escape. It was as if the lowlands of Ecsed were only ten kilometers after Donaueschingen, and the water, flowing in a thousand directions, were suddenly to stop in its tracks. A pretty puddle, loads of valuable waterbirds. Still, it's just not the same.

The "handsome count," László, died, the empire fell on the shoulders of the seventeen-year-old Pál, and all around sharks hungry for the spoils, from brother-in-law Nádasdy to the Court. How fortunate for us that by then the great cardinal Pázmány had returned to the bosom of his one true, Catholic God, the only one he seemed inclined, but only just, to accept and acknowledge as his superior.

# 54.

As if starting off to a matinee or a noneventful soccer game, so did László and his cousins set off, upon the invitation of Captain General Ádám Forgách of Érsekújvár, to the county of Nyitra, to punish a band of marauding Turks. (Obviously, the Turks must have called us marauders, too—except, of course, in Turkish.) They successfully freed the Christian prisoners taken by the pagan horde, but there was a heavy price to pay. Eight members of our family fought in the battle, and four of them died on the battlefield, on one day, on one field, in one hour.

Meanwhile, young Master Pál was sulking in the castle at

Sempte. Though he begged and beseeched his brother that he might accompany him to camp, which would not have been an unaccustomed request—*virtu* too must be learned firsthand—undaunted, as if driven by a premonition, László refused to allow it.

When the sad news reached him that after a heroic fight his older brother fell in battle, in the twinkling of an eye the youthful Palkó turned into Pál, the young master into a lord, a great lord, the adolescent into a mature male. He grew vertiginous with fear and the need to act. His entire being shriveled up. He found himself on the verge of a nervous stomach and a fainting spell. But the moment passed. It passed, or else he shooed it away, and he calmly sat down to dinner. He had the table set for his brother László too but for himself not, as at other times, on his brother's left, but at the upper end of the table, facing him. There sat the two brothers, at one table, one absence, the other presence. Their older cousin, Farkas, on László's right at other times, now on Pál's right, one of the most important figures of the family machinery, a real *éminence grise,* brilliant, obliging, modest, without issue—according to the *Chronicle of Löcse,* a gentleman of respectable and noble character, and a kind heart. He had busied himself with the family's legal affairs even in Count Miklós's time, later becoming László's legal advisor, and with the death of the Palatine, the overseer of the education of his orphans.

He regarded the new head of the family with pride. Pál sent an immediate dispatch to the captains of the Esterházy castles of Lánzsér, Lakompa, Regéc, Bicse and Pápa, his strict orders being carried on quick-footed steeds that until further notice they must let no strangers enter the castle. Master Farkas managed things so that the new head of the family should feel he is in charge. Pál knew that everyone must think he is in charge, and so he suffered the helping hand of his experienced relative to continue resting on his shoulder.

Upon waking the following morn did they proceed in search

of the bodies and did come upon the ill-fated László, with masters Ferenc, Tamás and Gáspár, all of whom fell most valiantly in the service of the gods and their homeland. Of the servants of ill-fated László fifty fell upon the field of battle, and many besides suffered grievous wounds. They found the bodies ravaged, each and every one, only on the body of his ill-fated brother the shirt, footwear and breeches having been spared. Also, there were twenty-five wounds upon him, some from bullets, others stabs, yet others slashes. His military gear can be reconstructed to satisfaction partly from his steward's diary, partly after the cuirass and headpiece in the Museum of Military History in Vienna. My deceased brother wore a short, ample leather shirt over the simple black breastplate. There was a leopard-skin cover on the back of his steed. His saddle, harness, round shield, mace and sword with Damascus blade were adorned with inlays of turquoise and pearls. Atop his black helmet encased in an aigrette of precious stones there flew a bouquet of crane feathers divided in three to suit his rank as captain general and a pair of exquisitely wrought French guns, carefully loaded with powder, were tied to his saddlebow. None of which helped him; having sunk into quagmire, his horse fell, and he fought on having alighted from his horse. As it can be seen on the breastplate on display in the museum, a bullet entered his lower body by ripping a piece from the hem of the plate. This probably caused his death.

From Sempte they hurried on to Frakno, where all the servants of the castle and the turnkeys were obliged to swear their fidelity. He also consorted with his sweet affianced Orsolya (Orsicska), so they could pray together for the living and the dead— their dead kin and their living selves. Also, with the leadership of Count Farkas the intricate maneuvers to stave off trouble were begun, the gist of which was, in part, the clarification of the ownership of the various portions of the estate (*cf.,* for example, the handling of the dominions owned by lien), and in part curbing the voracious appetite of Ferenc Nádasdy, who was the husband of our elder sister Anna, a brother-in-law, a relative, but this did not prevent him—eh, it didn't prevent him from doing anything!, when in the meantime, in his hypocritical way, he had Drentwett, his silversmith from Augsburg, fabricate a splendid ceremonial plate in honor of the heroes of Vezekény. Farkas needed all his cleverness in order to keep the voracious appetite for property of the future Lord Chief Justice in check.

Also, there was the permission to be obtained from Rome for nuptials with the very, very closely related Orsolya; the family was able to win the good graces of the lady Dona Olympia Maldachini, the powerful sister-in-law of Pope Innocent IX, whereupon Master Farkas wrote in the expenses column: one thousand golden thalers.

## 55.

The war council decided that the potential hostages, Grandmother and little Mátyás, should go on a little pleasure ride, so to speak. It feels good to say it: little Mátyás; it feels good to talk about our father as a child, not in order to gain the upper hand, on the contrary; in this way it feels as if we could withdraw ourselves from the seemingly obligatory Oedipalities, or at least, that the first few steps in that direction can be taken, and that it is possible, at long last it is possible, to pamper our father, which otherwise can't be done even with the best kinds, not even with friendly, amiable fathers, and even with a friendly, amiable friend only just a bit, a little bit, and with circumspection.

A pleasure ride, the council reiterated; they'd have even winked, had they not considered it vulgar. They squinted, they wrinkled their brows, they raised their eyebrows. (The family had always distinguished itself in brow raising—"though its original

spirit had paled, there can be no doubt that in brow raising . . ."
They were especially masters of the asymmetrical, skeptical variety. My grandfather had no peer, the very epitome of the *genre*, and though my father was in possession of the requisite playfulness of the facial muscles, he could at best imitate his father, even if impeccably, see? this is how I'd raise my brow, if I'd raise it, and he raised it. Third-generation weakling, not only can't I raise mine, I can't even pull them together. To be perfectly honest, I hardly have eyebrows. In case of profuse sweat, they're of no use to me at all . . . )

Also my grandfather would be the driver, they decided slyly, so there'd be no one to betray the "flight into Egypt," as they referred to it in their letters by way of a secret code.

## 56.

A letter writer can't imagine, because if he could, he would rather not write the letter, preferring to cut off his hand instead, break his pen in two and spill the ink, he'd rather *go* there or break off the *relationship,* if only he knew how helpless and humiliated you become when illicit hands fiddle with your letter. (Those in the know said that they got steamed open at the No. 7 Central Post Office.) A man using the telephone is in the same predicament. He can't really imagine that they're listening in on his conversation. Assumptions abound, of course, romantic notions. But how far removed they are from the simple, dreary truth!

There is probably no family who in the sixties did not think that their phone was being bugged, or who did not notice small, suspicious signs where the envelope was sealed. This without regard to gender, religion, or worldview, one might say.

"It's only natural," my mother laughed, but I was appalled. "If they can't arrest you, throw you in jail, shoot you in the head,

what can these poor people fall back on, if not a bit of spying?"
And then, those pitiful attempts, too, at covering the phone with a
pullover, or carrying it into the bathroom! Every tap turned on,
the toiled flushed—they can't hear, we can't hear.

Everyone in the whole world thinks they can outsmart the
wiretapper. A mistake. You can always outsmart something, even
someone's brain, but whose? . . . A wiretapper is not a person, a
human being, not an intellect that can be outwitted. Because they
don't take their own weakness into account, by their very nature,
preventive measures are arrogant. And arrogance, when weak, is
hateful. Whenever my parents used the phone (since they assumed that they were being bugged, they always meta-phoned), I
covered my eyes with my hands so I wouldn't have to see, and
covered my ears so I wouldn't have to hear them. As if they didn't
exist. What petty, ridiculous narrow-mindedness, what shits my
parents are. I sobbed. Infantile, pathetic.

Preventive measures fall into two groups. One derives from
the arrogance of self-censorship. It assumes that you can guess
what may be a subject for wiretapping, and what not. How clever,
circumspect and—just a bit ashamed because of it—authoritarian
our father must have thought himself every time he thundered at
us, "That's not a topic for the phone!"

Enough to make you cry for shame.

As if wiretapping made a distinction between important and
not important. We mustn't say church, anthem, or schilling, but
can safely say bell, song, and inkling. Darkness slowly descended
on us, so many fluttering red flakes, stop, go no further!, as if it
were that simple! As if the odious wiretapper, like an odious spider, were weaving his odious cobweb around his victim. The
wiretapper is weaving his web. Baseness. Baseness is spreading. It
is this baseness that I saw.

The other preventive measure derives from the arrogance inherent in freedom. It assumes that nothing matters, you can say

whatever you want, *those people* will do what they feel like anyway. Consequently, you can also do what *you* feel like. You can say whatever you want, and they can go lick your a . . . clean.

By his nature, my father belonged to the first group, but like everyone else, at times he slipped into the second, either because he was weary, or because all that self-imposed discipline was too much for him, and this was his way of remembering freedom. At such times he began joking with his anonymous partner, apologizing for holding him up, et cetera. The usual thing. Meanwhile, he'd talk out at us in a sort of stage whisper, as if to make sure we understood what he was up to. I'd never heard my mother laugh so hard. So-called preventive measures can't do without an audience, a grateful audience, so that whoever is listening in should feel ashamed. I felt so ashamed, I could have died.

Once I just couldn't bear to listen anymore and I ran to the phone and slammed down the receiver. My father was so shocked, he forgot to slap me on the mouth.

"What was that all about, son?" he asked softly, surprised. And I, sobbing, threw my arms around him, pressing him close, closer. The buckle of his belt burrowed into my face.


## 57.


Hundreds and hundreds—millions!—of buckles found their way into our apartment at the time. Like a colorful army of bugs, they slithered about, blue, red, white, black. They wormed their way into everything. We came upon them in the kitchen, among the plates, in the toilet, the beds, the pillowcases, school bags, and out in the garden, too. We had just moved back to Budapest, and nobody made much of an effort to hire my father. Not everyone was with them yet who was not against them (*cf.* Kádár!), not to mention the fact that my father was against them. But then Uncle

Juszuf Tóth hired him—how my mother hated the man!—first to work with the plastic buckles, then to lay down wooden floors. I don't know why my father kept bringing all that plastic junk home. As extra remuneration? We even took them to school to barter with. A bit of PR for Papi. But just the buckle, without the belt.

If only he'd worked in a chocolate factory! Or the slaughter-house. The big brother of vegetable store Feri always brought tripe and gave them away to the neighbors. Mother was so re-pulsed, she wouldn't take any, even out of courtesy.

"I understand, Aunt Lilike. Aunt Lilike is pleased to look down her nose on simple food."

Careless use of language got my mother's dander up every time. Our use of gotta and gonna and the like electrified her.

"Listen to me, Mr. Tóni. First. Don't call me Aunt Lilike."

"I understand, Aunt Lilike. But why is Aunt Lilike pleased to call me, Mr. Tóni?"

"How old are you, Mr. Tóni?"

"Twenty. Nineteen."

"Well, that's why." Mother waved an arm. "Also, don't use please like that, in that ingratiating manner."

"It doesn't please you?"

"It doesn't please me."

"Let's skip it, Aunt Lilike. I can't talk like Aunt Lilike pleases, while Aunt Lilike isn't pleased with the tripe. I get it. You think it smells. But it doesn't. You gotta rinse it well. I can show you how, and so can Mutter."

"And also, Mr. Tóni, don't say Mutter. Your mother is not your Mutter."

Tóni was the unfortunate target of the preaching that was aimed at us, except he (naturally) listened to our mother, unlike (naturally) us.

"In one ear, out the other!" Spot on.

"Mutter, Vater, I see what you're at. But this time you're wrong . . ." and here he paused, drew a deep breath, closed, then opened his eyes, then spit it out: "Aunt Lilike, if you please!" He sounded jubilant.

This was one of the few times I had ever seen someone looking at my mother as a woman. (She had a permanent, secret admirer, Uncle Zoli, but it was so secret, he wasn't aware of it himself: his glance either pleaded or felt sorry for himself—but for such things you don't need a woman.) Mother was weary of Tóni and pleased with him, too.

"I see, you're a man to be reckoned with. Sit down, I'll order some tea. But kindly leave *that thing* outside."

I'll order some, I'll have them bring some. She'd usually say it like this, then go and get it herself. She wasn't joking. It's just that her life can be circumscribed by this light joke: a lady of breeding who—having been a workhorse—continued to work like a beast of burden all her days.

"My family needs me for a servant." So what else is new?

Outside the tripe, inside the tea, steaming, biscuits, napkins, sugar cubes, silver spoon. Tóni was in seventh heaven. There's nothing he wouldn't have done for our mother. Tripe, for one thing. He kept bringing her tripe. Later we talked him into tenderloin. But before that, it was marrowbone.

## 58.

Tóni's adoring, five-and-dime novel glance made me first think that my mother is a woman, and when the bone marrow came, that my father is a man. That this is what a man is like. He procures, solves, provides, divides.

"The midnight predators gather for the kill," our father

announced mock-heroically, then sat down at the kitchen table with ceremony, the pot in front of him. We crowded around him, buzzing and craning our neck, so we shouldn't miss anything. "Take your places," he said looking at us with make-believe severity and then, like a chief physician at the operating table (or a priest conducting mass), he raised his two hands, "The scalpel, sweetheart!" he said to mother, who did and did not take part in the show. She was happy that we were happy, we, her children, and also the man who at that moment was busy pretending that life is beautiful and exciting, and he the master of all he surveys, the benefactor of the small group for whose benefit he was demonstrating that this beauty and excitement is everywhere at all times, just look, even in a bone, a leg of beef!

"Towel!" At which to our surprise, our mother—a surprise, time and time again a surprise—handed him not one of the much-used kitchen towels, there were even old diapers among them!, but a bright and shiny white heavy damask towel, on which we could clearly make out the embroidered twelve-branched crown, *hence* a Károlyi inheritance. Our father was surprised, too, and threw our mother a questioning gaze—we watched them with gaping mouths, like gods, our chance to take a peek at Olympus: our mother nodded, yes, yes, at which our father wrapped the towel around his left wrist with admirable dexterity, first whipping it up into the air, where it floated in the kitchen sky like a bird, a white dove of peace, what else (according to Little Huszár the dove of peace is not even a dove, but a turtledove, which is like a prickle and a thorn, there's no rose without a prickle, peace-turtledove), then the towel began its leisurely descent and wrapped itself around Papi's wrist, and he plunged into the pot for the bone. We heaved a sigh, oh, oh, what now?; in the twinkling of an eye our best kitchen towel became *used*, filthy, covered with grease, brownish and sloshy; we gave a look of alarm, oh, what has become of it, we wailed, or would have liked to, but we were just being taught that it's no good being overscrupulous, we were learning something about doing things on a grand scale, and also, perhaps, that there's a price to be paid for this wonderful turtledove-like gesture; it requires many things—this ancient towel, and also our mother's hands, spoiled with washing, so that she could wash this again, too; in short, that our father's conjuring trick had in it the interplay of the personal and the impersonal, of the present and the past.

And then, the enormous quarry in our father's enormous hand as he held it suspended above the plate put there expressly for him; he raised his right hand, made a fist, and . . . and struck! But where? Not, as we had expected, down on the bone, but on his own hand! We watched this, too, with mouths agape. Well, I'll be! Of course, when you combine folk wisdom with the laws of physics . . . Usually, a large chunky piece slithered out in response to the first blow, the sign we were waiting for; we quickly sat down around the table, and the excited, if not nervous, activity took its precipitous start.

"Quick! Quick! The bread!" our father said excitedly, because the toast was somehow always late, just a bit, but late. Always. "Hot! You gotta eat it hot!"

The first bite was his. Our mother cut off a butter yellow, quivering slice, a medallion, from the best piece, then sprinkled it with salt, paprika and black pepper in that order, handing it to our father as if giving him the Sacrament. He took it to himself with his eyes closed, ecstatically, swallowed it, waited, waited for the aftertaste, then nodded:

"Go ahead. It's not poisoned."

We had to be quick so the marrow wouldn't harden, as if the worst that could happen in the whole wide world was hardened bone marrow. If it hardens, we lose. Something like that. So we plunged into it. And then, at the last moment, we realized, we remembered, we, the children, and also the man and father, that Mami hadn't had any yet. And then she got some, of course; we offered her our own, nothing but the leftovers by then, the darker, tattered bits, which doesn't mean it's no good, and our mother liked it, too.

## 59.

We didn't believe for a minute that Mami didn't like breast meat and preferred the wings or the parson's nose every time; the truth willed out, it reared its ugly head. ("Horse's head, or parts of it, can be used for soup. It's a bit sweeter than one's used to, so it takes more seasoning, that's the secret," our aunt said. Our mother made a face.) We knew she was doing it for us, that she was *devoting* herself, sacrificing herself for us, and we thought this is how it should be, that's what mothers are for, to make sacrifices. When we'll be mothers, we'll make sacrifices, too. Or not. Besides, what's wrong with wings?

On the other hand, we didn't just believe but knew for a fact that our father's favorite delicacy was that barely edible, sour, hard, dark *thing*, cheap chocolate of the bitter variety. The problem was created by wicked or unenlightened guests, and before we could have a disheartened and ungracious go at it, our father grabbed it away from us and started munching it, pleased as pie. He even got it all over his face. We watched. It seemed nearly as good as cognac-cherry kisses.

Once—this was later—when our guests didn't bring us chocolates anymore, if they brought anything at all, I wanted to surprise him for his birthday (or Christmas?) with bitter chocolate. There was none in the shops just then, and I walked my feet to the bone until at last (on a tip from the center half of the Kőbánya Meat Co. soccer team) I found some in Kőbánya. I was proud of myself. I'm not a talented gift giver, but this time I had succeeded. I was inordinately proud of myself, and handed it to Father with a beaming smile.

"Hm," Father said with reserve as his fingers groped around the treasure. I told him what difficulties I had obtaining it. "Hm." I couldn't imagine what I'd done wrong this time.

"Your favorite sweet, is it not?" I said to stifle a mild curse. And then it turned out ("I'll tell you whose favorite sweet it is!") that bitter chocolates for him were the bishop's nose! When I told the others, they wouldn't believe me.

"But he even used to smudge it all over his face, he was so happy!"

But in the end, we didn't take offense at this about-face of his, we ignored it. Refused to believe it. And he went on receiving the bitter chocolates ("a bitter joke"). The only thing that had changed was that now, when we gave it to him, we couldn't look him in the eye.

## 60.

Besides plastic belt buckles, we also had industrial-size reserves of kid-skin gloves. Aunt Mia gave mother a pair of kid gloves every Christmas, a pair of glacé kid gloves made in the city of Vienna by Hoffer on the Juden Gasse, even during our forced resettlement. She also received a pair for her anniversary, which came to two pairs of glacé kid gloves per year.

Our mother hadn't quite reached twenty pairs yet, but almost, when she laid the gloves out in front of her, and she cut and sewed and snipped and—because that's what was needed just then—she turned them into toilet paper holders. Toilet paper holders from Aunt Mia's kid-skin gloves! For once, we were let in on the secret. So the responsibility should be spread all around?

"What happens if Auntie comes to visit?" we agonized. Her not being able to see was no consolation. She saw whatever she wanted to. She didn't need her eyes to see!

"First of all, she's not coming, because they won't give her an entry permit. Our people's democracy is scared stiff of Mia tante's antirevolutionary fervor," our parents said, trying to make light of it. Plus, in order to reassure themselves.

We imagined Auntie riding in at the head of her antirevolutionary forces, speaking with a slight aristocratic burr, because she spoke with a slight aristocratic burr, declaring martial law, then looking in the eyes of the commies with sympathy, and saying in all seriousness:

"Káh-dáhrrr's had it, bohys!"

"But what if she gets the permit?" we persevered, taking the pulse of the approaching goulash-Communism.

"A lady of breeding does not use the bathroom when she's a guest," my father said severely. (We have an aunt, the wife of one of our uncles, who for months after her wedding would return to her parental home to do her number two. A lady of breeding, indeed.) Still, he was worried, too, it seemed.

"Fear not, ye fainthearted ones," our mother declared, shaking her head with satisfaction, "this is such impudence, she wouldn't even dream that her beautiful gloves could be put to . . . that I'd . . . for the toilet . . . I won't even say it."

She looked around with pride. She'd paid something of her own back to the Esterházy family. Nonetheless, one toilet paper holder was painted with polka dots, and she also saved a pair of gloves for show. Just in case.

# 61.

I embraced my father round the waist—an ancient oak, Rákóczi's very own!—and the plastic belt buckle pressed into my face.

"Papi, darling, you know not what you do, please don't do it, I don't want them to hear everything, they mustn't hear everything," I sobbed, whimpered, blubbered, hiccuped, I hiccuped up the words, "they're animals, animals, Papi, dear, you have no idea, they tape all your words and play it back, sometimes on fast forward, sometimes slowed down, and they have a good laugh at it in there, Papi, forgive me."

My father scorned this sort of moping, he'd had enough, and pushed me away. Brushed me off, to be precise. This sort of tearful outburst never occurred again. In this respect I am like him: disciplined.

# 62.

The palace staff were shocked—and as my great-grandfather and family noted mischievously—they looked upon this newest aristocratic whimsy with disapproval, namely, that in these danger-fraught times the "palace" should be planning an excursion. And to make matters worse, they're leaving the old Excellency behind to fend for himself. Old man Tóth, who'd been in the service of the family for two hundred years by then, grumbled the most of anybody. (Immediately at the outset of said service, for some reason which documents do not reveal, but a letter written by Szidónia Pálffy to her sister-in-law, Mária Eck, in 1717 makes clear, they were given the extraordinary privilege of calling their Christened son after the son of the count. They called all their firstborn

Menyhért. As my ancestress Szidónia wrote, a year and a half after his birth, the first Tóth who went by this name "died from a horrible disease." No one could say what the horrible disease was.)

Going to the dogs, this was Menyhért Tóth's favorite expression. The country's going to the dogs, the crops, the young tomato plants.

"Letting His Excellency go to the dogs. I never heard of such a thing," he grumbled. The old servant had picked up the scent of the game, but not being able to make heads or tails out of it, disapproved. As far as he was concerned, a dramatic turn of events was a dramatic turn of events, and a tragedy was a tragedy, and anyone who thinks this way will always have the answer, or if not, he doesn't miss it, because the current of his life flows in a secure riverbed. There is a reason for everything; life has an order to it, even if it is difficult. This order, the Tóths', my great-grandfather and his family also insisted upon. It would have been foolish not to. But they knew that it did not come from God, but from themselves, or—what amounts to the same thing—their fathers and grandfathers.

While carefully readying the Esterházy buggy, Menyus Tóth continued to grumble, he couldn't figure out why the old Excellency was smiling so merrily, and why he was putting up with such indulgence.

The baggage and my father's set of underwear did not take up much room in the buggy, that goes without saying. (At least, it wasn't a briefcase!) Tóth and the others were busy packing, while the Count and his family, like an amateur acting company, were pretending that they were about to go on a pleasant day trip. They waved, they shouted, they brandished their handkerchiefs, they said enthusiastic good-byes, and so did Count Cziráky. Great-grandfather's furrow neighbor, who was there at the time. (Furrow neighbor, oh, God!)

# 63.

He died of a horrible disease: (Uncle) Menyus, my father's younger brother, he died of a horrible disease at the age of thirty-two, of polio during the epidemic of 1954. The antiserum, the Salk, was thrown on the market three weeks after his death. It was only a matter of three weeks! He resembled my father, but this didn't cast as large a shadow over his life as over his older brother's. I know him only from his pictures, where he is always laughing. I've met people who, when they found out who I am, said, "I loved your uncle," then took a good look—at me. ("I didn't visit him in the hospital. I was scared. I had a child by then. I was afraid, even though he was expecting me. I was too young. I was scared." "Don't cry.") I saw his letter. I recognized the words. They sounded like family.

His breathing muscles became paralyzed, and he had to be taken up to Pest in an iron lung. My father called an ambulance, but the medics didn't think the case was serious. My father cursed, which he almost never did.

Iron lung, we heard these words repeatedly at the time. It scared us. We tried to imagine it, but there's no imagining it—the fine, fragile, intricate inside of the lung, and a cast-iron stove, together.

Our parents said that Grandmother wouldn't leave her room for days, she just prayed and cried. (In which case, my birth wasn't the last time she cried, but for the first time, and for Uncle Menyus, the last. But no, forget it, you can't put a tag on crying.) When they were alone, they said that Grandmother had lost her mind, specifically, our mother said it, our father just shook his head.

"How can you talk like that, madame?" At times they used the formal form of address with each other, at others the informal. (Either one could be a sign either of tenderness or of chastisement.)

"I wasn't insulting Mama, I was just talking about her."

"Well, not like that. If that's the only way, don't say anything."

"Come, now, Mati, dear . . . She is talking with the angels, it's right here in her letter. She's not even talking, she's negotiating in order to receive news of Menyus . . . Mama has become a veritable Swedenborg . . . She's sitting in the cemetery, combing her hair . . ."

"Kindly desist, madame, I need to go to the toilet. I hate you so much right now for what you said!" Later he added by way of placating her, "It's the Degenfeld line," (i.e., the possibly exaggerated attention to the dead, et cetera).

Grandmother conversed with the angels for a long time. After a while, the local adobe Gypsies joined in as mediators, promising her a direct line to the angels and—after their remuneration was raised—to the tragically deceased young count himself. As far as we know, the remunerations were made in the form of the family jewels. As far as we know, that's how our stock was depleted.

# 64.

We could play swing with Father, because he was strong, but not with Grandfather. Grandfather's hand wasn't up to it. His hand was like Aunt Mia's—delicate, bony, silky, and smooth, made for kissing, not swinging. Still, we could play swing with him now and then. We would sit with him on the ledge of the stone fence.

"Swing-a-ling," I said, Hungary's former prime minister nodded gravely, and we began to dangle our legs. ("After he lost everything he had, your grandfather became a reasonably nice human being." An aunt on the maternal side of the family.)

"Swing-a-ling," he repeated, adding something about French history as such. Grandfather gave much reflection to things *as such*. He discussed things either with his friend who was living nearby "in captivity"—they exchanged letters in which they re-animated parts of the past in the minutest detail (did they have pangs of conscience? I don't think so, alas)—or with me.

"French history is like a theater performance where the viewers outnumber the participants. That is why it seems less than serious—from a distance. Hungarians are under the impression that the stage is empty, and so talk about bygone, illustrious performances out in the lobby. This is why Hungarians appear to be the most conceited people in the world—from up close. From a distance, they don't look like anything."


## 65.


There was the ancient family, hamming it up, watching for the effect. A memorable failure. That's the nice thing about the theater, everything comes to light. The servants stood around the yard without stirring, watching their masters' efforts with icy stares. No one is a hero in the eyes of his servants. According to Grandfather, this was the only revolutionary moment—as such—in all of 1919, and this, too, came about only because of their own blundering.

A Menyus Tóth, a Menyus Tóth fate.

"Giddyap," the driver, my grandfather, shouted. Before he turned onto the alley lined with ancient linden trees he unexpectedly turned the horses around and made an elegant circle in front of the palace. The actors smiled broadly, my little baby father was bawling, the people were standing around disdainfully.

Since there was a danger that my grandfather's tall, lean and elegant figure would be recognized despite his driver's clothes—a gentleman remains a gentleman even in hell, this is how they knew that they were in hell now—thirty or forty kilometers from Csákvár he took leave of his own, lest he endanger the safety of the "holy family," and took off in the opposite direction. There remained my grandmother, the infant, and—and his Kindsfau. Though the family subsequently spoke of this going into hiding as the moment of extreme peril, it could still accommodate a Kindsfrau. They didn't know much about peril, they were as yet unfamiliar with the twentieth century. They talked about all sorts of things, themselves, the country, the past, but they were unfamiliar with the profound silence of the twentieth century. Like all those who believe that their fate is in their own hands, they too were inclined to talk of their fate as if they were talking about a kitten: yes, yes, we know, sometimes it scratches, the cute little kitten . . . kitty, kitty, kitty . . .

Fate in hand—my father didn't know this feeling. He knew only the silence.

Having been accustomed to the comfort of genteel households, the Kindsfrau found more and more objectionables in the adverse circumstances of their outing. A couple of days later, she left my father high and dry. The first woman to leave him (her name is lost to history).

"Your Excellency, I have spent more than three springs in the service of the family, and I must insist on a certain standard,"— at which point she made a finicky gesture all round: the light pouring down on the picturesque clearing on a slant, like in some religious painting, in the distance, ancient oak trees, lush, overhanging vegetation shimmering in a thousand hues of green, you can't imagine anything more beautiful, though not a grand salon to be sure—"oh, and not first and foremost in the interest of my own safety, or comfort, no, but driven by the esteem and appreciation I share with the entire nation, and which binds me, both in my person and in my status, to this illustrious family."

Grandmother listened agape to this woman so jealously protective of the family's good name.

"Just think, Your Excellency, where the world is heading if anything can happen, even to an Esterházy servant!"

The governess was right. She understood the absurdity of the situation better than Grandmother, who, of course, was not in the least interested in the situation; a person watching the performance from their own box is not interested in the alleged abuses and corrupt practices with respect to the tickets. The governess was worried that they had taken the theater away from above her head. Grandmother didn't care. She looked up, saw the starry sky, and saw that it was good.

"I shouted some light words of abuse at her all the same," Grandmother said, but what it was she didn't specify. Great-grandfather was inordinately proud of her: proud that the Good Lord blessed the little lady with so much fortitude and equanimity, that when, with the approach of the terror troops she finally returned to the palace and alighted from the cart and turned into Countess Margit once again, everyone could see that she really had come back from some tranquil pleasure trip, and was not some nameless dame sneaking out of her hiding place like an animal of prey.

Grandmother had stayed in the wild alone; she nursed her son and tended to him, and she washed his diapers. They found refuge in our hunting lodges and looked for shelter at the parsonages. In the Vértes, they were on home ground.

As for my great-grandfather, he came to the comforting conclusion that in this particular case, to speak of the degeneration of the aristocracy was not yet timely.

# CHAPTER TWO

## 66.

Father Vili, some Vilmos or other, I think it was. Anyway, on one of our family outings we visited the parish priest of Gesztes who, at the time my father was in hiding, was a young chaplain there. He called our father Count, which we thought was great. We thought they were doing it for fun. They could've never fooled Mrs. Váradi, though. She'd have seen at a glance that the reactionary clergy, arm in arm with the reactionary oligarchy, were in cahoots, spreading their contagion. He called our mother Countess, but it was off key, out of place, Mami's countenance, too, showed her annoyance and discomfort. It felt exaggerated, untimely. Not so with Papi.

We dropped in without prior notice, but it was taken for granted all around that we'd be staying for lunch. The Reverend Father immediately told his housekeeper that she should—and with a laugh he gestured as if cutting his own throat—get working on two frying pullets.

"Cucumber salad, parsley potatoes!" he said, winking at us. Also, he brought wine and poured. "A drop for the young master, too," he said, and winked again. Our mother protested weakly, but she wasn't thinking of me as much as of my father.

"Wait till lunch," she attempted.

But she knew that if men want to drink, they drink. We drank. Then the parson went to change, because he was in his civvies. I was even reluctant to greet him with a "Praised be the Lord." The second we were alone, our parents began to whisper, as if they were in school. Especially Mami.

"What are we going to do till noon?"

Our father was in high spirits.

"Don't fret, ye fainthearted ones. Your Heavenly Father . . ." and he thrust a finger in the direction of the parson's room. My mother waved him off, then glanced at her watch. "What about visiting the castle before lunch?"

"Oy vey! Oy vey!" we wailed, raising our eyes to heaven, "don't tell us, the gothic barns!" These excursions were always planned with our educational edification in mind. Our mother guided us through the history of Hungarian art with a hard hand, the estates in Ócsa, Lébény, Ják, Zsámbék, Esztergom, the minaret in Eger. This country, we admitted with a heavy heart, has something beautiful everywhere you turn. And which, alas, we must pay close attention to. The "gothic barn" sigh summarized this unwelcome harshness of life.

"Excellent idea!" our father said, grinning at us—a rash gesture, but there you are. Swimming along with the tide, of course, just like us, the difference being that he didn't have a grownup appended to him. Mami waved him off again. Our little sister, the little traitor, climbed into her lap.

If, I thought, a pullet is the same thing as a hen, we're in deep shit, because it's Friday, and you can't have meat on Friday. In those days chicken was more expensive and desirable than plain meat; we rarely had it, and I liked it a lot. Still I couldn't help but speak up. When he was young, my father wasn't allowed to speak until spoken to, he wasn't allowed to talk about himself, he was not allowed to ask a question of a grownup, especially not relating to food (he was not allowed to praise food, either, it would have meant the right to an opinion—and thus the possibility of criticism). The parson smiled when he heard my question.

"Very true, very astute,"—meanwhile, he was buttoning up his frock—"an excellent observation, the young master is explicating an important problem!"

I didn't like this man. I even resented—"home ground"!—that he didn't call *me* Count. Why not? Either, or. After all, we are on our way to our former castle, are we not?! I will see to it. I will have a talk with his bishop. He needs to be taught his manners.

He was now sanctimoniously playing for time, like a magician preparing his knockout clincher. (Uncle Sanctity, this is how we called one of our sanctimonious high school teachers; he was a nice man, he taught art history, and he was always so taken by all that *lot* of beauty that was his to stuff into our heads, he could hardly breathe, he panted.)

"Our young friend,"—that'll be the day!—"thanks to your painstaking upbringing,"—a nod toward my mother, who evidenced a grating smile (just like the kid gloves, my mother's annoyance could at times take on industrial proportions; her expression took the most varied forms, the finest nuances of body language, including the rich play of the eyes—that dull sparkle!, you cringe just looking into them, those clammy endorsements, which nip every initiative in the bud at the moment of their conception, and the silences, the muteness, the speechlessness . . . ); he very astutely called our attention to something that—naturally—we never forgot ourselves.

And with that he pulled the rabbit out of the hat (it being Friday, carp would have been more suitable), the gist of which was that it is his anointed right and choice to give absolution from fasting, provided it is called for, which obligation is not binding on the young gentlemen to begin with, but should it bring on an attack of conscience, then: see above.

I didn't believe him. He just wanted to stuff himself with meat, and we were his alibi.

"It's Friday. I don't eat meat on Friday," I said contemptuously, and I thought that I would surely end up in heaven, not like these people here! Someone should go check if he's really a priest in the first place. (*Agent provocateur*. Mother had such a sonorous way of saying it . . . ) I glanced at Father. Nothing. The parson came over to me and stroked my head.

"Don't be so severe."

My father poured himself more wine. Ezerjó from Mór, while Mother began urging us to start off for the castle.

Our mother was always counting us, like so many ducklings, to see if we're all there. One, two, three, four, and as number five, she pointed a finger at our father, but she never said out loud, five. One, two, three, four, stop.

Oh, my beloved . . . stop!

## 67.

There were three castles by the name of Gesztes in the country: one in Gömör, one in Trencsén County, and this one here, in Komárom County. But even Kesthely is distantly related to Gesztes: at one time, it was Gesztel. The word "*geszt*" refers to the hard, inner core of a tree, its heartwood. Possibly, the first builder had a castle designed to be as sturdy and solid as the heartwood of a beech.

A cliché, but our father knew everything, or so it seemed to us. For instance, he knew all the kings of Hungary—which is pretty much everything to begin with. But he didn't just know facts; he could place everything in time; for instance, that when Charles V was *there*, who was *here*, and that he was the nephew of Catherine of Aragon, against whom her husband King Henry VIII started divorce proceedings just then ("Why just then?" "Not just then, *then.*"), when our King Lajos drowned in the River Csele at Bokány. And as soon as Ferdinand I died, Shakespeare was born. Not a bad deal. He didn't talk like a teacher, he didn't want us to remember anything (our mother was as happy as a lark if we said, if we threw it in her face: Ghirlandaio or Pollaiuolo); our father wanted nothing, he just told the stories and talked, more for his own sake than ours, though if we hadn't been there, he wouldn't have talked. Which made what he was talking about real. In school only mathematics was real, the other subjects I considered at times interesting, at times banal examples of animal training. He said things the way we say it is raining—provided it is raining. But having said that, we're not thinking of the umbrella, that it would come in handy now, nor the crops, about how badly they need the rain.

68.

Father didn't always talk like this—often he didn't talk at all—but Grandmother did. She always saw three or four hundred years at once, in the morning, and on Wednesday, too—for the moment disregarding eternity, which is even more than four hundred years. Everything—events, people, and especially losses and defeats—she saw in this light.

There was a radio interview with her once, a sociological survey, past and present, counts and servants in the light of the present—rather surprisingly, though in keeping with the nature of the Kádár regime. It's just that this nature took its time revealing itself, and also, in keeping with this nature, and being reluctant to see it for what it was, the nation too took its time. People diverted their gaze, they'd seen more than enough already, and now they said, what we've got is what we've got, *que sera sera,* just let's not talk about it, let's not be on familiar terms with it, let's not know its nature. Not to mention the fact that there really was no knowing what's what, what's what at any one time, because the yeses shifting into nos acting as yeses are neither nos (yeses), nor yeses (nos), and they're not even maybes (maybes), but in the end something happens just the same, or happened, yes, no, maybe.

Toward the end of the show they asked the participants what they would wish for, what their three wishes might be. Health, a larger pension, the majority said sensibly, and peace. My grandmother said something a little bit different.

The first: I wish my entire family good health. The second: I wish my only surviving son good health, good progress in his work, and joy in his children. The third, greatest wish: Hungary's good progress and the accomplishment of its historical mission.

No one except for Grandmother would have thought to wish the country anything good back then, it seems to me. The nation belongs to the Communists, the people of the nation thought, who'd be stupid or cynical enough to bother to think about what belongs to the Communists, they should rot in hell, besides, we'll steal back whatever we can.

My grandmother could see further, that's how her eyes were adjusted.

For instance, the Soviet army was in the country "temporarily," and she took this seriously, she felt that it had meaning, she saw the relationship between permanence and temporarity in her own way, Hungary was here three hundred years ago and it will be here three hundred years hence, the country is not like a bake shop; you can gobble up all the cream puffs in one afternoon, but it's not that easy to take possession of a country, to expropriate it, while overzealous initiatives such as this Communism here, whose basic tenet, by the way, is to be commended, it's *upright*, these, by their very nature, do not last long. Of course, by *long* she meant something different, she didn't measure it by her own lifetime, she didn't consider it of particular significance. (Which is dangerous, if you ask me, because it goes to follow that she didn't consider my life of particular significance either, of which we were given ample proof when we were made the subjects of her legendary, harsh punishments.) To her thirty years were thirty years and not an infinitude (my father called the infamous Thirty Years War the longest war in history), the Turks did not keep the country under the yoke for an eternity, but for 150 years, which is a lot, and which is not good, which is whatever you want to call it, but that's the fate of all nations, from time to time they're put in bondage for 150 years, at other times they put others in bondage for 150 years, being a nation is nothing to write home about, a nation's destiny is hard because subjection is hard and victory is hard, humiliation is hard, and so is *gloire*. Countries deserve our pity, especially the one we call ours. Be that as it may, it is not possible to think of people, our son and grandchildren, without thinking of the country as well, which is ours even when it does not belong to us and things are not as they should be just now and are going from bad to worse, and not because it is more and more difficult to live, it's not, it's easier, they've just started portioning, but because the state of the nation, its spirit, brings the worst out of people, it's this worst that constitutes the state of things, our own growing evil which is impersonal all the same, our national evil, and this is why one must wish the country good progress, in short, in our own interest, and not from the half-sincere (half-insincere) bowing of the head to lofty ideologies.


## 69.


Oroszlány, NPO, this is what we had to write on the letters we sent Grandmother. Nearest post office, this sounded as intriguing as if Grandmother were living at the end of the world or beyond.

We had to write her regularly, postcards, not letters, open post-office postcards, and she sent the same to us. The notes we received and sent were incredibly dull. She wrote about the weather and the corn, and we—well, we basically wrote about the same thing.

She lived in Majk, so she was our Majk Granny, as opposed to our Pest Granny, who lived on Monitor Street.

The palace at Majk was originally built for a monastic order, the Camalduls. My younger brother and I had a Camaldul game we played whenever we were on the point of fighting or arguing. Grandmother told us that they "quit" the Benedictines and weren't allowed to talk to each other. Playing Camaldul meant that the one to start the game would stand at attention, then take a big, emphatic step forward, as if quitting the Benedictines, and then you couldn't talk to him. My brother was better at keeping silent than I was, though he went about it in a pretty underhanded manner. In the middle of an argument he'd suddenly quit the Benedictines, and there I stood, left to the dogs with my clever argument. When this happened, I behaved not unlike Joseph II, whose actions I'd rather not comment on just now. Suffice it to say that he was the monarch who suppressed the Camalduls.

They were also called the White Friars because they wore white robes with an apron in front and back held round the waist with a friar's rope. They usually wore sandals, at times boots; they shaved off the crown of their heads, in the back their hair was cut short and in the round, and they had long beards. They lived in the cells that surrounded the main building. One of my ancestors had built it for them (he didn't know he was also building it for my grandmother). There were four rooms in the house, a bedroom, workshop, pantry, a small chapel, and a very long corridor. Plus a small yard. You couldn't see the neighbors. The friars were released from their vow of silence for three days, summer and winter. What did they have to say to each other then, I wonder?

What did they talk about for three days? If they were ill, they put a pot out in the window, that's how the Brothers who were not yet ordained knew that there was something wrong.

In the summer, or when our mother was in labor, we spent a lot of time with Grandmother. We learned the meaning of work from her. We saw that our father was always working, but we wouldn't have liked to learn from him, because he just sat at his desk and translated, which would have meant that we would have to study a lot. Mommy tried a more direct method, but how, I ask you? Shopping in the grocery store, weeding the garden, this is not serious men's work (our sister's expression!), and we never did it of our own accord. Worst of all, we didn't get paid for it.

At Grandmother's the brunt of the work was sawing and carrying water. We had to bring water from the pump well in two old, white, aristocratic jugs, for fifty fillérs, this was the best deal, but finite. On the other hand, there seemed to be an unlimited supply of wood to be sawed. We were paid according to how thick it was, while the knobbiness came under special consideration, and a certain type of beech wood that's very hard, these things meant an extra charge. The thickness could be ten fillérs, twenty fillérs, fifty fillérs, one forint and two forints. We were allowed to determine the size ourselves, and we never cheated. We checked up on one another, though. To this day, no matter where, no matter when, I can tell at a glance how many fillérs a tree trunk is worth.

In contestable cases, Grandmother had the last word, severe but generous, meaning that she never used a tape measure or anything. On the other hand, she was not impressed by the fact that we didn't cheat.

Although they took everything away from the family after '45, thanks to Grandfather's anti-German sentiments they left him a couple of holds, half of which Grandmother rented out, that's how she came by potatoes, vegetables, and fruit. Kati the cow had a stall in the old ice cellar. She was tended by Grandmother's younger sister, Aunt Emma, though nobody called her that, just Timby. We envied her her name. She looked just like Great-grandfather, the ultraconservative antirevolutionary force whom we could see every day on a photograph. Timby's goodness was apparent even to us children, possibly because she was good through and through; in the morning she went to work in the forestry, in the evening she came home, went to see Kati, ate dinner, looked through the English society papers, then went to bed. There was a quiet, vegetable goodness in her. Unless, of course, we misjudged her. Once she left two windows open and a tornado-like draft swept through the corridor, which was the most important area of the house, kitchen, salon and dining room in one.

"There's an icy wind blowing from your direction!" Grandmother commented, and Timby shot back merrily:

"No matter, let it blow!"

We learned this, too—no matter, let it blow.

Besides the cow there were also dogs (dachshunds and fox terriers), cats, uncounted, and fleas, counted. In the morning, we competed to see who had more bites. We counted one another's without cheating, especially around the waist, at the height of the rubber waistband of our pajama bottoms. At first we were caught off guard. But Grandmother waved it off:

"Just a little itch."

Upon which we said, still off guard:

"But Grandmother! It itches!"

Stalemate. Our little sister outdid us in the flea-catching department, because she persevered and had long nails. ("Squeak," we called her, and also "Pipsqueak.")

"Disgusting," she said when she heard them pop under her nail.

"One of God's creatures," Grandmother thundered.

Even the marshland of Ecsed was one of God's creatures! We hated that even more than the fleas! A flea, at least, is honest; cowardly, jumpy-bumpy, but honest. You knew where you stood. A bite is a bite, an itch is an itch. And a scratch a scratch. Not so the marshland of Ecsed! An evildoer! Inscrutable! A thief! One of Great-grandfather's estates was located nearby, that's why Grandmother was familiar with it. Grandfather told stories as if he were dictating, Grandmother as if she were writing. She didn't like telling stories, so she made notes, or *thumbnail sketches,* on which she meticulously insisted ever after, stubbornly word for word, and except for what was written, she would not speak. If we persisted in our questions, she'd look in her notes, do a quick search, then throw up her arms:

"It's not here."

Just like a real writer.

The marshland was good arable land, but dangerous, because it caught fire easily. Once she visited the still smoldering land with her father, and she could feel the heat through her boots. A ditch had to be dug all around the incandescent area to put a fire out. But only the winter snow could put the fire out completely. Once two oxen died from the smoke. Two oxen dying of smoke poisoning, now that's impressive!

## 70.

"I don't want French!" my four-year-old Grandmother cried ferociously, then flung herself down in the pristine Hungarian snow, and there she remained. The French governess (new) ran to tell on her. Great-grandfather came chiding. Grandmother spoke four languages as if they were her mother tongue, though she could only read and write Latin. Droves of tourists visited Majk, including foreigners, and she obligingly offered information about the palace and its environs in the appropriate world language. In her black clothes, her ubiquitous cotton stockings and raincoat, she looked like any other peasant woman around those parts. Her bent shoulders, which became more and more bent with time, made her look like a witch. At least, that's how I imagined a witch, except wicked. I tried, but I could never imagine Grandmother as wicked.

When her grandfather (a Károlyi, no doubt) became paralyzed, he had to use a wheelchair, and his faithful butler, Anti Bokor, wheeled him around. The children were afraid of him. Not so Grandmother. One evening, quite suddenly, he couldn't talk anymore. What I mean is, he talked, but you couldn't understand what he was saying. Nothing. Not even a guess. Great-grandmother Degenfeld (if that's who she was to us) asked him what he'd said and got a raging frenzy in return. The family stood there in shock, and could say nothing. Lots of guests, a big, awkward scene. And then the old man turned to his little granddaughter, and asked her something in this new, unfamiliar language. Clearly something important. Expecting an answer. Grandmother looked around. The grownups bowed their heads, each and every one. What was she to do now? She had a gibberish language that no one knew, she used it to speak to the plants and the animals, and to God. She couldn't give that away. But just then she saw a tear roll down her father's severe countenance, and she began to talk, *pettitoes feetikin gang.* She gave Grandfather her secret. He nodded happily.

But then, a little later, of course, he died. (His dog Pateau followed him soon after.) Grandmother's tears would not stop flowing. Great-grandmother Melinda suggested that they call a doctor, but Great-grandfather said no. He went to his daughter's room, took her head in his hands, and whispered, not so much softly as timidly:

"*Pettitoes feetikin gang!*" The tears stopped flowing.

"Your grandmother (was) ferociously Hungarian," I heard people say, neither criticism nor praise, just a simple statement of fact. Ferociously Hungarian as a *terminus technicus*. Blood does not turn to water. Secretly we were hoping that we were also ferociously Hungarian.

The Károlyis made a career for themselves much quicker than the Esterházys. By 1387 Merhard Károlyi is granted *jus gladii;* by King Sigismund's time they're barons, and they weren't given their ancient castle, they built it themselves, which they pointed out at every opportunity, and regarded us and others like us, who danced attendance on the Court, as no better than civil servants. Great lords in a small fish pond. From the Diet they proceeded not to Vienna, but as quick as they could, to Szatmár.

By the eighteenth century this changes, they make their appearance at Court, their golden fleece is growing, too. They get in line but stick out, too—they're holding on to their antiquity, great lords, ancient, independent. Great-grandfather accepts a national appointment (he's prime minister several times), but only as long as it does not clash with his innermost, jealously guarded principles. If it does, he gets out, he doesn't care a rat's arse about so-called political interests. He's not a civil servant politician who attains to privileges through his position. He feels that privileges are his birthright, he can afford not to take advantage of all of them. Besides, he's wealthy enough to pay for his comfort out of his own purse. His lifestyle is not dependent on his various political appointments.

Strictly speaking, he was a "rural gentleman," a squire. His unbounded puritanism had in it not only the dignity of the ancient

Magyar nobility, but also something bourgeois, haute bourgeois, like the frugal and wealthy burghers of the Hanseatic towns. He was made of the same hardwood—don't ask me how many fillérs' worth—as his ancestor, Krisztina Barkóczy who, when they were granted the title of counts, wrote her husband, Sándor Károlyi, asking what such things were good for? Why add a new coat of arms to their ancient nobility? We've had a nice coat of arms all along, now we'd just have to have new seals made, and engravers cost money.

Laci, the son-in-law of my grandmother's younger sister, annoyed his mother-in-law by repeatedly saying that there were so many Károlyi intermarriages because no one else was good enough for them. When they were among themselves, the Károlyis would confidentially ascertain that as a matter of fact there was no one better than them in all of Hungary.

For their part, ever since the time of Palatine Miklós, the Esterházys made Europe their playground, that's where they played ready or not, here I come! Seen in this context, their having been descended from the Salamon clan was not as important—it was taken for granted—as Kaplony was to the Károlyis. The Esterházys didn't bother their head about who and what sort they are.

Who and what sort.

72.

The tombstones of Damjanich and Lahner, who were among the thirteen generals executed in Arad in 1849 after the debacle of the Hungarian freedom fights, are in the park at Mácsa. This transpired because György Károlyi, Grandmother's great-grandfather, bought—he felt like buying, so he bought—the property of a certain Diodor Csernovics, who said that he was Damjanich's brother-in-law. After the execution, Csernovics sent one of his trusted men to Arad to the place where the execution took place to retrieve the remains of his brother-in-law. However, because two of the dead men had the same beard, the trusted man brought both of them back with him. An acquaintance of Grandmother at Mácsa tended the grave. She even sent a photograph. We still have it. When Grandmother went out into the countryside with her family, they could see the mountains of Arad, including the castle of Világos, which reminded them of King Mátyás, who had his uncle, Mihály Szilágyi, imprisoned there.

Grandmother was ten years old when she had to recite a poem at one of the functions of the Tulip Movement, the brainchild of Mihály Károlyi's mother-in-law, Ella Zichy (and a *bel esprit* if ever there was one). People who wanted to keep up with the latest fashion wore tulip pins on their dresses or a tulip button on the lapel of their coats—a pledge that they would buy only Hungarian products. The jewelers of Váci utca made tulips adorned with rubies and emeralds and the hatmakers fitted out their ladies' hats with tulips. Of course, this did not prevent the society ladies from buying their gowns in Paris or Vienna, or ordering their children's sailor suits from London. Anyway, Grandmother's younger sister, Laci's mother-in-law, was so afraid that her older sister might forget her lines, that in her fright she hid under a table. They could hardly get her out. But the recital went like a dream:

> *The Magyars have a flower, proud and patriotic.*
> *Its petal red, its leaves pure green.*
> *Let us hail her, it's our Tulip, our very own*
> *sweet Queen.*

Which is as much as she can remember.

The only Hungarian poem I know by heart without slipping up is the one I had to memorize when I was staying with Grandmother. She wrote it down on a small sheet of graph paper torn from a block of notes. There was no special reason, unless that ancient Károlyi reason. Here it is:

*We've seen enough of Turk and Tatar*
*had our share of grief and woe,*
*they did abound!*
*We groaned under the heavy yoke*
*and woe, we bled, we suffered,*
*yet survived!*
*But since the German hordes*
*are on us, our strength's depleted,*
*that's the truth.*
*We pray you Lord, do take from us*
*this hateful kit and cadoodle*
*multitude!*

I know it word for word, without tripping up, even once.


## 73.


Grandmother, we saw, went to mass every morning throughout the summer, the seven a.m. mass. We often went along as altar boys. The front pew was reserved for the family. This was the patron's pew. There are churches where the sign is still up, then whoever wants to—and can—goes and sits there. After mass, the chaplain hurried off (on his motorcycle) to Gánt. He had five churches in his charge, so he was always in a hurry and had to change clothes on the run. But after mass he always exchanged a few words with Grandmother. ("That was my oasis.")

We also saw Grandmother talking to priests—at her place, on the street, by the lake, at the post office at Oroszlány (that certain

NPO). It was as if Grandmother had placed the Church back into the world, and into society, the country—among the people. The priests were kept as well hidden as the Russian soldiers. You couldn't see them. Barracks, churches: that's where they belong. Plus people's hearts, I might add.

Grandmother had no aspirations of national proportions for the Church, she just acted normally, she had norms, and like that. We, on the other hand, were just having fun, practicing the sin of perk and presumptuousness, when we greeted the priests we knew as loud as we could. On the Number 34 bus, for instance, my younger brother and I spotted our chaplain, he in the back, we up front, with an appreciable distance between us.

"Praised be!" my brother shouted toward the back, while I hurled out at him in a scream, as if we were fighting:

"Our Lord Jesus Christ!"

We had just broken with the post-'56 social compromise, that's what this loud, public display conveyed. We were just saying hello, we must say hello to people we know, we said to ourselves in our own defense. The grownups pretended not to hear. Many of them became extraordinarily involved in the landscape. As for the chaplain, he turned crimson. By the way, this is one reason why they were being hidden, because they were hiding themselves as well. Just like everybody else.

"Shut up, son, if you know what's good for you!" a woman next to us said, boiling over with animosity. She didn't look at us either, but that wasn't from fear.

Grandmother carried on regular correspondence with the parish priests of the former family estates, Környe, Kecskéd, Várgesztes, Csákvár, et cetera. It would have been easy as pie to fabricate a charge against her: clerical reactionism in cahoots with their former lords and masters, planning to overthrow the government. The letters were about serious topics—subjects for upcoming sermons, or an exchange of views on abstract theological questions (honoring, in the meantime, Pope Urban VIII's edict enjoining the legates to discuss only one subject per letter). Many years previously she had made the acquaintance of Cardinal Pacelli (Grandfather was president of the Committee of Finance of the Principal Plenary Committee of the Eucharistic Congress), and they corresponded regularly later, too, when he was the Pope.

My grandmother corresponded with the Pope—in Latin.

She never showed her emotions, she always held herself in check, with two exceptions: if anyone spoke about her dead son Menyus, or Jenő Pacelli. From time to time she'd take out the big, red memorial album of the 38th Congress, and we'd have to look through it. She stood over us, a black exclamation mark, making sure . . . —I couldn't tell you what she was making sure of, possibly herself, or was this her way of finding an opportunity to look without arousing suspicion at the thing she wanted to see, whatever that may have been? But no, that's highly unlikely. Sentimentality and nostalgia were not in her nature.

She never endeared herself to us, she never called us by our pet names. Her goodness was aloof. She treated every physical relationship, or touch, with ceremony, the way she'd embrace us with all her might when we met, and cracked our bones, or later, at parting, the way she'd draw a cross on our foreheads, God be with you!, this is what she invariably said. The touch of her thumb felt nice and warm.

To tell the truth, I wasn't particularly impressed with the chief potentate with the metal-rimmed glasses and severe eyes. He seemed unhappy to me, and I didn't trust unhappy people, not even back then. Of course, being unhappy is no one's fault, but showing it, the fact that he's letting it show, is. *Kindly hide it!* I told Grandmother as much. Her severity did not frighten us. It made us equals. No, not equals, just free.

# 74.

We were free to talk anything but nonsense, we were free to work, to help; we were free to play, provided it was playtime; we were free to spend every moment of the day in a constructive way, and we were not free to lie. Lying constituted the greatest of all sins, any degree or form of lying, and it was no use putting on a weasel face, trying to turn things inside and out, something we were really good at—if we had it coming, we had it coming. At our Majk Granny, the moment of truth struck again and again, cuckoo!, cuckoo!, day and night.

The punishments were severe. And just, need we add. But this "just didn't" interest us, even though it is generally of great interest to a child, because the severity was so great, of such proportions, that time and time again, the sheer surprise of it took our breath away. There we stood, gaping. Which meant that we never discovered the iron consistency behind the punishment, whereas it would have done us great service.

For instance, who would have thought, or gauged, that the assertion that something or someone is God's creature could have such far-flung consequences—that this something or someone mustn't be flung over the fence, for instance? It was part of the nature of said fence that it was built of stone (the patron and founder allowed the stones from the Roman ruins on the outskirts of Környe "and also the carved stones from the buildings standing in the form of a corridor at some distance from our castle at Gesztes" to be "freely carried off" for the construction of the recluse); in short, it was impenetrable to the eye, the original intent being to isolate the monks from the world and from one another, while now—if not the intent, yet the effect of said impenetrability was that, depending on the trajectory, after a time the creature of God propelled over the fence could no longer be seen, except by the mind's eye, and we couldn't even check to see if the folk belief whereby this particular creature of God always fell on its feet was true or not. On the other hand, we could make excited bets about how long said creature, not being blessed with wings, would stay in the air, because even with our eyes closed we could ascertain and enjoy the—one might say—sacred moment when it touched the ground. In this we were not unlike the mine-throwing gunners, counting, as if in a trance, one, two, three, squeak, or in this particular instance, crack.

Our sister had it over us because I, for one, was restrained by the cats' concreteness, the fact that the cats had names, this was the worst;—yes, when all is said and done, the fact that they're God's creatures, whereas this left her cold; she cared only for the flinging as such, the graceful curve of the trajectory, and the blissful seconds of counting.

Gradually, the airspace above the yard was filled with flying cats, like so many singing birds. Being found out was just a matter of time. And time caught up with us. Grandmother asked no questions, she just ordered us into her room. She didn't ask what had happened, she knew, or who it was, it was us, all three of us; the ratio of participation, the "who" and "how high" did not interest her, nor did pangs of conscience count as a mitigating circumstance. In short, she was not interested in the details. She was holding a dog whip.

"What's that?" our sister asked, because she always had to ask everything.

"A dog whip," Grandmother said by way of information, which we noted with relief; after all we were not dogs, even if in his lighter moments our father would call us that. Nor could we discover on Grandmother's face the elemental fury that she proceeded to unleash upon us. We couldn't see her face by then, which is probably a good thing. We cringed under the whip. Each of us received two lashes. By the time we realized what was happening, the storm had blown over.

We felt a pleasant tingle run down our backs, an agreeable and curious twinge. We burst out laughing. Not so Grandmother. On the other hand, our laughter did not anger her. She was not angry with us. She was simply performing her duty to hate our faults, and not us—a prompting that came from within, and it came with ease. Though who knows . . . But she knew that the tingle would soon be replaced by a painful, burning throb, a shooting pain, and we'd have finger-thick welts on our backs, as if we were cut in half along the whip line, and were sure to fall apart into the bargain. We hardly dared move. This was the strangest of all, this new way of moving, as if we were sneaking away—away from Grandmother, the law, or ourselves? It was not a good feeling.

Only one other time did a cat fly at Majk. And what a flight it was! One got to understand Icarus. Father came to visit us, a big day!, and we had lunch together, according to form, the way it's done at peasant houses, with Grandmother at the stove, and us, men, seated at the table in a gentlemanly manner, on either side of the washing machine that served as a table. All at once a cat, one of an army of cats, licked the food on Father's plate. I was well trained in cat matters by then, and kept quiet. Father kept quiet, too, except his eyes flashed. He grabbed the cat, and with one wide sweep of the arm flung it out, up, up and away through the long corridor and into the yard. By the tail. But first swinging it jauntily over his head. God's creature goes flying straight along the corridor, heading outside, from the dimness into the light, screeching like the devil, its legs flailed out in four directions. It was a heartwarming sight, and I glanced at my father, my great, big, strong, darling daddy, and I was so proud.

At which a small, dark wind began to stir by the side of the stove.

"Mátyás!" came the icy sound. "For your information, Mátyás, a cat is one of God's creatures, too!"

She gave her son such a dressing-down, he was suddenly no bigger than myself. It wasn't bad, the two children together like that, by the side of the washing machine. He didn't get a whipping, but he had to apologize to the cat. I wonder which is better (or worse).

There was something heroic in the whip—though only in hindsight. (Not so the dog, ha, ha!) Not so the room detention! We didn't even know what detention was, though we were to find out soon enough. And yet, it all began so innocently. Grandmother—we might as well be aboveboard about this—was a lousy cook. But it didn't matter. When we were hungry, and we were always hungry, we ate everything, except that sorrel thing, because even Kati the cow wouldn't have touched it, it tasted so bitter. Or if she had, she would have regurgitated it. Just like us. But since we couldn't very well go into this sort of detail, we begged off due to a shared, all-round tummy ache, a sort of tummy ache epidemic.

She gave us a piercing look.

"So you have a tummy ache?" she asked simply. The question seemed of such importance to her, we didn't dare answer her (in so many words), we just nodded our heads.

"In that case, get into bed, all of you!"

In bed till the evening? That sounded like fun. And come morning, we'd get up . . . Now it was her turn to nod, what I mean is, shake her head. A bad sign. On the third day, it being Sunday, they'd have a parachute show at the airport in Kecskéd. Kecskéd? We weren't even allowed out into the yard, from where we could have at least seen something of the jumps. At which we broke into bitter tears, we were sorry for what we'd done, et cetera, et cetera.

"Stop it this instant," Grandmother said softly. And we stopped.


## 75.

I was studying the picture of the unhappy cardinal, but I was soon made to move on. Grandmother would point to a line or a caption, and I was expected to read it out loud.

"His regal bearing belies . . . ," or: "What majesty, dignity, wisdom and genius!"

It was a lot better than having to translate and read Chemise, in gothic letters. His shadow disappeared, or whatever. Another Péter. On the other hand, at least I learned to read gothic letters. I can even write them.

Sneaking a look from the red album, I saw Grandmother smile. For a brief moment, like a passing shadow, I saw a smile on her countenance, and suddenly I understood that unhappiness must be put on display only so that there could be a face like hers.


## 76.

Grandmother was always praying. When she had nothing to do, she fell immediately to praying. Or more likely, the other way around, she stopped praying because of her pressing duties. If indeed she stopped . . . ! We could see her sitting in the armchair in her room or on the chair by the kitchen stove, huddled up, her eyes closed, in black, her rosaries or prayer book in her hands. Which looked like Papi's hands, a wide man's hands, except with more knobs.

"Were you praying, Grandmother?"

"Yes, child, I was praying."

She had the same laughing, ironic squint as Papi, yet irony was foreign to her nature: she never made remarks—the *sine qua non* of irony; instead she went into action, she *did* something. Either something good, or something useful, or something good and useful. She was the least affected of the family by being bundled or chucked out of her old life, while she alone kept one of the basic family traits, the doing ("a family of busy bees"). She did not keep her aristocratic ways, because she never had any. None. One wonders how she and Grandfather ever got on. But then, their lives were not about each other. Though when I think of all the things that had to be done in common . . . Apart from being ferociously Hungarian, this too may have weighed in the balance when in '56 she refused to move to Austria with Grandfather.

"And what were you praying, Grandmother?"

"What? A good question . . . You ask good questions. One of these days you will also have to answer them." I blushed to the roots of my hair. I felt that Grandmother could see right through me, and I had strong views on being seen. "Still, if you must know, I'm praying for you, child, I'm praying for you," and she measured me up and down with her eye.

I like people praying for me, I have always liked it. I thought of it like some fabulously remote Swiss bank account which is and is not, but whether it is or is not, it accumulates. You don't even have to think about it, and it grows. I never once forgot to say the blessing at the end of mass, *benedictat vos omnipotens Deus,* cross, *Pater et Filius et Spiritus Sanctus,* Amen. The accumulation of capital. A classical Pharisaic thought. I understood the sum and substance of classical Pharisaic thought at an early age, the need to play it safe, the fact that the world is not guided by love but by love's commandment, what I mean is, various commands in general, God's commandments, and if we keep them, or a fair portion or percent of them, then, in the spirit of an unwritten contract, we attain to salvation, not like those others who don't give a hoot, or if they do, the percentage is not adequate, or they drink and cavort to excess or are slothful, as a result of which they, as opposed to us, incur eternal damnation.

May God Almighty bless you. Every time the priest said this to *me,* I blushed. I took every word of this sentence seriously, I had to take it seriously, and I felt, too, that now I was thoroughly blessed, and that's one of the reasons I blushed, that it should be so easy. I just had to attend mass, and God Almighty would devote His time just then, that Sunday morning, to me. Without Him or His severe deputies checking to see if I qualified, or if I was deserving of the blessing at all, He did it, He gave me His blessing.

As far as I was concerned, this was so awesome (prodigious!) and incredible, I had to protect myself, my body started protecting itself, concretely, my brain or my intellect (that's a body, too), and suddenly I didn't know anymore what it meant to bless someone; like when we repeat a word over and over again until its meaning is suddenly absorbed, or dissolved in vapor, and turns into a magic spell, that's what happened to me, abracadabra.

I asked Father for the dictionary. To bless: to ask a blessing on someone. Under blessing I found what I was hoping for: divine favor coming from God, grace. I also looked up grace, which at first frightened me, release from retribution. In short, all it means is that they generously desist from putting you to the sword? But then the divine love or favor of God was offered up as a second choice, which put my mind at rest.

In short, I was accumulating God's divine love and grace in that far-distant, imaginary bank account. I imagined that even if I was making a fool of myself, even if my idea was contrary to the essence of divine love, still, every time I attend mass I am blessed, I am given a blessing, what I mean is, I get a bit of divine assistance and am not put to the sword but am forgiven for my sins into the bargain, said forgiveness hopefully also pertaining to this sanctimonious stockpiling of mine—in short, it's more okay than not, I thought.

That's the first time I *turned* the pages of a dictionary. I shot a glance or two in Father's direction, hoping he'd praise me, but he didn't. I wonder why (not).

"Are you quite finished?"

"Yes, Papi, if you please."

"Then hand it back to me."


## 77.


My other major (concretely: disappointing) dictionary (reference book) experience involved the big Brehm, *Love in the Animal Kingdom*. The volume on mammals was missing. I knew almost everything about the love life of the ant, the wasp, the fish and the mollusk, what goes where, which secretions, salivas and pollens get lodged in which cavities, and in what manner, and I would have liked to crown my knowledge, I wanted to be initiated into the great secret up and including the long-tailed monkey, at least. I managed to study up on whales, but after that, nothing. They tried to tell me that they're mammals, too. Oh, sure!

I can't remember having been enlightened about sex at all. Mami tried to initiate us into the mystery of conception, but when she reached the pollination of the pistils, she stopped short, and so did we, because we insisted on being told—and in concrete terms, Mami!—where the pistil was and who had it, but also objecting in our father's name that he might be doing the pollinating, that he might pollinate anyone *inside*. Our father would never do a thing like that, he never has, and he never will. I never told my mother how disgusting I thought this image was (or was I merely repulsed by the word "pistil"?). By way of a compromise we suggested that we stick to the old, traditional explanation, crane, cabbage.

At which Mami turned us out of the kitchen.

Mami didn't have it easy. For some reason, when they were three and four, my younger brother and sister wanted to know if she was still a virgin. Actually, they knew she was. They just wanted it confirmed.

"Mami, are you still a virgin?" they asked tactfully.

I bet they were thinking of the Virgin Mary, partly because they (we) discovered a resemblance on a number of pictures, and because Mami owned a light blue cloak that she had to slip into in such a funny way, as if she were wrapping the flap of a tent around her shoulders, and this made her look just like the Virgin Mary. The other reason was that as everybody knows, the Virgin Mary is the best mother in the whole wide world, and our mother was also the best mother in the whole wide world. One who wouldn't want to disappoint her children. (By the way, she insisted that we get the point of the joke according to which the Virgin Mary has the same last name as ours. —Raphael.)

At this I pulled her aside self-importantly, it's silly, it's too much, sooner or later the truth will out, because, Mami dear, the truth always wills out, and then it'd do more harm than if we had to swallow the bitter pill of looking things straight in . . . The little eager beaver. Mother gave me a weary look, then a flippant shrug, an adolescent girl's shrug. The only thing missing was the chewing gum.

## 78.

I even had a missal. Nice and big. Gold initials. Colored pictures. The works. And also a stand to go with it, a music rack, a reminder that our mother had once learned to play the piano (though she never played afterward, ever). I held mass standing in front of the music rack.

*Dominus vobiscum.*

*Et cum spiritu tuo.*

*My brothers in Christ.*

It's the real thing. I don't know where it's from. An old family inheritance, probably. I had a smaller one, too, more like a prayer book. My Majk Granny gave it to me. According to the inscription I'm the second owner. The first was Uncle Marcel, who received it for Christmas—St. Nicholaus's Day, 1932—the one who disappeared in World War II. (He didn't die, he disappeared. It was considered a serious offense if we got it wrong. Worse, even, than the cat, except we weren't punished for it, that's what made it worse. If we got it wrong, it stayed like that, it stayed bad. Our mother would correct us, too, but her heart wasn't in it, she'd given up. It was interesting to see how much more upset she'd get by some breach of grammar. Whereas it was a man's memory up against a word!)

According to the inscription, I was given the book on St. Stephen's Day in 1959. There stood my full name, just like Uncle Marcel's. Twenty-seven years had passed between the two inscriptions, but Grandmother's penmanship had not faltered, it was just as sweeping and light handed. The only difference was in the two *y*'s. The top one, the younger, you might say, was more sophisticated; not who if not I sophisticated, not even overly self-assured; still, there was nothing to dampen its spirit, you can tell. The black ink, too, adds ceremony to the appearance of the script—the leg of the *y* plunges under in a curve, leaning slightly to the right, it's rightist, then after a quick loop it picks up speed, it sweeps back almost to the base of the *h,* then turns back around; those lovely old pens, they convey the impulse of the letters, the act of writing, the writer!; in the curve the line thickens, becomes darker, and then, galloping like the wind, cutting across itself, soars up to the sky, so that it can start turning into the letter *M*. My own *y* wouldn't have the guts to tie itself to the *P* like that. It finishes itself off down below. There is no wavering, no confusion, just a touch of the superfluous, like when—attention!—we underline something three times.

Walking around and reading this book, this I liked. I could see myself from the outside, and the person I saw appealed to me. I liked him. A boy pure of soul and joyful, intelligent and handsome (his good looks further enhanced by the big black proportions of the book); he is not a priest and yet, unintentionally, as it were, he is a servant of God, a man who leads a holy life. I liked repeating the Latin of the Confiteor, *et vos frates orare pro me ad Dominum Deum nostrum,* and in Hungarian, *Péter*'s betrayal, over and over again, *dico tibi, Petre* (that's still Latin): I say unto you, Péter, before the cock crow, thou shalt deny me thrice. I liked this part, and also what came afterward, that it came to pass, and that the cock crowed *just then.*

*Cantavit Gallus.*

## 79.

Papi was tipsy, but just barely. When he's tipsy, he's the sweetest, the dearest Papi in the whole wide world. His eyes are not yet veiled over. They gleam and sparkle, and when he looks at you, you can see the whole sparkling, brilliant world in his eyes. It's so good to be alive!, that's what you see in them, all this *much*, which is further enhanced . . . —all right, shaded. Mother's shade fell over this sparkle or, with slight exaggeration, elemental gleam—a shot of brandy will make it dandy?—when impatient and anxious, she wanted to herd us toward the castle of Gesztes.

"Just a drop more, Countess!"

Mother decided to ignore the priest's words, but Father nodded, all right. He was not about to resist temptation, he was willing to make the sacrifice and take unto himself this not bad, yet middling muscatel. So it wasn't Ezerjó from Mór after all.

"Pour some for the future, too, Father, for the youth of the nation," he ordered the priest as if he were a waiter.

"Matika, please, don't do this. Leave the child out of it."

Mother was hissing between her teeth. Pleading and demanding in one breath. Practice makes perfect, my brethren! The others made themselves scarce, but I stayed, because I was curious. Also, I wanted the wine. White on Friday is all right, white with the fish.

"Just a drop, Excellency!"

"Don't call me Excellency," Mother shot back leaping to her feet and making for the door. Father bowed his head. A muscle twitched on his face. But no, it wasn't a twitch, it was more like a throb, a sign of extreme agitation. His lips drew into a thin line, and he ground his teeth. The jawbones, we said to one another when this happened, a warning that from here on in, everybody better watch themselves. But who was to watch themselves this time? Mami? Who was just making her exit?

"You will stay right here," Father said in stifled tones, as if to himself. It was scary! Meanwhile, the parson was pouring the wine, some for me, too.

"Whatever you say, dear," Mother said turning back nimbly, as if she were on stage, or in company, "Father, if you don't mind, I'd like to give that muscat ottonel a closer look myself."

The parson is all bustle, my father is all smiles, and as for yours truly, I'm so confused, I'm about to faint. I drank my wine in one gulp. They laughed. No, no, young man, et cetera. I saw my mother drink wine on only two occasions. This was one of the two. She should have done it more often. My father wouldn't have been left on his own so much.

"Well, into the breach, dear friends!" my father now said, all sweetness and smiles, as if it weren't him who just a minute before told Mother with cold authority and brute force to stay put. I didn't understand how anyone could leap back and forth on the scale of emotions like this.

And now the parson. He was waving us good-bye like a housewife, I swear.


## 80.


"The world's somber seas are boiling o'er . . ." Our father stopped and shot a questioning glance at us.

"Omagyar!" we shot back frightened, afraid of trouble.

"Morons! Not omagyar, but o! Magyar!" Still, he wasn't angry. Our father didn't just know everything, he even knew the poet Berzsenyi, inside and out. We loved Dániel Berzsenyi more than anybody because we saw that he made our father happy, and we thought that he must've been a happy fellow too, a playful, Mozart-like genius. As far as we were concerned, the melancholy version they laid on us in school was a Communist conspiracy, even though by then Papi had pretty much stopped reciting his poems.

The excursion "up the mountain" thrilled Mami too. What can I say. Our mother was in love with mountains. She would have liked nothing better than to live in Slovenia, or Switzerland. Or Norway. The Carpathians. Mountains are the dwelling places of the gods and of beauty. She was on familiar terms with them. She knew them by name, as if they were people. When we played geography and it came to mountains, she had no peer, even though we usually wouldn't accept her overly exotic solutions. Outhouse Mountain, for one. We didn't even argue. We just laughed it off. Sure! Outhouse! What else is new?

"Don't try and outhouse us, Mother dear, those days are past!"

She was hurt. Unexpectedly and deeply. Her sadness seemed to say that we'd just renounced the past, or repudiated the Carpathians and Transylvania—all of former Hungary. (In our family we never said Greater Hungary. It is *still* great, our father kept telling us.) Our mother's assessment of the situation was correct; the Outhouse Mountain chain was as remote to us as the Big Dipper, just a fabulous, distant word that we found on the map later on—an indication that there was *something* behind it after all—still, it was like accepting the Big Dipper for a mountain. It didn't feel right humiliating our upright mother with such an easy handout.

"Know what, Mami? You can have the Bakony. The Bakony is a real mountain. We'll settle for Bakony."

"But children, that doesn't begin with an *o*."

"O!" we said, alarmed. "In that case we cannot accept it, after all. What a shame!" Then we laughed. "Let's not get bogged down, it's just a game. As for you, madame, you lost!"

Our mother (not to mention our father) hailed from Transdanubia, root and all, and when she spoke, she used those beautiful, aspirant *e*'s. A mountain for her was not the same as for the Transylvanians. In Hungary, where by Hungary I mean Hungary, anything that's higher than a ditch is a mountain. The footpath leading to the castle had hardly begun its incline when Mami started panting, oh, the view, it's fabulous! Despite her love of mountains, she wasn't thinking of the mountains, though, but of us, always of us. Our father thought of us only with good reason. This impressed us. We were partial to our father because we wanted to gain his approval. This was not the case with Mami. We paid little attention to her. We saw that every moment of every day, she belonged entirely to us.

Still, the incline, the possibility of a mountain, thrilled her. Yonder!, she said excitedly.

"Yonder! See . . ."

"Yes, we know, Ararat," we shot back.

". . . that delicate silhouette of the mountain chain whose grayish contours hail from a painting, as it were."

Hail and as it were; and that those *yonder* mountains have names too and people climb them. They all have names and they all get climbed. She said this with obvious relish. Our father listened with a smug smile.

"Mountains certainly are not wasted on you." And he giggled.

Our mother combined beauty with art and with nature, and all three with man. Once she was done, she presented beauty to us on a plate as the proof of God's existence. Beauty as ample proof of the Lord. Her belief in God differed from Grandmother's not in its unerring strength or constancy, but in its innocence. Grandmother wouldn't have known what to do with an expression like proof of God. She wouldn't have understood the dilemma, is there, isn't there, as if we were bickering over whether there's such a thing as the Danube or that (certain, concrete) corn on the toes. Grandmother's rationality did not endanger the innocence of her immortal soul. *Deus semper maior.* God is always greater. This was her motto. Mami didn't want to prove anything either, she was just showing (for our benefit) another way of seeing the Danube, especially since we're living by its shores and cross from one side to the other twice a day.

On those relentless get to know your country outings, it wasn't the country she was showing us, but the beauty. She was showing us the beautiful, something our father never concerned himself with. Or else, he didn't say. He spoke about what *is*, about the *here*, about what we have here, in this country, King Mátyás, brown coal, corns, *libera nos, Domine.*

For a while Papi put up with the hails and yonders, but then he flung Berzsenyi into the fray.

"O, budding seed of Árpád, thou Prime Magyar!" he roared. Our mother, questioningly: Me? Our father, embracing her: "Why dost thou tremble on my bosom, oh why, reluctant maiden fair?" Our mother, with another grimace: Me?

Eventually, with many a bend in the road, we reached the castle ruins. At one time it couldn't have been easy to occupy. Now it had been overgrown by weed and socialism. We spotted some dwarfed acacias hardly taller than the bushes, plus the mediocre, menial buildings of the State Tourist Agency. Our father led us to one of the taller peaks, on one side the unsightly hybrid, the vision of decay, dilapidation, degenerate and stunted growth, and in front of us, down below, a wide panorama, the disarming Transdanubian landscape with its curvaceous, leaping lines, its generous, Pannonian riches, as if nature could not be corrupted, appropriated, monopolized, as if it belonged to us still, and not the commies.

This is the totality our father was lightheartedly pointing out.

"But o, all things under the sky doth end this way!," whereupon we turned back toward the ruins and the tourist lodge, whereupon Papi waved an arm, annoyed, "Let's try again," and with a wave, wider now, indicated where we were to look: "But o, all things under the sky doth end this way!" He looked militantly to see if we were looking at this beautiful, seemingly inviolate terrain. "The iron fist of Time doth wreak havoc with it all: noble Illyon is gone, the might of proud Carthago, Rome and Babylon, gone, all gone."

But by the time he reached the point where Rome has had it and Babylon was not to be counted on either anymore, he sounded sad, disappointed.

## 81

Still on flat terrain, back at the bottom of the hill, I'd made up my mind that I was drunk. I was drunk for the first time in my life, and through no fault of my own. The idea was suggested to me by the fleeting spell of giddiness I experienced when I stepped outside the cool parsonage. Or was it the archetypal drive to imitate our father?

I started by staggering and tripping and rolling my eyes, the way it's done in a silent film. My sister gave out a squeamish yell. Mother waved it off. Stop the silly nonsense. Father was marching up front with my youngest brother sitting round his neck, singing.

"But I'm dizzy, and everything is indistinct before my eyes, and oh, my legs do tremble most inordinately!"

Mother touched my forehead.

"You're not feverish," she said with a frown.

"I know," I said in all seriousness. "I'm drunk!"

Her face clouded over. She waited a bit, as if wanting to make absolutely certain she heard right. And then—and then, she did nothing. This nothing—silence, sadness, chagrin, solitude—it was as if she'd slapped me. Never in all my life had I been slapped so hard.

Hurt to the quick, I refused to budge. I just wanted Papi to take me round his neck, and I knew that with regard to being taken up round his neck I was a borderline case, but this was no ordinary situation, this situation came about through no fault of my own . . . They didn't believe me. They looked right through me. On what basis? By what right? They saw when the priest made me drink. A small boy like me. How could they know . . . nobody, there's nobody in the world who could know that I'm not really drunk, that I have to help the tottering along a bit.

Only I know that. Nobody else has any reason to doubt it, nobody on Earth, and that includes the Good Lord. Nobody. And with that, I sprawled facedown into the sheep droppings.

I pressed my head against the warm soil. It was as it is written: The fruit of the naked earth lay parched under the sun's golden rays. Literally. They can't *not* believe what I'm telling them. It's not possible. Even God can't do what is not possible. He may be omniscient. But, for instance, can He divide by zero?

They didn't even turn around. My sister tried once or twice, but Mother tugged at her, and they proceeded on.

"You can't possibly know, there's no way you could possibly know that I'm lying," I sobbed. "You have no right!" Meanwhile, they were receding into the distance.

82.

The second time I saw Mother drink wine was when Grandfather died in Vienna and they wouldn't let Father attend the funeral. They said that it would be against State interests. Fuck them!

The mourning didn't show on him, on my father. He walked a little more off center and breathed differently, that's all. Also, he wore a black mourning band on his jacket and overcoat. Mother was at her sewing. The doorbell rang. A mourning band is a practical thing, a warning, beware, the dog bites. Our dog didn't bite. What we saw was what we always saw: he was sitting in the back room, typing. (Later, when they brought the gas into our house and the grownup room was emptied of furniture, you could see the worn-down parquet floor under the writing desk. Through the years he'd practically scooped out a ditch with his feet. The whole apartment was veritably plowed under. They broke up the parquet floor, they dug ditches for the pipes, and these piles of earth looked so out of place *inside,* they seemed so aggressive,

you'd think there was a war on in our home and these were communication trenches. The soil that was dug up was packed earth,
not *real* soil, it had been brought here from someplace else, that's
why you couldn't build cellars anywhere in the neighborhood.)

I went to get the door, but the mailman wouldn't give me the
registered mail from the Interior Ministry. I ran back in. Mother
was about to get to her feet when Father, jawbone!, growled:

"My son will get it."

Mother had somehow been left out of this thing altogether.
Left out of the organizing, the helping, the mourning. Now she
was being left out even more. We were leaving her out. Father
consulted with his mother, discussed things with his brother; they
telephoned, they exchanged letters; there was no room left for
our mother, no role for her to play in recent events. She couldn't
even help, whereas it was always she who did the helping. It
struck us how grateful our father was for any small sign of our
childish sorrow. When our little sister whimpered dutifully he
embraced her so passionately we didn't know what to make of it.
But only these father relationships were in evidence—the man
who had died was his father, and he was ours. Mami had no place
in the show. (She made serious, futile efforts not to take offense.)

I spoke to the mailman in a new tone of voice. I spoke as never
before, as my father's son. His deputy. As if death had elevated me,
too, to new heights.

"Father is in no condition to come to the door. I will sign for
him," I said and I took the pen from the mailman's hand. "There's
been a death in the family," I added pointedly. The frightened
mailman did as he was told.

"Poor Doctor!" he said, calling back over his shoulder as he
made himself scarce.

When I reentered, Mother, like a valet, was about to take the
letter from me. I wouldn't relinquish it, though, and took it to
Father. There she was, lingering behind again, again with no part

548

to play in the scene. Father took out the paper knife with the ivory handle and with great care, almost with enjoyment, but at all events theatrically, he opened the letter, glanced at it, took in the contents at a glance, threw the letter on the table, on top of the typewriter, lowered his head, and was shaken with sobs.

The paper knife in his hand was shaking, too, like a murderer, a parricide who has just realized the full import of his sin, and relents. That's when the meaning of Grandfather's death hit me. It meant that from then on, there'd be no one to stand between my father and death. That knife in his hand, that's his death, from now on there's no way not to think of it, they're standing side by side.

From the side, sobbing, I threw myself at him, crying, blubbering, my nose running, begging, pleading.

"Papi, please, don't, oh please don't die, sir," I cried clinging to his neck. He held me and cradled me like a baby.

"But it's part of my plans," he whispered. "I will die by-and-by, and you will bury me."

By-and-by, he said, sometimes he said by-and-by, you will have to think about it by-and-by, but not just yet. And I sobbed. After a while Mother peeled me off of him, but she didn't take me out but bundled me into an easy chair, went up to Father, took my place, embraced him, led him to the bed, like an invalid, covered him with the checkered blanket, kissed him, then the two of us tiptoed out of the room.

In the evening we saw them drinking in the kitchen, and later, in my dream, Father thanked me ceremoniously, a bit awkwardly for my heartfelt sobs.

"Thank you, son."

# 83.

I closed my eyes so I wouldn't have to see the parched grasshoppers. From close up a grasshopper is highly implausible. I pretended I was sleeping, as if the drink—see, I told you!—had taken me off my feet. I didn't even have an audience. But still. Who needs an audience to lie? Eventually, the shepherd found me.

"The parsonage," I said weakly by way of the solution to the puzzle. Like a log or a sack, he threw me across his shoulder.

"Here you go," he said to the parson, unceremoniously pulling me off his back and leaning me up against the outside wall. No one's ever given me as little thought as this shepherd.

The parson was generous enough to believe my tale, so I was generous enough to taste his fried chicken. He laid me down in his room. Some time later Mother looked in on me and gave me the silent, scornful once-over with her eye. For his part, Father said thoughtfully:

"It's nothing to fool around with, son. Besides, getting drunk, it's not that easy"—and ever so gently, he closed the door behind him, as if the state of drunkenness were some sort of knowledge one attained only by walking down a long and bumpy road, like in the joke, when in the tavern the father has his son try some schnapps with a sting to it, and the son spits it out with a snort, disgusting!, and his father says to him, so now you know what it's like, go home and tell your mother I'm not here for my health! Like that.

I lay in the darkened room because it was fun. Actually, it wasn't. Not that much. To my surprise, the parson looked in on me too, and asked if I'd like to make confession. At first I thought I'd scream so loud all the windows would break, then I thought I'd order him out of the room, as if I were my own grandfather.

Then I didn't think anything at all, but turned to the wall as if I were sleeping or wasn't even there. Only the taste of the cucumber salad in my mouth told me that I was. But the clergyman couldn't have known that, and he tiptoed out of the room—in the name of brotherly love, I fear.

# CHAPTER THREE

## 84.

I heartily disliked outings, but I disliked going on walks even more. I inherited this from my father (this is what I inherited from my father). We—my father and I—walked only when we had to.

In the summer of 1938 my father had to, or so he felt. His heart was brimming over. My mother was still not resigned, but she walked, too. The woodland and the meadow were drowsy with the heat. Such heat was not typical of Transdanubia. The sky was like a huge glass bell. Or more like a glass pane. Level, boundless, forlorn, strewn with sand from above, and with gravel and semolina, for at times the scorching sky above their heads turned dim, at others ruffled or grainy. They didn't look for shade. It would have made no difference.

They reached the top of a tallish hill that afforded a full panorama all around. Transdanubia is beautiful. As far as the eye could see, everything was waiting for my father, everything there would be his one day. But neither he nor the girl by his side were thinking about that just then. My father didn't think about it because it would have never occurred to him that everything was not his as far as the eye could see, because everything around those parts always belonged to them as far as the eye could see, and he was the firstborn, next in line for the estate, a *grand seigneur,* even as a child.

## 85.

Actually, that's not true. Never in his life, not for the fraction of a second, was my father a *grand seigneur.* His rare displays of haughtiness were the haughtiness of the spirit. His anger or intolerance came not from the power he had, not from the disregard of others inherent in power, but from his intolerance of stupidity, sophistry, and the irrational—his repugnance of it. Still, there was in his habit and constitution, his boyish leanness, an open and obvious nobility which, coupled with the irony nurtured by respect for rationality, leaves the world free to read all sorts of things into it, the *grand,* the *seigneur,* the count.

My father was born into one of the most illustrious families, but he never had an iota of power, ever. (Not even over us.) After the war he had—how shall I put it—no power *von Haus aus,* they bereft him of everything, the *von,* the *Haus,* the *aus.* As for before the war . . . I was about to say that he had had no time to practice his power, but that wouldn't be quite true; there's always time, because a breathful of time is enough for a man to show that he is one of the privileged few.

What man could tally the countless sweet associations that a Hungarian of old was heir to when my father's name passed his lips?

My grandmother's family, for one, did not tally them. They did not bring my father and his siblings up with a view to their privileges. On the contrary; they reminded them not of their name, but of their duties. They bound them forcefully to the quotidian, lest their imagination fly away with them.

Grandfather's wealth was eclipsed only by his reputation (which spread beyond the borders of the country) and yet, especially after 1919, he led the life of an industrious country squire. He didn't reflect upon the affairs of his large estate with an eye (or ear) to the sweet associations, but to the everyday practicalities. In forty-five, for instance—a highly unhistorical attitude!—he disapproved of the partitioning of the land not because it would have left him homeless and destitute, but because small farms are not efficient. Like a joke, he brought up the example of the Russian kolkhoz. He kept at Prime Minister Mihály Károlyi about this, too. They didn't see eye to eye at all, but my grandfather never turned away from him completely, and even helped the Károlyis when they were forced to flee. When the Communists came into power, guards were stationed in front of the Károlyi residence to protect and keep an eye on him. Accordingly, Grandfather always paid his visits through the garden in the back, climbing in through his Red relative's window (the nephew of Grandmother's father and mother, too), so they could discuss "things" over lunch. They didn't see eye to eye on anything. Grandfather thought that the Communists' land reform was better than Károlyi's. Károlyi couldn't figure this out. Grandfather's principles were dictated by his principles.

"Your grandfather was a smart man who got lost in the details," Mrs. Károlyi later said.

"Something that certainly can't be said of Károlyi," Father shot back equivocally, "*he* never knew *where* he got lost."

My father took offense at Károlyi's naïveté, and thus did not see that this naïveté was in a class of its own. My Aunt Carla refers to him only as "that elderly *roué*," or profligate.

# 86.

My father's family lived in accordance with a strict daily schedule. Grandmother had pronounced views with respect to her children's upbringing. In those days even parents who loved their children passionately felt it their bounden duty to break the will of their offspring, to teach them humility and obedience—not unlike the way wild horses are tamed. From time to time Grandmother would wax enthusiastic over some new, fashionable theory. When this happened, she couldn't wait to try it out, especially on her eldest son. One of her basic principles was that children must be trained to withstand the vagaries of the weather—in short, that they must get used to the cold. She put my father out in the open in subzero temperatures with hardly any clothes at all. Even his diapers were changed outdoors. Those present watched aghast as his little purple legs thrashed about in the icy air. Later she swore by the teachings of a famous German physician by the name of Kneipp, and every morning the children had to wade in their bare feet through the ice-cold stream that trickled through the nearby pinewoods. The fashionable exercise was called *wassertreten,* water treading. They were not allowed to wear socks or gloves, ever, not even in a raging snowstorm. Once Uncle Charlie, who thanks to his strong English lavender cologne was easily recognizable even with one's eyes closed (and with one's eyes open, from his gorgeous blue silk La Vallière cravats), saw that the children's hands and cheeks had turned blue from the cold and asked, concerned, if they didn't feel uncomfortable in their summer clothes in late November. The children felt that the question was intrusive. But my father straightened up, and with dignity and inimitable Spanish pride shot back:

"We're no sissies!"

I don't wear a hat or gloves either, but there is no theory behind it anymore.

The other, primary mainstay of severity was Fräulein Irén Fuhrmann, who struck terror in our hearts, and whom we inherited from the Andrássys. She had seen old man Gyula, *le beau pendu,* the handsome hanged man (whom, as we know, in his absence the Imperial law courts sentenced to be hung in effigy), and worshiped him like a demigod. She didn't seem to have a gender, because though she was clearly not a man, she was even less of a woman. She was German by origin, and a perfect bluestocking. You couldn't imagine anything more blue or more stocking. We all had to accommodate ourselves to her impulsive, hysterical moods, even Grandmother, because Fräulein Fuhrmann represented the glorious past. Though she hailed from southern Germany, in her affections and worldview she was inimitably Prussian, and as such, held Hungarians in disdain. Naturally, she did not show this in front of Grandfather. But she made up for it with my father and the rest of the children.

*"Von der Barbarei in die Dekadenz seid ihr gefallen; die Zivilisation habt ihr überschritten,"* she was fond of saying. (Having bypassed civilization, we were supposed to have fallen straight from barbarity into decadence!)

Whenever strangers took her for a simple governess, she flew off the handle. When Grandfather and Grandmother were away, she felt humiliated because she had to take her meals in the children's room, even though she ate at a separate table set up next to theirs. Haydn didn't make such a fuss over it.

"German philosophy was her hobbyhorse. She made your father and the others read Schopenhauer, Kant and Nietzsche even before they could spell," Aunt Carla said gleefully. "But thank God, she concluded that I was *kulturunfähig,* incapable of taking in culture of any kind."

Until their fourteenth birthday, the children ate their meals separately with their tutor or governess. They could not even take part in the dinners. Once in a while Carla could sit at the table, so there wouldn't be thirteen. The grownups held other people's superstitions in regard.

When the vineyard at Aszár was renewed, the vine-stock cuttings were used to heat the stove, and the older children were allowed to stay up and tend the fire, so they didn't have to go to bed early. There was a sheet of paper in the children's room with instructions: "Brushing your teeth, three times a day: three minutes. Washing your hands: four minutes. Getting dressed: seven minutes. In the morning, a cold bath (15 degrees Réaumur), in the evening a hot bath (20 degrees Réaumur). Five minutes allowed in the bathtub each time."

There was iron discipline at the table, too. For instance, the children couldn't drink water till after their meal. Carla asked for water. She didn't get it. At which she threw up. She could throw up like a pro. If the lettuce had been sprayed or the wine had sulfur in it, she wasted no time at all. Not that she needed a reason.

"It's not worth your trouble trying to poison me, my dears," she was fond of saying later, and she laughed uproariously.

She threw up for two straight weeks, but in vain, she didn't get her water, because it was not a question of hygiene, it was a question of etiquette. She was already getting her meals from Grandmother's kitchen by then, because Grandmother got specially prepared food, better made, or better tasting. She threw that up, too, but would still not get water before a meal. Proper table manners counted above all things.

## 87

More of a gourmand than a gourmet, Great-grandmother Schwarzenberg loved to eat, which is to say that from time to time, she ate like a pig. You'd think that princesses just picked at their food like birds. But she gorged herself, then took to bed and dieted for three days. Then came another "bloodwurst, liver-wurst, sour cabbage" attack, and she succumbed. She couldn't help herself. (She always said to Father and the other children, *"Mangez du pain, mes enfants, sinon vous sentirez les renards,"* i.e., they better eat bread with their meat if they don't want to smell like a fox.) Sometimes everyone in the palace, regardless of social stand-ing, got the runs from the sulfur—*colera nostra* was how Great-grandmother called it. She liked to use this epithet, and the others liked quoting it. Another stomach-related expression of hers was the *schnelle mafix*. The reference is obvious, except for the mafix—a black hole in the family chronicles.

She walked with a stick because once, in her youth, when she drove through a riverbed, she turned over with her cart and her knee got stuck between the spokes of the wheel and got crushed, and they didn't know how to treat things like that properly back then. Great-grandmother was suffering "from a stubborn injury," we might say. From then on she went everywhere with two ponies that she drove herself, and a light carriage, she sitting up front, with Tubik standing behind her. (From the forties, it was an automobile and a chauffeur.) Tubik was not a weakling, but he was scrawny, which is not a small thing because Great-grand-mother drove like the devil and kept turning over with the cart, and she was also big—as big as a guardsman, one might say. (Her brother was serving in the Viennese Guard.) I remember Great-grandmother sitting out on the porch when we were forcibly resettled. She wore black and she towered over us, *i.e.*, in all her guardsman-size, like a terrible Queen Mother—anyway, Tubik was able to turn the cart around, but not always Great-grandmother, and then he'd have to unhitch one of the ponies, and go get help.

Great-grandmother was an honorary firefighter. Once she saw that a house was on fire on the village outskirts. The honorary in her stood at attention, and she drove to the fire station even more swiftly than usual, jumped (climbed) off, and reported the fire according to regulations.

"Kindly sit down, Your Excellency!"

"*Nicht* Excellency, *Feuer!*" which afterward became a favorite saying with the firemen as well as us.

88.

The monotony and hardship of rural life was alleviated by the regular hunting parties. The season began with the belling in September. But the boys were given guns with real bullets only after their eighteenth birthday, though they were allowed to hunt for small game, rabbits, pheasants, and snipes (for the information of the uninitiated, with a fowling piece). Once in a while, Carla was allowed to go with Grandfather on the hunt. ("Were you his favorite child?" "You might say that.") She had to be right on time, though. If she was late, she was left behind without a second thought. Carla is (supposed to have been) punctual ever since. They invited people for the belling on Grandfather's legendarily short postcards: *Tuesday shooting for hinds. M.*

This is the only pretension that remained to our father, who went to the belling every year around September. (Not to shoot, just to listen.) It made him extraordinarily mysterious, as if our father were submerging himself in some strange, exotic world. He put on sundry pieces of green and brown clothing, heavy shoes, gray socks, a backpack, or better yet, rucksack. You'd think he was going to a masked ball, or better still, incognito. Our very own King Mátyás, among the masses. Mami assisted him in silence. Preparations were under way days before Papi's departure. Papi went around his business with exceptional good cheer, said cheer coming to a head in the imitation of the belling. It was pure magic. Sometimes in the house, and sometimes out in the garden, our father cupped his hands to his mouth and let out a loud and triumphant bellow.

The three of us children were all agog. We were proud of our father, proud that he was such a huge and magnificent animal. If we were out in the garden, we would even hide ourselves so we wouldn't scare him off. A deer is very sensitive and prone (to take flight). If we count ourselves as deer, then the garden has the ideal 3:1 mating ratio (in favor of the bucks). Our younger sister may look fragile, but she is more like a wild boar, trampling noisily over everything in her path.

"Can we go shoot Papi?" she asks. Our father keeps mum. No roaring. No bellowing. No belling. "Is it all right if we shoot you, sir?"

"No. I don't think so. I'd rather you didn't." Which brought the belling season to an end for the year, and we gave our sister a good thrashing.

By the way, the stag hunts were resumed only after 1925, because in the chaotic postwar years the stock had been almost completely depleted, partly by the soldiers returning from the war, and partly by the people of the nearby villages. The wild boars got off though. There were always enough left, no matter what, so hunting packs continued unabated from October through February.

Grandfather invited only first-class hunters, but he had a special aversion to braggarts, the Gascons, the Münchhausens. The following actually happened to him: he was invited somewhere (to old Prince Philip, at Pusztavacs, Prince Philip Josias, Duke of Saxony, Coburg and Gotha, to shoot for small game), and the men gathered in the castle the night before the hunt. A diplomat from the Balkans—who clearly had no idea that the rest of the company were excellent, tried-and-true hunters—had the word, and he launched into a loud braggadocio in broken German.

"Your Highness, I be ze very good hunter. There vere many ducks to me, five hundred in one night I shoot, but only ze drake, I do not to shoot at ze hen! Your Highness vill see tomorrow . . . wiz my two Brovnings, one hundred pheasants vith ze right, one hundred pheasants vith ze left . . . provided zere are enough pheasants!"

Géza Nemeskéri-Kiss, who enjoyed a countrywide reputation as a hunter, was standing in front of Grandfather. Like one tortured by cramps, he started doubling up, this civilian bombastic verbiage hurt, and he practically shrank under the pain and the helplessness. Grandfather put a sympathetic hand on his shoulder. He felt that this man was very close to him just now. His brother, Uncle Sanyi Nemeskéri-Kiss, brought us a slingshot once. He'd made it especially for us with great care, out of cherry wood and a leather band. A veritable work of art. A grownup making a slingshot, that's something we could appreciate. We'd shoot at the poplars, the birds, the sparrows sitting on the electric lines, and then—nothing to be proud of—blindly and at random into the factory yard next to our house, where we must have hit something in the bull's-eye. The maintenance authorities from the factory came to check all the houses in the neighborhood. We were in school, and our mother insisted heroically that we were innocent. (She lied.) Actually, it was the slingshot she respected, Uncle Sanyi's *"Prachtstück"* masterpiece.

"Will Your Royal Highness allow me," Grandfather cut in abruptly, "to tell the tale of an exciting hunting adventure from the Carpathians?"

"Kindly proceed."

Grandfather put on a grave expression, then launched into it. Except for his speeches in Parliament, he hadn't talked at such length in years.

"When I went stalking in the Carpathian wilderness once, unaccompanied, as was my wont, my path was cut off by a deep, rocky precipice between whose bounds flowed a rushing mountain stream. Need I say? In that trackless wilderness there is no bridge, but at last I came upon a huge, felled pine whose trunk happened to be lying across the precipice. I had no choice. I used that ancient pine in lieu of a bridge. Having emptied my shotgun, I placed it on my shoulder, and carefully began traversing the huge pine trunk. I had hardly reached the middle of the makeshift bridge when to my utmost horror, a gigantic bear appeared from behind the bushes opposite, and on the same tree trunk over which I was attempting to cross the deep ravine, he started toward me . . ."

The guests were listening intently, especially the hero from the Balkans, who had even forgotten the Riesling in his glass.

"Imagine my situation, gentlemen . . . with an empty shotgun on my back! There was nothing for it, I had to turn back. But no sooner had I turned back . . . no easy feat, gentlemen, if one doesn't grow up in a circus . . . when what do I see?"

"What? What?!"

"I see another bear, even bigger than the first, in front of me, which, having followed my tracks, and growling ferociously, steps on the other end of the trunk!"

The hair-raising story had even the real hunters in its grip, but the Münchhausen of the Balkans, trembling, mesmerized with excitement, cut in excitedly:

"Und vat to you zen happen?"

"Und zen," my grandfather said with his customary cool, "the bears had me for dinner."

## 89.

My father was far more interested in the far less glamorous and far less socially acceptable game of soccer. What I mean is, if it's acceptable, look to the plebeian or, in the worst-case scenario, the proli. Oh, our mother would wail, why this rough and primitive sport? If we must choose, why not tennis? Tennis is refined. It is for gentlemen. We could dress in white, and not these shoddy Silesia-cloth pants. White becomes us. Our mother's pleas fell on deaf ears.

As did my former high school teacher's, who was aghast when he heard that from time to time I wouldn't be able to make it to the extracurricular philosophy class, for which he'd just singled me out, because of soccer. I don't think he even understood what I was talking about.

"Is that so?" he said, and shook his head, saddened and vexed. "That can't be. It's absurd."

He looked just like Pope Pius XII, except without the power. But there was the same faint ivory color, the same thin, frail physique, unrelenting sadness and wire-rimmed glasses, aloofness and preoccupation, as if he were someplace else, as if he were constantly at his prayers. I don't think this transient, earthly life suited him, and this made him irritable; he was filled with permanent, mild irritability, which scared me; but the hypothetical, one might say tangible relationship with the heavens attracted me; his sadness, mixed with the chagrin, was beautiful, and I liked that; but there was a hint of threat in it, too, which I didn't like.

He seemed to be using the formal mode of address as he spoke to me.

"If you want to make something of yourself, sir . . ."

We were standing in the corridor of the monastery, in the blinding half-light, and I felt a lump in my throat. Never, ever, had anyone taken me this seriously before. Very rightly, the teacher did not address the fifteen-year-old boy as his equal. We were not equals. He regarded me slightly from above, with a touch of *hauteur*, and because he constantly pinned his eyes on the transcendental, a touch of rigidity, too. Also, an awareness of the respect due to his position, this too was part of his constitution. Still, he considered me a free man. He spoke to me with respect. He showed me the respect due to a free individual. In short, his love of God manifested itself in the attention he paid me. His profound faith was rooted in the seriousness with which he addressed me, which in turn was rooted in his love of the Lord.

I saw nothing of interest in my person that could have interested him, but he did, and so he invited me to go see him for a series of what you might call philosophical discussion. Sunday morning's no good, I said, that's the championship.

"The *what*, sir?"

He sounded confused. At a loss. His confusion made me feel ashamed, and now, confused myself, counterconfused, you might say, quickly, far too eagerly, unduly out of proportion, I started explaining the order of the championship sponsored by the Budapest Soccer League and then, in a narrative manner, I continued with the customs, the foreseeable likelihood of what time Sunday's game would begin and, apologetically, how I, personally, don't even like playing in the morning. For one thing, it's too much like a junior league game.

"Did you say . . . *junior?!*"

Which stopped me cold. Effectively. Two dejections, a head-on collision.

That's when he said that if I want to make something of myself, I must choose, either something, or soccer. He could read the answer in my eyes.

## 90.

Our father—we have his word on it—played right wing on the village team.

"I was fast, yes, fast."

We knew we could be impertinent with regard to the subject, the swift-footed right-winger took it in stride. Between two soccer games, which meant the meadow, we played in front of our house. We either played without a goalpost because we were short of room, or else our sister stood in the improvised gate, and we kicked the ball to her. Which more often than not brought with it what we came to call the Goliath-plague, because from time to time the ball landed in the neighbor's yard, and we had to go to their garden gate and shout Aunt Goliath! After a while, we called the kicks that went out of bounds Aunt Goliaths. She scared us. She was not one to ingratiate herself, and the ball didn't help matters any (I wonder why?). Besides, she had trouble walking. She walked with a sort of shuffle. She shuffled over to the ball reluctantly, then shuffled back to the gate, opened it, and handed the ball back as if it were a watermelon, all the while never taking her eyes off of us. She never railed at us, she never showed any emotion, which made us feel as if she were always watching. When she spoke, she spoke to us as if we were grownups, and that scared us, too. Consequently, we could never Aunt Goliath more than twice in one afternoon, and if we did, we went in delegation to our father—provided he was at home, of course—and requested that he kindly retrieve the thing that we had lost. He always came without a word of complaint, as if it were his duty.

The Goliaths were good neighbors. But people said they were Communists. Uncle Goliath was an *old* Communist, a foundry worker and trade-union man, while Aunt Goliath was a *new* Communist, a post-'56 career. We couldn't reconcile good and Communist, and didn't believe our mother, who tried to warn us away from them. These people can't be Communists because Communists have hoofs, or they're like Mrs. Váradi. (Later I heard that they kept reporting us to the authorities while day in and day out, they were chatting with us about the condition of the sidewalk. I also heard that this wasn't true. And also, that it happened the other way around, that they were being reported on all the time, out of revenge, because Aunt Goliath was a big shot, and big shots have lots of enemies.)

Once he was outside, our father would often join our game, and we obliged him, all the while letting him feel that our good-will had its temporal limits (we were anxious to go on with the game *properly*), and Father didn't force the issue. He knew that professionally speaking, we were not on par.

Banal as it may be, I will never forget the time my father commented, as if by way of an aside—who to?, where to?, why?—that I played better than he ever did. Ever. I made him repeat it. He repeated it.

"You play better, old boy, than I ever did. Than I ever could," and he drew himself up proudly.

I couldn't see what he had to be proud about. I'm the one who should be proud, I thought, and over his dead body, too! Never, either before or after, did it ever occur to me that I should be better than my father. But then and there, I thought that I was better than him. That I'd beaten him.

"I beat you."

A sweet, tingling sensation.

Except, seeing me swell up, facile, like a turkey-cock, my father's look of surprise disturbed the moment; and shaken, I thought that no, there's no way of beating him. There is no playing field for that. Or if there is, there's no game. Or if there's a game, there's no goalpost. Or if there's a goalpost, there's no referee to decide. Or if there's a referee, that's him.

But I didn't really care about this who beats whom thing, except for the afternoon when that sentence passed his lips, and when, by the way, I wore studded shoes for the first time. Veritable antiques—three-quarter-high ankle-boot-like things—they had once belonged to Lambi Fischer, Father's former teammate who, if my memory serves me right, was on the management of the famous Fradi team, and by all accounts a person of consequence in the world of soccer, and one day he would come to see me, to see how talented I was, even more talented than my father; in short, my life was on the up and up, and me only eleven; I've reached a certain level already, my father's. We have no illusions about it, but still . . . I tried to store the moment away—the muddy street, my sister's impatient grimace by the goalpost, the unfamiliar weight of the Lambi shoes. In short, I know something special, I concluded, and put the moment under lock and key.

During our soccer games, anything was possible. When we played, we were the bosses, and our father submitted himself to this exceptional order of things.

"Tell us, Father. If someone did not pass the ball to that certain swift-footed, celebrated right-winger, was he duly brought before the feudal headsman to suffer under the swing of his feudal broadsword?"

We passed, we dribbled—five o'clock tea!—while he watched his budding aristocratic saplings with pleasure. I don't remember his watching us with pleasure at any other time, except on the soccer field. We were never as close to him as there, in front of the house, between two Aunt Goliaths; our relationship was suddenly imbued with a loving lightheartedness and elemental joy, while all the time we couldn't wait for him to go back to his typing. On the other hand, we didn't wait for it *very* much. Not very much, just naturally.

Our parents never told us about the fabulous, fairy-tale world that Aunt Goliath and her kind hived off of us, and so we never thought about it. They didn't keep mum because they were careful (God forbid the children should get used to it!), or because they were neglectful; on the contrary, they must have thought that the (family) tradition was so powerful, they could afford to neglect it. Why nurse it like a weak sapling, when it's an ancient oak? (Just by way of an example.) The facile disregard could have just as easily been replaced by facile regard; it's the facile that counted; if you felt like it you talked, if you felt like it you didn't, you couldn't go wrong. Still, there was a difference between my father's and my mother's not talking—the former didn't, the latter wouldn't.

Only Mami's older sister Bogyi, never Aunt Bogyi, just Bogyica, Bóbikó, who wore a velvet ribbon à la Winterhalter round her neck, talked about the old glory. But her point of view was exceedingly one-sided. Since my maternal grandfather was in my paternal grandfather's service as the steward of the estate, Bogyica's comments (they never added up to stories) pointed mainly to how nobly and valiantly Apik Grandfather stood up to Count Móric Grandfather, of which—on the whole—very little made any sense.

Still, during these easygoing soccer afternoons in front of the house, there were two things we wanted to hear about, the question of *just gladii,* but especially, Father dear, what's the story with the landlord's right to the first night, the *jus primae noctis?* What was the story back then, and what is it now? ("*This* you have a head for! Not like the Seven Deadly Sins or the battle of Lepantó. I bet you've never even heard of it!" "The battle of Belgrade!" "Simpletons!") When they abolished it, the people's democracy

568

made a big mistake. Indubitably. Our father chuckled. Which made us feel as if it hadn't been abolished *completely* after all. Was there hope that Mrs. Várady's head would be severed from her shoulder? We could invite the whole village to watch. Or use the whipping post. Of course, we'd need a village first. Though the school would do just as well. Or the seventh grade, at least! We could always decide later if it's to be the *just* or the *primae*. Either way, we win.

The historical constellation, however, stood as follows: the parents of my father's soccer pals had at one time been in the employ of the estate—that is to say, they had been entirely dependent on us. Which led to numerous complications, as you can imagine. For one thing, the swift-footed right-winger used the informal form of address with the left halfback (or *half*, as they were called then), the son of Knapp, the deaf tailor (the same Knapp the deaf tailor who in '49 made a pair of corduroy work pants for Aunt Carla—"fine, prewar material, Countess, not Communist!"—who in order to help out her mother and father, took on coal and firewood delivery in the district. A twenty-year-old nobody of a girl, everyone thought she wouldn't last, but she did. Even the old Slovak carter, the doyen of carters, approved of Aunt Carla's pants, saying it's about time you got somethin' proper on you, it's about time!, because till then it was nothing but a fashion show, checkered sailor suit, indeed! However, the authorities had a different view on fashion, and when—as was only to be expected—they sent Aunt Carla to a forced labor camp on trumped-up charges, they brought this up against her, too, that she dresses like this in order to make people feel sorry for her. She was supposed to have "schemed to make people forget that she's a countess"), and so they called one another by their first names, Matyi, Dodó. During the rabbit hunt in winter, the same halfback, a beater then and there, greeted Mr. Kelemen (Pista Kelemen), the severe

Master of the Hunt who hired, better yet, called in the beaters, with due respect, hat in hand, then proceeded to chat and laugh along with that *other* father of mine, whom just a moment before, hat in hand, the Master of the Hunt had greeted with even more due respect. Those hats (my father's excepted) were constantly in motion.

In short, I'm better. I wanted to hear it again. And Father repeated lightly:

"You're better."

It was soon afterward that he said that beautiful (and highly quotable) sentence, whose facile wit hid . . . well, it hid a lot of things.

"For a time I was my father's son," thus spoke my father, "but by now, I'm more and more my son's father."

"How about me? How about me?" our sister asked, rolling her eyes self-righteously.

"Yours too, of course," our father nodded, then sneakily, unexpectedly, toed the ball into the goal.

Which I'd rather not comment on, professionally.


## 91.

In order to do justice to the occasion, Grandfather had a Château Margaux 1787 brought up from the cellar, this for the formal dinner given in honor of Father's graduation or birthday. Grandfather kept good wines, not many, but all selected with discernment and care.

(When the Russians came in—they came in several times; for two whole months, the front line kept shifting back and forth in the vicinity of Csákvár, hand in hand with a great deal of horror—the first measure my Grandfather took was to have the wine barrels drained. The village concluded that its lord and master had gone mad. But Grandfather knew all about war, and he knew all about drunken soldiers. The village knew as much as he, but letting wine go to waste like that, well, that just isn't right! How true. But neither is war. Or who knows. Besides, Grandfather wouldn't hurt the best or finest bottles either.

"Either they'll survive, or else the Ivans will drink them. To their health! Bordeaux won't do them any harm, anyway," he murmured with transparent generosity. But they didn't drink it. They discovered it too late. The Germans were on their way back, and there was no time. What little time remained was barely enough to mow down the bottles. To kill them.

"Asians," the *grand seigneur* hissed between his teeth.

My grandfather lost a lot. He lost everything, all that he possessed. He lost his son, too, in the war. But nothing pained him as much as this. He didn't take anything to heart as much as those couple of bottles (some with cognac), because he could find no explanation for it, whereas he could have. All it would have required was a bit of looking.)

The wine that was served was so ancient, alas, that it had solidified and had to be scooped onto small plates and eaten with a knife and fork. They ate the wine with a knife and fork! Just like in America! Wine experts say it's out of the question, it's not possible. But it's too late. I can't let go of this image, the Germans occupy Czechoslovakia and so on and so forth, the fireworks erupt, and in the meanwhile, under the dark, Hungarian village sky, in the castle lit up for a celebration, my father, a damask napkin with an embroidered white crown tucked under his chin, is eating wine with a knife and fork—nibbling and munching time itself. They even got a little tipsy.

# 92.

For his graduation present, his father sent my father on a Norwegian cruise. Time he saw the world. He was chaperoned by a distant, somewhat older cousin (Onkel Pali)—another branch, tribal love in action. We heard all sorts of fanciful, absurd things about the ship, that it's got several levels, it's got a pool and a tennis court. We especially resented this last one. A boat is a boat. This tennis court was so impertinent, we couldn't even think of it as a lie, or a boast, we just waved it off, as if our father were our classmate. Or schoolmate. (Later we saw a picture of the Titanic. So what? So let him have the last word!) They luxury-cruised up and down the Skagerrak and the Kattegat. Once they took a boat ride to a small nearby island; cliffs, picnic, wicker baskets with shrimp, white wine, fresh bread. On one of the cliffs a woman was sunbathing in the nude. Everyone pretended they didn't see. But my father saw. It was the first time he'd seen a nude woman all in one piece. The boat heaved itself over the big waves. My father trembled.

"I'm frightened," he said out loud. The Norwegian sailors continued rowing. "Gentlemen," Father announced, as if it were a discovery, "I find that I am frightened." *"Mine herrer, jeg er redd."* He had a way with words. He could suddenly feel the infinite might of the sea, the fact that he was now at the mercy of the ocean, whereas he was just not familiar with it. A classical God-experience sneaking in through the back door. He also came to understand that whether it's a flatboat or an ocean liner with a tennis court, it's all the same. These two things happened to him on the grand tour of Norway—fear and nudity, and God.

The sunbathing woman was past the first blush of youth.

# 93.

"Provincial. I'm still far too provincial."

It wasn't until he started college that he learned how little he knew. And also what a great deal. He first came face-to-face with the immense, unfamiliar world of knowledge in the large library of the castle at Majk, which took up two spacious rooms. First he flung himself on Verne's books. He veritably gobbled them up, one after the other, never suspecting that for the most part, the vividly imagined fantasies would, in fifty years' time, become reality. Next he immersed himself in Gaborian's detective novels. But the book that he found most interesting because of its strange, bizarre atmosphere was Captain Marryat's *Ghost Ship.* (He never used a bookmarker. "One knows where one's at.")

But later, up on the balcony, where the great eighteenth-century authors were lined up side by side, he discovered something which at first impressed him with its sheer bulk and dignified cover: the *Encyclopédie.* His scent led him in the right direction. The first article that he opened to was the chapter entitled "Dieu," by Voltaire. Did he really want to learn something about God, or did the volume open there because the former Esterházys repeatedly opened it there, we don't know. (I don't know.)

Did our family need Voltaire to tell them about God? I wouldn't bet on it.

# 94.

So then. There they were, my father and my mother, strolling on the open plain by the edge of the forest (in the Vértes Mountains) languid from the heat, and neither thought that as far as the eye could see, everything would one day be my father's. Father didn't think it because if everything is yours, you can't think about everything, there's no *place* to think it, and also, what for; and Mother didn't think it because she had already thought about it the night before.

This transpired when Menyus Tóth, young Menyus, who was my father's butler since my father turned sixteen, was sent from the castle. Would Mademoiselle Lili feel inclined to take a stroll with Master Mátyás? That's when she thought of it, while she asked the boy to wait to check her schedule; this is what she thought, that here, as far as the eye could see, everything belongs to the young offshoot, and do her eyes want to see as far as that in this place?

"Fine, Menyus. Kindly tell him I'll be there."

The boy did not move. Mother tilted her head questioningly to the side, at which the young butler grew hot all over, and skedaddled away like a rabbit or some other timid animal.

Our mother was four years older than our father, which they kept from us for a long time; specifically, Mami kept it from us, and she was right to do so, because when we found out, we were really shocked, and condemned her for her sudden aging on us which, to add insult to injury, she did behind our back. As far as we were concerned, married couples are of the same age, anything else is perverse. Grandfather is fifteen years older than Grandmother, but it's best not to go into that, we said, and rolled our eyes piously. As for the woman being older than the man, there's no such thing. It was the tardy revelation of the secret that steered us into this impossible pass. She might have been born earlier, but she's not older, my brother attempted. But then we started learning mathematics.

The year my father graduated coincided with the year Mami finished her teacher's training. According to Bogyica, Papi— sometimes she also calls him Papi which, regardless of the context, was music to my ears—was always hanging out at their place, not so much because of Mami, but because of the general good mood, from which I was supposed to understand (I understood) that *up in the castle* life was cold and without feeling, not like at their place. They also danced a lot because Apik had a victrola brought from Győr. A gramophone. Bogyica said gramophone the way Mami said *tahksi* and *rehcahmié*.

"Matika didn't get enough love. His Excellency, your grandfather, I'm sorry to say, loved no one, while your grandmother loved only the dead. That's the truth."

I didn't believe a word my beautiful aunt said.

My father's clothes, to say the least, gave no indication of this "as far as the eye can see" business.

"You've grown out of your pants, I see," the young woman said abruptly. She said this instead of laughing, instead of laughing at him. Father gave himself the once-over with some surprise. The piece of clothing under discussion did, indeed, end above the ankle, though the huge, boot-like lace-up shoes almost reached it even so.

After a while, he shrugged. "They'll do."

We were familiar with this practical indifference, this sensible negligence of his. Our father had no relationship to the beautiful (not even his own). That's the Majk grandmother line.

A policewoman, a lieutenant, born Countess H., told me that she'd danced with my father, and that my father was a lousy dancer, and also a lousy dresser, and she ran her fingers through my hair. I was eight at the time, but unlike my father—given the slightest provocation—I always threw whatever beauty I could muster into the fray. Countess (Lieutenant) H. was wild about my hair.

"We laughed a lot at your father! You should have heard him protest! High tie-ups are very practical in a village, he said, and the fact that it does not quadrate with city fashion, I'm quoting him *ver batim,* quadrate!, is not a consideration with his mother when she acquires clothes for him. Good Lord, a Spartan grandmother!"

"They'll do," my father said again, "they were my father's."

Mami laughed all the same.

"His tailor died," she giggled.

"Who? What?!" father said with a blush, for it rarely happened that he didn't understand something.

"The decent fellow seems to have met his end before he could have completed this noble piece of clothing which, as we see, has been serving the family for generations, and has handsomely survived not a few signorial backsides. Poor fellow, he died before he could have achieved his illustrious masterpiece, the so-called *long pair of pants!*"

"You are making fun of me," father noted with amusement.

"Just a bit, Your Excellency."

The young teacher's sad eyes looked my father up and down. She found the young man in front of her attractive, the stalwart contours of his face, his wide, horn-rimmed glasses, which lent an air of helplessness to his entire being, his lean figure, and the playful eyes that at the same time seemed just a tad unreliable. She even put the tailor of the tragic fate down to his credit. She felt a palpitation in her heart when she thought that possibly she would have something to do with this man, and she felt a palpitation in her heart, too, when she thought that she would have nothing to do with him. As for my father, he saw none of this as he continued his lighthearted banter.

"See? This only *looks* like a forest. But it's much more of a park, really. A park that tends toward a forest."

"Papist reasoning . . . It is what it is and it isn't, but only to make it what it is that much more. On the other hand, we, Protestants . . ."

"I know, I know. You protest!"

576

Mother was mortified. She shot him a look. She wasn't used to such frivolity. At home, in her family, even jokes were serious. They carried profound meaning, and if at all possible, they were meant to teach people a lesson. Witticisms were out, puns were out. Except for humor. They were afraid of people who lacked a sense of humor. My father's family, on the other hand, were afraid of nothing and of no one, even if they didn't feel like talking about it. What they didn't feel like talking about they didn't talk about. Consequently, it did not exist. Only what you talk about exists. My mother's family talked about everything, this is how they were courageous. My father's family talked only about what they felt like talking about, and this is how *they* were courageous.

In place of the palpitations, instead of them, Mother now felt nothing but scorn in her heart. Her face turned purple with emotion, her body felt hot, and . . . and deep down, inside, there throbbed a minuscule, icy something. Frightened, she touched her breast. She would have liked to massage it away. She didn't know yet that these two feelings would be with her for the rest of her life, that everything about her and inside her would change, her colors, her words, her smell, but these two feelings would hold out to the end: the adoration and the scorn, plus what follows from them—a touch of pity.

"We Protestants"—Mother wasn't even a Protestant, only Grandfather!—"prefer to see things for what they are. Eye to eye."

Their eyes met. At this moment, my father entertained some very pleasant thoughts about the world, about everything as far as the eye could see. My mother didn't concern herself with father's seeing, although he was seeing in earnest; and also, she wanted to finish saying what she had to say. This, too, she learned at home; not the willfulness, but the need for completion. My father's family considered fragments complete, too; they knew that a fragment is not a fragment because it is missing something, but because of what it contains. My mother's family suffered from fragmentation; anything that was not complete pained them, anything and everything that's merely a leftover, a fraction, a residue, a residual, a clipping, a shaving, a paring, a scrap, a morsel, a bite, a crust, a crumb, a snatch, a chip, a snip, a snippet, a giblet, a colon, a cutlet, a chop, sediment or flip-flop, anything fragmentary or truncated, while for Papi's family everything that exists, that *is*, is interesting.

"A forest is a forest," the young teacher concluded severely.

Father laughed wholeheartedly. We never experienced this laugh in its pure form, only his smile, which is never clear-cut, it is complicated by numerous transpositions and tends toward the enigmatic. But this full, shrill laughter, which comes from the guts . . . we heard it, but only when he was tipsy, and so it frightened us, which seemed especially sad because laughter, if anything, is about the lack of fear. It is a Homeric outburst.

"A forest is a forest no doubt, chère mademoiselle," and he pressed Mother's hand who, angered by the cheapness of the gesture and by her appreciating it nonetheless, even though she heartily detested anything cheap and didn't even deign to give it a fleeting thought, turned pale, "a forest is a forest, naturally. But the words . . . whether a word is just a word, that's the question."

Mother couldn't understand the youthful count, neither his easy, wholehearted laughter, nor this sanctimonious edging up to words. Her family did not talk about words, they used them. As far as they were concerned, words were not the object of speech or of discussion (whereby they spared themselves a number of inconveniences to be sure; they circumvented them). They used words and respected them like a master builder respects his tools, a mason his trowel, the painter his brush; they nurtured and maintained them, picking through them expertly (or with sensitivity, as they said back then), squeamishly and furiously, but in any case, always with passion, and not merely with an eye to practicality and usefulness; they went through them with hate, love, and tenderness. They felt responsible. They had much to lose. There was a stake to their use of words.

On the other hand, my father—specifically, my grandfather and his family—never felt that they had anything to lose since (repetition!) they had so much that they had every reason to think they couldn't lose it all, for everything can't be lost, only a lot. But if you lose a lot from this everything, there's still everything left. Accordingly, everything remains the same, and accordingly, it is not worth thinking about. Later, when historical happenstance took from them everything they possessed, this line of reasoning came full circle: if you have nothing, no matter how much of it you may lose, the same amount remains. Accordingly, everything remains the same. And—teetering on the brink of a great big nothing—they concluded that it's something not worth thinking about, and they either marched out to the potato patch to rake the potatoes (having taken on the work for half the yield), or else sat out on the porch and quietly reflected on the vagaries of fortune.

They approached words differently, too. If, as above, we regard words as so many work tools, we might say that they regarded themselves as work tools, too—the trowel, the brush. Also, the other way around: if they thought of themselves as artisans, or craftsmen, they also thought of words as such, as their equals, to the extent, at least, that those and they cannot be separated one from the other—the hand about to pull up the wall, the mason's hand, doesn't show, nor the hand of the painter about to paint over it, and it goes without saying that the universal hand that was supposed to have created the world doesn't show either. It is being pulled up, it is being painted; they didn't so much use words as struggled and wrestled with them (who's who?), and so the plank where as artisans they could have secured a foothold, the ladder they could have climbed as painters were nonexistent, nor were they in possession (so they didn't possess everything after all?) of the metaphysical sunglasses through which they could have glanced at the full, bright sky (Grandmother excepting). There was no distance between themselves and the world; they kept finding themselves embroiled in the world, of which the words that describe the world and the space between the words formed a part.

The young man was thinking of proximity, the young woman of distance.


## 95.


The wasp, on the other hand, wasn't thinking at all. It acted on impulse. It'd been keeping its incredible, multifaceted eye on the couple for some time, notably, the swaying yellow skirt caught its eye, the colorful giant bell as it flip-flopped among the green trees, the two bell hammers swinging inside, ding-dong, ding-dong. The summer of '38 seemed promising. The hot July sun urged the fruit to early maturity, and the wasp sipped the syrupy leaves sanguinely. But never had it seen a pear this big before, though by then it had flown across much of the (blunted) triangle of Kőhányás-Zsémlye-Bíborkapuszta; it had been to the Edit manor, left fallow that year; it knew the famous, straight-as-an-arrow linden-lined alley leading to the castle (over which even Metternich had rode once—true, because he'd lost his way, and that's why. He couldn't find his bearings as easily in Asia as on the European political dance floor. Later, the Russian troops also drove down the alley, though in their case the expression "lost their way" is not applicable; specifically, in '45 the Russians and the Germans took turns occupying the castle, the latter carrying off furniture, objects of art, paintings and vases on the basis of careful cataloging, conscientiously, being careful of the objects in the manner of gentlemen. For their part, the Russians acted from the heart. They were sticklers for cleanliness. For instance, they didn't shit on the floor, but demolished the rococo porcelain stoves with the green-leaved Herend Esterházy-pattern down to midheight, and used them, and they carefully paved the muddy path leading to the outhouse with heavy leather-bound volumes of suitable size—they walked all over the "Dieu," and for weeks grilled sheep cut down the middle inside the burning grand pianos). In short, it (the wasp) had led an adventurous life.

Was it a wood, a solitary or a colonial wasp, who is to say? Certainly, I couldn't. But based on what transpired, it was most probably an ichneumon, a so-called probing wasp.

It's relationship to human beings was ambivalent to begin with. Its mother kept issuing hysterical warnings against them, in all probability having mistaken themselves for bees. Bees are the ones that sting only once, because if they sting, they die—and they sting. Bees are like the Japanese. Real risk takers. If lured by cakes, honey, or apple juice, the wasp happened to fly too near to people, they began sawing the air in a ridiculous manner, and it could see the fear and disgust on their faces. Which stirred its interest. The vehement brandishing of the arms did nothing to make either of the pair relax, and so the decision was up to the multijointed legs (hands) of the wasp: either to nobly fly off in search of new songs, cakes, honey, or apple juice, or immediately, ------, like a dive bomber, or better yet, a dive bomb, ------, and bull's-eye!

To the surprise of them both (in fact, all three), my father seized my mother's wrist; he grabbed it like an acrobat, and began whirling her round and round, the skirt shot up as far as the eye could see, a merry-go-round, and the two of them, the country fair, the stall keeper, the carousel, the small carousel seats with the chains, and they the joyfully strolling Mari Törőcsik and Imre Soós from the movie, except they couldn't have known that at the time. My father was strong. He was playing with the young teacher, playing in earnest, the way only a young man knows how. My mother, on the other hand, didn't like games.

What I mean is, she liked games, she liked playing cards, and parlor games in general; she liked sitting with Apik of an evening on the spacious verandah, and also with the boys, her two enchanting, promising brothers, one younger, the other older; she liked brain gym and cultural quizzes, she liked to play geography and Monopoly, and could easily give herself over to the world of games—except all the time she knew that she's *there,* in that world, in that game, and not there, on the verandah. But whenever she found herself unexpectedly involved in something, being involved by others without previous notice in something whose rules were unfamiliar to her, whose rules may not have even been clear-cut, or worse yet, were nonexistent, that made her go off the deep end. (The Count and his family had a different slant on this, saying: we're being tossed back and forth between everything and nothing, in short, we're playing; we are not the world behind the mirror, where things have no weight and there is no night and no day, nor are we the world in front of the mirror— nor are we the mirror.)

"If I were to let go of you now, you'd go whirligiging out of the world," my father shouted merrily.

"Well, then, don't let go, silly boy," the young woman thought, and though she let out something like a giggle and a sigh, she said only that he shouldn't be so flippant. She clearly shared the popular mistaken notion that games lack seriousness, that they're silly, a joke, infantile, immature and childish.

*Z------!* What a to-do! The wasp hadn't counted on it. The yellow bell was floating above the world, the two clappers were dangling in the sweet darkness so as to take his breath away. Even his . . . But what really pained him was the circumstance that being an arthropod, he lacked a heart which now, taken off guard by the quick flood of joy, could have beaten faster. Then after my father had rather roughly lifted my mother out and up from this spin, giving her a whirl and spinning her within the spin (like the astronaut game at the Amusement Park), and taken off guard by the quick flood of joy Mother screamed happily, then, in that joyful, screaming whirligig of an instant, the wasp ------ under the bell, ding-dong, ding-dong, ding-dong bell!, what celestial chimes!, and there was no up and there was no down, there was no light and there was no darkness, for a second the celestial harmonies of the sky shot through the cleavage of the boughs of the summer oak, after which nothing but the earthly remained, an even more delicious, suffocating darkness, a wet materiality, and the flesh, and the merging of the flesh, to bite a piece out of it, to consume it, to gobble it up, to take possession and unite, to plunge, to delve, be annihilated, be hers, be mine, be!

And when it sank its triumphant dart into the delicate mound or, better yet, the wooded terrain just turning from mound to hollow—a *novice* terrain, a dark gully, Turnkey's Hollow!—when it bore itself into the flesh redolent with perfumed spices, never before had it penetrated flesh this deep or this tempestuously, in such earnest, advancing through the strangeness molecule by molecule, making it his own, and thereby familiar—it was suddenly and simultaneously gripped by the yearning for annihilation and eternal life. But it was too late to decide—provided that decision had been at all possible—for it was about to wrench himself free of the trembling soil of his sweet damnation when half of its body snapped off (assuming for now that the dart is up front, just like a beast of prey's, tusk and fang, face-to-face, and not in the back, quietly slipping from the tip of the abdomen, without the slightest dignity, incidentally and murderously), the wings were still moving, taking who? what? out into the light. Head reeling, in the last moment of life, the wasp could feel itself doubled, subject and predicate, inside and outside, both, and then, the eternal longing having been satisfied, it fell to the ground.

The summer had come to an end.

My mother was not a crybaby. On the contrary. But now she let out such a horrendous scream that my light-headed (spellbound) father nearly released her hand, in which case, as we know, my mother would have gone whirligiging out of the world as if shot from a sling, up, up and away over the oak—away, toward far-off Kecskéd, Kömlőd, and Nagyigmánd, over Tornyó and Csordakút, and over all the rest, through the airspace of nothing but family holdings as far as the eye could see.

The lord in perpetuity of Csákvár and Majk trampled the wasp, the piece of wasp circling round him, into the ground, then took matters into his own hands. He laid my mother who—as if intoxicated by the wasp's sting—was in a daze, down on the soft, shady grass under the tree, turned her on her side, hiked up her skirt, and found himself face-to-face with the remaining half of the wasp, this tragic, yet as we have seen, also happy leftover.

"Lilike," he whispered with dark sobriety, "I must now extract the poisonous substance," and then he proceeded to do all the things the wasp managed, and managed not to do.

I don't know how many moments of such perfection they had in their lives, but I could surely count them on the fingers of two hands. Which is as much as I know about the sex lives of my parents.


# 96.


Father was satisfied, mother was pale as they sauntered back toward the castle and the manor house. At the juncture before they reached the lakes, where a mill had once stood, mother abruptly let out a yelp:

"No."

"No what?" the young man said with a grin.

"No."

My father didn't take it to heart. We know perfectly well how a no can turn into a yes on a quiet night, how lips that had been stubborn and tight in the evening can pucker up ever so sweetly by dawn. These were the thoughts my father was thinking, a bunch of silly nonsense. On the other hand, as he took a whiff of the air, he felt that the vision and scent of Turnkey's Hollow would be with him the rest of his days, and in this he was not disappointed.

But he didn't see my mother the next day, or the day after that. She got married to some man called Horváth or Szabó, six of one, half a dozen of the other—which she kept a secret, just like her age, as if she'd excised a couple of years out of her life—a man who the day after the wedding joined the army and proceeded to die a hero's death on the Russian front without delay, which later we considered commendable and tactful of him, namely, that this man, a stranger, did not wish to take our father's place after all, our father's, whom we wouldn't have exchanged for anyone in the whole wide world.

Ten years later, when my mother and my father met again, you'd have had to be blind to think that as far as the eye could see, everything still belonged to him.

# CHAPTER FOUR

## 97.

What's to be done when the world around you is about to collapse, the earth opens up, the rivers overflow their bounds, but
dry out, too, the sky is cleft in twain, and the stars fall into it, and
the sun, too, and it grows as dark as the inside of a garbage pail,
and in the salon the Murano chandelier, which sheds its gleaming
light in a thousand directions all at once, begins to sway? Whereas
our grandfather had brought it back from the time he was ambassador. What I mean is Grandfather's grandfather.

In the thirties, Grandfather visited Rome on several occasions,
and Ambassador Villani introduced him to Mussolini. (The same
Villani who was later forcibly resettled in the town of Mező-
berény, not far from us. Come rain or come shine, Grandfather
and he met every third Sunday of the month—once again, the
former ruling class was up to its ears in intrigue—and Villani
read to him from his fascinating notes, which he'd jotted down
in Rome.) Since Grandfather praised the splendid palace, like a
proud and enthusiastic tourist guide, the Duce showed him
around (*Mappa mondo*).

"*Si, si, Eccelenza, la mia casa paterna,*" Grandfather commented
from time to time, which the Duce didn't understand until he was

told that my grandfather's father, may he rest in peace, was born within its walls in 1855, when the building housed the Austrian Embassy to the Vatican. But then he really understood.

The branches of a family tree can reach far and wide, weaving a net through time and space, creating personal contact with the past and the world at large. Consequently, an aristocrat, who is not tied to the present, and who is not tied to his country, or is, but is not tied hand and foot, can't be thinking that his country and culture "begin and end with Joseph II."

If he is honest and has eyes, he will see that this is not his world anymore, and yet it seems as if he were the one still holding it together. As if. In short, if he is honest and sees into the bargain, he will pose the question: what's the use? But no. Anyone asking what's the use is either a revolutionary, or a prey to depression. Besides, if there's no use in it as such, there is still work to be done. They go about their business as if nothing had happened (whereas it did! it did!)—or, failing all else, there's always the having of a good time, embedded as it may be in an obligatory sense of resignation.

I am—basically—talking about Grandfather. Grandfather had an incisive intelligence. He was as fabulously wealthy as the hero of a Jókai novel, incredibly powerful and influential ("where he went, there was no pardon to be had"), and also highly respected. And yet, he seemed to be standing on the sidelines. And yet, no one could have said that he's not participating in the game. And yet, he was not cynical. He was aware of his so-called historical responsibility.

Shortly before his death, Prime Minister Gyula Gömbös sent word to Grandfather that he'd like to show him his peach grove at Tétény. Grandfather couldn't abide Gömbös, hated him like the boils ("we were far removed from each other personally"), nor was he attached to peaches with anything like inordinate passion. But he went all the same. He found a very sick man fully aware of his condition. Walking tired him, so after a short stroll, they sat down "in the hall of the handsome villa." All around, along the walls, on the tops of the low bookcases, keys to cities and all sorts of diplomas, a whole collection. Gömbös talked about the recent past with melancholy and resignation, expressing his regret that Grandfather and his friends had misunderstood him.

"It is understandable, is it not," Grandfather nodded curtly. He looked at the sick man. He was going to die. How much easier it is to talk to him now, like this. "You see, when I go home after a public appearance where I am applauded, I don't see in my salon what you see"—and Grandfather made an involuntary gesture (derogatory)—"I see the portrait of one of Prince Rákóczi's companions in distress at Rodostó, let's say, or the Prince Primate crowning the Hungarian King, let's say, or the Chancellor countersigning the Edict of Tolerance, let's say, the one that was Napoleon's choice for king and minister of foreign affairs in forty-eight. I see it because it is there for me to see. I see my grandfather's portrait, who overthrew Schmerling, and when I think of them, I can't be at all certain that they would have applauded me. You, my honored friend, come home after one of your successful speeches or daring feats, and what do you see?" He looked around with another wave of the hand (derogatory). "You see all these documents attesting to your appointments, and you see tributes by the dozens, and thus you can hardly doubt the correctness and durability of your actions." Grandfather saw that Gömbös wasn't paying attention, but he went on with what he had to say. It felt good talking frankly like this. "What you don't know, my friend, and this is what kept us apart, is that a sense of historical responsibility is one thing, and the fleeting adulation of personal accomplishment quite another. These affect a person in very different ways. Provided," and here my Grandfather smiled, "that you can tell one from the other!"

Gömbös had grown tired by then, and in October (of 1936) he

died. At parting, he surprised Grandfather with a large glass jar of peach preserves. A ten-liter, mammoth jar. "Typical of Gömbös's caprice."

Later, during our forced resettlement, my mother generally used the "gömbös," as the preserve jar came to be called, for dill pickles. I can still see the fragile dill parachutes. Then, one day it fell on my head and was shattered into a thousand pieces. There were a lot of people, I remember, guests, and Father removed twenty-seven splinters from my eye. They watched in silence as Father went through his motions like a doctor.

"You could have been blinded twenty-seven times over!" he later said with pride, "twenty-seven times!"

"Finished!" he announced after a time, and the guests applauded. Papi wiped his forehead, then had a shot of brandy. In this instance, there was no question of historical responsibility; only the fleeting adulation due to personal accomplishment. He was pleased. As for me, I became superfluous for the night.

<h1 style="text-align:center">98.</h1>

Grandfather was not an essayist of history, but its philologist. He became member of the Upper House at a tender age and, though this was not the norm, right away he was made junior member of the committee in charge of the common affairs of the Monarchy, headquartered in Vienna. He was on the appropriations subcommittee. Assistant delegate, appropriations sub, or even top, or top-top, but always something of the sort: irreproachable, businesslike dealings with small practical matters while the existence and honor of a nation was the stake. While the question pertains to the existence of God, the answer is limited to the number of "Hail Marys" imposed as forgiveness for our sins.

Will there be war? This was in the air at the time. The very first day, the youthful member of the subcommittee is going through the documents and suddenly the question of the coal supply of the battle fleet "popped into his head" (i.e., whether the coal indicated in the records existed de facto). He did not suspect the wasp's nest he'd disturbed. There was no coal, how could there be; instead, they'd bought arms, which became a delicate bone of contention between the Belvedere and the Fleet. They had to suspend the session in order to come up with a delicate answer to the indelicate question.

"Ask before you ask," was Prime Minister Wekerle's paternal advice.

The delegates were given an elegant lunch in the Burg, followed by the Imperial *cercle,* where being addressed was considered a great honor. Having formed a semicircle, the Hungarian gentlemen waited for the king to walk around. Being a new man, and thinking it out of the question that the king would address him, Grandfather stood to the side so that—as a passive observer—he could have a good look at the proceedings.

Francis Joseph comes in, looks around like a severe, contentious head clerk, spots my twenty-somethingish grandfather, and without greeting anyone makes straight for him. The others step aside to clear the way. Seeing that he's alone in the middle and therefore in the way, Grandfather panics and steps aside, too, and is back in line with the others. Chagrined, the king changes direction and makes for him again, hurriedly, impatiently. The delegates make way for him again, Grandfather backing up along with them. As if drawn by a magnet, the king turns toward him again and shouts:

"*Halt endlich!*" then, part of the same gesture, he gives him a gracious smile. "Your grandfather was a faithful subject of mine. I expect no less of you," and with that he turns to the senior members of the company.

After the *cercle,* the others congratulated him, "That was a neat retreat, Móric."

"Good show, my boy," Wekerle said with a wink.

Grandfather studied the accounts, the contracts, the statements, the reports, and if he didn't understand something—a characteristic of men with brains—he would ask. Wekerle and Tisza brushed him off. They were practiced at it. Fine, but what if they don't sign the Serbian contract in time, Grandfather interpolated with the Prime Minister.

"In that case, I will take the Greek calendar as authentic. I will gain thirteen days, while the Serbs will feel honored," Wekerle smiled slyly.

The House had a good laugh at the annihilating response to the young man's disagreeable inquisitiveness. At other times he'd question Tisza in great detail, and at length. He can't get out of answering this one! And he did, for ten whole seconds.

"Fine, fine," the great Tisza nodded. "I am reminded of a question from the shorter catechism: If you believe, avow and aver all this, what good is it to you?!" and he sat down. Chuckles from right, left, and center.

Day by day, the world was steadily collapsing, and my grandfather could watch it from up close. With its characteristically terse and rigid understatements providing the marginal notes, as it were, his life seemed to be one continuous annotation to history. Sometimes not enough is enough, sometimes it is too much, but always, it is more than nothing. This is what he said. And also that things are either small, or they appear significant.

## 99.

"My notes may (or may not) prove the veracity of Prince Ligne's contention, to wit, that people quickly grow tired of the good, look for something better, find something worse, then insist on it ever after for fear of something still worse to come.

After the assassination at Sarajevo, some of us who knew the deceased accompanied the funeral train to Artstetten (on the left bank of the Danube, by St. Pölten). A stormy night. Court circles: general disapproval. It seems to me that if the funeral had been conducted with more ceremony, the leaders of the great powers could have met, and the history of the world could have taken a different turn. (Comment: the history of the world *never* takes a *different* turn.) As things stood, though, only the '*An meine Völker*' came and I enlisted in the army. My younger brother Alajos died on the battlefield.

I was given leave to attend Francis Joseph's funeral. There was something uncommonly dreary about this historical act, the way we laid in the grave and buried the Monarchy without knowing it. On the way back from Vienna, my life was spared by pure luck, as I happened to be traveling via Marcheggen and not Bruck, where Thallóczy, department head of the Ministry of Finance, was the victim of a train accident, and I would have surely traveled with him in the Pullman car.

Francis Joseph is by far the most insignificant dead man in the history of the world.

During the coronation I had the honor of accompanying the crown for three days, from the Castle vault to the Coronation Church, there and back, there and back.

To my surprise, I was appointed Privy Councilor.

The short stay and hasty departure of the royal couple made a bad impression all around.

A less known fact—early January 1917, rumors of an all-out submarine war. Danger of the U.S. joining the war, and contradictions re. the records of 1916 December 12. I wanted to make an interpolation. It was the custom to inform the Prime Minister in advance. Tisza shared my concerns, he told me that he himself was very much against it and had indicated as much to Chancellor Bethman-Hollweg, but the Germans turned a deaf ear. Resigned, he commented that as things stand, he'd have to take the odium of this decision on himself. He requested that I waive the interpolation. I waived it.

In the spring of 1917, I was called up to Pest. In Pest, Tisza offered a ministerial portfolio to István Bethlen and myself. No agreement was reached. At best, we'd have become political hostages of the discontented factions. I wish to note that the royal decree re. the franchise was prompted by the so-called Prussian *Osterbotschaft* proclamation, which brought in the reform there.

Then in June, as an answer to a crisis that had been brewing for months—and for want of anyone better—I was appointed to form a new government and to establish universal suffrage. In the early morning of June 12 I was ordered in for an audience, where His Majesty announced his intentions. I said no. Two more audiences in the course of the day. Finally, I agreed to head a minority government. On a weak footing from the word go. As I was waiting for His Majesty in the antechamber for the third time, I ran into Baron Nagy, the Hungarian head of the Cabinet Bureau, who'd just left His Majesty, with a bunch of files under his arm, and he asked me, "Have you any idea, Your Excellency, what is going on here today?!"

Not wishing to do without Andrássy's wise counsel, I requested that he be a minister *a latere.* He agreed, then at the last moment, reneged. I don't wish to go into the unforeseen reversals of fortune again involved in setting up a cabinet except to say that I had every reason to believe that the position of Min. of Cult. would not be below Apponyi's dignity, and that in the fall he could be my successor. I was disappointed, and so was he.

•   •   •

In the summer of 1917, the German Emperor, in Laxenburg. I have to present myself. The Iron Cross first class meant for me is lying on William II's desk. From the word go, the atmosphere like ice. Unpleasant. Also, me having to stand throughout. The Emperor expressed his disapproval of various Hungarian and Austrian affairs of state. He had nothing to do with either, I had nothing to do with the latter. I told him. His eyes flashed so murderously, I could hardly suppress a laugh. Whereas it wasn't funny. His Majesty was not happy that his Prime Minister hated him so.

The Emperor called us to account in icy tones, re., for instance, Kramař's having been granted clemency. I said, (a) it's Austria's internal affair, and I'm the Hungarian Prime Minister, (b) if he wishes to hear details for military reasons, he should turn to Prime Minister Seidler. He didn't like that. When I mentioned the efficacy of ending the war, he turned indignant.

'It seems you have no idea of the military situation!'

'Indeed, Your Majesty, the Western front, how shall I put it, is a blank spot for me.'

'Did you know that the French lose so many horses a day due to the pestilence?'

'This is the first I've heard of it, Your Majesty. Alas, in nineteen-fourteen Marshall Joffre used requisitioned taxicabs.'

At which, even more pointedly: 'Have you any idea the decision my general staff is forcing on me? I must choose between capturing Paris or Calais.' (Incredible! On July 6, 1917!) As if a young boy were bragging. With a slight bow, I said:

'May the effectuation pose no greater difficulty for Your Majesty than the choice.'

The Emperor gave me a long look. Had I anything to lose, I would have lost it all.

'*Genug, danke.*'

Just then a decoration fell off his chest, producing a sharp, shrill sound and I stepped back, whereupon His Majesty—to this day I don't know why—bent down to pick it up. But just then Bárczy, the secretary, leapt to the spot and, as if in a circus, they bumped heads.

'Idiot,' the Emperor said, waving an arm.

A most peculiar scene, indeed. What reflex could have made him bend down like that? I certainly didn't think of it. (By the way, years later, at Dorn, the Emperor mentioned 'the young man's *frech* and impertinent response.') I remained standing where I was, and the cross that was meant for me remained on top of the Emperor's desk. At the Court luncheon that followed, poor Bárczy thought I'd forgotten to pin it on, so he went and obtained one. When I whispered to him that I didn't get it in the first place, he couldn't decide if it was proper for him to wear his. I put his mind at ease. (Wasn't difficult.) Later, via the Budapest consulate, they sent along a second (!) class medal, *sans* commentary. Nor was I called to Germany while I was in office, not once. (In his book, *The Tragedy of Europe,* Ashmed Bartlett, English journalist, distorted the scene when he described it.)

Much ado. A German naval delegation looked me up in Buda with a view to convincing me of the efficacy of an ocean block-ade. (They knew I was against it, they knew that formerly Tisza had talked me out of bringing it up in Parliament. Tisza was against it too, but only I knew that.) They rolled big, impressive, colorful maps out in front of me, they knelt down beside them on the floor, but I was not willing. Afterward Bárczy said I was right, the Hungarian prime minister mustn't do that. I informed him that I remained standing as a private individual with a knee problem.

They showed me on the map where they'd blocked off the

Mediterranean, the North and the Eastern Sea, the La Manche and the St. George Channels. I naïvely asked about the area stretching from Brest to Bordeaux. They shook their heads. Three cheers in hindsight!

By August, the time was ripe for me to resign (so that in time for the fall session of Parliament a consolidated government could be formed). Since he was the head of the majority party, Tisza was the first person I informed about my resignation. We also discussed my successor. Among others, I mentioned Klebelsberg, who was Tisza's secretary of state. Tisza didn't respond. He turned away and looked out the window. He said nothing. Neither did I. Then at long last:

'No, no, he won't do.'

My silence turned into surprise. Then slowly, as if he were about to reveal something of the utmost importance and of great consequence, he said:

'Do you know what he did to me?' Good old Klebelsberg, I couldn't imagine what he could have done to Tisza, who then turned away from the window: 'For a full year he let me believe he's a Calvinist!'

Indeed, that won't do at all! Needless to say, someone else became my successor despite the fact that in June he (Andrássy) left me high and dry. But possibly, this is what influenced the King.

Because political upheavals and visits to the front made it difficult for His Majesty to come to Pest, I made several trips to Reichenau and Baden. (Second class, which many people didn't understand, and even brought it up against me. The second-class wagon goes to the same place, I said. This made them think I was a miser.) In order to avoid calling attention to myself, I got off someplace after Bruck and took an automobile to Court, where discretion was not the better part of valor, and so certain things reached my ears that should have come to my prime ministerial ears to begin with, e.g., the French peace talks between Revertera and Prinz Sixtus."

## 100.

Once in the early 1960s we spent the summer with Nicolas Graf Revertera, Nicolas Graf Revertera's son. They happened to be next in line to absolve our obligation to "spend the summer with a quasi-rural cousin." Gothic Styrian countryside, rushing mountain stream (we "rode" atop it on a rubber mattress, which had its dangers, if you ask me, while Tante laughed and cheered us on from the shore, driving along and competing on her jeep), a wild, primeval landscape, mountains with their heads in the clouds, rock climbing. (Once we pushed a boulder the size of an armchair down into the valley; it bounded down like a ball, the toy of a giant, bounding higher and higher over the peacefully grazing herd of cattle at the bottom of the valley, crashing headlong into the trees opposite and hitting home like a meteor. We got scared. There was nobody there. You can be terribly alone on the top of such a big mountain, or mountain ridge, and we couldn't help thinking that we were close to the sky. My brother and I didn't say a word to each other, we kneeled down in the profound silence that came in the wake of the stone and made confession; we confessed the rolling stone, but it was no good, we felt that we'd sinned, we'd damaged the mountain.)

The castle! As I conjure up images from my childhood, it's not a building I see, but details; a room here and there, somewhere else part of a hallway that doesn't connect any rooms, just on its own, no more than a fragment in my memories. This is how everything is scattered within—rooms, stone steps that descended in such intricate ways, and also the narrow spiral staircases; you circled around in their half-light like blood in your veins. Tower rooms, high-hanging balconies, unexpected verandahs that you reached through miniature entryways—all this is still with me and I shall carry it with me for the rest of my days. The image of this house, it's like something that has plunged into me from some great height, and when it touched ground inside, it was shattered into bits.

Onkel looked like Jean Gabin. He was a taciturn and handsome old man, monumental, like an ancient oak. He let me go hunting with him. Roe-buck. I had to keep two steps behind. When he stopped, I stopped. At such times, I may have napped, it was so early in the morning. When he pulled the trigger, he hit the mark. It made me proud. I saw myself in the place of the hunter. The glance of a deer, they say, is the most human of all the animals, human and sad. But it's the flies I remember, there were always flies on or around one's eyes. In German hunting terminology, blood is not *Blut*, but *Schweiss*. At first I was corrected (every time), later praised (every time).

My brand-new jeans rubbed at the thighs. The oak didn't complain, but from time to time he threw me a pointed look over his shoulder, at which I held my legs farther apart, and for a while, tried walking like that. Admittedly, no one saw me like that except for the deer, but not for long. But soon I walked regular again, and then I started rubbing again, and got that look again. But maybe I got it all mixed up and it wasn't Revertera. We wouldn't talk for hours on end. Being together and not talking, this was unfamiliar to me. Till then I kept quiet only when I was alone.

We got back to the castle again around ten-thirty, when we had an *ample* breakfast, then I took a nap. In the afternoon we went for snipe. No, in the evening. Busy working days.

# 101.

"Having been convinced that this was not mere hearsay. I decided I'd go and present myself. Three possibilities: (1) Clarify the situation with His Majesty. No problem, but it would prejudice the outcome of future talks and would embarrass His Majesty. Why would he continue to have further confidence in the responsible Prime Minister, if such talks could be kept a secret from him. (2) Simpler still: resign without getting further information. The Crown's confidence has been shaken, I cannot accept responsibility for talks that were kept from me, and a minister without responsibility: pure nonsense. (If it fails, let it fail, if it succeeds, so much the better.) (3) More complicated: since for some reason they were kept from me, I cannot decide if the outcome of the talks will be successful or not, and am not in a position to cover for His Majesty should the outcome be undesirable.

On the occasion of my farewell appearance—I'd given my state of health and my chronic sleep disturbance as the cause—His Majesty was surprisingly generous. He must have suspected that I had suspected a thing or two. He recommended me for the highest award which, though showing my gratitude, I declined and instead requested that as an expression of his continuing confidence in me, he should follow my advice one last time and inform the German Crown Prince in writing about the necessity of a Belgian and Elsace-Lotharingian restitution, without which peace would not be forthcoming. Also, that full victory would demand a great deal of blood, and is uncertain into the bargain. He did so (though in a more politic manner than I had suggested, without mentioning Belgium), and Count Ledochowsky, colonel and aide-de-camp, took it to the Kronprinz. (Prinz Sixtus published the letter in his book, p. 277.)

I quit my velvet chair feeling I had done something worthwhile. Being fully aware of the modern *'secret de roi,'* I was hoping to cover the King with the letter and also, should the venture go astray, the 'I said so back in the summer of 1917' could prove a handy (bona fide) alibi. However, during the Chernin–Clemenceau dispute in May 1918, they forgot about the letter because they considered it 'out of date,' whereas it would have made a lot of embarrassing explanations quite unnecessary. I resigned from my post as minister without portfolio in Wekerle's government for the second time in eight months. I could not go along with the explanations fabricated for the sake of the public.

The 10th government crisis that broke out presented me with the opportunity to come out strongly against His Majesty's intention to give up the throne—politically inconsistent, militarily catastrophic—while from the point of view of political law and dynamics, taking into consideration that the heir to the throne was underage, it was also ill-advised. (Napoleon I, Charles X.)

Back to the farewell audience of August 1917. Though he'd deserted me and His Majesty did not consider him *too* dependable, I advocated Andrássy as my successor. The appointment fell to Wekerle (thanks to Daruváry's intervention, no doubt), who was an expert tactician, but did not enjoy His Majesty's good graces, who'd made Francis Ferdinand's antipathies his own. (The F.F.–Wekerle antipathy was mutual.) I attempted to bring His Majesty around. But seeing that he could not be swayed, I stressed the importance of trust. In times of war, especially. (In January, I was asked to join the government specifically to check up on Wekerle. Awkward.)

His Majesty sounded me out: what would happen if 'by way of

trial' Károlyi were given the appointment? I had neglected to mention him.

'He would request Your Majesty to resign over the telephone'—which happened on November 18th. We laughed. There was no reason to. In the summer of 1918—I had resigned from active politics almost completely in the meantime—I ran into Marshall Böhm-Ermolli in Vienna. (I had served under him as a volunteer: as Prime Minister, I had repeatedly proposed his person to His Majesty for inspecting the Italian front.) He was headed to the King in Baden. On Michaeler Platz we were joined by former Minister of Foreign Affairs Burian.

They saw the situation in a dark light.

'The worst part of it is that even the Germans have no confidence in a victory anymore.' I called up an acquaintance of mine in Pest. Wanted to see some big shots [sic!] in the evening, if possible. I took the five o'clock express, and by ten several of us were sitting around dinner. Later Tisza joined us as well.

'It is possible,' I propose to him, 'that the war will not end in victory. In any event, it is nearing its end. It is time to think about a peace treaty. Transylvania and Croatia and possibly the northern counties should be brought up during peace negotiations. We should start reflecting and taking measures to ensure their autonomy. Otherwise we will lose them.'

'Could you repeat what you just said, Móric?' he asked. He sounded annoyed.

'Otherwise, we will lose them.'

He looked at me with such surprise and animosity, you'd think that the partition of the country was my idea. What in fact followed neither of us could have foreseen—the parade of historical folly, lack of vision, and horrendous selfishness.

'The union of Transylvania and Croatia's constitutional standing are Hungary's internal affairs, and as such cannot form part of any international negotiation.'

I mentioned to him that not long ago, when I was in Prague, I saw the so-called ethnographic map of Hungary, more or less with the later Trianon borders.

'Ridiculous,' he said, 'that would bring Geszt (the Tisza estates) under Romania!'

Again we laughed, and Geszt fell to Romania. (It didn't fall there, it remained in Hungary, 870 meters from the frontier.) Any further 'reflection and taking of measures' seemed futile, and I went back home to the village. Tisza's eyes were opened only after his trip to Sarajevo. His undaunted respect for reality led him to make the following fatal statement on October 16, 1918:

'I must agree with Count Károlyi. We have lost the war.'

This statement legitimized Károlyi, my wife's elder cousin, an antidynastic defeatist who subsequently became president of the Republic in 1918, then handed power over to the Communist Béla Kun, leaving his country to fend for itself, while he left it by car on July 4, 1919 (with my help), returning only on May 8, 1946, when it no longer involved a risk. Many people hoped that he would fight for the bourgeois democracy of 1918. Instead, he represented the proletarian dictatorship in Paris, though truth to tell, he later took up Rajk's cause, and resigned. He suffered no financial drawback, and died in his own home, while his 'people' . . . but I'd rather not go into that. His passionate destructiveness did not spare him either, neither his person, nor his memory. *Conduire ne puis, suivre ne daigne.* This is how I had characterized him years before.

In early October 1918. Burian ordered Tisza, Andrássy and Apponyi, with whom I was well acquainted, to Vienna to discuss the proposal for a cease-fire to be presented to President Wilson. It was tragic and intensely painful for me to see and hear these three distinguished gentlemen, who had played leading roles in Hungarian politics during the previous twenty to thirty years, and who had been desperately at odds with each other many times, to see them during the final hours of their country. [As for me, this is how I see my grandfather . . . ] Tisza was under the stranglehold effect of his visit to Sarajevo, the melancholy Andrássy was witnessing the destruction of his father's great accomplishments, while Apponyi had to concede that his country's independence and self-reliance, for which he had fought all his life, could be realized only through substantial territorial losses. Having participated in some of the discussions, I could not share in the general optimism regarding Wilson's swift and more or less favorable response.

I had had a glimpse or two into the witch's cauldron of the Monarchy's politics, which was anything but dualistic. The signs of decay were already in evidence when the corpse was still alive.

United States of Austria? (Herron Lammasch, February 1918.) If this is what they wanted, Wilson and the others would have taken the time to see to the conditions. Never in the history of the world has a council of four had such enormous power in their hands, the fate of hundreds of millions. The dismemberment of the Donauraum was a success (revenge, reprisal, *Gloire et Revanche*, hang the Kaiser, etc.—these were Clemenceau's leitmotifs), but despite the unlimited power and possibilities, they couldn't come up with a new, lasting configuration. (Something the Congress of Vienna had managed before them: it created the 19th century. It may not have been a big deal, a *Prachtstück*, but something, all the same.) Hitler, Stalin, brown and red dictatorships, this is the annihilating consequence of Versailles-Trianon. The proof of politics is in the pudding.

On the other hand, one wonders whether a confederate

state—basically, a Danube Confederation as envisaged by Lajos Kossuth—could have worked. Might not foreign irredentist propaganda and the domestic right to self-determination have escalated the centrifugal effect? And in parts of Hungary, especially, how would the Hungarians, who'd have found themselves in the minority, have reached, et cetera.

However, this is entirely hypothetical.

On the other hand, the Republic of Councils was not hypothetical. Awkward. Social ideas worth considering and not entirely to be rejected in the greatest chaos, spiced with infinite stupidity and, to put it mildly, human weakness. Also, difficult times personally—my wife, the daughter of the president of the anti-Bolshevik government at Szeged. People's commissar Hamburger was kind enough to congratulate me as the husband of the most valuable hostage of the Republic of Councils. A doubtful commendation. For a short time I was also in prison, as the guest of the Lenin boys in the Batthyányi cellar, Cherni and Co., leaving my wife and our firstborn to fend for themselves. [That's Papi! My papi! My papi's born! Here it is, in writing!]

The regime following the Republic of Councils put me under quarantine both socially and politically, but at the very least, relegated me to the sidelines. My efforts with respect to universal suffrage fell under criticism, and my attitude under Bolshevism was also criticized, both publicly and in private. This especially because in early August 1919, I interceded with General Gorton in the interest of giving free passage to the people's commissars, including Béla Kun, who was one of the most loathsome fellows I had ever met. Especially the Sacher brigade (Hungarian aristocrats who held their 'meetings' in the Sacher in Vienna) criticized me heatedly. So much water under the bridge, which is a *lot* of water . . . Having been called before Honor Tribunals, I was given

604

# 61.

I embraced my father round the waist—an ancient oak, Rákóczi's very own!—and the plastic belt buckle pressed into my face.

"Papi, darling, you know not what you do, please don't do it, I don't want them to hear everything, they mustn't hear everything," I sobbed, whimpered, blubbered, hiccuped, I hiccuped up the words, "they're animals, animals, Papi, dear, you have no idea, they tape all your words and play it back, sometimes on fast forward, sometimes slowed down, and they have a good laugh at it in there, Papi, forgive me."

My father scorned this sort of moping, he'd had enough, and pushed me away. Brushed me off, to be precise. This sort of tearful outburst never occurred again. In this respect I am like him: disciplined.

# 62.

The palace staff were shocked—and as my great-grandfather and family noted mischievously—they looked upon this newest aristocratic whimsy with disapproval, namely, that in these danger-fraught times the "palace" should be planning an excursion. And to make matters worse, they're leaving the old Excellency behind to fend for himself. Old man Tóth, who'd been in the service of the family for two hundred years by then, grumbled the most of anybody. (Immediately at the outset of said service, for some reason which documents do not reveal, but a letter written by Szidónia Pálffy to her sister-in-law, Mária Eck, in 1717 makes clear, they were given the extraordinary privilege of calling their Christened son after the son of the count. They called all their firstborn troops without jeopardizing the dynasty once and for all in Hungary. In Tatabánya the miners gave me a heated locomotive. (We became 'acquainted' during the Republic of Councils when they set up an independent Soviet. They wanted nothing to do with Béla Kun.) Bia–Torbágy, Budaörs, the military didn't stop me, side streets to Buda, to A. I gave him the message, along with my opinion.

Nothing came of it.

The legitimists disapproved and criticized my stand on this many times, and in large numbers.

As I said, I withdrew from politics until at a public meeting around 1930, for no apparent reason, Prime Minister Bethlen called me 'the quartermaster of the Bolsheviks.' Alas, twenty years later, when my estates were nationalized and I was forced to relocate, they forgot to credit me with it. History is a careless accountant of the receipts and expenditures columns. Its columns are different from ours, from the people's, I fear.

In response, I ran for representative in Tapolca and was voted in. (So that after ten years as Prime Minister, I should be able to witness Bethlen's fall from power. Though he undoubtedly consolidated Horthy's regime, he did not deserve his sad end either.) Instead of practical politics, I spent my time checking appropriations accounts and budgets, in words and in writing. Closed committee debates, big addresses in front of large audiences—these are not for me. I became member of Committee No. 33, which reviewed the coercive measures. There were six or eight of us in opposition. Still, we were able to accomplish one or two things, especially with respect to the Jewish question, and in concrete cases, even to intervene.

As a member of the Defense Committee, I repeatedly espoused the view that although we are well armed, we had no allies at the hub of the Slavic-German axis, and also, we suffered enough losses in 1914–18, and should therefore stay out of the games big powers play.

In early 1938 Austrian Minister of Foreign Affairs Schuschnigg, Guido Schmidt and Count Ciano were here to negotiate. Franco's acknowledgment, Italy's withdrawal from the League of Nations, et cetera. At a dinner my wife was sitting between Ciano and Schmidt [Grandmother hemmed in by the world powers!?]. According to Ciano's diaries (Bern, 1946, p. 87), my wife made no bones about the Italians being responsible for Hungary's subdivision, and that it's easy to take a country apart, but very difficult to put it back together again. Whether she said this or not I don't know. But when Ciano asked, leaning over the pike with Orly sauce, why I didn't visit Rome during my term in office, she said:

'Italy's actions at the time made it quite impossible.' Then she added something pointed about loyalty between allies.

Be that as it may, I remember perfectly well that at the coronation of Pope Pius XII (which I attended in the company of Gyula Czapik, former Prime Minister Károly Huszár and Zsembery in March 1939, but which did not carry as much weight as an historical hiatus, nor as much symbolic significance as the funeral of Queen Victoria or Emperor Francis Joseph, both of which I witnessed), Ciano stepped up to me on the podium, and confidentially whispered in my ear that the entry of the Germans into Czechoslovakia was just around the corner. Then he added, *'Rassurez Madame que nous n'y sommes pour rien,'* whether he then added, *'cette fois,'* I no longer recall.

Having returned to my hotel, a telegram from Stockholm awaited me with the news of my younger brother Ferenc's death. (A brain tumor that had gone undetected. He was one of Olivercrona's patients.)

·  ·  ·

On a dark, damp November night, a black automobile stopped in front of my castle. Prime Minister Pál Teleki alighted, unaccompanied. He was a friend from my youth. In 1917 I had appointed him head of the welfare organization for veterans, and he subsequently became an adherent of the Szeged Line.

Hungary had joined the Tripartite Accords just three days previously (Nov. 23, 1940). Having returned from the Belvedere, Teleki gave an elegiac speech, something which for those not in the know must have seemed strange. On this particular night, too, he appeared to be in exceedingly low spirits. We were still sipping the Château Lafite '28, a gift from my cousin. He complained about his minister of foreign affairs Csáky [my beautiful Aunt Irmi's former husband!], that he'd gone too far in the matter of the German minorities. He told me about his meeting with Hitler at Belvedere.

'That madman is bent on bathing Europe in blood!'

Word for word, that madman is bent on bathing Europe in blood. He also said that he was feeling—crazy as it may sound—that Hitler was bent on launching an attack against the Soviet Union, a dual front, German defeat, Hungary the theater of operations. We talked at length—at Laffitte-length—about the situation, and concluded that we must sign a friendship and nonaggression pact with the Soviets. Hitler couldn't take offense publicly, for at this time he was an ally of the Soviets, and should he attack Russia in the spring nonetheless, there'd be a theoretical—though highly unlikely—possibility for neutrality (Finland). Several weeks later the news came: the naval banner with a hammer and sickle cannot be raised in Szeged. Ah, *bitte* . . . Whereas a pact like that would have come in handy in Yalta.

This thought did not disappear without a trace, it seems, or maybe the war situation got worse. In either case, after Teleki died,

Bethlen and my humble self were repeatedly ordered to Horthy's presence.

The Regent had the idée fixe that the war would end with 'a round table *Konferenz*,' and since he held on to this idea even after Casablanca (January 1943) and Roosevelt's 'unconditional surrender,' I can only assume that he thought Hitler wouldn't last till the end of the war. Be that as it may, he seemed disappointed over the debacle of July 20, 1944.

I remember coming from the Castle with Bethlen once, who said in German:

'*Dem Menschen ist nicht zu helfen.*' Humanity is past redemption.

Not that he or I were in a better pass ourselves. In late March 1941 I attended Lajos Staud's funeral. I'd been a guest in his home many times during Béla Kun's reign. Several people of note were in evidence. I heard someone say that Hungary wanted to join the German *einmarsch* on Yugoslavia, where the pro-German government had collapsed. I tried to reach Prime Minister Teleki, but ended up in the painful position of having to send him a no-nonsense letter with the information about the proposed attack, calling it an ignominious act without peer, et cetera.

I asked for an immediate audience.

It was granted. Teleki was distraught. He said that the army was coercing him, which would mean war with the West, et cetera, but he couldn't see a way out, except suicide.

'That'll make the country think! It'll bring the country to its senses!'

For a long time I said nothing which, or so it seemed to me then, he understood. Then I made him promise to forget it, a suicide results in touching funeral orations, nothing more. He promised. However, if Horthy doesn't veto our involvement, he's going to resign. To his face, Horthy was against the occupation, but he never issued an order to that effect. Shoulder to shoulder, we were once again marching to our doom.

During the war crimes tribunals of 1945–46, at Bárdossy's I think, there was mention of Teleki's alleged farewell letter to Horthy. I will continue hoping till the end of my life that it was apocryphal, because certain expressions contained therein ('igno-minious act without peer,' et cetera) were word for word the same as the phrases in the letter I had written to him.

At the end of June 1941, I heard from a reliable source (General B., head of the Finance subgroup) that the offensive against the Germans was about to be launched. I rushed to see Prime Minis-ter Bárdossy.

'We want to follow the Germans into the quagmire? Is that it?'

He categorically denied it. He said it was out of the question, and in the spirit of a chiefs-of-staff proposition, the Council of Ministers had just brought a decision to the contrary. Relieved, I returned to my castle. Then a couple of days later (June 27, 1941), I heard about Hungary's declaration of war over the radio. I rushed back to Bárdossy. Reproaches, recriminations, et cetera.

'Yes,' he said looking me in the eye, 'the military would have rebelled if we had stayed idle again. It is impossible to mobilize for years and not take action. It is impossible to talk about an enemy for years without doing something about it.'

I asked Defense Minister Bartha if he was fully aware of the consequences of such a move.

'Naturally. This was our last chance to join.' And join they did, thoroughly, without our knowledge, without consulting us, and in the face of the law.

The bombing of Kassa, which served as the excuse for the decla-ration of war, was the work of the Germans. First Lieutenant Krúdy, the director of the airport, assured me of this over and over. I was interred with him at Kőhida. Then we were both deported to Heves County in 1951. I don't believe that anybody asked Horthy, or that he had a say in this. The General Staff, Werth & Co., had grown far too strong, making all sorts of promises to Hitler, of which the government, and Horthy personally, could have known very little.

A small detail: on December 12, 1941, upon orders from Hitler [Hittler: for some reason Grandfather always wrote it with two t's] a tragicomic declaration of war on the United States. Ignoring it, we met with members of the Embassy same as before. One of the diplomatic wives was painting the Horthy family, visiting the Castle as before, ignoring the state of war. Before Christmas she asked me if I would go with her to buy a frame. She was looking for a frame bearing the Hungarian crown.

'Why? What for?'

'I just painted the Admiral, you see, and I have a good sketch of the painting, and I will soon have to leave your beautiful country, Móric, and once I've left, I'd like to make a present of it to Otto (i.e., Otto von Habsburg). *He'll be so pleased!*'

Oh, that delicate American *feel* for our European embroilments!

Something of more weighty historical interest. At the December 16th, 1941, session of Parliament, where ignoring the agenda, Bárdossy got up and announced the declaration of war made without consulting Parliament, Zoltán Tildy, head of the Smallholders, gave a speech. Without wasting a single word on what he'd just heard, without protesting against this manner of declaring war or demanding the immediate remedy to their not being consulted—he lauded Horthy and the recapture of Bácska in the spring, as if he were making a toast at a party. (Bárdossy was sentenced and executed in 1946 precisely because of these things—

the annexation of Bácska, and the declaration of war without consulting Parliament. At the time, the selfsame Tildy was Prime Minister and President of the Republic with the right to grant clemency. In any case, the transcript of the above-mentioned session became restricted material under his term of office (or was it destroyed?). —His role in 1956 didn't do anybody much good either. He was sentenced to six years in prison.)"

## 102.

The strong, intricate mechanism of the pruning shears, the fascinating beauty of the springs, the stalks, twigs, fruit trees cut on the bias, the pipe, the smoke, the smell, the brown, checkered (Esterházy checks?) breeches, the gray cotton socks, the beard and the pink silken lips: this is what I remember of the "pruning afternoons" Grandfather and I spent together. He liked me to be around as he worked because I was a quiet, well-behaved child, I knew how to be quiet, and liked it, too. I didn't bother him either in his work or in his ongoing monologues. It was as if he were telling his stories to me: not my father, but me.

"Bárdossy was as smart as they come. Astute and quick-witted. Which led him astray. There was no way to understand this century through logic."

"Does it hurt?" Grandfather gave me a look of surprise. I think he must have thought, does this century hurt him? He didn't answer, while I was thinking of the tree, whether the pruning pains the tree.

"Apponyi, on the other hand, was full of good intentions. He could find something good even in Clemenceau. Good intentions are not enough."

"And what was Grandfather not enough in?"

"What makes you think I was not enough?"

I pointed up at the burned-down half wing of the castle, then "down" at his darned pullover. He nodded ("I see your point, child").

"I was too short on determination and too long on patience."

<br>

## 103.

"In early 1942 I was seated next to Ribbentrop at a dinner. He talked a lot of rubbish. He's spectacularly ignorant about history. He's 'completely' sure of victory, *'sein Führer'* has already forecast a Soviet defeat (October 3, 1941: *Der Gagner gebrochen und nie sich erheben wird)*—the enemy is beaten and can never pull itself together again, he's taken over the direction of the military, England will lose India, the U.S. is just bluffing (this was his way of bluffing with me), German-Soviet relations had deteriorated because of us, Hungarians, because with the Second Vienna Awards, the new Romanian borders, guaranteed to please us, stood in the way of a Russian offensive to the south via Focsani, et cetera. Was he really so naïve as to try and make me believe it? (According to the transcripts of the Nuremberg trials, their plans for an offensive had been drawn up much earlier.) Our exchange was strained and drew the frightened ears of the table.

I said to him that perhaps the bombing of Belgrade might have also taken the wind out of Stalin's sails. The Russians are such sentimentalists.

'Excuse me?!'

And furthermore, I can't comprehend, because it's incomprehensible, why his (*sein*) Führer, instead of liberating the various Soviet states who hate the Muscovite yoke, forges them into one with requisitions and strict police measures to give them a name, thereby inadvertently training partisans. He let it past his ears.

Over coffee at the end of the meal (the bitter end), he told me some things about the events surrounding the Molotov talks held in a Berlin bomb shelter, the sporadic British air raid, while I told him about my first and last audience with Kaiser Wilhelm, and requested that he let his (*seinem*) Führer know. At which he blew his top. Many people looked up, though many did just the opposite, veritably disappearing inside their coffee cups.

'But Count, how can you compare Wilhelm II with mine (*meinem*) Führer?!' Then he turned to the man sitting next to him and didn't talk to me for the rest of the evening. The waiters were standing by. They were waiting to clear off the table.

On the other hand, thanks to this scandalous conversation, I didn't have to reject Horthy outright, who had just then taken the curious idea into his head to recommend me, among others, as a possible successor to Bárdossy, whom he'd been wanting to get rid of for some time (and in which he succeeded in March 1942). Needless to say, the dinner had made me persona non grata.

In 1942, after the disgraceful Novisad episode, I saw Horthy.

'What a shame that I hadn't been granted the title of *vitéz*,' I said to him.

'Oh. But it's still not too late . . .' He hadn't a clue what I was driving at.

'Oh, but it's too late for *me*,' I said, 'because had I been a *vitéz* before Novisad, I could have resigned now. But, never mind. I don't think I'll ask.'

And that's how it was. I never asked, even if the not asking hadn't quite taken the shape I had envisaged.

Italian capitulation, after the fall of Mussolini (1943), at Horthy's. One partner left the alliance. We should do likewise. I brought up the example of Prussian General Yorck with Napoleon, the Convention of Taurrogen, 1812. He was in complete agreement. He was especially excited by the reference to Taurrogen. He made me repeat it twice, then overflowing with a profusion of gratitude, saw me to the door. Disproportionate. Later I found out that Bethlen had already looked him up in Kenderes, where he spoke in a similar spirit, and received a similar promise. (So Bethlen wrote Kállay, too.) Yet again, I returned to the village reassured, and yet again, I had to hear over the radio the exact opposite: new divisions had been directed to the eastern front.

In August 1943, Tildy, Peyer, Rassay and myself ask Kállay to declare Budapest an open city. We're still deep into the discussion when the sirens scream. We go down to the ministerial shelter. The supreme command of the army are already there. For some reason, they're surprised by the new arrivals, us. They're quick to reassure us that they're only bombing Wiener Neustadt. Right away, I'm reassured: my younger sister was an army nurse there! [The ravishingly beautiful, blind Mia Tant!] Nothing comes of the open city.

As the bombing of Budapest escalated, the diplomats were appointed to so-called 'alternate lodgings.' I was assigned the nunciature, where Papal nuncio Rotta was quartered with me from March 1944. He was a God-fearing man, whose piety, I might add, surpassed his political gifts. In the case of Msg. Verolino, his *uditore,* this was the other way around. Following long and cumbersome negotiations (my father-in-law and Bishop Apor, who was later killed, took it upon themselves to help exert pressure) he was willing, not as nuncio, but as the head, or doyen, of the diplomatic corps, to exert his influence with Horthy (who withdrew for weeks at the time) and the Swedish king, asking them to bring pressure on Hitler against the further deportation of the Jews. In Pest, the deportations stopped.

On October 15 the nuncio was informed that Horthy's wife

would like to request asylum at the nunciature. She would have set off immediately, but having been informed, the Germans stopped her twenty kilometers from Csákvár, and turned her back. Rotta was a heavy tea drinker. On that particular day, he had outdone himself.

When the situation seemed all but lost, a so-called Crown Council was held in the royal castle. Several former prime ministers (my father-in-law, et cetera), with the Chief of Staff and two or three generals. (In late August Romania also seceded and declared war on us, whereby we remained Hitler's last satellite. Henchmen, they said later. But in any case, the last.)

On September 8, 1944, a lengthy meeting—Bethlen, who was hiding in the countryside, in the uniform of a full colonel, plus ten or twelve others.

'The Russians will march in when and where they wish,' Chief of Staff Vörös informed us. 'A couple of days ago General Guderian told me confidentially that they're not going to turn the war around with the V-2s.'

Bethlen issued an uncategorical call for an immediate cease-fire. Everyone else in the same spirit, more or less. Two comments from me.

'Why do they ask for our opinion in this desperate situation, when they didn't ask after Kassa either, just went head on at the Soviets? An immediate cease-fire! I do not wish to see the bitter gratification whereby raising their hats like hotel porters, discredited generals should have to be telling me again, 'You are right, Your Excellency!'

'You are right, Your Excellency,' Bethlen said with a dour smile.

Later that night I reached Csákvár with the news that the decisive step would be taken on the morrow. But it wasn't. Again, it wasn't. Even at the eleventh hour, five weeks had to go by before Horthy's radio address. Too late, toned down. He didn't say that he'd signed a cease-fire, but that he *would*, when the publishing abroad of the accomplished fact would have prevented the actions of the Szálasi rabble. And even this was retracted in the bathroom (!) up in the Castle, when Horthy, though *vi ac metu,* to be sure, asked for Hitler's protection, and handed power over to Szálasi. Like Károlyi to Kun in 1919. It is regrettable that the Hacha became the model for the Knight of the Order of Theresa and not Moscado [?] (Toledo).

On the other hand, without the capitulation, Hitler's counter-measures and deportations would have been graver that they were. There might even have been a civil war lead by Szálasi and supported by the Germans against Horthy and the Russians! Also probably a lighter, more friendly Russian occupation, and certainly better chances at the peace talks. If anyone were to reproach us, i.e., Horthy, with the Benelux, Danish or Norwegian examples, the geographical situation and the sea can't be ignored. *Rebus sic stantibus,* everything according to its own circumstances.

I know from one of the participants that without the knowledge of Lakatos, who was then Prime Minister, and on direct orders from Horthy, on October 11, four weeks after the Crown Council, a preliminary cease-fire agreement was signed by Géza Teleki (Pál's son), Faragho, a certain Szentiványi, et cetera, in Moscow. Ciphered material re. above with Vattay. Thanks to this agreement, Stalin didn't have Horthy brought before a tribunal as a war criminal, though for political reasons, four of his prime ministers died of unnatural causes within five years.

In November 1944 I was confidentially told that I was on the Germans' list of deportees. I readied myself, I waited. Awkward. The Gestapo had me arrested, Sopronkőhida, along with Mindszenty (at the time bishop of Veszprém), László Rajk, Pali Jávor (inflammation of the gums!), Bajcsy-Zsilinszky. From Christmas the executions were stepped up, but since Kőhida was maintained for common criminals and not political prisoners, whose life expectancy, as we know, is not long, both the gallows and the executioner were missing from the basic furnishings. The former was improvised in a barn by the outbuildings, while to make up for the latter, they found a man condemned as a common criminal, a ventriloquist. Until we learned about his latest occupation, he had been entertaining us in the evening with his art, but later this stopped.

I had former Prime Minister Lakatos, who was biding his time there, too, for a while, to relate to me the history of the Admiral's manuscript, the one he signed in the bathroom in October. It was not edifying.

Two shocking executions. One around 9 o'clock on December 24 (!), that of my Parliamentary colleague Bajcsy-Zsilinszky; a dreamer, as good-intentioned as they come, a consummate optimist. For instance, that first Schuschnigg, then the Poles wouldn't let the Germans into their country. Just two days before his death he reassured me that the Anglo-Saxons wouldn't stand for this *justizmord*. The other was Niky Odescalchi's, who'd gotten lost with his aeroplane.

We didn't have it bad physically, but the specially set up military tribunal kept 'promising' the rope.

I was interrogated. They accused me of many things in minute detail, quoting certain of my comments at the Crown Council meeting of September 8 *verbatim* ('If they didn't ask when we entered the war, why would they, et cetera'); treason and cowardice,

I heard, was taken for granted because I had demanded a cease-fire, and throughout the war I was supposed to have acted in a disloyal manner vis-à-vis Hitler (which, after all, I could not deny).

I never came before the tribunal though. To escape from the approaching Russians, they drove us to Bavaria, *per pedes,* then cattle cars. Plus one night in Mauthausen.

The end of the war found me in Bavaria, at a peasant's, in a mill. The cow was just calving, and we were assisting. The Allied troops were heading east, and the soldiers waved. Was it to us, or the cow?

Despite advice to the contrary, I took my son Mátyás, whom the end of the war also found there, and we went back to Pest. A scene of devastation. I had to participate as a witness in the trials of the war criminals. I had to be on hand at all times, practically under house arrest. With the exception of the anti-Semitic Jewish executioners Baky and Endre, I felt sympathy with respect to those condemned *ab ovo.* I answered only what they asked, and as sparing of words as possible. Unfortunately, the questions were precise and comprehensive. They relied on the notes of Under-Secretary of State Bárczy, a sort of transition between *Wharheit* and *Dichtung,* truth and poetry. For months in Pest, I had to be 'available' by phone. It was one of the most painful and awkward experiences of my life."

104.

"Sándor Márai was also subpoenaed (along with Grandfather) for István Antal's trial, held in the Markó Street building of the People's Tribunal. On the way, he meets Bárczy von Bárcziháza, another witness. They were hanging people every week by then out in the yard, sometimes every day. Ten years was considered clemency. One floor down, they had just granted Szombathelyi clemency in this manner. On this particular day, a couple of minutes before their arrival, they were just hanging Endre and Baky. Bárczy, the ring leader, dressed with impeccable elegance, was chatting as he walked down the corridor. The rabble, who had congregated for the smell of blood, were staring out the windows. On their way back, they saw the two hanged men through an open window. Their faces had been covered by then.

'Oh, Endre!' Bárczy said lightly, as if greeting an acquaintance. Except for a *lorgnon* in his hand, we might be in the cellar of the Conciergerie.

The witnesses arrived one by one, including several interesting members of the *ancien régime:* the lawyer Vladár, who succeeded Antal as Minister of Justice, and who was leaning against the window frame, smoking a pipe. He said of Endre that he was 'an unfortunate fellow' who had been 'a fine public administration professional, especially at Gödöllő.' In reality, he was a drunk and a sadist, a madman fired by all the despotism of the petty noble careerist.

Grandfather arrived almost in rags, a crushed hat, knee breeches. Even so, he was the most elegant man in the city. Or possibly, because of it. He gave a gentle smile when Márai warned him:

'Today we're just the witnesses, but tomorrow we might be the defendants.'

'The Germans deported me, my friend, and now I can't find the Aiglon letters at Csákvár. A great pity. Besides, the family lived at Csákvár for two hundred and fifty years. A rare thing.' But now he'd lost everything, and was staying with the actor Pál Jávor as a subtenant.

He is quiet and cheerful, a rare example of the gentleman, Márai thought. They waited for hours until they were called. Around noon, my grandfather said:

'Don't you find this is insane?'

'Yes,' Márai said, 'insane.' "

# CHAPTER FIVE

## 105.

When asked why they didn't go *out West*, aristocrats mostly gave an awkward shrug, or with recourse to some witticism, tried to hide something, their own confusion, possibly pain, and if they'd come down in the world, their self-pity. "Zsiga wanted to go, but Széchenyi wouldn't let him," the great hunter Zsigmond Széchenyi was supposed to have told Kádár. "Why should *I* go? Let *them* go!," or, "Since fate has dropped (!) me here, I might as well stay," and so on.

Father never gave an answer either that made any sense. Maybe it's this way: if you have to ask, there is no answer. An answer is possible only where there is no question. Certainly, they never asked themselves this question, as if their decision had been reflex-like, biological. Their remaining here seemed to go so thoroughly against their basic interests, it was so thoroughly meaningless (as far as the country and the community were concerned), that the person asking had every right to be curious. A gentleman is never surprised. Yet this question and their consequent remaining here surprised people all the same.

As they trudged back from Bavaria, my father and grandfather met relatives (including the one who had my name) going the

622

other way, and these relatives invited them to go along. Grandfather courteously declined:

"I want to find out what's going on first."

## 106.

With the war in mind, we asked our father if he'd killed anybody. If he'd killed a man. As usual, our younger sister spoke for us all. There we stood, like organ pipes.

"Tell us, Papi, please, have you killed a man?"

Our little sister had a way with grownups. For instance, she never greeted anyone with the usual "Kiss the hand." Good morning, good day, this is what she said with a slight parody to her seriousness, and the grownups tried to smile it off, but could not distance themselves from the consequences; they didn't speak to her like a child. On the phone, for example, many people didn't dare use the familiar form with her.

"*Au revoir, mademoiselle.*"

"*Au levoil,*" because she couldn't quite manage her *r*'s yet.

Our sister always stood out from her surroundings. Our father never. If, to give you an example, he walked into a tavern, he immediately became like everybody else. There was *something* about his bearing and about his brow, to be sure, but the people weren't afraid to go up to him; he was obviously a regular and not a stranger. Perfect mimicry. On the way to Grandmother's we had to change trains at Felső-Galla, and wait for the connecting train in the buffet. As he entered, father would immediately pull himself in, then apart, then reassemble himself, gulp down his beer straight from the bottle, call the bartender by his first name, and give the waitress one of those smiles. One time, two drunks were sitting on beer crates pushed up against each other by the wall, young, with stubble and missing teeth. You could tell at a glance that they'd been drunk for years. Belching, grinning, good-humored and friendly, they yelped at my sister:

"Hi there, old boy."

Her answer wasn't haughty, just formal; it wasn't unsociable, just courteous, in a place where courtesy could not be easily understood. She turned toward them, and nodded in all seriousness:

"How do you do."

The men turned grave. I don't know what this lean little blonde could have reminded them of, but frightened, they huddled up against each other on their crates.


## 107.

I was familiar with that railway station, too. We were waiting for the bus to Oroszlány. Ikarus, rear engine. One time the bus slid into a ditch and nearly turned over. Its position was precarious, to say the least, and we had to climb up to the door, and jump down. My father was standing outside, helping the people, especially (?) the women, explaining to every passenger individually that *in all probability* the driver must have been bitten by a wasp, and that's why he lost control of the bus. Wasp, driver, control, he must have said it at least fifty times. I felt ashamed. I'd never seen my father so eager before. As if he were toadying up to the others. For a long time afterward rear engine Ikarus buses frightened me.

We were sitting by an iron-framed table in the garden. Father ordered beer after beer. Concretely, five. I know of five. Father *slapped* the beer: he slapped the foam from out of the mug, a powerful swing of the arm, as if he were playing tennis, which ended in a quick, small flick of the wrist not allowed in tennis. We liked this, my father and I. The beers were a golden yellow, smelly, and bitter. I couldn't imagine why my poor father was torturing himself with this awful, bitter brew.

"Beer is beautiful." Father laughed, drawing a mustache under my nose with the foam. I made a face. "Try it." I gave in. Carefully, as if I were tasting horse piss, which as we know, is always tasted with due caution, I took a sip, and immediately heaved it up and spit it out.

"What you just said doesn't sound too convincing, sir," I said in my confusion, and made a solemn promise—how well I remember the moment!—that I would never drink beer again in all my life. It doesn't make sense. I went to pee (as if I'd had some beer), then I wandered off until I found myself among the tracks. I scuttled past gigantic locomotives, big as animals. You could feel the heat radiating from them. They droned, they whinnied, they panted, living beings, really, so-called Kálmán Kandó locomotives. Then the loudspeaker said my name. The radio said my name. I broke out in a sweat. The iron monsters scared me. Also, I was afraid to move. I stood among the rails, the locomotives nearly catching my side. I was scared stiff.

"Your father is worried about you," the railroad worker who found me said unhurriedly. He put a hand on my shoulder. I nearly buckled under it. We strolled along like two old friends. When he saw me, my father leaped up from the scrawny table, his gestures exaggerated, overeager and helter-skelter, as if he were sawing through the air.

"Watch it, son," the unhurried and weary railroad worker whispered, gently letting go of my shoulder, like someone who'd rather not get too close to the lackluster eyes and helter-skelter gestures. I gritted my teeth and turned on him:

"I'm nobody's son!"

My lips trembled. The man shrugged and disappeared inside the station building. My father hugged me to him eagerly, as if he were eager to let people see that he's eagerly hugging me, which scared me. I thought he was going to slap me, and turning from him, I snapped my head and knocked off his glasses, whereupon he really did slap me, whereupon peace and quiet was restored once again for the day.

## 108.

"Tell us, Papi, please, have you killed a man?"

We waited to see what would happen. But he hadn't. At least, that's what he said, that he hadn't, and he looked at us endearingly, like one in the know. If the question we asked Father was a good one, sometimes he'd notice. Again and again, he'd notice us. We saw this amused look of surprise in his eyes many times, as if he were surprised, pleasantly surprised that we're his children, and he our father.

It was a disappointment to learn that he hadn't killed anybody. Why, then, did he bother to go to war? Pál Kinizsi killed people! It's the only way to save the nation! Maybe he got off because Grandfather pulled some strings.

"In short, you would have liked me to have had killed some-one?"

We did not want to go into this "to have had" business, and we didn't want to go into the killing. It's just that we would have liked our father to be in the war movie playing in our heads.

We didn't dare say anything, but we nodded intently.

"What about the poor fellow whom, for the sake of argument, I might have killed? Have you thought about him?"

This "for the sake of argument" was again over our heads, but we indicated that no, we hadn't thought about him.

"How about his children, who might be of the same age as you?"

Unmoved, we shook our heads, no, no, we hadn't thought about them either.

"But for all we know, they might be studying the same thing as you!" Papi cried in desperation. Strange. Could he have been hoping that if we have the same thing in our heads, we'd be more sympathetic, that the absurdity of the situation would be more apparent to us? But we had strange ideas in our heads.

"The child of a fascist is also a fascist!" I shouted.

Father looked abashed, like someone who'd been punched in the stomach. We knew we'd made a mistake. We'd hurt him profoundly, except we didn't know how or why.

"What in your opinion is a fascist." Our father was so desperate, the interrogative sentence turned into a statement.

"A fascist is a fascist," I countered.

"The Germans," my brother said, coming to my aid.

"But we . . . But we were also on the side of the Germans!"

His tone frightened us. For one thing, he talked to us as if we were grownups, for another, you could tell by his looks that in this argument with adults, his position was precarious, and that scared us. But what frightened us most was the fact that we were supposed to have fought on the same team as the Germans, i.e., the fascists. Miklós Horthy, yes maybe. But we, Hungarians? Never! That's crazy! The Germans put Grandfather in jail, while his son, our father, need we add, is in league with the selfsame Germans as a soldier? That's ridiculous!

"Well, that's how it was!" Papi shouted, and stamped his foot impetuously, like a princess.

But by then we were not paying attention. Even the ridiculous has its limits.

## 109.

From this day forth, you will not know this man. Even before our mother let this sentence pass her lips, or even before she thought it, because she couldn't have (on the contrary!), we went and asked him.

"What do you young gentlemen wish to know?" he asked, raising his eyebrows.

Whether he's killed a man.

"As you young gentlemen wish," he said with a bow in our direction. "That's what it's all about, is it not? You have to have war from time to time, so humanity can lie back and relax again."

But we didn't like this answer either. We didn't like it if someone hadn't kill a man, and we didn't like it if he had. We dropped the Second World War.

"Can't hurt, can't mend," we said, and shrugged.


## 110.

We said it only because our father said it all the time (not so Mommy, it was an Esterházy expression); still we never understood what this "can't hurt, can't mend" was supposed to mean.

It's from a delightful and profound family anecdote. Under the service of our ancestor Károly, the Bishop of Eger, the peasants had learned to lay down everything—hoe, scythe, hat—and kneel if they saw the Count's coach, so the Bishop could bless them.

What they must have been hissing between their faithful teeth while they were being blessed is anybody's guess. There's a lampoon from the year 1765 with a passage about Károly, though it doesn't describe him at all:

*Bishop E.'s intent on gain,*
*Shoving it in the mouths of Youths again and again.*
*And adding insult to all the injury,*
*Heaping gain on gain, repeatedly*
*He doubles his tithes unabashedly.*
*Good Shepherd, who art here your Flock to smother,*
*May the living daylight leave you, and no other*
*May you lie faceup, the sooner the better.*

Thirty-four years pursuant to said good wishes did the living day-light leave the illustrious relative, and his cold body was de facto laid faceup. He was one of the pioneers of the pioneering eigh-teenth century. Pápa and Eger would not be the same without him. He had many disputes with Emperor Joseph II and was sup-posed to have written his name with an *sz* to set himself off from the branch of the family serving the Viennese Court. At which the Emperor warned him that if he insists on being refractory, he'd deprive him of his bishop's title, and where would he be in that case?!. He shrugged (bishops don't shrug) and addressed his earthly master thus:

"In that case I would go home, where I'd be a lord just the same."

He was a lord and a gentleman, but lords and gentlemen die too, and so he died.

When his heir, the young nephew, drove through the gentle slopes of Eger—*vulgo:* the estate—for the first time, he was sur-prised and puzzled by all that kneeling.

*"Herr Graf,"* the steward, a certain Pál Törő, whispered. He had been hired years ago by Bishop Károly out of the goodness of his Catholic heart, because when the Calvinist church of Mezőtúr was occupied by order of the Bishop of Vác—rah-rah-rah, Counter-Reformation!, give 'em their due, men of the cloth!— with his sword, this Törő cut off the hand of the man who tried

to lock up the church by force. (But it's not true what got around, that Károly, of all people, was the Bishop of Vác, because he became bishop only in 1759, *ergo* in 1754 it was either not the Bishop of Vác who had it closed, or else it was not my Uncle. So much for the facts.)

"Herr Graf, give 'em your blessing."

No way, not him, he's not competent in that area, *Unsinn* (German in the original).

"You gotta," said Törő, and raised his heavy, brown eyes on his new lord and master. (He'd remained a Protestant at heart.)

The youthful Esterházy could make neither heads nor tails of the strange old man he'd "inherited." In fact, he couldn't make heads or tails out of anything here, not the language, not the gestures of the people, not the country as a whole. Vienna he understood, Wiener Neustadt, too, not that it left much to the imagination. But from then on—east of the Leithe—he understood nothing. He couldn't understand the mud, the dirt roads, the poverty, the itinerant Gypsies, the overriding pride of the Hungarians, their eagerness to take offense.

What the Hungarians want, the young man thought as he glanced into the eyes of the wild old man—"I'm going to dismiss him!"—could hardly be dismissed if there were at least thirty million of them. But as things stand, it's quite ridiculous, really. (By the way, years later—during the nineteenth century, I might add—having become acquainted with the beauty of the country, strolling over the enchanting hills of the countryside, the mysterious valley of the River Szajla, he relented somewhat and felt that he now had a better understanding of the overheated emotions and grand yearnings of the Magyars. *Ich habe mich ein wenig mit ihren Superlativen ausgesöhnt*—that he'd come to understand their superlatives.)

He had stomach cramps, so he looked irate. Then he remembered a certain lovely Mrs. Kovács. Or Horváth. Or is that the same? With the atrocious accent. Then next he thought that from now on he's Hungarian too. At which he gave a timid laugh.

Pál Törő may not have registered every nuance on the finely chiseled, though weakly countenance of his lord.

"Hey, what're you waitin' for?" the old Magyar grumbled, and when he saw that the Count still had no inkling of what was expected of him, he quickly grabbed hold, gave him a shake, you gotta, he hissed, and with a shove, he had him veritably hanging from the coach, hanging on display. A great sigh rose from among the stacks, and the field glistened yellow. It was the sigh of people who'd been waiting with growing annoyance, yet with the patience of centuries, people who did not know what to make of the unaccustomed pause. "The origin of every revolution is the 'void' in which we are compelled to look at ourselves," the youthful Goethe had written his father. More wit than depth, but charming just the same. And also, can depth be charming, his father had scribbled in the margin. Nothing is as powerful as the truth, and the smallest truth is powerful, too.

"Your blessing," Pál Törő panted from behind, as if prompting an actor who has forgotten his lines, "give 'em your blessing!"

At which the Count raised his finely wrought, lean, pale hand and without the least sign of conviction, drew a cross in the air. Happy now, the people crossed themselves, too, while he grumbled:

"*Nützt nicht, schadet nicht,*" can't hurt, can't mend, and from then on whenever he rode out, he always acted likewise, and with the exception of Pál Törő, this occasioned general satisfaction all around.

## 111

When I had the argument with the Huszár brothers about who is a Labanc, because according to them, we're pro-Habsburg Labanc loyalists, but not according to me, and also they're supposed to be anti-Habsburg Kuruc patriots, and I asked why, they said it's because they're poor, at which I said so are we, at which they had no more to say, and I had nothing more to say either, and when I got home, I asked my mother if we're poor.

"What do you think?" She didn't even look up, didn't even glance my way. As if she were annoyed because I was questioning their poverty and the heavy load she had to carry because of it. I asked Father too who, to my surprise, fell to thinking about it. As opposed to Mother, he looked around the room with interest— where are we? what's going on?

"Well . . . at this point in time I wouldn't call it rich." And he also said that poor is not the opposite of rich. The not-rich are not necessarily poor. The poor are farther down the scale. They're destitute. The poor are poorer than the poor. "No, son, we're not poor, we're just living in poverty."

Our father was constantly inattentive, which he tried to hide behind his obligingness and attentiveness. Still, he was never quite *there*. We'd reach out, and paw the air. At times the air would take our father's shape. It seemed to me that with this "poor versus living in poverty" thing our father was suggesting that for some mysterious reason it is easier for us to be poor this way than if we had chosen it of our own free will, for our amusement, as it were, and could suspend it at will.

"I wouldn't go that far," our father nodded. He was in high spirits. My perplexity amused him. He also said that during our forcible resettlement, knowing that we'd been the victims of injustice made the hardship easier to bear. The outer concomitants of defeat were supposed to be hiding a moral victory.

"Difficult is difficult," a woman's voice called in from the kitchen.

## 112.

Once in her despair, because she had nothing to feed us and couldn't ask anyone for food anymore, my mother took to stealing. She stole potatoes and got caught. She cried. Later I saw her cry many times, but always because of our father (and once because of me). For this once, she was crying for herself.

There she was, out on the porch, crying her heart out. As if to a great lord, or king, did the people of the house come before her presence, excepting Uncle Pista, its lord and master (i.e., its peasant) who, in keeping with the escalating class struggle (1951), was serving his well-earned kulak sentence at the Hatvan jail. He was locked up for hiding produce, or for slaughtering a pig in secret, or because of an untidy yard (a piece of straw by the well)—you could be locked up for anything, anything at all. Cause and effect did not stand in the strict archaic relationship the ancient Greeks had in mind. Cause and effect were not in a cause-and-effect relationship, but a legal one.

"I never understood," thus our mother, "why the Communist state thought it paramount to legitimize their obvious flagrant injustices with the instruments of the law. Why isn't it enough to finish Rajk off? Why do they insist on a confession?"

"A European tradition," Father said as if to no one in particular. "The Inquisition did likewise. The only way to crush one's principles is along with the backbone."

Annu, the oldest daughter of the family, also showed up. Her hair reached down to her waist, and she had a skin problem on her face, her very beautiful face, a puzzling, purple patch. Mami had found her a doctor, because she was afraid and too ashamed to go. She stroked Mother's hair.

"Don't take it to heart, Aunt Lilike!"

Her mother, Aunt Rozi, brought a little hot chicken soup, as if to a sickbed.

"Eat, Lilike. You must eat. You must."

Mami sniffled, spooned her soup, sucked on the chicken leg. Papi was sitting tactfully in front of her, by her feet. From time to time he reached up and stroked her hand.

Pista junior showed up, too, and looked at Mother with his big round eyes. As always, he came to show his respect.

More than ten years later, at the Sugar Plant of Hatvan, Pista junior got involved in an embezzlement scheme.

"A swindle, a swindle," my aunt Bogyica giggled, as if she approved, or as if this were some happy, fun thing, a prank—though it is more likely that her constant readiness to gloat over other people's misfortune had found a target for itself. She was completely devoid of a sense of humor, and now her innate sense of irony found itself thrust into the arms of gloating. ("So then, in marched those nice Russians, right? I refuse to get trapped in that cul-de-sac of whether they raped my sister-in-law or whether she was asking for it . . .")

Late at night, when people never ring our doorbell, someone rang our doorbell. A delegation showed up from Hort, men in white shirts and black hats, as if setting off for mass, and women in suits, as if they were going to a (compulsory) holiday show at the culture center. Though I listened as hard as I could (need I say), I heard only the one sentence over and over again:

"Doctor, sir, you must help Pista. You must help Pista, Doctor!"

But my father couldn't help, and Pista junior was thrown in jail, and the people of Hort could never quite forgive him. Surely he could have done something, if only he had wanted to. They couldn't imagine that my father had as little right to want anything as they. If not less.

When everyone in the house had been to talk to Mother, but to no avail—Mother was whimpering, Father was sitting on the ground—the whole thing started all over again, and everyone (with the exception of Uncle Pista) came as they had done before, Annu, Aunt Rozi, repeating themselves and their gestures, assuring my mother that it's no big deal, it's all right, it's perfectly all right, others have been driven to do the same by extremity.

But though they (the aggrieved party) kept saying that it was all right, it wasn't. It wasn't all right at all. Eventually, everyone forgot. They forgot, and my mother forgot, even my father forgot. And in my own way, so did I.


## 113.


We felt that there was a mystery behind our attitude to poverty, that something was not right. For all practical purposes—this is how we saw it—we were poor, and our clothes shabby. (For years we thought that children's clothes were used to begin with, that there's no such thing as new children's clothes.) We didn't go on vacation, the rugs were threadbare, meat was a rarity and chicken rarer still—but we never thought of this. But no, that's not how it was. We didn't even see this poverty. For one thing, they hid it from us, our mother hid it from us, and for another, we had everything we needed, which must have meant that what we had we looked upon as everything. Our father did not concern himself with it, we were not aware of it, while the balance was provided by our mother, who would not have liked the moral whatnot that comes with poverty to go to waste. If she's working like a beast of burden, people should at least feel sorry for her. Or possibly, she wanted even less: since she's working like a beast of burden, at least. Since.

Still, there were indications that in practice this poverty was resting on shaky foundations. The cooking, for instance. It was poor, but *how*! Let's not beat about the bush. Our mother remained a slave to hors d'oeuvres, even in our forced resettlement. Of course, we denied this hors d'oeuvre business in front of our classmates. Why get involved in hopeless explanations? Green peppers or tomatoes stuffed with cottage cheese and dill, or just a boiled onion with mayonnaise, canned liver paté tuned up with sour cream and thyme—something. For the sake of appearances. Our mother could make something out of almost nothing. No, not just something, but something beautiful. In every sphere of life she was at war with anything ugly, anything that lacked shape. Hard semolina pudding from goat's milk and grits, which she then flattened out, baked, cut into rounds, then stacked them up with jam between the layers. This was the Tower of Babel. We could talk to our heart's delight then, partly pure nonsense, partly gibberish (obvious wisdom). Duck *sans orange*. Who wants more sansorange? (Déclassé humor.) In short, hors d'oeuvres and *dolce*. *La dolce vita.*

"A little *dolce*? *Pur la bon buss.*"

As if we had a choice, this double sentence was always forthcoming.

But there was no denying the tomato juice with pepper, nutmeg, ginger and ground orange peel, when available. We loved it. Our friends made faces and pushed the plate away.

"You're putting on airs!"

When it came to food, there might have been a touch of the *précieux* in us. We were proud of our taste buds.

Still, from time to time we reproached our mother for cooking too much *like a lady*. I'd be hard put to say what we meant by this. Maybe that in our home the potato soup was not as nice and greasy, and there were no big chunks of onion swimming on top like in other homes. It was pale, with sour cream. *À la française,* our mother said. She made us onion soup, too. And to go with the meat—we didn't see this anywhere else either—a bit of something sweet, for contrast, baked fruit, or her legendary *sauce piquant* made with common mustard and just as common jam.

Still, the worst of all was the silver cutlery, the fact that we ate with the silver cutlery every day, not only on Sunday or holidays.

"Why?"

"Because that's all we've got," our father grinned. Our mother shook her head. The weight of the silver got imbedded in our hands. When we were invited somewhere, or at school, our hands could hardly switch to aluminum.

"What's the matter, can't you eat properly?" A too light hand is hasty and helter-skelter, it spills things, it makes you eat like a pig. We didn't say anything. But later we were caught red-handed. It happened at the swimming pool. We would've been caught red-handed even without the silver cutlery.

We spent most of the summer at the pool across from our house. We went in the morning and stayed until it closed. We could've had something from the buffet, but that's expensive, or we could've taken bread with us, like we took to school, with butter and green pepper slices, and at times we did, each wrapped separately in a napkin. But come noon, it had to be a hot meal. If at all possible, we ate at noon, this is what we brought with us from our compulsory resettlement and the village—church bell, lunch, century after century. In short, at noon we dropped whatever we were doing—soccer, swimming, flirting—and headed for the fence, where our mother was waiting with the food can, because one must eat, and one must eat regularly, and do justice to the meal. Accordingly, one of the food compartments held napkins and the only cutlery we had at home, that certain ancestral cutlery. There we sat side by side, knife of silver, fork of silver—

which looked even more bizarre among the half-naked bodies—
Bless these Thy gifts, most gracious God, from whom all goodness
springs, make clean our hearts and feed our souls with good and
joyful things. And there stood our friends around us, disdainfully
watching our green bean (!) salad with dill.

These lunches did not help our assimilation with the working
class.

114.

I know not my shores, runs a line from an Ahmatova poem. Like
the great Russian and very Soviet rivers, my father's life had also
been diverted. I know not my shores. My father never said this,
not because he knew his shores, but because he didn't look. For
the first twenty years of his life, there was nothing to look at. A
firstborn son has well-defined duties. Everything progressed
nicely, smoothly, according to form, along its appointed path. The
length of the trousers may have possibly been shorter than one
would have expected from the Count of Galánta, the Lord in Perpetuity and Commander of the castle of Frakno, the Member in
Perpetuity of the Hungarian Upper House, and the heir to the
entail. Twenty years on the aristocratic threshing floor: can't hurt,
can't mend.

In a war you don't go looking around.

And later, by the time he could have taken a look round, we
know what had happened. My father never gave it a second
thought. He never looked to see what his life could have been
like, and what his present life was a replacement for. He took
things in stride. What you see is what you get.

## 115

His real life began when he remembered Miss Lili again, who was a widow by then and an elementary school teacher. My mother behaved like someone who needs to be convinced of something, that was her way of being head over heels in love with my father (carousel, wasp), while my father behaved like a young man head over heels in love, because he was a young man head over heels in love.

He was even willing to sit through a ballet. Generally speaking, he shared mother's cultural interests enthusiastically. He went with her to the Museum of Fine Arts, the Music Academy, the theater. He even told us about this as proof of his love when we later asked about its roots.

"I even went to the ballet!" he bragged, proud as a peacock.

In return, *en revanche* (as Mother said it, *reh-vansh*), an eye for an eye, mother went to soccer games. Or was taken. She definitely went once. For some reason, our father often talked to her about the great Henni, the Fradi goalie. Consequently, our mother knew all about Henni, but next to nothing about the game itself, unless that the goals scored, and so, when Újpest kicked a ball into the Fradi gate, to Henni, meaning us, Mother leaped jubilantly to her feet in the midst of a flock of shocked Fradi fans, and shouted goal! goal!, as a bunch of tired, melancholy men's eyes were pinned on her, and in his shame, Father buried his face in his hands. We heard this repeatedly, especially in Mother's proud account. We, football children and Fradi fans, looked at her the same way all those green-and-white-hearted, poor Fradi-Hungarians had done.

# 116.

Classical father-son icon: my father and me at the soccer games.
We saw the seventeen-year-old Albert play at Üllői Road. His
first time. That brief, expectant silence in the stadium, when genius suddenly manifests itself. His head was bandaged. Something
must have happened during the first halftime, but we weren't
there.

"The one in the turban," my father said looking around significantly, "we're going to be hearing about that boy." He said so,
way back then!

We did everything as we were supposed to. We bought sunflower seeds and pumpkin seeds before the game, either in paper
bags, or else, turning to the side, possibly opening a coat pocket,
showing where the seeds should go. Then during intermission,
we hurried—no, we ran, without exception, we always broke
into a run. Father grabbed my hand and dragged me along, and I
floated behind, higher and higher, like a coat or a fairy, so we
could be at the head of the line at the buffet, but without missing
a single moment of the game. We looked down on people who
started for the buffet before it was time. I drank the ubiquitous
Bambi (later I heard the technical term for this alcohol-free concoction of questionable origin and socialist aims: horse spittle),
and Father drank beer. One or two mugs. Three. I was given instructions at home to try and prevent him from having the second, but certainly, the third.

"Papi, I beg you, sir, don't drink any more," I begged him
once. But he gave me a look that effectively stopped me from attempting it ever again. Not even when it came to the fourth—
provided there was a fourth. (He drank his fourth beer either
because our team won, and he was ecstatic, or because it lost, and

he felt lame and helpless. When it was a tie game, he had his fourth beer in order to formulate an expert opinion.) I would follow him in silence, sometimes even to the pub, though I didn't like that and I was scared, because Father became morose and unpredictable. But up to and including the third beer his mood picked up, and that I liked.

The hot dogs and baked sausages they served with big dollops of mustard that we bought during intermission we would take back to our seats. We liked the look of the empty field. The empty field is beautiful. I remember those tastes very well, the sunflower seed stuck between my teeth, the horse spittle, the greasy paprika sausage with mustard, the tobacco smoke, and that *close* smell of beer. —And below us, that beautiful green square with the white lines and circles inside.

Heaven must be like this, Father. Good food and beauty, I thought.

But my concocted heaven was far too Catholic, it seems, because I had to pay dearly for it, redeeming it with pain. Every time, without exception, I got a horrible headache or migraine accompanied by nausea. But only after a game. We were swept along by the crowd down the stairs, Father glanced at me, I nodded, at which point we rushed to the first toilet we could find, he stood by the urinal, while I waited for an empty booth. Like that. This waiting seemed so forced to me, I didn't like it. Afterward, Father always said:

"You're pale."

Always. He was impatient, but he tried to hide it. Like an attack, that's what this migraine headache was like. It began in the middle of the second inning, around the twentieth or twenty-fifth minute, and came to an end with the vomiting (except that I was a bit pale). I insisted on the hot dog and baked sausage despite the fact that I was destined to see them again in pieces inside the toilet bowl. Just once, against the heroically struggling Tatabánya team, my head started up by the end of intermission, and accordingly, everything happened sooner, with people leaping out of the way, laughing and disgusted.

"Shit, son, don't drink so much!"

This time Father didn't hide his impatience and came immediately to my aid.

"Go away! Can't you see he's ill? You think we're doing this for our amusement?!" and with a rough gesture, he wiped my mouth. It hurt. His shirtsleeve got soiled, but he didn't care. He wasn't squeamish about anything physical. I'd never seen anything physical, ever, repulse him.

Except once.

## 117.

Our mother's family wasn't too keen on this marriage. They were afraid of Father and his family, even though by 1947–48 the working relationship between the grandfathers had been terminated. Still, they must have remembered a thing or two. At the same time, no one could accuse Mother of wanting to feather her nest. That would have pointed to a very bad sense of timing, as by then, Father had nothing left except for his beautiful eyes.

He was born Endre, but everyone called him Plop. (There was a quickly maturing pear tree in the huge orchard at Nagyszent-jános, and when he was a very small boy, Uncle Plop was supposed to have toddled over to the tree, dragging his small chair with him, and would sit there for hours, watching the pears, and when one fell to the ground, he'd nod and say: plop! Until the age of four, this was the only word he ever said, plop!) In short, Plop, who was Mother's younger brother, came back from the front in 1947, and he was against it too, even though he liked my father. They were born the same year, started university in Budapest at the same time, and attended the Ludovika military academy together.

They also went out into the night together. The Tabán bar in Hadnagy Street, and a waitress called Micike.

"We spent a fortune, ten or fifteen pengős. Meanwhile, our hands met under the table, alighting on Micike. We laughed, all three of us. What else could we have done?"

This is what Uncle Plop said to his favorite older sister: "Don't forget. A family of aristocrats would rather have their son marry a whore than a girl from a family of poor aristocrats. They're a liberal family. But they squander their liberality on one another. No matter what they may say, they will always look down their noses on you. Especially your future father-in-law. A poodle with a poodle, a puli with a puli, and don't you ever forget it."

Uncle Plop was strict, or rather, pedantic, or rather, he was a man of principle who adhered to his principles. He held principles on education, too, principles based on underlying principles, in the spirit of which he kept chiding our mother because of our education, which according to him went wrong from the get-go. He was going to show her. For some reason, Mami didn't laugh him off, and she didn't shoo him off, but gave him a free hand, if a small one.

As his first move, Uncle Plop introduced the so-called Black Book, a black notebook in which he entered our omissions, mistakes, impertinences and various manifestations of indolence, and also, on the same line, the appropriate (imposed) punishment (prohibitions, payments in kind), followed by a note to the effect that we had served our punishment.

We adhered to this new, unfamiliar military order stoically, with equanimity. Our mother looked on surprised and averse. She was not used to quite so *much* help.

Though we were used to doing the shopping, we were handed a slip with a list of things to buy, and in parentheses what to buy if we can't find it. There was no cause for worry. We knew every-thing. Ten rolls, two kilos of bread, two hundred grams bologna, never potato-meal sausage. She even wrote Pick instead of winter salami (but in the shop we asked for winter, it's the only kind they had). Even so, we rarely bought any, and never sliced, but in one piece. Mother would slice it herself. Only she was allowed to do it, not even Father, because everyone (would have) sliced it too thick. Once—sinning in secret—I chewed on a piece one cen-timeter thick, falling on it as if it were common sausage, or bread. It didn't taste like anything I knew. A bad conscience will influ-ence the taste buds, as will the fascination of sin.

I never saw slices as thin as my mother's. A veritable miracle. The sun shone right through them! There was a strict rule about how many could go on a slice of bread. With Uncle Plop it would have been some percentage, obviously—what percentage of the surface of the bread could be covered, and so on. And we'd have had to make calculations into the bargain. Later, while I was in high school, I used to visit him, as he put it, to learn higher math-ematics. His brain worked more like an engineer's than a mathe-matician's, but he kept it neatly ordered, which benefited me. On the other hand, he didn't mind so much when we (he) couldn't solve some of the problems. Only I was shocked.

Unfortunately, a person can always tell how much of the salami is rightfully his. One thing is for certain: the slices could not touch or cover one another, and you couldn't cut yourself a slice of bread bigger, but just enough for three rounds. Our sister, who liked riddles—all in all, she liked to use her head—enjoyed rack-ing her brain (if one and a half squirrels eat one and a half nuts in one and a half days, how many nuts do nine squirrels eat in nine days), raised the question, how big is the ideal slice of bread, where lies the best quotient for the use of the salami, where would its ideal placement be? But this was not worth thinking about, because a roll was ideal—half of a buttered roll (the butter could just barely pass over the small "holes"), a slice of green pepper, and a full, round slice of salami.

Apart from the Black Book, there was also the Proper Eating Contest, another of Uncle Plop's brilliant didactic triumphs. He had the theoretical considerations contingent upon eating all worked out along with a system of marking to harmonize with it. How one should hold one's knife and fork (not at the neck), spoon goes to the mouth, and not the mouth to the spoon, the hands never under the table, elbows close to the body (to practice, we actually had to eat with a book under each armpit), and water only after the soup. The jury—our parents and the brains behind the operation—walked around the table with stern expressions. They were taking notes, making faces, nodding, and clearly enjoying themselves. Thinking it amusing. But they didn't have eyes to see that we were not amused. We were anxious and uptight. We wanted to win, whereas when eating, you should be only wanting to eat.

## 118.

As both Bogyica and Uncle Plop were proud of saying (Mother would not comment), my maternal grandfather was not a drunkard, just a man who liked to have a good time. Not a drunkard, just a reveler, i.e., he was a disciplined man, but he loved life. At the White Ship in Győr he used to dance on the table with Deske Nyári and his Gypsy band providing the music. But even then he'd get up at the crack of dawn, have lunch exactly at twelve-thirty, followed by the post office, newspaper, a half-hour nap. Every evening, issuing orders to the tenant farmers, the stewards, the bailiff's assistants. Twenty-seven thousand holds of forest and twice as many holds of nonforests were under his care, because this is how much the other grandfather owned. A responsible job. Talking to the chemist at Magyaróvár about the proper artificial fertilizer. Checking on the average yield at the milk farm at Forna. Renegotiating the contract with the tenant Wittman. He played tarot, for small stakes. The children rarely saw their parents. The boarding school would allow just one visit home per month. He never once hit the children, that was Grandmother's job. Grandmother used to slap them around.

We never got to see this severity, only the terrified sadness of old age that was nestled in her profound, deep-set, walnut brown eyes. She turned ugly in her old age, as if her face were only half carved, and there appeared new, rough-hewn surfaces, rough, broken planes. This was especially glaring in the light of Bogyikó's beauty. But she was sweet. A sweet grandmother.

Then one day to the next, she forgot how to cook. She stood in the kitchen, took out a pan, put it back, picked up the salt shaker, put it back.

"I'm sorry, my darling," she said giggling to Bogyika, "I forgot! I've forgotten everything!" As if she were admitting some childish prank, some amusing practical joke.

Later, she couldn't recognize people either. She got the living and the dead confused. Step by step, she also became paranoid. Specifically, she was convinced that Mami was after her hide. We supported this suspicion of hers wholeheartedly, delivering up many small evidences of the above-mentioned lady's depravity. In our eyes our mother was so good and perfect that it was great fun talking about her as if she were evil. This was so far removed from the truth, it was so preposterous, that we thought of our secret smear campaign as a bashful declaration of love. We collected so many good absurdities, we had a great old time! Grandmother was more than happy to oblige. It gave her a new lease on life. We even promised her a gun, for self-defense. At which she said, out of the blue:

"I insist on a Smith & Wesson .38, little ones!"

We didn't know where she got that.

119.

János (Nepomuk) IV, Csesznek branch, Chamberlain, Lord Lieutenant of Hunyad and Zaránd, later Veszprém County, Privy Counselor, Deputy Master Chief Commissioner, member of the Crowned Hope box of the Viennese Freemasons, took to wife Countess Ágnes Bánffy of Losoncz, the daughter of Count Dénes and Baroness Ágnes Barcsay of Nagybarcsa, Queen Maria Theresa's goddaughter and foster child, this on June 10, 1777, at Schönbrunn.

Incidentally, at one time during his term of office in Veszprém County, the former relative staved off the election of Deputy Lord Lieutenant János Horváth of Kocs with so much zeal that he infuriated the electoral deputies, namely, the noble gentlemen of Szentgál, turning them so thoroughly against himself that the latter, threatening to beat the living daylights out of him, broke down the doors of the County Hall assembly room, and physical violence was avoided only because with the outraged electorate at his heels, János quickly sneaked out a side door in the company of his faithful Master of the Hunt and made for the rest room. But just as they reached the door, their pursuers caught up with them, and tore off a sleeve of János's short, fur-lined *mente* coat, whereupon the Master of the Hunt brandished his drawn knife and, pushing our grandfather through the door, put an end to the chase.

Ágnes's father was Catholic, her mother Protestant, who as

part of her marriage vows signed a letter of mutual concession to the effect that children issuing from the marriage would (as is only right) be brought up in the Catholic faith. But she had her wits about her. As Chancellor of Transylvania, the father was away most of the time (in Vienna), and the mother tried to force her daughter to marry a Protestant person—or man. When the wool fell from off the eyes of the Chancellor, he called upon his wife to hand over their daughter to him, which his wife denied him, and more. Bánffy attempted to make the "Protestant devil" see the light, but in vain. At which he led an assault against his own house with a force of arms, and freeing his daughter, conducted her to his mother in Vienna. There she was christened a Catholic, the Queen took it upon herself to be her godmother, and she became the wedded wife of my relative János. Their wedding was held in the imperial chapel at Schönbrunn. The dowry and the supper at Schönbrunn was a gift from the Queen. (Details of the nuptial ceremony can be found in the letter written by lady-in-waiting Countess Mihály Michna, née Baroness Latonselle Dessfeigny, to the Bánffy family. A red velvet pillow from the gilt carriage, a present from the Queen, is still extant.)

Now then: their daughter, Josefa, no, Marianna, who married a Ruspoli prince, couldn't speak a word of Hungarian. This aunt of mine stood by the window of her palace in Rome, surrounded by all those Ruspolis, her glance taking in the rooftops of the Vatican. Then she turned around, and with impeccable pronunciation, with only the *r*'s rolled perhaps a bit too hard, the way it's done in Cegléd, let's say, she said:

"*Őry Jánosnak árnyékában jó ülni*"—It is good to rest in the shadow of János Őry.

Not a word of Hungarian, before or after. She was buried at Vignanello, in the Ruspoli crypt.

"*Őry (Őri?) Jánosnak árnyékában jó ülni.*" We never knew where she got that.

# 120.

When he was in a good mood, Grandfather whistled beautifully. He liked to have Mother sit in his lap. But once in his anger, he threw the coffee cup against the wall. (The cold sour-cherry soup was hot. Strange. Because when the hot soup was cold, he always joked: Did a wind blow through the kitchen? A storm, a breeze, a hurricane?! 'Cause there had to be *something* . . . ) But next day, by way of appeasement, he ordered a twenty-four-place dinner set from Vienna. He commanded respect. The boys didn't oppose him, ever. As Apik wishes. As Apik thinks best. According to Bogyica and the other children, though they were worlds apart in wealth, he was much more generous than our other grandfather.

"You couldn't even *talk* to His Excellency," was Bogyica's ascerbic comment.

"That's not true," my father said, bowing his head as if in shame.

At the Ludovika military academy, Imre Jóni was Uncle Plop's class officer.

"Grant me leave. My father is dying."

"Leave granted. But if your father is not dying, I'm having you put behind bars!"

My grandfather passed away on October 4, 1940, at seven o'clock in the evening. His four children stood by his bedside, waiting for seven o'clock. At the moment of his death, Mamili went out of her mind and cursed God.

She cursed God.

The children were so terrified, they cried.

They never mentioned it again. When my sister ferreted this out, she hurried to Grandmother to ask. Our sister is big on questions, this is how she is brave, and this is how she is a coward.

Grandmother blushed, then smiled, then shook her head.

"What are you talking about, little one? Why don't I go make you some crêpes?"

She made the most incredibly light and tasty crêpes. She could also flip them. Never, in any other situation, was there anything playful about her, not even anything joyful, except there in the kitchen, with the crêpes.

But later, she forgot the crêpes, too.


121.


Were we children born of love, each of us asked separately, playing our parents off against each other, you might say. But our question came too late. It no longer made sense.


122.


It would not be strictly correct to say that as opposed to Mother's family, Father's family was gung-ho about their marriage, because this gung-ho would have meant my grandfather, who was neither gung, nor ho, nor, indeed, anything else.

Which is surprising. As if he didn't care about my father's future.

Not so Grandmother.

She paid a formal visit to my mother to talk her into the marriage, who didn't need any talking into. Still Grandmother was right in thinking that my mother was wavering. At the time Mother was living with Mamili, Bogyica and the others, across from the Király Baths. Grandmother got herself all dolled up, something she had never done before. Bogyica was laughing up her sleeve. She made her famous delicious café for the negotiating parties. Mother was annoyed by her sister's arrogance. *She* wasn't laughing.

She was scared. Was she scared of everything? Or not yet? Not at the time? Was she back then the way she looks on her photographs? ("I am a lady, the heroine of my own life. Such was my decision.") Usually, we saw only her unexciting "I am a mother, I am a martyr" face; it was through this that at times we could catch a glimpse of—how shall I describe it—my sister's face, the face of a reckless, mischievous, yet calm woman. It's wild physical disharmony was glaring especially in comparison to Bogyikó, who was as beautiful as if she'd stepped out of the pages of a magazine, just like Mia tant'. In the fifties, her lady-like elegance stood as ample proof of the evanescence of the dictatorship of the proletariat. She was incapable of being anything but elegant and breathtakingly beautiful. On the other hand, in diametrical opposition to all this, she wouldn't and couldn't do anything that went against the rules. Our mother used to mention disdainfully that when she was baking a cake, her older sister always measured out the ingredients to the gram. Then she shrugged and added:

"Of course, yours are incomparably better than mine."

It was a surprise visit. Grandmother didn't give prior notice. Bogyica opened the door for her. She brushed passed her as if she were the chambermaid. My mother was reading, and when Grandmother stopped on the threshold to give her a good look, she—she did nothing. She went on reading as if she hadn't noticed. She misunderstood my grandmother who, as if about to launch the Charge of the Light Brigade, took two wide leaps like some tiger or other wild animal, and was by my mother's side, her ubiquitous black raincoat flapping behind her like those Bolshevik banners in those Bolshevik films. Then just as unexpectedly she squatted down, took Mami's hand, and stroked it. They said nothing. Each liked the feel of the other's hand.

"Please don't leave my son."

They sat around Bogyikó's coffee in silence.

Grandmother had come to beg, but when she saw that my mother would love my father till the end of time, she cut her visit short. She was concerned about her son, not her daughter-in-law. She always took my mother just a bit for granted. For instance, she never talked about her, only when talking about our father. About us. But she wrote her a letter, more precisely, an open postcard, every single week. When she heard that our mother was studying French ("refreshing her French"), she wrote to her in French, and when, for a short time, English, then in English.

"Is the pen on the table," we asked, strict but fair.

"*Oui,* le pen, it is on the table!" our mother shouted, *vraiment* happy. This is one thing she was always willing to do.

The postcards were invariably about the same thing—short, matter-of-fact reports about how she and her younger sister were getting on, followed by an analysis of the weather forecast from the point of view of agriculture as a whole—is it good for the country, all this rain—and possibly something too about the international situation, with special regard to the Kennedys and the Pope.


## 123.


Historical self-recrimination and a bad conscience? The anti-Habsburg Kuruc reflexes? The dual upbringing? Be that as it may, for many years I was under the impression that driven by self-interest and compliantly following the call of the times, we took advantage of the tailwind of the Counter-Reformation four hundred years in the past, and switched over to the Papists; that this, plus two prudent marriages, had bolstered the family ramparts.

I'm not saying I found anything wrong with this. Everyone, every rich person, every millionaire says ("there are no rich men anymore, just millionaires") that though he is an honest man, let's not go into his first million. Dagger, poignard, marriage, adultery, the yellow corpses of tax officers in the murky waters of the Thames, et cetera, this is all part of the package, it seems. Why should we be any different?

And I suppose we weren't. Notwithstanding, my ancestor Miklós converted to Catholicism not from worldly ambition but faith, conviction and heart—on account of his deepest convictions. For one thing, it brought him nothing but disadvantages for years.

Family lore has preserved a scene which, by all odds, never took place, one confirmed by a number of sources (one), in which the irate and very Protestant father chases his Catholic son from the house.

It was not unusual at the time for Protestant families to educate their sons at Catholic institutions, mostly the Jesuits. As there were no Protestant schools nearby, Miklós, the future illustrious palatine, studied at Vágsellye near Galánta. Interestingly enough, they were not afraid of the Jesuits, whereas if a Jesuit grabs hold of someone, he's not about to let go . . . Hungarian Protestantism was young and proud, the Protestants had confidence in themselves and in a Protestant providence. God's ways—and the ways of young men—however, are inscrutable. The century hadn't yet turned when news came that the young man had "gone over," whereupon his maternal uncle, the great lord, future Palatine (1608) István Illésházy, and a militant Protestant, ordered him back home to Galánta forthwith. (This arm in arm with his father Ferenc, "a clever head councilor.")

Upon his arrival, his father, who was sitting at the table, was supposed to have slammed his spoon into the soup bowl so vehemently that the soup spattered all the way to where Miklós stood. "Yes!" he cried when he was asked whether he had indeed converted to Catholicism. Indeed he had. Furthermore, he had every intention of dying as one.

I see no impediment to that, his father bellowed, flinging a number of plates at his head.

"Of my ten sons, I have given you as tithe and levy to the devil!" His father further threatened that he'd have his brains bashed out of him, have him punished a dozen times over, then be done with him. At last he alighted from his place at the table, and had his son ignominiously chased from the premises.

The youthful Miklós took his punishment with equanimity, and making no answer to his father, he went and knelt by a tree out in the garden in front of the house, and amid profuse tears, he thanked the Lord most piously for bringing such suffering on his head in exchange for his true faith. Then amid a torrent of tears, and showering him with her blessings, did his mother watch him walk away across the meadow on foot, saying, among other things:

"My dear son, you of all the others were born of the pain of thine mother. Go with the holy blessing of the Lord our God." This is how they took their tearful farewell of each other. He never saw his father again, who was still alive in 1603, but on this side of that year, his name no longer appearing in the documents, it is probable that he passed on around 1604.

Still, it is true that his nuptials with the widow Mágocsy, née Baroness Orsolya Dersffy, imparted not a little momentum to his brilliant career. On the other hand, any further hearsay that would insinuate a marriage of convenience is nothing but the calumny of the Protestant "publicists," of whom János Szalárdi and Máté Sepsi Lackó were the ringleaders. In his historical memoirs, the latter takes for granted that any Protestant lord and aristocrat could have met his end in only one manner—being poisoned by the Papists. (The victims included Bálint Homonnai and his son István, and also Ferenc Mágochy.)

Be that as it may, the Mágocsy relative, Archbishop Pázmány, found nothing reprehensible in the circumstances. (Pázmány's mother, Margit Massai of Haraklány, was the younger sister of Eulália Massai, the second wife of Gáspár Mágochy.) Nor did György Drugeth, nor the Jesuits in Bratislava.

It got around that even before the husband passed away there was a certain amount of spooning and canoodling, and that before they took their wedding vows they were supposed to have cohabited, and that being unable to bear children, the elderly Orsolya bought concubines for Miklós, partly out of the goodness of her heart, and partly to produce an heir.

Let us take a good look at this one thing, at least, namely, that our ancestress was older than our ancestor. Let us crush this base Protestant spitefulness at the root! If we leaf through—and why should we not—the records of the general assembly of Sopron County, we can read there a protest against the use of a pasture of the Lánzsér dominion, initiated in the name of "Her Excellency, the maiden Orsolya Császár," dated January 7, 1586. In short, Orsolya Dersffy's mother was not yet married. Since Mágochy was born in 1582 and Uncle Miklós in 1583, and Aunt Orsolya not before 1586, the latter could not have been older than the former. *Quod erat demonstrandum,* I rest my case.


## 124.


As for my parents' marriage, that too imparted a not unappreciable momentum to the life of the man in question, even though subsequently, it did not reach dizzying heights, to say the least. On the other hand, as opposed to Dersffy Grandmother, Mother was older than Father.

Needless to say, the marriage was looked upon as a serious *mésalliance*, even though there was no rank anymore or, to put it another way, everyone, everyone who mattered, was below rank.

On the other hand, anyone who brings a firstborn into the world, especially a male, is considered a person of rank, and on a certain day in April, smack in the middle of the century, I did my bit to improve my mother's social standing.

My mother wanted a simple Christening. She didn't give a fig about her prestige, even though later we constantly witnessed her hopeless struggle, her invisible combat, with my father's invisible family. On this particular occasion, however, she was thinking of God, not of the family. The family, however, was thinking of us all, and in this particular instance, even our father was helpless—the ancient customs proved stronger than him, and the Church claimed me, promptly, and with due ceremony.

I howled.

"Oh, the little infidel!"

I howled in my ancient layette wrought at the edges with spun gold and beribboned with the yellow and blue family colors, while the faithful servant of the Church registered, not without a show of piety (it comes with the job, like lower back pain for miners), the increase in the congregation.

Needless to say, we supported the Church *ex officio* as well. Every Sunday for centuries we took our place in the patron's pew during mass. (I've sat in a patron's pew, too, reserved for me, as it were, even though I could no longer practice my right to appoint the parish priest.) We were an intricate network, need I add; we'd given famous bishops to the Clergy, including an archbishop. It was a natural and continual relationship, which could even survive the fact that our Ferenc supported the initial reform drives of Joseph II, while our bishop, Károly, fumigated it, except after a while Joe threw all restraint to the wind, and there was no following him.

As we have seen, of the family, our Majk grandmother embodied this practical-minded, amicable—and thus, critical—relationship. As a result, unlike those who, in accordance with basically French tradition, regarded the hand of the Church as a hairy, greasy paw, or else a powdered, evil, bony hand of power and authority, I have come to feel about the Church as I feel about the dentist: contrary to custom, I am not afraid of it.

## 125.

The reason: we used to go for treatment to Uncle Laci Baynok, Bogyica's brother-in-law, her husband's older brother, who looked a lot like Vittorio de Sica, except not as much as his younger brother.

I wasn't afraid because for one thing, he had delicate hands (the lack of pain is an important element in any exchange of views), and for another, treatment was presented (sold) to us as part of a family visit of sorts, with the grownups drinking coffee and *engaging* in *discourse* (including my father!), while the three of us, our younger sister included, tried (in secret) to spend as much time as possible with the painting of a nude. We kept throwing innocent glances *in a certain direction* as we leafed through old prewar magazines, the society paper *Társaság,* and the theatrical magazine *Színházi Élet,* neatly bound together by the year. At such times, Aunt Flóra, Uncle Laci's wife, whom we were not allowed to call Auntie because she'd think we were looking down our noses at her, and so we didn't call her anything at all, and who was Jewish and was missing a lower arm, though she moved it and kept it still so cleverly that nobody noticed, nor did we ever bring it up, neither the one nor the other, and who died amid unspeakable suffering when she began rotting from the arm up, invariably said the same thing:

"*Színházi Élet?* That's Zoltán Egyed's paper. He was a clever, intelligent and distinguished Jew." Just this. Invariably.

Allegedly—our mother alleged to it—the nude was of her.

"How would you know?" our father grinned as if he'd painted the painting himself, or as if he'd been the brush.

We behaved exceptionally well on these afternoons, as if Uncle Plop had coached us. Which is to say that we were a bit scared, after all. Also, we were bored with the whole thing, or at least, in part, and so, from time to time, from the back, from the direction of the salon, getting ahead of the real ("ordinary") waiting patients, we'd go to look in on Uncle Laci, to say hello, so to speak, and find out how he's doing, and then, as if by way of an afterthought, he'd have a look at our teeth. "Fangs," he called them.

"That's your father's plaque! A weak-gummed family!" Stuff like that.

Though this had nothing to do with it, when I was admitted to the Piarists, my tooth, one of my eyeteeth, suddenly started to grow like a rabbit's that didn't eat enough carrots, or a wolf's that didn't eat enough rabbit. Uncle Laci's father had just died. He was one hundred years old. He had beehives up in Hüvösvölgy. Once he lost the queen bee on the train. The train had to stop at Ceglédbercel. The Ceglédbercel affair! My appointment fell to the day of the funeral.

"That's quite an avant-garde idea from an eyetooth," he said softly as deep in thought he tapped the tooth. He'd pulled his white coat over his suit. He wore beautiful Italian silk ties. A veritable fortune, our mother said. She made snide remarks about Uncle Laci. There were a number of reasons for this. She scorned them, because Uncle Laci and his wife would fight from time to time. What was worse, they'd even talk about it in company, as if it were a proof of their love for each other. Also, she disdained them because after the war they made a living as cardsharps (which they denied, but in vain), and furthermore, on these visits, our father flirted openly with Aunt Flóra, and our mother wanted Uncle Laci to do something about it, or against it, but didn't. As far as we could tell, our mother was very friendly with Aunt Flóra. They were nice to each other and always smiled. During the siege, when they occupied the same apartment and bomb shelter for two months, Aunt Flóra taught Mami to play with puppets.

"A funeral is not an avant-garde genre," and he kept tapping my tooth. "Good. The Piarists, that's good. *Vernünftig*. The Piarists will bring out what's in you. At your age, that's what you need. They're a teaching order. Poor and severe. They know that knowledge is limited and must be nurtured and respected. They're modern and open to new ideas. They're not as entrenched in their ways as the Franciscans, but they're not as pleasant either. Also, they're not as power hungry as the Jesuits. Of course, now they can aspire all they want, they're glad to be alive. Which is more of a Franciscan program, of course. The Piarists spend all their time thinking. Does that hurt? I see it hurts. We must wait to see what it wants. This, son, is a tooth with a will. Let's not aggravate it. And don't laugh for a while!"

He sat down across from me on a small chair that could swivel around like a piano stool.

"I've never seen you like this. I see the whole country with half-open mouths. All that darkness in those mouths! . . . Do you smoke?" I didn't. That's when I started not smoking. "The Piarists. That's good. Good and reliable. Like a tweed suit. Of course, there are no tweeds anymore . . . They last, though . . . Christenings, funerals. These are best left to the Catholics. People have stopped ordering tailor-made suits . . . As if it were possible to guess ahead of time what a man is like. Clothing factories! *Contradictio in adjecto,* son! The Piarists will do the declension for you.

Of course, in your family everyone is Catholic, from *A* to *Z*. Cap à pied. Backward and forward. Though come to think of it, there's your mother! With a letter of mutual concession, I assume. In which case, only from *A* to *M*, or *M* to *Z*. Birth, death . . . Keep to the beaten track. Only what's been tried. Catholics think in terms of the theater. It works. A well-oiled machine. Works smoothly, without a hitch. Catholicism works without a hitch. Not much catharsis, but they don't seem to mind. They go in at seven and come out at a quarter to ten. Helps pass the time . . . If you ever need to, you can safely lean on your Catholicism!"

I didn't dare say anything, but I didn't dare keep quiet for too long either. At first I nodded, fine, I'll lean on it. Then I asked whether he did so too.

Whether from time to time he also did some leaning.

"Leaning? On what?" he smiled. He was handsome, and he knew it.

There was a third brother, Uncle Dodó, Doh-di, as Bogyica said, as if she were chanting. He didn't have a hint of de Sica in him, and people said his selfishness and miserliness defy the imagination ("*Schmutzig,* son, a *schmutzig* son of a . . . !"), and that he lets women support him, elderly women, though by now he's pretty much caught up with them himself.

"Also, he's always going on outings with those old bags! Nothing like healthy living! He doesn't want to die. What a *common* thought! Ordinary! And he's always wearing green kneesocks on his outings!"

Uncle Laci's smile would have made any woman sigh. But only I was on hand.

"Lean on what?"

"Well, as you said, sir. On Catholicism."

"Let him that's *got* it lean on it." He thumbed my knee. "The only religion I'd join is a religion that says that the Creator is laughing at what He's created. In which the Creator is a *mocking* god. Things would be so much simpler if we'd only accept this mocking god. Christianity has no laughter . . . I . . . I have nothing." He stroked my knee. "I am the richest of them all."

I didn't understand. After a while, I asked cautiously:

"Are you Protestant?"

He whispered, as if giving away a secret:

"Oh, even better. An atheist."

"Oy!" I heard myself say.

"But don't tell them," and he made a wide sweep of the arm, as if to indicate the whole world. "Sometimes it's necessary to submerge oneself in the medicinal waters of self-pity, but not too much. It's like onanism: it has a certain *je ne sais quoi* to it. Still, it's . . . it's not to God's liking." No one can pronounce the name of the Lord as lovingly as an atheist. I saw Parliament through the window. We fell silent. Then he embraced my legs and leaned his head on my knees. I looked at him from the roomy dentist's chair, from above, as if from a throne. After a long silence he said:

"My God, my God." Pause. "It is a beautiful thing when your father dies. You will see, it is beautiful. Except the bees, what's to become of the bees?"

I stroked his shoulder.

And all the time, my eyetooth, it must have been growing steadily.


126.


Everyone at my baptism went about his business. The servant of the Church ministered, the Good Lord registered (with certain reservations?) the multiplication of His flock, and my father began his adventurous life as a father. He grinned at me, then enthusiastically, in accordance with the ritual of baptism, renounced the devil and all his works in my name. (Being a father is a mystery. Without the knowledge of the participants, mysterious questions give way to mysterious answers. Being a father is difficult because you cannot prepare for it. What *can* be learned about being a father, what can be accomplished with good intentions and sensitivity, is of little or no interest. I didn't know this at the time. But my father did. What *he* didn't know was that in the end, we, all of us, are found out.)

My mother's countenance, beleaguered by happiness (me! me!), was nonetheless clouded over by the accustomed gloom, the one that all the mothers in our family who—need we say—are not born Esterházys are prey to (though once in a while, one branch would help out another, even if not nearly as often as the Károlyis, who in their Puritan arrogance would have preferred to choose only from among themselves, they couldn't go wrong with that), and are thus outsiders *after all*, even though—need we point out—without them the branch would dry out, break off, wither away.

My mother—Infant in arm, a proud mother, the classical Madonna pose—felt that the Lord God was like an unpleasant, presumptuous brother-in-law, or maybe mother-in-law, but no, more like her elder sister, but no, more like our father-in-law's elder sister, an aunt, a gigantic *tante*, a giantess, whose glance holds the lives of the "intruder" in check. The intricate web of the aunties hovered intrepidly above the heads of the family, on their faces not the envy of the infertile, but severity and knowledge. They were the guardians of order, the guardians of an unspoken inner—and it seems, unfathomable—family order beyond words. They were not weak old maids; my mother could not enjoy such easy satisfaction as, looking askance, we once again caught sight of the huge, colorful, wide-brimmed *shaded* hats, to which everything was made to match severely and inevitably, everything, the eye shadows, the lipsticks, the belt buckles, the patterns on the handbags, the soles of the shoes.

Not an easy order, this.

If we go back in time, we can shudder even more: a nineteenth-century dress, buttoned to the chin, black, closed, made in Vienna, a *muttermörder,* though presumably they're not wearing them there anymore—a piece of clothing like that could represent the authority and unavoidable disapprobation of the aunts on its own, and so on, backward in time, without relief, first in this, then in the next century, until we find ourselves facing the taffeta vest embroidered in gold worn by the Palatine's younger sister which, with the exception of Mondays, can be seen on the mezzanine of the Museum of Applied Arts in Budapest. On every similar piece of clothing and object, from Bogyica's lipstick to Zsófia Illésházy's rouge, this unmistakable family metaphysics, this archaic etiquette, is there for the asking.

"We renounce him! We renounce him!," the members of the family chanted, grinning mischievously. We were writing 1950, or someone was, at any rate. It was clear what they were thinking. We could still be effortlessly elegant for one Sunday, to the extent of a baptism, scandalously distinguished. Proud, haughty. The centuries of rightful possession were still nearby, we could still feel how it tasted. We did not feel the taste of privation, of absence. (I, for one, didn't even feel the taste of a pacifier. Mother insisted that her children grow up in a pacifier-free environment. She felt that a pacifier is vulgar, and she wanted to protect us from all things vulgar, poor dear . . . )

"Still, two thousand years are two thousand years," they nodded toward the altar with satisfaction. "This Commie *virschaft, alles mit allem,* won't last thirty years on the outside, if that. It is not surprising if now—repugnant and inconvenient as it may be—certain harum-scarum elements"—imagine this with aristocratic affectation!, *hah-rum scah-rum,* and you will understand the genesis of proletarian discontent—"are desperately trying to make up the difference, which is impossible, of course, even according to the elementary rules of mathematics."

Politically neutral, I continued bawling, though at that point it would have been hard to prove. Aunt Mia held me under the baptismal water. Excited, she forgot she was holding me and let me slip into the baptismal font, a total immersion of the Protestant type. The altar boy assisting the priest quickly plucked me from the font and restored me to my mother, who sobbed and clutched me, dripping, to her bosom. The priest laughed, he'd never witnessed anything like this before. This here is a regular little Baptist now, he said, who hardly needed him. My father growled like a watchdog. Let no man slander his child and call him Protestant.

"Quiet, man, you're in God's house."

I was up to here at the very start with holy water. It was summer. It felt good.

## 127.

I had a dream (a revery), and in this dream (or revery) I asked the Lord about my father. I inquired. Put out feelers. Plied Him. About what He is like. I wanted to know what He is like. Better to be safe than sorry. This is how I spent my time in my mother's belly. But despite my repeated urging, the Lord wouldn't give me a straight answer. He's no fortune-teller (He said, in the sonorous, stentorial tones of the actor Imre Sinkovits as a young man). But I'm not asking about my future. I'm asking what my father is going to be like. At this He giggled like an adolescent. What, indeed? In retrospect it seems to me that the Good Lord was cunningly talking to me the way my father would later on, possibly so that I'd get used to it, used to that tone.

But I wanted Him to tell me, and not just indicate or intimate, but to tell me straight out about my father and this Hungary we call Hungary—tell me what I should expect.

But no. He suggested instead that I try to imagine my father. I shrugged—a storm in a cup of embryonic fluid. Oh, it's not that important, I'll manage without it. No. I should try to imagine him. Paint him on the canvas of my imagination. Or its wall. Cut him out of pulp paper and color him. (This is the etymological connection between pulp paper and Papi.) I should make a silhouette à la Goethe with a pair of scissors. Don't be afraid of Goethe, he won't bite. Or putty. Yes, putty might be the best thing. It may not be classical as far as materials go, but at least it's easy to work with. Pliable. In short, I should roll him, knead him, squeeze him. Who? My father. Put him on a pedestal, paint his portrait, take his picture. Gather up and paste together the photo that my mother once tore into a thousand pieces in her rage. When? In times to come.

And also, I should make sketches, drawings, oil paintings.

My father as an etching, an aquarelle, a silk screen print. My father as a caricature, a landscape, a battle scene. The battle scene would come off best as a film, actually, with the forbidding warriors appearing between my father's strands of hair, on the edge of the dense wood, in the early-morning fog, then they'd come out marching, slowly, carefully, with dignity, over the wide-open space of the forehead. I would carefully raise myself in the steed Challenger's saddle, not arrogant, just happy, said steed having been gifted to me by the great lord Pázmány, the highly ambitious cardinal of the bright intellect, gifted out of love and calculation, because in him these two were fused into one—self-interest, cunning, and true saintly goodness.

# 128.

But it was not a dream wherein once—just once—like two troublemakers, we locked horns. Not with Pázmány, with my father. When? We were still attending the Fradi soccer games, though not together anymore. In any case, way after the Peace of Westphalia. Wheezing, I stood before him, who, a blue moon, looked very much like a father just then.

"You are dead wrong, sir, if you mean to interfere with my plans," I said, having resorted to the formal mode of address without realizing. We had just started using the familiar form with each other around that time. But when he's simply my father and I am simply his son, a child, then I talk just like a child, a vestige of past times. "Not if you stand on your head, sir, not then!"

My unexpected firmness impressed me. I had been a relatively peaceful adolescent. I didn't trouble others much because "others" didn't trouble me much either. I was lonely, as far as that goes, I felt alone, but I didn't know where to point the blame. I didn't talk much but kept silent, and Father responded with silence, which I acknowledged with silent irritation.

The old man smiled, and the so-called laughing lines ran together on his forehead. (After a while we children switched from Father to old man, and he pretended, not too convincingly, that he disapproved, and his being proud was just a lapse.) This mobility of the forehead, its liveliness, gave the impression that my father was deep in thought, weighing things, deliberating. The wrinkles lead one to assume a certain attentiveness and an immense skepticism of sorts, which could easily be mistaken for overbearing pride.

I noticed the same thing about myself later on, how in a certain gesture or sentence, which I meant to be friendly, emphatically pleasant, sometimes even exceptionally reassuring, there would appear something of my father's irony and aloofness, which can make people feel uneasy or frustrated, even when I don't want this to happen or, to put it another way, when this is what I don't want to happen.

My father's occasional bumptiousness, his close-mouthed pretend omniscience, could have made me hit the ceiling (I didn't). I didn't realize I was the cause: if I leave him be, he's never like this. He's like this only when I'm bent on getting him to deliver the goods. He doesn't like delivering the goods. Or maybe he hasn't got goods to deliver. Or there's all kinds, he's got his, I've got mine, and when he comes out with his, I don't even notice.

"All you do is complicate my life!" I shouted with youthful fervor and fear into his face. My vehemence surprised me, as if it weren't me talking. But it was. Besides, it was impossible to have a proper, classical fight with my father anyway. For one thing, Grandfather's icy aristocratism would instantly surface in him, fighting, that's for servants!, and you, itching to challenge him, automatically and on the double end up sharing this view at the first raising of his brow. And for another, he generally avoided conflict of all sorts, he extricated himself from altercation; he shook his head almost imperceptibly, the crow's-feet stirring around the eyes, the wrinkles of squinting merriment; his eyes gleamed, as if to indicate a smile, which was itself the smile, and softly, *he moved out of range.*

(He and Mother never fought much either. When he was in a bad way, i.e., he was drinking—"he was stinking drunk"—and didn't come home, not much, even then. Surely, this also depended on our mother, who was of two minds about whether she wanted to know what she knew but would have liked not knowing.

Our sister found a thin, white, so-called notebook. Dirty, stained, soiled, faded from the light. It was produced by the Fűzfő

667

Paper Mill at 0.50 forints a throw, and one of us had written on it with a child's hand, Sketch Book, then immediately crossed it out. On the back is the alphabet in printed letters, illustrating how it is done: from *Aa* to *Zszs*, then: Punctuation:.?,;:" ", then the imperative to be taken to heart: The outer form of everything you write should be done with care and be presentable! Budapest, Sept. 4, 1963.

Our mother must have snitched the notebook from us. It's got practical notations, a list of clothing given to Bogyikó or received from her, the money paid out to Margitka, dishwashing, ironing (from which it turns out that she got ten forints per hour), expenses, lines of figures (with sum totals). Every single entry is also crossed out, indicating that it's been taken care of. In the back of the notebook, proceeding from the back toward the front, our mother painstakingly noted down "your father's goings-on," date, hour, minute, event. I'd rather not go into it. But there, too, this is what was evident, this two-mindedness; surely, she needed to make a record so that later she couldn't pretend that these "things" never happened. Needless (?) to say, Father denied everything. He deemed the rebukes unjustified and highly exaggerated, but promised he'd never do it again. From time to time we heard whispers to this effect. But what won't happen *again*, we wondered, if the thing that brought the rebukes never happened in the first place. In these notes of hers, our mother wouldn't write out the words. She was obviously afraid of the words, of recording things through words, and she was afraid of the empty lines, too, the gaping emptiness as a form of self-deception. Ex.: *dn.*: this meant that he's drunk as a noot; *lips.*: that his shirt had lipstick on it, or he did.)

In this nearly nonexistent argument I gave a brief outline—for Papi's sake, who wasn't listening—of my plans, with special reference to the program relating to our shared memories, from the choir of angels to stewed knuckles, from Péter Pázmány to my prick, from my mother to my father, and also—a beautiful thought—that everyone else's memory is mine, too, and also his, and my brother's and sister's, the neighbors', and the voluntary cop's, too, they're mine, all mine . . . I was having my say.

"You will never grow up," he cut in abruptly. I detected a sense of pride in his voice, which I had no choice but to attribute to my person as a backhanded compliment to me, or as a tribute to my position as a child. "You will always be a child, and I will always be your father." Pause. Then, as if delivering the clincher and enjoying it: "Until I die."

I think I shrugged. And then, as if clowning and tripping over himself, my father launched into an explanation, to wit, for your information, and just in case, young man, common memories are not built atop a secure rock, and also, that even though my caring parents caringly named me Petrus at my Christening, they're no Rock of Gibraltar, they are standing in a quagmire, the putrid, boggy, churning, gaseous, nightmarish wasteland whose name is death.

He kissed me.

"Death is the mortar holding our common memories together, pumpkinhead."

Two troublemakers making trouble.

# CHAPTER SIX

## 129.

When in May 1951, the forced resettlements started in Budapest, my parents took it all in stride. There was no need to worry or be unduly alarmed; it was just the usual thing all over again: if all is lost, there is nothing to lose, which is a freedom of sorts, after all, but worse comes to worse, it can provide the illusion of freedom. Though I hadn't yet lost anything personally, I was not worried either, nor unduly alarmed, because I thought—and what else could I have thought?—that it was only natural, that that's what life is like, that you get dragged out of your crib, strangers burst in, screaming and shouting, hurried packing, scurrying about, the night is dark, truck, gasoline fumes, then more strangers, more screaming, my father's impassive countenance, my mother's tears, then the tears dry up and she never cries anymore, or hardly ever, and if this is the way things are, then what's the use of worrying or feeling unduly alarmed?

I had no idea when I first laid eyes on it that Budapest was the city of fear. Fear held my native town in thrall, it held everything in thrall; there was nothing but this fear, the winding Castle streets, the promenades, the foul outskirts and elegant avenues ("the avenues that once bore the names of your uncles")—everything. With its "hideous, colossal, festering ass" fear and trembling had engulfed the city. My crib offered a spectacular view of Blood Meadow and the Castle. A choice spot. My first home was a villa in Buda situated on a steep lot, as if the house had grown out of the ground not far from the steps named after our King Csaba, on the side of the hill that bore the name of the ill-fated traitor Martinovics.

After the convent where they had been given room and board was disbanded by the authorities—and which, unless I am much mistaken, had been established by us, the family—Great-grandmother Schwarzenberg and Aunt Mia came to live with us. The ubiquitous dark glasses that Aunt Mia wore enhanced rather than concealed her beauty. A famous actress trying to hide from prying eyes. Like that. Yet there was nothing of the actress in her, and her beauty, too, had faded (or had always been faded, which is a contradiction, of course). No man ever approached her as a man. The only bond of affection she held was for her brother, my grandfather. She wanted to devote her life to him, but he wouldn't have it. Wouldn't hear of it. Joining a convent seemed the logical thing to do, except she didn't want to dedicate herself to Christ either, neither as his servant, nor as his betrothed. She didn't have enough warmth of heart even for that. Which left pecuniary support. In her desperation, Aunt Mia tried to hide her lack of warmth, hide it behind kindness. To no avail. Whereupon we, children, being equally desperate, did our utmost to reassure her that we loved her. Our mutual desperations were a fine match for each other, I think. On the other hand, she had the softest hands in the whole wide world. Like a weak little bird's. We took hold of her hand; she did not object, and we slid it up and down our cheeks. Meanwhile, she was supposed to be teaching us German.

## 130

I had a distant, fascinating and intriguing uncle, Miklós Szebek, whom everyone called Roberto, as if he were an Italian gigolo, except my mother. She always called him Miklós, formally, Miklós, Miklós, if you please, always like that—and later my father, who wouldn't call him anything, "he did not speak his name."

From time to time he also lived with us. He had his own mattress ("my, my!, this is real horse hair!, it's first-class horse hair, this!"). At first he slept in my room, but my mother was always worried about how I'm faring there in that distant room, or just wanted to be with me and didn't want my time to pass without her company. (Later, when there were many of us, time passed all over the place, and Mother no longer could—or would—supervise this passing, though truth to tell, she was past worrying by then; she couldn't worry about four children, it would have driven her mad; with four children you can only hope, which is sometimes enough, if it's enough.) Anyway, she moved in with me and slept on the mattress, and Roberto moved into the conjugal bed with Father. They had a good laugh over it—all three of them. Originally, Roberto was supposed to be my godfather, since he'd done such a good job as a witness at the wedding. But he demurred.

"You don't want someone like me for a godfather," he said in chilly tones, and blushed.

## 131

For a long time I was under the impression that the evil piece of paper asking us if we would kindly oblige the authorities by getting the hell out of our home in twenty-four hours and proceed to our newly appointed place of residence, which brought with it not only the moral benefit of teaching the enemy of the people— that being yours truly (the eviction papers were accidentally addressed to me, but my parents pretended not to notice)—a lesson, but a more practical benefit as well, since it made a perfectly nice apartment free and available, concretely for the people, and more concretely, for Comrade J.G., may the pox take him. In short, everyone stood to benefit; we regained our moral balance, while the people, et cetera, et cetera. The point is that for some time I was under the impression that the eviction order came on June 16, 1951.

June 16 is the correct date, but so is July 16, it being the last day of evictions. The very last. Which means that they dangled a carrot in front of my parents' noses, as a result of which the worst that could happen in a dictatorship happened; they started to hope.

But this never happened again.

132.

"Excuse me, Your Excellency, old Mr. Nuszbaum is here. He wishes to speak with Your Excellency." Mrs. Artúr, Mrs. Gábor Artúr, that was the name of Grandfather's housekeeper in Pest. Grandfather's place of residence was officially in Pest, and so he was also asked to join us. Grandmother stayed in Majk.

"*Properly speaking,* I'm a descendant of Görgey," Mrs. Artúr whispered confidentially to Grandfather, ignorant of the fact that you couldn't whisper confidentially to Grandfather; at least, there was no one in the world who was in a position to want—or dare—whisper anything confidentially in his ear. Grandfather was shocked.

"Görgey. Of course. As you wish." But Mrs. Artúr idolized

him and couldn't do enough for him (soft-boiled eggs, et cetera). On this day, the day of his forcible resettlement, she kept breaking into tears.

"Who is this Nuszbaum?"

"The grocer from Lövőház Street. Don't you remember him?"

"No."

"He insists on speaking with Your Excellency. Can I send him in?"

"Can't he make it another time? Next Thursday afternoon, let's say, during five o'clock tea in Hort, at the kulak's house, where I am transferring my living quarters."

"Please don't bring that up," Mrs. Artúr whimpered. "Poor old man, he's very agitated. Let me show him in."

Grandfather nods, Mrs. Artúr shows, Mr. Nuszbaum enters, bows low, greets Grandfather, Grandfather gives him the cautious go-ahead.

"How do you do."

"I'm Mór Nuszbaum. Don't you remember me? Of course, you can't expect an Esterházy count to remember a Nuszbaum." When Grandfather came back from POW camp, he stood in line at the Jewish Federation aid office. They look at his name. Móric. Fine. Mother's name, Schwarzenberg. Fine. *Nu*. Móric, old boy, how did you manage to get this handsome family name?

"What do you want, Mr. Nuszbaum?"

"So you know I'm called Nuszbaum."

"You just told me."

"Oh, yes, of course."

"What can I do for you, Mr. Nuszbaum?"

"I'm not here from *achrem*, sir . . ."

"Achrem? Wait a moment . . . During First World War I served a couple of years in Galicia. My younger brother Alajos died on the battlefield there. But I don't remember an Achrem . . ."

"That's not a city, sir, if you please. I mean, *achrem*. *Achrem* is this!" And with a sort of "in the chest from behind" convoluted gesture, he scratched his left ear with his right hand. "If you see what I mean."

"Possibly," said Grandfather flatly.

"In short, I'm not here from *achrem*."

"You can come from wherever you please, just come to the point!" Grandfather yelled impatiently from atop the half-packed suitcases.

"Who is this Nuszbaum, I ask? A nobody! A great big nonentity, if you please, compared to an Esterházy. Kindly tell me the truth. Am I not right?"

"I don't know what you are getting at." Grandfather was beginning to feel uncomfortable.

"I heard about the painful situation Your Excellency is experiencing. Nobody knows better than I, oh, the pain! It's been in my blood for five thousand years, this running helter-skelter, grabbing what little you have and fleeing, always, God only knows where. We know all about it, sir. My grandfather, when he was fleeing Galicia . . . And all that Old Testament wandering, forty years in the desert, all that bother and vexation, sir, it's right here in my blood . . ."

"If you don't mind, Mr. Nuszbaum, could we please get down to business? Provided you have any."

"Oh, dear, what a foolish old man, the way I'm carrying on, keeping Your Excellency from your work."

"Well, as a matter of fact . . ."

"But before I come to the point, I just want to say, please don't judge us by that man Mátyás Rákosi. We don't like it . . ." He also committed the same *faux pas* as the housekeeper; he started whispering. "He's got his nerve—*azes!*"

"Oh," said Grandfather, and they plunged headlong into a deep silence. "Well, dear Mr. Nuszbaum, it's been a pleasure."

"Wait! Wait! I haven't even started what I came for."

"In that case, could you make it short?"

"I'll try. But you know, sir, before I plucked up the courage to come here, I was thinking that Your Excellency will have me thrown out."

"Now that you mention it . . ."

"Because when I learned that Your Excellency will be deported tomorrow, I put together a small package. Here it is. And please don't throw me out with it!"

"What on earth is it?" Grandfather asked, not crediting his ears.

"I've been to hell and back with my family. I know what a man needs at a time like this. This is a package like that, sir, if you please. I put it together myself. Please trust my experience."

Grandfather turned very angry. He didn't have much practice in dealing with people not of his rank. At the moment, what he resented most about the new times was the new relationships.

"I hope you don't imagine that I will accept this charity package . . ."

Nuszbaum cradled the package to his bosom as he approached Grandfather.

"Take it, Your Excellency, I beg you!" They looked silently at each other. "Do you want to hear? When in 1944 the Arrow Cross drove us away with the yellow star on our chest, Your Excellency was just walking along Lövőház Street. You were wearing a herringbone suit, had a walking stick in your hand and a gray hat on your head." I was familiar with these from Hort, where Grandfather wore them every Sunday, herringbone, walking stick, gray hat, that's how he attended church. The Party secretary tried to prohibit it, especially the walking stick, but he couldn't because there was freedom of religion. I was scared, scared of the herringbone; I didn't dare touch the jacket in case it pricked me, but in reality I was afraid I'd choke on it, because I'd learned by then that you can choke on fish bone. "And then Your Excellency stopped on the edge of the sidewalk, and as we passed by on the road . . . with a beautiful gesture, you raised your hat to us!"

"I don't recall . . . But it's really nothing, nothing at all . . ."

"Nothing? I will never forget it! Have you any idea what it meant to me then and there, in my condition? I felt like a human being again! Do you understand? A human being! I straightened up and stared into the face of the Arrow Cross man with the machine gun!"

"That just shows your strength of character, Mr. Nuszbaum . . ."

"No, sir, no. That public raising of the hat gave me strength to survive the horrors to come. My entire family perished. To the last man!"

This 'to the last man,' it's some sort of Jewish tradition, my grandfather thought. A family of aristocrats can't perish to the last man. Somehow, someone *always* survives. Four men dying on the same battlefield within one hour, yes, but to the last man? No. That's how their arithmetic works.

"To the last man! You can't imagine how often I thought of that gesture with the hat. That then and there, on Lövőház Street, a man gave me back my self-respect!" Mr. Nuszbaum was panting heavily. He wiped his forehead with a handkerchief. Then exhausted, he said, "In short, this is what I wished to say. That I'm indebted to Your Excellency."

"But why is it that you mention it now, after so many years?"

"I would have liked to many times, but my nerve failed me. But now . . . I feel . . . I feel we're closer."

"No," my grandfather said inaudibly, giving way to despair.

"That we're closer . . . possibly . . ." At the door, he turned back: "May my God bless you, Your Excellency!"

Curtain down.

"I'd be better off if this Nuszbaum were God. Obviously, I'd be much better off."

## 133.

Bill of lading serial number 0111263, series X of the Trucking Company for the Conveyance of Goods was filled in in pencil. License plate number: YT-404. Load-carrying capacity: 4 tons. Load-carrying capacity of trailer: ___ Way bill number: 013601. Order number: 31252. The carting contract is liable to the schedule of fees and the Vehicle Operating Regulations. Place of lading: Budapest. Place of unloading: Hort, Heves County. Forwarder (consignor) my father, with an *sz* and *i*, address: XIIth district, et cetera, place of residence (?!): same. Consignee: here, father's signature, with doctor, awe-inspiring, inimitable. Asterisk, footnote at the bottom: Fill out only in case of inter-city trucking. Which made this inter-city trucking. At the bottom the heavily framed space is for the registration of the forwarder (consignor) (i.e., my father).

Type of packaging: not filled in. Number of packages: not filled in. Type of consignment: personal effects. Declared weight in quintals: not filled in. Confirmed weight (outside of the heavily framed space!): not filled in.

Separate agreements, other notations (ex.: re. loading and unloading, route designation, equipment): not filled in. Attachments: not filled in. Name of person (company) paying the bill of lading: the same. Address and residence: the same. Account number: cash, and under it the highly respected forwarder's (consignor's) one might say revolutionary signature once again, the first letter tore through the paper in several places, this powerful and grand *D* is no joke, whereas it is only the *d* for doctor, but very much part of the name. You'd think it was there instead of the count; but when I mentioned this to him, he looked at me as if I'd lost my mind, as if our family had thrown in its lot only and exclusively with the peasant uprisings (György Dózsa's grandson, et cetera), anonymously. Anyone who has ever come face-to-face with my father's *D* has a higher regard for him, a man to be reckoned with. Forging is out of the question, I practiced for years and came up with nothing but paltry imitations. I admire him for this *D*. I often asked him, just for the fun of it, for my enjoyment, to write down his name, our name, the pen gliding up and down for seconds, to the right and left loops thrown in for good measure, double somersault and a Swedish leap, but not haphazardly, mind you, but according to a perfectly choreographed and emotionally charged plan—(after '45 Father worked for the Commerical Bank for two years, foreign correspondence, that's where he "got into the practice of it")—and suddenly there it was, this strange, wild calligraphy once more, which didn't remind me even remotely of the name I write, what I have to write, and yet is the same, an ecstatic, transcendental version. The impressive initials—which aren't even "us"—he flips in a thinning, insignificant little tail, the superfluous remains of the name, this is how ambitious intention is thwarted by irresolute will.

The truck is to show up on July 16, 1951, at 21:00; persons conveyed, with an *sz* and *i*, my father, my mother, and me, ages: thirty, thirty, one, which was not strictly true, father was thirty-two, and mother thirty-five. Among the persons conveyed there's also a policeman hailing from Gödöllő, age thirty-five, Török Street.

The calculation of charges can be found outside of the heavy frame. According to the bill, the truck did 71 kilometers, for which the charge was 484 forints; trailer: not filled out; load back, charge for waiting; not filled out. Going uphill (the slope at Gödöllő, I imagine, the infamous "horseshoe" was still there then), 10 kilometers, that's 40 forints. They didn't charge for dirt roads, there was no snow surcharge, not even a disinfecting fee; on the other hand, there was a charge for showing up: 34 forints. That comes to 558, i.e., five hundred fifty-eight good old Hungarian forints. Accepted and confirmed by me, László Meszes, truck driver. Branch office stamp, signature, place and time when bill of lading was filled out. No. 1. Comm Min.—511133. Athenaeum Printing Co.

On the back, like a title: Confirmation of work done. Subtitle or genre designation: László Meszes. Copy; the carbon paper's light, bluish stains smudged the sheet—as if the night were falling, and it's impossible to tell whether we're seeing the earth or the sky. The paper reveals that the truck left the garage—interesting; they wrote it like this, garage, in English, I wonder why—at 19:40, on the letterhead it says: from garage to garage, as if to say, from soul to soul; the kilometer gauge stood at: 37,620. It reached us at eight-thirty p.m., having come 14 kilometers (empty, as the heading emphatically points out). They got us loaded up in two hours, we loaded up in two hours, and we left at a quarter to eleven.

After a brief consultation, my father decided to call a cab for (great) Grandmother and Aunt Mia. Interesting—no one saw anything unusual in this, not even later. After all, being resettled by cab! A touch of pride and arrogance, at least! But no, nothing except for practical thinking, plus the absurdity of the very thought of the two elderly ladies traveling on a truck! Aunt Mia up on the loading platform, yes, that's pretty fantastic. Taking a cab is not. Just expensive.

The policeman was assigned the driver's cab; he acted decently, or better, still, matter-of-factly, without sympathy, just like a valet, an English butler; he helped us load, he spoke softly and to the point, from time to time addressing a word or two to my mother.

"No, not that, you won't need that. That, yes."

He said it gruffly, in a manner that did not call for gratitude, you could even hate him if you chose. Mother didn't want to sit up front, so Father ended up sitting next to the policeman, and I in my mother's lap. To this day I can smell that Csepel truck, the smell of the diesel fuel. (This, to me, is what the taste of a piece of madeleine in the tea was to Proust.)

Mami sat on the loading platform. A gentle summer's night enveloped her. She leaned back into the red cedar easy chair and lit up—we liked Mami's smoking, we anticipated, watched for and admired the gesture as she inhaled, blissfully lowering her lashes, as she exhaled the smoke with a merry little sigh, for a moment the entire delicate and doubtful ceremony conjuring up behind her the elegant haute bourgeois world that had never quite existed; she flung her long, handsome legs, Bogyica's, across each other, as if she were sitting in a huge, celestial salon (in motion).

Also, she sang quietly to herself.

She was pulled down toward the earth by the fatigue which from then on never left her. The loading had been a success, she was pleased, *carpe diem,* she enjoyed the moment. Now and then she waved merrily to the taxidriver, whereupon Grandmother gave a dismissive wave of the hand. Mother pretended she didn't see. She put one across the Esterházys every chance she got— which isn't true like this in the least, because she never put anything across her children as *such,* though from time to time she'd do them mischief just the same.

In short, Princess Schwarzenberg was helplessly, desperately waving to them that they should stop, she's got something to say, but Mother ignored her all the way to Hatvan, where they finally stopped. The policeman knew an alehouse that was still open, and the men gulped down some cheap schnapps. The policeman— András Juhász—back into the silent mask of the English butler.

Great-grandmother past her ninetieth birthday by then, but still hardy and imperious, magisterial, and the size of a baroque wardrobe. She spoke mostly German. I don't know where I got it, but I was under the impression that she was the king of the Czechs, or had been, except for some reason, it was now on hold. I was afraid of her because she would look right through me, as if I were invisible. Only once did she not look right through me, when her eyes came to stop on my hand. She raised and turned it contemptuously.

"These fingers are suited for playing German music, but Chopin never!" And she dropped my hand like a sack of hot potatoes.

Later in Hort, wrapped in a heavy black shawl like a peasant, she was moved out onto the porch, into the sun, where she sat till the evening, until she was enveloped in shade. She had to be moved by the hour. My fear disappeared when once she let out some gas, and I was standing beside her. Her face remained impassive. Screaming with laughter, I ran away. The king of the Czechs waved her stick at me. Big deal. Who are the Czechs, anyway? Besides, by then, or still, I was a peasant who had shaken off, or was in the act of shaking off, the yoke of the past centuries.

"Matyi, please! *Bitte!*" she said, ordering my father to her in that gentle Hatvan night. Unobtrusively, with nothing but the slight motion of her brow, she indicated the policeman. Everybody was looking at them. "I've hear said," Great-grandmother whispered, "that the menservants of the sultan who are taken into his service because of their beauty"—and at this juncture there was that motion of the brow again aimed at András Juhász, "and whose numbers are legion, are dismissed when they reach twenty-two."

She stared fixedly at Father, who nodded, then sighed, then nodded again. Then Great-grandmother changed the subject, venting her surprise and indignation that Father should have organized this outing when the visibility is so poor. She likes these merry picnics, but this one—and she swung out her arms, nothing, *nichts, Matyi lieber, nichts,* she sees nothing of the landscape, whereas if her memory serves her right, this hilly region of northern Hungary is utterly charming. She'd taken part in an imperial hunt once, but no, the Emperor wasn't there . . .

"King," my father grunted.

Except, that poor Elizabeth! Still, it's really most inconsiderate. Poor Mia, for her it is probably all the same, oh, the eternal realm of Darkness, and the truck, too, puffing its fumes right under her nose.

Father lowered his head and earnestly begged his grandmother to forgive him. Indeed, everything is not *quite* as it should be.

"Forgive me, Grandmother."

The redoubtable Schwarzenberg princess smiled and stroked father's head.

*"In Ordnung, bist ein braver Bube,"* she said, then added dreamily, *"Ein Ehemann ist eine schöne Sache,"* it's all right, he's a good boy, and a husband is a fine thing.

Mother stayed on the red cedar, she was singing, she'd had a shot of the schnapps too—one of the few times that she drank with my father, who through the years became more and more lonely, he and his drink.

"What, may I ask, are you drinking?" Great-grandmother demanded. Father would have liked to hide it. "Show it to me!"

"This is not for Grandmother, Grandmother, if you please," he said. He was worried.

"Let me be the judge of that. Besides, what is this policeman doing here? I don't like the police."

"Grandmother!"

"Stop whispering. It's bad manners. I didn't like them before, when they wore those feathers, and I like them even less now!"

She took the schnapps from Father's hand and smelled it. *"Mein lieber,* this is dreadful."

"Yes, Grandmother, dreadful."

But by then the old lady had downed the drink like a regular coachman.

"Dreadful, indeed, son. Thank you." She glanced about her, as if she'd just noticed the truck loaded to capacity with furniture, with my mother sitting atop, softly singing to herself.

"Lili," Great-grandmother said. She was shocked.

Pause.

"Let's go. We'll be late," the driver said.

"That is out of the question, young man. I can't possibly be late for dinner, and if I am, the rest of the company are too early!" She kept looking from the policeman to the driver to my mother on top of the truck. "At times the appropriation of land, the confiscation of furniture, jail and other forms of punishment may be called for, I admit." She took a whiff of the glass. "But putting aside the administration of justice for a moment, the law and necessity, I can't help but be surprised time and time again at the sight of how brutally people treat other people. Brutally."

The three men said nothing.

"All right, *allez, allez,* let's go!" And also, that this time they'd be going ahead of us because they don't smell as bad as we. In a pack, the least smelly heads the hunt.

And so it was. But sometimes the cab went too fast and we flashed our headlights at them, but at first they misunderstood and stepped on the gas with us lumbersomely trying to catch up, and Mother laughing and screaming in the back, and with me holding on to Father's knee as if the grownups were playing car race as we swayed right and left in the profound night of the Great Hungarian Plain. Or wasn't it the Great Hungarian Plain?

We had to turn left off of the road to Gyöngyös. The wheels squeaked and squealed and Great-grandmother waved wildly for us to catch up, if we can. We could see her laughing. We'd never seen her like this. I even said:

"Great-grandmother is laughing."

"Mind your manners, son." My father's words smelled of schnapps, but unlike Mother, I wasn't bothered by it. On the contrary. On the other hand, I didn't like the smell of next morning's wine, the breath, it's so stale, sour, and cold. But fresh pálinka smell is warm and heady and strong. Papi-strong.

A long, straight road led us into the main square. We watched the sky turn red and then blue, as if they'd lit a bonfire to welcome us. But it was only a house on fire. The birds, too, began to chirp and sing. They must have thought the day was breaking.

"Is this hell?" I asked.

"No," said father briskly.

In the bizarre light we could see strange creatures standing in the fields, looking at us.

"What are they, Father?"

"Cows, son."

"What are cows, Father?"

"Cows are cows, son."

As we drove farther along the brightening road, there were other creatures in the fields, white, furry creatures with four legs.

"What are they, Father?"

"Sheep, son."

"What are sheep, Father?"

Angry, Father pulled me closer on his knee, as if trying to ram me into the ground, barking at me, will I never stop asking questions?

"Sheep are sheep, cows are cows, and that over there is a goat. A goat is a goat. A goat gives milk, the sheep gives wool, and the cow gives everything. What else in God's name do you want to know?"

I started crying because Father never talked like that, never

685

spoke sharply to us. Father may have been strong, but that day he was also worn out.

Father may have been worn out, but as soon as we reached the main square, he jumped off the cab, called to the driver (the policeman kept to himself), and quickly got in line with the firefighters to pass the water buckets.

A man in uniform stepped up to him. "Who are you?"

Father's spirits were high from this work, and from the helping.

"The house is on fire," he said offhandedly and was about to pass the bucket, but the policeman grabbed his arm. The water spilled out. "The house is on fire." Then he added, by way of explanation, "the fire doesn't ask you who you are."

There was a woman standing next to him. Obviously, she had no time to pin up her hair, but had pulled it together with a rubber band. She started screaming with laughter. The catastrophe, the fire, liberated the people. They forgot that they were afraid. They stopped what they were doing, and laughing, repeated the stranger's words, the fire doesn't ask you who you are, ha-ha-ha. The policeman shifted his feet nervously. His name was Lajos Feuer, that's why everybody was laughing. By then *our* cop had come over as well, and the two whispered something to each other. We were cleared.

We arrived at our designated place of residence at 1:30. The kilometer gauge stood at 37.705. Freight designation: personal effects, weight: 40 quintals. Number of trips: I. Leaving Hort at 3:00, time spent: 6:30. And bottom right: dispatcher's stamp (with trade name) and a signature: that energetic, awe-inspiring handwriting again, the invincible scorpion that begins with a gigantic *D* and turns back upon itself.

## 134

Old man Pista Simon was waiting at the gate.

"The Simons?" the driver asked.

"That's us," he said, never once taking his eyes off my father.

"István Simon the kulak?" our policeman asked for the sake of accuracy, his tone official for the first time.

"You could say that," the old peasant shrugged, and continued eyeing my father, who had alighted just then from the high cab of the truck. But before he could swing into action (taking me down or, what is even better, putting me round his neck), old man Pista rushed over to him and . . .

"Welcome, Count," he bellowed, grabbed Father's hand, and kissed it with a loud smack. Father was so surprised he didn't resist, while the old man kept repeating how happy he was and what an honor (as he later said in the village, the finest person from Pest at the home of the finest peasant), and he doesn't know what he's done to deserve it, he'd never met such a great gentleman in all his life, he's never shook hands with such a great gentleman. At last, Father felt his own awkwardness.

"All right, Uncle Simon, all right!" he said, and grabbed the old man by the shoulder, as if trying to make a drunken man stand up straight. "We're not alone," he added quietly.

A woman was standing inside by the kitchen stove. It was Aunt Rozi. She was cooking something, but when we entered, she didn't turn around.

"You kissed his hand?" she grumbled to the stove, but audibly all the same. Our little column stopped in its tracks. "You kissed his hand?!"

"Yes," Uncle Pista said softly, also to the stove, or into thin air. He was angry. "Yes, yes! It's only right and proper!"

"You're an idiot," Aunt Rozi said, showing even more of her back than before. She was making a late-night dinner for us, eggs with onion, green pepper and sausage, from eggs whose yolks were bright yellow.

Me and the two elderly ladies were put to bed. Once in bed, Great-grandmother ordered Father to her bedside.

"You did well, dear. *Hort, das ist wirklich schön einen richtigen Hort zu besitzen . . .*" Hort is a treasure, a refuge, a haven, an asylum. Hort is not only beautiful, it is also safe. "An asylum! Good work, son."

"No, Grandmother, it is not good. Nothing is," my father, who was again dead tired and nothing but tired, grunted. "This here, Grandmother, this whole thing . . . is . . . it's *in Hungarian*."


## 135.


Right away, just a day, just a moment after the institution of the land reform, a delegation of men came to see my father from the village. They've thought it over, and they've come to the solid conclusion that they don't need the bit of land they can each have, they'd rather give it back to His Excellency, the Count (Papi), who should go on managing and overseeing it, it'd worked out so well before. My father regarded these serious, grownup men for some time, decked out as if they were off to the Easter resurrection parade, their boots as shiny as a mirror, their white shirts buttoned up to the collar, in their hands their black hats, which each was crushing between his fingers.

There was silence. Father had listened graciously while they had finished saying what they had come to say. Then one of them, Dodi Knapp's father, broke out:

"Kindly say somethin'! Ya gotta say somethin'. Ya mustn't shame us like this!"

"Fine, fine," my father said slowly, enjoying what he was about to say. "Just tell me, friends, have you made arrangements?"

"What sort a arrangements, Your Excellency?"

"Visiting arrangements."

"Visitin' arrangements for where?" the men asked, impatient and puzzled, looking at each other for the answer.

"The Ávó, where else?"

Hearing the word "Ávó," the men huddled closer together.

"Why do you say a thing like that, Your Excellency?"

"I say a thing like that because, what do you think? If you men do what you propose, how much time would the Ávó need before they came and arrested me? No time at all. Then you could come visit me in the jail house. That's why the arrangements are important . . . Or were you not planning to visit?"

The men looked at each other again, but no one wanted to answer the question. They were loath to commit themselves. Also, they didn't like the conditional. If it is this or that, yes, but this they didn't like, they thought it was irresponsible, compared to the declarative. They were familiar only with what was.

"In that case, Your Excellency must advise us what to do."

Father gave a quick shrug. The men took offense. Disappointed, they left. Later, Grandfather disappointed them as well by favoring the farmers' cooperatives. He felt that parceling out the land into dwarf holdings made no sense.

"It makes no sense!" Sense was Grandfather's guiding principle, the most important sacrament. He couldn't make heads or tails of the ancient yearning of the Hungarian peasant for land because he never hungered after land himself, he had enough of his own. Then later, when in a sudden fit of ill-considered democratic fervor he attempted to convince a peasant of the superiority of the new ways, of the advantages of working a set number of hours in unison with others just like a clerk, and that the yield would be greater, et cetera, et cetera, the cautious peasant didn't want to say either yes or no, but by way of an answer pointed at a bird flying overhead. He didn't dare speak about freedom, but he had the courage to point out its symbol . . .

## 136.

My mother was brought up with an eye to practicality. Mamili put the girls to work. They learned to cook and bake early on, and though cleaning was the servants' job, for half a year they had to do that too ("you must learn, dear, what to expect of the staff"). Household chores plus culture, religion plus public education with a bit of dancing thrown in, they knew everything young ladies of breeding should know.

Father, too, was brought up for the same thing, i.e., for life. Except, they were both brought up for a different sort of life. Being forcibly resettled had not figured in their plans. I'm not saying that their upbringing did not oppose the view that this was the best of all possible worlds, it's just that they never thought that what came to pass could conceivably come to pass.

If anything saved my mother, it was not her education, nor her perseverance, fortitude or sense of responsibility, but her sense of refinement which she regarded as part of Creation, and she held on to this conviction of hers forever after with effortless ease and single-mindedness of purpose. Bogyikó too had a respect for form—and it worked fine for some time—but it was missing the personal touch. My beautiful aunt never burst her bounds; she exercised restraint in all things, even in her truly breathtaking beauty. Life gave Mother a quiet life, but that was hers, lock, stock, and barrel.

These are her napkins, her place mats painted with her two hands, her seating cards, her handwritten menus (the legendary cardboard menu cards from the very bottom of life, elegant, and in French, Hort. 26.4.1951, Grandfather's banquet in honor of his seventieth birthday, held out on the porch, *carré de porc rôti,* because Aunt Rozi got us pork from an illegal slaughter; and the horrid bull's blood, the Château Torro Rosso!), her unobtrusive, refined way of speaking—these saved the family from a decline of sorts. Which is an overstatement, of course. (It saved it from nothing.) Father took all this in stride. Having been surrounded by refinement all his life, he couldn't care less about it. Couldn't appreciate it. Didn't even notice. He regarded my mother's ambition, the forthright individuality of her refinement, with suspicion. Had he a grain of pride in him, it would have been with outright condescension.

My father never looked down on anyone, which is how he was an aristocrat. My grandfather looked down on everyone, which is how he was an aristocrat.

As for me, I just keep blinking my eye.


## 137.


When my brother fell ill, or was it Uncle Menyus?, Papi went up to Pest a number of times. The bus left at 14:30, it reached Engels Square at 16:10, started back at 18:55, and by eight-thirty he was back at his appointed residence. He was never caught. Once he laughed and told Grandfather that he'd forgotten to buy a ticket on the bus, but nobody asked him for it.

"You went without a ticket?"

"I did, indeed," my father said proudly. And also, that he took a bath in a bathtub! After a year! In hot water! And he even had ice cream. "And also, I got five tons of the cheapest lignite. And also railway sleepers for kindling! I think the sleepers are identical with the ones Menyus laid down in 1944." He stretched himself tall. "I have always liked doing what felt good, or if I couldn't, I liked what I was doing to feel good." And he grinned.

"You went without a ticket?"

Only now did Papi notice Grandfather's severe expression. He nodded, yes, without a ticket, as luck would have it. At which Grandfather nodded too.

"In that case, as luck would have it, you will now go to the bus station, son, buy a ticket, and tear it up."

"And . . . ?"

"That's it."

"Shall I bring it back?"

"What for?"

"To show you."

"What for?"

He went, he bought it, he tore it up. Order was restored.

Apropos this order, Grandfather was eating chocolate. He was sitting in his easy chair behind the curtain, eating in secret. I asked him to give me some.

"Please give me some."

"An Esterházy does not beg."

"All right, then don't give me some."

And lo and behold, he didn't.


## 138.


The dictatorship of the proletariat came up with a plan—cunning, they hoped. They had calculated that the forcible resettlements to the countryside would make the peasants, who were the ideological allies of the working class, hate the ruling class, who had oppressed them for centuries and were rotten to the core besides—hate them not only more than ever, but this time, in the spirit of Party policy. The plan was a whopping failure.

The exact opposite happened. The peasants and the ruling class were overwhelmed by a feeling of undifferentiated solidarity. ("Go kneel in the second pew countin' from the confessional, you'll find something there, for a quick Lord's Prayer." "You never ate so much chicken in your lives, have ya, son, as back then?") For instance, the awkward circumstance that they had to share their already crowded homes with strangers they blamed on the Communists without giving it a second thought. Some even considered it an honor.

Consequently, we were given their one good room, the so-called *clean* room, whereas theoretically we should have been living (making amends) in the shed attached to the house that was full of chicken shit and resisted any attempt at heating. When inspection time came, the authorities didn't neglect to notice.

"There's plenty a room all around," Uncle Pista said, but did not look the man from the council in the eye.

"Have it your way, Simon," the young man shrugged, "but beware of the consequences!"

These people couldn't get a sentence out edgewise without making it sound like a threat. Pass the salt. I have a headache. It is your turn to take the boy to kindergarten. Your uncle was shot today. This, however, was more habit than outright malice, because they *did* intimidate people all the time, regardless of what they were saying, thinking, or fabricating. That's dictatorship: the certainty of intimidation and the certainty of fear, $i + f$, intimidation plus fear, that's dictatorship for you. But it's not like one half of the nation is intimidating the other half, or the powers that be are intimidating everyone, because there's something contingent upon all this, a howling, horrifying uncertainty, because the one who is doing the intimidating is also intimidated, and the one being intimidated intimidates others in turn. The strictly delineated roles are obscured to the outer limits, everyone intimidates and everyone fears, and all the time there are executioners and there are victims, and the two are clearly distinguishable, the one from the other.

At one time seven of us had to make do—and so seven of us made do—with the twenty-five square meters of the "clean" room. We divided the room in two with a gray blanket. The realm in the back, beyond the blanket (and the Seven Seas) belonged to Grandfather, all of it, with everyone agreeing that it was only fair. He did too, though I'm not sure about Mami, who wouldn't say. Grandfather was not a man to be defied. (Of course, that depends on what we mean by defiance. Human defiance on a grand scale cannot be checked.)

Uncle Pista Simon and family (including defiant Aunt Rozi) were even afraid to turn to him. To turn to him in words. Whereas compared to his usual self, by then Grandfather had turned into a warmhearted, kind old gentleman. When he engaged his "hosts" in conversation, sticking to factual, general subjects on agriculture, they ran away, bashfully hiding their faces. Grandfather shook his head. He never did figure out what he'd done wrong.

Everyone called Mother by her first name. They didn't think of her as a gentleman, not even a gentlewoman or a lady of breeding (though *that* she was, as far as that went), but first and foremost, as a mother. To prove the point, there I was, wailing; besides, she was big with my younger brother by then, or was in a blessed state, it was too early to tell which. They called my father Doctor. Uncle Pista opted for Count, but Father talked him out of it. The old man chewed this over, then smiling slyly nodded, fine.

"What's so funny, Pista, old buddy?"

"Nothing, *Doctor*, sir." And Pista winked at the word "doctor."

"Only a fool would laugh at nothing, ain't that true, Pista, old buddy?"

"That's very true, *Doctor,* sir." And there came another wink.

"Something in your eye, old buddy?" Father asked pointedly, whereupon a silence ensued. "In that case, old friend, tell me what's in place of that nothing, otherwise I'll be forced to conclude . . . understand me?"

The old man let out a chuckle and brought his hand up to hide his lips.

"Sure, sure . . . *Doc . . . tor.*"

They talked as if they were afraid of being overheard. Uncle Pista circled round and round what he would not say and enjoyed it, while Father, as if he were stuck inside an old Transylvanian anecdote, tried his hand at some imaginary peasant language, talking the way people used to talk in Pest when telling old stories of the simple folk. Meanwhile, the old kulak laughed up his sleeve, thinking he'd gotten the better of the secret police, because even though he said doctor, he was thinking count.

"Besides, seein' how we all feel the same way in the village," and he winked again, "we *all* say Doctor, in which case this *doctor* also means *count,* but they can't have nothin' on us, 'cause we all say doctor!"

On a purely linguistic plane Uncle Pista was right—the faultless implementation of a faultless thought: they can't have nothin' on you. Later on, though, it became evident to all concerned that they can always have *something* on you, and do. Uncle Pista, too, was soon arrested on some fabricated charge, not that a dictatorship needs fabricated charges, or only rarely; what they need is fabricated laws, the kind that can't be adhered to, and who decides whether they're being adhered to or not? What impressive scope for action!

He was behind bars for a year. After his release he was no longer laughing. He was weeping.

"Look what they done to me, Doctor," he said, holding his hands up to my father. My father saw nothing out of the ordinary.

Nice, strong peasant hands. "They're white, Doctor, *white!* Oh, the shame of it!"

Uncle Pista hadn't worked for a year, and his hands looked it. This is what he was showing my father, this shame. By then my father had proper, tanned, rough, swarthy hands. His fingers were so strong, you could use them for a swing. We held on to his index finger—our hands could hardly encircle it—as he swung us back and forth.

My brother was born in September. He had such a big head, or grew one, people came from all over to look, and in December, at the age of ninety, Great-grandmother died.

She owned a silver cane with a hippopotamus head (Uncle Charlie brought it from Africa, or so they said, along with his chronic scrofulous conjunctivitis, both a gift from some minor king). When she tapped it, we had to run to her and kneel, or whatever. She used to sit on a throne-like chair, and we had to kiss her hand.

"Stop pawing me, I'm not dying."

In the end, she suffered a stroke. She was conscious of what was going on around her, and she understood what we were saying, but the line of communication between her thoughts and her words had been severed. She tried her best, though. One day at lunch she looked at me and said, "Pass the salt." I passed the salt. Her face was drenched in sweat. She began gesticulating with her trembling hand. Her eyes filled with tears, and she kept saying, "Not that! The salt! The salt!"

Overcome by fear and pity, I looked with bewilderment at Aunt Mia, who'd been looking after Great-grandmother. Biting her lips and pale as a ghost, Aunt Mia first stared into space, then at the others, who were shifting uncomfortably in their seats, then passed the toothpicks, the paprika, the soup tureen.

"Not that! The salt! The salt!"

At which, stupid and tactless as I was, instead of crying, my tears gave way to laughter.

"*Mistviech!*" Aunt Mia shouted at me, "*Schweinehund! Marsch hinaus!*"

For days afterward I wouldn't look anyone in the eye and hated Aunt Mia more than anything in the world because she was right. Ever since, mourning and tragedy bring laughter instead of tears. Who knows. Maybe it's some sort of atavism. For all I know, I might be descended from a tribe that weep when they're happy and laugh when something ails them. I'm never as merry and high-spirited as when I'm feeling low.

Later Great-grandmother stopped talking altogether. She didn't even say salt. When a shadow fell over her, she let out a yelp, and someone would move her chair back into the sun. By the afternoon she'd progress from the brick-floored porch onto the soil in the yard. The soil doesn't respond to tapping. Great-grandmother couldn't tap with her stick anymore. This is what killed her, I think, that her power over others was irrevocably gone. What will become of the Czechs now? And the Crown? Papi will have to see to it. He hasn't much time, of course. He leaves in the early morning, and when he comes home, he's exhausted and sits on the porch, or verandah, he sits in the dark of night alone, just sits there, with no one daring to talk to him, not even Grandfather. Only my mother. He's as lonely as a king weighed down by the pressing travails of the realm, yet for all that he seems to be a king who is a subject, too, and this sort of thing takes the wind out of a king's sails. Then he abruptly springs to his feet, the hens, like so many frightened courtiers, scurry off, his ermine robe sweeps along the cool stone of the porch, and by the time he reaches his bed, he is fast asleep.

At times, he fell asleep even before I did, which filled me with pride.

## 139

Once in a while, if we were careful we could sneak up to him and ask him for a story. But if our timing was not opportune he brushed us off like cats or shooed us away like ducklings, so he wouldn't step on them. (Once—though not because of this—my brother threw the ducklings down the hatch in the outhouse. "I love the way they *screeched*.")

Most of his stories were about the heroic Huns. Or was it Magyars? Prince Csaba, and how the hooves of his steed were covered with star dust. He could even imitate the clapping of the hooves when Prince Csaba was riding on pavement, heading for Gyöngyös, let's say, or Hatvan. In the beating of hooves on pavement my father has no peer. We learned it from him, and I can do it, too. But only he could do an entire brass band with cymbals, bugles or what have you. There must've been six of them at least (*i.e.*, the band). But he had to be in a jolly good mood, or had to have some drink in him.

"Hay is for horses, straw is for cows, milk is for piggy-wiggs, and wash for old sows."

"As Dolly was milkin' her cow one day, Tom took out his pipe and began for to play, so Doll and the cow danced round and round till the milk pail was broke and crashed to the ground."

By then, we also knew all about cows. A cow is a cow, is a cow, ha–ha!

Each of us had our own tale. Mine was Prince Csaba and the star dust, my little brother's the seven-league boots, my sister's the tetanus shot (ha–ha–ha). Each of us had our own story. At least, that's how I saw it. My brother talks a lot, he'll talk to everyone (even now). Our sister, on the other hand, cries all the time either because she's got a mid-ear infection, and that's why, or she's got stomach cramps, and that's why, or neither, and that's why. I make funny faces for her, so she'll stop crying. I place a leaf on my head and let it fall down. Our sister laughs and laughs. I push the pram round the yard and in front of the house, people on our street come to look, a baby carriage with springs, a real aristocratic carriage!, while my brother is on the swings with the grocer's Frédi and I hear him tell him about Prince Csaba's star dust, and he's clicking his tongue, see, this is what Prince Csaba's steed does on the asphalt when they go to Gyöngyös or Hatvan.

I tell him to stop telling that story, it's my story. It's my story, and my story is my history. He won't stop. I push him and he cries, waah, waah, then Frédi pushes me, with my story in his head, at which point everything goes black in my head and I run at him with fists and knees and feet . . .

"Hey, stop, stop," but I won't because I can't, I don't know how, and if I stop, they'll take my story from me and tell it from now on instead of me. Frédi pushes me away and runs off yelling.

"The Count tried to kill me!" he screams. "The Count tried to kill me!"

I don't know what to do because I never tried to kill anyone before and my brother in his swing is frightened, he cries.

"Don't kill me, brother, dear, I beg you, don't kill me, spare me, please."

He looks so helpless I put my arms around him and help him off the swing. He hugs me.

"I won't tell your story anymore, I promise," he whispers in my ear, his breath hot. "I won't tell Frédi about Prince Csaba."

I want to laugh but I can't because my sister is crying in her pram again and it's gotten dark outside and what's the use of trying to make funny faces and letting leaves fall off your head when they can't see you in the dark?

In the evening, Mother asks what I did to that poor grocer boy.

"His mother was here. A lovely woman. I don't know what we'd do without her."

My brother comes to my aid, I had no intention of killing Frédi, and I didn't want to kill him either, probably I didn't want to kill anyone at all. Our father shushes him up and takes him on his lap, "giddyap, giddyap," riding him on his knee.

My mother says, "Go over to Frédi's and tell him you're sorry."

But Father cuts in, "Do you *want* to tell Frédi you're sorry?"

"No."

My parents look at each other.

"Frédi is a good boy. He was only pushing your little brother on the swing. Isn't that right?"

"He was trying to steal my star dust story."

"Oh, now," Papi says, looking me steadily in the eye. "Frédi doesn't care about the Prince Csaba story. It's *ganz egal* to him. He has his own story. Hundreds of stories. Frédi is Jewish."

"What's Jewish?"

Father laughs. "Jewish is . . . Jewish is people with their own stories. They don't need Prince Csaba. They have Moses. They have Samson."

"What's Samson?"

"If you go and talk to Frédi, I'll tell you about Samson later."

But he never did.


### 140.


About eleven years later, my brother was walking down Szent István Boulevard arm in arm with my mother. They were just passing the Luxor Café. My brother had grown fifteen centimeters that year. He took Mother's arm. They were pretending that Mami is a mature woman, and he a young man. Mami's belly hadn't grown distended yet, and she didn't wear a wig, and sometimes she even got decked out. We liked her bright yellow, sexy suit best, especially with the turban that went with it. That turban was like her smoking. It showed us someone else than we were used to seeing day in and day out.

She would even wink, discreetly, hardly noticeably, with her left eye. She usually played this game with me on the local train, as if we were strangers, and she was giving me the eye. A fun game. I didn't feel jealous of my younger brother. He loved our mother more than I did because he loved her despite our father, loved her *in spite* of him, which I couldn't do. Still, I always felt that I was in a special position because even though our mother didn't love me more than the *others,* she was clearly grateful to me because when I was born, she was happy. Not necessarily because of it, but happy all the same. This is why I didn't feel jealous of anyone, neither my brother's exclusive and therefore greater love, nor our sister, who had to be loved the most (middle-ear infection, et cetera.).

In front of the Luxor a well-dressed man wearing a dove gray overcoat and a soft dove gray borselino came over to them. He appeared to be a man of the world until he opened his mouth, because as soon as he did so, his unpleasantly obsequious, servile and insincere manner overpowered everything else. Dove gray is powerless against an insincere man.

"My respects, Your Excellency, kiss the hand, if you please, and the young Count as well. I assume this is the young Count. My respects to him, too, if you will permit."

My brother didn't bat an eye. He'd never heard a human being talk like this before, except in the movies. ("Silent movies.") But he'd never heard our mother talk like this either.

"Kelemen!" she roared like a fishmonger. The man literally pulled in his neck. "Where's the silver?! Where's the furniture? The pots and pans?!" The man kept shrinking. "The Dumas fils!"

*Fisss,* you should have heard her thunder. Our mother was beside herself. My brother wouldn't let go of her arm, he was afraid she'd lurch at this Kelemen guy. "And the collected works of Jókai? The old clock? Vekerdy's old clock?" She was raging. *"Jerger Schachuhr Robust Genau Geräuscharm Seit Jahrzehnten!!!"*

"Don't, Mami, please don't!"

"And the gramophone? His Master's Voice?" This for the benefit of my brother, in parentheses. "And Aunt Emma's bed? The one she died in?!" She was panting. "Return the silver this instant, you thieving rascal."

A quick, painful, haughty and dignified expression flickered across the thieving rascal's face. Bowing profusely, he started backing off there, in public, as if acting in accord with strict Spanish etiquette.

"I am doing all I can, Your Excellency, I am doing all I can, and we have every reason to hope that I will succeed, I assure you. Good-bye, good-bye . . ." He stopped, he bowed, in my brother's direction, too, then quickly turned on his heel and with a back slightly bent scurried off in the direction of the Western Railway Station.

The scene wore Mother out. She was panting, her eyes were flashing with anger. Back then, on the day of their forced resettlement, my parents took part of their belongings to the lawyer Kelemen, would he kindly safe-keep it for them until they return; the silver, the silver platters, wine goblets, the tureens decorated with lion's heads, the Vermeil set, the candelabra ("chased"!), they must've weighed at least two quintals. Three. Two or three. We never saw them again. It proved to be one of the most efficient means of squandering the family silver. I wonder why our father didn't beat it out of him. Why didn't he grab him by the throat or apply pressure in some other way? I wish I knew.

There's a tumbler, by all appearances a simple tumbler, with a note inside it bearing Mother's handwriting: *This tumbler belonged*

*to Róza Deli's, Ádám Mányoki's mother. It is FD because Róza's father*
*was called Ferenc. It is not silver, but due to its age, is valuable all the same.*
*The pattern is called a cloud pattern. I had it appraised by the museum, it*
*is appr. 400 yrs. old.*

"What a contemptible Jew!" Mother hissed between her teeth in front of the Luxor. My younger brother walked by her side without batting an eye (again). He was taller than my mother, who shook her head as if she'd just realized what she'd said. "I don't have anything against Jews, only impudent and dishonest people, among whom there are a remarkable number of Jews."

## 141.

The grownups in our family got used to doing manual labor very quickly. It just so happened that they were up to it, and they wanted to do it, too. Most of the people from Pest were of a different opinion. They took offense because they'd been offended, and as for physical labor, they looked down on it. My father, as I said, looked down on nothing.

By day two, people could sign up with the church construction crew as unskilled laborers. Interesting that they allowed it back then, the building of the church. The parish priest had been expecting my father and invited him in for a chat, offered him a drink, and attempted to talk him out of the lowly task of mixing mortar, at which fox-like, stalking his prey—he enjoyed such games—my father posed the rhetorical question, to wit, whether one could say that there's a difference between one sort of work and another if it served the Lord, and whether he, as a member of his family, was not duty bound to carry on what his forebears (not ancestors, mind, but forebears) had done for centuries before him, and come to the aid of the Church, if as a palatine, then as a palatine, if as an unskilled laborer, then as an unskilled laborer. The reverend father found this line of reasoning noble and incontrovertible, and so they drank another round of schnapps.

Later they rented a piece of land fifty-fifty on Andris Hill and on the Keller estate. Hoeing potatoes. ("You're a mighty handsome woman. Your backside's big enough for two rows of potatoes.") They looked soused from exhaustion as they tottered home. Palms cracked, the skin in shreds, in spots scraped down to the flesh, but at least this was tangible, a pain that could be understood, that made sense. But what was this thing that went beyond fatigue and exhaustion, what this crushing defeat of the body, the feeling that there is nothing but the body, and that you're one with your body, your pain, your despair, what is this?

"It's called work," Aunt Rozi said to the kitchen stove.

My father kept pressing his back dramatically like an old woman.

"Oh, oh, it's killing me!" And he attempted a laugh.

Aunt Rozi did not turn around; as always, she was busy over the stove, for there was always something to keep her busy over the stove.

"You'll survive," she said, like one speaking from experience.

"What did you say, Aunt Rozi?" my father said sharply, for he had no liking for conflict and always tried to avoid it by smoothing things over.

"All I said, Count, is that hoeing potatoes won't kill you, Count."

"Hush, now," Uncle Pista said, hushing her with typical male cowardice.

"Don't you hush me, what're you hushing me for?"

To me, Aunt Rozi looked like an old woman. She must've been around fifty, a peasant woman who wore her hair up in a bun, obese, with layers of underskirt. Her cheeks glistened with anger. As for her eyes, they always sparkled, which added a certain beauty to her, but be that as it may, it certainly set her apart.

"If it's Count, then it's Count. It's Count. What do you want from me?! Doctor this and Doctor that, who d'you think you're kidding? Yourself? Him? The Ávó?"

She spoke the Palots dialect, which became my mother tongue, too, ávó, auwh-waooh, it sounded like a bark, a pained whimper.

"A count,"—and at this juncture she jerked her head back and shot a glance at my father as if to confirm that she was telling the truth—"a count's got no business raking." Or did she turn just at this point? "Raking ain't for gentlefolk."

Silence fell over the kitchen. It was tantamount to saying that my father's family had no business being there. My father stood around uncomfortably; there was no one to argue with; there was nothing to be said.

"Now, now, Rozi dear," Uncle Pista said, trying to set things right, "the doctor and his family, they're not . . . they're not . . ." And he fell silent.

"They're not *what*?!" his wife pounced back, as if my father and mother weren't there. Mother ran out to the clean room in tears, it was full of people (us), at which she ran out again, out to the yard, and the garden beyond. Frightened, Uncle Pista toddled in place, like someone practicing a dance step (beginners' course), while unperturbed, Aunt Rozi watched the young woman run amok.

"What's the matter, Aunt Rozi?" my father piped.

"Nothing," Aunt Rozi said turning back to her stove, "what makes you think anything's the matter, Count?"

Again, there was nothing for him to say.

For over a week they didn't speak to each other, except in greeting. (Not even Uncle Pista!) At sunrise, my father would go out to the potato patch with the others, at sundown they dragged themselves back, they wrapped their hands in rags, like lepers, Mother pushing her bulging belly before her, cooking all sorts of horrible *stuff* in the summer kitchen outside—she hadn't yet mastered the art of cooking a meal from nothing (she would!); in the morning they said hello and in the evening they said hello, but never asked for help, and never got any. Obviously, this couldn't go on much longer, but my parents were young, and in a certain sense, spoiled. They thought their strength would hold out indefinitely.

Then one night, when my father reeled into the kitchen, Aunt Rozi said to the stove, "You're raking too fast, *Doctor.*"

"It needs to be done slower?"

"The point isn't slower, it's the rhythm. In keeping with your heartbeat, Doctor." And a crimson fire flushed her cheeks.

From then on, she helped every way she could—how to hold the rake, how to wind the foot rag round the foot, what needs raking, what needs just a thinning out, what's a flat spade, and how to tell if a goose is fat (there's a protrusion under its wing, in the "armpit," and not till then!), how to make corn mash. And corn fritters. And rye cakes.

"You can make food out of anything, Lilike, and like it. Take it from me, I know," Aunt Rozi said this with a certain desperation, and her eyes sparkled something fierce.

For instance, there was the case of the poppy seed noodles. They were supposed to be my favorite. They were supposed to keep body and soul together, or whatnot.

"I'll masticate some poppy seed noodles for the child, Lilike."

Lilike thanked her. She didn't know what mastication was. My father knew, but he wouldn't say.

"Will you tell me, Aunt Rozi, what masticating is? Will you show me how?"

"Masticating is masticating, what's there to show?"

But she showed her just the same. She stuck out her tongue like an oven peel, as if she were sticking her tongue out at Mother, though she was just trying to show her the progress she was making.

"Lots of saliva, Lilike, that's the secret. That'll make it nice and soft and silky. See how silky this mastication is, Lilike?"

Like a countess to the title born (which she wasn't), my mother fainted dead away. Her one and only son and this revolting, dark gooey pulp of saliva?! Father wrapped her in his arms and smiling (what the heck, he was laughing for all he was worth) removed her from the kitchen—a socialist Gregory Peck.

Later my mother became a masticator of some note herself.


## 142.

Our bread allowance, belonging to the lowest caste, intellectual plus class enemy, was 250 grams, and even so, only after the rest of the people got theirs. Sometimes I went along with Grandfather. I held his hand. He was always smoking a pipe. We went to the back of the line and stayed there, because if anyone came, they'd get in front of us. If they didn't, Mrs. Kenderesi, the loud-mouthed shopkeeper, comrade shopkeeper and wife of the council president, was there to remind them.

"Those of you from Pest get in the back!" At which we ended up in the back of the line once again. We had to wait even if there was no line, partly because they couldn't tell us anymore to move to the back of the line, and partly because someone who was more deserving of the bread than we might show up, and just about everyone was considered more deserving of the bread than we were.

The smell of bread, its fragrance, is heavenly, and so my younger brother and I didn't agree with our classification. Besides, my younger brother didn't consider himself a citizen of Pest, he'd been born in Gyöngyös and had never crossed the village limit. (Once Bogyica sneaked him up to Pest, but no one knew that here—what clearer indication of the revolution of the wheel of history, a wheel which, as we know, cannot be turned back—the progression in our places of birth: Budapest, Gyöngyös, Budapest.) As for me, I insisted on the Lord's Prayer and demanded our daily bread. We howled. The mixed run of customers in the mixed-goods store listened to our concert with mixed emotions.

"Give them biscuits!" Mrs. Kenderesi yelped at the shop assistant, which prompted Grandfather to compose a brief essay in which he provided a short outline of history as such, and then—or possibly as a part of said outline—he drew a parallel between Marie Antoinette's cake ("If there's no bread, let them eat cake!") and Mrs. Kenderesi's biscuits, *back then cakes, now biscuits*; in the evening he read it out to us but no one listened, a fact that Grandfather noted with satisfaction; on the one hand, he pretended not to notice, on the other, it confirmed him in his skepticism vis-à-vis the world, and the following day he hastened to send a copy of the essay to Károly Rassay, a former political associate who was "in detention nearby" (*epitethon ornans*), and who in turn sent him an enlightened, detailed and encouraging response. They corresponded on a regular basis; like two chess players, they reanalyzed past political situations (would Imrédy have fallen if Grandfather's friend had not produced documents in 1939 proving that Imrédy was partly of Jewish descent, et cetera), critically and self-critically, in the minutest detail, taking into account obscure facts known only to the two of them. In order to confound the authorities, they wrote under a pseudonym. Good show.

Mrs. Kenderesi, that old bitch, cheated as well. When she put the bread on the scales, the wrapping paper hung down on her side by the counter where she thought no one could see, then she put her weight on the paper, pulling on it, so you were lucky if you got half of what you were supposed to get, one-half kilo instead of one, one kilo instead of two, et cetera, and nobody would say anything, because she was the council president's wife. There were as many Rákosi and Stalin pictures hanging on the wall of the shop as there were of the Virgin Mary and the Sacred Heart of Jesus before.

"She used to be on her knees in St. Joseph's chapel clacking her rosary beads and breathing like a virgin martyr. Now it's the Party Headquarters. The old bitch!"

My mother knew that Mrs. Kenderesi was the council president's wife, but she didn't know what it meant to be council president, or what it meant to be his wife. The first time she came back from the shop, she started yelling even before she got to the house, "Aunt Rozi! Aunt Rozi! Is this supposed to be a kilo? Is this *pittance* a kilo?"

Aunt Rozi turned to her kitchen stove.

"Half a kilo, Lilike, half a kilo."

Mother insisted on using the scales.

"What for, Lilike?"

Lilike wanted to weigh the bread. It was 540 grams.

"Do you see? Do you see?"

"I see."

At which there was again nothing to be said.

The next time my mother stood on line and Mrs. Kenderesi weighed out the half-a-kilo kilo for Annu Arany, she lay a sheet of newspaper on the scale, poured on flour from a large bag, sifting it, sifting it, here you are, a kilo of flour, at which Mother called from the back that she didn't think so, that's a very small kilo of flour.

Mrs. Kenderesi flushed and glared.

"Are you accusing me? You of all people accusing *me*?"

"Ah, no, dear, sweet Comrade Kenderesi, how can you think

such a thing?" Ingratiating as a bag of fleas, Mother was. "Just that I think there was a little accident, if you will,"—this must have been the only time in her life when she used this vulgar phrase, and did so with relish!—"the way your hip was pressed against the scale, but what *am* I saying, it was the newspaper."

The women continued to wait on line quietly, they couldn't understand this thin woman from Pest, what she was up to. They stared into space. Not so Annu Arany, who glanced proudly at Mother.

"God forbid I should accuse you," Mother said with emphasis on the word God, and how clearly it rang out stripped of its immediate context; "God forbid, Mrs. Comrade Kenderesi, Comrade Kenderesi's wife . . . oh, dear me, and is that your money I see on the floor there?"

Mrs. Kenderesi stepped back quickly and the needle on the scale jumped and quivered.

"What money?" she said until she looked at Mother and knew. Mother smiled.

"Oh, dear, must be the trick of the shadows," Mother said and smiled at the scales. There was a mistake right enough, the needle hovered just over the half-a-kilo mark.

"That scale gives me no end of trouble," Mrs. Comrade Kenderesi said.

"I'm sure it does," Mother said.

"But my conscience is clear."

"I'm sure it is. Your reputation is well known in these parts."

"I try to be a good Communist."

"Try? God knows . . ."—short pause—"I speak the truth, you don't have to try, dear, for you're well known for having a kind heart and I was wondering if there might not be in this morally irreproachable shop some morally irreproachable sweets for these morally irreproachable children?"

"Well, now, I'm not a millionaire, but here . . ."

710

"God bless you, Mrs. Comrade Kenderesi, you're the living proof of the strength of democracy, and I know it's asking a lot but could you possibly lend me a couple of cigarettes?"

"I'm not here to supply luxuries."

"If you could see your way, ma'am, I assure you, your generosity, which rests on such strong principles, will weigh heavily in the balance . . . what I mean to say, the scales."

"All right, all right. One time for the cigarettes and one time only!"

"God bless you, and I'm sorry you have so much trouble with those nasty scales."

Out on the street Mother said to Annu, "A lady does not smoke on the street," and coughing, took a deep drag on her cigarette. By the time they reached home, Aunt Rozi had heard all about it.

"You should be more careful in future, Lilike."

"Thank you," Mother said, smiling triumphantly, "I will." But she wasn't.

## 143.

"Don't, Doctor, you'll just smudge it up," they told Father when, during time off from threshing (there's no time off from threshing!) he was about to wipe his face. "Leave it be."

The people from Pest were assigned to one brigade (low capacity, bad jobs badly paid, but they worked badly, too). However, my father was soon advanced up the rung and put into a regular group, their own. He was a good worker, though he never learned how. He accommodated himself. His body accommodated itself, too. It did and it did not.

There he stands, atop the threshing machine. He's the feeder, the chaff flying all over the place like so many tiny bugs. His youthful body, slender, fragile, bends every which way, his strong and fragile body, as if the wind was up, bending like a reed, weighed down by hardship, the hardship of work. He straightens up, feels his lower back. He's wearing dungarees, a checked flannel shirt, a brown beret, like everyone else there (except for his shoes, because he was always particular about his shoes). And yet, it's as if the trembling, grumbling, dusty, clattering threshing machine were a huge ship, a luxurious ocean liner in a sea of wheat, a Titanic voraciously gulping up the sea from beneath itself, mowing it down, and my father standing on the captain's deck, except he's not the captain, that would be an exaggeration, he's more like a silhouette, a fine, hovering insubstantiality. Work had made him the equal of the peasants, while this insubstantial gracefulness of his body made him lonely.

Later he was put in charge of poling, which is one of the most difficult jobs. It requires a special aptitude; talent, perseverance, strength and courage will not suffice. With a "full" fork in hand, you have to run up the ladder to the top of the stack in one go. My father did it so well, with such exceptional ease, that the others watched with mouths agape the way he ran up to the top of the stacks laughing, as if he'd been training for it all his life. He'd reached thirty, he was almost the same age as Christ.

There was also the melon. Streaked Zardecki, a lovely name. Years later, too, Father selected the melon for us, knocking on it and feeling it to the horror of the vegetable vendors. The melon brigades would also go to the distant melon fields. They lived in huts dug into the soil. Sometimes we'd go visit. We loved the hut, it was like a playhouse, except we were scared of what we'd find, because the men drank a lot.

"Pali Nagy, he's your father's ill genius."

In 1954 the Danube flooded the melon field, and the melons floated down the stream like so many soccer balls!

## 144.

If a man is mean-spirited, it's better if he's also stupid. This Kenderesi was not stupid. He concocted the idea of assigning Father to the police to check up on the peasants re. the compulsory delivery of the produce. My father had "to sweep the attic clean," as they called it back then. To resist and be in cahoots with the peasants was out of the question. His cell was ready and waiting at the prison in Hatvan, they kept reminding him.

"It's waiting, Count, keep that in mind." And also, that a new broom sweeps clean.

The people knew this too and said it's all right, Doctor, but—repetition!—it wasn't. For one thing, I got spat on in the street. I didn't tell anybody. He could have refused the sweeping, I thought back then. But he didn't.


## 145.

March 5, 1953, was the first time Roberto called me majoresco, which made a lot of sense to me. A majoresco is clearly someone who wanders around the *major*, or manor, a great deal, which accorded with the facts, because the fields rented on a fifty-fifty basis on Andris Hill and also the Kelemen field north of the village fell toward Gyöngyös, where one of the manors stood, and where I used to play a lot by myself, tied to a long, thin rope, which is not as brutal and cruel as it may first sound, just practical, though I tried to give my parents pangs of conscience all the same, putting on a pained expression and rubbing my ankle in the evening, it's swollen, I said, but no use, they were so exhausted by then, there was no place for pangs or anything else, for that matter.

Majoresco. This word suggested strength, surprising strength. It was the first time I could feel a word interfere with the universe. When he called me majoresco Roberto talked to me differently, because I seemed to be a different person; I was said to be someone else, and so I was. I was not surprised when my playmates called me count, clearly meant to be derogatory, I even shot back weakly at first, Who're you calling count?, because we'd heard that Grandfather had been a count, and Papi was one too when he was young, but then he stopped, or got banned; be that as it may, it was a thing of the past. But in our youthful world this had no significance, being called count had no consequence, it didn't improve my prestige or my chances, though it didn't hurt either, it just seemed a special means of differentiation. The borderline between differentiation and stigmatization is narrow indeed.

Still, it was a sign—like the silver tableware and Mami's cooking—that there was something wrong with the family to which I belonged. But the fact that my name is an omen, a sign, a portentous sign, didn't worry me for a long time. The stamp on our foreheads was on full, glaring display, but we didn't think of it as portentous, we thought that it was natural, you're always stamped, one way or another, you always have to count on being hassled, either because your name is Kovács, or because you attend Sunday school. Later there were four Kovácses in the class, and the teachers thought it highly amusing to say, And now it is Kovács's turn to stand up and give us the answer!, and they smiled up their sleeve and the time passed, and the poor Kovácses, including the poorest Kovács among them, trembled with fear.

## 146

I was the only student from my class attending Bible studies. Attending Bible studies was not the problem, the clerical influence on my mind wasn't the problem, the weakening of the stronghold of materialism wasn't the problem. The problem was the signing up. It was bad for statistics. Since there was freedom of religion because they said there was freedom of religion, there was a so-called school Bible course, a regularly scheduled Bible class held in school. Religious parents decided to let sleeping dogs lie, and in keeping with the spirit of the times, did not challenge the (purely) theoretical gesture made by the people's democracy with regard to freedom. Instead, without further ado, they sent their offsprings, who were clamoring for moral gratification, to the local parsonage to receive religious instruction. May the Lord have what is the Lord's, and may the Emperor also have what is the Lord's—seeing how everything is the Emperor's to begin with.

But for some reason my mother wouldn't let sleeping dogs lie. She was not a hero—she was not a small-time rebel, I fear—nor was she motivated by the beauty, discipline and ethics inherent in being a guiding light; it was more like the feeling that it's all the same or, on the contrary, since it's been posted that students could sign up for Bible class on Monday between one and one-fifteen (they switched it from Tuesday the last moment, let the info. get around if it could!), why not take it at face value, and not as a provocation, and not as a piece of daredevilry, but with a touch of ennui, lethargic perseverance? Why not do it without casting frightened glances around? Why not throw the obligatory caution to the wind as if we were normal people? In a dictatorship, to be normal is dangerous. It is tantamount to madness.

It was such a little thing, really. It was as the saying goes: my parents ignored the little things, and as for the big things, they didn't count. I was never a Little Drummer nor a Young Pioneer—and later our high school didn't have a local Communist Youth League. The Piarist fathers neglected to start one. For some unfathomable reason, they were not in favor of it. The Gypsy boy Jani Oláh wasn't one either, and Stern wasn't either. Nobody ever called him by his first name (Pityu). He was supposed to be a Jew. Little Huszár heard it from his brother. We had no idea what a Jew was. It had something to do with his nose. But we couldn't be sure that that's why he couldn't be a Little Drummer. These are real labels, but they didn't seem real to me. I wasn't left out of anything except the Little Drummer meetings, for which everyone envied me, and they couldn't give me bad marks (and didn't want to, either), and they couldn't leave me off the class soccer team. And what else was there?

## 147.

Sitting and playing keepie-uppies with a chestnut (football jargon: keeping the ball in the air with short, repeated kicks)—no one in school was as good at it as me. Standing was another matter. But sitting down, definitely. I was the champ. I don't know why. Even my shinbone had a thing for anything round. Be that as it may, all I had to do was keep my leg up with my foot flexed, of course, like a Lepeshinskaya, let the ball or chestnut fall on it, either peeled or with the shell still on, and it pretty much started bouncing on its own.

I played for small stakes, and never for money—milk, poppy seed rolls, hot chocolate, whatever I needed just then. (In the summer, down by Lake Balaton, at the friendly beach games, it was spinach, but no meat.) I didn't win all the time, but mostly. I sat by the wall on the bench during the main recess, and waited for "clients." Little Huszár was my secretary, which was a post requiring great tact and expertise, because he selected or drummed up the volunteers, agreed on the terms, which in the case of the upperclassmen was usually a tricky business. It was a confidential post, he had to keep to the mutually agreed upon principles, i.e., that it's the game that counts, not the gain, and still, we must keep our heads and not be our own enemy, et cetera. Like a spider, I sat and waited.

There was another problem. It seemed expedient to keep the financial rewards of our little game a secret from the grownups. Little Huszár attended to business, for which he received 40 percent of the take, a reasonable sum, if you ask me. At first the 40 percent put a strain on our relationship, but I didn't notice. For one thing, Little Huszár didn't know what 40 percent was, and when I explained four out of ten, he looked at me with genuine bewilderment. Why four, why four *exactly,* and what has four to do with forty. Besides, he wanted half. I, however, didn't think this was fair. I was motivated not by pecuniary gain but the recognition of my own know-how. Also, practically speaking, 40 percent is nearly half.

I wouldn't want you to get the wrong idea, though. Little Huszár, Huszi, was neither my orderly nor my servant; our relationship had nothing of the master-servant about it. Two equals brought their know-how into the business, the major difference being that I was sitting while he was standing, which goes without saying. If I had been as good at keeping the chestnut in the air standing up, I'd have also been standing, which also goes without saying.

And so, in the early 1960s I sat around in the school yard by the base of the stone fence during main recess, with no thought to Nikita Sergeyevich Khrushchev's mounting problems, the nature of which entailed wheat plus the Chinese, when a long, black shadow fell over me, a soft, autumnal shadow cast by Big Huszár;

and right away I knew that I was about to experience mounting problems of my own. Except, I was in the dark about their nature.

Big Huszár brought fear and trembling to the hearts of students and faculty alike, plus Little Huszár. Plus me, which goes without saying. He was wild, unruly and unpredictable, bloodthirsty, dumb as an ox, but also infernally cunning, strong and intractable. He had failed three times already, so just like Mami and Papi, he had nothing to lose either.

In short, Big Huszár was a free man. Which is not necessarily a good thing when you're in public school. His facial hair was growing out, he drank, he skipped classes (without an excuse, no less!). He was supposed to be working, loading coal carts at the Southern Station. His parents were divorced but shared an apartment. His mother drank like a fish (I knew her, Aunt Ilike, thin and mummy-like, as if a stocking that was too small for her had been pulled over the dark-brown skin on her head. She greeted me in a deep drawl that startled me, and with a courtesy that came off as out of place and unjustified, Good day, son. Also, she bowed her head, as if I were not just a child). When they ran out of money, Big Huszár had to pitch in. But at the time the only thing you could see from all this was that Big Huszár was a savage brute.

For fifty fillérs he'd eat a fly, for one forint you could take a picture of the cadaver on his tongue, for five forints and an apple (Starking), he'd bite a mouse in two. He never worked with outsourced mice, he liked to catch his own.

I was frightened, but I did not stand up. Main recess was mine, and the chestnut, and the keepie-uppies; mine and Young Huszár's, who was standing to the side, but without being sufficiently frightened—and something he'd never done in my presence before, he was dribbling a chestnut. Interesting. Only now did I see how alike they were. Big Huszár did the talking, as if he were Little Huszár's private secretary. I should have found a secretary for myself, too, but couldn't, and this proved fatal.

Basically, the problem was not the 40 percent, but what the 40 percent was 40 percent *of*. Because what right have I got stopping his younger brother? Curbing him? Why don't I give free rein to his many and varied ideas, like the keepie-uppies auction, which could be run like a betting office, and prices would go skyrocketing in no time at all?

"The Great Bear. The Evening Star," he added, threateningly.

I didn't know what he was driving at, honest I didn't. What prices? And why would they rocket sky-high? Also, what would they do once they got there?

"You're a moron," Big Huszár said with a resigned nod of the head. It wasn't even worth his while punching me in the nose. Still, he was definitely after something. I shook my head with conviction. I saw no reason to consider myself a moron. Well, I am, and a colossal one at that, flinging good money out the window like this, with both hands! My ability to take imagery literally I had discovered early on, and so now I could think only of my two hands, in the act of flinging—twins, obviously—going from client to client, flinging the money out the window. Not a bad career. Profession: two fists.

Little Huszár's expression was a blank. I couldn't read anything off it, especially anything encouraging. Still, it was to him rather than his brother that I said that we're just having fun.

"With your prick in the dust!" his brother shouted, and he caught the thorny chestnut in midair like a tennis ball, squeezing it with his bare hand. I winced. "What do you mean, just having fun?!"

I don't think he was expecting an answer, but he got one anyway. I had done a considerable amount of thinking about games, I had to; about the tension, i.e., that everyone considers a game an unserious business, inferior, *nothing but a game*, whereas my experience told me just the opposite. I was practically always playing, because I was either playing soccer, or I was reading. I became

719

fully submerged in the world of the book, though I rarely identified with any of the characters; I never aspired to be Gergő Bornemissza from *The Stars of Eger*, or Vicuska, or Boka, or Nemecsek, or David Copperfield. But I became submerged in the book itself. In short, not the time of the Turkish occupation or Budapest at the time of the *belle époque*, but the new terrain that was made up of several things: the book itself, the concrete object, the style of the letters, the quality of the paper, the condition of the dust jacket, on it the author's picture (his eyes!), and also, what the book was about, hot, sweating horses, foggy mornings, a bishop's-purple Catholic glint of the eye, the frozen Balaton, a London slum, the exotic improbability of an island in the Pacific, and also the situation in which I was reading the book, standing on the bus, lying in bed sick (stewed cherries, chocolate bars!), in the early morning, just after opening my eyes, or just before falling asleep, under my desk during class, mixing the excitement inside me with the excitement outside, Fagin contra Mrs. Váradi—but I'm going to stop here, mixing is not the right word, it's misleading, because it's the inside and the outside that stops existing, the game stopped it from existing, whether I was playing soccer or reading, or daydreaming (basically, I was freeing Évi Katona Rácz from various perils, lions, thieves, eighth-graders); these events were not situated in what we call the real world, like an island, easily distinguished from it, outside, inside, no, because they were the real world to me, completely, without limitation, there being nothing except what is real.

This is why—namely, from simple self-interest—that I took games seriously. I knew perfectly well that a lost game was not the end of the world, but telling ourselves in the middle of a game that once it's over, what happened on the field won't matter anymore, we won't care because we must go do our lessons and eat our dinner—I considered this ridiculous, and above all, impossible. The imagination is no laughing matter, I reflected.

It was a bouquet of such reflections that I now handed the two Huszárs, specifically, that when I'm sitting at the base of the brick wall dribbling the chestnut, I am the person who is sitting at the base of the brick wall dribbling the chestnut, that's all!, get it?!, that's all there is to it!, and in comparison to this, the winnings, the gain, is secondary, inconsequential, a mere afterthought, only the game matters, the game is everything, and outside of this everything, there is nothing.

"Isn't that right?" I chortled.

Little Huszár said nothing. A painful grimace rippled across his big, round countenance. What I said caused him physical pain. This pain suddenly turned him into a little boy, too. I sprang to my feet. They drew back. The little one began to speak still from within that drawing back. No dummy, I knew it all along.

He reasoned that it's right as far as that goes, because, as far as that goes, I'm sitting by the base of the brick wall while he's not sitting by the base of the brick wall, I'm doing keepie-uppies with the chestnut while he's not doing keepie-uppies with the chestnut, and far be it from him to take offense at it, nor is he saying that sitting is preferable to standing, that it'd be better to sit where I'm sitting and to do what I'm doing instead of standing and doing what he's doing, except, and with that except came the crux of the matter, if we call this whole thing a game, then he has no choice but to conclude that . . . —when excited, he spoke in grownup sentences, just like his older brother—that he and I are playing different games, ergo that everything is different, too, and outside of this everything there really is nothing, except what falls outside the bounds of my everything and ergo does not exist, could easy as pie fall inside the bounds of his everything, something demanding the greatest of attention, and so, to use my own words—up yours, buddy, and I had the distinct impression that I'm stronger than they, that I'm stronger than the both of them, separately or taken together—in short, that this is no laughing matter.

Every time he heard the word "game" Big Huszár gave a twitch as if he'd been struck. Little Huszár was right, and this confused me; there's no peeping out of everything into nothing. So what next? The big one had been trying to say something for some time; he gaped, just about launched into it, but checked himself each time, until he spit out what he had to say with the coarse passion of rage, helplessness, and spite: "You're nothing but a damn *Labanc!*"

I knew that this was not true, my family had not been pro-Habsburg loyalists, because Uncle Pattyi played in the film called *Rákóczi's Lieutenant,* he rode the horse instead of Rákóczi's lieutenant, who was played by Tibor Bitskey, and the stuntman for an anti-Habsburg Kuruc is a Kuruc himself. Besides, what exactly did he mean by "you"?

"Your whole family, who else? No use protesting. We learned in school how you oppressed the people. You learned it too!"

"Who oppressed the people?" I yelped, though without full conviction, since the subject never came up at home, I couldn't help thinking that maybe we really did oppress them.

"Who . . . ?" Big Huszár didn't know what he was talking about either. "Who? *You!*"

"Are you referring to me?" No response. At which I lashed out at him. "Or my little sister, the one in nursery school? *We* oppressed the people? Is that it?"

Again, calm as a grownup, Little Huszár interjected.

"Not your younger brother or anything like that, but your father, and his father, and his father before him!"

"What about you, or your father's father? He could've oppressed them, too!"

They spoke in unison.

"We don't have any."

"That's impossible. Everybody's got to have a family."

"Not us. We got only us and our parents. But they're divorced."

"We got only us, too, me, my brother and sister and my parents, except they're not divorced. Sometimes they fight, though."

All of a sudden, the two Huszárs were so cock-sure of themselves. Could the tables have turned without my noticing?

"That's a lie! You're not just you, you're all of you! You're the whole family, and not just the ones living now, but the dukes and princes, too. The whole lot!" And Big Huszár let out a horse laugh. "That's what I call everything, old buddy!"

"If that's the case, what does that make you?"

"Nothing," said Little Huszár.

"Kuruc," said Big Huszár.

"What makes you a Kuruc?"

"Poverty."

"We're poor, too."

At which there was no more to be said on either side, neither theirs nor mine; I retrieved the crushed chestnut from Big Huszár's hand, and sat back down by the base of the brick wall once again.

# CHAPTER SEVEN

## 148.

My name didn't interfere (much) with my life. It made its presence felt, but it didn't bully me, and it didn't blind me. On the other hand, it was great for anecdotes.

For instance, once they turned on me on the bus because in the big (profane) crowd, I was making squeamish faces, silently hating the whole thing, and also, somebody stepped on my foot—if I don't like it, why don't I take a cab—at which I continued my affected ways, at which that certain sentence came, why am I so squeamish, who do I think I am, the Prince?, and *here followed the name,* "my father's fine name." I had just received my first I.D. papers. I shoved them under the man's nose. (I didn't feel like launching into the distinction between a prince and a count.) He read it syllable by syllable. Basically, he couldn't believe his eyes. He shrugged. The thing had no effect on him, he just stopped talking.

In those days, when asked if I was related, I said no, I'm not related, I am *them.* I didn't say it with pride or arrogance (although it must have sounded that way); I said it matter-of-factly, I am not *related* to my family, I am part of my family, I am one of them, I'm them.

But mostly I answered in haste, which confused them, and they just fell (hastily) silent; it would have indeed been simpler to take a cab—or a hansom.

## 149.

It (my name) acted up only in the army. There was a different time reckoning in the barracks; specifically, the times were different, younger by fifteen or twenty years. In this way, I had a chance to experience firsthand what it must have been like to live with my name in a real dictatorship. (Lousy.) Like the man from Mars, that's how they stared at me; as for me, I wasn't afraid yet, because I didn't know I should be. (Not true. I knew perfectly well, except I kept forgetting; I was scared, then forgot, I was scared, then forgot; that's dictatorship, I was scared and I forgot. I sinned against one of the Commandments by being afraid and then forgetting. I was afraid on my own, no witnesses, which made it easier to forget that I was afraid.) I was plunged into this *thing* after high school graduation, with no safety net.

"Well, Count," said the young army doctor amicably, "I see you got just one prick, like the rest of us mortals."

"*Indeed, I do, sir,*" I said, the reserved yet cooperative scion of the house, in my best English, nodding and raising my balls with the tact of a soccer pro, "but I got *two balls!*"

The doctor shot me a look, his boyish face pink and gleaming as if he'd also just graduated, his bushy, black eyebrows drawn together, lending a certain severity to his face, said severity being offset by his perpetual girlish smile. When I got dressed, he waved me over.

"You mind if I call you by your first name?" I was on my guard. What was he getting at? "My mother is a Nádasdy!" he announced in a semiwhisper, grabbing my elbow on both sides.

What he said must have been very important, both proof and disclosure. I listened with animosity. I seemed to recall that the Nádasdys were related, but for one thing, who wasn't related, and for another, that certain bygone Ferenc Nádasdy had perfidiously stabbed us in the back, hadn't he? Playing the relative to our face, he got our Aunt Júlia for his wife, then when we were in dire straits, tried to get his hands on our estates. Of course, he was later duly beheaded, and then we got *his* estates. Oh, highly esteemed relative of mine, what a pleasure to meet you!

The young doctor spoke in an excited whisper. Do I know what the army is all about? I mustn't go thinking it's to defend the homeland, tra-la-la, tra-la-la (??), or . . . and here he lowered his voice even further . . . the socialist camp. Give me the "my mother is a Nádasdy" approach anytime!

"Intehr-nah-tionahl-ism," he whispered with the same drawn-out *ah* Mami used when she said tahxi, take a tahxi. He laughed. "Just one thing counts. You. Or us, the young people, to bring us to our knees, to teach us who"—and he lowered his voice further still—"is the boss."

Then he held forth in a whisper about the nature of dictatorship and fear, that a dictatorship is scared, too, but that just makes things worse for us underlings. A dictatorship should walk around with head held high and not prowling like this, like the one here. I couldn't make heads or tails out of what he was getting at. Whose prowling where with head held high? I saw a Nádasdy girl in my mind's eye, her hair let down, galloping like Lady Godiva o'er the misty plain in the wake of a prowling dictatorship.

"Watch yourself, old boy," the doctor, who was still in transition between boy and man, said, gently sliding his hand down my arm, his palm silky-smooth, like Aunt Mia's, then embarrassed, trying to annul the gesture. I didn't understand a word of what he was saying, and I couldn't have cared less. But later, if I felt I was

726

riding a high horse (not the Nádasdy girl's), if I felt that I was acting too much on my inclinations, I recalled this strange, grownup
boy's shy warning: watch yourself, old boy.


150.


There were more than enough people watching me to begin
with. Gyula Szabó and I made a pair on two iron beds pushed up
against each other. He was an easygoing village boy studying to be
a math and physics teacher, bony with a strong physique, a blond
crew cut, a girlish, turned-up nose, but rough, pitted, pockmarked skin, daring yet cautious; he carried out his orders without griping, he had what most of us adolescent adults, who were
dreaming of a bright future (college without admittance exams!)
lacked, a sense of seriousness. Nobody fucked with him, not even
the meanest officer.

It wasn't a confession and it wasn't a disclosure—he saw nothing secretive or hush-hush about it—he just told me because it
happened, and because it concerned me. He didn't take sides, he
wasn't outraged or apologetic; if anything, he seemed annoyed.
He regarded everything not directly related to manual labor with
suspicion. In that case, why was he going to attend college? Because he was very smart, and his parents back home didn't want it
to go to waste—something that Gyula, with his down-to-earth
peasant mentality, found only natural. Besides, teaching is almost
manual labor.

He told me that the major from Military Intelligence called
him in to ask about me. He asked him to tell him things because
clearly, he must hear things—what I say, who I talk to and what
about—because Gyula mustn't go thinking I've changed, you
can't make a silk purse out of a sow's ear, and Gyula better be on

727

his guard and stay vigilant, because Gyula is the true son of the people, he must always keep that in mind, whereas I am not a true son of the people, and Gyula had better keep that in mind, too, and he better think of his father, the destitute cotter, his grandfather ditto, for all we know, Gyula's family might have suffered under the Esterházy yoke. Gyula's from Transdanubia, and need he remind him, that meant the Esterházys, and that meant there was no crying mercy.

"No mercy you say? In Transdanubia?" I asked in surprise. Does it follow then that there's mercy *here*? Still, I knew that the only thing that followed from this is that if there is mercy here, then this is not Transdanubia. (We were stationed in the deepest depths of the Great Plain, in the mysteriously named Hódmezővásárhely. Peasant Paris.)

"No. No mercy," Gyula grumbled, *back there* we were up to our old tricks.

"Excuse me?"

He's just repeating what the major told him, he doesn't know what it's supposed to mean.

That we ruled the roost?

Yeh, that must be it, because the major's father, the major said, had seven other brothers and sisters, and the only reason they were born in seven castles belonging to the family is that two of them were twins. There they were, in my mind's eye, the destitute cotters as pair of twins coming into the world with a chip on their shoulder, bawling, vigilant, in the various Esterházy castles.

"What exactly are you driving at, Gyula my sweet?"

"That I gotta inform on you, asshole!"

"Inform? On me?"

He waved me off. It's not *me* we're talking about but him, it's him that's gotta write a report every night about what I did all day. Except he doesn't know. Furthermore, he couldn't care less. Furthermore, he wouldn't know even if he cared, because I'm in town playing soccer all day.

"How am I supposed to inform on you when the most basic conditions are missing," he asked sober and despondent.

151.

Practically the minute we got there they drove us out to the big expanse of a meadow behind the barracks popularly known as the Great Hungarian Plain and made us play soccer, about forty of us all at the same time, in nothing but a pair of pants, no shoes. I liked this near nakedness. It meant that we were out of uniform.

I was not on bad terms with my body, but not on the best of terms either. I wasn't prone to anxiety either, just irritated, annoyed. This strained relationship had a triple source. One had to do with soccer. I wasn't good enough physically. I wasn't bad either, but my body was no help. It refused to deliver that extra added plus. When my speed needed improving, it took thousands of practice springs, and when I was low on stamina, I jogged up and down the long, dark paths of Csillaghegy. I hated it. Really and truly hated it! I didn't like admitting to myself that a talent for soccer goes hand in hand with a talented body. I had to make it perform by brute force.

My helplessness offended me. And also my nose. When I was around fourteen it started growing, a source of dissatisfaction for years to come. From time to time I measured it (no easy task, forehead, the root of the nose, the ridge, where it stops, where it starts, and no cheating), and I studied it with a complex system of mirrors. The thing would not let me rest. Then three years later, from one moment to the next, the nose resentment stopped. Maybe I came to realize that my nose was me, too.

Ditto for my so-called manhood. They're not annexed to me, a tendon, an ankle, a cartilage (torn), a muscle, my nose, my prick: they're me. I thought of myself as part of Creation. And, Catholic, though all I understood of Catholic ethics is that we're all sinners, and sin means breaking the Sixth Commandment, i.e., fornication, i.e., masturbation, or as it is said in Confession, breaking the Sixth Commandment on your own. On your own. I considered all this fuss about my prick ridiculous, but awesome, too, and from time to time extended it or narrowed it down to my whole body.

Also, I got to thinking. If from time to time I didn't transgress "on my own" I'd be innocent as a newborn lamb and I'd have nothing to confess, which is clearly—one might say patently—absurd. It was thanks to my sinful body—the gratifying, pagan sense of gratitude flooded over me more than once—that I grew into a morally substantial human being.

### 152.

There I stood on that vast plain in my bare feet, grinning like a half-wit, so full of pleasure I can remember it to this day, a sated body, united (so to speak) with nature, the grass tickling the soles of my feet, the gentle breezes of the Great Plain nuzzling the legs of my pants; for a fleeting moment there I was, oblivious of the strange, menacing world bound on my destruction.

Going barefoot was pure ecstasy, not only because it was the implicit symbol of civilian life (there's no such thing as a barefooted soldier), but also because our boots had chafed our feet by then, the perimeters of the wounds were inflamed and bright red with pus oozing out of it in spots. Foot rags, when Sputniks are circling in space! To wind a foot rag properly and expertly around your foot is by no means impossible, but there's a point in your life when, like some pernicious living thing, this piece of cloth appears unexpectedly gnarled up in some hidden recess of your boot with just one thing in mind, to bite into everything it can find, the unsightly wounds on your heels, the wrinkled crevices between your toes, the circles below your ankles. We also had to learn how to walk in boots: like two enormous stone balls, you don't step out, you swing out.

As if there were eight or ten referees (umpires), veterans from the soccer team were walking around the field smoking and seizing us up—a herd of cattle.

"You, there! You! And you!"

If they pointed at you, your name was taken down. It reminded me of *Two Half Times in Hell*, where the concentration camp team plays against the German guards, and it's in their interest to lose, but their dignity gets the better of them. One heck of a movie.

For the space of a brief sigh I also thought of dignity, the dignity of soccer. It is impossible to play ball with forty men on the field, it is theoretically impossible even if we enlarge the field proportionally, a different, unfamiliar choreography comes into play, points of convergence foreign to its nature, a sort of Brown movement that looks, or looked, very much like a combination of running amok over the meadow and playing pool; the particles, kept in irregular motion, on the basis of whose movement it is possible to determine the so-called Loschmidt integer, also known as the Avogadro integer (*cf.* shrimp with avogadro) were fighting for their very lives (we were fighting for our very lives) just like in that movie.

I quickly got the hang of the field, but soccer is a team game, whereas this was anything but a team, a bunch of sops pitted against one another, made to run all over the place. I stood around a bit longer in my barefooted happiness, but then the life force stirred within and I started chasing the ball as if I were attending a fox hunt, hay ho tally ho!, and when I caught up, suddenly I was the fox, the prey, with the entire pack at my heels, I throw a glance sideways, I see a short black Gypsy by my side naked to the waist, so he's one of us, it's time to pass the ball, but I opt for just one more dodge, I manage it and I don't, they catch up, and wrestle me to the ground.

There I sat, down, way down, on the ground, with the little black guy standing over me.

"Ah was in the clear," he softly commented, gave me a searching look, then jogged back to his place. As if there was a back to jog to! In short, he gave the game its due. A nice Gypsy boy, Gyuri Máté, by far the best wing I ever had the pleasure of knowing, quiet and not argumentative, a born soccer player. If—a professional hazard—he ever kicked anyone, it had to be an accident. It (practically) pained him more than it did his victim.

"Aw, I'm so sohwry, pal, aw, I'm so sohwry," he'd say chanting plaintively when this happened, taken aback and frightened each time. He couldn't understand why his opponent fell into a rage. It was because of the goodness. The goodness was written all over him. It gleamed in his eyes.

Indeed, he was in the clear. I turned purple from shame. I hated the guy that was me there, at the time, the one who dishonored the game. I did not submit to its rules, I gave way to alien, outside promptings, I wanted to please. I felt awful. From then on I didn't do a dodge, I didn't go on a fox hunt. When I had the ball, I passed it immediately as they tell you.

True, they also tell you to take responsibility for every movement you make.

Gradually, the sweat dried up on me.

One of the officers beckoned me over. If my name had barely brushed past me till then, at this point, from this moment on, it kept knocking me down. Slapping me in the back. As if it were dark, and suddenly, from all directions, you never knew from where, it bashed me in the head, pinched me in the arm, pulled my ear, twisted my nose and pressed an elephant kiss on my thigh.

"Who? Me?" I asked in round-eyed surprise, and just to be on the safe side, pointed a finger at myself. Then came the sentence.

"No. The Prince . . ." That *was* a surprise. I laughed. Loud. From the guts. "What's so funny, soldier? Standing there, laughing. Who'd you think you are, Beckenbauer? Who the fuck are you?"

I took the question seriously. Indeed, who am I? My hair had been cut the day before. Touching the back of my head, the unfamiliar nakedness scared me. A naked snail. Or the naked snail's neck. They've even taken my neck from me. Also, with my hair cut, my nose grew longer, and I caught myself studying its shadow again, whereas I thought I'd licked the habit. The bright September sun was beating down on us. In the distance a pole well was bobbing up and down, a postcard, the Great Magyar Puszta in Technicolor, and in the meantime, the corporal shouting, yelling at the top of his lungs, though more from curiosity than anger. Or anger, but not rage. Who do I think I am? There was a team before me, the Hunyadi Sports Club, and there's gonna be a team after me, too, the Hunyadi Sports Club, but an army team's no gentlemen's club, you gotta exert yourself, put everything you got into it, plow the field—interesting how those involved in soccer always end up using sportswriters' clichés when they talk: pass the ball into the net, slip your hide past the defense, launch an assault on the penalty area. You gotta exert yourself, sweetheart, and not stand around like a marquis to the title born—I didn't bat an eye—and if I don't feel like playing I should say so, it's all right, it's a free country.

"Your name?"

I didn't want to tell him. For the first time in my life I felt I'd be

733

better off with any other name, Kovács, for instance, or Rosenkrantz, or even von Zichy. Anything. It was uncanny. I could feel the scent of betrayal in my nostrils.

"Don't you have a name?"

"I'd like to go back to the field," and I went back to the field.

"You're hopeless, snail head. But I'll get you yet," the corporal droned behind my back, sweet as molasses.

The far end of the field was boggy, deep, a quagmire; those who ended up there took horrendous falls, slipping right and left like in a cartoon film. The officers laughed.

"Was 'e satisfied with ya?" Gyuri Máté asked laughing on the run, then passed me the ball, and I passed it right back, as I was supposed to, then made for the no-man's-land, the quagmire, as I was supposed to.

It was the same supposed to.

## 153.

On August 26, 1652, my relative László's horse, Challenger, had a fatal slipup in the quagmire.

Was this the same supposed to?

## 154.

Out on the field I felt as if I were riding through town in Challenger's saddle—a handsome Turkish horse, chestnut and a stud, by the way—cutting a dashing figure, knowing my worth, a warrior, fearless, the town's benefactor, I fling a couple of thallers among the people, the horse's hooves going clip-clap clip-clap as if my father were providing the special effects, and I fling kisses of commiseration to the Gypsy girls (*in concreto,* mostly whores).

Out on the field I dashed about, frisky as a colt, driving myself, pressing forward, luxuriating, laughing. This freedom and flight was everything, and I was inordinately grateful to the God of the Game for making me so happy. Thanks to my exaltation they must have thought I was soft in the head. But I proved to be a reliable defense, a classical, solid right half, a good cover. I could always be relied on to cover my man.

As I was getting dressed, pulling on the new regulation uniform of the Hungarian People's Army, piece by piece, the good cheer and laughter abandoned me. I hated the cap most of all. It made my head itch. Also, I looked ugly in it, and by the time I was back in gear, I was once again that melancholy, doleful figure who was not the least to my liking, a skinny, uniformed stranger with the shaven nape I caught a glimpse of now and then in shop windows or car windows, someone I would have liked to keep at a distance—from women especially, one look at them, and the rain began to fall, and in the winter, the snow, plus sleet, which froze over by the morning, and in front of the Kovács Szántó statue the cars crashed into one another; it's hard to tell who's at fault, everyone's cursing and the insurance people refuse to pay.


## 155.


But I found a safe haven in town, a civilian lair where I didn't have to be on my own like some animal, like in the pub where I hid out if I could leave the barracks on the pretext—sometimes actually true—that I had to go for soccer training, a home where I was always welcome, where they were glad to see and feed me. We kept eating and eating. Eating was everything—a sign of respect, attention, proof that they'd been expecting me.

They were in awe of my name—there were whispered exchanges with the woman next door behind my back—but only just so. They were proud that someone *like me* would come to see them. They couldn't have made a bigger fuss if I'd been a real honest to goodness count, heir in perpetuity of Csákvár and Gesztes, et cetera, I'm sorry to say. Disconcerting. My faithful subjects, betraying sorry signs of political unreliability. The Communists are turning the world into a bunch of *lumpen*. Or is it simply due to the Great Plain, where poverty makes people slow and resistant to change? Transdanubia is different. Order, hierarchy. The Great Plain is churlish, simple. (Possibly, also more honest. But no. Being up front and being honest, they're not the same.)

People respected my uniform, and this surprised me. Playing soldier turned my stomach. I found it repulsive, repugnant. I felt nothing but fear and disdain. A bad joke. But people must have made a mental connection with the Hussars, valor, homeland, the defense of the homeland. I was surprised, but I didn't argue. I sat back and enjoyed the misunderstanding.

I ended up here thanks to Aunt Margit, who cooked, ironed, and did odd jobs for my mother (for ten forints an hour). I considered her an insincere and sly person who could bake incredible sweets, vanilla crescents and candied and chocolate rounds, and then she'd reach the dizzying heights of a grandmother. I didn't like her but was surprised when I learned that she didn't like me either, that she had enough guts not to like me, considering her cowardice.

A sly servant, I thought. A menial. She spoke humbly to everyone, and if my father spoke to her once in a great while, because generally he took no notice of her, this great honor made her tremble, and she turned red from head to toe.

"How are you, Margitka?"

"Oh, Count, you're much too kind," she panted, which drove Father up the wall.

"Not at all," he said between his teeth, "not in the least!," and he gave a nervous shake of the head (the jawbones!).

From time to time Margitka grabbed the old count's hand (*fifty years!*), bent over and gave it a loud smack.

"What are you doing, woman!" my father cried, unable to hide his disgust, whereupon—I saw it myself several times—Margitka took the reins and from below, from the kissing of the hand, she looked up squint-eyed—sly dog!—and I might go so far as to say insolent, yes, but in any case, with the same fervent disgust as my father's, and said, still to his hand:

"I'm so sorry, Count," and she kissed that beautiful hand once more.

Father took some of the tea cakes and, munching them, went back to the safe haven of his desk.

It was this Aunt Margit's younger sister who lived in Hód-mezővásárhely. Her name was Ilus, but nobody called her aunt. Like fire and water. The way she held her head, nose in the air, shoulders pulled back a touch, her instep held affectedly like a steed's, or a thoroughbred's, her eyes mischievous, kind, with just a glint of superciliousness—Ilus was pride personified. Her husband, Uncle József, was two meters tall and straight as a ramrod. He had been a gendarme under the old regime ("where was I to go with a frame like mine?"), and he liked talking about it. They loved each other. They spoke the soft, rolling local dialect and bit into the hot red paprika the way others bite into a red apple.

"Some mohre, deahr haart?" Iluska asked as the tears flowed down her cheeks.

This "deahr haart" felt good. I was afraid to bite into these wild and unruly plants, the cherry peppers, and the thin ones called the cat's weenie, but I sprinkled a generous amount of the poison green rounds on my omelet and added paprika to the stew, for the sheer pleasure of it, because I wanted to, that was obvious, and not because I wanted to show off or be polite—which they noted with mute appreciation. They wouldn't have thought that the finicky, dyspeptic city boy sitting at their table was up to it. I had my father to thank for my newly gained respectability. He taught me how to handle hot paprika (goulash).

We ate a lot. (You can get drunk on food, too. It can be intoxicating, too.) Sometimes we also had a drink.

"To the infinite power of destiny," Uncle Józsi said, providing the cue, and we had to stand up. They held their pinky out, like an ass's ear. Elegant. We had good times. I had good meals, well-seasoned greasy ribs, fresh sausage that tasted of the living hog, paprika salami, headcheese, which they called *svártli,* and of course, chicken exquisitely seasoned with paprika and made into a stew served with dumplings, and also fried pullet and eggs, soft and scrambled and sunny-side up, always made with stewed onions.

Uncle Józsi committed suicide. He hanged himself.

"I can't make it out, deahr haart, I can't make it out."

From then on, Ilonka paid more visits to Pest. The two sisters couldn't abide each other.

"Oh, her?!" and they waved a hand. Except, Ilus also laughed. And she wouldn't take the metro.

"Prohper peohple shouldn't goh into the belly of the earth, Pehter deahr," she said, and called a cab. Her older sister never took a cab in her life. Proper people don't take cabs, she would have thought, had she entertained thoughts of this kind. Then they moved in together.

"It's hell, deahr haart."

## 156

I found a slip, like Socrates' debt of a cock, among my mother's things: Margitka 150 forints. I paid her a visit. She had trouble breathing, she kept panting and wheezing. She interrupted her intake of breath with the mute gaping of her mouth, creating pauses where all things lose meaning. My glance fell on the carefully framed picture of my mother standing on a small bedside table, a rare, laughing picture. I'd never seen it.

"What's this?" I yelled at her.

"You know perfectly well!" Margitka nodded, squinting like an old (wary) cat, giving me the eye. She thought that I ought to know something, that was clear. Clearly, I should know something. "You know perfectly well!" This time she was screeching. But as her glance slid from me to the picture, her expression underwent a dramatic change. It softened, it took on a rosy hue, red and white patches slid up and down her neck. She was panting differently, too. She'd put me out of her mind. "Oh, why did you die?!" She grabbed the picture and smothered it with kisses.

I couldn't help thinking of the saliva in Margitka's old mouth which was now slathered—exaggeration—all over my mother's face. And also the back of her hand. In short, I was working through my father's sentiments and repugnance. It was droll, strange, and terrifying, all at the same time. Jealousy, loathing and filial gratitude, all jumbled together. Oh, the intricate web of relationships that confronts you already at the moment of your birth! Being a father, a mother, a child, how complex it all is, what a baffling structure a family is, cosseting and nakedness, security and vulnerability, its ebb and flow, give and take, stroke and slap.

"Oh, my beauty, my precious, the light of my life, why did you leave us? Why did you forsake me?" She saw me standing there. The touch of cruelty came back to her cheeks. "Why didn't you leave me provided for?" she hissed into my face.

Silence. Then timidly I asked what I'd asked the captain on the side of the soccer field:

"Who? Me?"

This was the same me. The question came less from self-centeredness than the suspicion that one can't always be sure.

Scornful, Margitka waved me off.

"You? *You?!*" The "oo" sound narrowed her cheeks, the sense of disdain, pity and surprise lent a contemptuous pucker to her lips. "No of course not. Her! Your mother. Why didn't she provide for me? Is that how little Aunt Margit meant to her? It oughtn't have taken much appending a shack to the house, a pigsty for an old woman, it oughtn't have taken much! I would've stayed in your service till my dying day, but I wasn't wanted no more." She was wheezing again. I felt no compassion. She grabbed my hand. "I'm a nobody, Count, what good am I on my own?"

I pulled my hand away. Again, I found myself in my father's place. She wagged her index finger at me, cursing, it was terrible, like a witch in a fairy tale.

"Of course, you was always like this, even as a boy. Hoity-toity. Holier than thou. I've kept an eye on you, even if you don't like it. You think I don't see? I'm not dumb just because I do ironing and clean plates, I'm not dumb . . . Never an honest word out a ya . . . the way you fawned . . . As Aunt Margit thinks best, thinks best!, don't make me laugh . . . I remember right enough! What sort a talk is that?! You was even ashamed when your ma sent me to school to get you, tryin' first not to see, then makin' like you just noticed, playing Little Lord Fauntleroy, phew!, like a little knight! . . . Oh is that you, dear Aunt Margit! . . . Oh it sure as hell is, may the pox take you and your priggish kind, except I didn't say it because I was scared, scared a ya and nothin' but a child. Scared of a child, can you beat that?"

I stood there and shrugged.

"I was always scared a you all . . . but most of all, I was scared a your pa . . . the way that tall, handsome man came outta his study, I nearly peed in my pants . . . Once I accidentally spilled the water for tea just before he came into the kitchen and he thought it was one a you and he says, which idiot was that? Of course, you laughed. Which idiot? Me, I said right away, it's best to confess this sort of thing right away. And he started hemming and hawing and said, In that case . . . naturally . . . ah-hum . . . how are you, Margitka? I hear it to this day: In that case . . . naturally . . . ah-hum . . . how are you, Margitka? The first time I laid eyes on him, your pa was so handsome I knew I'd never forget him, ever, and that scared me, too, this never . . . I ain't felt nothing like it before . . . Never's such an enormity a time . . . I never thought on it before . . . Don't worry, you don't look a bit like 'im . . . Your ma, my Lilike, she was the only person I wasn't afraid of 'cause she was such a dear, good woman. None a you deserved her . . . a saint . . . I was scared a you too."

She looked me proudly in the eye, the first and the last time I saw her proud. I pulled myself up to my full height. The lord of all I survey.

"I thought you was a count, like your pa!" She waved a dismissive hand. "You didn't even want my cake." That's not true, I thought, but I'm not saying. "Of course you was always like that, arrogant, clever, conceited. Wouldn't touch the pie, though it was groaning under the weight a the morello cherries . . ."

"Groaning? Who? The pie?"

". . . or the sweet noodles. Not the pie, not the noodles."

"With walnuts," I said, indulging my reveries.

"And now who am I supposed to serve? I'd a served, I'd done it till me last breath." She grinned. "Or your last breath . . . You're

741

not a real count. A real count makes sure he's served . . . You think I don't see how you're even proud of it? Proud a being your own servant? Is that what you think humility is all about? That's no humility for a count. A proper count don't go abandoning his folk like that. There's no lack a servants! Around here everybody's a servant. They made servant out a everybody, except your pa. Nobody could make a servant outta him, he's on a pedestal. They can't touch him . . . People get abandoned, that's why this country is bad. It's a bad country."

She practically spit the end out as if it were meant for me, as if I were this bad country. She'd never talked like this before, she never talked this real. Who would have thought that Margitka is a real person? Or that she could love? I better make a note of this, I thought. She put the picture back on the table, a gesture of dismissal. I forgot all about the 150 forints. But she didn't. I gave her two hundred. She nodded.

## 157.

At first I thought my name would be good here, too, a good source of anecdotes, and what could go wrong in a Hungarian anecdote?

Once in the middle of a political seminar—the refuge of forbidden naps—I was startled awake by hearing my name called, I jumped up and saluted according to form, whereas it was just the heroic Tibor Szamuely languishing on an Esterházy estate, and I'd misunderstood. In short, the lecturer had said:

"Esterházy estate." And snapping to attention, shouting enthusiastically, I said, "Present!"

This could have been taken as provocation, but following the cue from my innocent, sleepy face, they concluded I was just an idiot. They were as unprepared for my name as I was. Nothing came of it. Nothing comes of nothing, I thought, and nothing came of nothing. Later, though, when something did come of something, I learned soon enough that though nothing comes of nothing, anything may come of anything.

For instance, nothing came of it when I had to put my parents' and grandparents' occupation down on a form. Landowners, I confessed, but it had to be more concrete. They needed to know how many holds, but I saw the column on the form, and knew it wouldn't be big enough, there was no way I could write in all the zeroes. I told them, and they roared at me for a while, though I was just trying to help.

Also: The regulations allow the storage of two books in the small bedside table. But my Majk Granny decided that the time had come for me to read the nineteenth century, and she sent me the whole Cheap Library series, about twenty volumes, Stendhal, Balzac, Turgenev, Flaubert, everyone, and I read them all conscientiously. (Once in the early fifties, "culture propagandists" showed up at Lóránt Basch's house. Seeing all the books, one of the young, naïve propagandists sighed, oh, so many beautiful books!, at which the old man, angrily: And you might as well know, I read them all!)

You can actually fit twenty books in, though it went against regulations. The captain couldn't believe his eyes when he reconnoitered this small, but well appointed workers' library during one of his rounds. It took his breath away. In order to alleviate his mild nausea, he grabbed the stand as if it were a cat or a small kitten, by the neck, and started shaking it, and the world literature came tumbling out, out and under, until the captain calmed down, Stendhal, Balzac, Turgenev calmed him down.

He was panting, but he looked at me with something akin to gratitude. He was straightforward, he didn't set perfidious traps for

743

us, but if we fell into one, he swooped down on us. He screamed a lot, too, but his bark was worse than his bite. Now he whispered my name lovingly, and closed his eyes. What did he see, I wonder? Then he softly whispered my name again.

"Esterházy. Take. Note. This is not. A reading man's army."

I grinned, I took note, this is not a reading man's army. Indeed it is not. He assigned me some impossible task, but the nature of the inflicted punishment was just as I thought. Bagatelle.

## 158.

Self-denunciation. There were few things I enjoyed half as much. I plunged into the genre head-on—head-on, as if in a daze. I was inventing my life. I felt no sense of responsibility. I was not cynical, my considerations were purely esthetic.

Like a Lego castle or a dress-up doll, I took my life apart into little pieces with relish, flinging the bits about helter-skelter, aggrandizing some, reducing others, making still others disappear, mixing the real with the imaginary, treating the imaginary as real and the real as imaginary, and vice versa; I embedded sincere confessions inside wholly fallacious frames, and padded white lies with events anyone could safely confirm.

It was almost as pleasant as being out on the soccer field. Almost. I couldn't have said what made it different, nor did I care. I didn't even notice in the midst of my daily revels, which reached their epitome during the quiet evening dictations, that Gyula was watching me with growing antipathy, if not horror.

I paced up and down, the way it's done in the movies when someone is in the throes of creation; I considered and reconsidered, I flung my hands in the air, I yelled—I had a grand old time.

"New paragraph, sweetheart. Next the target individual,

parentheses, private, capital E period, close parentheses, where-upon he did bathe his nobly carved hose, no, nose, in the last rays of the setting sun, don't write that down, asshole!, in short: made defamatory . . . let's leave the Latin in, let them wreck their feeble brains . . . defamatory remarks about the socialist armed forces as such, namely . . . Or should it be to wit?"

"Namely."

"Namely, that it sucks."

"Enough for tonight," my partner grumbled without betraying the least sign of appreciation.

"No, no, Gyula, my angel. The secret police made their bed, now let them lie in it. They will get no mercy from me. New paragraph! Today I happened upon . . . Are you listening, Gyu-lus?! Without me, when would you have ever *happened upon* any-thing? At most, found . . . Continue. I happened upon a letter that the target individual had sequestered under his pillow . . ."

I stopped and shot my partner a look of pained disappoint-ment.

"What a louse you are, Gyula, going through my things like that! And my father's letter, of all things . . . !"

"Up yours!" the blond boy threatened, springing to his feet.

But there was no stopping me, an explorer inebriated by the discovery of writing. I dictated, and when I made some excep-tionally pleasing change in the world, giggled. I had just gotten myself involved with a father, in a devil-may-care manner with a devil-may-care father, frivolously with a frivolous father.

"New paragraph. My dear son, we are of one blood, and so I think it likely that you will commit your father's mistakes. If this should happen, try to wriggle out of the various delicate situations promptly and with honor, as I have done in my time." And also that the dear son should pay particular attention to three things in case of war: obey the orders of his superiors, care for the well-being of his subjects, and his horse. His commanders will take care of his enemies. "Et cetera, your loving father. Your loving father. How do you like that, my pet?"

Eyes bulging out of their sockets, Gyula glared at me and shuddered. Frightened, I stepped back. What's going on?

"What loving father are you talking about, asshole?!" he hissed and began tearing at the results of the day's labors. He tugged and pulled at the sheets of paper. And for my information, I'm not going to get him involved in this shit, this sordid, low-minded treason, I'm not going to make an abject informer out of him, he knows that's what this complicated nonsense is all about. He's no hero, but everything's got its limits. He's not doing this anymore, he can't take it anymore.

He tore the report into thumb-size pieces. You'd think it was snowing. Then his hands were empty.

"But Gyula, my sweet, it's just a game! We're just playing," I whispered, taken aback.

"You know who you can fucking play with!" he roared spitefully, and began retching.


## 159.


That's when I thought of him first since he'd left the country, this was the first time I'd thought of Roberto. But only in passing. It's history, so much water under the bridge.

Between January of 1957 and June 1963 we saw each other almost every month. If he couldn't make it, he sent word. But since we had to keep it a secret from my parents, it took some doing. Actually, it didn't, because the school janitor was our go-between. Roberto sent short letters in small pink envelopes.

"An affair of the heart?" the overworked janitor commented.

My dear Petár, Your Excellency, this was the form of address he invariably used. I liked it. It made me smile.

"You better not open that letter in front of me, son." There was in the janitor's voice a hint—no, not of menace, but something very close to it. A sense of power over me, as if it were within his means to hand out a reprimand.

Though they were about the cancellation of our next meeting, I liked these letters and I liked these meetings, a bit the way you like being called upon in class when you know the answer. In short, I was happy, and I was scared, too. Excited. Lying to my parents like this, over the long haul and not just on occasion, and not for the thrill of it, was exciting. I said I was going for my English lesson. Once my father said, *how are you,* but before I could answer (I was planning to say *senk you, very vell*), thereby suffering disclosure, he warned me not to say anything, just smile. I didn't. Neither did he.

There was in my meetings with Roberto something vertiginous, as if I were dreaming. Or been whacked on the head. As if my head ached. My head ached a lot, this too was part of my inheritance. I had to fend for myself back then. I couldn't very well discuss this thing with children (schoolmates, my brother), and I couldn't very well discuss it with my father, I was in no position to do so; I wouldn't have wanted to remind him of those terrible days anyway. I wanted him to forget, as if nothing had ever happened. Nothing. My presence was reminder enough, so I tried to keep out of the way. For her part, Mami hated Roberto with such a passion, she wouldn't have believed that I'd been seeing him.

In short, I couldn't talk about our meetings with anyone else but him. That's the way things were, and I saw nothing wrong with that. In my eyes, he was a real uncle. An uncle knows almost everything a father does, except it's better, because you don't have to draw conclusions from it all the time. You can never enjoy a father 100 percent like you can an uncle. That's what he's there for. On the other hand, they are seldom important, which takes away from the enjoyment value.

We always met in the same place, a café on Üllői Road across from the Museum of Applied Arts, the sheep outside, the wolf within, the sixties outside, we within. We met there because the first time and several times later, too, after our chat or my report, we'd cross over to the museum. Roberto could arrange anything, the storeroom and the restoration workshop, too, and he showed me the family treasures stored there. Flasks, plates, goblets adorned with *lavalière* drops and rosettes, beautiful pitchers, ceremonial arms, centerpieces wrought of ostrich eggs and silver, chalices ornate with ivory reliefs, "crucifix watches," coral rosaries and agate pears, objets d'art in relief, carved of ivory. So many things! I must see it for myself.

I saw it. I didn't feel anything.

Of course, by then I usually had a terrible headache, and I was tired.

In the café Roberto drank cognac, fine Hungarian Lánchíd cognac, and when he leaned close to me, I could feel the mélange of tobacco and cognac and warmth. It felt good, inhaling it. (When he drank, my father was usually cold and sour, which isn't as nice.) Initially, the first two or three times, we just talked with no particular aim in mind. I told him what happened to us during the past couple of weeks, and I tried to provide as detailed a description of my father in particular as I possibly could. Later on I even took notes so I wouldn't leave out the smallest detail that Roberto might find interesting, and he, for his part, would interrupt me with questions, taking notes of his own until eventually he also asked for mine.

"I hope they're not molesting the family."

He was thinking of the police, I knew, and said, no.

I liked our meetings. Still, with the passing of time, an indistinct feeling of unease took hold of me, as if I were closer to him than my father, and this worried me, so I suggested that we should stop seeing each other, or at least not as often.

Resentfully he looked up, then away. After a while, he heaved a sigh. He put his hand on mine. He's extremely pleased that I'm so honest and aboveboard with him, because honesty is important. It's not even a character trait, but a gift. Still, he would like to add that there is no need to say everything that's on one's mind all the time, being able to hold one's tongue is important, too, and I should keep that in mind for the future, though admittedly, honesty is basic to our relationship, too, it is the foundation on which mutual respect, esteem and love can flourish, and he knows that at times it is precisely in the interest of our meetings—in short, in my father's interest—that I am compelled to lie at home, and he has no doubt how this must make me suffer. (It didn't. I always tried to lie as *briefly* as I could. I didn't make things up, I just did what I had to do, soberly and briefly, so I could go to Üllői Road.) He appreciates my honesty, still, let's keep to the well-trodden path—without realizing, surely, he pressed my hand hard against the tabletop, it hurt—and I should just try to imagine how awkward it would be de facto if these, my notes, were to land in my mother's hands somehow, how *difficult* it would be to explain this *thing*, because this thing is highly complex and not black or white, because the world is an intricate interplay of intricate overtones, though by all odds he should be saying—and he ran a finger over my palm—that it's my father who is complex, it is his complexity that has brought about this situation, but let's not talk about it anymore. He hopes I understand what he is getting at, and he's astonished how quickly I've grown into a little adult; with slight exaggeration, we'll be drinking to our health with cognac before long; and being reassured by my maturity, he'd like to be so bold as to add that in a certain sense it'd be too late to back down now anyway, what's past is past, it can't be undone, history is not a command performance, a bargain sale where you can return the merchandise, and I shouldn't brood, the fact that the question came up proves how close I am to my father, and naturally, to him as well, he hopes; still, there's no need to weigh things, only what had to happen happened, and because the threads run together in his hands, who is a friend of the family even if we think otherwise at this time, things don't happen in a vacuum, everything is . . . secured. As for the notes, there's no need for me to worry, he'd mentioned them purely as a theoretical possibility, and he gives me his personal assurance that they will never fall into the wrong hands.

My hand was all wrinkled up. I thought of the terror that seized me on the morning of November 5, 1956. I tried to conjure it up, but in vain. Here in the café it felt like an island with just the two of us, and through transposition, my father. If I want it's a secret, if I want it's honesty, dry land is at a great distance, and since this depends exclusively on me, I do not feel the need to report *out there* on my islander's life.

And all the time, in the murky depths of the café, his French piqué vest iridescent, there stood a young waiter casting furtive looks my way. Though his fingers were wrapping the silverware in napkins, he was looking askance at us. . . .

## 160.

Have I gone completely mad, Major Molnár inquired, overcome as always by elemental weariness whenever he had to say my name. He could hardly get to the end, he ran out of breath, the *z* wouldn't buzz, the *á* wouldn't gape, the *y* wouldn't end with a flourish, just a soft fade, a yawn, as if the male branch of the family had died out already.

He was a political officer, a soccer fan, the guardian angel of the soccer players, smart, cynical. He treated us well, but we had to be on our guard. He was not to be trusted. On the other hand, he was inordinately vain and spiteful.

Also, where do I think I am? In school? At some literary jerk-off? But since he's on my side, he's going to enlighten me about where I am. In the armed forces of the Hungarian People's Republic, asshole! And is he correct in assuming that I think everyone here is an idiot.

"What can I say?"

"What can I say, Comrade Major! This is the army, not five o'clock tea."

"Yes, sir, Comrade Major."

His tone suddenly changed, as if up till then we'd merely been fooling around, but from there on in, the fun was over.

"Who're you trying to fool, you prick. They knew all along that you write those reports."

The suddenness of the revelation made my head reel. I had not counted on it. Never in my life had I felt so keenly that I'd made a mistake and the mistake could not be remedied. The mistake is rolling me along in front of it, like when you botch up a penalty kick. You've kicked off already, everything's already decided, except it isn't evident yet, and nothing but the bitter and fruitless prayer remains to undo it. Oh, please, it's just a game, please don't be mad at me! I didn't mean it!

"They know everything."

"But . . . but why?"

"Not why, but everything."

I saw the same contempt in his eyes as in Gyula's, except there I also saw horror, and here, only boredom. My own eyes I couldn't see. The major's attractive face was already worked over by drink, a slight pudginess was in evidence, not to mention the color and consistency. My stomach turned. Could everything I'd been dictating to this accidental Gyula of mine be true? True in that banal and tedious sense that it really happened? Suddenly I became a participant of everything around me, my own story, which laughing and giggling I thought up night after night, and the history of the nation, which I didn't know who thought up. Certainly, it was far from amusing.

# CHAPTER EIGHT

## 161.

Our mother was high on fatigue and she was high on stamina. Again and again her reserves of stamina surprised us. When you're a mother of four, the strength available to you is not enough. A bit more is always needed, and if there's a bit more, a bit more is needed still. However, this fact implies neither the presence of hope, nor of despair.

Our mother's strengths manifested themselves on a wide scale. There was everything: girlish caprice, levity and laughter, tight-lipped endurance, strength as a jovial surplus, self-control, and the reliability of a beast of burden. But later we discovered that a mother's strength is only almost infinite.

Our mother's evening performances were not preceded by preparation of any sort, not even the previous night's performance. Each seemed to be the first, a premier, surprising, astonishing, mysterious yet natural, like a miracle, unavoidable, yet not contingent on anything, especially on the day that was just coming to an end.

It was contingent on our mother, and she—need we say—was contingent on nothing.

She made no preparations, gave no explanations, did not attempt to talk us into it, did not organize anything—she'd have made a lousy cultural organizer in a factory; instead, when the time came, she let us know. She let each of us know in turn, she stepped up to each of us individually, whispered something in our ear, one after the other, first the people of the household, Uncle Pista, Aunt Rozi, Annu, Little Pista, then, taking a deep breath, her father-in-law (she didn't whisper, but stopped in front of him, nodded, and said very softly, "Papa, please . . ."), Aunt Mia, before she got very ill, Great-grandmother, and the children.

She also whispered something to Papi, but as if it weren't the same thing she'd whispered to us—a beaming man's face from the early fifties!

She also whispered in our ear that we should bring something to sit on, a chair, a kitchen stool, a joint stool, a pillow, a wicker, a throne, and sit here and there. Everyone followed her instructions, no one thought of complaining. The people of the house obeyed silently, even Grandfather, though *his* face didn't burn with enthusiasm; smoking his pipe, he looked on with stoical goodwill and wry attentiveness.

An excited bustle centered around the seating arrangements took its start, not unlike our TV watching later in the sixties. Then, once the audience had taken their places—there was also a buzz, which subsequently died down—and it was nice and quiet, Mami launched into the show: either she read out loud, or she played puppet theater. Even when she read out loud she held a puppet in her hand, as if it were doing the reading. What? I don't remember. Dickens, Conrad, *The Little Prince*. She never held a performance in the same place twice, sometimes it was in the "clean" room we occupied, sometimes the kitchen, sometimes the back of the yard (next to the dung heap). If it was in our room, she played puppets from behind Grandfather's dividing blanket. Otherwise, she used Uncle Pista's "prison rug." He had two meters and seventy centimeters to pace up and down, up and down in his cell, and the old man, his legs, his body, his heart, settled into this distance, and when he was released, he bought a rug (according to Mami, not as ugly as all that), two meters and seventy centimeters long, and every evening before going to bed, he walked up and down, up and down on it. Aunt Rozi cried.

The performance never lasted longer than thirty minutes, and when it was over, everyone laughed like children, including the children.

## 162.

Evening had not yet come, but it was already dark, the hours turning ink blue, it was March 5, 1953, the people fell silent, Great-grandmother Schwarzenberg was dead, but I was still afraid of her. Or was I? If you don't know whether you're afraid or not, you're afraid. It got dark earlier, a heavy, billowing snow cloud lay over the sky, an unnatural dimness hovered over the village, like when they cleverly turn the stage dark with artful lighting.

We were waiting for the snow. Mami arranged it so that we'd think of the window as the stage. She said nothing, she just looked out into the dark without moving, and only when unexpectedly big flakes of snow began to fall unexpectedly even though we'd been expecting it, she lowered her head with a great show of modesty, i.e., with false modesty, like a director satisfied with the players. The snow was falling in two different patterns—here, closer to us, on a slant, there, farther off, in lozenges and possibly tetrahedrons, and the air became dimensional (three). The flakes melted as soon as they hit the ground.

We were extraordinarily pleased with our mother's beautiful, original and intriguing production—the snowstorm.

Roberto had a way of dropping in, and he always managed to make a special occasion of himself. Whenever he walked through the door, it was Sunday. Everyone liked him. Whether my father or my mother liked him more would be hard to say. My mother regained her youth by his side, they frolicked like children, they were like brother and sister. My father, on the other hand, watched and studied his friend like a wise old man. They almost never talked in front of the others; they moved off and conversed in a whisper.

This time he came with the snowstorm. He didn't just show up, he burst in then—as if putting on the brakes—grabbed the doorjamb, looked around, then softly, practically spitting out the words, he said:

"Get out."

He was drunk. The people of the household disappeared in a flash. The snow ended, my mother's production ended. But this time, no one laughed.

"You must excuse me, Uncle Móric," Roberto said with a nod toward my grandfather, who couldn't abide drunks, and proceeded to sequester himself in his suite behind the blanket. My parents were shocked. Their friend threw himself in Grandfather's easy chair, and like someone startled awake from a dream, began reassuring us—and for some reason, especially me, majoresco this and majoresco that, and how is the young gentleman, and has the young gentleman thought about the future yet, which has turned in my favor now that the political constellation has changed. And that my time has come. The time of the majoresco.

From which I concluded that from now on I'd be tied up to a tree in the manor like before, wandering only as far as the rope would let me. Consequently, I greeted the news of Stalin's death with subdued good cheer. Also, I didn't even know who he was.

"*Lehunyta szemét a szemét,*" Roberto said with a grin, then he too proceeded to close his eyes. But first he winked at me, "An untranslatable pun."

"He was a great rascal, may he rest in peace," my mother nodded. They had had no idea why Roberto was so excited. They hadn't been glued to Radio Free Europe day in and day out, and they hadn't been waiting for the Americans, they were waiting for the night (day in and day out). They were overwhelmed with work, the struggle for survival, and you couldn't see Stalin from there.

"A dictatorship needs a tyrant to hold it together, don't you see?" Roberto said, waving his arms about.

"Far be it from me, to spoil the fun," Father said good-naturedly.


## 163.


*Mensch ängere dich nicht.* Aunt Mia played this game with a vengeance none of us could match. She never spared us, not once, not ever. She knocked down whatever could be knocked down with obvious, ungodly relish in the following manner: she'd swing her own man in front of the enemy a couple of times as if she hadn't quite decided yet, as if there were a glimmer of hope—and there is so much hope in a child!—then with a short flick of the wrist, as if she were ringing a bell, she'd flick the man off the board without further ado, veritably beheading it, all the while pinning her searching glance on her victim's countenance. She always managed to win, and then she'd say:

*"Mensch ängere dich nicht,"* adding, *"ängere,* with an umlaut!" My younger brother usually broke into tears, as if the umlaut had done him in.

Roberto stood the men up, threw the dice, then moved helter-skelter, but always so he'd knock down a red man.

"Here's the red, where's the red? Off with the red!," giving the reds an Aunt Mia–style what for. "Out! Get out! Away with you! We've had enough!"

My parents watched and laughed.

"We want to play too! We want to play too!"

They ended up thrashing the reds in unison. This "*Mensch*" is the same game as our "who laughs last." Father ran on about how apt the German and Hungarian expressions were. The West, the eternal winner, can afford to view the situation from the vantage point of the loser, comforting him, the loser, with amiable generosity, don't take it to heart, old man, *ängere dich nicht,* it's just a game, and besides, easy come, easy go, this time you lose, next time you win. The direction and position of the Hungarian, however, is not clear, as if it were just a naïve inquiry, a theoretical gathering of information, who *does* laugh last? But no, this is the loser's question, because a loser puts his hopes in the future, we've got what we've got, whatever happens happens, but in the end it's going to be my turn to laugh, I am the one who is going to laugh at everyone else, because this is all that counts: who laughs last.

"You're so talkative today, Mati dear," Mami commented with a touch of sadness.

Roberto screamed with laughter.

"Laughter," he shouted, "you see, old man, it's the laughter that counts! So then, who laughs last?" Meanwhile, scornful, he kept striking the red men off the board. "I do! We do! We laugh, old man, and not them. Not that filthy bunch."

My father (a bad habit) fell to thinking.

"Why? Is *this* the end?"


## 164.


Two and a half years later, in October 1956, there *was* a sudden end of sorts, but nobody laughed. (Correction: at the end of the end "they" laughed.) All the same, the red men were struck off the board just like Roberto had shown us. We were living in

Csobánka by then—by then and still then—because those who'd been forcibly resettled were later free to choose a place of residence (the sedentary lifestyle of the serfs had ceased the century before), anywhere except Budapest. Having been forcibly shipped out of Budapest, they didn't have a permanent address there, and so could not go back. In short, if the problem hadn't existed in the first place, the solution would have been a cinch.

When in May 1954 we entered the dim basement apartment in Csobánka where our mother had to keep a washbowl against the wall which by evening was filled up with water—for some reason, I thought of it with outright pride, the *full* washbowl as the measure of our misery and privation—Mami was waiting for us. We were standing on the threshold, holding our father's hand on both sides, and the room was chock-full of toys, like in a fairy tale. A teddy bear (frayed!) was sitting propped up majestically in the middle, next to it a rubber ball with polka dots, and what later proved to be the best toy of all, a train strung together with fishing wire out of empty sardine cans (yellow, Danish). We used to pull it along in the sand or the wood shavings, whereby we had instant rails as well, which from then on we were told to respect (the exciting interplay of freedom and restraint).

Because of all this, plus the elevated expressions on our parents' faces, we thought it was Christmas. We didn't care about the warm weather, but where was the tree? The Christmas tree? We stood around, exasperated. Our mother had just finished the laundry and had hung it out to dry on the fir tree near to the house—colorful shirts, underwear, red, blue, yellow, white. There, she pointed, there's the tree, see, there it is!

My brother and I exchanged looks. I was going to do the talking.

"In that case, would Mother kindly tell little Jesus that he should have brought that Christmas tree inside the house, where it belongs."

But it's so beautiful and tall.

True. Still, little Jesus should have thought of that before.

But we've never had such a big Christmas tree.

True. Nevertheless, we cannot accept this sort of *bad grace* from little Jesus.

At this our father slammed his fist on the table with such brute force that the glasses and the cutlery trembled for some time. He was thirty-five years old. Midway on life's journey he was made aware that he had strayed into a dark forest.


# 165.


First he was employed as a seasonal share watermelon grower at the Red Star Farmers Cooperative in Békásmegyer. That's where we saw those fantastic huts dug into the ground. Pleasantly cool even in the most stifling heat. As if Father and the other men had built them for fun, each a sort of sand castle. Even better, because you could hide inside. Pali Nagy and he worked together as a pair. He was our father's "ill genius." Bogyica said that they "tippled together" far too often. Tippled. Oh, how I hated that word. Uncle Pali liked to joke. Also, he had a great big gold tooth in his mouth.

"He's a gold mine!"

We knew he couldn't be the same age as Papi. He was much older. All you had to do was look at him. Still, he had the same pleasant *pálinka* smell, a nice schnapps smell.

After the melon thing, Papi was hired by the Budapest Road Maintenance Company as an unskilled laborer. He mended roads. We liked that. We were proud, and we said so every chance we got that he's a road mender. Our beloved father is someone to reckon with, he's a road mender! A road mender isn't just a scraper. He's not a chicken that goes around scraping, but more like a cowboy that wanders freely along the roads making sure they're all right, as if a road were a fine horse, sometimes from the Muraköz, sometimes an Arabian thoroughbred, clip-clop, and from time to time he gives his horse's neck a pat, good boy, Charlie, there's a good boy! The road to Pomáz was built by our father too, and so was the service road to Csobánka. What I mean to say, he didn't *have* them built, he took care of them. He repaired them. He filled in the potholes with bitumen, patched up the shoulders, weeded the ditches. He mended everything beautifully—a sight for sore eyes.

Sometimes when he worked nearby, my brother and I would sneak a look (on the sly). We were awfully proud of him. Naked to the waist, he smoothed out the bitumen, while black streaks of dirt slithered down his body. From nearby someone would bellow at him now and then, *fuck it, Count, don't you fuck it up again!* Beads of sweat glistened on his back and around his waist and also his forehead. He wiped it off with his lower arm and fixed his glasses—a professor naked to the waist, smart and strong, too, that was clear, brains and brawn like the Greeks about whom Mami used to read to us, because we refused to read on our own. We wanted to be road menders like Papi, so what was the use of reading? If we must, we'll wear glasses (re. the brains), *guileful Odysseus*, we heard her read; but most of all we wanted to work with bitumen. But our mother must have misunderstood something because she started crying while we started laughing. The two brought about an equilibrium of sorts.

When we were young, we saw grownups cry a lot.

Sometimes Papi didn't come home for the night because they were working too far away, or "they forgot to dispatch a truck" to cart the workers home, and so the men slept in a trailer. We didn't think the trailer was as great as the dugout hut. On the other hand, it moved. A moving room!

(I have a remarkable piece of paper, torn in half, legal size, with French squares, from 1952, bearing a stamp, "Road Maintenance Co., Székesfehérvár, Bridge Building, Környe. Supervisory Board for Work Affairs." The letter was written in pencil. Móric Esterházy, Majkpuszta, Castle. For the building of the bridge at Majkpuszta we need 1 or 2 night watchmen, preferably living nearby. If you can take this job on kindly look up our group supervisor or the foreman of the masons at the site. The work is 12 hrs. per day and lasts appr. 4 weeks. Payment: 2 forints per hour. During your term of service you will have to stay in the shack set up at the site. Heating permitted. Please respond.

Who could have possibly imagined a letter like this, let's say, back in 1917? No spiteful Communist brain could have dared go so far. The guillotine yes, but a night watchman?!)

If he didn't come home, that was good because we could wait for him to come home, when will Papi come home already!, and then he'd come, and we'd be happy, especially Mami. (Later she was not happy, though. Later she just waited, and she continued waiting even after Papi was home, and we made this waiting our own, and we couldn't tell anymore whether we were happy or not.) We were all happy except for the twins, because they were too small to be happy.

Babies are not like young animals. Young animals know how to be happy or sad. A dog or a goat, for instance. We've got a goat out back, a bearded professor. We tried milking it but we couldn't, or it wouldn't let us, it held back its milk. Babies are more like plants, though the twins cried a lot all the same because they kept on getting earaches in their middle ear. They always got the same illness. If a cold, then a cold, if the middle ear thing, then that. That's how twins are. When they're old enough for potato noodles we'll see if it's still share and share alike. Or when it comes to us. But most of all, how will they act with each other?

Because if it's going to be love, will they love each other more and more, until they merge into one like certain stars (re. the Kulin & Róka textbook)? Or if it's hate, one the other, and the other the one, even more, will they cancel each other out? But it was not to be.

# 166.

We were sick all the time, though I wasn't sick as often as the others, the twins especially. You'd think they had to share everything with each other, including their strength. Once my younger brother had to be sneaked up to Budapest to Doctor Szlávik at the clinic because he had whooping cough and it surpassed the local doctor's know-how. He didn't know whooping cough when he saw it.

Bogyica took the smuggling on herself. (It had worked at Hort.) They got on the bus, and when the policeman came to check the passengers, Bogyica handed him her I.D. It had a child (our cousin) entered in it. The policeman looked Bogyica up and down, then he looked my brother up and down.

"Is this your son?"

Bogyika sighed a deep yes, smiling like an actress who is pretending that she is smiling like an actress. The policeman closed the I.D., then flipped it in the air, fanning it. Bogyikó realized she'd been found out. Her son was six years older than my brother. She promptly cut the double smile short. She'd been scared all along, but now it showed. At this point the policeman spoke up, as if he were afraid of this very beautiful woman's fear.

"The child is smallish, *considering*."

"He's sick," Bogyikó said with animosity.

"You'd better get him to a doctor then, ma'am!" He was about to hand back the I.D., but my aunt was faster than him and grabbed for it. Except the policeman hadn't released it yet, which made it appear as if they were engaged in a struggle.

"Excuse me," the young man said kindly.

"As you wish," Bogyica answered, but her manner was so cold, the window was covered up with frost. She hadn't meant to do it, except the fear was bouncing back and forth, and she couldn't make sense of herself anymore. She acted on reflex, and this is how it came out—haughty, arrogant, "as you wish!" She looked out the window over the heavily wrapped head of the child, which wasn't easy, considering the frost.

"Shit," the policeman grumbled. He was thinking that he should have followed regulations and made this hoity-toity dame and her brood get off. No need gentrifying herself up to Budapest. They've got a proper doctor in town. He's good enough for everybody else. But he said nothing and got off the bus. He couldn't make sense of himself either anymore.

## 167.

A motorcycle with a sidecar was a frequent guest, on (and inside) it two *sweet* men, Uncle Sanyi Vadász and Uncle Miska Kozák, who was completely bald, though he was still young. Both of them worked in the printing shop with Mami after the war.

A huge garden, more like a park, was attached to the house. There was even a stream in the back. We lived in the basement downstairs, but we could have the run of the garden as if it belonged to us. Whenever the BMW showed up all of us walked down to the clearing by the stream, laid a blanket on the grass, the BMW brought grilled chicken, wine, a picnic!, a merry summer picnic!

A summer picnic in October. The grownups were drinking

wine and we lemonade. But we were allowed to clink glasses. Then we fried bacon. Papi (always) ended up with the prettiest piece, though he slashed the rind for us too, but it wouldn't open up like it did for him, like a crown with its points outstretched. They kept telling us not to fry the bacon over the flame, just the embers. We couldn't figure out why and didn't take the sound advice. Mami smoked a cigarette, puffing, puffing, while Miska Kozák and Sanyi Vadász flirted with her.

I think that our parents were still young just then. Not so later that night.

The twins were given onion boiled in milk, which Mami had learned how to make from Aunt Rozi. You cut an onion in half, drop it into the boiling milk with a bit of butter, sprinkle the whole thing with pepper. It's good when you're sick. I tried to force it on the twins, but they wouldn't eat it. We liked playing with them because they moved and they made sounds. But Mami called us to order, they're not toys, but we could see very well that she and Papi played with them a lot themselves.

But now the grownups were playing separately in a bunch, listening to one another and the trickle of the stream, immersed in their friendship. (Once or twice Roberto showed up too, but he and the two men didn't get along. This hurt Mami's feelings very much.) I saw that one of the twins wasn't acting like the other, because she wasn't acting in any way at all.

"Has she still got a fever?" Mami asked, laughing, as if I were not I, but the doctor.

"She's very quiet and she's a wee bit cold."

I didn't dare repeat it. I felt a sense of solemnity. This was the first time I'd seen a dead man from up close. It took some time before Mother responded to the terror in my voice. Screaming, she leaped to the child, pressed her close, kissed her repeatedly without thinking, then started running toward the house.

"No! No! No!" she cried.

She didn't stop by the house, though, and continued running. We took Papi's strong, warm hands, one on each side, like we used to. Everyone stood rooted to the ground. Then the two friends took off after Mother. They jumped on the BMW as if it were a horse and swaying right and left, vanished down the garden path from before our eyes.

"Lilike! Lilike!" they shouted from the motorbike, but Mother couldn't see or hear, she was howling as loud as she could, pressing one of the twins close to her bosom, running down the village street. People thought she was running amok. At first the doctor wouldn't open the door for her because he thought that must be the revolutionaries trying to get to him; his son was with the Ávó, and though he kept saying it was the green *border guard* Ávó, the Ávó's the Ávó.

"She's dead," he said blankly,

Mother lurched, grabbed his collar like a man, and started shaking and strangling him.

"You scoundrel, you filthy ávó man! Cure her this instant!"

Uncle Sanyi and Uncle Miska had to hold her down. They were a poor match for her.

"Hold her tight!" the frightened doctor ordered, then gave her a sedative in the arm.


## 168.


I tried to comfort our father.

"It's just one twin now with a middle-ear infection."

"What?!" our father cried out, but then he didn't hit me after all. He just looked at me with disgust. In this great tragedy, our feelings got all mixed up.

"*Mid*-ear," my brother said helpfully. Everyone loved him, he was so beautiful.

In the middle of the night we were startled awake by our father's crying. He was sitting on the floor by the empty baby bed, half leaning over the side, as if sheltering or burying it under his body, and he was sobbing so his heart would break. He'd taken off his glasses, which made his face look empty and like a stranger's. It was stained with tears, as if dirty snow had melted over it. He was blubbering and hiccuping (as if he'd been drinking). He wailed, covered the wooden bars with kisses, oh-oh-oh-oh, then he pressed his forehead against the bars, his hand hanging limp over the top like the broken wing of a bird. The bars left a mark on his forehead.

"My darling baby, my sweet baby, my darling baby." It was terrible to hear.

Our mother lay on the bed without making a sound. That, too, was terrible to hear.

My brother and I usually slept in the white iron bed head to foot, but now it was side by side. He stroked me.

"See?" he said pointing at our father, "how much he loves us? When we die, he's going to cry like that for us too."

We fell asleep in each other's arms.

"She's very quiet and she's a wee bit cold," I mumbled as I fell asleep.

Later on no one in the family ever mentioned the other twin, the twins, either directly or indirectly, ever.


# 169.

A white coffin. While Mami and Papi were at the funeral, Aunt Irmi had to watch us. She was even more beautiful than Bogyica, which we wouldn't believe until we saw her. She spoke with a German accent. She was born in Graz, but she was also forced to resettle, because her second husband, Uncle Józsi Prónay, was related to the Prónay of the special Prónay detachment that went around the country in 1920 hanging Communists, or those who were called Communist, or those who were presumed to be Communists, or those who could presumably be called Communist.

Also, her first husband was Foreign Minister István Csáky. She told us all about the tragedy many times, but made us promise to be as silent as the grave.

"Keep silent, *süsse* dears, like the grave diggers, *also wie gesagt*," and she raised a finger to her lips which (already back then) she painted with brown lipstick.

When, having signed the agreement on Yugoslavia, they were coming back together from Hitler in Berchtesgaden, the white-gloved waiters were serving fish in the dining car. But Irmike didn't like fish. This is what saved her.

"Being the minister's wife, I could afford the luxury of choosing." she said to us by way of warning and explanation, and we knew in a flash that we wanted to end up as ministers' wives.

Papi and she always spoke German to each other. She had tears in her eyes when she spoke about her first husband, tears and smiles, and she spoke about him a great deal. At such times Uncle Józsi leaned forward to listen, as if it were the first time he was hearing it, as if hoping that this time the ill-fated Csáky might get off. But he didn't, because one of the waiters, a Gestapo man, mixed ground glass into the aspic (*pron.* ah-spic). They got rid of him in this complicated manner because ground glass makes the kidneys bleed and the cause can't be determined, and so poor Csáky died in the hospital two weeks later of "natural causes." (Hitler didn't like Csáky's friendly overture with Yugoslavia.) We kept as silent as the grave (diggers).

Her coffees were as famous as Bogyica's. We used to go up on the hill to their house for coffee. A major ceremony, a sleight of hand. As a full-fledged participant, I had coffee with milk brought fresh from Aunt Mariska, still warm and sometimes as fine as heavy cream. But the grownups had a mélange of sorts too, coffee made from beans, of medium strength but delicious, perked in double flasks, plus a mixture of chicory (red label) and Frank coffee. (A small roll wrapped in yellow paper? Made up of pressed rounds? In spots the barley chaff glimmered through. Or was it the other way around? Was the chicory this pastille?) Under the lower of the two flasks there was a small alcohol burner with a wick. The water was in this one. When it boiled, it rose into the upper, cup-shaped flask through the neck and through the ground coffee sprinkled into the filter—grinding, roasting here at home, courtesy of Uncle Józsi—then they removed the flame and as it cooled, the liquid dripped back down, a brownish black. They repeated this procedure two more times. At its base the glass tube was encased in paraffin which fit into the mouth of the bottom flask like a cork. The upper, cup-shaped flask was open.

When the masterpiece was ready, Irmike would sigh:

"The moments of drinking coffee are the only truly edifying moments in my life."

At which Uncle Józsi added, like a line of poetry:

"Ay, the moments of reflection and relaxation."

At which Irmike shot up a hand to her lips:

"Oh my God! I hope nobody's trying to tell the truth! *Gehört sich nicht,* it's such bad manners."

At home, Mami and Papi did a laughing imitation:

"The moments of re-lax-a-tion!," and making fun of himself, Papi added:

"On the other hand, the coffee is impeccable! *Grand cru!*"

Once the magic contraption blew up. It gave off a loud pop. Nothing awful transpired, except everything was covered with brownish-black stains. The grownups giggled. They didn't dare come out and say it looked like shit. Shit that hit the fan. And so, we didn't either. When Uncle Józsi died in sixty something, Aunt

Irmi emigrated and ended her days in an old age home in Graz. She left many books with gothic script behind at our place with "Csáky" ex librises.

*"Es gehört sich nicht!"* I hear you.


# 170.


The village was slow and sluggish in responding to the revolution, though later it got its share of revenge as surely as if, with flying banners, flags cut out in the middle, it had ecstatically celebrated the thing it had anticipated with fear. Though possibly more was afoot, except we didn't notice. In my father's autobiography dated 9 February 1959 he makes the following statement: "With respect to my behavior during the antirevolution, the relevant authorities have once again found nothing objectionable."

They found nothing objectionable. Once again. Fuck them!

They didn't leave the apartment. My mother was crying quietly to herself, she couldn't figure out what was happening. Father was glued to the radio. Uncle Sanyi Vadász and Uncle Miska Kozák showed up. They tried to console Mother, but without paying much attention to her; on the other hand, they tried very hard to persuade Father to come join them and participate in the shaping of the country's future, which was just then being decided.

Father had a ready answer, that was clear. No, on the contrary, he shouldn't participate in this thing at all, he really mustn't. He's not saying that he doesn't approve 100 percent, and then he hasn't said half. After all, it's his revolution, too. But this revolution is made so admirable and sensational by the fact that those very people in whose name the horrors of the past years had been perpetrated have now taken up arms—in short, the people—and though they've neglected to ask for his consent, he'd also become one of the people by now and is still the people at this very moment, and will continue to be the people from here on in. Or the son of the people, if you will. (Grandfather, for instance, never became the son of the people. He couldn't have even if he'd tried. But he didn't.) Still, if he were to legitimize his position and were to participate in the revolution of the people, he'd turn back into a count in the twinkling of an eye, a *grand seigneur,* a ruling class that's had its day, and he'd cast a shadow over this great event. Cardinal Mindszenty too would be well advised to limit himself to praying for the revolution and resigning himself to heaven.

Uncle Sanyi and Uncle Miska listened to this exegesis (impatiently), gave my father a manly hug, and my mother, too, and trotted off on the BMW. What's become of them?

By the way, an emblematic Red Cross truck was standing in front of our house, too. My father didn't even look up as he sent the driver away. Only afterward did he say what he'd say later at soccer games if we made a bad pass, what we heard him shout so often from the bleachers: Who to? Where to? Why? On that indifferent November dawn he said it just a bit differently and much more quietly:

"What for? Where to? Why?"

### 171.

Still, something must have happened in the village, because from one day to the next the grading system in school changed. It did an about-face, and one became the best mark, a five, the way it had been before the war. Our teacher wrote it on the blackboard: 1—excellent, 2—good, 3—average (the average didn't change, average is always average, it's average), 4—satisfactory, 5—unsatisfactory.

Five is unsatisfactory? We laughed it off. We laughed at me, too, ha-ha-ha, a student with all fives!, and the others pointed at me, though by then I'd been a one for two whole minutes at least. All they had to do was glance at the blackboard, and they did. But they didn't take it seriously, and who could blame them? You can't go around switching words back and forth on a whim. Words need getting used to.

I was an exceptionally good student. I studied all the time. I thought that that's what school was for. I did my homework even in elementary school, which was not at all usual. Even my brother and sister looked down their noses at me because of it. They considered it a sign of stupidity. But only my sister was smarter than me maybe, clever, because she got top grades with zero homework, something I don't think I could have done. Anyway, probably not, because I never had the nerve to try it. It never entered my mind *not* to do the homework to the best of my ability.

As a consequence of all the passion and artlessness I often received fives, including right after October 23, a five five. But when the fives became ones, instead of changing the fives to ones, for the sake of simplicity they struck them off the record, and so they went to waste.

This is the situation I was attempting to rectify the entire afternoon of Sunday, November 4. Aunt Klotild, from whom we were renting the apartment, was helping me. All I remember of Uncle Varga is what I heard, that he was the chief of the nail smiths, but I don't remember anymore what that means. Aunt Klotild and Mami were born the same year, but Aunt Klotild was an old woman. Her teeth were missing and she was ashamed of her dentures because they made her lisp, so she hardly dared open her mouth. I turned to her for help because I couldn't turn to Mami, who'd been silent for days. She put the food in front of us without saying a word, then lay down fully clothed. There was no comforting her. Besides, we didn't dare. Sometimes Papi would sit by her side, but he didn't say anything either.

For three fives you got a big five, a five made of cardboard, a piece of cardboard on which our teacher drew a red five with a magical red pen, and I took it into my head that in order to restore order in the universe, I, or we, would make (or I'd have made) a one out of cardboard for the fives that had gone down the drain. I told Aunt Klotild I lost it. She mixed together a nice red color. When she finished, she stroked my head and softly said the title of the Móra short story:

"Pétör the Cheat."

I was going to take the one to school the next day. Considering the historical circumstances, my timing was definitely off, and the red one-as-five never made it to school. Had it done so, it would have been a one once again, though still red, to be sure.

## 172.

Early in the morning we were startled awake by a loud banging at the door.

In wintertime Papi gets out of bed at six and starts up the two iron stoves (coke and compressed slack). Half asleep, we catch a glimpse as he crosses the room without his coat, his shirt collar turned up as if it were a light spring day, a heavy fur cap pulled over his head, ember flickering on the tip of the cigarette between his lips. (We had fur caps too. My brother's was brown, soft and fuzzy, and he liked wearing it. Mine you couldn't stroke like that. Besides, it made my scalp itch. I didn't like it at all.)

"Go back to sleep, puppies," Papi growls if he sees us moving.

He never does it ahead of time, he never prepares the kindling the night before, he only chops it up in the morning. Quite an art. He holds the axe by the base with one hand, carving with it as if it were a jackknife, as if he were drawing an aquarelle with a rough brush dipped in whitewash. After a couple of strikes the log won't stand up on its own anymore, and then one's clever, handy, and all-knowing daddy steadies the log with his left hand, hop!, releases it, and in that bit of eternity he cleaves it in two with a small, firm and precise flick of the wrist. Later there isn't even that little eternity, and either the index finger of the left hand steadies the log, at which juncture you can come down on it from a shorter distance, or the left hand grips it at the bottom, at which point the arm is free, but you have to watch so the axe won't run past you.

Mami gets out of bed at six-thirty (in summer at six), and we get up at seven, when everything is ready, warm, and the breakfast on the table. When I'm going to be a father, I'm going to cut kindling wood too when everybody's still asleep and the house is gently breathing, and I'm going to make it warm. They won't know how it happened, but the warmth, it'll suddenly be *there.* (A couple of years later they put ready-made Tüker-brand kindling on the market, then they brought the gas into the house. Now when morning comes, the warmth is something that's there of its own accord.)

As if someone had gone at our door with an axe.

"Open up! Open up!"

As if huge, vicious angels were trying to turn us into Tüker-brand kindling. Papi stumbles along in his pajamas, his hair standing up all over the place, it's always like this in the morning, but we only see it on Sunday. Today is Monday. (*Ein Struwelpeter,* we said later, no, no, he said, a bit later than that.) It stands up on two sides as if he had wings, but the real mess is in the back, a haystack, pillow-tousled, and up front—and this is truly incredible—it hangs down over his forehead as if it were combed that way, an idiot child's, or the Roman emperor's. He sees us watching and stops.

"Open up, or we break down the door!"

"Don't be afraid, puppies!"

774

"We are not afraid, sir!" we shout in unison, because we see nothing but him now, our funny, silly, sleepy Roman emperor in his sliding pajamas, just him, nothing else, so what reason would we have to be afraid? We look defiantly at him. Reassuringly. If we're not afraid, he mustn't be afraid either! Then, in the midst of the threatening noise, he comes over to us (there's not another person in the world, Mami included, who would have dared to do this, or could have, who could have made time like this for us; any person with a sound mind would have turned to the door); he touches us, me on the cheek, my brother on the head, then he gives a short laugh, which takes us by surprise.

"Oh, so you're not afraid? I wouldn't go that far."

You'd think it was from a film the way the soldiers come pouring in. They must've received special training in occupying a dangerous and hostile children's room, rushing all over the place, flattening themselves against the wall, covering the front guard. My brother and I are impressed. We watch their maneuvers with mouths agape, and when they finish their business and have clearly occupied our home without shedding blood or taking victims—and in a matter of seconds at that!—bringing the enemy to his knees, the two of us break into applause, and our mother comes over to us, pulling her robe together against the cold as if she'd grabbed herself by the scruff, and reprimands us:

"Stop it this instant!"

Papi is by the door. We've never seen him like this, his face pale, careworn, the lines falling off it as if it weren't there, as if he were just renting it. Out on the porch in Hort, in the night, his imperial face must have been like this, but this face now is even darker, it has darker shadows. Still, after they've all trooped in and he sticks his head out the door to take a peek outside, he seems almost lighthearted. Or if it's fear, it's fear from a comedy.

Following in the wake of the soldiers as if he'd been left behind or is tardy, an awkward civilian walks in, a blond man wearing glasses. He is young and he looks like a teacher, except he's nicer and more amicable. Still from the comedy, he pats Father on the shoulder who, for his part, is still peering out, watching.

"The house is surrounded," he announces, as if Papi were checking, or looking for an escape route. Our father straightens up and nods.

"Good show." Good show. He says it again and again. The clincher to a joke?

"Be careful, Mati dear," Mami whispers, but only we hear, Papi does not hear this declaration of love (and never, neither before nor after, would we ever hear a declaration of love from either of them again).

After his initial surprise the young man looks at Father with pity and says softly, off the record:

"Don't be afraid, sir. There's no need to be afraid. The Russian comrades are searching all the houses in the village, looking for counterrevolutionaries."

"Good show," Father nods again.

"*Shto? Shto?*" one of the Russians says, pricking up his ears. He's the boss, though they all look alike and they're all young. But still, you can tell. Until he spoke, we looked only at their uniforms and guns, not their faces. Taken aback, my brother whispers to Mami:

"Mami, they're Chinese."

"*Shto? Shto?*" the boss asks turning to us.

Mother shakes her head for all she's worth, you'd think she'll never stop, nothing, nothing, no one said anything, no one's thinking anything, we're not here, we're nowhere, you go on working, doing what you're doing, looking around, we'll close our eyes.

We have to get out of bed. We're standing by our mother's and father's side, as if we were on the gym line in school. My brother is not afraid, but I tell him not to be afraid anyway, because they don't execute people inside houses.

"*Shto? Shto?*"

I know by now what he's saying and I answer him. I tell him that I said to my little brother, because he's my little brother, not to be afraid, because there's no such thing as an in-house execution, then I look at the man wearing glasses to translate, and to my surprise, he does. The boss laughs, then says something. But this time he is not laughing.

"Are there hidden arms in the house?" my translator translates.

"No," Father says promptly.

"Yes," my brother says promptly.

For some reason, this needs no translation. Everyone understands. Without having to be told, the soldiers aim their guns at us. Is it possible that my information is wrong, and there is such a thing as an in-house execution? Can an execution squad be set up anywhere? The Chinese are clearly in awe of my brother. My father, however, has stopped being afraid. He is raging, the jawbones are at work.

"*Idy suda,*" the commander says gravely.

The *idy suda* makes Mother shiver, and she throws her arms around us. Now it's our turn to be afraid.

"Don't be afraid, ma'am, it's just a routine check. It's all right," the interpreter says. He's lying. He's scared, too, which is nice of him.

"*Idy suda,*" the Chinese says again.

"No! Never! He's staying with me!" our mother screams into my ear, as she draws us closer to her bosom.

"You might at least lower those guns," Papi comments softly, which makes everyone nervous. He tells us the same thing. We can play with a gun if we feel we must, but we mustn't aim it at each other.

"One human being does not aim a gun at another human being." He made it sound like a point of etiquette. In the evening we brush our teeth, during the day, we do not aim guns at people.

"But what if the Ishmaelites and/or the Malachites should attack the homeland?" our sister once inquired of our father.

"That's another story," our father said ungraciously.

My brother likes the limelight. He frees himself from Mother's heroic embrace and makes for the dresser. Our sister, the eternal rebel, is shouting after him for all she's worth. The commander waves an arm. One of the Chinese—a strange sight—goes after my tottering little brother, who stops by the dresser. He is on tiptoes.

"In there."

"Who is in there?" the man in the glasses asks nervously.

"Shut up!" the Chinese roars. Clearly, he's got a gift for languages. My brother turns around. He is terrified, poor thing, you can tell by the look in his eyes. He leans down. The soldier moves in unison with him. And he pulls out my popgun. The rat. The soldier slaps him, though it's not quite a slap, more like a flick of the wrist, a breeze brushing past. At which the boss reprimands him severely. Screams at him. The interpreter heaves a sigh of relief, then turns to my father.

"The Russian comrades have a great respect for children."

"Good show," Father nods. As for my brother, I'm glad to see that he's going to get what's coming to him, I just have to wait it out.

"*Shto? Shto?*"

"*Dietyi! Dietyi!*"

"*Da, da.*"

The Russians tramp all over the house and the garden (and later the whole country). Just to be on the safe side, one of the Chinese is left in the kitchen. Our mother is feeding us. Our father is not eating. He's standing by the wall like a schoolboy, clasping the polka-dotted coffee cup in his hand, the jawbones at work. Mami offers the soldier a slice of bread and butter.

"Voulay vous a slice of hleb?"

A sweet gesture, a coarse-grained resentful voice. Like one who'd been pinched, our father wheels around.

"You're feeding him? You're feeding this man?!"

The Chinese catches on. These guys take to the language like a duck to water.

"He's hungry," our mother says in the same dim, dejected tone of voice.

We hear a round of gunfire outside. Our hungry Chinese promptly aims his gun at us, all the while casting a look of surprise at the slice of bread in Mother's hand. Then he gestures with his gun for us to go stand by the beds again. (He's not Chinese, he's Asian, our mother corrected us, but we checked the map, and China is Asia. Shaking her head, Mother had no choice but to accept it. Needless to say, our sister, the little know-it-all, objected that China is Asia, but Asia is not China. Ridiculous. It's not ridiculous. Every Chinese is Asian, but not every Asian is Chinese. We didn't follow. Everybody that's in the room now is a human being, see?, but not all human beings are in the room. For instance, Aunt Klotild, because she's upstairs. Get it? Yes, we lied.)

We're standing by the beds.

I take my little brother's hand and make a solemn promise never to forgive him, ever, for this warm, well-padded little hand, which he held out to me to hold. The interpreter comes running in. He says something to the soldier. The soldier, a nice young man *otherwise,* roars with laughter, then he explains that we have nothing to worry about, they just shot the goat by mistake.

"Good show," our father says with a nod of appreciation.

I can feel my brother's hand slip from mine.

"George?!"

His voice, which is calling them to account, trails off. Father nods and grins. Mother strokes my brother's head. He's got a nice, round head, very strokable, but he pulls himself away and with his head down, in imitation of George, he barges at the man in the glasses to butt him. The soldier does not move. He watches and laughs.

Papi hadn't been working for days. He rode his bike over to Pomáz, then without accomplishing what he'd gone for, he turned around. ("The dictatorship of the proletariat is on hold, Count!") But I had to go to school, and so I went.

The soldiers stop me by the garden gate. They're Hungarian. They want to see my school bag. I show them my school bag. I try not to be impertinent. These days it doesn't take much to get a slap by mistake. Or like poor and very smelly George, a round of bullets. Still, I show them my books and notebooks from a high horse.

"What's this?" The soldier asking the question is even taller than Papi, which is quite an accomplishment. Then, very like a cautious customs officer, he takes my cardboard one, my red five turned one, the Klotild version, in his hand. I turn red, as if that piece of cardboard would give everything away. The soldier looks distrustfully down at me. I launch into an explanation. This here is a five, a big five, because three small fives, that's one big five, and since my three small five's are worth . . .

"Take it easy, kid. I won't hurt your five. I got a kid your age at home. *Voilà* . . . ," and smiling like a magician, he raises the cardboard up in the air, he wants to make good what he'd done against his stupid son, and lo and behold, see?, it's not a five at all, but a one, a splinter, a stake, a tree trunk (but you know that!), and he will now, because in certain situations a soldier can do what a father can't, in short, he's going to tear it up and make it disappear, *voilà*.

I let out a yell, Oh!, I think of all the meticulous attention to detail that cheating requires, the determination, the concentration, the ingenuity, the orchestration, the color, the curves cut with the manicure scissors . . . Too late.

The soldier and Papi get bored with it; they get bored with me. Still, he has me pull off my shoes to see what I'm taking with me. All we find is my feet. He gestures for me to scram. As I go, I hear him whisper:

"Little prick."

This scares me, and I break into a run, though I look back to see if they're catching up, if these two words are catching up with me. I run as if I were running away from a bullet that's been fired. Which means either that I'm dreaming, or one more second, and I'm about to die.

The latter of the two eventualities transpired.


# 173.


My father isn't prone to headaches. Nothing ever pains him, not even those incredibly thick, curvaceous varicose veins on his legs which we were allowed to touch only on special occasions, though sometimes our fingers would run down them just like that, for no reason. Or else we played river.

"Duna, Tisza, Thames and Gulley, let's give Dad a run for his money!"

"Duna, Tisza, Thames and Gulley, Dad can't give you a run for your money," the head of the family responded, getting at the heart of the problem.

Or else we played train, and where the varicose vein disappeared, that was the tunnel. Our father's legs were multipurpose paternal legs.

I inherited my propensity for headache from my mother, mine

being better than hers to the extent that mine never lasts longer than a day. It goes away with sleep, and I almost never wake up with a headache. Hers would sometimes last for a week, but only once in a great while would she allow herself the luxury of lying down. At such times she'd lie in bed behind closed drapes. The light hurt her eyes (which we didn't realize for a long time because for years we lived in apartments where the sun never shone in the window). Also, she didn't sleep because she couldn't, the ache hurt too much. Besides, we wouldn't leave her in peace, how's this, how's that, we asked timidly but constantly, where does this go, what should we do with that? She continued in charge of the household, even in the dark.

But mine was also worse than hers because as I've mentioned already, mine came with vomiting, and wherever and whenever we talked about this, there was always someone, Mami, Bogyica, Irmike, anyone, who'd say significantly: migraine. Always. There was even praise in this, so young, *practically* a child, and he's already suffering from migraine. (*"So jung und schön ein Zichy."*)

On this particular day we were told in school that we'd go back to the old system—the ones would be fives, the twos fours, the threes threes . . .

"So the threes stay?"

Her face ashen, our teacher went on with the list, the fours are twos, the fives ones.

"I am not going to write this on the board," she said. Her name was Mária Katona.

It's really simple. All we have to know is that a one is a one. I repeat. A one is a one, a two is a two, and so on and so forth. And there we were, thinking that this was only natural.

## 174

When it was headache time, I scurried home, because I preferred throwing up at home. Luckily, the vomiting always started when I reached home. But not this time.

The church bell had just tolled noon and the main square was full of people. Men. I'm standing behind wide, black shoulders as if I were in the back row, as if it's the only place I could still get tickets for. I can't see what's happening onstage. There's an unaccustomed, heavy silence, as if no one were breathing. The men are attending to something onstage; they're not clapping, they're not whistling, and they're not excited, they're just watching. I'm trying to make my way among the coats, but can't. That's when I learned that black is not a uniform color. Sometimes it is dark blue.

"Get on home, son."

It's too late, I won't make it home in time to throw up. I stagger into the small Post Office yard, lean against the wall. I see the saltpeter stains from up close. I'm gripped by a terrible bout of vomiting, everything comes out, I'm throwing myself up out of myself, my saliva dripping. I even press my backside together, it'd like to come from there, too, it'd like to come from everywhere. It's coming through my nose, a piece of carrot is hanging from my nose.

It stinks. I stink.

When I return to the square, the crowd is just breaking up. Made to disperse.

"Okay, everybody, disperse!"

What I see, what I see there, in the middle, boggles the mind. Besides learning about the black, that's where I learned what it means to turn to stone. As if Grandfather were looking at me, I look and I turn to stone. I see them scrape my father up off the ground, jerk him up, tugging, then shove him inside a police car and fling his coat after him, as if it were yet another arrested individual. The police car circles round once. It heads toward me. I'm scared. In the middle of the square a policeman picks a pair of glasses up off the ground. I can clearly see as the policeman beckons, the car stops right in front of me, there's my father sitting behind the pane, staring rigidly ahead, his face his Sunday morning face, when we're playing, it is without glasses, naked, slightly unfamiliar, slightly younger-looking. I'm standing. I'm very frightened, I'm afraid to move. Papi, dear, I'm sorry I couldn't save you this time, but I promise to save you in the future, always. I will get you out of everywhere. I will sneak behind the driver in my light moccasins and quickly, without a sound, cut his throat as I disable his partner with one blow. Excuse me, sir, for being late, but I was held up, I say to you. You nod, put your glasses back on. Thank you, son, nice work. Then we mount our waiting horses and head for the woods of Grand Arrogance. Wipe your slippery hands in my horse's mane, son.

They roll down the window from inside. The policeman flings the glasses through the window. They laugh. Tires squeaking, the car speeds off toward the service road to Pomáz.

## 175.

I played good sibling the whole afternoon. Be good to one another, children, our parents kept reminding us, because what will this world come to otherwise. In order to please them, from time to time we did as we were told and we were good to one another. We would take turns being good, not that any of us clamored for the privilege. Being good is hard work. It takes tact and you have to pay attention, besides of which it's deadly dull, besides of which it clearly doesn't lead anywhere, except maybe the improvement in the state of the universe. It clearly wasn't worth the effort. Why are they making such a big deal out of it, we wondered, and why are they so pleased afterward, exchanging looks, smiling from ear to ear, ugggh!

Clearly, they were not just after a bit of peace and quiet. (They must have known that with this many children it's *theoretically* impossible anyway.) If it's peace they wanted, or more concretely, quiet, they had us play *silent lions*. We saw through their scheming machinations, but we didn't mind, because it was such a good game. When we were lions we could prowl around the apartment ominous and threatening, even wild, meaning on all fours, but quietly, without a sound, because the Creator, or so we were slyly told, took away from us (as lions) the ability to growl. We would have liked to know if there really *are* silent lions, or if we're the only ones.

"Oh, of course, naturally," our father mumbled. But we saw that he didn't have a clue.

"Because if there's no such thing for real in nature, Father dear, then we're not for real either, in which case, and in consequence, there's no such game either! A human being can't be the product of his own imagination!" Thus our sister, with a martial gleam in her eye. But Papi put an end to the dispute in his customary fashion—with an all-knowing smile indicating that once, once in the future, we would have to find the answer through our own resources. (We loved this our own resources; my, my, what a great big resource you've got!, et cetera.) What we say may be true, or it may not be true, or both, or neither, in which case, it's a third.

We were of two minds about this smile. We didn't like it because we wanted answers. Simple answers to simple questions. Who is a good person? Who is a bad person? When and where could we have a proper talk with God, but this time, for real. We didn't want much, just straight answers, and not this smile. The cat that swallowed the canary. But we also liked it because we could see interest and attentiveness on our father's face, as if he were hoping to learn something from us, poor dear.

Sometimes they'd make allowances. The 10 percent silence, for instance—the 10 percent silence, or the Tithe, as our mother called it (the reference went right over our heads)—which allowed for a soft growl. When it came to growling, Papi was the best. The menace issued from the depths of his throat in a gurgle of waves, and in such a subdued pianissimo that it could have passed for just 5 percent, but so terrifying, that we ran to Mami for shelter who, in the worst-case scenario, impassively called out to our father not to scare the children, but if we were lucky, she banged us on the head with her front haunches, letting out her red killer claws—which caught nature by surprise, let me tell you! Then she ruthlessly pushed us away while she growled, the wings of her nose trembling, her lips pulled back, and the terrifying teeth of the lioness were bared. We were terrified.

It was so good, this terror!

"Papi, Papi, help! Leo the lion's in the kitchen!" we screamed, running back to him for safety and embracing him around the leg as if it were a tree trunk suited for hiding. But oh! It's not a tree, but the majestic and hungry leg of the lion king! And back we scurried to the kitchen for our very lives.

"Oh, oh, Mami, dearest, et cetera, et cetera!"

There was no knowing whether we'd been caught helpless between two lines of fire, or whether our mother would wheel around this time (she spent a lot of time standing by the stove, just like Aunt Rozi) and lovingly, like someone playing at being a happy mother—and one eventuality was better than the other— calm us theatrically, oh, my dears, do calm down, there's no lion here, you know perfectly well lions are native to Africa; but then as she embraces us she growls menacingly, and we want to run, but she won't let us, changes gears and is all sweetness and light again, and she says, all the while searching our faces, what we're used to hearing from our father:

"What's up, puppies? Is the world too much for you?"

## 176.

Our father rarely played with us. It was difficult to get him into a playing situation. We took it in stride. But when we managed to talk him into it after all, we were doubly delighted. How I loved it when he threw me up in the air, then caught me! Even when we were "great big louts" we'd ask him to do it. Our favorite was the *Mistike's papa* production. (Who was this Mistike, I wonder? Or mistake? But that's unlikely.) It involved the following: we climbed on top of the furniture, the table, too (though maybe not in our shoes), bowed to the audience (quantity was not the issue), then waved to our sideman, who made the official announcement.

"And now, Ladies and Gentlemen,"—he cleared his throat so that all present (quantity was not the issue), should realize the gravity and the danger inherent in the moment—"Mistike's papa!," and when we heard papa, we leaped up into the sky air, from where the sideman, our father, would pluck us out. Mami didn't like it.

We didn't like the nighttime lion game. If Papi came home late and was drunk, then sometimes, depending on how much he'd had to drink, he was in the mood for games. He didn't care, he got us out of bed.

"Puppies and patriots, get up! Your country calls!"

It was no use begging, he would not relent. Crying just made things worse. It's best not to do anything, and I mean anything at such times, only and exclusively what he wants. The start is not bad—except, we're sleepy—the way he leaps from bed to bed, crying *hic sunt leonès,* and he sniffs and pants, fooling around, and that's good because it's amusing, and everything would be great if only we weren't so frightened, but we're frightened, even though he's playing with us at last.

"A forint for everyone who promises to die for his country!" He takes it right back. "No. A weak generation. Not a penny, not one. It's gotta come from the heart!"

By this point we have to stand at attention, either in the middle of the room, shivering with cold, the worst-case scenario, or if we are lucky, on the bed. My brother could sleep standing up, he could serve his country even as he stood. Still, because of the soft mattress, we were unsteady on our feet.

"A true Magyar does not wobble while taking an oath!"

Once I asked him what a true Magyar was. I took the wobbling as my point of reference, and since I wobbled because of the mattress and my father wobbled because of drink, I couldn't get very far in my head. My father looked at me as if I'd killed somebody, or worse. He took a step toward me.

"Oh, Papi, sir, please don't!"

A mistake. He took another step. At which I shut my eyes.

"Please get better, Papi dear," I said to myself, "and that stupid country, too!," and I yelled, "A true Magyar does not wobble while taking an oath!"

You can cry with your eyes closed. I could hear him stop, as if I'd said a magic spell.

"That's the spirit, son. Go on, take the oath! I had no idea I had two such admirable sons. This is not how you started out, Petár, dear."

*This* Petár I hated, he used it only when he was drunk. Later I could tell what he'd had to drink, what it took for him to say it, to make him go as far as this Petár. After swearing allegiance to the country, we sang the Anthem or (depending on what he'd had to drink) the "Rákóczi March." (For a long time, at soccer games, after the national Anthem and the inevitable "rah-rah Magyars!," I'd say to myself, solemnly, ceremoniously, and very deep down, a true Magyar does not wobble while taking an oath!) Father accompanied the "Rákóczi March" by imitating an entire band. We liked this even more than the "hay is for horses" song, especially the part about cannon thunder, sword rattle, it's what makes a Magyar march off to battle!

Fired by patriotic fervor, we were shouting enthusiastically by then. Not so our father, who was overcome by patriotic gloom.

"It's what makes a Magyar march off to battle!" he stammered with infinite gloom. In an instant he forgot us, though he called back to me, "Just make sure, Petár, dear, just make sure they don't arrest you in your own home!," then he sat down at the table and softly, overcome by emotion, he began to sing Irish patriotic songs. He'd learned them from Grandfather, who'd picked them up at Oxford while he was a student there. Back then, they were considered entertaining, impudent, revolutionary.

He sang either the Roddy McCorley or the Kevin Barry. The latter was the louder of the two.

> *Just a lad of eighteen summers*
> *Sure there's no one can deny*
> *As he marched to death that morning*
> *How he held his head on high.*

There came a knock at the door. It was Uncle Varga.

"Oh, Doctor, for God's sake, it's three in the morning. You'll have the whole house woke with the wailing."

"It's all right, Dani, I'm only teaching the boys how to die for their country."

"They can do that tomorrow, can't they? They can die for their country in the daytime."

"But it's urgent, Dani, very urgent. Time is pressing," and with that he throws his arms across and embraces himself, closer, closer. It's scary.

"I know, Doctor. But they're only children. Babies. You go to bed now like a decent man."

"Bed?!" Our father sniffles, we're at attention, ready to die for our country, if only we could get Uncle Varga out of here so he wouldn't see us like this, so he couldn't feel sorry for us the next day, and Aunt Klotild shouldn't stroke us with that suffering face of hers. She even gives us a praline from her secret chocolate reserves.

"My poor dears!" and *voilà,* out comes a chocolate-covered almond. If we could get to the almond without Papi's late-night horror scenes, if we could only do it, this would be a beautiful world indeed.

"What am I to do in bed, Dani? When her little face is there day and night, her curly black hair and lovely blue eyes. Oh, Dani, what will I do? Was it the hunger that killed her, Dani?"

"Of course not. Lilike was nursing her and a baby that's nursed is not hungry. God took her. He has his reasons."

"One more song, old friend, before I go to bed."

"Good night, Doctor."

"My little chickadees! Monkey tails! Christians! To arms! Time for a song." We started in on the song, from the lungs.

*Yung Rodimekkorlie goes todie*
*Onzebridge ov Toome todahj.*

"You'll die for the country, won't you, boys?"

"Yes, Papi, dear, we'll die." We're on the verge of tears, the corners of our lips hanging down, though we'll gladly die for the country, but still, it's us doing the dying. On the other hand, by now our father is in high spirits again.

"Fine. And we'll all meet your little sister in heaven, won't we, boys?"

"No. Yes. Oh. We will."

My brother is leaning against the table leg, sleeping on his feet. My father lifts him, staggers across the room—he wobbles: a true Magyar, it seems, stops wobbling only when he's taking an oath— and puts him on the bed next to Mami. I climb in too, and Papi, still in his clothes, lies beside me. I'm hoping he'll put his arm around me, because sometimes he throws his arms around me, but he goes on singing the Rodimekkorlie and talking to our little sister, the other twin who is not.

"Oh, my little curly-haired, blue-eyed love, I will dress you in silks, I will clad you in purple, I will cover you in velvet, and we will go to the Savoy together."

He falls silent, but he's not sleeping, I can hear that he's not sleeping. When I finally fall asleep, dawn is on the horizon.

177.

But things get even worse when our mother tries to come between us.

"Will you kindly leave those poor innocent children out of it!"

She's sitting at the kitchen table, shaking, her hair hanging damp, her face wet.

"Can't you leave them alone. Go to bed. Why must you make fools of these innocent children." It's the only time we're innocent, at other times, never. She comes over to us. "Go back to bed," she tells us.

We stay put, we know everything, what I mean is not everything, that's why we're scared; we don't know a thing, but we make a move as if we're about to move so Mother won't think we're on Daddy's side. At night we're not on anybody's side, partly because they're like strangers (as if they were playing a role—well), partly because we'd draw the short end of the stick and the other would take revenge, our father instantly, erratically, going for the jugular, while our mother would wait till the following day to get back at us for our betrayal in a much more refined manner. One is worse than the other, and the other is worse, too.

This give-and-take caused a rift between us all the same. Some of us tended to one side—our sister toward our father, my brother toward our mother. The lines of affiliation were not strictly drawn, they were soft, pliable, easily crossed. Nevertheless, each of us had our favorites. Sometimes I favored one side, sometimes the other. There's no comparing loves. Nor was my situation made less equivocal when I cleverly tried it the other way around and asked not who it is I love more, but who I miss more.

I miss everybody.

"I want them up," our father says. "I want them standing where they are. I want them ready for the day Hungary will be free. Don't interfere. Go to sleep, you saint. It's these children that'll carry the flame! Or am I mistaken?" We are not always ready for our cue. "Or am I mistaken?"

"Yes. No. We'll carry it."

"Go to bed. Your father's gone pure stone berserk."

We don't move, just enough to look as if. Papi starts putting on his clothes.

"Don't you dare leave the house!" our mother threatens, jumping to her feet. "Don't you try walking out, or you'll regret the day!"

"Poor, poor day," Papi says with a grin, and wraps his scarf round his neck. He glances at us. He turns grave. "And my poor country."

And yet we're standing more or less at attention, hardly wobbling at all.

## 178

"Sing. Sing. Sing!"

"No."

"Sing, or you'll regret the day."

"Don't do this, Matika."

"Don't Matika me, damn you . . ."

"Jesus Christ."

"Don't jesuschrist me, and don't cry. Just sing. Did you hear?! I'm not about to say it again. Don't cry. I'll help you. I'm going to look for beaver. Now say it. Say it after me. I'm going to look for beaver . . . say it, damn you . . ."

"I'm going to look for beaver."

"That's the spirit, sweetheart."

"Don't sweetheart me."

"Why shouldn't I sweetheart you, sweetheart?"

"Sweetheart your . . . whores."

"Fine. Sweetheart. The next line."

"I can't."

"Sure you can. You can do it, you saint."

"Matika, please. Stop it."

"And hump her till her cunt's in fever!"

"No."

"And hump her till her cunt's in fever!"

"Disgusting."

"Well?!"

"And hump her till her cunt's in fever!"

"That a girl, sweetheart. And now, the two lines together!"

"I'm going to look for beaver, and hump her . . . till her . . . cut's . . ."

"Cunt! Say it properly. And loud!"

"Cunt."

"Is that what you call cunt? That's not cunt, that's shit. Cunt!"

"Cunt."

"Fuck it, that's not a cunt, that's a whimper . . . It's no use talking to you . . . You think it's disgusting . . . All right, let's try the other. I'm going to look for duck."

"I can't take this anymore."

"Sure you can, sure you can, sing it, damn you, or I'll bang you and your brood to kingdom come! Sing, you saint, sing, or you'll regret it."

"I'm going to hunt for duck till I get my flying fuck."

"Good. That was real good singing. See? You can do it if you try. Once more, without the song."

"I'm going to hunt for duck till I get my flying fuck."

"That was beautiful. You're improving, sweetheart. Getting better by the minute . . . Don't cry . . . It's all right . . . Sing it here, into my ear, nice and soft. Or my neck . . . I'm going to hunt for . . . It makes no difference, now, does it? Beaver or duck . . ."

In teachers college Mami majored in singing. She sang like an angel. With feeling.

## 179.

Good siblingship was a much more subtle idea that we'd given it credit for. Being a good brother (or sister) involves not just—or not primarily—some sort of general goodness, a humanitarian gesture, a show of restraint, good will and meekness with a pinch of unctuousness thrown in for good measure. Being a good brother or sister means you have to love. A good brother or sister is a good brother or sister. You can't be a good brother or sister on your own, you're dependent on each other, and it's no use staggering your resources and making the other do it, it sticks. A lousy underhanded trick, if ever there was one.

I practiced good siblingship the entire afternoon of November 5. It's easier after a good vomit. Also, I was scared. (God, I was scared so much in those days!) I was scared of what I saw, and also of what I didn't. What I saw I pretended was just a dream though I knew it wasn't. I could clearly remember the piece of carrot, the glasses with their splayed sides, my father's frozen expression, the horses, the hill of Nagy-Kevély in the background, but because no one knew about these things beside me, not even Papi (!), I pretended it was just a dream.

I kept mum about my dream. But Mother too must have had a dream of her own, because as if I weren't even there she kept pacing back and forth, chain-smoking. The pacing back and forth we didn't like, but the smoking we liked. After a while she couldn't stay inside anymore and went out to the garden, where she continued pacing.

Uncle Varga was a decent sort, except he didn't like Aunt Klotild chatting (too much) with Mami, said it might lead to complications. But he went to the nail smith's a lot, and then Aunt Klotild would come talk with Mami, and also to help out. We looked down on her because she was missing her teeth. We thought she was a witch bereft of her powers. We laughed at her. I think she knew. When we were making my revolutionary red one, she kept giving me a pained look of reproach. Needless to say, I wasn't laughing then because I wanted something from her. Uncle Varga is her second husband. Her first husband died at the River Don.

She joined Mother in the garden, and they strolled arm in arm, like two friends.

"You mustn't fret, dear. You're better off waiting. I'm not saying it helps, but what else is there? When someone leaves or they're taken away you must wait for them and then either they'll come back, or they're brought back, either with their shield, or on it, you know, like the Gracchus legionnaires. You must wait as forcefully as the force used to take away the person you're waiting for." Suddenly they switched to the familiar form of address. "Wait with humility, Lili, dear, wait with passion and vigilance. Relentlessly. The person that's disappeared may talk. But you must wait tight-lipped, weighing every word, the spoken and the unspoken, listening backward and forward in time, discovering the pathways leading into the thicket, looking for the secret road signs that the other might have missed as he cut a path through the jungle of his fate. You must never wait contemptuously or half-heartedly, like someone invited to a heavenly banquet who then picks at his food with the tip of the fork. Wait elegantly, with generosity of heart. Wait as if you were waiting for your last moment on death row, the one the turnkey has granted you. Wait for all you're worth, because waiting is the greatest gift we humans have. Just think, Lili dear! Only man knows how to wait."

"And dogs," Mother added offhandedly.

She's saying this (Aunt Klotild said) because she knows all about waiting. She's had her share of waiting. As Béla's wife she'd grown accustomed to the bitterness and painful pleasure of waiting. Who is Béla? Aunt Klotild shook her head as if to say, think. Mother slapped a hand on her forehead, oh, I'm sorry, and now she understands everything.

She understood nothing. She waited in her own terrifying manner, which we subsequently came to know intimately, in all its guises. (There's frightened waiting and there's humiliated waiting. In the former version, whoever is waiting is afraid, afraid for the other or afraid for himself or—rarely—for some other reason. In the latter version, whoever is waiting is humiliated through the act of waiting. Aunt Klotild was talking about the first, my mother was practicing the second.)

By late afternoon Mami had calmed down. She was so quiet,

796

you'd think she'd joined the good brother (or sister) movement. On the other hand, good siblingship, it's not something you can do indefinitely, like staying under water. You can handle your own somehow. But seeing the humanitarian exertion on the rosy cheeks of your poor unfortunate adversary, radiating from goodness, when all you should be doing is playing with the building blocks—well, at such times you feel an overpowering urge to surreptitiously pull the bottom-most block from under the tower just as the other is about to crown the top with the last, winning triangle. Needless to say, being all too familiar with the ways of the world, the other suspects that the lower-most blocks don't slip out of place of their own accord, that they've got to be *made* to slip out; and so, instantaneously with the horrendous crashing sound which makes our mother wince as if she'd been struck, she plucks a block out of the air and directs it toward the shinbone of the culprit, who gives a kick in consequence, et cetera, et cetera, as a result of which the tower collapses several times over, and now the sound of two, not one, wild and desperate cries, or screams are heard, like "someone being skinned alive."

At such times, one of us was bound to get slapped, concretely, my younger brother. If there was the slightest doubt, he got the slaps as sure as a juggler's box, both the rational, practical motherly as well as the rare but cardinal, symbolic, fatherly slaps. For one thing, he really was a so-called lively child, "mischievous," "a little rascal," for another, I was able to hold on to my good brother expression for just a split second longer.

"Little traitor," my mother said succinctly. But this did not change the compass reading of the slaps.

After a while whenever we heard the persecutorial question, "Who was that?" my sister and I would automatically say that it was my brother, who for his part—sometimes because it was the truth—would deny, refute, disaffirm and disavow everything, standing on the defensive, arguing his cause, thereby getting himself deeper and deeper into the mire. Pitiful to behold. I watched with a pained smile, poor guy, humiliating himself in this way, grabbing after straws instead of owning up to his truly abhorable deed like a man. Curious. My brother never took offense at this flood of injustice; on the contrary, he submitted to his fate with pride. Later, when this was brought up, he'd dismiss the memory with a shrug. That's what I call true brotherly love.

## 180.

Before any of us good brothers (or, if we include Mother, sisters) could have so much as touched that imaginary, yet omnipresent building block, Roberto came to visit us as he'd done in the past (to kick that proverbial building block from under us with his boot in earnest, making everything come tumbling down in deadly silence).

I knew instantly that he'd brought news of my father.

He barged in in his usual manner, without knocking, just like the authorities, or as if this were his home.

"Oh, Miklós!" my mother shouted, and threw her arms round his neck. He threw his arms around her, too, holding her and rocking her back and forth. Our mother always greeted him this way, except she wasn't always this terrified, and our father too was missing from the scene. He used to watch his friend with an indulgent grin, waiting, with a pretense at impatience, when is it going to be his turn for a hug?

Now there was just one hug.

Roberto greeted us with the usual courtesy, the young counts, the little countess, the majoresco, just as he always did. My brother grinned, I glowed, my sister kept mum.

When he leaned down to pat us, I could tell that he'd had too much to drink. I never said that my father was drunk, not even to myself—he's tipsy, he's high, he's soused, he's pissed, he's pickled. There were the expressions I was used to hearing. And also, that he's in a state. At first, our mother was ashamed of our father's drinking. Later this changed, and she began to be ashamed of herself, and later still the time came when nobody felt ashamed of himself in front of anyone or anything, and nothing remained but the enduring. Until not even that.

"Say that again!" Mother said indignantly out in the kitchen. They were always playing, but not this time. We could hear Roberto saying something in his deep, resonant voice. "Get out of my house!" Mother hissed between her teeth.

"You can't mean that, Lili, dear, you can't be serious," he laughed. "You really want to turn me out? Make a persona non grata of me?"

"Get out!"

Silence. We listen breathlessly. There seemed to have been a scuffle, then silence.

"You're overreacting, Your Excellency!"

"Are you threatening me? You have the nerve to threaten me?!"

"Absurd, my dear. That's absurd."

Roberto slammed the door shut behind him the way Father used to, though rarely.

Mami came back in slowly, dragging her feet, bent as if she were about to collapse. We hardly recognized her, her face was pale and red, all at the same time. She looked weak, but when she spoke, she sounded determined, her voice fortified with the power of anger. Her eyes sparkled, as if she were blaming us along with Roberto. (She'd given us one of those "oh, you men" looks.)

"Do you know who that man was?" We nodded gravely. "From this day forth, you do not know him!"

My brother didn't understand how we cannot know somebody we know, because we can only not know somebody we do not know. Of course, that's not what we were told. We were told that from that day on we were not to know somebody, i.e., to act *as if* we didn't know him, even though we did. As if. We spent all night practicing. One of us was Roberto and the other didn't know him. Then we switched. As we practiced, we also came to realize that whoever we don't know from this day forth we must also hate, and we mustn't talk to him.

But why should we hate Roberto?

Our sister, the little brat, either didn't understand anything, or she was on to everything from the start, because when we let her join in the game from pure generosity of heart and it was her turn and we didn't know her, she burst into tears.

Mami did, too, in the other room.

Before we went to sleep, we had to pray for Papi.

"Why? Did he die?" my brother asked bravely and logically, whereupon he got a Papi-style backhanded slap from Mother. My brother who, contrary to me, because I made the extent of my pain or injustice known immediately, never cried, now burst into tears. Mami hugged him. She didn't make an exception of him (she didn't make an exception of any of us, unless maybe a little bit of me, because I was her first); strangers would coddle him, too, they stroked his curly locks and soft, brown skin. My brother is beautiful, and people like that a lot. Not much, just a little, but I was jealous of him for a long time.

When we finished our prayers, I asked if we're going to pray for Roberto. Mother's eyes flashed, then she left us. Just to be on the safe side we threw in a Hail Mary for Roberto. Our mother believed in God. It's just that she couldn't understand why she should have to suffer so much.

"The original sin, my good woman, the original sin," we grinned as we came back from Bible class, "indeed, indeed, the expulsion from Paradise, and also, the sweat of your brow. You should have thought of it before, Mami dear, it's too late now."

My mother never saw Roberto again. I saw him the following day. It might have been better not to see him, but then I wouldn't have seen my father either.


181.


I was not afraid. I said to myself that I'd already used up the fear I should be feeling—because the predicament I was now in clearly called for a modicum of fear—previous day, in front of the post office. When I walked through the school gate to head for the third-grade soccer game (I did this every day; they let me join the team!), the two bullies who dragged my father off the day before walked up to me. It was so much like a film, I got on my high horse again. I thought I had one over them.

They said, Come with us, kid, get in, and I said, Don't call me kid, I have a proper name. Besides, this is not the best place, with everybody looking.

I turned away and headed for their car, a Pobeda, which was standing by the curb with its motor running. The third-graders didn't dare call after me, but I saw that they saw. They were looking, so they must have seen. The two policemen followed behind awkwardly. Clearly, they'd made a mistake, they were supposed to grab me "without making a scene," otherwise they would have gone straight to the principal. But they were waiting here instead, without making a scene, as everyone could see. Either, or.

I didn't know if I should get in up front or in the back, which made me afraid, after all.

I want to say good-bye to my mother.

They hollered with laughter.

"Well, well, the hero of the family!"

Their belly laugh made my fear disappear once again, though by then I just about had enough of this seesawing. What's going on? Am I afraid, or am I not afraid? I pressed my lips together, the way I'd seen my father do.

I sang the Kossuth song and Rodimekkorlie and Kevinberrie and also hay is for horses, straw is for cows in Father's key, a silent lion, of course. Those guys up front had no idea of the majestic beast threatening their puny little lives. I would have liked to sing the Anthem but I couldn't stand up. I'll have to consult Father about what to do in case of obstacles such as this. Under a hanging tree it's easy, because you have to stand at attention to begin with. But what about a sitting room, or a sitting bath, as even its name indicates?

I got on my knees and looked out the oval back window. The Oszoly cliff, it's like a face, a head, a somebody, and it was looking at me. Since I was on my knees, I decided to pray.

"Sit," they snapped at me, as if I were a dog.

### 182.

Never in my life was I as happy to see anyone as I was to see Roberto then. The car stopped in front of police headquarters in Szentendre, and they said I should stay put. I sang some more, and I trembled some more, too. It was either singing or crying, but since I couldn't cry, I was even more—no, not scared, but I felt the way I felt on the main square in Csobánka. I was rooted to the ground. My head didn't ache.

"Come with me, Your Excellency!" The door next to me is opened, Roberto bends forward to servile depths, I recognize his midnight blue head of hair. He's balding, if only slightly. This is the first time I notice it.

"Sweet Roberto!" I throw myself round his neck, forgetting Mother's warning; later, I'm thinking, later I'll make time for that, too, the not knowing him. But now I'm going to hug him and bury my head in his neck. Sweet Roberto.

He puts me down faster than I'd anticipated. Let's go.

"Are we fleeing?" I say, tiptoeing after him.

"In a sense," he says without looking back.

"Should we run?"

He stops, looks back, no, let's not. It wouldn't help.

"I understand," I say, because I don't understand anything. Nor do I want to, a first for me. I'd left my schoolbag in the car. Roberto waves it off, which I could take as a sign that I'll never have to go to school again, but I'm not all that happy, due to the already mentioned *musterkind* considerations. A wonderchild.

I can't catch up. Roberto is always two steps ahead of me. We're trotting past rows of houses along narrow streets, first up-hill, then down, until we find ourselves by the Danube. It's big. We walk down to the water. If we were horses we could have a drink now, I think. The sun is shining, a cool wind is blowing, we're walking up and down like two old friends. Or two grownups. I try to take big strides. To keep in step. I'm waiting. He wants to tell me something. We're standing facing the Danube.

"Do you know what politics is?"

Sure. The Ruskies and the Commies. He curls his lip. There's no knowing whether he's smiling or smirking, and if he's smirk-ing, who at.

Well, this here is a question of politics. They've turned Papi into a question of politics. It makes no difference now who did what or didn't, he knows that my father's a careful fellow, he curls his lip, he couldn't have done much, obviously, obviously, he didn't do anything, but the question right now is who could have done what, it's the could have that counts, it's the could have that's dangerous, what *is* is not dangerous, what is is never danger-

803

ous insofar as, in theory, it can always be caught red-handed; what is is the least problematic, he might be sentenced to a year, or two, or a hundred, or none. The regulations, or laws, as they used to be called, spell out clearly what's to be done.

But this could have is another kettle of fish!

The could have can't be brought to trial, it slips out of the grip of regulations, proclamations and decrees, and though we may know everything about the person in question, all we know is this everything, meaning, only what *can* be known; they know who my father used to talk with and meet back in the village and outside the village, where he works, whom he sees in that makeshift wooden shack by the road, that shanty, the trailer, but no need going into details, there's no need for me to know everything, the world of grownups isn't quite like it may seem from a child's perspective; in short, that's *all* they know, the everything, but now Papi must be helped over from the could have to the is, and that's the crux of the problem, to turn the could have into the is; but we both know how stubborn my father is, he knows, and I know—I don't, my brother's the one who is stubborn, and also George, the goat, but now he's not stubborn either anymore, isn't that so?, but can grownups be stubborn, too?—in short, my father is stubborn, which is understandable, after all, he's a sovereign human being, he insists on what, according to his views, he must insist on, and he's not taking this amiss, how could he, besides, the point isn't to judge him but to help him, in which case it would be ridiculous to accuse him of the thing without which there'd be nothing to talk about in the first place, because he wouldn't be needing help.

Still, he's surprised at him because, after all, what is it that they want from that outstanding man, my father?

"Who?"

"Don't interrupt."

Just a signature, a gesture, a sign. Life is not black and white, and my father won't be any more honorable if he refuses. A person shouldn't pretend to be more immaculate than he is. Life is neither pure nor filthy, neither rotten nor majestic, it goes on, it flows, it wants to flow and to go on. Also, it's not inconceivable that he could get work to suit his qualifications, which no one would think of questioning, they're first-class qualifications! It's not martyrs and road menders with two college diplomas that the country needs, and every man who suffers is a danger to the public. He doesn't have to renounce anything and he doesn't have to lie, after all, you can't build a country with humiliated people. All he's got to do is sign, he signed too right away, and he's not ashamed to own up to it, just an innocent game, but it happened, and what's past is past, maybe I remember it, too, one remembers what one chooses to remember, one can remember anything at all!, namely, that once they celebrated Stalin's death, he and my father, and maybe even my mother . . .

"Leave her out of this!"

"Don't shout. I'm talking."

. . . They were playing who laughs last which, in honor of that day of mourning they'd revised a bit, because they didn't laugh at the end, but at Stalin, and they knocked only the red men off the board. In short, the game went against the reds. That's all there is to it, that's what he's got to sign. Besides, isn't that what it was like?, it was exactly like that!, and that's all they want, just a gesture that he's not against them, and though he keeps saying to him *Mensch, ärgere dich nicht,* my father refuses. He refuses to listen.

Well, if he refuses, so be it.

We resume our silent walk along the riverbank. I sneak a look at him from below. I can't detect any grownup impatience on his face, and yet he's not finished with me yet, I can tell. It's like my brother's when he's about to cry. My brother laughs a lot, but he can cry at will. My brother knows a lot of things.

"It's not that simple."

"What?"

"This 'so be it' of yours. If it turns into a political question, it's not that simple. These people, they won't take no for an answer."

"Who?"

"Politics . . . they want the signature." He laughs. Roberto usually laughs at himself. Now he's laughing for my benefit.

"And what do *you* want?"

"I want to help your father."

"Thank you." I remember the warning. But what can I do, I'm standing here, and I know him. I know this man.

"However, I cannot do it on my own, as you see. For some reason, he won't trust me implicitly. But he trusts you. You're his son. Blood of his blood. The majoresco."

We're standing on the shore. The Danube is strong, it is flowing. I look at this man as if he were my father. I'd never helped my father before. I could help with the kindling, possibly, but it's dangerous because of the axe. Besides, I'm still sleeping. When the stream overflowed its bed and the water had to be kept at bay with sandbags so it wouldn't sweep away the greenhouse, Uncle Varga's "work of a lifetime," that was another instance I could have helped, but they chased me away. Out on the melon field too we were underfoot. It's difficult to help a father, because it's difficult getting close enough to him. Once we went to early-morning mass together at Advent, in boots and fur hats with the snow crunching under our feet, like in a tale. Our breaths froze in midair. The shepherds on their way to the Infant in Bethlehem. And then the branch of a fir tree knocked off Papi's hat. Poor man, the way he grabbed for it, it was silly, as if he were slapping his forehead because he'd forgotten something. Oh, I just remembered, my fur hat!, like that. And I picked it up and he thanked me. That's helping, isn't it? Helping Mami is easy. It's even too much. The wide range of shopping (we're not allowed to buy the meat, she always buys it herself), weeding, collecting twigs, washing socks, doing the dishes, babysitting, picking lamb's lettuce on Galina Hill. Helping Mami is a cinch, it is inevitable, but there's nothing interesting about it.

"What must I do?"

"Sign for him."

"What?"

"What, what . . . A piece of paper."

"What piece of paper?"

Roberto impatiently smooths back his hair. I realize I'm asking the wrong question, it's out of place. Or who knows. He's flapping his hands like a bird its wings. Don't fly away, dear Roberto! Just something about that parlor game, but only what happened, it's of no consequence, just a gesture . . . You remember, he who laughs last. And he laughs. As for me, I ask what Father had asked years before, namely, is this then the end.

"No." The smile stays put on his face like a shadow. "It's just the beginning."

"Is that all? A signature?"

"That's all."

"No big deal."

"I don't want to give you the wrong impression." I look up at him, he straight out, at the water. "A signature is a big deal. A great big deal. That's your name there. Your name is there forever. Your name. The name of your family. This name has been on countless papers and documents throughout the centuries, deeds of foundation, peace treaties, appointments, sentences, sometimes determining the fate of whole nations . . . A signature does not lose its validity."

I listen to this with pride, especially the part about validity, and also that this will satisfy them. I don't ask who anymore, politics, obviously, the Commies and the Ruskies. But whoever it is, if they get what they want, they'll leave my father be.

But where exactly is my father?

That's neither here nor there. He's fine. Actually, he isn't.

"Is he with the police?"

"Yes."

But what does he, Roberto, have to do with the police?

He's got nothing to do with the police, he's got something to do with us, with my father, and those who are still in trouble, who are rowing in the same boat.

"Fine. How many signatures do you need?"

"That's the spirit, Your Excellency. Here, in the lap of the Carpathians, without humor you're as good as dead."


# 183.

Better to die a hero than to live your life as a moral nonentity, we know. Two and two makes four. But to perish like a sucker? Because of a misunderstanding? Unnecessarily? A country that needs heroes is unfortunate, and it's this misfortune we want to avoid. Roberto puts his arm around my shoulder. It feels nice. I have butterflies in my stomach.


# 184.

They'd given my father a terrible beating, they'd slapped him around like a child, they'd beaten him like a horse, and in their first rage kicked in his kidneys, then methodically kicked his whole body and especially the soles of his feet—which I learned only later.

We're standing in an office of sorts, or a glass cage, one wall is made of glass. Inside, beyond it, a man is lying on a bunker. I know it's him. I'm watching him from the glass case. The secretary is typing. She didn't look up when we came in and I said hello, but Roberto didn't. The glass reflects, and I can see the outside, meaning ourselves, and the inside, too, meaning him. I'm so close, my breath fogs up the glass pane.

"Go on already," Roberto roars at me gruffly from behind. I turn around. I hardly recognize him. I don't understand what he wants me to do. Crash through the glass? The woman looks up. Her face is hairy, downy, and in the strong sunlight these pieces of down cover her face like a fine, blond fur. Ugly. She indicates the small door by the corner with her head. It feels like I have to enter an animal cage. I enter. My present fear, too, is directed at the wild animal, that maybe he'll leap at me. I approach carefully. But just as at a certain point the magnet draws the iron to it, I suddenly find myself at the cot, kneeling by the side of the body. He seems to be asleep. It never enters my mind that he may have died.

Which is a lie. Every time we saw him sleep with his mouth half open, his jaws dropped, his cheeks hollow, death-like in his immobility, we were terrified, again and again. We saw him sleep only on Sunday. (Sometimes in the afternoon too, unexpectedly, but then we didn't really see him because we weren't allowed to go into the inner, or "grownup" room.) On Sunday he was the last to get up. Honor the day of the Lord! We could relate to that. It meant that for once Papi could sleep late. Late, but not too late, because we'd wake him up. The greatest favor was when we could get in next to him. This was even better than getting in next to Mami, though we liked that too.

"Papi, Papi, Papi dear," I try to wake him, as if it were Sunday. I'm afraid to touch him. He does not move. He does not even raise his head. Only now do I notice that his eyes are open. But he doesn't move his eyes either. His lips are cracked, and there's a bleeding cut. "Father! Father! Please!"

Roberto knocks on the glass—not so loud, not so eagerly, and besides, hurry up. I don't know what to do or say. He (my father) knows everything anyway. Which makes it difficult to pray, too, because he looks at me and he knows everything. But now he's not looking at me. He's not moving. No part of him is moving— his body, his face, his eyes.

"I signed that paper so you could get out of here."

I can't go on with what I have to say. I see him huddled, his hands pressed between his locked knees. I stroke his face. He gives a start. A shiver runs through his body. He turns toward me but does not look at me. He looks everywhere, above, to the side, and through me, everywhere, except at me.

He is trying to spit with all his might.

He is trying to spit at me.

What's this spitting? What are you spitting for? Please stop spitting. Spitting is easy. Which is not true. Spitting is not easy for him. The saliva, heavy with blood, does not want to leave his lips. It is sliding down his jaw.

I wipe it off. I wipe the blood and saliva off his face. I wipe the spit meant for me off his face. Please stop spitting, sir. You must leave this place, but you can't do it on your own. Roberto could have helped. But obviously, you don't know him either anymore. Just like Mami. Fine. But I am here, and you must know me, sir. I am your son.

I am your son. This thought makes me blush. It makes me blush scarlet from hatred. But then I feel the fear again. Don't worry, Papi darling, it wasn't difficult, don't worry, it's over and done with, the bastards, everything will be all right in spite of them, these scoundrels thought they could defeat us, they thought they could bring you to your knees, blackmail you, the villains thought everything belongs to them, even you! But they can't touch you, Father!

He's trying to spit. I wait. I wipe it off.

810

I didn't understand why he couldn't come with me right away. He's got to stay another day, they said, for the sake of appearances. Roberto takes me in the police car to the service road leading to Csobánka.

"You must walk from here. Also, there's no need to tell your mother everything. However, I leave that up to you."

## 185.

When he tried to spit on me (he was disgusted by his own saliva!), he said a fascinating, rare word: shitpulp. A word unseen by the eye, unheard by the ear. A shitpulp, that I'm shitpulp.

"And from now on, so shall you remain."

## 186.

"Where were you?"

"In school."

I got a horrendous slap, the size of which you've never seen. All the slaps my mother never dared give, they were all included, and also those to come; she continued beating me, first with her bare hands, her fists, then the broom handle. I didn't resist much, except for shielding my head. I didn't cry, I didn't speak, I didn't beg. She shouted horrible words; she was beside herself, a stranger raving at me, striking me with all her might. She was strong. Possibly, this is when she was the strongest in all her life. From here on, her strength began to wane.

I was panting too, and then I felt tired. The beating hurt, I wasn't used to it, and so I couldn't even feel happy that this beating forged a secret bond between my father and me. When I got into bed, my limbs were heavy with pleasurable fatigue, as if I'd been at play all day. Or as if I'd been helping my father. My brother and sister came to sit by my bed, and they stroked me. I fell into a deep sleep.

<br>

## 187.

When I woke up in the morning, fear had me by the throat. It was like nothing I'd known before. It wasn't even the throat but the stomach and the lungs and the heart. The fear was tugging and churning and pulling at my insides as I struggled to breathe, and the translucent, crystal-clear fear of sin flooded over me. Or more like a dark elation in reverse. This time I wasn't afraid of someone or something, but of everything. A brand-new feeling: I hated myself, and I feared the Lord.

Whereas we'd got on so splendidly before. Before, in His fight against me, the Lord was on my side. But now I feared He'd ask me what I'd done, and I feared that He might not ask me anything. That no one would ask me anything. Suddenly, I was terrified of everything, because I saw this everything as terrifying; God is terrifying: what does He want from me?, and the not-God is even more terrifying, if possible; does no one want anything of me? Is there no place to appeal?

Whether He exists or not, I was left alone with Him. *Deus semper maior, Deus sember maior,* I kept repeating. We'd been on easy, amicable give-and-take bartering terms till then. I thought that if I behave, meaning that I help Mami (weeding, et cetera) and I don't beat my brother and sister over the head unless it's absolutely necessary and I go to church regularly to assist as an altar boy, I have Him eating out of the palm of my hand. *This is the way it is,* I thought, that He's dancing to my tune, because I'm singing His song.

I began to pray, deep down inside, in secret, so no one should see. But no one was looking. No one, there was no one. Please, God . . . —I press and squeeze my eyes together, my lips, my nose, by whole body—please have pity on me.

Take pity on me. This is what I realized, this is what the feeling of guilt pervading every bone in my body made me realize, this blunted panic and fear so much like pain, yes, this was it, I realized that this time I shouldn't be asking or begging or coaxing or wheedling as I'd done before, looking for the most advantageous vantage points for begging but—throwing all caution to the wind—I must turn to Him in supplication. I implore You. Don't take Your revenge on me and don't experiment with me and don't put me to the test to see how I'd fare in adversity, how I'd suffer Your blows. I will do everything to understand You, I promise.

There I go, wheeling and dealing again.

Flood waves of nausea and fever and trembling come over me, my countenance afire. What I realized—it was surprising and shocking—that no one is going to help me except for God, not my father and not my mother, nor Roberto, not my brother and not my sister—no one, except for Him. And here I was, thinking I was helping Him by going to church regularly! Also, if He doesn't help me, I'll have to live with this dark nausea. But how can I trust Him if He's not the way I'd imagined Him for myself? And yet I must trust Him, because otherwise I cannot go on living. One can't live in fear. But do I trust Him because I have faith in Him, or because I have no choice? Because all other options would be worse? (This was my big God-experience of November 5, 1956.)

I decided that every morning I would wake up with this sentence: Take pity on me! Every morning these would be the first words out of my mouth. The first thoughts of my heart go up to You, Lord. Take pity on me. I kept this up for a pretty long time. Then in late November they switched gym class to before eight o'clock, and then the first sentence became: where are my sneakers?

Where are my sneakers, take pity on me.

# 188.

At first, I make a quick detour to church before school to say my sentences on bended knees.

"Is anything the matter?" the parish priest asked after a couple of days. My parents knew him well, Father Zsigmond, but everyone called him Zsigibigi, even Mother, who'd blush at her frivolity every time she did so.

"Just praying," and I blushed, too.

He looked at me kindly, then nodded.

"Sin makes the Lord," he said, and stroked my head.

# 189.

When he came home two days later in his checked shirt, his broken glasses, and strange alterations on his face and handsome forehead, my father made the same stroking gesture.

I was afraid to look at him, but eventually I looked, I looked in his eye. Father's double, I thought, because thanks to Uncle Plop, we knew all about doubles.

"I dropped them," our father said in answer to my brother's touching question, "I dropped them," he said, then took his glasses off and looked, turning them around in his hand. Three parallel furrows cut across his brows. Father, please. Forgive me.

# CHAPTER NINE

## 190.

I finished first grade in Csobánka. I lived with Aunt Irmi. I drank coffee with her and leafed through books with gothic lettering. Then we found ourselves back in Budapest, and I finally had my own room. We in the family called it the gas chamber. For some reason that's where they'd installed the gas meter, and apparently, there's no gas meter without leakage, and the persistent, faint odor of almonds pervaded the bit of space one could hardly call a room. It wasn't even some distant cubbyhole but a corridor, because it served as the access to the bathroom, and so it combined all the inconveniences of a neglected space as well as a popular one.

On the other side of the wall, which was the grownup room, stood an out-of-service stove covered in brick and edged in white. The grated flue, more like a hole, was over my bed, that's where the warmth, the heat, must have come from at one time. Now it was the other way around; it seemed as if it had been put there expressly to air the place out because of the gas.

The lozenge-shaped iron grid looked like the grid of a confessional. I made confessions, and I heard confessions, too.

I could hear a lot of things, especially at night. Or at least partly.

A Penelope, my mother's life was spent waiting for our father. Willy-nilly, we got embroiled in this waiting too, waiting as a lack of trust, hysteria, obsession, hurt, hate, anxiety turned to hate, fear turned to anxiety. Our mother was always suspicious, and the suspicion consumed her. After a while we left her alone with her waiting and went to sleep because we were growing, and growing children need their sleep.

I didn't have to wake with a start in the middle of the night—or rarely. The noises filtering in through the iron grating—the strangled whispers, the sudden flare-up of word snippets, words with impenetrable meaning, more rarely crying, too, from dramatic motherly blubbering through whimpering and coarse, silent male sobbing, the slamming of doors and the resonating boom of falling plaster—these sounds can be taken as part of your dreams for only so long, as if you weren't hearing right. Beggars can't be choosers, you deceive yourself as best you can.

## 191.

But one evening the sounds that came filtering in through my confessional were of a type I'd have never dreamed of. The whole thing was so implausible, I knew immediately it was no dream.

The Emperor, come to visit my father.

A Habsburg (i.e., one piece of Habsburg) had come in the night unexpectedly, under the assumed name of Müller.

"Müller," smiled the son of the last Hungarian king (*nix* emperor after all).

"Your Majesty," I heard my father say.

What the prince wanted is a mystery. He'd come to visit his faithful country. His faithful family. His faithful subject (thinking that the son of a faithful subject must be faithful too). He'd come to take his bearings. That's how they do it, first they take their bearings. We have a fine tradition of princes in disguise, but what remained of it back then, in that anxiety-filled chilly night (and years) was visible on Father's face only after the high dignitaries had departed.

There was an entourage in grayish-green Austrian suits with horn buttons and perfumes that, to our (Eastern European) noses, smelled uncommonly strong. The air of the gas chamber also changed as the smell of royalty filtered in. These indistinguishable men were whispering through the entire visit loud enough for me to hear, and they kept an eye out, too: they checked the blinds, whether each is properly let down, and even pulled the curtains to; they walked around, peeping, moving things, rearranging things with expansive, self-important gestures, like the secret police in silent films. They moved about the place, snooping, as if it belonged to them, or had received orders from a very high place.

My mother was also speaking in a whisper (only my father and the Prince spoke in their normal voices). But basically, she kept busy. She put up coffee and stormed through my space on her way to the bathroom to put out clean towels and refresh her lipstick. (In my father's opinion she was too eager and should have leaned more heavily on the Kossuth-type republican traditions of the Hungarian landed gentry.) And surprisingly, it wasn't our mother but our father who remembered us, and from time to time asked the strangers to quiet down because we were sleeping. He was watching over us, and we didn't wake up. (My daddy can watch his children the way no one can.) He was not discourteous, just reserved, reflective, flexing his muscles in a long-forgotten role.

When they were alone again and my father had seen the Habsburgs to the door—the whole thing didn't last more than half an hour—my mother giggled:

817

"What was that all about?"

"*Nicht der Rede wert,*"—Bagatelle, our father said with a sleepy stretch, still from inside the previous language.


## 192.


"Servus, Matyi, old boy," the parquet floor polisher and authorized enemy Juszuf Tóth said. (After a time the regime could even afford authorized enemies.) He was a *maszek,* a private entrepreneur, the former left-back of the village soccer team. He called my father by his first name with pride and emphasis. He'd come by the privilege twenty-some-odd years before, the first in his family to do so, though they (they and we) had lived in the same village for centuries.

"How are you, old boy?"

My father gave him an honest answer. Juszuf slapped him in the back, something he wouldn't have dared before, as if they'd tended pigs together. (As a matter of fact, they did tend pigs together. As a consequence of Grandmother's strict views on education, the little counts had to do this, too. "Some people watch pigs, some people keep pigs, and some are pigs," et cetera.) He offered to help. It was not the peasant that stirred in him, though a *bit* of the griffin from the family's coat of arms cast a shadow on their relationship, namely, that it'll come in handy when the proper order of the world is restored (though he knew what everyone knew, that nothing would be restored here, nothing is ever continued here, everything always has to begin from scratch); nor was his offer of help prompted by some mysterious surplus of courage, a sudden upsurge of recklessness, namely that he, Juszuf Tóth, private entrepreneur and superannuated left-back, thumbs his nose at the present, this shoddy everything, because he couldn't have thumbed his nose at the present, because it can't be done. If all there is is the present, there's no place to thumb your nose *from*.

If anything, Tóth was a petit bourgeois, a special Hungarian hotchpotch, Hungarian chaff. ("Politics kept pulling and tugging at people until the twelve-place dinner service was broken.") He took a risk hiring my father, not much, but still. On the other hand, as if in compensation, he paid him less than a regular worker. Regarded from the perspective of the class struggle, counts are more remunerative.

"Put it here, friend," and Father did.

He wasn't quite sure what they'd agreed on, but he had no choice. An unskilled laborer who helps lay parquet floors gets up at four-thirty in the morning, carries the buffing machine like a hump, preparing the ground. Initially a certain amount of awkwardness is permissible, and my father took full advantage of the opportunity. He burned the brush, kept breaking the counter laths, and repeatedly got his foot in the floor polish tin. But when he crashed the beautifully aligned parquet pyramid to the floor, and having no familiarity with its order, only its shape, put it back together, packing it up in a helter-skelter manner, his friend Juszuf lost patience. This here is no charity ball, it's work.

Father looked at his benefactor with profound melancholy.

The latter was shocked by his helplessness. He had no idea that things were that bad, and since he was constitutionally a good man (he's constitutionally a good man and thickset), by which I mean that he didn't use the bad in him if he didn't have to, he attempted to console my father, saying that there won't be a *problem*. Actually, he was consoling himself. My father's unabashed naked self-revelation, a product of his helplessness, took him by surprise. He wasn't used to it.

Gradually, my father learned all about parquet floors. Later, because Juszuf switched to it, it was time for plastic moldings. But by then he'd also started translating, first only from German, then from English, too, then from French, then into German, and English, and French, and then all over the place, backward and forward, initially as a ghost writer, without using his name—and all the while his work papers, the guarantee of his safety, were with the parquet floor polisher, plastic molder, and former left-back. A friend. A true friend.

## 193.

My father's life had regained a semblance of normalcy. A semblance, but not normalcy, not a proper normalcy, whereby the question begged to be asked, to wit, what's with this normalcy? Could it be more difficult to bear the bearable than the unbearable, because in the case of the former we must ask, what is it that we are bearing, whereas if we bear the unbearable, the question—a luxury—doesn't come up, because there's nothing but the bearing.

It was at this time that my father became solitary in earnest. From now on I will always see him sitting behind his desk, typing. The clatter of the keys booms through the universe, filling up every nook and cranny, reaching every distant bay and hidden cove, this shoddy, relentless banging that is more of a wheeze or a rattle in the throat than the indifferent noise of a machine, a smothered cry and supplication sating all of Creation, this last, resounding sound of my father's life, this horrible and horribly botched, banal, frightful, bad and expiatory note, this piece of helplessness, uniqueness and wholeness.

The moment of real solitude was not him standing on the melon patch, a peasant among peasants, glancing frightened into the camera, but this one. Like the country, he had nothing left either, just the present, and he was not used to this solitude, this historical solitude in the least, which in an underhanded manner was personally his, the Good Lord had it tailor-made for him, and when he glanced into this solitude, the mirror of this voracious present that had gobbled everything up, it showed him nothing but a man, fortyish, a born somebody who is nowhere, who has arrived nowhere, who is not, and if he is, what's the use?

We were helpless to change this solitude. None of us could, not a jot. (I, for one, bored him to death!) Also, it was not good for him to look in this mirror, it was better for him to stand around cheap, dim taverns, that was better for him.

A desk, the ceaseless clatter of the typewriter, plus this sour half-light: this was all.

## 194.

After Mária-Polixéna-Erzsébet-Romána, Mia tant' to us, applied for and received her emigration papers, from time to time she'd descend on us from Vienna in the guise of a family visit. A guest brings double joy—first when she comes, and second when she goes. So we were happy when she came, even though it meant a lot of work because we had to present a variant of good sibling-ship, with an emphasis on good manners, our piety, and our studies. We did it more from routine than enthusiasm. Still, we didn't make faces too often, for which Mother seemed inordinately grateful, because the visit was to check up on them, too, how well the family is *holding out* on this hostile terrain, whether the fortress is still intact. A source of tension, considering that it reminded my parents of something they wished to remember as well as to forget, though my father, who was most intimately involved in the problem, immediately came over to our side, "placing himself off bounds," *aprés lui le déluge*. Besides, father's side of the family was ill suited to keeping to form, because they *were* the form and so could not address the problem from *outside*. The job of preservation fell to my mother, who went about her duty conscientiously—conscientiously, terrified, persevering courage. The rest of us took it in stride.

We couldn't play with Aunt Mia's blindness the way we could with Grandmother's arteriosclerosis. We had a lot of fun with that, and our mother never stopped us, which we—mistakenly— took as a sign of consent.

"You should be ashamed of yourselves!" she said later with tears in her eyes. But we weren't.

"God should be ashamed of Himself," our sister whispered for our benefit, but thinking this might be too much, we fearfully told her to shut up.

Besides, we didn't believe that Aunt Mia was blind. We didn't dare cock a snook at her, either to her face, or behind her back. All in all, her presence brought a dramatic improvement in our manners. When she went back to Vienna, which back then was as far from here as the Moon, this is what remained behind her—our improved manners, plus the joy that comes when a guest leaves.

195.

Plus the coupons for foreigners. Visiting capitalist relatives were obligated to buy restaurant coupons valid only in certain earmarked and exclusive restaurants, mostly in Budapest. These coupons had to be paid for even if, like Mária-Polixéna-et-cetera, they were staying with their families and were provided with bed and board.

"Play humble pie, then fleece them clean," Father said as he counted the coupons. You'd think they were worth millions, by the grin on his face. "A distasteful national tradition. Fawning on strangers, then robbing them blind." He said this as if he'd done the robbing himself.

We'd been robbed blind by then. But the fawning remained, and we were set on reaping the harvest. *Sabirati urozhai.* We learned all about it in school. We ate up the coupons. I'd never seen my father as enchanting, strong and cheerful as during these illegal family Sunday brunches, or as he called them, swindle brunches. We glanced at him and we knew and we saw that the life ahead of us would be just like him: enchanting, strong, cheerful.

"*Also,*" our father commanded in the morning. "*Auf, auf zum fröhlichen Jagen,* kleine good-for-nothings. *Avanti,* my dears!"

On these merry outings we had to speak German, but no, not speak, converse. This was the grand yet simple idea behind the harvesting: we passed ourselves off as foreigners. Promoted ourselves to a coupon-rich territory. How risky was this? I wouldn't know. In principle, certainly. Except there were no principles. Except in this way anything could be consequent upon anything—in principle. Except it was turning into a decidedly practical world just then; except the practical was, if not governed, yet threatened by principles—in practice. We were defrauding the state, and under socialism, this was tantamount to mortal sin. But this was becoming the sort of socialism where there were—for all practical purposes—no mortal sins. A couple of Lord's Prayers, and you were off the hook. (And all the while, the wild frenzy of the Inquisition was still in your bones . . . )

By the way, the Church also accommodated itself to this piddling about. Our parish priest wasn't at all happy when Mother signed us up for Bible studies at school, the only one to do so.

"Your Excellency . . ."

"Don't call me Your Excellency!"

". . . Your Excellency, why bang your head against the wall, if you know what I mean."

Mami knew and she didn't.

"The priest is right," my father said, "you can't slap shit around."

On these coupon Sundays we were freedom personified. A secret society for freedom. Of course this necessitated that we give ourselves up, that we be not we. Never mind. We were not about to split hairs, and made a stately entry into the Kárpátia Restaurant, let's say.

And right away there came toward us . . . well, a morose, mean-spirited wretch of a man, not a waiter but a catering-sphere laborer, a pariah, a disgrace to the profession. Morose and hungry for revenge—at the moment, this hunger was the only thing binding him to gastronomy. But before he could begin to unload his burden of frustration and fatigue on us, our father took command, veritably flying onto the scene as the light spring breeze made his coat flap, floating in his wake like a cape.

"*Grüss Gott!*" he cried joyously, and we mischievously echoed him, "*Grüssgott, grüssgott!*"

Oh, that *Gott!* All guilty smiles, our mother repeated it after us, ohgotting like the echo at Tihany. The name of God did not pass our lips in a whisper, slipping out inadvertently as it were—oh, dear, we hope no one hears except for the Good Lord, of course—but loud and clear for all to hear, as if it were natural. We hadn't had a bite to eat yet, and already our father had reinstated God and made Him natural, and he did so with ease, by way of an aside, as it were, and not with the anxiety-riddled courage of the nonexistent Catholic opposition—in short, it was not an act of courage or of cowardice, but the cheer that comes, of its own accord, from faith.

It was around this time that Budapest ceased to be. The city had stopped remembering itself. It disappeared. It was lost to sight, you couldn't see where it was, where it came from, or where it was headed. Some restaurants, however, lagged behind the city and the people. The Kárpátia, too, remembered a world of the past and turned into its own insipid parody simultaneously; no longer conjuring up anything, it could do only one thing, rub your—or your father's—nose into the present.

Freedom begets freedom. Old and new reflexes stirred to life in the wretch approaching us, like the waiter who notices not everyone indiscriminately, but the important, *essential* customers right away, bells begin to ring inside, the silver bells of the snob and the servant, the forgotten repressed melodies of the dignity of service as well as those of the creature of the new age, the thief, the scoundrel, the crook, the petty thief who'd spotted his prey.

He wouldn't have necessarily jumped at hearing German, it could easily be a second-class German, a peanut gallery GDR; even a Czech is better, an ermine gentleman from Prague, Goot'n tahg, auf veederscene, get lost, find a luncheonette, but hold on, mate, this here's no goot'n tahg coming at you but a pure-bred *grüss gott*, a *vertigli* Austrian, a cousin, *common in evribodi,* though his coat is misleading, at first glance it's like something from the Red October Clothing Factory, that's the West for you, this understated simplicity, this "as if"-ness; judging by his coat the guy could be Hungarian, a contemporary Hungarian, but the way he walked it, that sweep, the springtime flapping of the coat, only a foreigner can walk in like that; a Hungarian today is either droopy, his coat hanging on him, a withered, autumn leaf, or these VIP nobodies, they don't even wear a coat, just arrogance, the driver pulls them up to the revolving door; but this forehead is something else, you won't find a forehead like this anywhere on this side of the Leithe—and he's bowing and scraping for our benefit, he's swarming and droning and buzzing, yahvohl, bitteshine, come in my little ducklings, gootte platz, commen zee and Feri fuck it what's keeping the menu?

"*Vati! Vati! Was bedeuter* Feri you prick!"

"Overplayed," our father said under his breath.


## 196.

My brother is a born hotelier. He likes people, even if not wholly without self-interest. He loves to talk with a passion, to chat people up; even as a child he liked to walk the street and like an adult, have a friendly tête-à-tête with the neighbors; he speaks several languages and is always after something. He has so-called plans for the future. This is how he ended up working in a hotel. He worked his way through the hierarchy, from elevator boy to bellhop, from bellhop to concièrge. Not the first one to do so, but still. It was something. And also, he was a trusted insider, because two gentlemen showed up in the manager's office and asked to see him. The assistant director shifted in place awkwardly.

"Congratulations, Comrade, continue the good work. The Comrades want a word with you."

For a while my brother listened to the comradely words, correct in their own way, just barely ingratiating, i.e., barely threatening, but sedate, rather, what must be must be, nor was there a sense of complicity, though they didn't talk straight either, they had every reason, for instance, to assume that my brother knew about the "shower room" where the West German hunters were put, and which received its name from the wiretapping devices that looked like showerheads. My brother listened to this ceaseless blather that bored the speaker as well as the listener re. the new responsibility that came with his new post ("The fuckers made a sly remark about you, too, thinking I'd fall for it"); and though he's very practical-minded, it took him a while to see the light, but when he did, he understood right away that although it may not look it, these people now want everything from him, they want his whole life, and he started shaking his big round head; he wouldn't have liked giving them his whole life, he had so many plans for it back then; but he liked working at the hotel; he knew he was appreciated, he felt his power growing, and he liked using it; he felt that he was a man born to rule and would not lose his head, but put his power to good use.

And then he smiled.

The assistant director also smiled, while the faces of the two comrades crinkled into a smile of sorts. They fell silent. Four smiling men. And in this silence the youngest of them spoke up, softly, sweetly, more of a big adolescent than a grown man.

"Oh, valiant sirs in shining armor, go fuck your spurs and fuck your honor!" Then, no count, just the perfect bellhop, he bowed elegantly and left the scene.

"I'll be," muttered the stupefied assistant director.

But they didn't pursue him, they let him be. (Of course, he had to leave the hotel. A pity. He liked it there.)


## 197.


The coupon outing was incontrovertible proof of the advisability of learning languages. Tangible proof. Thus our parents. We didn't mind. Waxed enthusiastic, in fact, especially because (as things stood) our father was in no position to correct us linguistically. Otherwise always and everybody: courteously, relentlessly, without pity. He was constitutionally allergic to bad conjugation. He came down with hepatitis, or whatever. (Or was that from drink? Ha-ha.) He didn't spare our mother either, since it was not about our mother, but conjugation. Now she was as free as we were to show off, weaving her way through the *der-die-das* thickets without fear of the consequences.

We children were a sure ace of spades in the subterfuge, though to tell the truth, more because of the leather knee pants than our familiarity with German. My parents wanted to take no chances when, despite the cool, unpleasantly breezy late March weather, they made us wear our lederhosen.

The lederhosen is a curious invention, a stranger, by its very nature, to the healthy Hungarian collective consciousness, and thus also a stranger to us. We eyed it with suspicion. On the other hand it was as Western back then as a plastic raincoat or blue jeans. Besides, a gentleman is never surprised at anything. Still, am I a Bavarian peasant boy smelling of cows?

But we wore them anyway. The lederhosen reveals its real nature and qualities in the wearing. It has two indigenous varieties: the shiny and the chafed. My brother had a shiny pair, and I the chafed. I don't remember my sister's, only her thin, spindly legs as they dangled out of it, like spider legs. The lederhosen has a wonderful characteristic: it doesn't get dirty. It can't, it is not capable; it is theoretically out of the question; what in the case of a pair of wool pants is scandalous, and in the case of jeans, after a while leads to self-deception, in the case of lederhosen is called patina. Oh, the heavenly joy of wiping your filthy, greasy hands directly and publicly in your lederhosen!

"That's how they do it," we said to our skeptical mother when she objected, and referred her (a genealogical botch-up!) to the Austrian branch of the family. Also, with time the leather pants gradually come to maturity. Time as it is transformed to beauty, that's the lederhosen.

We considered it our moral responsibility to eat up the coupons. ("We're not leaving them to *these* people!"). Which meant that we were morally bound to choose expensive dishes. At first we were ashamed of ourselves. A gentleman does not concern himself with the price.

"Unless," our father quipped, "he's short of liquid assets. Temporarily, of course!"

Still, with time, a new, hitherto unfamiliar, pleasant sensation caught up with us—the sweet delirium of wealth. It was a stranger to us, but we caught on in no time. We quickly learned that money, just like the lack of money, has its limitations, and the fact that we couldn't have green beans without meat, only with haunch of venison in mushroom sauce, violated our independence. But who cared! We let our parents know that in case they should hesitate on moral grounds, we have the answer: it is better to be rich than poor.

We even had frog legs, I excitedly yes, my brother adamantly no, while our sister never knew what hit her. We started humming a tune, but due to our bad choice of language, were quickly put on hold.

*"Virágéknál ég a világ, sütik már a rántott békát, zimmezumm, zimmezumm, recefice bumbumbum!"* Poor Virágs, their house on fire, and they gotta eat fried frog legs, tra-la-la, tra-la-la, lah-de-dah-de lah-lah-lah.

And there we were, thinking all the time that the Virágs were poor! No wonder. What can you expect of a folk song?

"It smells. This smells," our sister commented as timidly as if she hadn't opened her mouth in five years. We leaned over the corpse. Indeed. Even our father—who never thought anything was spoiled and gobbled up the slightly stale leftovers, the spoiled vegetable stews, the milks of questionable provenance, the suspicious-looking eggs with relish—was forced to admit to the smell. (Our mother used to say that eggs don't even have to smell. They become inedible on mere suspicion. "Just like cardinals," Papi commented with a grin. "Not only must they be above reproach, their reputation must be above reproach as well," and he gobbled up the compromised chicken egg. He had eggs every morning. Back then there wasn't such a thing as cholesterol.)

Poor frog legs. They smelled to high heaven. Maybe the refrigerator, that certain famous Saratov brand, went off the blink. We had one at home. Rattled like a tractor. But it's not the rattling that counts, it's the cold that counts, and no one's as good at cold as the Russians, our father opined. Our mother shrugged. In spirit she'd got stuck with the Bosch. Besides, for all we knew, from revolutionary—sorry, antirevolutionary considerations—the frogs went bad on purpose, in order to cast a shadow on the good reputation of socialism.

If that was what they were after, they succeeded.

Like always, our mother would have liked to avoid a scandal because of the frog legs, whereas our father wouldn't have liked to avoid a scandal. Afterward at home my brother and I practiced (with sorry success) that light yet emphatic gesture, threatening yet elegant, like an aside and yet annihilating, with which Papi beckoned the waiter over and addressed some words to him, whereupon the latter scurried off, frowning and alarmed, only to return with a big fat man in tow.

Our father sat on his throne without moving a muscle, waiting. We understood that we must not speak, lest he fall out of his role. But he managed to wink at us. Mami was worried, and she infected us, too, except for my sister, whose curiosity invariably got the better of her.

"Out of the question, *mein Herr*," the fat man said with a shake of the head as he approached. He looked like someone who was used to being in command; it was not advisable to provoke him, you could tell. But that it wasn't advisable to provoke our father either we hadn't seen before until that moment. "Out of the question, *mein Herr!*" His German wasn't bad. He was waiting for our

830

father's response. It was like watching a Western. Our hero meets his match, a big, nasty man. They stare at each other, unblinking. A showdown.

Our father points gracefully at the corpses. His adversary inspects the frogs—my stupid brother had just begun peeling off the fried breading; my mother slaps his hand—then he looks up inquisitively.

*"Nun ja?!"*

*"Nun?! Ja?!* Is that all you have to say?" our father cries out and pushes back his chair with a squeak. All eyes are on us. "Is that all you have to say, *nun ja,* is that all that the manager, because you are the manager, are you not?, of an exclusive Budapest restaurant, because this is an exclusive Budapest restaurant, is it not?, who is furthermore in charge and is a real gourmand, are you not?, and damn it, what was I saying?!"

Our father was talking very loud in the crudest possible Viennese accent, as a consequence of which no one understood a single word of his tirade. In the ensuing silence our father repeated his light gesture:

*"Voilà, der Gstank!* Smell it!"

The nasty man raised the plate toward his nose timidly, as if it were a bomb set to go off.

*"Nun ja?"* my father smiled.

"Too much," my father's son sighed. (Motherly poke in the ribs.)

My father does not obstruct the various paths of retreat open to the maître d' but gives a satisfied nod instead, acknowledging that the other has noticed nothing out of the ordinary, though need he add, they offer their apologies, whereupon my father nods with redoubled satisfaction.

"It's on the house," the maître d' says between his teeth and has the waiter bring Zalai crab ragout with dill sauce—an unexpected turn of events whereby he nearly wins the battle, and we'd be stuck with the coupons! But father shows his hand, and orders champagne.

"Russian, son, because it's the best, is it not," and he winks at the waiter, who stares him down, his expression as dead-pan as he can make it.

The feeling of victory sweeps over the whole family.

"In moderation, Mati, dear," our mother whispers dutifully now and then, but she'd had a bit to drink herself.

At the end of the meal and after the coffee, our father waves the waiter over. His expression is careworn. The waiter's is humble, bristling with suppressed rage. No wonder. The spoiled frog legs are coming out of their pockets. They're going to be cried down. No disciplinary action, though.

*"Jawohl, Herr Doktor!"* This must've slipped in from Vienna, where everyone is Herr Doktor. But people wearing glasses, definitely.

"Listen, son. At this point in time I think we need a drink . . ."

"Oy!" (Mami).

*"Nicht oy,"* and he flashes such a charming smile at our mother that she instantly forgets everything, i.e., she remembers everything, the slim young man who used to make her go weak in the knees. "In short, son, bring us a smooth, round cognac, V.S.O.P. A.S.A.P.," he urges, patting the waiter's backside, like a horse, giddyap!, this for our mother's benefit who, throwing all her severity to the wind, including the linguistic one, pronounces herself ready to try the cognac, or at least dip her tongue into it.

"Dip it, sweetheart, dip it!"

"Me, too, me too!," we clamor, we also wanted to tip it, or dip it.

Also, a smooth, round cognac must be followed by a good, fine cigar.

"Nothing less than Havana, the bastion of the international

labor movement will do, son!" He closes his eyes. "Those huge, quivering, greasy thighs on which those sweet, hefty Cuban women roll the tobacco leaves! Take my word for it, son. The aroma, that inimitable aroma, comes from that awe-inspiring roll on the thighs!" After lengthy deliberation over the surprisingly wide selection, he choses Fidel Castro's favorite cigar, an Inter Muros Grandioso. "That Fidel is an ambitious young man. *Ein Mörder*. Inter Mörder Grandioso . . ."

"What the fuck do you take me for? Who the fuck do you think you are? A James, or something? You think you sucked the pyramids into shape? Well, go on, suck . . . You think I don't know what you're gabbing about, giving yourself airs, provoking us throughout the meal, what the fuck for?, because you got money? Well, I don't, and what of it? Lick my arse . . . the Russians this, and Moscow that, the labor movement, you think I don't know?, what the fuck do I care about the Russians and Moscow, it's just that they fucking care about us, and actually, I don't fucking not care either, because they bring the dough, they have to, it's still a lot cheaper than shooting people, they're the ones supporting us, you prick, and not you and your kind, fuck you. Where were you in fifty-six? Nowhere, that's where you were, nowhere. Austrians? What Austrians? There's no Austrians, there's no Austrians even less than there's no Hungarians. What's an Austrian? The Rapid plus the Austria Wien! They were here once, we learned it in school, one hundred fifty years of Turkish repression, four hundred years of Habsburg repression, that's all, may the pox take you, but I'm not angry, you prick, you'll dish it out in the end, you want to play the gentleman, and that takes money, if only we could've palmed Józsi's frogs off on you, he left them out too long, and kiss your arse till it blistered, the crab wasn't much better either, except we ladled that dill sauce over it, but never mind, my little Sunday Labanc, you puny, weak-chested German," the waiter thought and bowed obligingly.

We were just departing with everyone in attendance, both sides voicing their utmost satisfaction, when my brother tripped over a heavy fold in the thick carpeting, fell on his knees, and started bawling—in Hungarian. But by then it didn't matter.

"*Ach,* how quickly doth these critters take to your strange, exotic language, but never you mind, there'll be frog's legs yet to come, *nestpah, ohne* tra-la-la!"—and the good shepherd our father quickly herded us outside, out, out, out you go, where hand in hand, forming a chain, the five of us broke into a run, veritably floating in the direction of the nearby street bearing the name of Lajos Kossuth, as if we were playing "give us more soldiers, King!"

There we were, floating behind our father, like the back of his coat.


## 198.


When we reached Lajos Kossuth utca, our father stopped.

"My little angels," he chirped, so full of charm that the blood froze in our veins, "go on home, there's that lovely first-class number six bus, I have something to do."

Our mother looked at him as if he'd just killed a man, or ransacked a shop, a nobody, a piece of shit. Instinctively, we backed off. Our father decided not to decipher that look, and launched into an enthused and muddled disquisition about why it is of the essence that he go visit Juszuf Tóth. Come to think of it, we can go along if we like.

"Puppies, want to come along?"

"Yes, yes," we piped, the little idiots. Mami didn't move a muscle. It was bad, seeing her like this.

"Oh, bunny, don't look at me like that! You're absolutely right.

How silly of me. Just boring financial matters, or not even that. We need to hand in some papers to the Small Tradesmen's Association. They're all-powerful, you have no idea how powerful compared to . . . like an elephant to a flea . . ."

"And not a flea to an elephant," our sister pipes in helpfully.

"Indeed," Papi nods. He seems dejected.

This is the point where our mother starts pleading for all she's worth, he shouldn't do this, ruining this beautiful Sunday, et cetera, but she stops short, tottering precariously, should she be frank, threatening or submissive, she can't feel and she can't decide which would do the trick. None of the above. There is no ratio either that would work. And there isn't enough past experience or debacle that could teach us, because some terrible hope remains, always, that some piece of cleverness or a trick would get the better of a *drunken mind*. Except, it can't be done. This is what distinguishes (heavy) drinking, this uncertainty, insubstantiality, shadow world and bedazzlement, this will-o'-the-wisp and fairy light.

Our father as fairy light.

All at once, the fairy light (fiction and conjecture) turns on his heels and exits the scene; he doesn't plead, he doesn't justify, he doesn't explain, he flits away. Our mother takes off after him; my brother would like to, but I grab him from behind, you're not going anywhere, I say; I say it in a way that makes him obey. We're watching the two wildly gesticulating adults, no sound, a silhouette performance, a useless intermezzo. Our mother comes back smiling.

"Your father has some business to take care off. We're going home. *Allons, allons . . .*"

Honesty didn't work then, and it didn't work later.

## 199

Stopping short in your tracks was no better. Still, Mother does it, she keeps stopping short; consequently, our father walks several paces ahead of us, casting merry glances over his shoulder, like a smart horse.

He pulls the wagon. Pulls everything, everything and everyone. He doesn't stop short in his tracks, just slows his pace, then stops. He carefully slips out of the harness; he doesn't cast it off, his legs don't end up outside the traces; he removes the bridle—our mother embodies a suspicion-filled variety of waiting, her back is bent, like a cat's, she's grown ugly with waiting; he takes the bit from between his cheeks, it's glistening with foam in the March sun, then with a quick, adroit movement he slips out of the brow band, the blinders and curb chain, which roughs up his hair; we've seen photos of Einstein like this, hair in chaos, intellect in order, we laugh at the clownish muddle; finally, he pulls off the breast harness also and turns around, a cigar between his lips.

The sun is shining, the Inner City is busy, oh moment, tarry!

"Puppies!" my father huffs proudly, "for once we're taking a convenience called a taxicab home. I'm tired."

On the double, our mother calls out "Tahxi!" with her characteristic *ah*, because she realizes that this way nothing is bound to happen, because it's what doesn't happen that's good. (This was what defeated her, this "because," and this sort of "good.")

"I'm tired. You're tired too, are you not?" my mischievous father asks. A blushing virgin, Mami lowers her head. My parents are coy. We hardly ever caught them at it (through the years), unless to the extent of a kiss. We don't like listening to this teasing, it's more unpleasant than touching, whereas it's touching. Making fun of Mami, we launch into it ourselves:

"Tahxi! Tahxi!"

## 200.

He leans against the church wall, the Franciscans, he's about to heave up, our mother springs over, sits him gingerly on the stone ledge, my father's head keeps bobbing as if there were no muscles in his neck—the nodding muscle?—my mother keeps lifting him, then manages to lean him against the wall at long last. Is the head supporting the church or the church the head?

His forehead gleams with oil and sweat, his hair in knots, like sparrow feathers, our mother fishes a handkerchief out of the profound depths of her purse and spreads it over our father's face. We look on. We're bored.

The subject lies ready-made at our feet.

A stinging, sour smell issues from him. It reminds me of ammoniac. We approach, then back off. There's nothing but this smell.

"Our father, a colorless, odorless, stinging gas."

He recovers, sees nothing of us, tries to straighten up, brushes us off him; as he stands, he slips out of his coat, his shirttail flapping, hanging out of his pants.

To our surprise, he begins to dance.

One arm raised bent above his head, the other held tight behind his back, he takes up a posture, proud and defiant, raising his head high like a true Magyar, a flickering of ancient shepherds' fires in the blood, and he begins to spin round faster, faster, his waist pulled in, his hair floating, stamping his feet. Our mother merges herself into the church wall.

Father doesn't cause much of a stir. People throw him a cursory glance, a dissolute drunk, staggering.

"Come!" our mother says, reemerging from the church wall, brushing Father's coat aside. "We have no business here!" Then, gathering us under her arm, she starts off for the nearby Astoria.

It's not me, I'd been keeping a low profile, not agreeing, but resigned, but my brother, the confirmed mother party, who now slips out of her protective embrace and makes for my father, a whirling dervish, tapping and stamping his feet on the ground, doing the *csárdás* with a ghost. My brother looks on, then timidly attempts a step or two, moving along with my father, more and more along with him, catching the rhythm, the gesture, the dance. They're dancing frenziedly; my poor brother, he can hardly keep up, but then he takes the lead, calming the other down as if putting the brakes on an unruly horse, ho, ho, take it easy!, that's the spirit, my proud Challenger, easy does it, my treasure!, good horsie, a good horsie, he calms down, good, a good horsie.

Drenched in sweat, panting, they stop. Now what? My father reels, my brother stands below him, pushing and supporting him, a sack, back to the church wall. He sits. Slowly recovers. Exhausted, grateful, he glances at his son, my brother.

"Father, come."

No, no, he should come closer instead. Timidly, my brother shuffles a foot, my father shuts his eyes, as if he were sunbathing, indicating that he should come closer, closer still. By this time my brother is sorry he ever launched into it; he's on Mother's side again; blinking at her from over his shoulder, he'd like to come back to us. Barely raising his eyelids, Father peeks out, sees my brother's outline (it's as much as he ever saw of us), then quick as a flash, a rattlesnake, he lashes out and pulls my brother to him, who is so frightened, he's past crying or screaming, whereas he would very much like to cry and scream; he pulls him close, clutching him in his arms. My brother is panting with fear and fury; he's around father's neck; he sees the yellow, pockmarked church wall from up close. Father is stroking his hair.

"My treasure."

"Do not stroke me, sir! Stroke your . . ." No one ever dared finish a sentence like this.

"What's up, is that what you're asking, boy?"

"No! No!"

Now it's Father's turn to placate and cuddle my brother. Does he see the plaque on the church wall just above their heads? It indicates the water level during the great flood of 1838. The ice at Csepel Island piled up and forced the water back toward the city. They could easily be under water now, so they'd be well advised to start gaping like a fish, as if they had gills, the fish could be swimming past their ears, fat carps, swift breams, or just the ice floes, they could see the barges from below, and possibly the sky, with some murky blue filtering through, and they could see Mika Wesselényi, the heroic rescuer, though only from below, of course.

"Go on, son, gape, gape, oxygen is essential to life . . . I'm going to tear you apart, like a fish . . . The point is, old boy, that we're standing here high and dry and there's nothing. I am not, and you are not, and that goes double for your mother!, this temple is not here, and as for Liberation Square, that's not here with a vengeance, if anything, maybe our gills, we've still got our gills . . . no . . . if anything, it's those spoiled frog legs, I ate frog with your grandfather once, at the Bristol in Vienna . . . Veal, lamb, ba-a-a-a- . . . Your grandfather liked good food, while I generally go hungry. Either, or."

He's panting, struggling for air. Frightened, my brother turns his head away.

"The Szentkút country fair!" my father hollers. "Take a good look round, son! This here is the Szentkút country fair! I'll sing it for you."

Before my brother has a chance to protest, he pastes his huge, handsome, fatherly hand over his mouth.

"The fair at Szentkút cooked our goose . . ." The *oo* sound warbles gently, then gurgles in his throat. "Cooked our goose. Get it? Know what I'm saying it instead of? They stole our mule then let it loose . . . They wiped us out, that's what I'm saying . . . that there's nothing . . . not even the memory . . . Stole it, with all the trappings . . . You'd like to inherit, boy, wouldn't you? We started inheriting and inheriting and inheriting . . . this little piggy and that little piggy . . . until the last little piggy had none." He raises my little brother to face level and takes a long, hard look. "How old are you? Never mind. You'd like to be a count, it's written all over you. You like giving orders . . . and you always will . . . or will want to . . . How I hate it! My father, he knew how to give orders. Without a word. Just a flash of his eye. The way he'd stand there. No, not *there*. Just stand. The past. What's past is past . . . bagatelle . . . This is one thing I'll never understand . . . Not that there was anything good in them robbing us blind, mind you, because what's good in turning a ballroom into a barn? It's no good for me, and it's no good for the cows . . . They took everything, down to the last nail in the wall. Everything. The country . . . And with what finesse, pulling out their bag of tricks! As if the country had stolen itself from itself . . . And so it doesn't call their bluff, just fights on."

He lowers my little brother down round his neck.

"A wholesale plunder . . . Who? Is that what you're asking? There's nobody here but us, everything around is us. We've got nothing left but our father's . . ."—he stops short—". . . and wipe that grin off your face, son. Because I'm not going to say it. If it's one thing you're good at, it's grinning. When it comes to grinning, you're the best of the lot . . . Anyway, you know what I'm saying . . . it rhymes with fig . . . The inheritance . . . We've got nothing left but our father's tra-la, gonna harness that up to get us back home to our own little land, tra-la."

## 201.

At the word "home," with "land" trailing just behind, my father leaps up as if we'd found a solution, as if we were going home on that. He's coming along with us quietly, minding his manners, my mother, like a severe, out of sorts governess, leading the pack up front. And yet, when we enter the apartment, my father is already sitting by the Hermes Baby which is clattering steadily, like an automatic machine gun, he's pounding it, striking it, and the words come pouring out, going pit-a-pat on the white sheet, one in wake of the other, words that are not his own, nor were they ever, nor will they ever be.

"The fair at Szentkút was a fuck-up . . ." The up sound warbles gently, then gurgles in his throat. "A fuck-up. You understand fuck-up, don't you, son?"

# Comments

When you're working with sentences, you're in need of sentences. Sentences can come from a variety of places—some I overheard on the street, others were whispered in my ear, still others I read; you'll even find some that I made up by myself. These have a different status only at first glance. A sentence never stands in isolation; it is always intertextual. If I write down a yes, that is always just a bit the last word of Joyce's *Ulysses* as well. These borrowed words are interwoven into this text not for lack of my own but to show that literature is a commentary on our shared human experience. I entertain the romantic notion that novels stand in a congenial relationship to one another and help one another out. Therefore, as a sign of my gratitude as a colleague, I hasten to list below those from whom I have received direct help in this manner. In short, the novel contains verbatim quotes or quotes reworked and reshaped, sometimes no more than just a word, yes, or an adjectival phrase, or the space between two words, from the following: *

843

Mona Abaza, Endre Ady, Ibn Hazm Al-Andalusi, Sherwood Anderson, János Arany, Aziz Al-Azmehs, László Baránszky, Barlosky, Donald Barthelme★★ (!), Samuel Beckett, Saul Bellow, Walter Benjamin, László Berényi, Klaus Beyrer, Ádám Bodor, Borges, Péter Bornemissza, Gesine Bottomley, H. C. Buch, Italo Calvino, Camus, Daniel Charms, Chesterton, Cioran, Lars Clausen, Craig, A. L. Croutier, Béla Cselényi, Mary Daly, László Darvasi, Deutsch-Stix/Janik, Walter Dirks, János E., Günther Eich, Harald Eggebrechts, János Erdélyi, Gräfin Agnes Esterházy, Miklós Esterházy (my great-grandfather's diary from 1921), Móric Esterházy (my grandfather's handwritten notes from the inter-war years), Péter Esterházy (I was not loath to turn to myself for help either), Efim Etkind, Mordechai Feingold, Ferenc Fejtő, Jens Malte Fischer, Andrea Friedrich, Günther Bruno Fuchs, Dmitrij Galkovszkij, László Garaczi, Sigfried Gauch, Leopold Ginzburg, Natalia Ginzburg, Carlo Ginzburg, Goethe (because Goethe is present everywhere), Witold Gombrowicz, Nilüger Göle, Gábor Görgey, Péter Gothár, Anthony Grafton, György Granasztói, Pal Granasztói, Günther Grass, Graves, Greenblatt, Grillparzer, Valentin Gröbners, Balázs Győres, Thomas Hardy, HC CD Cover Text, Peter Härtling, Haydn, Johann Peter Hebel, Herbert Heckmann, Heidegger, Helmuth Heissenbüttel, Roland Hengstenberg, Eckhard Henscheid, Mrs. Horváth (the cook who lent me names of country dishes), Hölderlin, Bohumil Hrabal, Peer Hultberg, A. Huxley, Jackel, Venedikt V. Jerofeyev, Jochen Jung, James Joyce, Ernst Jünger, Franz Kafka, Yasunari Kawabata, Wim Kayzer, István Kemény, Paul Kersten, Hermann Kesten, Imre Kertész, Danilo Kiš, Tom Klaus, Otto Klemperer, Leszek Kolakowski, Fritz Kortner, Dezső Kosztolányi, Karl Kraus, Gyula Krúdy, Emil Kulcsár, La Bruyère, Renate Lachmann, Christine Landfried, György Láng, John Lee, Dénes Lengyel, Wolf Lepenies, Mario Vargas Llosa, Malacka, Mann (Erika, Golo, Klaus, Thomas), Manuela, Sándor Márai, Henrik Marcalli, Gabriel Marcel, Matthäus, Frank McCourt(!), Merényi-Bubics, László Mérő, Henry Miller, Petra Morsbach, Mozart, Moses, Vladimir Nabokov, Nádas, Sten Nadolny, Nizami, Cees Nooteboom, Hans Erich Nossack, Kenzaburo Oe, Ortega, Orwell, Samuel Osherson, Jürgen Osterhammel, Endre Papp (Bandi), Renato Pasta, Oskar Pastior, Péter Pázmány, Ida Péterfy, Josef Pieper, John M. Prausnitz, Gero von Randow, Ágnes Rapai, Hans Werener Richter, Eberhard Rieth, Rilke, Jennifer E. Robertson, Joseph Roth, Otto Sanders, Barbara Sanders, Schatzmann, Peter Schneider, Ingo Schulze, Julian Schutting, Barbara Sherberg, Spectaculum 46, Sprüche der Väter, Mandyam V. Srinivasan, Ezra N. Suleiman (How are you?), Magda Szabó, Béla Szász, László Szörényi, Georg Tabori, Imre Tóth, Toynbee, John Updike, Johannes Urzidil, Domokos Varga, István Vörös, Mihály Vörösmarty, Peter Wapnewski, Paul Watzlawicks, Wittgenstein, Benjamin Lee Whorf, Wilfried Wieck, Gabriele Wohmann, Hans Wollschläger, Conrad Ziegler.

*Péter Esterházy*

# *A SELECTED BIBLIOGRAPHY

| SOURCE | SENTENCE |
| --- | --- |
| Donald Barthelme | Book One, Sentence #113, #143, #144, #145, #146 |
| Samuel Beckett | Book One, Sentence #332 |
| Saul Bellow | Book One, Sentence #36 |
| Mary Daly | Book One, Sentence #238 |
| Natalia Ginzburg | Book One, Sentence #250, #354 |
| Witold Gombrowicz | Book One, Sentence #304; Book Two, Sentence #15 |

Venedikt Jerofeyev          Book One, Sentence #220

James Joyce                 Book One, Sentence #207

Danilo Kis                  Book One, Sentence #24

Leszek Kolakowski           Book One, Sentence #91

Frank McCourt               Book Two, Sentence #126,
                            #133, #139, #142, #167, #176

Vladimir Nabokov            Book One, Sentence #266

Joseph Roth                 Book One, Sentence #292

John Updike                 Book One, Sentence #370

★★I'd like to offer a special thanks to the Estate of Donald Barthelme for permission to quote extensively from *The Dead Father*, which I have done in Book One, Sentences #113, #143, #144, #145, #146 of *Celestial Harmonies*. It is because of my admiration for Donald Barthelme's writing that I have used parts of his *The Dead Father* interwoven with my own text. I appreciate the indulgence of the estate in this matter, and hope that the author too would approve of this borrowing.